Monks, Bandits, Lovers, and Immortals

Eleven Early Chinese Plays

MONKS, BANDITS, LOVERS, AND IMMORTALS

Eleven Early Chinese Plays

Edited and Translated,
with an Introduction, by

STEPHEN H. WEST
and WILT L. IDEMA

Hackett Publishing Company, Inc.
Indianapolis/Cambridge

15 14 13 12 11 10   1 2 3 4 5 6 7

For further information, please address:
  Hackett Publishing Company, Inc.
  P.O. Box 44937
  Indianapolis, IN 46244-0937

www.hackettpublishing.com

Cover design by Abigail Coyle
Text design inspired by Stephen H. West
Composition by Agnew's, Inc.
Printed at Sheridan Books, Inc.

Library of Congress Cataloging-in-Publication Data

Monks, bandits, lovers, and immortals : eleven early Chinese plays / edited and
translated with an introduction by Stephen H. West and Wilt L. Idema.
      p.   cm.
  Includes bibliographical references and index.
  ISBN 978-1-60384-200-6 (pbk.) — ISBN 978-1-60384-201-3 (cloth)
  1. Chinese drama—960–1644.   I. West, Stephen H.   II. Idema, W. L.
(Wilt L.)
  PL2592.5.M66   2010
  895.1′2408—dc22   2009045964

The paper used in this publication meets the minimum requirements of American National Standard for Information Sciences—Permanence of Paper for Printed Library Materials, ANSI Z39.48–1984.

∞

Contents

The Writing Club of Hangzhou

Support for Hackett titles, and information about forthcoming postings, can be found at
www.hackettpublishing.com.

Acknowledgments

We have been working together on the study of early Chinese drama now for more than thirty years, and this represents our third jointly authored book. We repeat here the statement in our first, *Chinese Theater 1100–1450*, that this is a truly "collaborative effort of both of us, for which we assume equal responsibility."

We continue our lifelong debt to our late teachers in the field of Chinese drama, Tanaka Kenji and James Irving Crump, but as we have grown older that debt has spread to many colleagues in the field who have offered stimulating advice and counsel: Tseng Yong-yih, Sun Chongtao, Wu Shuyin, Wang Chiu-kuei, Hua Wei, Wang Ayling, Cyril Birch, Dirk Jonker, and a host of others, as well as our drama students, He Yuming, Patricia Sieber, Karin Myhre, Robin Ruizendaal, Tan Tianyuan, and Shiamin Kwa. Most of all, however, we have always found it a joy to work together, and our working relationship has been marked by humor, patience, and an intellectual stimulation that has created expectations of a certain level of rigorous investigation of texts and a commensurate level of understanding of where those texts fit in middle-period history, culture, and literature.

In the preparation of the manuscript for publication, we would like to thank Jennifer Bussio (Tempe), Tan Tianyuan (Harvard), and also Rick Todhunter, Meera Dash, Abigail Coyle, Carrie Wagner, and all of their colleagues of Hackett Publishing Company.

Tempe, Arizona, and Cambridge, Massachusetts, 2009
Stephen H. West and Wilt L. Idema

Introduction

The Historical Background

For the average Westerner, the impression of the Chinese theater is primarily one of spectacle and cacophony. We are most often treated to Peking Opera or to Kun Opera, with their lavish costumes, well-articulated masks of facial paint, and string and percussion instruments. In eyes that are culturally attuned to a mimetic spoken drama or to the staging of the classical opera, Chinese opera seems strangely confusing. There are no props beyond a table or chair, stagehands walk freely back and forth on stage during the performance, and the audience pays little attention until the singing begins. But what is exotic to us is bedrock in Chinese culture. Drama, along with ritual and food, is one of the three major legs of ordinary Chinese life. And it has been so for a millennium.

The plays that are presented in this anthology all come from the early part of that thousand-year span, and all stem from specific places and specific times. They are documents that must be placed in historical context in order to understand their provenance, their social and cultural background, and their literary value. These dramas, first written in the period from 1250 to 1450 but often only preserved in much later revised versions, build on and reflect a living oral tradition of performance that already had a long history by the time they emerged. They therefore do not spring onto the stage fully formed and utterly new, but are a genre of writing that shares structures and language with earlier types of performance art. The commonalities they share are their structure—an alternation of prose and sung poetry; their language—a mixture of dense colloquial and simple classical Chinese; and their mode of presentation—one singer functioning both as a describing and judging narrator of events, and as a lyrical voice of the singer/protagonist's emotional and physical state. The differences are in certain modes of presentation—while other forms relate stories solely through the eyes of only one singer-storyteller, in plays other people populate the stage as secondary and interactive characters.

While the language and the basic structure of performance art—alternating prose and rhymed text—can be traced far back in time, at least to the so-called transformation tales (*bianwen*) of the eighth to the tenth centuries, *zaju*, or Northern drama, which accounts for the bulk of plays in this anthology, is part of a recognizable group of urban arts that flourished in the great cities of China from the late Tang (617–906) through the Song (960–1276) and beyond. Some of these forms begin as distinctly regional arts, but were transported to the cities, where they became mainstays of urban performance. As a progenitor of Northern drama, the most important art was one called "all keys and modes" (*zhugongdiao*), a long narrative *chantefable* that combined a variety of then-extant song forms that included short suites of individual songs in the same mode and all written to the same rhyme. *Zhugongdiao*, which seems to have originated in the Shanxi area, provided a nascent structure of musical suites that later *zaju* adapted as the organizing principle of individual acts, with each act eventually written as one long song-suite. There are two (partially) extant published examples of this form from the twelfth century, namely *The Story of Liu Zhiyuan in All Keys and Modes* (*Liu Zhiyuan zhugongdiao*) from the Linfen area of lower Shanxi, and *Master Dong's All Keys and Modes of the Story of the Western Wing* (*Dong Jieyuan Xixiang ji zhugongdiao*), the first full-fledged colloquial telling of the famous *Story of the Western Wing*, China's premier love story. Both of these texts have been translated fully into Western languages, and their stories would continue to be adapted for the stage throughout the later centuries.[1]

Other, nonmusical, entertainments found in this milieu were the so-called Song dynasty "variety show" (Song *zaju*) and Jin dynasty "performers' texts" (*yuanben*)—that is, farces and comical skits that employed an ensemble or small troupe of actors. These farces were popular both on the urban stage and in the imperial court where the two core role types of the ensemble—the butt (*fujing*) and the jester (*fumo*)—were a staple of court events organized around banquets, poetic competitions, and other social activities. These dramatic entertainments excelled in the use of jokes, cleverly rhymed poetry, and slapstick comedy. It is most likely from this early form of drama that *zaju* drama adapted both the custom of using role types (*jiaose*), rather than individualized characters, and the distribution of tasks among these role types. When the "all keys and modes" and these farces and skits merged in Northern China by the middle of the thirteenth century, the single singer (either a male or female *role type*) was retained from the long prosimetric narratives, and the play was fleshed out with the introduction of other actors who were given spoken parts in the dialogue, and who continued to perform comic skits on stage as a humorous leavening that was an expected part of performance. We have translated below a suite of songs that describe such a troupe on stage. Since the emergence of *zaju* neatly coincided with the establishment of the Mongol Yuan dynasty (1260–1368), *zaju* is often designated as "Yuan drama," but we have to realize that the genre most likely emerged before the establishment of that dynasty

---

1. See the section *Yuanben* and *Zhugongdiao* in Appendix 2: Bibliography and Suggested Readings.

and continued to flourish well into the later Ming. Simultaneously South China witnessed the emergence of its own local theater, the texts of which are known as "play text" (*xiwen*).

Urban Setting

While the structure of our Northern plays clearly derives from generic ante-cedents, the ideology behind the texts is overwhelmingly urban, representing in the beginning the social and cultural values of a distinct society of people. For the urban dweller, consumerism and the power of money had to a great extent leveled class interests and blurred the historical boundaries of a rigid ethical-hierarchical social system based on mastery of a set of canonical texts and success through the imperial examinations. We are fortunate to have in hand a description of the capital at Kaifeng, a city of over a million inhabitants in its heyday from 1000 to 1125, *Dreaming of Splendors Past: The Eastern Capital* (*Dongjing meng Hua lu*), finalized in 1147 and first published in 1187. This small text, which describes the capital from the point of view of a materially sophis-ticated man-about-town, is packed with dense descriptions of a city life in which entertainments are at the heart of everything: imperial rituals, religious holi-days, and seasonal holidays. But the text also gives a vivid description of special areas set aside for stages and performance in the center of the urban area near the imperial city:

From "Streets and Alleys at the Eastern Corner of the Imperial City"

A little further east one encounters the Calabash Stew Shop of the Xu Fam-ily. On the south side of the avenue is the Sang Family Tile Market, just north is the Central Tile Market, and next the Inner Tile Market. There are some fifty playhouses here, large and small. Among them the largest are the Tree Peony Theater, and Lotus Flower Theater of the Inner Tile Market and the Yaksha Theater and Elephant Theater of the Inner Tile Market. These can seat thousands of people. From the time of Ding Xianxian, Wang Tuanzi, and Seven Sages Zhang many people later performed here. In these tile markets are many things like purveyors of herbal simples, sellers of hexa-gram prognostications, hawkers of used clothing, those who wager on food and drink, cutters of paper designs, and singers of ditties. One can stay here all day and never be aware that it approaches evening.

These tile markets (called *washe* or *wazi*) were similar to the "floating world" (*ukiyo*) of Japanese cities, and they constituted a similar labyrinth of desire for city dwellers in China. Notorious as sites of gambling, prostitution, and way-ward will, they were described thusly in the early fourteenth century:

The meaning of *washe* is from the phrase, "they assemble like tiles stacking; they disassemble like tile stacks falling apart"—that is, it is easy to come together and easy to disperse. No one knows when the phrase began, but in the old capital [of Kaifeng] it was the site where people of worth and commoners were completely uninhibited and without restraint, and it was also the gate through which young wastrels passed to fritter away their time and come to total ruin.

The large theaters inside these tile markets presented a multitude of entertainments. *Dreaming of Splendors Past* has an interesting passage, called "Skills and Arts of the Capital Tile Markets" (*jing wa ji yi*) that provides a list not only of entertainments but of the entertainers who were most noted in the years 1117 to 1125. These included oral storytelling, singing, stick and string puppets, child wrestlers, dances, knife tricks, tumbling, twirling dishes on rods, twirling large pots with the feet, pole climbing, shadow theater, and *zhugongdiao* about foolish young students. According to our narrator, "The audiences of the various theaters never varied because of storms, cold, or heat," but remained constant in number.

The Theater

These entertainment districts drew a mélange of people, from providers of food, clothes-hawkers, parasites, and gamblers to rich young men who frittered away their family's fortune on female entertainers of all types and status. In this netherworld, crowded with sounds and smells of a life of the senses, a group of people might be seen milling around a doorway hung with bright banners announcing the day's plays, seeking entrance into the theaters. A few coppers got one in the door, inside of which one was surrounded by a maelstrom of people sitting on rising tiers of benches that expanded up and beyond the stage like large arcs cut from concentric circles. A description of the urban theater, a song-suite written in the late thirteenth century, gives us a partial view of what it was like. It begins as a parody of a country hick who comes to town to buy some paper items to be burnt in sacrifice.

"Country Cousin Knows Nothing about the Stage"

Du Shanfu

([BANSHE MODE:] To the tune *Shua hai'er*)
When winds are fair, rains are timely, and people secure and happy,
Nothing in the world equals the joy of us farming folk.
Mulberry, silkworms, and all five grains have been reaped to the full,
And the government offices ask for neither corvée nor tax in kind.

So my village asked me to repay our hearts' fervent wish,
And I came to town to buy some paper cash and incense.
I had just struck the main street and was about to cross,
When I saw a paper banner, scribbled all over, hanging down,
And below it a raucous gaggle of people the like I'd never seen before!

Distracted by the advertisements, written in characters that he cannot read, he soon has his coppers snapped up and is prodded into the theater by the shill at the entrance to the theater:

(*Sixth from Coda*)
I saw one among them, with his hand propped on a door made of
    posts,
Shouting out in a loud voice, "Welcome, welcome,
Latecomers, if it's packed there'll be no place to sit."
He said that the first half was a farce skit, "Sporting in the Wind and
    Moon,"
And the back half a playlet, performing the story of the actor Liu
    Shuahe.
He yelled out loud, "Easily the match of any roving players,
An equal in performance is truly hard to find."

In the eye of this human whirlpool was a stage, empty except for wooden benches that held the musicians with their simple but highly effective instruments—a drum, cymbals, wooden castanets, and some winds. As the clanging of the gongs and clacking of wood gained tempo a small troupe of actors—perhaps composed of an official, a desirable young woman, a mother distraught over the fate of her sons, and perhaps two chuckle-headed clowns—came on stage amid the sound of melon seeds cracking, the slurping of tea or wine, conversation, and the hubbub of those still finding their seats. The audience took notice of this motley crew's entrance, of their cadenced voices, witty dialogue, and japes and bawdy skit.

(*Fifth from Coda*)
He got two hundred coppers before he let me through—
In through the door and up a steep wooden slope I went,
Where I saw them sitting layer on layer, level on level, a circling peak.
Raise your head to look—why [the theater] is just like a bell tower!
But look down—it turns into a whirlpool of people.
I saw some girls sitting on a dais—
Now it was no ceremony for welcoming the spirits or parading the
    gods,
But they kept on banging on the drums and rattling their gongs.

(*Fourth from Coda*)
Then out comes a young girl, who made several turns,
Before long, leading out a whole pack.
There was a real bad apple in the bunch:
Dressed in a black kerchief, with a brush stuck through the top,
His whole face was limed white, and then brushed with ink-black
    lines.
I know how he probably got along!
His whole body
Head to toe was covered in a flowered cassock.

(*Third from Coda*)
He recited some poems and lyrics,
Voiced some rhapsodies and songs—
Not half bad!
His tongue ranged over heaven and earth without faltering—
He'd remembered so many clever words and flowery phrases!
Then, as he approached the end
And finished speaking,
He lowered his head and slapped his feet.
The prelude was finished and the main section about to begin.

(*Second from Coda*)
One of them was dressed as Squire Zhang,
And that other guy had changed into Little Brother Two.
They walked and walked and walked, saying they were on their way
    to town,
When they saw a girl standing under an awning.
Now that old guy began to lay plans; he wanted her as a wife.
So he made Little Brother Two try to make the match.
She only wanted beans and grain, rice and wheat,
She never asked about satin cloth or silky gauze.

(*First from Coda*)
First she made the Squire prance forward, but never to dare to mince
    back,
To lift his left foot, yet never dare lift the right,
Now back, now forth—all by her command.
Now the Squire's heart is really steaming,
And he smashes his flesh club on the ground so hard it splits
    in two!
I was so sure that it was his brain bag, his skull, that had cracked,

And that it would certainly give rise to depositions and court
   complaints,
When all of a sudden everyone really started laughing.

(*Coda*)
But I was suffering a bladder full of piss
That was bursting so I couldn't stand it—
Still, I stood as much and lasted as long I could because I really
   wanted to watch,
Just because that bald ass made me laugh so hard!

Here the second half of the performance is missing, unseen by the poor bump-kin who had to heed nature's call. It would have been a proper music drama in which an official, or more likely a young woman, would turn to the audience and, as the percussion swelled, would begin to sing while the onlookers would fall silent, rapt in the appreciation of her voice. This suite was written around the middle of the thirteenth century by an otherwise little-known poet, Du Shanfu (c. 1197–1270) and represents the stage at an early period of development. It shares many features with later stages: it was, except for the musicians, and perhaps a table or chair, empty. These few items served as tables, thrones, beds, and a variety of other uses. They were moved, sometimes while the arias were being sung, by stagehands dressed in subdued colors. There was no attempt at any realistic representation, and actors often broke study to address the audience directly.

The stage jutted out into the audience and was visible from three sides. At the rear were two "ghost door paths" (*guimen dao*) that led back into the green room. All actors entered and exited through these two doors. Despite this simplicity, the stage directions of plays show a wealth of detailed action. Many of these were mimed to songs that described what was going on and symbolic props were frequently used: red handkerchiefs spilled out on stage to represent blood or stick horses were used to replicate cavalry, etc. Only the clown used makeup, a minimal application of white and black for the eyes. Costumes, however, were stipulated for each role type and these were both markers of their role and their social status; the emphasis was clearly on essentialized social and theatrical types. But our information on exactly what costumes actors wore is shaped by context—we have elaborate descriptions of costumes in Ming manuscripts from the imperial palace, but only stage directions and occasional visual representations before that.

One of the best of those images is a famous wall painting, dated 1324, found in a temple in Shanxi (Fig. 1). This shows the actress Zhongduxiu and her troupe. A careful comparison of this with the end of Act 1 of the drama *Zhongli of the Han Leads Lan Caihe to Enlightenment*, which we have translated below,

Fig. 1. Wall painting from Mingyang Wang temple

will provide some detail of the way that the stage was laid out: a cloth backdrop was hung with a valance over it on the outside that could be used to advertise the actors, the play, or the theater. In the mural the valance reads "Zhongduxiu, Actress of the Grand Guild Performed Here." Two other cloth pieces, called "spirit pictures," were hung on the backdrop. In the mural, they show a person brandishing a short sword on the left and a dragon on the right.

The Actors

Eleven people are represented in the mural. The front row shows the actors themselves. Zhongduxiu is in the middle, dressed in the formal clothing of a scholar or official. The two persons on either end of the first row are, judging by the size of their feet, also females who are performing male roles, here either servants or guards of some kind. The gender of the performer and the gender of the character did not have to match, and in fact a major source about actresses from that period indicates that women often performed many types of male roles. The two characters that were usually male were the comic (*jing*) and the second male (*ermo*), a residual artifact of the butt (*fujing*) and jester (*fumo*) of the playlets. Here these roles are on Zhongduxiu's right and left respectively. Musicians are shown in the back—one female with clappers, a person of indeterminate sex playing a flute, and a male drummer. Another male, with a heavy beard, and a female holding the fan complete the ensemble. On close examination all of the beards, except for the drummer's, appear to be false. From the "ghost doors" another female, part of a larger backstage crew, peers out toward the audience.

This mural corresponds closely to what we know about the troupes of early theater. From the painting, and from the play *Zhongli of the Han Leads Lan Caihe to Enlightenment*, we can judge that the average troupe had fifteen to twenty members. These included the actors, musicians, and stagehands. The model of organization was an extended family and actual members could be married or blood relatives, but did not have to be so. Each troupe usually had a single "star" performer who played the leading role, either male or female. The female role type was called a *dan*, and the male, *mo*. We know from contemporary sources that women and men both played either role. As we mentioned above, it was not the gender of the player, but of the role type that dictated the gendered performance on stage. Actresses often played the part of handsome young men as well as women, and vice versa. A single role type, whether male or female, sang all of the arias. This leading performer could change characters and appear in any number of costumes and as a number of characters, but except in cases where the role type dissembled on stage by cross-dressing, the gender of the role type stayed the same. Some plays, in which the *mo* or *dan* played a different role in every act, may well have been written as a vehicle for a specific actor or actress to display his or her versatility. The other major role type was the *jing*, or "comic," who tended to play both comic and malevolent characters. Several other role types were distributed among members of the troupe to fill out the roles with subsets of characters dressed to define a social role or hierarchy, or level of seniority:

	Female (*dan*)	Male (*mo*)	Comic-Villain (*jing*)
Zheng: Lead	*Zhengdan* female lead	*Zhengmo* male lead	——
Wai: Extra	*Waidan* extra female	*Waimo* extra male	*Waijing* extra comic
Er: Second	*Erdan* second female	*Ermo* Second male	*Erjing* second comic
Hua: Flowery	*Huadan* flowery female	——	——
Ruan: Weak	——	*Ruanmo* soft male	——
Lao: Old	*Laodan* old female	*Laomo* old male	——
Tie: Added	*Tiedan* added female	——	*Tiejing* added comic
Chong: Opening	——	*Chongmo* opening male	——

TABLE I. Typical Role Types in Northern Drama (*zaju*)

The names of other ancillary role types are based on actual names or positions, precisely in the way that English denotes "everyman" as "John Doe":

Meixiang	"Apricot Fragrance": a maid
sai Lu yi	"Equal of the Physician of Lu": quack doctor
Zhang Qian	"Zhang Thousand (= John Smith)": a yamen official
Li Wan	"Li Ten-Thousand (= Bill Brown)": a yamen official

by age status:

lai'er	Child
lao bu	A harridan, old hag, madam

or by occupation:

dian xiao'er	Tavern owner, innkeeper
kuaizi	Executioner

or by position:

jiatou	Emperor
gu	Official
kongmu	Clerk
jiangjun	General
cu	Soldier

and so forth.

Formal Features of Northern Drama

Northern drama (*zaju*) is marked by several formal characteristics. As we noted above, songs were normally sung by one role type, and the scripts were designated as "female role type scripts" (*danben*) or "male role type scripts" (*moben*). The play was composed of four individual song suites, each suite comprised of a series of single-stanza songs written to the same musical mode, all arranged according to a predetermined pattern. The suite was always concluded with a coda that marked the formal end of the suite and the act. Sometimes a short sequence of one song and coda, called a "wedge" (*xiezi*), either began the play or was inserted before the second or third act. The musical structure of the play was so clear that originally there was no necessity of written designations for each act in the scripts. Leaving the end of a print line clear when the scene was finished, and jumping to the next line to begin the next, however, carefully denoted scenes within each act. Later, Ming editors made formal breaks between each of the four (rarely five) distinctly numbered acts, numbered each act, and identified the wedge as well. They also added an entry and exit scene for each act. The musical modes chosen for each of the acts was a matter of convention, but readers of this volume will note that virtually all first acts begin with the *xianlü* mode, and that there is a strong preference for *shuangdiao* mode in the fourth act. Each suite was written to the same rhyme, and the sequence of songs within each suite, which could run to some length (but was usually eight to twelve songs), was conventional but not absolutely regular. So, the reader will notice that there are some similarities in the arrangement of song titles within the suites of each act to the same mode, but that the sequence varies from play to play. Earlier editions will have shorter fourth acts than later editions. At the end of some plays a "dispersal" scene is noted, which was a short postlude the actors presented as the audience left. These were sometimes used as celebratory moments, as in the play below, *Rescriptor-in-Waiting Bao Thrice Investigates the Butterfly Dream*, where the troupe turns to deliver a paean to the court.

Editions and Social Background

It is impossible to discuss the social background of these dramas without reference to the history of editions. The two-hundred-plus Yuan and early Ming Northern dramas that are extant stem from a variety of sources: early commercial editions, private vanity editions from a Ming prince, manuscript texts from the Ming imperial court, later commercial texts based on those manuscripts, and highly-edited editions from the very late Ming. This history not only reflects a three-hundred-year movement through time, but also one upward in the social register. While the early texts stem directly from production scripts, later ones are essentially closet dramas—reading editions heavily subject to the ideology of high culture, especially Confucianism, in their rewriting by sixteenth and seventeenth century editors. Thus, to discuss the society and culture they reflect means referring to a complicated calculus of time, social register, intended audience, and background of the editors.

The Earliest Period

The earliest stratum of text consists of thirty independent Yuan printings of Northern comedies that have been grouped together since the eighteenth century and become known by the collective title of "thirty *zaju* in Yuan editions" (*Yuankan zaju sanshi zhong*). As a set of texts stored together, they can be traced back to the library of a Ming scholar, bibliophile, and dramatist, Li Kaixian (1502–68). The plays subsequently passed from his hands through those of other private collectors until they wound up in the library of the famous bibliophile and scholar Luo Zhenyu (1866–1940), who made them available to his protégé Wang Guowei (1877–1927), the first modern historian of Yuan drama. Following the establishment of the Chinese Republic in 1911, Luo and Wang spent some years in Japan, where a new generation of sinologists actively pursued the study of Chinese fiction and drama. The plays were loaned to Kyoto University, which published them in 1915 in an attractive but flawed woodblock facsimile edition (despite the fact that one of the most renowned specialist woodblock cutters was brought over from China for the job). The original thirty plays were later donated to the newly established Peiping Library and are now held by the Beijing National Library. They have been photolithographically reprinted in several modern collections, and at least three modern monographs have been devoted to their collation.

Although the genre of *zaju* is primarily associated with the large cities of Northern China, only four of the texts claim to have been printed in Dadu (present-day Beijing), the capital of the Yuan. Almost a double number of plays (seven) claim to derive from Hangzhou, the former capital of the Southern Song capital and then one of the major printing centers of China. Moreover, as the center of the Yuan administration of the former Southern Song territories, it also housed a large population of northerners in the first half of the fourteenth century, who favored their own regional form of drama over local drama in the south. While the majority of plays carry no indication concerning the place of printing, it seems plausible to assume that in majority these plays stem from Hangzhou too. Some texts advertise themselves as *xinkan* (newly printed); others carry the legend *xinbian* (newly composed). Either phrase can refer either to an original work or a revised edition. The physical appearance of the woodblock printings reflects a craftsmanship that ranges from good to very poor. The orthography is that common to other Yuan texts, although the quality of the printing can actually change in a significant way even within a single edition. As a body, there is a remarkable variety among the texts in terms of the number and clarity of stage directions, the use of characters for their sound, rather than their meaning, and the quality of printing. These remain difficult texts to decipher, and indeed none of the modern transcriptions and studies agree on what every written character in the text means.

None of the *Yuankan* plays bears an attribution of authorship. All attempts to assign authorship to these plays is done by scholars and bibliophiles on the basis of later editions that bear an author's name, through musical formularies, or through bibliographies. Some of the thirty plays in Yuan editions are not found in later sources; in some other cases the titles as found in the Yuan editions and those in these catalogues are not fully identical, making any identification tentative. The lack of ascribed authorship in the earliest texts surely indicates that plays were not yet conceived of as belonging to an authorial identity in the same way that other forms of literature were. This suggests that, like other performance texts, they were embedded in a matrix of corporate textual negotiations and live production. As such, they were documents from a highly fluid tradition and any single printed edition captured only a single moment in a mutable and living tradition of performance. Such written texts may be seen as a static snapshot in a long process of evolution, not as particular moment of creation *ab nihilo.*

The printed plays are of two kinds: five of the thirty plays only consist of the four suites of arias of the lead performer and have no (or extremely few) appended "plot prompts" (*guanmu*), which in the context of the *Yuankan* texts mean stage directions and cue lines. The other twenty-five plays not only present the arias but also print stage directions, cue lines, and some incidental prose dialogue. Despite the fact that these fuller editions contain no prose dialogue for the secondary characters in the play, some of them still claim to be *diben* (full editions) or *zuben* (complete editions), a designation we take to refer to the fact that they reproduce the arias in their entirety. Modern scholars, however, used to editions that have been prepared for reading and that provide full dialogue for all characters, have strangely found these editions "defective" and have wondered in print why the plays were printed in such a format. The most persuasive explanation is that the plays were not primarily printed for the benefit of performers or readers but for the benefit of listeners. Many members of the audience, then as now, may have had trouble following the dense lyrics of the arias as sung in performance. In contemporary China it is normal practice when traditional plays are performed to project the text of the arias alongside or over the stage. These texts may have performed the same function for listeners in the urban theater of the early capitals. This would also explain why so many more texts were printed in Hangzhou than in Dadu: while Hangzhou may have been a minor center of *zaju* performance, its audience rarely had a full command of the Northern dialect in which the plays were composed and performed. In order to provide the audience with a text of the arias, the printers made use of the most complete texts at their disposal—the role text of the male lead or female lead: "female texts" (*danben*) or "male texts" (*moben*), scripts written for a single dramatic lead. A close look at the stage directions will confirm this. For instance, the following is from the opening passage of *A Beauty Pining in Her Boudoir: The Pavilion for Praying to the Moon*:

> After WANG ZHEN *and* MOTHER *have entered and spoken — after being summoned — and after you enter dressed as* WANG RUILAN *together with* MEIXIANG *— act out greeting* WANG ZHEN. *After* WANG ZHEN *has spoken — act out parting, emotionally. Act out offering the cup:* Father, you are so old. Please be careful on your trip. *After* WANG ZHEN *speaks — act out wiping away your tears:*

This short passage reflects the grammatical structure of the stage directions, in which a moderate imperative follows clauses marked by the particle for completed action, indicating that these directions are written only for the actor or actress who is going to play the female lead. Spoken lines are cue lines for the arias that follow; above, the cue line "Father, you are so old. Please be careful on your trip" leads into a song of parting between father and daughter:

> Rolling up the earth, a wild wind blows frontier sands;
> Sunlit in the sparse wood, evening crows caw.
> I offer to you this cup of "flowing sunset" filled to overflowing.
> If I could but detain you half a moment—
> For, in a moment's space we will be far apart, each at an edge of
>   heaven.
>
> (*Reprise*)
> About to depart, your whip urges on the skinny nag.

After WANG ZHEN *has spoken:*

> What you will see are "white bones strewn like hemp across the
>   Central Plain."
> Even though, during this campaign,
> You bear the burden of "heaven collapsing and earth crumbling
>   away,"
> You must think of us, mother and daughter, and come home soon.

No other characters are given speaking lines in the plays, and no stage directions are written for them. Such stage directions that mention other players are clearly for the convenience of the lead role: they provide the sequence and types of other actors' performances. This allows the lead role to keep track of stage appearances, to enter at the correct moment, and to properly time his or her performance. This practice accurately reflects what we know of the structure of early acting troupes, which, although comprising a "family" of actors, were usually supported by a single star performer. Other members of the acting troupe—the secondary characters, the comic, etc.—probably had only fixed scenes to perform, or smaller parts of dialogue that could be easily memorized. The arias represented different problems for the lead singer—in addition to being a complicated mixture of linguistic register and metrical requirements, they had to be sung, not spoken. Other performances on stage were easier to manage: they were stock routines or set speeches. Even fuller texts from the later period that write out all monologue and dialogue in fact often note the presentation of many of these stock routines only in stage directions, for instance, "here the comic and the clown perform the skit of the 'Battling Quacks.'" It is only texts that, intended for performance at court during the Ming, had to be inspected by the court censors prior to performance, that fully write out all of the spoken parts (including the repetition of information) and routines.

There can be little doubt, then, that the early texts had close ties to performance and represent works of a completely different nature than dramas found in the later collections. One indication of this is that, of the sixteen plays that are known in more than one edition, the *Yuankan* text, with a few exceptions, will always have a significantly larger number of arias when compared with their later counterparts. The performance of the lead singer was more substantially and proportionally highlighted.

As fragmentary as these plays are, they represent an earlier tradition of textual production, and are artifacts of a time before drama had passed through the hands of court or literati editors. These texts were not subject to an ideological rewrite in order to make them conform to the Confucian norms and values of the elite and, since they appealed to a broad spectrum of Yuan society from high to low, they certainly reflect popular culture of their time. They are more outspoken in their representation of what we might term the "common" world— a world of crime, sex, violence, and love, in which the latitudes of behavior are quite wide. The language is more directly citical and less squeamish about portraying violence in politics and the corruptibility of humans.

In those cases in which the same play can be found in both the *Yuankan* and later texts, one can very clearly see the differences between early editions and those of the late Ming. One minor difference is the consistent inclusion and careful marking in later plays of so-called "padding words" (*chenzi*) in arias. It would, of course, be wrong to automatically assume that these *chenzi* were not a feature of earlier performances; they were simply not written into the script. A much more major difference in later texts is the extensive increase of the texts for the secondary characters, and this increase substantially fleshes out their part. This change in textual format may be seen as a product of two converging phenomena: the first was the collection and production of texts at the Ming imperial (or provincial royal) court; the second, the pressures brought to bear as plays were moved off the stage and onto the desk.

Plays by a Ming Prince

Zhu Youdun (1398–1439), also known as the Exemplary Prince of Zhou, was a grandson of the founding emperor of the Ming. He lived the majority of his life in his family's hereditary princely estate in Kaifeng, except for a brief period of exile in Yunnan, because of the internecine fighting in the royal family. He lived for the most part a life of extraordinary luxury, but also one beset by the ever-present possibility of a reversal of fortune due to shifting alliances among the emperors' sons, grandsons, and cousins. He was a man of wide interests and accomplishments: he wrote poetry in several forms, composed music, painted, and practiced calligraphy. He was also a great fan of peonies, planting thousands of them in his residence and making them constant topics of his poems, plays, and paintings.

Zhu wrote and personally published thirty-one plays that can be divided roughly into two groups. The first are those that were written to celebrate birthdays or other festive events in the palace. As can be expected from plays about birthdays and anniversaries, these placed the mythology of Daoism (and sometimes Buddhism) in the foreground, emphasizing the pursuit of immortality on the one hand and the ephemeral nature of physical existence on the other. These were celebratory hothouse plays that required a large cast and elaborate costumes. They were extravagant productions, short on plot and playing free and easy with the strict rules of Northern drama. The one-singer rule was often broken by actors singing in duet or in groups, and by the staging of elaborate dances. A far more interesting group of plays are those centered squarely in the secular world and dealing with the mundane, for instance prostitutes, merchants, or bandits (two of which we have translated in this volume).

Zhu's plays are the first known to have contained both the texts of songs as well as the prose dialogue. He was quite aware of the novelty of this publishing innovation and every title of his thirty-one plays is followed by the term "with complete dialogue" (*quanbin*). His proud statement fudges a bit, however, since the dramas do not contain the entire spoken text. For instance each stage entry of a major character usually involves a short repetition of action to that point, as a way of bringing new arrivals up to speed. These are simply marked in the text by two shorthand characters meaning "so on and so forth" (*yunyun*). Stock jester-and-butt comic scenes, specialties of secondary roles, are simply noted, "perform X skit here." This is a practice that would be followed by later commercial editions. Still, the editions are the only early dramas known to have stemmed from the author's hand as he intended and, since they provide a relatively complete text, they are a rare source for the study of staging and performance.

Li Kaixian and the *Revised Plays by Yuan Masters*

Near the end of his life Li Kaixian sponsored the publication of a collection of *zaju* entitled *Revised Plays by Yuan Masters* (*Gaiding Yuanxian chuanqi*). Six of the printed sixteen *zaju* survive. Inaccessible for most of the twentieth century, these plays have been rediscovered and reprinted in recent years. Four of the six feature an emperor as one of its characters despite the fact that the portrayal on stage of an emperor had been repeatedly forbidden in the early decades of the Ming. A comparison of one play that has been preserved both as one of the "thirty *zaju* in Yuan editions" and as one of the extant plays from *Revised Plays by Yuan Masters* strongly suggests that at least some of the plays in *Revised Plays* had been edited on the basis of editions from the Yuan. If so, the plays in *Revised Plays* would provide us with editions of Yuan plays by Ming editors that, unlike those to be mentioned below, had not passed through the imperial palace of the Ming. It would appear that Li Kaixian and his collaborators kept all the arias from the original editions, and facilitated reading by providing a simple dialogue to guide the reader, since those dialogues were missing in the lead actor scripts of the "thirty Yuan editions." As a result, when compared with other edited Ming texts, the plays in *Revised Plays* tend to have more arias in each suite and a less developed dialogue than the plays revised to be performed in the palace. Li Kaixian's editions of *zaju* were often reprinted in later collections. Of the two plays on emperors that we have included in our selection, Bai Pu's *Rain on the Wutong Tree* represents the *Revised Plays*, and the edition of Ma Zhiyuan's *A Lone Goose in Autumn over the Palaces of Han* we have used also probably derives from the editions from Li Kaixian's enterprise.

Palace Editions and Their Printed Offshoots:
Zaju New and Ancient Copied and Collated in the Maiwang Studio

Between 1612 and 1617, a little-known scholar from Jiangsu, Zhao Qimei (1553–1624), collected in his studio the *Maiwang guan*, hundreds of editions of *zaju* from a variety of sources. They included manuscripts from the Ming palace that had been used in either the Office of Drum and Bell (*Zhonggu si*) or the Court Entertainment Bureau (*Jiaofang si*) and a variety of printed editions from the late sixteenth and early seventeenth centuries. The original number of plays contained in his collection is unknown. Upon his death, his library, which contained the dramas, passed into the hands of a fellow scholar Qian Qianyi (1582–1664), who was also a renowned book collector. His libraries unfortunately fell victim to fires, but he managed to pass along to his grandson, Qian Zeng, some 340 plays. Qian Zeng (1629–1701) stored these dramatic texts in his library, which was known as the Yeshi Garden. He scrupulously listed the titles of these plays in his library catalogue, and the collection of dramas became known through time as "Northern Dramas New and Ancient Long Stored in the Yeshi Garden" (*Yeshi yuan jiuzang gujin zaju*). They later passed through other collectors' hands until rediscovered in Shanghai by the modern scholar Zheng Zhenduo (1898–1958) and others in 1938. Sadly, only 242 plays remained, two of which are duplicated in different editions. Of the 240 titles, 105 are attributed to Yuan or late Yuan–early Ming playwrights, and the other 135 to dramatists of the Ming. Seventy of these dramas are in woodblock editions: fifteen in *The Anthology of Northern Dramas New and Ancient* (*Gujin zaju xuan*) by a certain Xijizi and fifty-five from the *Zaju from the Hands of Famous Authors* (*Gu mingjia zaju*), which is discussed below. The other 172 plays are in manuscript editions: 157 from the Ming palace and 15 from the hand of a certain Yu Xiaogu from Shandong.

Nearly all of these plays have undergone editing and annotation at the hand of Zhao Qimei, who collated the palace editions, or collated printed text against the palace manuscripts. Of these texts, 120 have appended lists of props, including weapons, costumes, masks, beards, etc., that are used in each act (called *quanguan*). Since these were originally appended to the palace editions, it gives us an excellent idea of how players were costumed during the Ming, but it also may reflect the culmination of a tradition that stretches back into the earlier dynasty.

These plays were originally centralized at the Ming court, where they were stored in the imperial archives (*neifu*), which was essentially a lending library for court performances. Eventually, these plays were copied out and sent out to the imperial princes (like Zhu Youdun), and from there they found their way into the hands of literati and aficionados. Eventually printers succeeded in laying hold of them, regularized their format, carved them on blocks, and brought new printings to the commercial market. Evidence clearly shows that virtually all of the commercial editions of the late Ming, with the possible exception of the *zaju* printed by Li Kaixian as the *Revised Plays*, are either based on or owe a substantial debt to the palace editions.

The manuscript editions completely reproduce every stage direction and every bit of dialogue. This complete scripting of performance points to a radically different acting group than the family troupes that staffed the commercial theater in the Yuan. While the family companies were organized around a single star for whom the texts were primarily written, every actor of the court troupes was the best available for each particular role. In such an environment, each person would surely demand an equal amount of stage time, and this resulted in the consequent diminution of the lead singer's role.

While the extensive dialogues of subcharacters that mark the palace editions are pared down and some of the redundancies of plot restatements are omitted in the commercially printed collections based on palace manuscripts, they still reflect a tendency toward completeness, and the dialogue is written out for each character. Moreover, the late Ming commercial editions regularize the printing format of drama and make changes to earlier texts. For instance the *Yuankan* plays and those by Zhu Youdun do not divide the play into discrete acts (*zhe*), which are otherwise clearly marked by the musical structure of the arias. Late Ming editions carefully separated the drama into "acts" (*zhe*), but in the process they did away with a practice of earlier editions, which was to leave the end of a line blank when an individual scene was concluded. They do, however, continue the convention of putting sung text in larger characters and spoken text in smaller graphs. Arias are written in larger size characters and individual lines start at the top of the page. Spoken text is written out in smaller characters and dropped a two-character space below the top of the page. In one respect, this regularization was the logical conclusion of the practice begun by Zhu Youdun, who was the first to carefully separate sung and spoken passages. But it also marks the move of dramatic text from the stage (where scene division is important) to the desk: delineated acts form a logical unit of text and the extensive stage directions serve the reader as rhetorical narrative guides. The regularization of format was a necessity brought about by reading practices, not performance.

Zaju from the Hands of Famous Authors (Gu mingjia zaju)

Published in 1588, this work is noted as edited by the "Immortal Scribe of Yuyang" (*Yuyang xianshi*). The seal of *Yuyang xianshi* is found imprinted on another edition of dramas, one edited by Wang Jide (d. 1623), and this has led some scholars to attribute this edition to Wang, a famous critic and playwright. Others attribute the collection to a certain Chen Yujiao (1544–1611). Still others suggest that the compiler may have simply been a book dealer who used the name *Yuyang xianshi* as a false attribution to spur sales. The collection first appeared as two separate issues, the *Zaju from the Hands of Famous Authors* (*Gu mingjia zaju*), which contained forty plays and the *Newly Supplemented Zaju from the Hands of Famous Authors* (*Xinxu gu mingjia zaju*), which probably contained another forty. Of these eighty plays, sixty-five are still extant: fifty-five in the *Maiwang Studio* collection, and thirteen found in fragments of the collection that exist outside of the *Maiwang Studio* collection (three plays are duplicate). Other sixteenth- and seventeenth-century collections (see below) show considerable rewriting at the hands of literati editors, who changed the plays to accord with the aesthetics of lyric poetry and the newly risen *chuanqi* drama form. But the *Gu mingjia* edition clearly is more conservative in its editorial conventions and in making changes to language and structure, which suggests that it was probably an edition produced for the popular reading market.

Zang Maoxun and the *Yuanqu xuan*

No anthology of *zaju* has been more influential than Zang Maoxun's (1550–1620) *Selection of Yuan Plays* (*Yuanqu xuan*), also known by its alternate title as *One Hundred Plays by Yuan Authors* (*Yuanren baizhong qu*). Published in two installments in 1615–16, it quickly supplanted all earlier anthologies and for centuries informed the expectations of readers and scholars about what, precisely, a *zaju* printed edition should look like. Even today, after the discovery of a variety of other—and quite different—editions, it is the most commonly used collection of early *zaju*. It is, to some extent, unfortunate that his edition of the plays are so readily accepted as authentic versions since Zang introduced into the texts a different aesthetic and a different language, rewriting both the arias and the plain speech in the text to conform to contemporary dramatic practice and language and to accommodate the tastes of demanding upper-class readers.

Zang Maoxun came from Changxing, in the most northern reaches of modern Zhejiang, on the southwestern shore of Lake Taihu. His was a well-established local literati family, related by marriage to some of the most prestigious families of the realm. Zang's father, Zang Jinfang, obtained the Advanced Scholar degree in 1543 and occupied a variety of official positions in the capital at Beijing and in the provinces before passing away in 1568. Zang Maoxun spent the first few years of his life in the capital, but returned in his twenties to Changxing, where he studied for the examinations. He passed the local examination in 1573 and, after two unsuccessful attempts, passed the Advanced Scholar examination (barely) in 1580. He served briefly as Instructor in the prefectural school at Jingzhou and as a District Magistrate of Yiling before being promoted to Erudite in the National University. In Nanjing, his scandalous lifestyle and preference for young boys came under attack by the Director of the National University, who asked via memorial to have Zang removed. Zang was cashiered and returned to Changxing, where he retired from any further official service.

He spent the rest of his life traveling constantly through the Jiangnan region, keeping in touch with his many friends, among whom were such eminent dramatists as Tang Xianzu (1550–1616), author of *The Peony Pavilion*. In his later years, he turned to writing and publishing for profit to supplement the income from his family's estate. He published two large anthologies of early poetry and versions of Southern-style plays he revised (including those by Tang), but he gained fame primarily through his publication of *A Selection of Yuan Plays*. His own writings were collected shortly after his death as the *Collection of Fubao Hall* (*Fubao tang ji*). Some of the letters in that collection contain a meager amount of information on his publishing and collecting activities.

Unlike many of his contemporaries in the drama publishing business, Zang was not a dramatist. No plays are attributed to him, but he was very involved in the contemporary drama scene as a critic, editor, and publisher. The core of his critical writing on drama is found in the two prefaces he wrote for his *Yuanqu xuan*. There, he betrays a low opinion of the Southern drama that was popular in his time because it had strayed so far from its origins in the Yuan. As he said, "Now Southern plays fill the world and everyone calls himself 'an author'; yet they do not understand how far they are from Yuan playwrights." His primary objection was that too many plays were written by "famous writers" (*mingjia*) rather than by "professionals" (*hangjia*), and these famous writers were far more concerned with euphuistic rhetoric than with stagecraft and performance. The professional to Zang was not merely an actor, but a literatus with a deep understanding of the theatrical métier and some practical experience in acting. Most of all, the professional understood that early *zaju* provided the model and inspiration for writing arias. The constituents of this model were that "sentiment and language must accord in a subtle way with character and situation," that "plots had to be tight and integral," and that "poetic prosody and musical modes have to match." In order to present proper examples of these features, Zang Maoxun presented an anthology of superior *zaju*—heavily edited by him—to exemplify the criteria. As noted below, there is a certain irony to this stance, considering the extent of his changes to the literary style of plays.

The texts for his anthology were culled from *zaju* that were in the possession of his family, were available in contemporary commercial editions, or were from a private collection of more than two hundred manuscript editions. Zang borrowed this latter group in 1613 in Macheng (in the northeast corner of Hubei) from a hereditary military officer with the Brocade Guard in the capital. His collection was based on manuscript editions held in the eunuch agency in charge of theatrical entertainments in the imperial palace. Thus, while there may be some instances where Zang had access to earlier editions, it appears that the overwhelming majority of his texts derive directly or indirectly from stage versions of *zaju* used in the imperial palace during the Ming. He did not simply print the plays as he found them, but subjected them to extensive revisions that, in his own words, "removed superfluous verbiage and altered them on the basis of my own idea of what had been written incorrectly, taking pride in my grasp of the superior wisdom of the Yuan authors." Almost from the time that the *Selection of Yuan Plays* appeared, the liberties he took with texts have been subject to heavy criticism.

However, it is easy to see why Zang Maoxun's anthology immediately came to dominate the market. Earlier editions, printed during the Wanli period (1573–1619), were often of very poor quality. Zang offered his fellow Jiangnan literati a superior production that surpassed all of its predecessors both in scale and quality of format. His one hundred plays, for the most part, are the finest quality plays, and represented well the products of the "four great masters of Yuan *zaju*" (*Yuan zaju si da jia*), Guan Hanqing, Zheng Guangzu, Ma Zhiyuan, and Bai Pu. The plays themselves were prefaced by an extensive anthology of earlier writing on dramatic criticism, and each play was begun with a two- or four-block woodcut illustration of the highest quality. The text of each play has been carefully collated and both dialogue and songs were presented in a large, neat, and easily readable type. Sound glosses were provided for characters that were unknown to Southern readers, or that had uncommon pronunciations. Internal contradictions were removed from the plot and offenses against correct literary taste, such as incorrect allusions and faulty parallelisms, were corrected. He turned contemporary stage versions of early *zaju* into perfect reading materials for sophisticated gentlemen and educated womenfolk. Because of the high readability of the texts of *zaju* edited by Zang for his *Yuanqu xuan*, the text has had many admirers through the centuries, and it has been accepted without question as the preferred text for literary readings. However, after the appearance and publication of other editions, including earlier works from the Yuan, his arbitrary changes have come under increasing attack in scholarship.

For a balanced evaluation of the extent and nature of the changes introduced by Zang Maoxun, we must take a closer look at his actual editorial practice. This is possible now, since eighty-five of the plays in the *Yuanqu xuan* exist in other printed or manuscript versions. Zang made several important types of changes in order to standardize all of his texts. He regularized editorial conventions by restoring the separation of dialogue and arias through the use of different text sizes. He also divided the plays into acts and wedges. He added dialogue or stage directions that appeared to him to be incomplete in other editions, he changed tune titles that were incorrect, incomplete, or which used an uncommon variant for their name. He also changed what he perceived to be scribal errors. He also altered the plots in many plays to bring about a tighter resolution, resulting in an extraordinary expansion of the fourth acts: of the 222 arias that Zang himself composed and added to the texts, 116 are added to the fourth act. This betrays, ironically, the influence of contemporary Southern drama, which conventionally concluded with a grand reunion scene. Zang also retouched many of the arias, effecting changes in the structure of the *qu* form to make it more closely resemble the tradition of *ci*-lyric writing that was favored by literati writers. For instance, there are many places in earlier versions that can freely employ either quasi-parallel or non-parallel lines in the arias. In some cases it was even stipulated that parallelism was *not* to be used. Zang freely altered all of these and changed all of them to strict parallel couplets. He also changed the rhyme patterns of the lyrics, winnowing out some older mistakes, but also forcing passages in which rhyme was either unnecessary or optional into rhymed lines. He also cut out a sizable number of songs from the plays.

Zang fleshed out the dialogue of the plays, the linguistic mortar between the bricks of the arias. In doing so, he created a better context for the songs, but he also replaced older colloquial and grammatical forms with those of his own time. This is roughly equivalent to replacing the words of Renaissance English drama with those of the nineteenth century. In making these changes, Zang may have been emboldened by his belief that Yuan dynasty authors only wrote the song lyrics, and that actors improvised the dialogue. He may also have acted on his mistaken assumption that the plays had been written as examination assignments for the Advanced Scholar degree, with the result that authors ran out of time and inspiration after the third act, leaving Act 4 flaccid and incomplete.

His changes were not always purely textual in nature and also affected the values embodied in the plays and their meaning. The palace editions of the plays, upon which practically all commercial editions of the Ming are based, had already removed much of the blatant violence, outspoken social criticism, and bawdy vitality of the Yuan dynasty texts, but Zang went a step further in emphasizing Confucian values as the source for action and de-emphasizing greed and lust as human motivation. He wrote into the plays the ideal values of the dominant literary culture, which may account for the success of his anthology as much as its beautiful textual format and literary enhancements. More importantly, he presented a canonical version of readable texts that were identified as works by individual authors. This accorded with the time-honored belief in Chinese literature that one could experience both the man and his time through his writing. Thus his texts bolstered the artifice that his editions allowed one to understand the writer's personal reaction to specific social and political situations. This fact, as much as the literary embellishments, turned the plays from scripts that originally were the product of collective social, cultural, and theatrical energies into reading literature that supposedly mirrored an individual psyche.

Yuan plays (Anon)	c. 1300–1350	30 plays
Zhu Youdun	c. 1420–1439	31
Revised Plays by Yuan Masters (Li Kaixian)	c. 1540–1560	16
Maiwang Editions (Zhao Qimei)	1612–1617	242
Northern Dramas New and Ancient	c. 1580–1610	15
Northern Dramas from the Hands of Famous Authors	1588	55
Imperial Palace manuscripts	c. 1400–1600	172
Yu Xiaogu manuscripts	15	
A Selection of Yuan Plays (Zang Maoxun)	1615–16	100

Table 2. Sources and Dates of Production for Editions Used

Southern Drama from the *Grand Canon of the Reign of Perpetual Joy*

In this anthology we have included one play, *Little Butcher Sun*, that belongs to a drama genre that in Chinese is most commonly designated as "Southern plays" (*nanxi*) or "written-out plays" (*xiwen*). The major difference between Northern *zaju* and Southern *xiwen* is that whereas in the former genre all the arias are assigned to one singer, in the latter all actors have singing roles. The tunes employed in Southern plays were popular Southern songs and were not organized into suites according to mode as in *zaju*. In general, Southern plays are of much greater length than *zaju*, severely limiting the possibility to include full plays in an anthology like this one.

Southern plays began as regional drama in the coastal areas of Eastern Zhejiang and then spread to the capital of Lin'an and beyond. In a work entitled *Trivial Talks (Weitan)*, Zhu Yunming (1460–1525) remarked,

> *Nanxi* appeared after the Xuanhe reign era of the Northern Song (1119–25), around the time of the "Southern Crossing" (c. 1125–26),[2] and it is designated as "Wenzhou comedy." I have seen old official documents and there was an official proscription by Zhao Hongfu that listed several titles, like *Chaste Maiden Zhao and Cai the Second Esquire (Zhao Zhennü Cai Erlang)* and others; but in fact there were not many.

Zhao Hongfu, otherwise an obscure person, was a lateral cousin of the emperor Guangzong, Zhao Dun, who ruled from 1190 to 1195. The simple fact that he issued such a proclamation banning performance of *nanxi* clearly indicates just how popular the form had become by the end of the twelfth century. Xu Wei (1521–93), the great Ming scholar and dramatist, also wrote in his work on theater, *A Sequential Record of Southern Lyrics (Nanci xulu)*,

> *Nanxi* began in the reign of Emperor Guangzong of the Song, and its first successes were those plays by Yongjia playwrights such as *Chaste Maiden Zhao* and [*The Heartbreaker*] *Wang Kui*. Some people say that it was already spreading everywhere during the Xuanhe reign period and actually reached its high point during the "Southern Crossing."

If we take these two late passages together (and trust them), we can construe that *nanxi* was created around 1120 in Wenzhou (i.e., the coastal area of modern Zhejiang) and that it had reached the capital of Lin'an (modern Hangzhou) by the 1190s. It then became the prevalent form over a wide range of Zhejiang and Fujian. By the end of the Southern Song (1276) it had even spread to Jiangxi, as witnessed by Liu Xun's (1240–1319) remarks in his "Biography of the Lyric Poet Wu Yongzhang": "By the Xianchun reign period (1265–75), Yongjia comedy (*Yongjia zaju*) had appeared. Vile youths altered [the genre]; thereafter lascivious singing became popular and 'correct sounds' ceased." Liu

---

2. When the Jurchen destroyed the Northern Song and the seat of government moved to the south.

Yiqing repeated this charge of lewdness in the semi-historical text, *Affairs from Qiantang* (*Qiantang yishi*), where the "written-out play on Wang Kui" appears in a list of plays that "teach lasciviousness" (*xiwen huiyin*). We may assume that Southern plays continued to flourish in China south of the Huai river during the Yuan, despite an almost total silence of our sources, which deal mostly with the more prestigious genre of *zaju*. While *zaju* made inroads into the South following the Mongol conquest of the area, it probably did not spread widely beyond major urban centers such as Hangzhou, where it may have primarily appealed to a large community of Northerners. It is also clear that Southern plays borrowed heavily from *zaju* when it came to plots, and some Southern plays experimented with the inclusion of Northern songs and song suites.

From various sources, we are able to deduce the titles of some 182 titles of known early *nanxi*, but almost none of these survive. A few preserved plays have survived in heavily revised editions from the sixteenth century, and some fifteenth-century printed editions have been unearthed in recent archaeological excavations. Three plays have been preserved in a single stray volume of the *Grand Canon of the Reign of Perpetual Joy* (*Yongle dadian*), a huge imperial compilation completed in 1407 of which only a limited number of volumes have survived the ravages of time, fire, and looting. These three plays are:

Zhang Xie zhuang yuan	*Top Scholar Zhang Xie*
Huanmen zidi cuoli shen	*A Playboy from a Noble House Opts for the Wrong Career*
Xiao Suntu	*Little Butcher Sun*

These three plays are known collectively as "three written-out plays from the *Grand Canon of the Reign of Perpetual Joy*" (*Yongle dadian xiwen sanzhong*). One among the three, *Top Scholar Zhang Xie*, is conventionally dated to the late Southern Song, although there is no hard evidence of its existence prior to 1407. The others are clearly Yuan. These three plays are the product of corporate authorship, produced by "talents" (*cairen*) of "writing societies" (*shuhui*). *Top Scholar Zhang* was written by the "Writing Society of the Nine Hills" (*jiushan shuhui*). *A Playboy from a Noble House* is noted as "newly compiled by talents of old Hangzhou" (*gu Hang cairen xinbian*). And *Little Butcher Sun* is a product of the "writing society of old Hangzhou" (*gu Hang shuhui*). These three plays together formed the last chapter of the large section of the *Yongle dadian* devoted to "written-out plays." It is not clear, however, to what extent they are representative of the genre in the fourteenth century, since it would appear from the still-extant table of contents that the average Southern play was much longer than any of these, occupying by themselves a single chapter.

The renowned scholar, educator, and painter Ye Gongchuo (1880–1968) discovered the volume that contains these plays in 1920 in a London second-hand bookshop. The plays were photomechanically reproduced in 1954 in the first series of the *Compendium of Old Editions of Drama* (*Guben xiqu congkan*). On each page are eight columns of text with two lines within each column. Smaller characters are used for the stage directions and larger characters for both spoken and sung lines.

As we can see from this short history of the editions, each set of plays has to be understood as a product of a particular place, a particular time, and a particular provenance. The earliest texts clearly stemmed from the theater itself and reflect the physical and social space that theater occupied. Products of an urban society, corporate and accretive in nature, their themes, language, and staging were tightly bound to the audience they served. As plays passed through the Ming palace, certain elements were removed. It was forbidden, for instance, to stage plays about emperors or about Confucius. Other elements were allowed to remain, and in the printed editions that stem from these scripts, we still find desire for sex, wealth, and power as motivating factors in plot development and characterization, although in diminished form. But the picture is much more complicated. While Northern drama was originally a product of the urban commercial stage, the second part of the thirteenth century witnessed a rise in textual production. This period coincided partly with the Mongol invasions and the abrogation of the civil service examinations, for which young scholars prepared themselves as the avenue to political and social success. It has often been argued that upon the suspension of the examinations, writers now saw writing not as a tool for social advancement through bureaucratic ranks, but something that could gain them economic and cultural capital. The standard interpretation by twentieth-century scholars of drama is that writers turned to such forms of writing, which had earlier been despised as low-brow, to vent their frustration at the depreciation of their social status caused by the suspension of the examinations as the primary route to official and scholarly success. One may well wonder, however, whether such a political explanation for the rise of drama is tenable. More likely is that the emergence of *zaju* as a new form in the urban theaters of Northern China may well have created an urgent need for scripts, and the demands to create long rhymed sets of songs were far beyond the powers of improvisation of even the most experienced actor or actress. Most of the successful playwrights were located in one of the few major cities in Northern China, and each of them wrote a substantial number of plays, of which in each case only a small number has been preserved. The authors of these plays are best seen as professional playwrights, working in close cooperation with the urban theater. Guan Hanqing, who was credited with sixty-seven plays and who was retrospectively proclaimed the "originator of *zaju*," is a good case in point. He held only minor office, and was involved not only with writing, but also with one of the best-known actresses of the time, as her paramour. Most likely he and others wrote on a commercial basis, very much like the prolific professional playwrights of Elizabethan London. Other authors seem to have written primarily for court production of *zaju*, and eventually the new form of drama may have even become a medium of self-expression—but such authors who wrote for these non-commercial venues usually are credited with a much smaller oeuvre than those who wrote for the urban theater. Court playwrights would get a new stimulus in the early decades of the Ming when Northern drama was adopted as the primary form of court drama. At this distance in time it is difficult to determine any substantial motive for writing the plays and all we can say is that some brilliant young men jumped at the opportunity provided by the needs of the theater, and as good playwrights used their work to reflect on their own society.

Two major points in the three-hundred-year history of textual production of Northern drama are visible in the texts that remain. The first is the break between the original Yuan editions and all those that follow. Early plays from the urban stage were conceived and executed by people who were intimately familiar with the social register of the characters they represented on stage. But, as educated writers, or Ming princes, began to write drama, a distance was created between characters on stage and text producers. As writing drama moved up the social scale, one might say they wrote "about" instead of "of" the people who occupied non-elite social niches. These literati writers may have been mavens of the pleasure quarters, but by virtue of their education and background, they were shielded from the quotidian pressures of the ordinary person. One of the major fallacies of much modern criticism is that it often views the characters created by such writers as true representations of the plebeian class, rather than as fictive creations by those who reside not only outside of, but oftentimes well above, that class.

The second major break occurs with the canonization of Zang Maoxun's *One Hundred Plays by Yuan Authors* as the textual representation of Yuan drama. His plays, which have been drastically revised and rewritten and in which the spoken language of earlier editions has been consistently winnowed out, have been accepted as "true" indicators of the social conditions of the Yuan under Mongol rule. Modern criticism has somehow seen the changes he wrought only as aesthetic despite the clear fact that his editing introduced a whole new ideology into the text. When the study of drama became a legitimate academic enterprise in the early twentieth century, and concurrently was established as an academic discipline, these plays were used in a nationalistic agenda to represent "the true voice" of the people, an unmediated reflection of a popular consciousness that would replace the high cultural values of the Confucian tradition and lead to progress and modernization. Marxist ideology that followed on the heels of this enlightenment agenda also stressed that these plays represented the voice of a repressed social and economic class, a true proletariat oppressed by a ruling feudal elite.

   In light of these historical trends and the provenance of each edition, it is important to understand that, as a group, these dramas represent no organic or unified social or cultural reality. They were written primarily as entertainment for the stage and later for reading. In terms of popularity, the closest parallel is perhaps something like the modern American theatrical musical: *The Sound of Music, Oklahoma*, or most particularly *West Side Story*, with the distinction that in the Chinese case the original plays were created by a corporate authorship. They were highly conventional, all making use of the same set of already exist-ing tunes for their arias. In this respect, they resemble such ballad operas of the West as Gray's *Beggar's Opera*. A skilled playwright made use of a small body of a few hundred tunes, divided over nine musical modes, and each made his own selection of tunes to be employed—within some very restrictive conventions. And, just as talented lyricists like Stephen Sondheim could be involved in writ-ing *West Side Story*, so the well-educated Chinese author could participate in the actual production of Northern plays. And, like *West Side Story*, they could adapt a story from the classical canon, finding within the two millennia of his-tory, poetry, stories, and tales of Chinese civilization their own *Romeo and Juliet*. In our quest for social and cultural understanding of these plays, we should exercise the same judgment that we would use in evaluating *West Side Story*: just how closely did the Jets of that play resemble the real gangs of New York streets?

A Finding List of Northern Dramas
in This Anthology by Editions

Table of Dynasties

SHANG c. 1460–1045 BC

ZHOU 1045–256 BC
    Western Zhou 1111–771 BC   Eastern Zhou 770–256 BC
    Spring and Autumn 722–421 BC   Warring States 480–221 BC

QIN 221–207 BC

HAN 202 BC–AD 220
    Western Han 202 BC–AD 9   Eastern Han 25–220

THREE KINGDOMS
    Wei 220–65   Wu 220–80   Shu-Han 221–63

WESTERN JIN 266–316

EASTERN JIN 317–420

NORTHERN AND SOUTHERN DYNASTIES 386–589
    Northern 386–581
    Northern Wei 386–534   Eastern Wei 534–50   Northern Qi 550–77
    Western Wei 535–57   Northern Zhou 557–81
    Southern 420–589
    Song 420–79   Qi 479–502   Liang 502–57   Chen 557–89

SUI 581–618

TANG 618–907

FIVE DYNASTIES 907–60
    Later Liang 907–23   Later Tang 923–36   Later Jin 936–47
    Later Han 947–50   Later Zhou 951–60

SONG 960–1279
    Northern Song 960–1127   Southern Song 1127–1279

LIAO 916–1125

JIN 1115–1234

YUAN 1260–1368

MING 1368–1644

QING 1644–1911

Conventions

As the Introduction indicates, there is a great disparity among the physical formats of the actual texts of the dramas that we have used. Consequently, there will be some inconsistencies in their presentation in translation. A typical *zaju* drama, stripped to its skeletal form, will have a title, a wedge (optional), and four acts, and conclude with a "title" and a "name." Each act will consist of a suite of songs in a single mode arranged in order, written to the same rhyme, concluded by a coda (*wei* or *sha*). For instance, in *Qiannü's Soul Leaves Her Body*, the structure looks thus:

Dazed behind the Green Ring Lattice, Qiannü's Soul Leaves Her Body

Wedge: XIANLÜ MODE:
  (*Shanghua shi*)
  (*Reprise*)

Act 1: XIANLÜ MODE:
  (*Dian jiangchun*)
  (*Hunjiang long*)
  (*You hulu*)
  (*Tianxia le*)
  (*Nuozha ling*)
  (*Que ta zhi*)
  (*Jisheng cao*)
  (*Cunli yagu*)
  (*Yuanhe ling*)
  (*Shangma jiao*)
  (*Sheng hulu*)
  (*Houting hua*)
  (*Liuye'er*)
  (*Zhuansha*)

Act 2: YUEDIAO MODE:
  (*Dou anchun*)
  (*Zihua'er xu*)
  (*Xiaotao hong*)
  (*Tiaoxiao ling*)
  (*Tusi'er*)
  (*Sheng Yaowang*)
  (*Malang'er*)
  (*Reprise*)
  (*Luosi niang*)
  (*Xueli mei*)
  (*Zihua'er xu*)
  (*Dongyuan le*)
  (*Mianda xu*)
  (*Zhuolusu*)
  (*Reprise*)
  (*Shouwei*)

Act 3: ZHONGLÜ MODE: Act 4: HUANGZHONG MODE:

Act 3: ZHONGLÜ MODE:	Act 4: HUANGZHONG MODE:
(*Fendie'er*)	(*Zui huayin*)
(*Zui chunfeng*)	(*Xi qianying*)
(*Ying xianke*)	(*Chu duizi*)
(*Hongxiuxie*)	(*Guadi feng*)
(*Putian le*)	(*Simenzi*)
(*Shiliu hua*)	(*Gu shuixianzi*)
(*Shang xiaolou*)	(*Zhai'er ling*)
(*Reprise*)	(*Reprise*)
(*Shi'er lou*)	(*Gua jinsuo*)
(*Yaomin ge*)	(*Weisheng*)
(*Shaopian*)	(*Ce zhuan'er*)
(*Shua hai'er*)	(*Zhuzhi ge*)
(*Sisha*)	(*Shuixianzi*)
(*Sansha*)	
(*Ersha*)	
(*Weisha*)	

TITLE AND   At the phoenix pylons an imperial summons urges one enlisted for the
NAME: examinations;
             The Song of Yang Pass sorrows one who sends the traveler on his way;

             Tuning his unadorned zither, Student Wang spells out his vexation;
             Dazed behind the green ring lattice, Qiannü's soul leaves her body.

With the following symbol, we identify cases where the original edition signals
the end of a scene by leaving the remainder of the line blank and skipping to the
top of the next line to begin a new scene:

We use brackets for several purposes: (1) to indicate a missing subject, (2) to
indicate a missing object, or (3) to add information that the Chinese infers but
does not state.

Within this overall structure are three basic kinds of text: stage directions,
plain speech, and lyric songs (translated as blank verse). Names, roles, and role
types appear in small capital letters, stage directions are in italics, arias are inset
three spaces, and padding words are inset six spaces in reduced type. Poems are
centered. Rhymed text from other forms of performance, for instance, the
"Stomping Song" of *Lan Caihe*, is inset two spaces and left-aligned. Tune titles
are in italics, and the mode to which the suite is written is in small capitals, as
in the following passage from *Butterfly Dream*:

(FATHER WANG *with* MOTHER WANG, *leading three* MALES, *enters:*)

The moon passes the fifteenth day—its beams grow dim,
A person reaches the middle of life—all affairs cease.

I am surnamed Wang and am a man of Zhongmou District here in Kaifeng Prefecture. I have five souls in my family—this is my wife here. None of the three sons we've spawned are willing to lead a farmer's life; all they do is read and write. Well, boys, just when do you think you'll "burst into prominence from your lowly position"? (ELDEST WANG:) O father and mother, "ones above," what's the benefit of being a farmer? If I "work till I'm wearied, toil till I'm tired" for ten long years, I'll be happy as a lark when I've won that one position! (FATHER WANG *and* MOTHER WANG *speak:*) Such a good son! (SECOND WANG *speaks:*) Father, mother—for this son, it's been

Ten years beneath the window and no one asked of me,
But a single success will raise me to fame and renown through the world!

(FATHER WANG *and* MOTHER WANG *speak:*) Such a good son! (THIRD WANG *speaks:*) O father above and mother underneath. (FATHER WANG:) What gibberish! How can your mother be underneath? (THIRD WANG *speaks:*) When I was young, I saw you sleeping in the same bed, with father on top and mother on the bottom! (FATHER WANG:) Just look at this twit! (THIRD WANG:) Father, mother, what I meant to say was, "Literary talent can establish the self!" (MOTHER WANG:) Papa, if it's a case like this, you'd better come up with a plan for our sons to establish their names for a long time! [*Sings:*]

([XIANLÜ MODE:] *Shanghua shi*)
　　Don't say
"Literary talent can establish the self,"
　　When, alas,
Our family fortune is in direst straits.
　　In vain
You have labored hard "beneath the cold window,"
　　For right now
The little people all over town
Are partial to the deceptive, not to what's true.

ROLE TYPES and *stage directions*

Recited doggerel, entrance and exit rhymed verse

Spoken text: dialogue, monlogue.

MODE and *tune title*

Lyrics

Padding words

There are some additions and exceptions to these rules. When the edition does not separate stage directions with parentheses but only with a large space, we use long dashes to separate the stage directions, as in the opening to *The Pavilion for Praying to the Moon*:

> *After* WANG ZHEN *and* MOTHER *have entered and spoken — after being summoned — and after you enter dressed as* WANG RUILAN *together with* MEIXIANG — *act out greeting* WANG ZHEN.

In *The Chalk Circle*, Zang Maoxun has added the phrase "continue in speech" (*daiyun*) to indicate the continuation of a thought in stylized speech:

> (*Sings:*)
> And after I had heated up a hot bowl of soup, then she said it lacked
>   salt and soy paste.
>   (*Continue in speech:*) She tricked me into getting some salt and soy
>   paste.
>
> (*Sings:*)
> Who ever expected her to secretly pour in poison herbs?
>   (*Continue in speech:*) And after only a spoonful or two of this soup,
>   the Magnate died. Sir, think about this—
>
> (*Sings:*)
> Why did she so quickly cremate the corpse and bury it in the wilds?

We have annotated the text primarily with students in mind. By the time these texts were created many of the gems of Chinese poetry had entered the colloquial lexicon and had become standard, even cliché, parts of ordinary speech. Unless a poem has special significance in the text, we have merely identified these passages by putting them in quotation marks. They function as a form of speech the Chinese call "set phrases" (*chengyu*) or "colloquial sayings" (*suyu*), which are handy aphorisms that are spoken to capture the moment linguistically as a precise category of behavior or feeling.

A glossary of characters for romanized Chinese terms and names may be found on the title support page at www.hackettpublishing.com.

I

Moving Heaven and Shaking Earth: The Injustice to Dou E

GUAN HANQING

Much ink has been spilled trying to identify Guan Hanqing (c. 1245–1322), the best-known of Yuan dramatists, and the period in which he lived. In a work called *The Register of Ghosts* (*Lugui bu*), a book that gives a short biography and bibliography of dramatists known to its author, Guan Hanqing is listed in the section entitled "Those famous nobles and men of talent of former generations who are already dead, but who have plays they compiled still circulating in the world." There he is identified in a single line, "a person from the capital Dadu, from a registered medical household, and having the sobriquet of *Jizhai sou*." Dadu, on the site of the inner city of modern Beijing, was the Mongol capital of China. Biographical records on Guan are scarce and succinct, providing little information beyond *The Register of Ghosts*. References to him in contemporary records are sparse. His name usually occurs along with Bai Pu (1226–after 1307), Ma Zhiyuan (1254?–1320?), and Zheng Guangzu (d. c. 1324) as a group known as "The Four Masters of Yuan Drama" (*Yuan zaju si da jia*). Taken together, the sources seem to point to a productive period from the middle to the end of the thirteenth century. Others have placed his birth as early as 1210 and his death as late as 1324, although the best of modern research places his birth between 1241 and 1250 and his death between 1320 and 1324.

Guan wrote some sixty-seven plays, eighteen of which are extant (although their attribution to him is not always well substantiated). His works cover virtually the entire thematic spectrum of Northern drama, with the exception of plays on religious conversion. His extant plays account for more than one-tenth of the entire extant corpus of the 162 plays assigned to the Yuan, and of the thirty original Yuan editions, he accounts for four, twice the number of any other playwright. He is perhaps best noted for his plays on women, on the travails of love, and on the vicissitudes of marriage. His heroines, three of whom are included in this anthology, include prostitutes, servants, compassionate mothers, and the poverty stricken. Under his pen, female characters emerge with a clarity and wit seldom seen in other plays. As one critic put it, his heroines are all "high-spirited, best not stirred up, self-willed, sharp-tongued, outspoken, unafraid, coarse and salty, yet lovable—like thorny wild roses." Indeed, thirteen of the eighteen plays attributed to Guan are scripts for a female lead.

Over the centuries, Guan has become lionized as the father of Chinese theater. Legends began as early as the Ming that he had been an actor, a gifted amateur who caroused with singsong girls and spent his years in the netherworld of brothels and entertainment that the Chinese call "the windy dust" (*fengchen*). But recent work has shown that this is a process that occurred retrospectively. A comparison of Guan's early textual corpus with later recensions, often edited by literati, shows a remarkable difference in rhetorical strategies and in linguistic practice. That is to say, this later image of Guan as king of the demimonde may have been an historical persona, created as a way to legitimize the tradition of theater and to make it a fit literati art. His place as a cultural hero has not been fixed solely by the interests of the past. He was lionized during the 1950s and the Cultural Revolution as a class hero, a spokesman for the urban and rural poor who were oppressed by the weight of Chinese feudalism and under the yoke of foreign domination by the Mongols.

Of all of Guan Hanqing's many heroines, none is created with more skill and can evoke more emotion than Dou Duanyun, better known as Dou E, "Beauty Dou." A young woman who before age twenty loses her mother and is sold by her father into a short-lived marriage of convenience, she suffers enormous torment in her life. Her father barters her to a moneylender, Madam Cai, to ransom a debt he owes Cai, but also to secure further funds to complete his quest for a government position. Madam Cai purchases Dou E to be her daughter-in-law, but her son dies soon after their marriage, and Madam Cai and Dou E live on as two widows. Transactions and indebtedness are the major focus of the characters' relationships within the play. A crooked physician (who is also an herbalist) owes money to Madam Cai and attempts to kill her to escape his debt, but he is thwarted by a father, Zhang, and his son, Donkey, who save the old woman. She in turn tries to repay this debt of kindness with money, but the two refuse economic reward and pressure her instead to marry the father and to persuade Dou E to marry the miscreant of a son. Dou E's refusal to capitulate to Madam Cai leads to a series of events in which the young woman is wrongfully accused of murdering her new "father-in-law" and is subsequently tortured, forced to confess, and executed. A woman of a respectable family who is powerless against men, whether boorish pursuer or corrupt official, Dou E is moreover in deep conflict with her mother-in-law. To fulfill her deathbed promises to her husband, Dou E must continue to serve Madam Cai as a filial daughter. Since wives are responsible for maintaining family sacrifices to their husband's family, this also means Dou E has to remain chaste. In Dou E's eyes, the old woman accedes to old Zhang's desire for marriage much too eagerly and then tries to entice Dou E to quit chaste widowhood and abandon promises to her husband so she can be "free" to marry Donkey. When Madam Cai's persuasion fails, Donkey plots to poison the old woman in order to remove any obstacle to simply taking Dou E. The plan runs awry, however, when his father drinks the poison instead. Donkey then accuses Dou E of poisoning his father and gives her a choice between two options: marry him or face accusations in court. She opts for the latter. In court she encounters corrupt officials who find it to their own economic advantage to torture her to extract a confession. But Dou E holds out and capitulates only after her mother-in-law is threatened with a beating.

Injustice is, of course, no stranger to the Chinese stage, but its force is magnified here both by the powerless position of women (even those with money) and by the inability of ethical behavior to bring order to everyday life. Dou E comes to the conclusion that death is the only way to sustain the promises she made and the only possible escape from the woes in this life. She thus submits to the executioner's axe, but only after pleading to Heaven to reveal that she was wronged. Her three famous oaths—that her blood will fly upward, that snow will fall in midsummer to cover her corpse, and that there will be a three-year drought—are fulfilled by Heaven. The final oath is responsible for reuniting Dou E's ghost with her father, now an incorruptible official. He punishes all miscreants involved in the case and rehabilitates Dou E's reputation as a "chaste and filial" woman. It is important to understand that love between father and daughter is not at issue in the culmination of the play. The father loves his daughter, but his major role is as a patriarch to restore honor to the family name. The relationship between the individual and the family in China is quite different than in traditional Western households. At the beginning of the play, for instance, despite the fact he loved his daughter, Dou Tianzhang had to sell her to raise money to take the examinations. He did not do so because of a selfish desire to personally excel—it was necessary to raise or maintain the family's status. Here, too, he is motivated by the need to clear her name more as a family member than as an individual agent.

The play probes deeply into traditional beliefs about the nature of injustice and the impartiality of cosmic law as evinced by Heaven. Like other plays, *The Injustice to Dou E* seems to show a commonly held opinion that personal injustice would most likely be remedied in a future life. This is a logical stance considering the lack of positive law and the importance of social determinants in the graded administration of legal punishments. Hierarchies of status, age, gender, and seniority were powerful factors in arbitration and legal decision-making. And, although intensely hierarchical social roles were supposedly tempered by ethical behavior and codes of compassion and responsibility, the source of those ethics was always the moral development of a single individual; human fallibility thus always opened the path to corruption. By forestalling any remedy until a future life, one could focus blame on people of social and political power who misapplied the law without calling the cosmic moral basis of the law, as exemplified by Heaven, into question. Injustice was the product of bad people, not a bad system; it was not crime or even torture that provoked Heaven, but its unjust use against the innocent.

Like many plays first dramatized during the Yuan, Guan's story of Dou E (*Moving Heaven and Shaking Earth: The Injustice to Dou E* [*Gantian dongdi: Dou E yuan*]) is created out of generic themes, historical incident as passed down in legend, and (some would say) out of the age-old tradition of social and political commentary. The historical story is that of an originally unnamed woman, "the filial woman of Donghai" (*Donghai xiaofu*), whose unjust death was believed to have brought on a drought. The story exists in several versions in Han dynasty and later texts. The tale as found in Gan Bao's (283–351) *Soushen ji* is perhaps the best-known:

> During the Han a filial wife in Donghai nurtured her mother-in-law with extreme care. Her mother-in-law said, "This woman suffers so to be attentive to me. I am already old. Why should I be so concerned for the years left to me that I would long encumber the young?" Thereupon, she hanged herself. The woman's daughter made this accusation to the officials: "That woman slew my mother." The officers took [the filial woman] into custody and thrashed her, torturing her with bitter ferocity to bring closure to the case. The filial woman could not stand the cruelty and pain, and falsely submitted to the charge. At that time Sir Yu (Yu *gong*) was Chief Jailer, and he said, "This woman nurtured her mother-in-law for more than a decade and was known far and wide for her filial behavior. Certainly, she did not commit the murder." The Grand Protector would not heed him. Sir Yu strove to get the case righted but could not prevail, so he collected the documents of imprisonment, wept in the offices, and departed.
>
> From that time afterward there was a severe drought in the Commandery, and it did not rain for three years. A new Grand Protector arrived and Sir Yu told him, "That filial woman should not have died. The previous Grand Protector slew her wrongly, and the calamity we suffer now derives from this." The Grand Protector then made sacrifice at the gravesite of the filial woman and took advantage of the occasion to mark her tomb. The heavens rained immediately and there was a great harvest that year.
>
> Elders have passed down what follows. That filial woman was named Zhou Qing. As Qing was about to die, one cart bore ten ten-foot bamboo

poles on which were suspended five banners [representing the colors of the Five Phases].[1] She spoke an oath to the multitude, "If I am guilty, I am willing to be slain and my blood should fall down as normal. If I have died wrongly, then my blood should flow up against gravity." As soon as the punishment ended, her blood—a greenish-yellow—went right up to the tip of each pole and then fell back to earth along each of the banner poles.

The play draws directly on the contents of this tale, which was probably handed down for centuries in a folk version either based on the historical text or coincidental with its transmission. Its didactic nature is clear, both a caveat to the wrongdoer (nothing goes undiscovered) and an assurance to those subject to injustice that wrongs will eventually be righted. It also introduces us to the figures of Sir Yu (Yu *gong*), the father of the Han minister Yu Dingguo (d. 40 BC), and to the Grand Protector (a prefect or magistrate). Sir Yu was renowned in his own day and in later times as a diligent investigator of crimes and a just judge. Beyond this triangle of righteous judge, Sir Yu, and venal prefect, a second official eventually appears to rectify the mistakes of the first. This structure is a distant archetype for the characters that populate what would later come to be called "case plays" (*gongan xiju*). These courtroom dramas are about perspicacious and incorrupt judges who use logic or superhuman intelligence to overturn wrongful verdicts, either in life or post mortem. They were extraordinarily popular in narrative and dramatic literature from the earliest records of their performance in Southern Song (c. 1125–1276) to an explosion of late Ming and Qing novels. Such bureaucratic heroes as Di Renjie (630–700, made famous in the west by Robert Van Gulik's Judge Dee mysteries) and Judge Bao—both derived from actual historical figures—matched more fictional creations such as Qian Ke, the clever magistrate who appears in two of Guan Hanqing's plays.[2]

In courtroom dramas the crime usually occurs early in the play, and it is committed by a character who violates one of the fundamental legal and moral prescriptions of society—the murder of a parent, sibling, spouse, or a person of high degree. The perpetrator creates a situation in which the crime is easily attributed to someone of inferior economic, social, political, or gender status, and when the innocent is sued in court, there is often a bribe exchanged or a love

---

1. These are the five elements earth, metal, water, wood, and fire, the interaction of which produces a change in the cosmos. Through a system of symbolic correlation, they align every event and thing in the cosmos in a fivefold system of classification. See Joseph Needham and Wang Ling, *Science and Civilization in China*, vol. 2 (Cambridge: Cambridge University Press, 1954), 216–63.

2. There are several rather weak attempts to claim that Qian Ke is based on a historical figure. None, however, are convincing.

relationship between the perpetrator and a clerk who "investigates" the case. The clerk inevitably works for a lazy and corrupt official. The wrongfully accused maintains her innocence until she can no longer bear the torture (or, as in the case of Dou E, an elderly family member is threatened with torture) and confesses to the crime. In some cases (as in *The Chalk Circle* and *The Butterfly Dream*, below) the accused is sent to a higher court, either a provincial center or sometimes the capital itself. There, a wise and incorrupt judge will sense an injustice and reinvestigate the case. Sometimes a verdict is reached locally. Some supernatural force, usually a ghost or a dream, manifests an event to enlighten the judge about the true nature of the case under review. But no matter whether he is actually investigating a case or interpreting signs from the supernatural, the crux of the reversal lies in the judge's clear intelligence and his ability to assess moral character.

It has long been a tradition to read courtroom dramas allegorically. A few of the characters who perpetrate crimes are high-ranking officials, and some scholars have made the case that these plays are veiled criticism of the Mongols who had conquered North China first in 1235 and ruled all of China by 1276. A more recent trend, in the middle of the twentieth century, was to read these plays as allegories of the suppression of the proletariat by the feudal ruling classes. What makes the plays so amenable to such allegorical readings is that they deal with the central issue of justice and morality. Since political position and the power to rule derive in Confucian thought from the moral formation of the individual, extended into the social and political world, evil and corruption were constant features of interaction between people and the government.

Dou E was certainly read as one of the harshest criticisms not only of human immorality, but also of corrupt local government and of the basic social and ethical codes of Confucianism. Its portrayal of Dou E's abandonment by her father, her prospect of chaste widowhood from the age of twenty to the end of her life, and the betrayal of her mother-in-law—all despite her filial behavior—question the most basic of Chinese ethical codes. These allegorical readings, however, tend to downplay the universal nature of the injustice and its link to Heaven.

The edition we have used is a regular four-act play from the *Gu mingjia* edition. There is a lengthy introductory scene at the beginning of the play that, in other editions, has been fleshed out by a suite of two songs to make it into a regular wedge. In other respects the play is completely regular. In his *Yuanqu xuan* version, Zang Maoxun has severely edited the play. He made small but significant changes to the text, heightening the filial nature of Dou E and making her motivation less driven by the personal torment of emotional deprivation brought on by an early widowhood. Zang has also fleshed out the ghost scene, which in

the *Gu mingjia* version is quite short. In Zang's edition, Dou E confronts each
of the principals in the case, and sings an aria to each. All other translated versions of the play have relied on Zang Maoxun's edition, and his rewriting is
usually accepted as part of the original play. It is clear, however, that he was in-
fluenced by dramatic conventions that existed at his time and by a refined sense
of poetry that was a product of growing literati involvement with editing and
production of dramatic scripts.

Dramatis personæ in order of appearance

Role type	Name, family role, or social role
Opening male lead	Madam Cai, mother-in-law (Cai Popo)
Old lady	Madam Cai, mother-in-law
Extra	Dou Shi (Dou Tianzhang), father; Overseer of Executions
Child	The young Dou E
Peerless Physician	Peerless (herbalist and apothecary)
Old man	Father Zhang
Second comic	Donkey Zhang (Zhang Lü'er)
Clown	Prefect of Chu
Zhang Qian	Zhang Qian, yamen clerk
Clown	Flagwaver, holder of head
Executioner	Executioner

Moving Heaven and Shaking Earth: The Injustice to Dou E

(OPENING MALE LEAD *enters, dressed as* MADAM CAI:)[3]

> Flowers have a day they will bloom again
> Humans have no years of second youth!

I am Madam Cai, a citizen of Chu Prefecture. Of the three of us who were in my family, my husband, unfortunately, passed away long ago, and I have just a single boy who is now eight years old. We two, mother and son, pass our days and months together in a rather well-to-do household. In Shanyang Commandery here lives a certain Scholar Dou, who asked last year to borrow five taels of silver. Now the interest and principal should amount to ten taels.[4] I've sought this silver several times, but he can't afford to pay me back. Now, Scholar Dou has a young daughter that I've had in mind to make my daughter-in-law and so balance out the debt of those ten taels. He said that today was an auspicious day to bring her to give to me. So, today I won't go out collecting debts, but just stay at home and wait. Scholar Dou should arrive any time now.

(DOU TIANZHANG *enters, leading* THE CHILD, DOU E [*and recites:*])

> In my belly I've tasted to the full every affair of the world,
> In my fate I've not been the equal of anyone under heaven!

I'm Dou Shi, also known as Tianzhang. My ancestors were residents of Jingzhao district of the capital, Chang'an. From my youth I practiced the studies of a Confucian and read much of the Odes and Documents.[5] But before I could

---

3. This is a rare instance that clearly demonstrates that male players portrayed female roles, although the text itself stems from the Eunuch Bureau and may represent only court practices. The *Green Bower Collection* (*Qinglou ji*), which describes the talents of actresses, makes it quite clear that women played male roles. But, because Xia Tingzhi (c. 1300–70), author of the *Green Bower Collection*, covered only actresses in his collection—he intended on writing a later work on famous actors—we cannot prove from his text that males played female roles on the urban stage, although we can surmise that that was the case.

4. This was the so-called "kid interest" (*yanggao li*), a form of taxation that doubled the amount of interest and principal every year.

5. The *Book of Odes* (*Shijing*) and the *Book of Documents* (*Shujing*) were two of the traditional Five Classics of the Confucian curriculum; here they are metonymic for the classical canon.

advance to seize either merit or fame my wife passed away, leaving me with this girl, whose childhood name is Duanyun. She's seven now, but was three when she lost her mother. I'm as poor as if I were scoured clean! Now, I'm living here in Shanyang Commandery in Chu Prefecture. There is a certain Madam Cai who lives alone with her son. She's a rich woman and since I had no traveling funds, I borrowed five taels of silver from her, a loan that now adds up to ten taels with interest and principal in like amount. She's asked me for it several times, but I have no way of repaying her. I never guessed that she would keep sending someone to persuade me to give her my girl for her daughter-in-law. Now the Spring Register shakes and the Examination Field opens[6] and I have to make my way to the capital to sit for the examinations. But, alas, I lack any travel money. I've no way out now but to give Duanyun to Madam Cai as a daughter-in-law. But, what proper daughter-in-law? It's clearly the same as selling her to pay off the ten taels that I borrowed before and to borrow a bit more beyond that—just enough to see me to the examinations will suffice. Oh, Duanyun, there's no other way out for your father! Well, as we've been talking, we've reached Madam Cai's house. Is Madam home?

(MADAM CAI:) Please come in and sit down, my scholar. I've been waiting a long time!

(*They act out greeting each other.* DOU:) I've brought my daughter straightaway to you today, Madam. Dare I say she'll become your daughter-in-law? Simply use her as you will. I have to go to sit for the examinations now and can only hope that you'll look after her. (MADAM CAI:) You owe me ten taels of silver, but I'm returning the loan documents to you now and in addition loaning you two more taels of silver for travel expenses. Please don't think it too insignificant an amount! (DOU:) Thank you, Madam. First I owed you so much silver and now you give me more for travel—this kind of kindness must be repaid another day. Madam, out of consideration for me—if my daughter ever acts the silly dolt please take her in hand. (MADAM CAI:) Just don't worry about it; I'll treat her as my own. (DOU *kneels and speaks:*) Madam, if Duanyun ever needs a beating, out of consideration for me, please just scold her. If she should be scolded, then just reprimand her lightly. Daughter, it won't be the same as when you were with me. As your father, I was capable of going easy on you. If you're ever naughty here, you're in for a beating or a scolding. After I leave now, will we ever see each other again? (*He acts out grieving.*)

---

6. The Spring Register (*chunbang*) was the list of successful candidates from the spring examinations for the degree of the Advanced Scholar (*jinshi*) that was held every three years.

Thrumming my sword, I harm myself with grief,[7]
In literary writings, I practice those of Confucius!
Unfortunately, my wife died before me,
And now father and child must also part!

(*Exits.*)

(MADAM CAI:) Scholar Dou has left his young girl here to be my daughter-in-law and gone off to the capital to take the examinations. I've nothing to do and better see to her.

(*Exits.*)

❊❊[8]

(PEERLESS PHYSICIAN *enters:*)

I practice medicine with all due care,
And dispense my simples according to the Basic Herbal;[9]
Dead ones I can't physick back to life,
But live ones I can physick dead away!

I'm Peerless Physician, and I run a raw simples shop here in Jing Prefecture. There's a Madam Cai in this city from whom I borrowed ten taels of silver, which now runs to twenty with principal and interest. She's come several times to ask for the money, but I don't have anything to give her. Well, if she doesn't come anymore, then that's it. But if she does come, I have another plan! I'll just sit here in the simples shop and see if anyone comes.

(MADAM CAI *enters:*) I am Madam Cai. Thirteen years ago Scholar Dou Tianzhang left his young daughter, Duanyun, with me as a daughter-in-law. I

---

7. This is a reference to the story of the Lord of Mengchang and Feng Xuan. Feng was enlisted as a retainer in the Lord of Mengchang's household, but was poor and unnoticed. One day he beat time on the hilt of his sword and sang, "Oh, long sword hilt, let us return; they serve food without fish." He was given fish to eat. Later he repeated his actions and sang, "Oh, long sword hilt, let us return; we go out but without a chariot." He was given a chariot. Finally, he sang, "Oh, long sword hilt, let us return; there is no way to maintain my family." The Lord of Mengchang finally employed him and Feng's wise actions on behalf of his lord provided him with a lifetime of security. Here, of course, the lament is not only that Dou Tianzhang is both unrecognized for the worthy man that he is, but also that he must desert his daughter, since he also is poor and without a way to keep his family intact.

8. This is the end of the first scene; in other editions, this has been fleshed out to include a short song suite and thereby function as the standard wedge that often occurs in Yuan drama.

9. "Basic Herbal" (*bencao*) is the generic name given to pharmacopoeia in China.

changed her name to Dou E. Who could have guessed that my son would die so soon after marriage? That was already three years ago, and my child Dou E has been a chaste widow since. I told her that I was going into the city to try and get my money from Peerless Physician. I've already reached his gate. Is Peerless Physician here? (PEERLESS:) Madam, I don't have any money in the house. Come with me to my country house so I can get some. (MADAM CAI:) I'll go with you. (*They act out walking.* PEERLESS:) We're out of the city! There's no one to the east, no one to the west! If I don't do it now, I'll never do it! I've brought a rope along. Oh, Madam, someone's calling you! (MADAM CAI:) Where?

(*He acts out strangling* MADAM CAI. OLD MAN *and* SECOND COMIC *act out racing on.* PEERLESS PHYSICIAN *hastily runs off.* OLD MAN *acts out saving* MADAM CAI. SECOND COMIC *speaks:*) Father, it's an old woman; she was almost strangled to death! (OLD MAN:) Madam, where are you from? What's your name? Why would someone want to strangle you? (MADAM CAI:) I am named Cai, and am from this city, where my daughter-in-law and I live. There's this Peerless Physician who owes me twenty taels of silver. He tricked me into coming outside the city where he tried to strangle me to death. I . . . if it weren't for you and brother here . . . how could my life have been saved? (SECOND COMIC:) Old one, did you hear her? She said that she has a daughter-in-law at home. If you want the woman, then I want her daughter-in-law. Tell her! (OLD MAN:) Madam, you've no husband, I've no wife. What do you think about being my old lady? (MADAM CAI:) What kind of talk is this? I'll give you a substantial sum of money as thanks! (SECOND COMIC:) If you're not willing, I'll strangle you myself! (MADAM CAI:) Brother, let me think it over a bit! (SECOND COMIC:) Think! If you go along with my old man, then I'll want your daughter-in-law. (MADAM CAI *says in aside:*) If I don't go along with you, then you'll strangle me! (*Speaks:*) Why don't the two of you, father and son, come home with me? (SECOND COMIC:) Let's go!

(*All exit.*)

(FEMALE LEAD *costumed as* DOU E *enters:*) I am Dou Duanyun, a person of Chu Prefecture. At three I lost my mother, at seven I was separated from my father. My father gave me to Madam Cai as a daughter-in-law and she changed my name to Dou E. At seventeen I was married to my husband, but unfortunately he passed away three years ago. Now, I'm twenty. There's a certain Peerless Physician in this town who owes us twenty taels of principal and interest. We've asked for it many times, but he's never given it back. Now, my mother-in-law has gone personally to collect it. Oh, Dou E, when will come the time that my fate shines through?

([XIANLÜ MODE:] *Dian jiangchun*)
A belly stuffed with idle sorrow,
Many years of suffering endured,
Steady in their presence:
There is no end, no cessation—
Morning, evening, it always remains.

(*Hunjiang long*)
In yellowing dusk and the whiteness of day,
Forgetting to eat, neglecting sleep—both frustrating.
What came last night in dreams
Lies today in the heart.
"Earth endures, heaven goes on and on":[10] that's hard enough to get
    through,
But old grievances and new vexations: when will they ever end?
These damned eyes suffer,
Sorrowing brows furrow,
Heartfelt thoughts knot in profusion:
Threads of my heart go on, and on, and on,
O when will this ever end?

(*You hulu*)
Did my eight signs[11] not say I should endure a whole life of worry?
Who else is there like me,
Who can find no end, no termination?
Isn't it said, after all, "A human heart will find it hard to flow forever
    like water?"
From the age of three, after my mother passed on,
And long after seven, when I separated from my father,
I married a man to share my life.
But, he too plucked out the shorter straw,
Leaving both mother and wife to guard their empty rooms.
Truly, who will ask after us, worry about us?

---

10. Reminiscent of the last couplet of Bo Juyi's famous "Song of Unending Sorrow," in which the souls of separated lovers, Emperor Xuanzong of the Tang [alive] and Yang the Precious Consort [dead] lament after meeting in a celestial journey:

Earth endures, heaven goes on and on, each has a time they will end,
But this vexation threads on and on, never snapping!

11. The "eight signs" are the eight heavenly stems and earthly branches of times associated with the year, month, day, and hour of her birth that are used for divination.

(*Tianxia le*)
Isn't it because in some former life I burned incense, but not to the
    end,[12]
So all the affairs of my future
Are wiped out with one brush stroke?[13]
I encourage all to hurry and cultivate their future lives in this one—
I will wait in service upon Madam
And keep filial chastity in my mourning—
My words will be fulfilled!

Madam went to collect debts. I wonder why she isn't back yet?

(FATHER ZHANG, MADAM CAI, DONKEY ZHANG *enter together.* MADAM CAI
speaks:) You, father and son, wait here by the door a second. I'll go in first.
(DONKEY ZHANG:) Mother, you go on in first and say that your son-in-law is
waiting at the door! (MADAM CAI *acts out greeting* DOU E. DOU E *speaks:*) Mother,
you're back. Do you want to eat? (MADAM CAI *acts out crying, speaks:*) Oh, child,
how can I tell you?

(*Yiban'er*) (DOU E *sings:*)
I see her tears overflow, spilling ceaselessly drop by drop,
Emotions held in check, but depressed and anxious from constant
    worry.
Here, I busily greet her, hurry to ask what's wrong,
There, she wants to explain it all.

(MADAM CAI:) How can I tell you?

Just look at her:
One-half hesitation, the other half shame!
Madam, why are you so vexed and weeping this way?

(MADAM CAI:) I went to ask the Peerless Physician for my money and he lured
me outside the city wall where he strangled me. Fortunately, a certain Mister
Zhang and his son, Donkey Zhang, saved my life. So, I summoned old Zhang
to be my husband—and that's why I'm so troubled. (DOU E:) You're off the
mark, Madam! Think again! We don't lack money in our house to use; and
you're old—why are you seeking a husband? (MADAM CAI:) Child, I had no
other choice! (DOU E:) Mother, listen to me!

---

12. The incomplete burning of incense refers to a common belief that one's hardships in this
life are the result of not worshipping the Buddha with all one's reverence in a former life; karma.
13. The "brush stroke" is that of the judicial attendants in the afterlife.

(*Houting hua*)
When the auspicious time comes, I'll worry for you,
When the marriage vows are made, I'll sorrow for you.
You can comb the bun at your neck, as white as frost and snow,
But how can you wear that embroidered head covering,[14] patterned
   with gold?
No wonder! True it is "a woman grown should not be kept,"
Now you're nigh unto sixty,
And when we each reach middle age, all affairs cease!
One stroke of the pen wipes away old favor and love,
Two minds are matched in a new husband and wife—
For no reason you'll make others split their mouths with
   laughter,
You'll make others split their mouths with laughter!

(*Qing ge'er*)
You have suffered more than she who fanned the grave dry,[15]
And you're sure no stripling of young bamboo shoot, either.
But all of a sudden you want to artfully sketch moth-like eyebrows to
   become a mate.
In the beginning your husband left you property,
Worried about you,
Gave you stew and gruel in all the seasons
And bound you round and round.[16]
All he ever hoped was that widow and orphan,
Without needing to rely or depend on others—
Mother and child—would reach old age!
O! Father-in-law, you went through it all in vain!

(MADAM CAI:) Oh, child, you have summoned a husband too today. Today they
both pass the gate![17] (DOU E:) Madam! If you want to summon a man, you
summon one! I definitely do not want a husband! Today has been chosen, and

---

14. I.e., the marriage hat.

15. As Zhuangzi was about to die, he made his wife promise not to remarry until the dirt on
his grave had dried. His wife met an attractive young man, and began to fan the dirt on the grave
so that it would dry and she could marry him. She did not realize, of course, that Zhuangzi had
turned himself into that very youth.

16. A term from the *Book of Odes* meaning both intimate and tender thoughts, but also
lovemaking.

17. "To pass the gate" is a term used for marriage, but most often of males who are taken into
a wife's family and who change their surnames to that of the wife's family.

I'm afraid they're going to pass the gate. (DONKEY ZHANG:) We've been summoned to pass the gate today.

> Hats, hats, are bright and shiny,
> Today we're to become bridegrooms;
> Hats, hats, are handsome and neat,
> Today we're to become the guests of honor.
> What fine husbands! What fine husbands! Not bad! Not bad!

(DOU E:) You jerk, stand back!

> (*Weisheng*) (*Sings:*)
> I think that women
> Should never believe what issues from the mouths of men!
> Look at what—heaven goes on and on, earth endures—
> What you have taken in: a boorish old bumpkin
> Who drags in some stubborn ass.
> Old favor and love has been wiped away with a single stroke.
> You should ponder what you have done—
> My father-in-law "ran the prefectures and knocked around the
>   provinces,"
> And worked so hard to wind up with a rock-solid fortune that lacks
>   nothing.
> Oh, father-in-law was who secured it for us,
> And now Donkey Zhang wants to enjoy it!
> This is a case of "One person plants the earth but someone else reaps
>   the harvest!"

> (*Exits.*)

(FATHER ZHANG *and* MADAM CAI *speak together:*) Old one, let's go have some wine.

> (*Exit.*)

(DONKEY ZHANG:) Dou E isn't willing, so is it all washed up? For better or worse, I'll make her my wife. I'll go and have some wine.

> (*Exits.*)

> [Act 2]

(PEERLESS PHYSICIAN *enters:*) I am Peerless Physician. When I lured Madam Cai outside the city to strangle her, I bumped into two guys who saved her. I'll open up my simples shop today and see who comes in. (DONKEY ZHANG *enters:*)

I am Donkey Zhang. That Dou E won't go along with me, but that old lady is sick now and I'm going to get some poisonous herbs to feed her. After I've poisoned her and she dies then that little wench, no matter what, will go along with me. Well, here's the simples shop. Brother Grand Physician, I've come for some herbs. (PEERLESS:) What kind of herbs are you looking for? (DONKEY ZHANG:) I'm looking for dosing-poison herbs! (PEERLESS:) Who'd dare compound poison herbs to give to you? You're a brash bastard! (DONKEY ZHANG:) You won't give me the herbs? Why not? (PEERLESS:) If I don't give them to you, what can you do to me? (DONKEY ZHANG *acts out dragging* PEERLESS, *speaks:*) Very well! Very well! Aren't you the one who tried to kill that old lady outside of the city? Do you think I don't recognize you? I'll drag you off to the magistrate's offices! (PEERLESS *speaks in a panic:*) Brother! Let go! I have the medicine! I have the medicine! (*Acts out turning over the medicine.*) (DONKEY ZHANG:) Since I have the medicine, I'll be off for home!

(*Exits.*)

(PEERLESS *speaks:*) So, it turns out that the guy who wanted the herbs was the very one who saved the old lady. Now that I've given him poison, I'm afraid I'm going to be implicated. There's no way I can keep the shop open now, so I'll just go off to Zhuo Prefecture for a while to peddle my herbs.

(*Exits.*)

(FATHER ZHANG *and* DONKEY ZHANG *enter, supporting* MADAM CAI. [FATHER ZHANG]:) Who would have thought that as soon as I moved into Madam Cai's house as her second husband she'd get so sick? It's all to my own bad fortune! Madam, if you can think of something you'd like to eat, just speak up. (MADAM CAI:) I'd like some mutton tripe soup to eat. (FATHER ZHANG:) Donkey Zhang, you call Dou E to make some mutton tripe soup for her mother-in-law! (DONKEY ZHANG:) Dou E! Madam would like some mutton tripe soup to eat—make some and bring it here as quick as you can! (DOU E *enters:*) I'm Dou E. Mother-in-law is not feeling well and would like some mutton tripe soup. I'll fix it for her myself. I can't help but think about how hard it is to keep watch over a woman's heart!

([NANGONG MODE:] *Yizhi hua*)
All they want is to sleep their whole lives behind mandarin duck
   curtains,
They're clearly not willing to spend half a night in an empty room.
First the wife of Master Zhang
And then the woman of Mister Li!
There's a particular brand of women who hang around together,

But never discuss how to run a proper family;
They only pick up all idle gossip,
Chat about their husbands or traps for catching phoenixes,[18]
Just show off their fund of irrational, vague lies.

(*Liangzhou*)
Could any of them mind a stove or clean the utensils like Madam
    Zhuo?[19]
Could any of them raise a tray level with their eyebrows like Meng
    Guang?[20]
These days there is a kind of vile woman
Whose talk is hard to figure,
Whose actions are hard to understand.
Old favor they turn away from to forget,
New love they favor and take a liking to!
On top of [their husbands'] graves the veins of earth are still fresh,
As they hang new clothes on their racks.[21]
Where are those who would travel the border regions to bring down
    the Great Wall with their weeping?[22]
Where are those who would happily throw themselves into the Great
    River where they wash silk?[23]

---

18. "To catch phoenixes" is to make an innocent fall for a trick and be trapped in a situation that brings harm to him or her.

19. Zhuo Wenjun was the wife of Sima Xiangru. They were extremely poor after they married, and she helped him run a wineshop in Chengdu. She has become one of the models of the perfect wife in Yuan drama; see Idema 1984.

20. Meng Guang was "fat, ugly, and dark-skinned" when she was married to Liang Hong at thirty. She dressed up in fine clothing for Liang, but he ignored her for seven days. He acknowledged her only after she had changed into normal workaday clothing, when he remarked, "This is Liang Hong's wife." They lived in reclusion in the mountains in the state of Wu. Liang hired himself out as a thresher and his wife, Meng Guang, would prepare him his dinner every night when he returned from work. She would present him his food by raising the serving tray "even with her eyebrows"; that is, showing him respect by not looking directly at him. Presenting the tray becomes a common phrase to indicate mutual respect and love between spouses.

21. That is, new marriage clothes or clothes she has bought to attract attention.

22. According to folk legend a certain Fan Qiliang was sent to work on the Great Wall during the reign of the First Emperor of the Qin. His wife, Meng Jiangnü, went to seek him, but he was dead. She wept so bitterly that the Great Wall crumbled to reveal his bones.

23. Wu Zixu was being pursued by troops of the state of Chu. He met a woman washing silk on the Yangzi. She gave him something to eat, and then he asked her that she not inform on him. To show her sincere resolve not to betray him, she threw herself into the river and drowned.

Where are those who would climb up the green mountain to be
    turned into insensate stone?[24]
Lamentable!
Shameful!
Women now do not have what it takes to be human!
Most only couple in lust, few have any resolve!
Those women who have come before shame them,
And there's no way they can say, "There are no footsteps for me to
    follow in!"

(DOU E:) The mutton tripe soup is finished, and I should take it in. (DONKEY
ZHANG:) Let me take it in. (*He acts out taking it, speaks:*) It lacks salt and vinegar. Go get some. (DOU E *makes a false exit.* DONKEY ZHANG *acts out putting the
herbs in.* DOU E *enters, speaks:*) Here's the salt and vinegar. (DONKEY ZHANG:)
Pour some in! (DOU E *sings:*)

You say
That it lacks salt, is missing vinegar, and has no taste at all,
And that I must add some seasoning, put in some pepper before it's
    smacking good.
I just want my mother to be healed swiftly:
Drinking a cup of ragout
Is better than sweet dew pouring over the body![25]
You three can still rejoice over your happy union!

(FATHER ZHANG:) Child, is the soup ready? (DONKEY ZHANG:) Yes, take it to
her. (FATHER ZHANG *takes the soup, speaks:*) Madam, eat a little soup. (MADAM
CAI:) I've troubled you. You eat a mouthful first, and then I'll eat. (FATHER
ZHANG:) You eat. (MADAM CAI:) You have some first. (FATHER ZHANG *acts out
eating,* DOU E *sings:*)

(*He xinlang*)
One says, "Old master, you eat first,"
One says, "Oh, Madam, you first."
I have a hard time listening to such talk—
No matter how hard I try, I can't keep myself from getting angry!

---

24. A faithful wife climbed a hill every day to look for her husband's return. She was finally
transformed into a *wangfu shi*, a "longing-for-husband stone."

25. It was believed that sweet dew rained from heaven in a prosperous reign, and that it
congealed into a sweet substance. If a person consumed it, then he or she would have immortal
life.

Those new marriage relations are all her happiness,
And she never thinks about the principled way of husband and wife
    from days before
When they were together always.
This woman's heart is like willow floss tossed by the wind;
She'd never be willing to become a "Husband-longing Stone."
Old favor can never come up to this new happy match!
All she wants is to be a wife for a hundred years.
Would she be willing to send winter clothes a thousand miles
    away?[26]

(FATHER ZHANG:) I ate this soup, and now I feel dizzy! (MADAM CAI:) Old one . . . how come you've gotten sick after eating this soup? (MADAM CAI *calls out, speaking:*) Old one, stay alert! Try to hang on! (*She acts out wailing.*) (DOU E *sings:*)

    (*Dou hama*)
    You're spending your vexation and worry on nothing.
    You don't understand:
    A human life or death
    Is just the wheel of transmigration!
    Affected by this kind of illness,
    Assailed by those ethers of the seasons,
    Or running into windy chills and summer sweats—
    Some die because of starvation, gluttony, work and labor—
    Everyone knows [the source] of his own symptoms![27]
    Human fate is linked to heaven, linked to earth;
    Can another person substitute for us?
    The years allotted to one have nothing to do with the life you are
        living!
    You were together for a few mornings, a few days
    As a single family sharing a single life,
    But there were no sheep or wine, bolts and rolls of cloth!
    There were no "flowered red" money packets or gifts of wealth![28]
    "Clenching fists, we make a life to pass our days,
    Opening our hands, it's as if we let it all go!"[29]

---

26. A reference again to Meng Jiangnü, who had sent her husband winter clothing before she learned that he was dead.

27. "The source of their symptoms" means what their lot is.

28. Traditional wedding gifts.

29. We take this to be a common saying, which in this case means: "You had some time together, but now he is dead and gone."

Don't you fear outsiders laughing at your shame?
It's not that I, Dou E, am recalcitrant or obstinate,
But I can't persuade you—one wise in the world's ways
Who weeps and wails, wails and weeps,
Who vexes heaven and troubles earth!
Humph! It would have been better had you been loathe to forsake
    the one from your youth—your first husband!

(FATHER ZHANG *acts out dying.* MADAM CAI *speaks:*) Oh, what shall we do? He's dead!

(DOU E *sings:*)

I really couldn't care at all,
Don't have a single tear of concern!
Don't let your mind be as if you're drunk,
Your intentions be as if you're doltish:
Your sentient soul flutters away,
Your hands wave, feet fly,
You weep and wail so!

(DONKEY ZHANG:) All right! You've poisoned my old man to death! You still want to end it clean? (MADAM CAI:) Child, I think you'd better go along with him! (DOU E:) Mother, how can you say such a thing? (*Sings:*)

(*Gewei*)
This guy manipulates my old mother to marry him off to me!
You murdered your father yourself, who are you trying to scare?

(MADAM CAI:) Just marry him! (DOU E [*sings:*])

For me, "A single horse finds it hard to carry two saddles!"[30]
Remember when your son was alive and we were husband and wife!
Now you would make me marry another?
I can't stomach that!

(DONKEY ZHANG:) Well, Dou E, you've killed my old man—do you want to settle it officially, or do you want to settle it privately? (DOU E:) What do you mean by settle it officially? Settle it privately? (DONKEY ZHANG:) If you want to settle it officially, then I'll drag you off to the yamen offices. You'll confess to the charge of murdering my old man. If you want to settle it privately, then you can become my old lady and I'll let you off! (DOU E:) There's no crime in my

---

30. A proper woman does not take a second husband.

heart, I'm happy to go to court with you! (DONKEY ZHANG *drags* DOU E *off as they exit.*)

✳✳

(CLOWN, *costumed as* OFFICIAL, *leads* RUNNERS *and enters:*)

> Most diligent and earnest when acting the official,
> I demand money from whoever comes to file a suit;
> If a superior should come to audit the files,
> On pretext of illness I stay at home behind locked doors!

I am the Prefect of Chu Prefecture. Today I'm ascending the hall to hold court. Zhang Qian, call the ranks![31] (ZHANG QIAN *acts out calling.* DONKEY ZHANG *enters dragging* DOU E, *speaks:*) I want to file a charge! I want to file a charge! (ZHANG QIAN *speaks:*) Come over here!

(*They act out greeting.* DOU E *and* DONKEY ZHANG *together act out kneeling.* CLOWN *also performs the act of kneeling, speaks:*) Please rise. (ZHANG QIAN:) Your honor, he is the one filing a charge, why are you kneeling to him? (PREFECT:) Don't you know that it is precisely those who come to file charges that are my mother and father? That they provide me food and clothing? (ZHANG QIAN *acts out responding.* PREFECT *speaks:*) Which of you is the plaintiff? Which the defendant? Speak in accordance with the truth! (DONKEY ZHANG:) I am the plaintiff, Donkey Zhang. I'm charging this woman with mixing up a poisonous concoction to kill my father. I pray that you will be my advocate. (PREFECT:) Which one put in the poison? (DOU E:) It has nothing to do with me! (DONKEY ZHANG:) And it certainly wasn't me! (PREFECT:) Well, it wasn't either of you; it must have been me. (DOU E *sings:*)

> (*Muyang guan*)
> O great one, you are as bright as a mirror, as pure as water,
> Reflect on the truth or falseness of my inward nature.
> This potage was originally full-spiced with the five flavors,
> I know nothing else about it!
> He made an excuse to taste it,
> And when his father ate it he got dizzy and passed out.
> I am making no absurd evasions in this court of law—
> Your honor! What would you have me groundlessly say?

---

31. The court runners and lower officials would open court by forming two ranks and calling out in a loud and solemn voice that court was in session.

(PREFECT:) "People are base creatures; if you don't beat them, they won't confess!" Zhang Qian, beat her for me! (ZHANG QIAN *acts out beating* DOU E. *He does it three times, he acts out spewing water on her.*[32] DOU E *sings:*)

> (*Ma yulang*)
> I can't bear this unfeeling club,
> Oh, mother,
> This is something you did all by yourself, who else is there to blame?
> I universally urge all women, who marry once or a second time,
> To consider my case a noted example.

> (*Gan huang'en*)
> Ai! Who cries and shouts so loud and fast?
> I can't stop wailing and weeping.
> My sentient soul just returns to me
> And I revive
> Only to fall dizzy and pass out.
> Struggling to get through a thousand kinds of beating and
>   whippings—
> Look at the fresh blood dripping and dropping—
> One stroke falls,
> One rivulet of blood,
> One layer of skin!

> (*Caicha ge*)
> I'm beaten until my earthly soul scatters, my sentient soul flies away,
> My fate covers the stones of the Yellow Springs.[33]
> Who will ever know the injustice in my bowels?
> I never poisoned my father-in-law, the crime for which I now face
>   responsibility.
> Your honor! I beg you to illuminate the truth of it with your bright
>   mirror!

(PREFECT:) Are you going to confess? (DOU E:) I really didn't poison him! (PREFECT:) If it wasn't you, then beat that old lady for me! (DOU E:) Stop, stop, stop! Don't beat my mother. I'll confess! It was I who poisoned father-in-law. (PREFECT:) Bring the cangue and cangue her up! Put her in death row! Take her tomorrow to the civic execution ground to carry out the sentence. (MADAM CAI:) Oh, Dou E, this pains me to death. It was all my doing that sends you to your death! (DOU E *sings:*)

---

32. The water was to revive her.
33. Yellow Springs was the Chinese Hades.

(*Weisheng*)
I'll turn into an injustice-carrying, grievance-bearing ghost without a
    head
But I'll never allow that sex-loving, wild, and lascivious thief with
    brazen face to go free;
I think that blue heaven
Cannot be deceived;
I think that the heart of men
Cannot be deceived.
An affair of injustice
Is known to heaven and earth.
I struggled to the end,
Fought to the finish,
But now it's turned out like this,
So what's left to say?
I was wronged and so confessed to poisoning my father-in-law to
    death.
Oh, mother, I dragged you in
To be beaten;
But can I allow you to be beaten?
If I don't die, how can I save you?

(*Exits.*)

(DONKEY ZHANG:) Tomorrow they'll kill Dou E, so I'll hang around the yamen
awhile.

(*Exits.*)

(MADAM CAI:) Tomorrow they'll kill Dou E in the marketplace. Oh, child. This
pains me to death!

(*Exits.*)

(PREFECT *speaks*:) Tomorrow I'll behead Dou E, but there's nothing left to do
today. Bring me my horse, I'm going home to have some wine.

(*Exits.*)

[Act 3]

(EXTRA, *costumed as* OVERSEER OF EXECUTIONS, *enters*:) I am the Overseer of
Executions, and today we carry out the sentences of the condemned. Seal off

the mouth of the alley and don't let anyone pass. (CLOWN *acts out striking three drum rolls and beating the gong three times.* EXECUTIONER *acts out grinding his blade.* EXECUTIONER *acts out waving the flag.* HOLDER OF THE HEAD *acts out sounding the drum and gong.* DOU E *enters wearing a cangue.* EXECUTIONER *speaks:*) Move a little faster, seal off the mouth of the alley! (DOU E *sings:*)

([ZHENGGONG MODE:] *Duanzheng hao*)
I've groundlessly run afoul of the emperor's law,
And all in a muddle suffer its punishment.
I utter a cry of "injustice"
To shake earth and startle heaven.
Heaven and earth are where I should bury my enmity!
O Heaven, you provide no ease for men!

(*Gun xiuqiu*)
There are a sun and a moon to appear day and night,
There are mountains and rivers to provide a mirror for past and
    present.
Heaven! Contrary to belief you do not discriminate the pure from
    the turbid—
And you clearly mix up Robber Zhi and Yan Yuan![34]
Those of virtue suffer poverty and want, and then are cut off short in
    life.
Those who create evil enjoy riches and wealth, and then are given
    extended years.
Heaven! You do nothing but fear the strong and cheat the weak.
I never suspected that heaven and earth would just push their boats
    along with the current![35]
Earth! You don't discriminate good from evil, and so how can you be
    earth?
Heaven! Today I bear wrongs, carry injustice, and grievously lay
    plaint to a heaven
That makes me speak alone, utter words alone in vain!

---

34. Robber Zhi was a notorious bandit often mentioned in classical texts. Yan Yuan was the brightest and most morally advanced of Confucius' disciples. See *Analects* 6.11: "What a worthy man was Yan Hui! Living in a narrow alley, subsisting on a basket of grain and a gourdful of water—other people could not have borne such hardship, yet it never spoiled Hui's joy. What a worthy man was Hui!" (trans. Slingerland 2003, p. 56).

35. That is, heaven and earth would simply go whichever way the current took them with no regard for righteousness.

(EXECUTIONER:) Dou E. Move along! You're going to be late. (DOU E sings:)

> (*Tang xiucai*)
> Me, wrenched by this cangue,
> Twisting left, slanting right,
> Me, pushed by people, falling forward, tilting back.
> Dou E has something to tell you, brother. . . .

(EXECUTIONER:) What do you want to say?

> If we go along the street ahead, I'll be stricken with enmity,
> But take the street behind and I'll die without grievance.
> I'm not just being willful!

(EXECUTIONER:) You're facing execution now and are on the way to the execution ground. What relatives do you have? (DOU E *sings:*)

> (*Daodao ling*)
> You push me on to the execution ground, and ask what relatives. . . .

(EXECUTIONER:) What do you mean by the front street? What do you mean the back street? (DOU E:)

> If we go by the front street . . . I beg of you, a little consideration,
> If I go by the back street. . . .
> I won't hold any grudges against you, brother!
> If I go by the front street . . . I fear mother will see me.

(EXECUTIONER:) You can't even be concerned with your own life now, why are you worried about her? (DOU E:) If she sees me wearing the cangue and locked in chains and on the way to the execution ground . . .

> It will make her uselessly die of anger, oh!
> Make her die of anger, oh!
> I plead with you, brother: as I approach this danger, please grant a
>   person a little ease.

(MADAM CAI *enters, speaks:*) Heavens! Aren't you my daughter-in-law? My child! Oh, this pains me to death! (EXECUTIONER *speaks:*) Old lady, stand back! (DOU E:) Have my mother-in-law come here so that I can give her some advice. (EXECUTIONER:) You, old lady, come forward! Your daughter-in-law has something to say to you. (MADAM CAI *speaks:*) O child, this is killing me. (DOU E:) Mother. It's all because you weren't feeling well and wanted some mutton tripe soup to eat. I fixed it and he said that it lacked salt and vinegar. Deceived by Donkey Zhang, I went to fetch some vinegar and salt, and then he put the poison in the soup. He made me take it to you to drink. No one expected you to give it to that old man to eat. In fact, his hope was to kill you in order to monopolize me as his wife—he never thought he'd wind up killing his old man. I was dragged off to the yamen and there, fearing implicating you, gave a false confession. Today I'm going to the execution ground. Oh, mother, any leftover rice gruel you might have, please pour out half a bowl for me to eat.[36] Any unburnt funeral money you have, kindle a bundle for Dou E.[37] Do this out of consideration for your dead son! (*Sings:*)

> (*Kuaihuo san*)
> Think on Dou E, who falsely bears this criminal sentence
> That will make of Dou E's head and body a corpse incomplete!
> Think on Dou E, who managed household affairs in days gone by,
> Mother! Think about Dou E, who had no father, lacked a mother.

> (*Baolao'er*)
> Think on Dou E, who has served mother-in-law these many years
> And, at each proper season, sacrifice one cup of cold gruel to me.

(MADAM CAI:) Rest assured, child. Oh, this is killing me! (DOU E:)

> Go to that place of execution, and spread some paper money on my
>   corpse
> Out of consideration for your son who has passed away.
> Weeping and wailing, wailing and weeping,
> Vexed and troubled, troubled and vexed,
> The ethers of my enmity rush against the heavens!
> I need not defend myself,
> Showing nothing, hiding nothing,
> I bear injustice, harbor grievance.

(EXECUTIONER:) Hey! Stand back, old lady, the time is here. (DOU E *acts out kneeling down.* EXECUTIONER *acts out opening the cangue.* DOU E:) Dou E beseeches the Overseer of Executions for a strip of clean matting. I have three things, that if you are willing to grant to Dou E, then she can die without enmity. I want two twelve-foot white banners hung aloft on the flag standards so that when the knife makes its pass and my head falls, a breast full of hot blood will not spill out on the ground but will fly up onto the white banners. If I've truly suffered an unjust wrong, then in these days of highest summer, let there fall an auspicious snow to cover over Dou E's corpse and head, and let Chu Prefecture suffer three years of drought!

---

36. The food was to be offered in sacrifice to her soul.

37. When Madam Cai makes sacrifice to her dead husband and son, she should burn some for Dou E as well.

(EXECUTIONER:) Shut up! What a thing to say! (EXECUTIONER *waves the flag,*
DOU E *sings:*)

> (*Weisheng*)
> Today, "a dumb woman takes her medicine and still suffers death."[38]
> "The plow ox suffers the whip for its master."

(EXECUTIONER:) It's getting dark. Ai! It's snowing! (EXECUTIONER *sweeps away
the snow, acts out praying to heaven.* EXECUTIONER, *waving the flag, acts out covering up.* DOU E:)

> When the frost fell they began to know to speak of Zou Yan,[39]
> When the snow flies then is displayed the injustice to Dou E!

(*The blade is run along the stone.* EXECUTIONER *cuts off her head.* DONKEY ZHANG
disposes of the corpse. EXECUTIONER *speaks:*) A great job! Let's go have some
wine.

> (*All respond in unison and exit. They exit bearing the corpse.*)

[Act 4]

(DOU TIANZHANG *enters:*) I am Dou Tianzhang. Thirteen years have already
passed since I parted from my daughter, Duanyun. After I arrived at the capital,
I passed the Advanced Scholar examination on the first try and was awarded
the post of Participant in Executive Affairs. I am incorruptible, capable, pure,
and upright, of the firmest and most unyielding integrity. Thanks to the grace
of our Sagely Ruler, who looked on me with favor, I have been given the rank of
Surveillance Commissioner of the Two Huai River Circuits. I go from place to
place to inspect prisons and audit records, and I have been empowered with the
Golden Plaque and the Sword of Authority so that I can investigate crooked
officials and corrupt clerks. I behead first and memorialize the crime later![40] I
am both happy and sad—happiness is holding a Censorial post, in charge of
punishments and sentences. Sadness is the fact of having given over my seven-
year-old Duanyun to Madam Cai as a daughter-in-law. After I assumed my

---

38. Is this an allusion to a story well-known in Yuan times? Or Dou E's description of her
silent acceptance of death?

39. One of the distant sources of this drama, this is the story of Zou Yan (c. 305–240 BC)
who was a loyal minister to his king. He was slandered and thrown into prison. He raised his
head to weep to heaven and in the middle of the summer it began to snow. This later becomes a
common allusion to injustices severe enough to evoke Heaven's displeasure.

40. He "beheads first" as opposed to the common practice of having all regional death sentences reviewed by the central government before execution.

post, I sent someone to Shanyang Commandery in Chu Prefecture to ask the whereabouts of Madam Cai's household. The neighbors there reported that Madam Cai moved that year to someplace else. Up to this point there has been no news. I have wept for my child, Duanyun, until my eyes are hazy and bedimmed, and worried and sorrowed over her until my hair has grown white. I've come to Yang Prefecture in Huainan, trying to find out why it hasn't rained for three years in Chu Prefecture. I'll rest awhile in this hall behind the Yang Prefectural Office. Zhang Qian, tell all officers and clerks in the offices that there is no levee today, but that we will meet early tomorrow.

(ZHANG QIAN:) All departmental secretaries and attached officials of the court! Today all are excused from attending, but we will meet early tomorrow. (TIAN-ZHANG:) Zhang Qian, tell the departmental secretaries that they should bring me any case files that need to be audited, and I'll review them by lamplight. (ZHANG QIAN *acts out bringing case files.* TIANZHANG:) Zhang Qian, set up a lamp for me. You've worn yourself out. Why not go get some rest! If I call you, then come; if I don't, then don't bother. (ZHANG QIAN *lights the lamp.*)

(*Exits.*)

(TIANZHANG:) I'll look over several of these cases first. A certain criminal, Dou E, poisoned her father-in-law to death. This is strange—the very first case I look at involves someone with the same surname as me. The crime of poisoning one's father-in-law lies among the sins of the "Ten Abominable Crimes."[41] Among those with my surname are some who don't fear the law! Well, this case is already closed so there's no need to look at it. I'll place this file at the bottom of the pile and look at another. But wait! All of a sudden there's a surge of dizziness. I'm getting old and I'm worn out from being on horseback. I'll steady myself on this desk and rest a bit. (*He acts out falling asleep.* GHOST DOU E *enters, sings:*)

([SHUANGDIAO MODE:] *Xinshui ling*)
Everyday I cry, stuck fast and weeping on the "Home-gazing
    Terrace,"[42]

---

41. These crimes are: to contemplate rebellion; to contemplate an act against the imperial tombs, temples, or palaces; to contemplate treason; a detestable act against parents or relatives; to lack moral values (concoct poisons, conjure evil spirits, slay the innocent); to be extremely disrespectful (steal imperial goods, harm the emperor); to lack filial piety; to lack concord (kill or beat distant relatives); to be unrighteous (kill a regional or local official, violate mourning for the husband, harm one's teacher); to have incestuous relations. See Shih Chung-wen 1972, pp. 235, 237, for a fuller explanation of this list.

42. The deceased pause on this terrace before being released into heaven, there to gaze back upon their family members. She cannot go any further because she has not had the proper sacrifices performed to release her soul.

Boiling over with anger, waiting for my enemy.
Now steadily slow, roaming in darkening fog,
Then keenly afoot, coming in a whirlwind,
Now locked in fog and buried in clouds:
I can pop up fast as a ghost!

(DOU E *gazes off into the air, speaks:*) Spirits of the door, those guardians of the gate, will not let me pass. . . . I am the daughter of the Surveillance Commissioner, Dou Tianzhang. Because my father does not know of my unjust death, I've come to cast it all in his dreams. (GHOST *acts out seeing her father and weeping.* TIANZHANG *also acts out weeping, speaks:*) My child, Duanyun, where are you? (DOU E *makes a false exit.* TIANZHANG *acts out awakening, speaks:*) How strange. I had just closed my eyes when I saw my daughter Duanyun in a dream—just as if she were in front of me . . . I'll look again at these cases. (GHOST *does the action of going over and manipulating the lamp.* TIANZHANG:) How strange! Just as I was getting ready to look at these cases, the lamp suddenly flared and then darkened. Zhang Qian is already asleep, so I'll have to trim it myself. (*He goes to the eastern side of the stage and does the action of trimming the lamp.* GHOST *acts out reversing the files.* TIANZHANG:) Well, I've trimmed the lamp so that it's brighter. Let's look a second time at the cases. There is a certain criminal, Dou E, who poisoned her father-in-law to death. How strange! This is the first case that I looked at and then placed at the bottom of the file! How can it be on top again? Well it's a closed case, so I'll put it back on the bottom and look at another file. (GHOST *acts out manipulating the lamp.* TIANZHANG:) Really weird! How come the lamp is flickering? I'll trim it again myself. (*He goes to the eastern side of the stage and does the action of trimming the lamp.* GHOST *acts out reversing the files.* TIANZHANG:) Well, I've trimmed the lamp so that it's brighter. Let's look at another case file. There is a certain criminal, Dou E, who poisoned her father-in-law to death. Humph! This is strange! I clearly put this case file at the bottom of the stack. How come, when I just went to trim the lamp, this thing winds up on top again? There must be a ghost in this hall behind the Yang Prefectural Office. Even if there is no ghost there is certainly an injustice in this affair! I'll put it at the bottom of the pile again and look at another case. (GHOST *acts out manipulating the lamp.* TIANZHANG:) This really is weird! Why is this lamp failing again? Now it's flaring and darkening. I'll bet there's a ghost manipulating it. I'll trim it once more. (*Goes to the eastern side and trims the lamp. Does the action of hurrying back.* GHOST *acts out reversing the files. They act out running into each other.* TIANZHANG *acts out drawing his sword, speaks:*) Aha! Aha! Aha! I said there was a ghost. You—ghost, I am the Imperial Surveillance Commissioner, Imperially dispatched from the central court, bearing the Golden

Tally and traveling by government horse! You come forward and I'll split you in two with this single blade! Zhang Qian, my son, lucky you are to be asleep. Everyone up, there is a ghost! There is a ghost! Ah, this frightens me to death. (GHOST DOU E sings:)

> (*Yan'er lou*)
> I see him guess time and time again with suspicious mind,
> While I, with weeping sounds, fill him with fright and wonder.
> Ai,
> O Dou Tianzhang, my father
> Receive Dou E's deep, deep obeisances.

(TIANZHANG:) You, ghost! You say that Dou Tianzhang is your father and that I should receive the bows of you, my daughter Dou E. You are surely mistaken. My daughter was named Duanyun, and became Madam Cai's daughter-in-law at seven. The names are different—how can you be my daughter? (GHOST DOU E:) Father, when you gave me to Madam Cai, she changed my name to Dou E. (TIANZHANG:) If you're my daughter Duanyun, I'll ask only one thing: are you the one who was punished for poisoning her father-in-law to death? (GHOST DOU E:) Yes, it was I, your daughter! (TIANZHANG:) Silence! You wretched wench! I cried so much for you that my eyes were blurry and sorrowed so much for you that my hair turned white. But you committed one of the Ten Repugnant Crimes and have been punished with execution. I now hold a high position in the Censorate and Secretariat, in charge of punishments and sentences, inspecting prisons and auditing files throughout the world, investigating crooked officials and corrupt clerks. You are my own daughter but were first to violate one of the Ten Repugnancies! If I couldn't control you, how can I control anyone else? I married you to another family, hoping that you would follow the Three Obediences and Four Virtues—the Three Obediences are to comply with the father when at home, to comply with the husband when married, to comply with the son after the death of your husband, these are the Three Obediences. The Four Virtues: to serve one's parents-in-law, to respect your husband, to harmonize your sisters-in-law, and to bring accord to the neighborhood—these are the Four Virtues. Now, not only do you not have any of the Three Obediences or the Four Virtues, but also you blindly committed one of the Ten Repugnant Crimes. Isn't it oft said, "You must have forethought in affairs lest you be troubled by remorse later?" In our Dou family there have been three generations with no male who has broken the law and five generations with no women who have remarried. Once having been given in marriage to follow your husband, then you should have practiced integrity, a sense of shame, benevolence, and righteousness. But you didn't even think about the Nine Loyalties and Three

Chastities.[43] Instead you violated one of the crimes of the Ten Repugnancies. You have destroyed our ancestral name with shame and have dragged my pure name into it. Tell me in detail the true facts now. Don't lie or make things up. Don't vary from the truth even the slightest as you relate it. If you do, then I'll dispatch a document about you to the Shrine of the City God, and assure that you will never assume human form again. I'll sentence you to the dark mountain to be a hungry ghost forever. (GHOST DOU E:) Stop your scolding, father! Cease your anger. Set aside for the moment your awe-provoking tiger- and wolf-like bearing. Listen to your daughter slowly tell it all to you once. At three I lost my mother, and at seven I was separated from my father. You gave me in marriage to Madam Cai as a daughter-in-law and she changed my name to Dou E. When I reached seventeen and was matched in matrimony to my husband, it was my misfortune to lose him, my husband from childhood, that very year. Madam and I have remained chaste widows. There was a certain Peerless Physician in Chu Prefecture who owed Madam twenty taels of white silver— principal and interest. My mother-in-law went to collect that silver, but she was lured outside the city walls where he tried to strangle her. Would he expect that he would run into a certain Donkey Zhang and his father, who saved my mother-in-law? That old Zhang asked, "Madam, who's at home?" My mother-in-law said, "There's no one home, just a widowed daughter-in-law, who is called Dou E." Old Zhang said, "Since you don't have anyone at home, then I'll make myself your husband. How about that?" My mother-in-law strongly resisted, and the two of them, father and son, said, "If you don't comply, then we'll strangle you!" My mother-in-law was frightened and couldn't help but go along. In truth, she was frightened into marriage and so she brought the two of them home to live with us. That Donkey Zhang tried to seduce your daughter many times, but I was determined not to assent. One day, my mother-in-law was sick and wanted some mutton tripe soup to eat. After I had fixed it, Donkey Zhang said, "Bring it here and let me taste it." He said, "Well, it's all right, but it lacks some salt and vinegar." He tricked me into going and getting some salt and vinegar and while I was gone he put in poison. He then told me to take it out, but my mother-in-law let old Zhang taste it first. As soon as he tasted it, his seven apertures ran with blood, and Old Zhang was poisoned to death. Then, Donkey Zhang said, "Dou E, you've killed my old man. Do you want to settle it publicly or do you want to settle it privately?" I said, "What do you mean settle it publicly or settle it privately?" He said, "If you want to settle it publicly, then I'll lay plaint at the yamen, and you'll repay my father's life with your own.

---

43. These appear not to be specifically enumerated virtues of a good wife, but are rather generalized numbers indicating the value of ardent chastity.

If you settle it privately, then you can just be my old lady." Then, your daughter said, "In three generations our household has had no man who has broken the law, and in five generations no woman who has remarried. 'A good horse does not wear two saddles, a virtuous wife does not change to a second husband!' To my death, I'll resist being your wife. I have a clear conscience. I would love to go to the yamen with you!" But there was no way to defend myself and I was dragged to the yamen offices. How could your daughter stand those triple beatings and sixfold interrogations? Or being strung up and bashed, stripped, and wrapped in rope? But even then I would not own up to any crime, even if beaten to death. Seeing that I would not confess, they wanted to beat my mother-in-law. Fearing that my mother-in-law was going to be beaten, I simply gave a false confession. This is how I came to be taken to the execution ground where I was executed. When I got to the execution ground, your daughter there made three oaths toward heaven. I wanted a twelve-foot piece of silk hung up on a flag standard, and when the blade made its pass, then my whole chest full of hot blood would not fall on the ground but would fly onto the white silk. If I was really a victim of injustice, then right away, in hottest summer, three feet of auspicious snow would cover your daughter's corpse. If they had wrongly persecuted your daughter, then this Chu Prefecture would suffer three years of drought. It came to pass that blood did fly up onto the white silk, it did snow in the sixth month of the year, and it did not rain for three years and not an inch of grass grew. It was all because of your daughter!

> Do not lay plaint to the yamen office, lay plaint to Heaven;
> The ethers of enmity within the heart mere words cannot express.
> Taking punishment on behalf of my mother, I could exercise filial piety;
> Ending my life because of my husband, I can be counted worthy.
> Three feet of auspicious snow covered my unstained corpse;
> One breast-full of fresh blood dyed the white silk.
> Frost fell before we noted the wrong done to Zou Yan,
> Snow flew just to reveal the injustice to Dou E!

(*Sings:*)

> (*Yan'er luo*)
> Your child never did it, though accused,
> And so my injustice and wrongs know no boundaries.
> I was unwilling to yield to another
> And thereby was dispatched to the execution ground.
> I would not shame my ancestors,
> And thereby destroy what was left from this life.

(*Desheng ling*)
Each and every day I hold fast to the Home-gazing Terrace,
My whole soul pained with enmity.
Father! Your sword of empowerment is keen enough to split a hair,
Today you are personally sent by the Sage's command
To investigate the facts until they are clear.
That bastard disordered ethical human relations and should rightly
     be destroyed,
And that creature should be slowly sliced ten thousand times!
Father! You take that confession I made and change it back again!

(TIANZHANG *weeps, speaks:*) Ai! My child wrongfully killed! Oh, this pains me to death. I won't ask you anything else but this: What is the cause of this three years of drought in Chu Prefecture? (GHOST DOU E *speaks:*) I am the cause! (TIANZHANG:) So, it was because of you all this time. Because of this daughter of mine, I am reminded of an ancient story: In the Han dynasty there was a filial woman who kept firm to her widowhood. Her mother-in-law hanged herself, but her daughter brought accusations that it was the filial woman who had killed her mother-in-law. The Grand Protector of Donghai slew the filial woman. Just because this one woman harbored an injustice, it did not rain for three years. Later, when Sir Yu reviewed the cases the filial woman clasped her case file to her breast and wept in front of the courtroom. Sir Yu rectified the documents and slew an ox to offer sacrifice at the filial woman's grave. Only then did the heavens allow a great rain to descend. In olden days the Grand Protector of Donghai wrongfully slew a filial woman of worthy actions. And just because of this one woman, it caused a dearth of rain for three years! This is exactly like the current situation! When tomorrow comes, I will be your advocate!

       A white haired father is afflicted with pain and grief!
     Wrongly slain and gone a young girl in her greening spring!

Child, it is getting light. You go back. When tomorrow comes, I will set your case plainly right! (GHOST DOU E *sings:*)

(*Weisheng*)
You take those crooked officials and corrupt clerks and destroy them
     all!
Imperially bestowed: a golden plaque and the sword of empower-
     ment, hair-splitting sharp
Can dispel the anxieties of one person,
And root out the calamity of the myriad citizens.

(*She acts turning her body, speaks:*) I've forgotten! Father! My mother-in-law is old and there is no one to care for her. (TIANZHANG:) What a filial and compliant daughter! (GHOST DOU E:)

> I enjoin you, my father, to move the grave of my mother[44] and care
>   with compassion for my mother-in-law,
> Take pity that she is old.
> Only after you have taken care of her, open up the case files
> And, on my behalf, rectify the criminal charges confessed to by one
>   wrongly slain.

(*Exits.*)

(TIANZHANG:) The day is dawning. Bring those officials and clerks from the Yang Prefectural Office, those who interrogated Dou E, bring them all here to me! (ZHANG QIAN:) I understand. (*He forces the officials,* CLERKS, MADAM CAI, *and* DONKEY ZHANG *on to greet him; they bow.* TIANZHANG:) Madam Cai, do you recognize me? (MADAM CAI:) I do not recognize you, your honor. (TIANZHANG:) Well, I am Dou Tianzhang. All of you, listen to my decision:

> Donkey Zhang conspired to murder his own father and deceive a
>   person of good standing—in the marketplace he shall be clearly
>   executed.
> Clerks and officials of Yang Prefecture mismanaged and went
>   contrary to criminal law—they shall be caned a hundred times
>   and never be employed again.
> Peerless Physician mixed the poisonous compound—he shall suffer
>   the blade at the Yunyang Marketplace.
> Madam Cai will be cared for in my own household,
> And Dou E's sentence shall be changed, purity restored to her name.

To follow through with this, take Donkey Zhang and decapitate him in the public streets; take these public officials and strip them of office, and then hold a great Jiao ceremony of the Waters and Land so that my daughter may transcend this world, cross over, and be reborn in heaven![45]

---

44. *Qianzangle an nainai enyang an popo*: this line presents a difficult case. *Nainai* in this context clearly means Dou E's biological mother; Zang Maoxun has deleted this line in his edition and conflated two lines together, *shouyang wo nainai*, "to receive and care for my foster mother."

45. This is a mixture of Buddhist and Daoist rituals: the purifying ritual of water and land of Buddhism (*shuilu zhai*) and a great offering feast (*jiao*) of the Daoists. The ritual was held to

TITLE AND NAME: An old lady who marries again is too crooked
hearted,
A virtuous girl who guards her chastity is strong
willed;

Bucking the wind and braving the snow, a ghost
without a head,
Moving heaven and shaking earth, the injustice to
Dou E.

---

pacify disruptive forces in the cosmos. Here it means more than simple funeral ritual; Dou Tianzhang must make sure that Dou E's spirit has been purified before it can cross over into the
afterlife.

2

Rescriptor-in-Waiting Bao
Thrice Investigates the Butterfly Dream

GUAN HANQING

Judge Bao is a literary figure that populates all of Chinese performing literature: drama, *chantefable*, Ming and Qing vernacular fiction, modern plays, movies, and television series. He is roughly based on a real historical figure, known
as Bao Zheng (999–1062), also known as Dragon Design Bao (Bao *Longtu*),
from his position as Academician in the Dragon Design Pavilion (*Longtu ge zhi
xueshi*), and as Rescriptor-in-Waiting in the Tianzhang Pavilion Bao (Bao *Daizhi*). From the biography of Bao Zheng in the official *Song History* we can
glimpse what would later be called "his iron face of impartiality" (*tiemian wusi*):

> He was summoned to be provisional Prefect of Kaifeng Superior Prefec-
> ture. . . . Bao held court with strength and resolution. Imperial relatives and
> eunuch officials all pulled their hands into their sleeves[1] because of him, and
> those who heard of him were all awestruck by him. People compared a smile
> from Judge Bao to the Yellow River running clear.[2] Even young children and
> women knew his name, and called him "Rescriptor-in-Waiting Bao." People
> of the capital spoke of him thusly, "Where bribes won't reach there is King
> Yama, Old Bao." According to long custom, those who sued in court did not
> need to go to the yamen to do so. Bao opened up the main gate, and made
> sure everyone had to come before him to explain everything about the case.
> None of his underling clerks dared cheat. Some eunuchs and powerful fami-
> lies had constructed gardens, the trees of which began to encroach on the
> Benefit the People River;[3] and for this reason the river became blocked, and
> it happened that the capital was flooded. So Bao tore them all down.

This short account, written about the same time that courtroom dramas were
in their heyday, provides the kernel of the characterization that was to make
Judge Bao such a powerful presence in literature. First is his fearless pursuit of

---

1. Dared not do things they should not.
2. The muddy Yellow River never runs clear.
3. This is the name of the canal that brought goods to the capital.

justice against, and even execution of, imperial relatives or powerful eunuchs who populated the emperor's personal bureaucracy. This fervor is carried over into literature where Bao is often portrayed as being in conflict with both fictional and historical men of power. His integrity and incorruptibility led to the overturning of cases that were badly handled or were tainted by outright corruption, particularly those in which a false accusation was made against a lower-class citizen to shut him or her up. Bao treated all people equally and did not waver in applying the law equitably. He was such a powerful figure that he was soon thought "to judge living humans in the daytime and their souls at night" (*ri duan yang ye duan yin*). Bao was apotheosized within a hundred years of his death. He was thought to be "master of a star" (*xingzhu*), that is, the reincarnation of a star-spirit, and as we see in *Little Butcher Sun* (see below), he was also believed to be President of the Court of Speedy Retribution, a high bureaucratic post in the netherworld below Mount Tai. As the quote from his official biography—"Where bribes won't reach there is King Yama, Old Bao" (*guanjie budao you Yanluo Bao lao*)—shows, in his lifetime Bao was already equated with King Yama, overseer of hell in Buddhism.

He was extremely popular in drama during the Yuan and Ming, and there are twelve plays extant in which Judge Bao appears, three of which are translated in this work:

Writing Club of Hangzhou	*Little Butcher Sun*
Guan Hanqing	*Rescriptor-in-Waiting Bao Thrice Investigates the Butterfly Dream*
Li Xingdao	*Rescriptor-in-Waiting Bao's Clever Trick: The Record of the Chalk Circle*

Four other plays exist in other translations:[4]

Zheng Tingyu	*Rescriptor-in-Waiting Bao's Clever Trick: The Flower in the Rear Courtyard*
Guan Hanqing	*Rescriptor-in-Waiting Bao: Selling Rice at Chenzhou*
Anonymous	*Ding-ding Dong-dong: The Ghost in the Pot*
Zeng Ruiqing	*Wang Yueying on Prime Eve: The Left-behind Shoe*[5]

Judge Bao figures prominently in other forms of performance literature and narrative fiction as well. Sixteen *chantefables* (*cihua*) in which the judge appears, published in the 1470s, were discovered in 1967 in a Ming tomb. These were written

---

4. For locations of other translations, see Appendix 3: A Partial List of Modern English Translations of Early Drama.

5. As *Die Geschichte vom zurückgelassenen Schuh* in Forke and Gimm 1978.

prosimetric narratives that adapted the rhetorical techniques of oral presentation. In the late sixteenth century, one hundred Judge Bao stories were assembled into a vernacular hundred-chapter novel called *The One Hundred Cases of Dragon Design Bao* (*Bao Longtu baijia gong'an*). A selection of sixty-four of these cases, now presented as a collection of short stories, replaced the novel, however, and enjoyed continuing popularity from the seventeenth to the nineteenth centuries. The popularity of Judge Bao continues, and there have been a number of movies and television series produced in China, Taiwan, and Hong Kong.

Butterfly Dream is part crime drama and part domestic play. As in *Injustice to Dou E*, Guan Hanqing has utilized his sources well and, as in that drama, this play's theme can be traced to a Han dynasty source. In this case it is an episode from *Legends of Exemplary Women* (*Lienü zhuan*), a text attributed to the great Han polymath Liu Xiang (77–6 BC), who also collected a version of the "Filial Woman of Donghai" in another of his works. The story is called "The Righteous Stepmother of Qi" (*Qi yi jimu*):

The righteous stepmother of Qi was the mother of two sons in Qi. During the time of King Xuan (319–300 BC) someone died from an altercation on a road. The local Agent investigated the body and it had suffered one fatal wound. Two brothers were standing beside the body and the Agent questioned them about it. The elder said, "I slew him." The younger one said, "It was not my elder brother, I am the one who slew him." As the one-year statute of limitations for judging a case ran out, the Agent was still unable to make a decision, so he explained his problem to the Prime Minister. The Minister could not make a decision, and he explained it to the King. The King said, "As the situation stands, if we pardon both, this is to release the one who is guilty. If we slay both, this is to execute the innocent. I have determined that their mother is capable of knowing the good and evil of her sons. Try interrogating the mother, and heed which one she desires to kill or to keep alive." The Minister summoned their mother and asked her this, "Your sons have slain a person, but each of the brothers wants to stand in the other's stead to die for the crime. The Agent could not decide [which was at fault] and explained it to the King. The King is benevolent and compassionate, so he asked which one the mother would desire to kill." Their mother wept and answered in response, "Slay the younger." The Minister accepted her words and then went on to ask her about it, "The younger is the one people dote on. You desire to slay him now—why?" The mother replied, "The younger is my own son, the elder the son of the first wife. When his father was ill and nearing death, he entrusted him to me, saying, 'Raise him well and look after him.' I replied, 'Agreed.' Now, once you have accepted the trust someone has placed in you and have given that person your agreement, then how can you simply forget that act of trust and not be true to your agreement? Moreover, to slay the elder and save the younger is to reject common righteousness because of personal love. To turn my back on his words and forget trust is to cheat the dead. To not be bound by my husband's words and to have already assented to them without really thinking, then how can I live in this world [i.e., How can I be considered a person]? Though I am certainly deeply attached to my child, could it be called right action [to save him]?" She wept until her lapels were soaked. The Minister entered and discussed it with the King. The King found her righteousness comely, and he considered her actions lofty. He pardoned both children, slaying neither, and honored the mother by naming her "Righteous Mother." The Gentleman says, "The righteous mother kept her word and loved righteousness. She was pure and concessive." The *Odes* say,[6] "A joyful and easy-going lord, / He is a pattern for every direction."

This tracing of sources is itself problematic, since we have no way of knowing the exact relationship of Han written sources or Yuan written sources to oral legend. Filial piety and righteousness are two of the basic concepts of Chinese family life. In the case of "The Filial Woman of Donghai," for instance, there are at least four different versions in Han texts. While it may be that three were copies of the first, we should remember that this was a world in which stories first of all circulated orally and, if written down, then only in manuscript. The power of oral exchange was far greater than in our own time. It could also happen, given the didactic nature of Chinese intellectuals, that textual stories would be used orally to instruct nonreaders. This would account, for instance, for the great number of stories from the classics that, like stories from the Bible in Western culture, reappear in popular culture, either as a direct retelling or in some structural or rhetorical recast of the original narrative. Guan may have adapted the stories from earlier texts or from oral retellings but in every case he has mined the basic story line for what is dramatic and crucial. Yet he has also changed the stories to his fancy when creating the dramas themselves.

The villain of *Butterfly Dream*, a certain Ge Biao, is sometimes said to be a Mongol, although there is nothing mentioned in the play to suggest that. He is only described as an imperial relative, and since the chronological setting of the

---

6. This first line is cited in several early texts (*Canon of Filial Piety*, *Mencius*, and *Traditions of Master Zuo*) and in historical sources thereafter. In each text one finds a matching line. It inevitably is used to refer to a lord who is "father and mother to the people," who is "loved by the spirits," or who "refuses to believe in slander." The structure of the lines is reminiscent of the poems of the *Book of Odes*, so it is often introduced with the same cliché, "the *Odes* say . . ." as a way of granting it authority

play is clearly not the Yuan, it is more likely that his station is accentuated to heighten Judge Bao's integrity. It is possible, of course, to read it as a criticism of Yuan law, in which Chinese citizens could take no revenge on any Mongol, even for slaying their parents. In native Chinese law, a person taking revenge for the murder of a parent could claim extenuating circumstance, particularly as in this case when the old father had been murdered simply out of malice. Since Judge Bao is usually acclaimed for his stand against the crimes of high officials and members of the royal family, his stratagem for saving the youngest son seems to be necessary to pander to a powerful family that is clamoring for revenge for the death of its own scion. One of the ways to sidestep the conflict between Judge Bao's reputation as being blind to status and his obvious conniving to spare the boy by offering up another victim instead is to read his plot as a direct criticism of Yuan law, which forces even those of highest integrity to stoop to cleverness instead of claiming moral high ground. This remains an intriguing but forced reading, favored by Chinese writers who are quick to attribute all of the social ills of the Yuan to the Mongols. Judge Bao must satisfy the common principle that a death has to be revenged, which he does by cleverly substituting the body of the horse thief. But in light of the totality of his representations, there is nothing here to suggest that Ge Biao is anything more than a symbol of people whose power put them beyond the reach of normal law.

The play in the *Gu mingjia* edition is a regular four-act play, with a wedge incorporated into the first act. As is normal with plays prior to *Yuanqu xuan*'s standardization of format, this long scene, which includes the *Shanghua shi* and *Reprise* normally found only in wedges, is not separated from Act 1. One anomaly of the play is at the end of the third act, when the condemned son, who has been portrayed as something of a witty simpleton during the whole play, breaks into song—a direct violation of all formal rules of the genre. It is, he says, his final song, and he should be allowed to sing it. This is one of the few moments in Guan Hanqing's plays in which such an emphatic rupture occurs in staging. No comparable example can be found in the thirty plays for which Yuan printings have been preserved, so it seems most likely that this scene was added in later times, when the roles of secondary characters were expanded at the Ming court.

Dramatis personæ in order of appearance

Role type	Name, family role, or social role
Old man	Father Wang
Female lead	Mother Wang
Male 1	Eldest Wang
Male 2	Second Wang
Male 3	Third Wang
Villain	Ge Biao
Supplemental male	Constable
Yamen runners	Yamen runners
Zhang Qian	Zhang Qian (yamen clerk)
Official	Judge Bao
Zhao	Pigheaded Ass Zhao (Zhao Wanlü), horse thief

Rescriptor-in-Waiting Bao Thrice Investigates the Butterfly Dream

[Act 1]

(FATHER WANG *with* MOTHER WANG, *leading three* MALES, *enters:*)

> The moon passes the fifteenth day—its beams grow dim,
> A person reaches the middle of life—all affairs cease.

I am surnamed Wang and am a man of Zhongmou District here in Kaifeng Prefecture. I have five souls in my family—this is my wife here. None of the three sons we've spawned are willing to lead a farmer's life; all they do is read and write. Well, boys, just when do you think you'll "burst into prominence from your lowly position"? (ELDEST WANG:) O father and mother, "ones above," what's the benefit of being a farmer? If I "work till I'm wearied, toil till I'm tired" for ten long years, I'll be happy as a lark when I've won that one position! (FATHER WANG *and* MOTHER WANG *speak:*) Such a good son! (SECOND WANG *speaks:*) Father, mother—for this son, it's been

> Ten years beneath the window and no one asked of me,
> But a single success will raise me to fame and renown through the world!

(FATHER WANG *and* MOTHER WANG *speak:*) Such a good son! (THIRD WANG *speaks:*) O father above and mother underneath. (FATHER WANG:) What gibberish! How can your mother be underneath?[7] (THIRD WANG *speaks:*) When I was young, I saw you sleeping in the same bed, with father on top and mother on the bottom! (FATHER WANG:) Just look at this twit! (THIRD WANG:) Father, mother, what I meant to say was, "Literary talent can establish the self!"[8] (MOTHER WANG:) Papa, if it's a case like this, you'd better come up with a plan for our sons to establish their names for a long time![9] [*Sings:*]

---

7. The phrase *fumu zaishang*, translated as "father and mother, ones above," is a term of respect that can also be understood to mean "father and mother on top."

8. A common saying; in full, "Study hard when you are young, for literary talent can establish the self."

9. The pun in these last two lines is on the phrase *lishen*, which literally means "to stand the body/self upright." The second level of translation would be: "(THIRD WANG [*speaks*]:) Father,

([XIANLÜ MODE:] *Shanghua shi*)

> Don't say
"Literary talent can establish the self,"
> When, alas,
Our family fortune is in direst straits.
> In vain
You have labored hard "beneath the cold window,"
> For right now
The little people all over town
Are partial to the deceptive, not to what's true.

(*Reprise*)

> They only
"Respect the clothing, not the man."
> While my
Words have never been partial in any way.
My three sons, when the spring examinations begin—
On what can they truly rely?
> How can
They all be capable of leaping the Dragon's Gate?[10]

(*They all exit.*)

(FATHER WANG *enters:*) I've come here to the main street to buy some paper and pens for my sons. I've run myself ragged. I'll just rest here a spell. (GE BIAO *enters:*)

> Generals and ministers are not born as such,
> A real man must vaunt his own strengths.

I am Ge Biao, and I'm from a powerful and influential family. I can kill others with no demand in return for my own life. I usually just wind up in jail. I've got nothing to do today, so I'll go cruise the main street. (*Acts out running into*

---

mother, what I meant to say was 'Literary talent makes a person stand upright' [i.e., not lie prone on the bed]. (FEMALE LEAD [*speaks*]:) Papa, if it's a case like this, you'd better come up with a plan for our sons to stand upright for a long time!"

10. A common idiom for passing the Advanced Scholar Examinations, found first in the *San Qin ji*: "Every year at the end of spring yellow carp from the ocean and all of the streams fight their way to a place just below the Dragon's Gate (located on the Yellow River). Seventy-two of them ascend the Gate every year, and when they first get into the passage clouds and rain soon follow closely behind them. From behind a heavenly fire sets their tails on fire and they transform into dragons."

FATHER WANG. GE BIAO:) Just who is this old fella, who thinks he can run into my horse's head? I'll just beat this old ass. (*Acts out beating* FATHER WANG, *who acts out dying, exits.* GE BIAO:) This old guy's faking his death to put one over on me. Horse, bite him! Horse, bite him! Trample him, horse, trample him! Fuck him, horse, fuck him!

(*Exits.*)

❋❋

(CONSTABLE *enters:*) Eldest Wang! Second Wang! Third Wang! Are you home? (*The three enter, speak:*) What are you calling for? (CONSTABLE:) I am the constable. Someone has killed your father on the main street. (*The three speak:*) It is really true? Mother, a calamity! (*All act out weeping.* THIRD WANG:) And just what whoreson killed my old man?[11] Mother, come here quickly. (MOTHER WANG:) Why are you so alarmed, children? (THIRD WANG:) Someone has killed our father. (MOTHER WANG:) Oh, how did this happen? ([*Sings*]:)

([XIANLÜ MODE:] *Dian jiangchun*)
Think carefully, think it through
Twice or thrice—
This strange, untoward, affair.
> I've run so hard
That my breath falters and my speech is thready,
> And I'm upset
That my ribs won't simply sprout a pair of wings.

(*Hunjiang long*)
> Ah, my husband
What have you done wrong to Heaven?
Seize that murdering criminal
And I'll seek to lay a charge against him!
> My husband never once
Made contact with the enemy outside the borders,
> And never
Ran afoul of anything public or private.
> If anything
Has happened to this weak and meek man of mine,
> I will
Take that overbearing good-for-nothing to court.

---

11. Literally, "which son of mine was it?" (*wo na er ye*); i.e., "I've had carnal knowledge of his mother."

Now I am
Crossing the main streets, coursing through the markets,
All the while scratching my cheeks and tweaking my ears,[12]
Wiping away my tears, rubbing the gum from my eyes.

(MOTHER WANG *acts out going to see the corpse.*)

(*You hulu*)
Just look at that
Place where he was wounded—a pit of purple mixed with blue,
Where his corpse is already laid out.
Well, you may have
Always worried before about our family fortune,
But couldn't have known yesterday that you were to die today—
We don't know today what befalls us tomorrow.
Your whole body defiled, limp, and bloody,
Your four limbs now cold, lank, and limp,
Your face, dry and yellow, looks like paper money—
In vain I call a long time.

(*Tianxia le*)
Beyond recovery, you've driven us to despair!
Our family fortune. . . .
Think carefully—
If the funeral cortege goes out tomorrow,
We won't even have a single packet of paper money.[13]
And we'll have our three children all alone with nothing to offer in
     sacrifice—
True it is, "A poor house manifests filial sons!"

(*The three speak:*) Mother, people say that it was Ge Biao who killed our father.
Let's go find that guy and drag him to the yamen to repay life with life!

(*Exit.*)

(*Nuozha ling*)
He was originally
A scholar of the Imperial College,[14]

---

12. Out of anxiety.

13. Funeral cash to burn at the funeral.

14. Every year officials selected the best students in the Imperial College (*Guozi xue*) to participate in both the standard Advanced Scholar examinations held by the Board of Rites and the special Palace Examination.

Could he have anticipated
Dying by another's fists?
And so now wind up
A corpse for autopsy on the main street?
Even if he's a high official
And we but an impoverished family of scholars,
We'll still have to submit our complaint!

(GE BIAO *enters*:) I am Ge Biao. I've had a few cups to drink, but there's nothing to do, so I'll go home for a while. (*The three enter*:) Isn't that the killer? Grab that guy! (*They act out grabbing him.*) Did you kill our father? (GE BIAO:) Yep, it was me. I'm not afraid of you. (MOTHER WANG:)

(*Que ta zhi*)
When we
Go to court,
Even such a sprig as you
Can't use your status as a "jade leaf or golden branch"
Of the royal family or imperial line—
Even if you were the grandson of a dragon or emperor's son,
If you kill a person
You'll still take it in court!

(*The three act out beating [him]. GE BIAO acts out dying. The three speak*:) This killer is feigning being drunk and won't get up. (MOTHER WANG:) I'll try and question him. (MOTHER WANG *acts out questioning him.*) Brother, what did my old man ever do to you to deserve to die by your hand? Why are you feigning being drunk and sleeping in the street? Enough of this! Get up! Get up! Aiya, you three have killed him! (THIRD WANG:) What a fine mess, I never laid a hand on him.

(*Jisheng cao*)
You should have
Thought what you were doing when you acted.
As it is,
What could you have been thinking?
The three of you
Have made a mess of right and wrong—
The three of you
Might have been right to beat him to death,
But the three of you
Have surely brought down a felony affair.
And

These two worthless "boys of the fresh wind and bright moon,"[15]
> Have destroyed you,
Three scholars of the Jade Hall and Gate of the Golden Horse.[16]

(MOTHER WANG *points to* GE BIAO *and sings:*)

(*Jinzhan'er*)
> I reckon then, that
You never stopped to consider
> That
It's forever a case of payment and revenge,
> Or that
Heaven is impartial with its retribution.
> All you wanted was
To act the bully on the street—
> Who could guess
You'd wind up a corpse laid out in a puddle of blood.
> True it is
"A general struck by a painful arrow will feel the same pain
As the one he fires at others gives!"

(*The three:*) We have no money, what will we use to go to court? (MOTHER
WANG:)

(*Zui zhong tian*)
> Every day we
"Have a gourd ladle of drink,
A wicker of food,"[17]
Some chopsticks,
A few spoons.
If we have to brandish cash when we get to court,
Unless we pawn a little useless writing . . .

---

15. Fresh Wind and Bright Moon are names of two lads who serve the immortals, used to refer to Ge Biao and old man Wang as dead fellows who make the living suffer.

16. Common reference to the literary men who surround the emperor. The Gate of the Golden Horse was one of the portals of the Han court. Flanked by two bronze horses it was where officials assembled when summoned to court. Han scholars were known as Academicians of the Gate of the Golden Horse. The Jade Hall was an earlier name for what eventually became the Hanlin Academy. The line is quoted from a congratulatory verse (*kouhao*) by the Song scholar Ouyang Xiu (1107–72), written to preface the performance of a comedy at a banquet he was attending with two friends (hence, "three scholars").

17. See *Injustice to Dou E*, n. 34. Here the passage refers to their poverty and by indirection to their moral self-sufficiency and happiness with their lot.

([MOTHER WANG:]) Even this won't save the day. If you

> Must die, then die today you must.
> Even though it's the crime of manslaughter,
> You'll leave behind a name for filial obedience!

(YAMEN RUNNERS *enter*:) Don't let them escape! Take those killers! (MOTHER WANG:)

> (*Jinzhan'er*)
> Bitterness on bitterness,
> My tears are spilling silky threads.
> This vexation has been bestowed by heaven.
>> They are
> Dragging us sideways, pulling us down—how can we protest?
>> On one side
> A chilling sight—my old man is lying there, a corpse;
>> On the other
> With eyes wide in fright, my children are done in.
>> Know this:
> "One receives fortune only once,
> But disaster comes time after time."

(YAMEN RUNNERS:) A killing is no small thing. Let's go off to see the judge. (MOTHER WANG *acts out grieving*:)

> (*Houting hua*)
> I know heaven will take no sides;
> Truly, every act is repaid or avenged.

([MOTHER WANG:]) "He with little hatred is no Gentleman, he without poison is no man!"[18]

> You weren't thinking at all.
> In this court case
> The three of you won't be able to stand the pain.
> You are assembled worthies, budding scholars[19]

---

18. That is, one must be hard-hearted and carry one's actions out to the end; here, to see revenge through to the end.

19. Although this portion of the text is printed in large characters, there is a possibility that these three lines are actually spoken text inserted within the sung lines of the aria (*daiyun*) to lead into "Who will leap the Dragon's Gate." These sentiments are expressed again in song at the end of the next aria, and it is standard practice to introduce topics in dialogue that are to be treated or even repeated in the sung portions.

Who were to leap the Dragon's Gate
And snap the cassia branch.
Because your father was wrongfully killed,
It was fitting that you take private retribution.
If you are taken by the court—
To investigate the true circumstances
And seek your depositions
They will use the head clamp[20]
And employ the finger presses.[21]

(*Liuye'er*)
       I never thought
This calamity would come from heaven,
       You
Beat him until he was a corpse laid out in a puddle of blood,
But right it was that you cleansed away your father's wrong.[22]
Even though you are sentenced to death
And sent to the Courts of Hell,
You will still earn a name for filial piety.

(YAMEN RUNNERS:) Off to the magistrate! (MOTHER WANG:) My sons, now that you've done this, what can we do? (*The three:*) What can we do, mother? (MOTHER WANG:)

(*Zhuansha*)
       Why did I tell you
To read the *Odes* and *Documents*?
To practice the classics and the histories?
       Because I
Wanted to emulate how Mencius' mother
Taught her child in days gone by.[23]
       Now incapable of
Clearly inscribing your family name on the Golden Plaque,
       Instead
Your names will be written out

---

20. A piece of hempen rope wrapped around the forehead and then tightened with a wooden stick.

21. Five slips of strung wood, inserted between the suspect's fingers and squeezed by tightening the string.

22. I.e., that you took vengeance for him.

23. Mencius' mother is known as a paragon of maternal love and concern. She moved her residence three times so that Mencius would be raised in the right environment.

On the "stave of crime."
> When it happened
It was an unpremeditated act.
If it is to be capital punishment,
It must be ratified by imperial decree,
And only one of you will pay with your life—
Certainly they can't cut off the Wang family sacrifices,[24]
Nor will they exterminate [all of the sons] in our family!

(*They exit together.*)

[Act 2]

(ZHANG QIAN *acts out walking, leading* YAMEN RUNNERS *to assemble for court.* ZHANG:) All horses and people in the court be at peace. Oyez. (JUDGE BAO *costumed as* RESCRIPTOR-IN-WAITING BAO *enters:*)

> *Dong, dong*, sounds the yamen drum,
> Public servants line up on the two sides;
> Of King Yama, at the Court of Life and Death,
> Of the Spirit of the Eastern Marchmount at the Soul-snatching Terrace.[25]

I am Bao Zheng, known also as Bao Xiwen. I am a man of Oldson Village in the District of Four Prospects, in Golden Measure Commandery, found in Lu Prefecture. I am an Academician, Rescriptor-in-Waiting at the Pavilion of Dragon Design, and have just been given commission as the Prefect of Kaifeng.[26] Now, I'd better get onto the dais and begin morning court. Zhang Qian, bring me any documents that need to be signed and sealed and I'll sign them and affix my seal on them. (ZHANG:) Clerks of the Six Bureaus, are there any documents that need to be signed and sealed? (*Act out responding from backstage.* ZHANG:) Why didn't you say so earlier? It's a good thing I asked you. Oyez. There is a case of the horse thief, Zhao the Pigheaded Ass, sent here from Suanzao District. (JUDGE BAO:) Bring him here for me. (YAMEN RUNNERS *act out making the prisoner kneel.* JUDGE BAO:) Take off that traveling cangue. You,

---

24. I.e., performed by male descendants on behalf of their ancestors.

25. The Eastern Marchmount, Taishan, was thought to be the abode of "The Grand Thearch of the Eastern Marchmount," overseer of the eighteen levels of hell, which consisted of seventy-two different bureaucratic offices. The second court, the Office for Apprehension and Investigation of Life and Death Cases was known as the Soul-snatching Terrace. Judge Bao was thought to be the Officer of Speedy Retribution; see *Little Butcher Sun*.

26. His rank as Rescriptor-in-Waiting is a court rank used to determine his status and salary. His office is as Prefect of Kaifeng, the capital of the Song dynasty.

are you Zhao the Pigheaded Ass? Did you steal that horse? (ZHAO:) Right, I stole the horse. (JUDGE BAO:) Zhang Qian, put on the long cangue and send him down to death row. ([ZHAO] *is pushed off stage.* JUDGE BAO:) I'm exhausted all of a sudden. Zhang Qian, don't you or the clerks of the Six Bureaus make any noise. I want to rest for a while. (ZHANG:) All runners and underlings, all clerks of the Two Corridors, make no ruckus! The prefect wants to take a nap. (JUDGE BAO *acts out laying his head on his desk and sleeping; acts out dreaming:*) Official affairs have really riled up my heart and I couldn't sleep if I wanted to. I'll wander around for a bit. Here I am at a little side door at the back of the prefectural compound. I'm opening up the door now. Let me take a look. Why, it turns out to be a fine flower garden. See how the hundred flowers blaze and glow, melding in harmony in the spring scene. There's a little pavilion with turned up eaves over there in that clump of flowers, and from the pavilion hangs a spider web. A butterfly is flying over the flowers and just got stuck in that web.

> I'm deeply moved to grief
> By this butterfly's sad plight.
> Don't say that only men alone die unpredictably,
> Even insects have wrongful deaths.

Ai, "even things that wriggle have sentience; all possess the Buddha nature." Here comes a larger butterfly to rescue it and set it free. Wait, here comes another small butterfly, and it's caught in the net, too. The big butterfly ought to rescue it, too. Strange, that large butterfly flew back and forth above the flowers, but didn't rescue it. And that little butterfly fluttered off leaving it there. The sage[27] has said, "Every human possesses the heart of compassion." If you won't save it, then wait for me, I will. (*Acts out releasing it.* ZHANG:) Sir, it is already noontime. (JUDGE BAO *acts out waking up, speaks:*) Every life hangs in the balance, even insects or butterflies. Zhang Qian, bring any sentenced prisoners that need review before me, and I will interrogate them. (ZHANG:) Clerks, bring out any sentenced prisoners who need review for interrogation. (*Act out responding from backstage.* ZHANG:) Oyez, Zhongmou District has dispatched a case of three brothers who assaulted and murdered a good citizen, Ge Biao. They have been dispatched here under guard. (JUDGE BAO:) How can common folk in a little district dare murder a good citizen? Have they arrived yet? (ZHANG:) They have arrived. (JUDGE BAO:) With a blow for each step, beat them into court. (ESCORTS *enter, driving three people on.* MOTHER WANG *enters, sings:*)

---

27. I.e., Mencius.

([NANLÜ MODE:] *Yizhi hua*)
> We've been escorted

To this Censorate that has no human feeling,[28]
> And have already reached

Kaifeng Prefecture, where abides the imperial law.
> These three

Undiscovered scholars
> Have been twisted alive

Into death row inmates under interrogation,
> And me vainly made

Skittish, heart sunk,
> Unable to still

The alarmed terror in my heart.
> True it is

"A criminal's gall is empty at bottom."
> I'm nearly compelled

To confess to this crime myself;
> For here are no equals

To the bailiffs and magistrate of our little place.

(*Liangzhou*)
> This

Kaifeng Prefecture—the king's laws are pure and just,
> And will not stoop to

The addlepated confusion of magistrate and clerks in Zhongmou
   District.
Pu-dong-dong, below the steps, the drum opens the court,
> Scaring me

Until my hands quiver and my feet shake,
> Unable to use

Dashing bravery and careless mind.[29]
> It alarms me so much

My spirit flies away and my soul disappears,
> Drives me so much

My strength is exhausted, my muscles turn limp.

---

28. "No human feeling" means both that it is impartial and that gifts or bribes (also called "human feeling" in Chinese) are to no avail. It is harsh but just and impartial.

29. Literally, "great gall and coarse heart" (*danda xincu*), i.e., to act impetuously without careful thought, here a nice play on the common saying (*danda xinxi*), "to act bravely after careful consideration."

This public case
Cannot be compared to the common or ordinary
         Because, to get to the center of it,
It means to suffer punishment or endure banishment.
Alas, alas, alas,
On the one hand my old man is a corpse laid out on the ground,
And what's more, more, more,
In dire straits children and mother are put in jail and tied up in the
    pen.
Ai, ai, ai,
I can foresee the brothers, suffering the knife, meeting punishment,
Will already be scared to death.
         Toward the edge of this petitioners' wall,
I will cock my ear and look with stealing eyes—
Who's ever seen such an office?
         Today's the day
And here's the place where fortune or calamity is determined, and
    truth and falsehood are set apart.

(MOTHER WANG, *with the crowd, act out seeing the official and kneeling.* ZHANG:)
Accused, face the court! (JUDGE BAO:) Zhang Qian, remove their traveling
cangues and give the escorts the proper endorsements to send them back.
([ZHANG] *acts out opening the cangue.* THIRD WANG:) Mother, brothers, let's go
home. (JUDGE BAO:) Where do you think you're going? Where's the similarity
between here and that Zhongmou District office of yours? Zhang Qian, these
three scoundrels are the murderers, but who's that old lady? Surely, she's a witness. If not, then she must have some relationship to these scoundrels. You, old
lady, what are these two to you? (MOTHER WANG:) These two are my older
children. (JUDGE BAO:) And the little one? (MOTHER WANG:) That's my third
child. (JUDGE BAO:) Quiet! You're no "Run the household by the right rules"
person! Consider how Mencius' mother taught her son—by carefully selecting
the neighbors to live next to,[30] or how mother Tao taught her child—by cutting
off her hair in order to treat his guest well,[31] or how Mother Chen taught her

---

30. See note 23.

31. Tao Kan's mother wove clothes for her son so that he could mingle with a higher class of
friends. After he had risen to become a district clerk, Tao Kan sent his mother some fine fish
paste. She sealed it back up and told him not to give her government provisions. Not only did it
not help her, it increased her anxiety. When a noble man visited Tao and was detained by a snowstorm, she cut up her sitting mat to feed to the noble's horse and cut off her hair to sell so she
could provide wine and food for a feast.

children—they wound up dressed in purple gowns and golden belts.[32] But you, you boorish wife, teach your children to murder good folk! Confess now, the truth!

> (*He xinlang*)
>> My children
> Are violators of public law who committed a horrible capital crime,
>> But those officials
> Do things neither human feeling nor reason can bear.
>> My children
> Should be pardoned for killing this person,
>> For we
> Are the black-haired masses, from humble origins, and ever poor.
>> I plead with you, father,
> Be an advocate for my children.
>> These three
> Have hit the books and studied from an early age,
>> And can only
> Rely on the lessons of the written canon
> That they put into practice as rites and righteousness.
>> How could they
> Devise a plan, a strategy,
> To lure someone else to harm?
> Under a hundred beatings, it's hard for them to explain clearly,
>> Haven't you heard
> "A third person destroys a major affair,
> Six ears cannot carry out a plan?"[33]

(JUDGE BAO:) If you don't beat them, they won't confess. Zhang Qian, beat them with all your strength. (MOTHER WANG *sings mournfully:*)

> (*Gewei*)
>> My children have run afoul
> Of Xiao He's severe law that calls for banishment, deportation,
>>   strangling, or beheading,
>> And for naught have read
> Confucius' sagely books that are full of reverence, restraint, warmth,
>>   and goodness.

---

32. A mother noted for her severity and uprightness, all of her three sons attained degrees and high rank.

33. I.e., there was no premeditation; more than two people cannot keep a secret.

Now beaten
Over their whole bodies—how can I watch?
So thoroughly thrashed
Their muscles are injured, their bones dislocated.
All more painful than
Suspending their hair from the rafters or piercing their thighs with
an awl.[34]
They
Never suffered this torture by their parent's hands.[35]

(JUDGE BAO:) One of you three must be the ringleader. Who was first to kill this man? (ELDEST WANG:) Mother had nothing to do with it. Neither did my brothers. I am the one who killed him. (SECOND WANG:) Father, mother had nothing to do with it. Neither did my brothers. I am the one who killed him. (THIRD WANG:) Father, O great one, mother had nothing to do with it. Neither did my brothers. And neither did I. (MOTHER WANG:) It has nothing to with any of my three children. Back then it was Ge Biao, the imperial relative, who first killed my husband. I couldn't stand the pain, and on the spur of the moment my anger got the best of me and I struggled with him, and killed him. It was, in truth, me. I killed him. (JUDGE BAO:) Nonsense! You confess, I confess, everyone confesses—it looks like a conspiracy to me. One of you, at any rate, will have to give up your life. Zhang Qian, really lay it on now. (MOTHER WANG:)

(*Dou hama*)
They are transfixed in silence—there's no one to rescue them,
Their eyes wide open—they suffer pain alive.
Children,
We'd better give him a confession.
I answer respectfully in front of you, sir.
That bastard bullied us[36]
And murdered my husband.
But now you investigate me, take this wife into custody—
You public officials are like wolves and tigers.
Your honor, still your anger! Cease your rage!
Not just hemp-wrapped clubs, head clamps, and finger presses
Are the punishments for intense and unending questions and
interrogation.

---

34. Steps taken by exemplary students to keep themselves awake to study.
35. Literally, "from their father's rice and mother's stew."
36. She's speaking now of Ge Biao.

What are the categories of your investigation
That call for beating them until they are soaked in blood?
The eldest brother gives voice to wrong, cries, "Injustice!"
But you, sir, make no attempt to hear an explanation.
Second brother endures a living hell on earth,
How can he bear such pain?
And the third brother is beaten most harshly—
And this ties my stomach in knots and hacks away at my heart.
> And here and over there, too,
We are frightened, scared, and skittish,
Eyeing each other again and again,
Back and forth we go,
Weeping and wailing, crying and bawling.
O Rescriptor-in-Waiting at the Dragon Design Pavilion, we are
> beaten to death by you!
> I recall now
When your father first said,
> "Isn't it true that
'Children and grandchildren make their own fortune'?"[37]
Now it's hard to swallow words or spit them out,
There's no way left to even breathe,
Except for short sighs and long moans—
A stomach of sadness like fire,
Tears of rain like pearls.

(JUDGE BAO:) Let me look at this writ that accompanied them. (*Acts out looking at it.*) Those clerks in Zhongmou are really inept. How come this writ says only, "Eldest Wang, Second Wang, and Third Wang murdered the good man Ge Biao?" Isn't there a single good secretary in the district offices? These three must have proper given names. And if not, then at least a child name. You, old lady, how do you call your eldest child? (MOTHER WANG:) He's called Goldlike. (JUDGE BAO:) And the second scoundrel? (MOTHER WANG:) He's called Ironlike. (JUDGE BAO:) And the third one here? (MOTHER WANG:) He's called Stonelike. (THIRD WANG:) -lyte. (JUDGE BAO:) What -lyte? (THIRD WANG:) Stone Acolyte. (JUDGE BAO:) It's clear they are murderers. For a peasant family to take such "hard" and unyielding names! It's clear that Goldlike was the murderer. (MOTHER WANG:)

---

37. Second line of the couplet: "So don't wear yourself out on behalf of them." Can either imply that children will do well without parents' concern, or that they will simply not repay the effort.

(*Muyang guan*)
>   If he's gold
> Then what's so hard about smelting him?

(JUDGE BAO:) Well, it must have been Stonelike who killed him? ([MOTHER WANG:])

>   If this one
> Is rock-solid can he be false?

(JUDGE BAO:) Well, it must have been Ironlike who killed him? ([MOTHER WANG:])

>   If this one
> Were iron could he withstand those "official laws like a furnace?"

(JUDGE BAO:) Beat these stubborn bags of bones. (MOTHER WANG:)

>   It's not that these children
> Are obstinate bags of bones;
> They really are harboring injustice and bearing wrongs.

(JUDGE BAO:) Zhang Qian, it's well said, "Those who murder owe a life; those who borrow must pay back their debts." Take out that eldest little bastard and let him pay with his life. (MOTHER WANG:)

> My eyes open in fright, I find no way to save him,
> Now surrounded and pushed down the stairs.
>   It makes
> It impossible for us to look at each other,
> For no matter what, there's no right way out.

O father Bao, Rescriptor-in-Waiting, you are so muddleheaded. (JUDGE BAO:) What did she say just as I was sending her eldest off to pay with his life? (ZHANG:) That woman grabbed the end of his cangue with her hands and said that you, father Bao, Rescriptor-in-Waiting, were muddleheaded. (JUDGE BAO:) Her? She said I was muddleheaded? Bring her over here. (MOTHER WANG *acts out kneeling.* JUDGE BAO:) Why did you say I was muddleheaded when I sent your eldest out to pay with his life? (MOTHER WANG:) Would I dare, sir, say you were muddleheaded? But, it's just that my eldest son is filial. If you kill him, then who will care for me in my old age? (JUDGE BAO:) Once his mother says he is filial all of the neighbors weigh in with testimony. Well, this is a case where I was wrong. Keep the eldest here to take care of her in her old age. Zhang Qian, have the second son pay with his life. (MOTHER WANG:)

(*Gewei*)
> On the one hand,
The eldest brother—concern for him ties my stomach in knots,
> On the other,
The second—he is so dear that my insides ache for him.
If someone has to pay with a life, then leave the children.
> I'd rather
You took this old woman!
But such harsh cruelty as this
Leaves no room to lay plaint—
All I can do is grab the end of the cangue with my hands,
And shout out, "Injustice!"

O father Bao, Rescriptor-in-Waiting, you are so muddleheaded. (JUDGE BAO:) Now what is she carrying on about? (ZHANG:) That woman said again that you, sir, are muddleheaded. (JUDGE BAO:) Bring her over here. (MOTHER WANG *acts out kneeling.* JUDGE BAO:) Look, woman, how come you said I am muddleheaded when I sent your second son out to pay with his life? (MOTHER WANG:) How could I dare say you, sir, were muddleheaded? But, it's just that my second son is a fine businessman. If you kill him, then who will care for me in my old age? (JUDGE BAO:) I said the eldest had to pay and you said he was filial. I said that the second had to pay and you said he was a fine businessman. Well, then, just *who* will pay life for life? (THIRD WANG *acts out putting on the cangue himself.* JUDGE BAO:) What are you doing? (THIRD WANG:) First brother won't be paying with life, second brother won't be paying with his, so all that's left is me. So, the best thing to do is to give you an early present. (JUDGE BAO:) Fine! Zhang Qian, take out the little one to pay with his life. ([ZHANG] *acts out pushing him and then turning him around.* JUDGE BAO:) You, lady—Is it all right to have the third one pay with his life? (MOTHER WANG:) It's fine. Isn't it said, "When three people walk together, the youngest is bound to suffer?" It's right for him to pay with his life. (JUDGE BAO:) And I'm not muddleheaded? (MOTHER WANG:) You, father, are not muddleheaded. (JUDGE BAO:) Quiet! Zhang Qian, bring him back. She almost put one over on me. Now I am setting a stepson loose! These two are your own sons by birth, aren't they? And this little aphid here is an adopted son who's being raised by you. You aren't very fond of him and so you'll let him pay with his life. Woman, if you answer correctly, I have a way out. If you answer wrongly, then don't think I'll cut you any slack. (MOTHER WANG:) All three are mine. What would you have me say? (JUDGE BAO:) If you won't tell the truth. . . . Zhang Qian, beat her for me. (MOTHER WANG:) Brother one, brother two, brother three, I'll say what I have to say—don't contradict

me. (JUDGE BAO:) Are these two elder ones your own birth sons? (MOTHER
WANG:)

> (*Muyang guan*)
> This child—
> Although I did not give him birth,
> I certainly suckled him.

(JUDGE BAO:) And the second one? ([MOTHER WANG:])

> This one—
> He was so young when I began raising him

(JUDGE BAO:) And that little one? ([MOTHER WANG:])

> This one here
> Is my own son,
> And those two there—
> Well, I am their stepmother.

(JUDGE BAO:) Woman, come here. You're doing it wrong. Have one of your
stepchildren pay with his life, and keep your own son to care for you in your old
age. Wouldn't that be better? (MOTHER WANG:) You, sir, are the one who's wrong.

> If I indifferently let one of the children of the first wife pay with his
>   life,
> Then I will display for all the evil heart of the stepmother.
>   If I imitate
> That heartless woman [who fanned the grave,][38]
>   Won't I be too ashamed
> To face the virtuous auntie of Lu.[39]

(JUDGE BAO:) Woman, you must make one of those three acknowledge that
they killed the man. (MOTHER WANG:)

> (*Hong shaoyao*)
> If my whole body was made of mouths, could I mislead you?
>   But I'm just like
> A gourd with no mouth.

---

38. See *Injustice to Dou E*, n. 15. Here, to spurn her promise to the dead husband to raise his
children.

39. A righteous woman of Lu who, when the state was attacked by Qi, fled with her child and
her nephew. About to be overtaken by Qi soldiers, she abandoned her own child and escaped
with her nephew. Qi generals, moved by her virtue, stopped their pursuit.

> You've beaten them
> Until their flesh is split and their muscles spill out, their skin
>   destroyed,
> And they are smeared and sullied with fresh blood—
> It's just like a living hell.[40]
> My three boys will all be sent to their deaths,
> You officials and ministers all rely on each other just like you were
>   relatives,
> So you'll surely side with nobility and relatives of the state!

(MOTHER WANG *acting out grieving*:)

(*Pusa Liangzhou*)
If the eldest son runs afoul of punishments,
Or the second separates from me along the paths of life and death,
Or the third returns to the Courts of Hell,
Then this damned old body of mine is left behind alone.
The eldest son is filial and understands the proper distances of the
   rites,
Second son can be left behind to manage the family affairs,
The third—say no more,
You shall pay with your life,
It is fitting that you go.
         The proverb says,
"When three people walk together, the youngest is bound to suffer."
Let the public officials shout and clamor!

(JUDGE BAO:) When I hear this woman speak I begin to believe the saying, "A good merchant hides his goods so well he appears to have nothing; a gentleman of overweening virtue has a countenance like the dull-witted." In this affair, I see that the mother is virtuous and the sons are completely filial. The mother is of the same class as mothers Tao and Meng, and the sons no different than Zengzi and Min Ziqian.[41] Now, I just had a dream when I took a nap. I just saw a small butterfly fall into a web and then be rescued by a larger one. The next one was just the same. But the last one fell into the net, too, and the larger butterfly didn't rescue it, even though it saw it fall. It just flew on away. I have a

---

40. That is, like a living representation of the Courts of Hell, often vividly portrayed in temple wall paintings, where victims are tortured, beaten, hacked, pierced with swords and awls, boiled in oil, and subjected to various other forms of punishments. This is not, therefore a summoning of a vague feeling of condemnation, but a reference to the intense physical punishment inflicted by the lictors of hell.

41. Two disciples of Confucius noted for their filial piety.

heart of compassion so I rescued the little butterfly from the net. This was Heaven, giving me a sign that foretold what was going to happen and that I should save this little fellow's life. Just now,

> I deduced the severity of the sentence based on codicils of law,
> And didn't understand that beyond the case lay other axes to grind.
> But how can we simply forget the killing of a good citizen?
> Isn't it said that one cannot let a criminal off lightly?
> So I first sent the oldest boy off to the execution ground,
> But because she said he was filial and could support her,
> I then sent the next one off to taste the blade.
> Then she said *he* could fulfill her daily needs by working for a living,
> And so I sent the youngest away to face the sentence,
> And she most happily sent him on his way.
> She showed naught but concern and kindness for her adopted sons,
> But no grief at all for her own flesh and blood.
> Virtue and obedience of this order should be rewarded with title and praise,
> Such ardent chasteness and excelling worthiness is fit for reward.
> Something just leapt to mind!
> Heaven caused my roaming dream soul to be first forewarned:
> Those three insects caught in the spider's web
> Equal the mother, the sons, and this official.
> Three times the stepmother has abandoned her own son:
> A perfect match to my noontime dream of butterflies.

Zhang Qian, throw them all into death row! (MOTHER WANG *acts out hurrying forward to clutch them:*)

> (*Shuixianzi*)
> I see them
> Pushed forward, pulled back, clinging to each other,
> For your sakes
> I grab the tip of the cangue and cry out, "Injustice!"
> With staring eyes they go out, once gone never to return.
> It makes me
> Feel powerless in a hundred ways.
> In such a mess as this
> Why not die?
> I'll follow you anyway,
> For, living or dead, I am at my end.
> Here
> I clutch their clothes tightly.

(ZHANG QIAN *pushes* MOTHER WANG *away, pushes the three boys offstage.* MOTHER WANG *sings:*)

(*Shouwei*)
>   Bao of the Dragon Design Hall
> Was always right on the money when judging cases in the past,
> But now as an official is no great shakes.
>   For no reason at all
> You sit in the Yellow Hall, and wear the Tiger Tally,[42]
> Receive glory and power, request salary and emolument.
>   While my sons—
> Their grave injustice and wrongs no concern of yours—
> Are cast into prison.
>   I'll act in desperation
> And rashly lay my plaint in the capital halls, in the offices of the
>   central government,
> And, beating on the walls of the imperial city, I'll drum out my
>   wrongs.[43]
> When I see the Simurgh Palanquin,[44] then I'll be impetuous and rash—
> A stupid old woman, I'll sing my tale of woe.
> And if there is still no one willing to be my advocate,
>   Then I'll best
> Find a proper death—
> You'll see no lonely widow, childless woman here.
>   Far better this
> Than being bereft with nowhere to turn,
> Pained and hurt, weeping and wailing, suffering torture while alive.

(*Exits.*)

(JUDGE BAO:) Zhang Qian, come here. What do you think of this? (ZHANG:) Do you think you've hit it right? (JUDGE BAO:) You loutish beast. Are my words ever wrong?

> I support the sagely and intelligent ruler of the present day,
>   Hoping to spread a pure reputation for all eternity.

---

42. The "Yellow Hall" is any position of authority; the Tiger Tally grants that position the power of life and death, executed without the necessity of imperial ratification.

43. A drum was placed at the entrance to the Imperial City, where common citizens could go and lay a complaint directly to high government officials.

44. Of the emperor.

If I can't see my way through this present case,
How can I sit in the southern court of Kaifeng Prefecture?

(*Exit together.*)

[Act 3]

(ZHANG QIAN *entering* [*with* LI WAN]:)[45]

In my hand I hold the ruthless club,
In my lapels hide the money of dripping tears.[46]
By light I trod the paths of wolves and tigers,
By night I sleep in the company of corpses.[47]

I am Zhang Qian. The three Wang brothers have been put on death row. I think I'll call the three of them out right now. (ELDEST WANG, SECOND WANG *enter*. [ELDEST]:) Brother, have pity on us! ([ZHANG]:) Carry that cangue over here, give him three strokes of the "Quelling Resistance Club." (*Act out beating three times.* ZHANG:) Where's that third one? (THIRD WANG *enters*:) I was here first! (ZHANG:) Li Wan, bring the rack over here, throw this belly-wrapping chain over them and cinch it down. (*Acts out cinching them down. The three act out crying out.* ZHANG:) Li Wan, go on home to eat, I'll look after them just in case the warden comes by. (MOTHER WANG *enters*:) All three of my sons have been put in prison and on death row. I've begged some leftover soup and scraps of food and I'll go give them some to eat.

([ZHENGGONG MODE:] *Duanzheng hao*)
Gazing far off at the prison of the condemned,
I've just left the Field of Mercy—[48]
Who dares say I'll slow by half a step?
From gate to gate I've begged, missing not a one,
And have sponged some leftover rice and mixed noodles.
    My children
Originally wanted to be Top Graduates,
To sit in the District Magistrate's hall,

---

45. Although not noted in stage directions, Li Wan (Li Ten-thousand) accompanies Zhang Qian (Zhang Thousand) on stage. Li Wan, like Zhang Qian, is a generalized stage name for a clerk.
46. I.e., bribes offered by the convicted.
47. I.e., he apprehends criminals by day and sleeps next to them in the jail at night.
48. Welfare centers set up by Buddhist monasteries for poor folk.

And request salary and emolument.

> Who has ever run as

Foul of the law as they?

> They never

Violated the three thousand codicils of the five penal codes.

> I

Am unwilling to eat,

Unwilling to wear good clothes,

And I sleep on ground scorched for warmth.

> Has anyone ever been

As poor and base as me?

> I am carrying on for Mother Chen[49]

And her proverb from olden days—

For sure she would "Never seek for noble rank and the riches of gold and jade,

But for sons and grandsons, and all worthy, each and every one."

I've taken all I can of this suffering.

(*Acts out arriving at the gate of the prison:*) Here I am already. I'll pull on this bell cord. (ZHANG:) That's probably the warden. I'll open up the door and see who it is. Who's ringing the bell? (MOTHER WANG:) I rang it. (ZHANG *acts out striking her:*) You boorish old woman! Is this your home? Why are you here? (MOTHER WANG:) I've brought some food for my boys. (ZHANG:) No lamp oil money, no bitter injustice money?[50] We live off our death-row inmates. If you've got any money, bring it out. (MOTHER WANG:) Have a heart, brother, have pity on me. My old man was murdered and my three sons are in cells for the condemned. I may eat breakfast, but never any dinner. I've begged through all of the backstreets for some leftover soup and scraps of food. I want to give them to my children to stave off their hunger. Have pity, brother.

> (*Tang xiucai*)
>
> The leftover soup and scraps of food I've begged I've reheated over and over,
>
> And the patched-up old padded jacket, I've worn right side and wrong side out.
>
> > Brother, let me give you these clothes. And these
>
> Old oversleeves I also give you, brother, as bitter injustice money.

---

49. See note 32.
50. Both are forms of bribes so jailors will treat the prisoners well.

(ZHANG:) I don't want your stuff. (MOTHER WANG:)

> Thank you, brother, for watching over them
> And keeping them whole.
> Please have pity on my children!

(ZHANG:) Their sentence has already been determined. I can't save them now. (MOTHER WANG:)

> (*Tuo bushan*)
> Alas, "one family, one fate"—
> My stomach is twisted into knots.
> One above, one below—
> Every word of each sentence is so full of suffering.
> One to the left, one to the right—
> I worry uneasily about each child.
> Every swipe of the hand is a handful
> Of teary rain flowing and falling.

> (*Zui taiping*)
> If you begin to enumerate their crimes,
> They truly do harbor injustice.
>   Here I
> Fret and worry, worry and fret, blame blue Heaven,
> And beg you, brother, to have pity.
>   Those three—
> Their wild and witless eyes wildly and frantically roll,
> And shivering, quivering hands tremblingly quake and shake.
> I am clueless, at wit's end, unable to save them:
> And it makes me so angry I'm bent over double.

(ZHANG:) I'll let you in. Let me close the door. (MOTHER WANG *acts out entering and seeing them:*) Oh, my children! (*They all act out grieving.* ELDEST WANG:) Why are you here, mother? (MOTHER WANG:) I've brought you some food. (MOTHER WANG, *in the direction of* ZHANG QIAN, *speaks:*) Brother, can't you let my children loose to eat? (ZHANG:) Don't you have hands? Woman, feed your children yourself. (MOTHER WANG *acts out feeding* ELDEST WANG *and* SECOND WANG:)

> (*Xiao heshang*)
> I, I, I run forward two or three steps,
> Take, take, take this food and urge them to eat.
> I, I, I scoop it all out one spoonful after another,
> You, you, you gobble it down,
> You, you, you moisten your throats.

(THIRD WANG:) Mom, can't I have something to eat, too? (MOTHER WANG:)

> Stone Acolyte, no matter what, mouthful by mouthful you choke this
> down.

(MOTHER WANG *acts out pouring all of the food on the ground, speaks:*) Elder
brother, I have a baked bun for you here. Eat it but don't let Stonelike see it. Second brother, I have a baked bun for you, too. Don't let Stonelike see you eat it.

> (*Daodao ling*)
> > These cadged
> Leftover soups and scraps of food
> > Can be no
> Thrice-sieved finest flour.
> > Don't think
> Of that elegant food and jadelike wine from the feast in the
> > Chalcedony Forest.[51]
> > Think back on
> Going out of Zhongmou County, nailed in your long cangue—
> > We certainly can't say,
> "We went in to don our robes in the Golden Hall."[52]
> Oh, it tortures me to think of it.
> So, so, so, so,
> I tell you wardens and jailers, don't bear any grudges.

Eldest son, I am leaving. Do you have anything to say? (ELDEST WANG:) Mother,
there is a copy of the *Four Books*[53] in the house. Sell it so you can buy some
funeral cash to burn for father. (MOTHER WANG:) Second brother, what do
you have to say? (SECOND WANG:) Mother, I have a copy of the *Mencius*. Sell it
and have some sutras and penitences read for father. (THIRD WANG, *crying,
speaks:*) I don't have anything to tell you. Just let me hug your head.[54] (MOTHER
WANG *acts out leaving.* ZHANG QIAN *speaks:*) Woman, do you want to be happy?

---

51. The Garden of the Chalcedony Forest (*Qionglin yuan*) was the site of the imperial banquet for successful candidates in the triennial national examinations. "Chalcedony" refers to the
bluish color of snow on pine trees.

52. To change from ordinary clothes into the robes of a successful examination candidate.

53. A collection, compiled in the Song, containing two essays, "Centrality and Commonality"
(*Zhongyong*) and "Great Learning" (*Daxue*)—originally chapters in the *Book of Rites* (*Liji*)—as
well as the *Mencius* and the *Analects*. These were staples of the curriculum of students and the
basic ethical texts of the time.

54. The line is at best a pun, at least ironic. The word we have translated "hug" means "to
squeeze" and is the same verb used for a head press used to torture prisoners into confession. The
line may also mean, "Just give me your head to squeeze."

(MOTHER WANG *speaks*:) Of course! (ZHANG QIAN *acts out going into the jail, speaks*:) Which one is the eldest? (ELDEST WANG *speaks*:) I am the oldest. (ZHANG QIAN *speaks*:) Go to the toilet. (ELDEST WANG *acts out leaving*. ZHANG QIAN:) Woman, this oldest one is filial. Take him out safely to care for you. Does it make you happy to see this son? (MOTHER WANG:) You bet I'm happy. (ZHANG QIAN:) I'll make you even happier. (*Acts out going into the jail, speaks*:) Who's the second son? (SECOND WANG *speaks*:) Me! (ZHANG QIAN:) Get up and go to the toilet. (SECOND WANG *acts out going to the toilet*. ZHANG QIAN:) Woman, I've given you another now, the second one, to make a livelihood for you. (MOTHER WANG:) Brother, what about the third child? (ZHANG QIAN:) Well, he'll be trussed up and hanged to repay his life for that of Ge Biao. Come to the foot of the wall early tomorrow morning and identify the corpse. (MOTHER WANG:)

> (*Shang xiaolou*)
>   These two
> Brothers he sets free and clear,
>   But the third one
> He pushes back inside.
>   And when I think
> How I suffered for him, that I bore him for nine months,
> Nursed him for three years. . . .
>   Well, it's better than letting the older two
> Suffer the corporal punishments of law
>   Or letting others say
> That I am a heartless stepmother
> Who is blind to goodness.
>
> (*Reprise*)
> All you ever wanted was to pay injustice with injustice,
> But you got caught up in something turned upside down.
> Had you never heard, "A murderer pays with his own life?"
> Or, "For every crime a punishment?"
> Or that you must "Die without resentment?"

(*Acts out looking at* THIRD WANG:)

>   And if I am too loathe deserting him now
>   It will make others say,
>   "Here's a stepmother
>   Who is pulling the wool over our eyes."

(ELDEST WANG *and* SECOND WANG): Mother, we can't bear to leave brother here. (MOTHER WANG:) Boys, go on home now and don't be upset about it.

(*Kuaihuo san*)
Let him die, so pitiful,
Let your little brother's life be lost to the Yellow Springs.

(*Acts out looking at* THIRD WANG *and grieving:*)

And let me turn away now and, unable to hold them back any longer,
    weep flowing tears.

(ELDEST WANG *and* SECOND WANG *act out grieving.*) (MOTHER WANG:) Enough,
enough! Let's go home

And let him die without resentment.

(*Chao Tianzi*)
                    I
Pity, truly pity
My son, so young—
When will we ever meet again?
                    Still it is better
Than letting all the lives of the former family cover the Yellow
    Springs,
                    Or senselessly
Stirring up the blame of later generations.
                    I have
Beaten my breast over it a hundred times
                    And it really
Tortures me with pain.
When tomorrow comes
"A single swipe of the knife will cut it in two"[55]—
His corpse lying out in the marketplace—
And I'll never see Stone's face again.

(*Weisheng*)
                    Before he that was father
Has even been offered a burnt packet of funeral cash,
                    He that is son
Already faces a penalty of death.
Can I ever see either father or son again?
If I should want to see them even once,

---

55. A common idiom meaning "it will be over in a flash"; of course with a special overtone
here.

                                    In
Dreams alone will come a reunion of mother and son.

                                (Exits.)

(ELDEST WANG *and* SECOND WANG *follow [their mother] and exit.* THIRD WANG *speaks:*) Brother Zhang Qian, where have my own brothers gone? (ZHANG QIAN:) It was the order of His Honor. Your brothers have been spared to take care of your mother. And you shall pay for Ge Biao's life with your own. (THIRD WANG:) You've spared my brothers to take care of my mother and I have to pay with my life! Well, let me put on these two other cangues, too. Even in death we three lean on each other. Brother, in what way will I die tomorrow? (ZHANG QIAN:) You'll be trussed and hanged, then thrown over that thirty-foot wall. (THIRD WANG:) Brother, be careful when you throw me over the wall, I've got some boils on my stomach. (ZHANG QIAN:) You'll surely die anyway. (THIRD WANG:)

(*Duanzheng hao*)
A belly stuffed from books I've read,

(ZHANG QIAN:) What are you doing, singing? (THIRD WANG:)

It's my finale!
I've mastered the *Book of Rites* and *Classic of Changes*.
Still, with frightened eyes, I see my allotted time draw to a close.
          What I hoped
Was to be an official, a minister, a person of glory and nobility,
          But today
I must give up both fame and fortune.

(*Gun xiuqiu*)
          Rescriptor-in-Waiting Bao—
He took even less effort than "the one who asked about the ox,"[56]
          My father—
He lacked the foresight and wisdom of "the one who instructed his sons."[57]

---

56. From the story of Minister Bing Ji of the Han. In early spring, he saw corpses of those beaten to death in the streets of the capital, but paid them no heed. His interest was aroused, however, by a panting ox, which he sent an underling to investigate. When criticized, he replied that the murder was not something under his jurisdiction. The panting cow, however, may have signaled hotter-than-normal weather, a sign that the harmonic balance of Heaven had been disrupted, thereby portending a similar disordering of the relationship between state institutions and Heaven.

57. Possibly a reference to a certain Dou Yujun, a doting father who taught his five sons so well that they all succeeded in the imperial examinations.

> And the budding scholar
Lacked the youthful bravado of "the one who inscribed his name on
the bridge"[58]
And, frightened, was bloodied by club and stave.

> Rescriptor-in-Waiting Bao—
You are also muddleheaded
And the clerks act as if they don't know it.

> On the sides of the hall,
The runners and constables line up,
Dignified and stern in appearance,
But on the whole, just a group of motherfuckers.
Being hanged out over the wall by the side of the jail
Is no "Single success to raise me to fame and renown through the
world!"
Zhang Qian, let me fuck your mother's crooked cunt!

(Exits.)

(ZHANG QIAN *follows him and exits.*)

[Act 4]

(THIRD WANG *enters, bearing corpse of* STUBBORN DONKEY ZHANG *on his back, and hides in a secure place.*) (ELDEST WANG *and* SECOND WANG *enter:*) We've come here with mother to seek out the corpse of third brother. Mother, move a little faster. (MOTHER WANG *enters:*) I've heard that my son, Stone, has been trussed up and hanged. The two brothers have gone to fetch the body and I've begged some paper cash so that I can cremate my son.

([SHUANGDIAO MODE:] *Xinshui ling*)
> Never before have I
Sneaked out of the city before dawn,
> Lest
Outsiders find out
And raise a ruckus.
> I've begged
A rag-tag passel of funeral cash,

---

58. On his departure from the city of Chengdu, Sima Xiangru, the noted Han poet, inscribed on the pillar of a bridge, "If I am not riding a tall four-horse carriage, I will not return across this bridge"; that is, if there is no success, there is no return. Sima Xiangru became the archetype of the lowly but soon-to-be-discovered genius and his statement a common linguistic piety of the examination-bound student.

And scrounged
A few stumpy ends of firewood.
      My son,
Won't get even a simple burial mat or carrying pole—[59]
Who would have expected such a fiery end?

(*Zhuma ting*)
      O child,
You, with your heart filled with vengeance,
Shall meet your father, cruelly slain, at the marker of worlds' divide.
      And should you meet,
Plot, you two, and execute a handy plan,
      To
Push that murderer off the "Home-gazing Terrace!"
The grotto-black skies of heaven are just turning white,
Stark, still quiet—this wild land beyond the walls.
Indistinct, hazy—there seems to be someone coming.
But as soon as I perceive who it is, it scares me to death.

(ELDEST WANG, SECOND WANG *enter, bearing corpse on their back:*) Mother, where are you? Here's third brother's corpse. (MOTHER WANG *acts out identifying the corpse and grieving:*)

(*Ye xing chuan*)
Scared, flustered, let us look at his face,
And his whole corpse smeared and smudged with blood.
      I'll
Hastily remove this hempen rope for you,
Quickly loosen your belt—
You boys, hurry over here and prop him up.

(*Gua yugou*)
      Help me
Hold his head still,
And close his jaw.
      On your behalf,
From a high terrace, I'll summon your soul back.
      "Ai, Stone,
In your haste, child, you lost your shoe."[60]
I call, but his gaze is evermore lost,

---

59. I.e., even the simplest of proper burial practices.
60. I.e., you lost your life.

My depression twists and grows,
My sorrow, unbearable.
> In vain it makes me

Weep and sob, cry and wail,
Grieve and lament, sorrow, feel full of woe.
> O Stone,

(*Gu meijiu*)
> I will

Force myself to rouse my worn-out spirit,
And call out your childhood name until it is clearly heard,
> "You,

Stone, filial and compliant, where do you now reside?"[61]
> You've

Cast your mommy away,
> And it makes me

Beat the skin of the earth in despair.

(*Taiping ling*)
> In vain it makes me

Weep and sob, cry and wail,
Thrash around on the ground in despair.
Nothing I do can summon you back
> And this assures

My life is ruined.
Burning with sorrow, I cannot endure, I cannot bear it.

O Stone. (THIRD WANG *enters and responds:*)[62] Here I am! (MOTHER WANG:)

I guess, and guess again, where is this reply coming from?
> Could it be

A mountain spirit or a water demon?

(THIRD WANG *enters:*) Mother, your son's right here. (MOTHER WANG *acts out being flustered:*) A ghost! A ghost! (THIRD WANG:) Don't be frightened, mother. It's your child, Stone. (MOTHER WANG:)

---

61. We believe this to be the incantation she is calling out to summon the soul.

62. This stage direction is rather unusual. Since Third Wang also enters below, this "enter" may be a false entrance, in which the player is visible to the audience, but not to the singer. Also, the term "respond" probably indicates a stage action rather than a simple verbal response. Since what is represented on stage is the actual ritual of summoning the soul, it would make great stage sense for the voice to be heard and the person to remain unseen. We should not overlook the fact that the line may also be read, "responds from above."

(*Feng ru song*)
If I go forward, it catches up behind,
> It scares me so much
That I tweak my ears and rub my cheeks.
> It makes me
Tremble and shake, hurry to bow before my child.
> On your behalf,
I'll arrange the sacrifice of Seven Sevens.[63]

(THIRD WANG:) Mother, I'm a person, I'm alive. (MOTHER WANG:)

If you're not a ghost, spill it all out quickly—how did you return?

(THIRD WANG:) His honor trussed up and hanged the horse thief, Pigheaded
Ass Zhao, and then made me drag him out here. He let your child off. (MOTHER
WANG:)

(*Chuan bo zhao*)
This disaster was only a moment of fate already on the wane
And I can already cut my sad worry adrift.
> I would have said that
My Stone had fallen into vast ocean—
> You elder brothers, don't be upset at me, but
What were you two doing?
Don't take offense at my words,
But how could you carry this corpse here without checking it?

(*Xiaohai fu'er*)
> You
Should have opened your eyes!
> Just
Whose corpse have you lugged here?
> You were neither
Happy as can be, stringing up fish on a willow osier,
> Nor were you
Dispatched by ghosts, or deputed by spirits.
> On your childhood name
Was a sentence of death,
So why have you suffered no harm?

(THIRD WANG:) All I know is that nothing happened. (MOTHER WANG:)

---

63. Seven sacrifices, one each every seven days, to liberate the souls of the dead into rebirth.

The proverb says,
"The truthful will always win out."
So, this corpse you've carried here by mistake
> Let's
Bury safely in the earth.

(JUDGE BAO *rushes on, speaks:*) Have you killed yet another? (MOTHER WANG *and the rest act out being flustered.* JUDGE BAO:) Don't be frightened. That's the horse thief Pigheaded Ass Zhao, who stood in your stead to repay the debt of Ge Biao's life. Now, you, the whole family, listen to the Emperor's decree:

> You, having been pampered citizens beneath the imperial sleeves,
> Possess the stuff to be stalwart ministers, to requite the state:
> The eldest brother shall go to follow affairs at court,
> The second shall wear regalia and insignia of high status.
> Stone shall become Prefect of Zhongmou,
> And your mother shall be enfeoffed as Lady of Stalwart Virtue.
> The state treasures righteous husbands and wives of integrity,
> And loves those filial children and compliant grandsons.
> The ruler of sagely light has bestowed these ranks in reward—
> Let us all gaze toward the palace gates to thank his beneficence.

(ALL *speak:*) Ten thousand years to the emperor! Tens of ten thousand years!
(MOTHER WANG:)

> (*Shuixianzi*)
> From the nine-layered heaven the document of pardon has flown—
> Let not the three of you resent the forced confessions any more.
>> We all
> Face the palace gates and quickly bow in respect,
> Our prayer only that the ruler of sagely light will live a thousand
>> times ten thousand years.
> That would be better than flowers sprouting afresh on withered
>> wood.
> This debt of pus and blood they have suffered to pay,
> And endured all the calamities of the prison's cell.
>> Today
> Ends the bitterness, now comes the sweet.

> (*Weisha*)
> We've just paid back our debt of terror,
> And from deepest darkness fought our way out of the fortress of lost
>> souls.

> We pray that our Rescriptor-in-Waiting Bao
> Will be arrayed among the Three Nobles of State,
> And rise a thousand ranks a day.
> You have proclaimed
> That the mother shall be made Lady of Stalwart Virtue,
> And the son, Prefect of Zhongmou District.
> You've pardoned mother and children, who will ever be unharmed,
> Old and young, who will have no more misfortune.
> All we pray
> Is that our Lord on the Dragon Throne will live ten thousand years.

TITLE: Imperial relative Ge, presuming on his power, commits a senseless
         act of violence,
         Pigheaded Ass Zhao, stealing a horse, sends himself to death.

NAME: Old Lady Wang, stalwart and virtuous, soothes her stepsons,
         Rescriptor-in-Waiting Bao thrice investigates the butterfly dream.

3

A Beauty Pining in Her Boudoir:
The Pavilion for Praying to the Moon

Guan Hanqing

A Beauty Pining in Her Boudoir: The Pavilion for Praying to the Moon (*Guiyuan jiaren baiyue ting*) is a regular Northern drama consisting of four song suites preceded by a wedge, all assigned to the female lead. No author is given for this play but, since the bibliographical sections of *The Register of Ghosts* and *A Formulary of Correct Rhymes for an Era of Great Peace* (*Taihe zhengyin pu*), a musical and prosodic study of *qu* lyrics written by Zhu Quan (1378–1448), both ascribe a play entitled *Baiyue ting* to Guan Hanqing, he is unanimously accepted as the author of this text. If in fact by Guan Hanqing, *The Pavilion for Praying to the Moon* is one of his finest works, allowing him to display to the full his talent for the portrayal of independent and strong-willed young women. A long-time stage favorite, the play remained in the *zaju* repertoire until the very end of the sixteenth century. Early on it was also adapted into the repertoire of Southern-style drama (*chuanqi*) under the title *Yougui ji* (*The Inner Quarters*) and became one of the more popular plays in this genre as well. This later adaptation has helped us by providing clues to the action of the Yuan play, and has provided as well the names of characters, which in the *Baiyue ting* are identified only by role types.

The background to the action of *The Pavilion for Praying to the Moon* is the Mongol attack of 1215 on the Central Capital (also known as Yanjing) of the Jin dynasty, located in the southwestern suburbs of modern Beijing. Since the play was written during the Yuan dynasty, the Mongol soldiers are referred to as "heavenly troops." The Jurchen, a Tungusic people who were also ancestors of the Manchus, founders of the Qing dynasty in 1644, established the Chinese Jin or "Golden" dynasty in 1115. After their conquest of the Northern Song capital of Bianliang (modern Kaifeng) in 1126, the Jurchen ruled all of China and Manchuria from the north shore of the Huai River to the steppes of Siberia. But Mongol military pressure, culminating in the sack of the Jin capital of Yanjing in 1215, eventually forced the Jin to transfer their seat of government to Bianliang, an event that provides the historical setting for this drama. In the opening wedge, the heroine Wang Ruilan and her mother send the family patriarch, Wang Zhen, a high court official, off to the war front. In Act 1, mother and daughter flee with the main populace when the capital is sacked. They are overtaken by government troops, panic, and lose sight of each other. Wang Ruilan encounters a student, Jiang Shilong, who is calling out the name of his sister, Ruilian, with whom he had lost contact in the same mêlée. Wang Ruilan, thinking he is calling her name, seeks him out. She decides to travel on together with him and for reasons of safety to pass herself off as his wife. A band of highwaymen capture them while they are en route (this incident is enacted in an opening scene of Act 1, left unwritten in our text), but it turns out that Jiang Shilong had earlier rescued the bandits' leader, Tuoman Xingfu, from the clutches of the authorities. Tuoman Xingfu proposes that Jiang Shilong join up with him, but Wang Ruilan urges Jiang to continue their journey to the new Southern Capital at Kaifeng.

Three months pass between the first and second acts. Wang Ruilan has fallen in love with Jiang Shilong and become his common-law wife. Act 2 opens at an inn in a small town where the couple has been forced to stay because Jiang Shilong has come down with an epidemic fever. In one of those common coincidences of the Yuan stage, as Ruilan sees off the local doctor who has just visited her husband, she bumps into her father, who happens to be passing by en route to Kaifeng. He forces her to desert the student and go away with him. Before being carried away, she declares her loyalty to Jiang Shilong and urges him to come find her in the Southern Capital after he recovers.

Act 3 also skips to a later time, after the political situation has stabilized to some extent and Wang Zhen has installed his family at the Southern Capital. We learn in this act that after being separated from her daughter, Ruilan's mother had met and adopted Jiang Shilong's sister Jiang Ruilian. So Wang Ruilan and Jiang Ruilian are now living together as sisters but are unaware of their common bond with Jiang Shilong until Jiang Ruilian secretly overhears Wang Ruilan pray to the moon to be reunited with her lover. This scene has given the play its name. Comparable midnight prayers to the moon are encountered in a number of coeval plays, perhaps the best-known to Western audiences being the garden scene in *Story of the Western Wing*, where Oriole makes a secret wish to marry student Zhang. When Wang Ruilan discloses to her adopted sister the name of her lover and the circumstances under which she had to leave him behind, her adoptive sister becomes quite upset. This leads Wang Ruilan at first to suspect Jiang Ruilian of being her lover's concubine but she soon realizes her mistake.

In the meantime, Jiang Shilong and his friend, Tuoman Xingfu, have also come to the new capital at Bianliang in order to take part in the examinations, Jiang in the civil examinations and Tuoman in the military. By the beginning of the final act both have passed their respective examinations as Top Graduates.

Wang Zhen arranges for the simultaneous marriage of his own daughter to the military top graduate and of his adoptive daughter to the civil top graduate. On the day selected for the joint wedding, Jiang Ruilian reproves Wang Ruilan for her willingness to marry someone other than her brother, whereupon Wang Ruilan laments the fact that she will be married to a brute soldier. When the bridegrooms arrive, Wang Ruilan immediately recognizes Jiang Shilong. The only option is to switch marriage partners, but Jiang Ruilian has been so scared by Wang Ruilan's description of the horrors of having a military man for a husband that she refuses to marry Tuoman Xingfu. She accepts him only after the arrival of an imperial emissary brings news of further promotions.

The Pavilion for Praying to the Moon is not based on any known source. Guan Hanqing may have made up the story himself or embellished an incident from (then still) recent history. The play is one of a small number that feature Jurchen characters. The Chinese surname, Wang ("king"), was commonly used in Chinese society by the Jurchen imperial clan, the Wanyan. To stress the fact that the Wangs are a non-Chinese family, the playwright has Wang Ruilan address her parents with the Jurchen words for father and mother (which we have translated as "Vati" and "Mutti"). The extremely rare surname "Tuoman" also is of non-Chinese origin and is recorded only for the Jin.

In plays that feature Jurchen, a clear ethnic stereotype is operative: Jurchen tend to be portrayed either as simple rustics, addicted to song and wine, or as strict disciplinarians, proud of their military tradition. The characterization of Wang Zhen clearly belongs to the latter category. His preference for a military man as a marriage candidate for his daughter must be interpreted as a preference for a Jurchen son-in-law, while his scorn of literary accomplishments hides his anti-Chinese sentiments. But while the elder generation of Jurchen may try to uphold the family tradition of manhood, the younger generation usually is represented as easily seduced by the lures of Chinese civilization. A very popular story with early playwrights was the tale of the young Jurchen nobleman falling in love with a Chinese actress despite parental opposition and running off with her.[1] In the case of *The Pavilion for Praying to the Moon*, the daughter of a high Jurchen official falls in love with a Chinese student and spurns a Jurchen military man. Mongols are rarely portrayed in Yuan dynasty *zaju*, and we may assume that plays featuring Jurchen were an important medium for venting ethnic antagonisms in Mongol China.

The element of ethnic bias adds extra spice to an otherwise already quite original love comedy. Notable elements are the wartime setting and the relatively

---

1. See *A Playboy from a Noble House Opts for the Wrong Career*, in Idema and West 1982.

complicated but, by Yuan drama standards, well-made plot. As in other love comedies all over the world, parental authority conflicts with youthful passion. Our heroine Wang Ruilan, once she has become aware of her love for Jiang Shilong, minces no words when her father separates her from her lover. However, it would appear that she and her father have agreed to keep silent about her affair when they get home: her adoptive sister does not know she has had a lover and only finds out by stealthily listening in on her prayers. Some modern critics have faulted the characterization of Wang Ruilan because by the opening of Act 4 she has submitted to the wedding arrangements made by her father. These critics prefer her characterization in the *Yougui ji*, in which she remains adamantly opposed to the marriage proposal, just like Jiang Shilong, until they become aware of each other's identity. Such critics would appear to impose too modern of a demand on Wang Ruilan, who, as is clear from Act 2, may not hesitate to speak her mind but does not have the strength or means effectively to oppose her father's will—at best she is only capable of passive resistance. Actually, Wang Ruilan's determined opposition to her father's wedding plans as found in the presently available editions of the *Yougui ji* appears to be a result of very late revisions to that play that reflect Neo-Confucian notions of loyalty and chastity.

Among Yuan printings of *zaju*, *The Pavilion for Praying to the Moon* is remarkable for its very detailed stage directions. A unique aspect of these stage directions is the great emphasis on the portrayal of quickly shifting moods and emotions by the heroine. Occasionally she is even instructed to act out two or more contradictory or complementary emotions at the same time. These stage directions lend a certain depth to the characterization that is missing from other preserved editions.

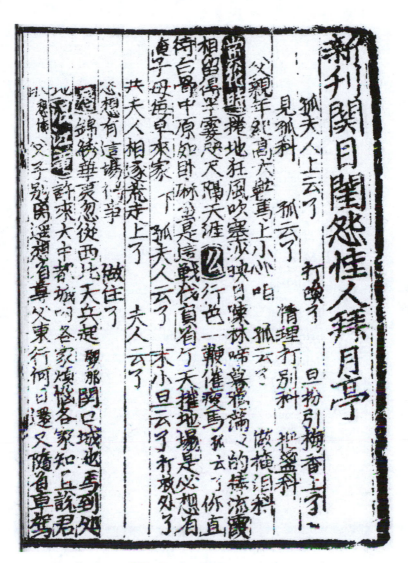

FIG. 2. The first page of *The Pavilion for Praying to the Moon* (page 83 in this volume), from an undated fourteenth-century edition

Dramatis personæ in order of appearance

Role type	Name, family role, or social role
Official	Wang Zhen
Lady	Wang Ruilan's mother
Female lead	Wang Ruilan
Meixiang	Meixiang, a maid
Male lead	Jiang Shilong
Little female	Jiang Ruilian
Extra male	Tuoman Xingfu, soldier
Innkeeper	Innkeeper
Physician	Physician
Cavalry scouts	Cavalry scouts
Matchmaker	Matchmaker

Newly Cut with Full Plot

A Beauty Pining in Her Boudoir:
The Pavilion for Praying to the Moon

[Wedge]

After WANG ZHEN *and* MOTHER *have entered and spoken — after being summoned — and after you enter dressed as* WANG RUILAN *together with* MEIXIANG — *act out greeting* WANG ZHEN. *After* WANG ZHEN *has spoken — act out parting, emotionally. Act out offering the cup:* Father, you are so old. Please be careful on your trip. *After* WANG ZHEN *speaks — act out wiping away your tears:*

> Rolling up the earth, a wild wind blows frontier sands;
> Sunlit in the sparse wood, evening crows caw.
> I offer to you this cup of "flowing sunset" filled to overflowing.
> If I could but detain you half a moment—
> For, in a moment's space we will be far apart, each at an edge of
>   heaven.

> (*Reprise*)
> About to depart, your whip urges on the skinny nag.

After WANG ZHEN *has spoken:*

> What you will see are "white bones strewn like hemp across the
>   Central Plain."
> Even though, during this campaign,
> You bear the burden of "heaven collapsing and earth crumbling away,"
> You must think of us, mother and daughter, and come home soon.

Exit.

[Act 1]

After WANG ZHEN *and* MOTHER *have spoken — after* JIANG SHILONG *and* JIANG RUILIAN *have spoken — after* TUOMAN XINGFU *is rescued — after entering together with* MOTHER *fleeing in panic — after* MOTHER *speaks:*[2] Who would have thought that such a disaster would occur? *After making up your mind:*

> ([XIANLÜ MODE:] *Dian jiangchun*)
> Over this brocade land of China and Barbaria
> Suddenly from the northwest
> Heavenly troops arose:
> > Observe
> How those walls and moats of border passes
> Turn to flattened land wherever their horses reach.

> (*Hunjiang long*)
> Within the walls of this oh-so-large Central Capital
> Every single family is beset with troubles known only to them.
> Let us speak for the moment of the lord and his ministers, now
> > scattered;
> > > Think how we,
> Father and daughter, have been separated.
> I long for my father far away on his eastern journey—when will he
> > return?
> We follow the imperial chariot, the imperial chariot on its flight to
> > the south[3]—when will we return?

After the MOTHER *has spoken — act out sighing:*

> This translucently clear, endlessly blue heaven understands, too, the
> > mind of man:
> Early autumn winds already sough and sigh
> And late rains are chillingly cold.

> (*You hulu*)
> Clear it is, "wind and rain press upon those who bid their old state
> > adieu,"
> Every step I take is one long sigh.
> Two streams of sorrowful tears drip from my cheeks,
> One drop of rain is caught between two tear-fed streams of
> > desperation.
> One gust of wind matches one long sigh.

---

2. All spoken and sung lines are those of the female lead. A colon marks the point in the stage directions at which the lead speaks or sings. Since only one person is represented in the play as a speaker, the text has omitted any stage direction that directs the lead to speak or sing.

3. To the new capital at Bianliang (Kaifeng).

Act out slipping and falling down: Ah!

>   Amidst a hundred worries, one step is one slip,
>>   Hei!
>   For every step I must raise my foot up once.
>   This one pair of embroidered shoes—I can't distinguish top from
>>   sole.
>   Thickly packed, gooey and sticky—they are covered with mud.
>
>   (*Tianxia le*)
>>   Mutti!
>   If you are so flustered and witless, how will we get anywhere?

After the MOTHER *has spoken* — *after you have made up your mind:*

>   Oh, under these low skies, the day is about to darken,
>   The easiest inn to reach is more than three miles away.
>   Windy rains above,
>   Muddy water below.
>>   Mutti!
>   Your slow and futile steps show that you're out of energy.

After MOTHER *has spoken* — *after speaking face to face to* MOTHER:

>   (*Zui fu gui*)
>>   Mutti!
>   I've broken all my new earrings into pieces,
>   And twisted my old hairpins apart at the joints.
>   I've ever so lightly pressed two rattan strips flat,[4]
>   And together with three pair of my heavy bracelets,
>   Sewn them into the thin brocade covering of the sash of my night
>>   clothes—
>   These I have tied tightly to my body.

After MOTHER *has spoken* — *after* CAVALRY SCOUTS *have entered and shouted* — *after* MOTHER *speaks* — *act out being frightened* — *after* MOTHER *speaks* — *exit* [*both*] *in a flash. After* JIANG RUILIAN *has entered* [*and after she has left*] — *and after you have simply entered* — *act out looking for the* MOTHER: Mutti! Mutti! *Act out shouting a number of times. Act out panicking. After* JIANG SHILONG *speaks* — *act out suddenly seeing* JIANG SHILONG *and being scared and embarrassed. After* JIANG SHILONG *has spoken* — *after striking a posture:* I've lost my mother and I'm looking for her. *After* JIANG SHILONG *speaks* — *act out making up your*

---

4. Probably gold jewelry hammered into the shape of woven rattan.

mind. After JIANG SHILONG *has spoken*: I've certainly never been left alone with a man to talk. But I'm in an impossible situation today. What should I do?

> (*Houting hua*)
> In the past if I heard someone suddenly bring up the topic of a
>   husband,
> I immediately left my seat,
> Silently bowed my neck,
> And blushed until my face turned red.
> But now I need to steel myself to it,
> It can't be avoided,
> I can't enlist any shyness or embarrassment.

After JIANG SHILONG *has spoken — smile enticingly at him:*

> (*Jinzhan'er*)
> You—brother and sister—have each gone east and west,
> And we—mother and daughter—have both been separated.
> If you won't feel shamed by it, brother, let me temporarily be your
>   sister.

After JIANG SHILONG *has spoken — I have thought it over!*

> You, brother, say, "If a man and a woman travel together in times of
>   war,
> Those who have a husband won't be carried off as plunder,
> But those without a man in the house will always fall victim."
> I've made up my mind!
> So, let it be,
> When no one asks, I'll act your sister for the while,
> When questioned, I'll say that I'm your wife.

After JIANG SHILONG *has spoken — act out traveling with* JIANG SHILONG. *After* TUOMAN XINGFU *has spoken — act out being scared. Follow* JIANG SHILONG *in greeting* TUOMAN XINGFU. *After* JIANG SHILONG *and* TUOMAN XINGFU *have recognized each other — after you have acted out — SPEAK:*[5] How can this student and this guy be brothers? *After having acted:*

> (*Zui fu gui*)
> You said your ancestors were acquainted with letters and ink
> And that you and your sister knew about calligraphy and books,

---

5. This single word stage direction is written in an extraordinarily large size. It may simply be an error in production of the woodblock. Otherwise, its meaning is unclear to us.

That your family tradition had been passed on to you,
That every generation had passed the examinations.
Are you relatives by sororal uncles? Fraternal uncles? Do you have
　　different mothers?
How come you have such a thieving brother?

After TUOMAN XINGFU *has spoken* — *after* JIANG SHILONG *has spoken*: Brother,
if you have a mind to do this, aren't you jumping to the wrong conclusion?

　　(Jinzhan'er)
　　You'd really rather throw those coarse brown sleevelets on your back[6]
　　Than wear the purple robes of court.
　　You consider a drinking bout in a bathhouse better than a society for
　　　　poetry.
　　To climb to the moon, there to pluck a cassia branch and become an
　　　　official, you find too slow,
　　And too late in coming, any fortune won from the tip of your writing
　　　　brush.
　　Now you see how quickly a knife blade can turn into money!
　　Now you want to learn how to set fires in high winds
　　And become an armed robber in the dark of the moon.

After JIANG SHILONG *has spoken* — *after* TUOMAN XINGFU *has acted*:[7] You
aren't used to drinking so much! *After* JIANG SHILONG *has spoken*: Don't drink,
I'm afraid you'll lose control after wine. *After* JIANG SHILONG *has spoken*:

　　(Zhuanwei)
　　Although it's a brother's heart
　　And an expression of his good will,
　　Your capacity for wine is limited, so beg off, drink only a little.
　　Although enjoyment and happiness may come like this,
　　You should still remember right from wrong.

Act out holding up JIANG SHILONG. *Act out thinking very hard*:

　　Ah!
　　I think back on it,
　　Everything I've done since my youth. . . .
　　In this topsy-turvy world I cannot act in the proper way.
　　Let us dissemble perfect accord,

---

6. Reddish-brown sleevelets worn by bandits.
7. Tuoman Xingfu lays on a banquet for them in his mountain lair.

Feign to be a single family,
And by this stratagem of escape, deceive this thief who breaks and
    enters.

[Act 2]

After the MOTHER *and* JIANG RUILIAN *have spoken — after* WANG ZHEN *has
spoken — after* INNKEEPER *has spoken — then, after you have entered supporting*
JIANG SHILONG — *after* JIANG SHILONG *has laid himself on the ground and acted:*
I've never suffered such misery in my life. *Act out heaving a sigh:*

([NANLÜ MODE:] *Yizhi hua*)
Buckler and spear have shaken the earth;
Rampant disaster has descended from heaven.
Hoping to return to father and mother, thrice thwarted,[8]
You have lost state and country in a single instant.
When dragons battle, minnows are sure to be injured,
But am I yet eager to bear this reduced and lonely lot?
You shouldn't have, but you did—
You took off your clothes,
And were infected by this rampant epidemic.

(*Liangzhou*)
It's just like a painful awl puncturing your temples,
A raging fire burning in your breast.
Your body is heavy, your limbs torpid, you can't turn your head,
Your mouth is dry, your tongue rough,
Your speech is slurred, you're raving.
To top it all off, I have no servants
And can't bother the neighbors.
It's just me, this single woman, alone
Who, day and night, administers his medicine and brews up his hot
    infusions.
        Ah,
The two of us deserted hearth and home,
        Oh, we
Stuck to it through the whole journey, battled wind and wave,
        Ai,

---

8. Literally, "three no-returns": no return without success, no return without establishing a name, no return without achieving something beneficial. Hence it means to be completely thwarted.

But never imagined in all those troubles, that you would be
    bedridden.
Suffering within, suffering without:
I would gladly tear out my heart and gall,
Exert all my strength and will,
To ask a practitioner to come,
But fear in a backwater like this, they are all quacks.
I can only hope that according to his lot his condition will not
    deteriorate
And he can slowly regain the proper flow of yin and yang.

After JIANG SHILONG *has spoken — after* INNKEEPER *has spoken — think long
and hard*: Well, let's try calling that physician and let him have a look. *After the*
PHYSICIAN *has entered and spoken — after you have made up your mind*: Doctor,
carefully take his pulse. *After* JIANG SHILONG *and* PHYSICIAN *have spoken —
act out praising him*:

> (*Muyang guan*)
> This physician is skilled in treatment
> Because his strength lies in diagnostics.
> He's on the mark nine times of ten and his prescriptions suit the
>   illness.
> "In this case, the fifth night will seem an acme
> But on the sixth it will still rise;
> If he has diarrhea, then it will take longer,
> But if you take the medicine, it will end in due course.
> Don't use those 'Pan-effective Marvelous Powders,'
> But have him take these 'Three-in-One Invigorating Infusions.'"

After the PHYSICIAN *has packaged the medicine — after seeing him to the door*: As
soon as he's better, we'll find a way to pay you, doctor. *After* WANG ZHEN *has
entered and spoken*: Isn't that him? *Act out calling* WANG ZHEN: Vati! Don't you
recognize me, Ruilan? *After* WANG ZHEN *has spoken*:

> (*He xinlang*)
> Since I last saw you in the Capital,
> The day you left court in great haste,
> How have you been, Vati?

After WANG ZHEN *has recognized you*:

> I've been thinking of nothing but you,
> Especially when we followed the imperial chariot south to Bianliang,
> When we didn't know whether to go or to stay.

Our family fortune was all abandoned,
Our servants had all fled,
Leaving a pair, mother and daughter, with no support.
From the morning that my body left the imperial Capital,
My dreaming soul has traveled every night to Liaoyang.

After WANG ZHEN *has spoken — act out grieving*: After the imperial entourage had started its journey, the whole population of the capital fled. We came out of the walls of the Capital along with everyone else. The heavens darkened that day, a strong wind was blowing, heavy rain was falling, and soon we couldn't keep up with the crowd. Then we were set upon by cavalry scouts and in the confusion we, mother and daughter, got separated. I don't know where mutti has gone. *After* JIANG SHILONG *has spoken — act being flustered. After* WANG ZHEN *has spoken — act being embarrassed*: It's your son-in-law who's ill. *After* WANG ZHEN *has spoken — after acting out telling the plot — after* WANG ZHEN *has spoken — act out being embarrassed.*

(*Muyang guan*)
Your child had no one on whom to rely,
No one to lean on,
And he really came to my rescue.

After WANG ZHEN *has spoken — after you have made up your mind*:

On that day I faced death,
It was a field of carnage before my eyes.
Sword and blade glistened brightly,
Men and horse were a confused mass.
        At that time
This rouge-cheeked girl in brocade silks
        Saw nothing anywhere but
Those white-faced lads on silver saddles.[9]

After WANG ZHEN *has spoken*: He's a student. *After* WANG ZHEN *has ordered* SOLDIERS *to drag you off — act being flustered, act being scared, act out grieving*. Vati! How can you be so cruel? *After acting out a state of panic*:

(*Dou hama*)
Father, it is just as if I had lived through the harshest winter month,
And had long hoped, long hoped for you, the Lord of the East—
        Hoping for
The sunburst of spring rays,

---

9. Jurchen military officers, who powdered their beards.

The pleasant warmth of east winds,
But, really!
Suddenly, frigid and freezing, snow falls on top of frost.

After JIANG SHILONG *speaks — act out panicking:*

Without the slightest feeling
They clutch my clothing tight and won't let me go.
Seeing someone on the edge of death lose their life
Anyone else in the world would feel upset,
But you are unwilling to show any compassion or concern—
Can I not sigh with grief?

After WANG ZHEN *has spoken:* Father, calm down, give Ruilan a little leeway so I can say a few words to him, and then you and I will go. *After* WANG ZHEN *has spoken:* Father, you don't know how kind he's been to me. *After* WANG ZHEN *has spoken:*

(*Ku huangtian*)
              Rather than
Robbers raping me. . . .
              Vati! Imagine!
How can I ever forget this kindness?
              Now you desert him—
Nowhere to turn to stay alive—
And simply split us apart.
Look at him, bedridden, crying so pitifully,
Left alone in his room in the inn, with no one to care for him.
The saying goes, "Can you hesitate after taking a hundred paces
     together?"
              How can you
Make me take my leave, open-eyed, without asking after him?

After acting out counseling JIANG SHILONG: Husband, my father is taking me away. Look after yourself well. *After* JIANG SHILONG *has spoken — act out being troubled:* Husband

This is all the evil doing of my father,
Don't blame your wife.

(*Wu ye ti*)
              Heaven!
In the blink of an eye, you have concentrated all the world's sorrow
     into this space between my brows,
And against this sorrow there is no defense.

After JIANG SHILONG *has spoken:*

> Once we have parted, please don't forget these words:
> "If your pulse takes a turn for the better,
> Please make sure to avoid a relapse."
> This purple-robed lord whose hailstorm is coming down,
> Doesn't recognize a white-clothed minister whose thunderstorm has
>   yet to come.[10]
> This one instant—boundless as heaven—
> We sigh as one in the same moment,
> Lost and forlorn in two separate places.

After JIANG SHILONG *has spoken* — WANG ZHEN *urges you on. After acting:*

> (*Sansha*)
> Husband, if you need to buy medicine, be ready to pawn your spring
>   gown.
> When you think about eating, defend against anything that might
>   harm you.

After JIANG SHILONG *has spoken* — *act out being troubled:*

> Don't hope for any trysts like those we've been having,
> But wait until you have completely recovered
> Then look for me in the side streets of Eastgate Way,
> And let us meet there once again.
> Here in this inn, you are reduced to a sick traveler;
> There on the posthouse road, I will be distraught and desolate.
>
> (*Ersha*)
>   Tomorrow morning
> By the gauze window you will hear the cockcrow at sunrise,
>   And I shall
> Halt my horse in the west wind to count the lines of geese.

After JIANG SHILONG *has spoken:* My husband, please don't worry.

> I only hope to find my mother in the Southern Capital.[11]
> I'd rather be a widow all alone,
> But I worry he'll try to force me,

---

10. Purple robes were those worn by highest officers of the realm. Students wore white gowns, so a "white-gowned" minister is a student destined for greatness, one whose name will shake the empire like a thunderstorm.

11. Bianliang.

Force me to find another man.
That prick better not even think about it!

After JIANG SHILONG *has spoken:* You are wrong.

> Jade steps, pearly screens, and painted chambers
> Are nothing extraordinary in my eyes.
>
> (*Shouwei*)
>> Don't assume that
> For the sake of kingfisher screens, red candles, and tasseled bed
>   curtains
>> I will reject your
> Yellow books, blue lamp, or snow-lit window.

After WANG ZHEN *speaks — after* JIANG SHILONG *speaks — after taking leave —*
act out counseling JIANG SHILONG:

> Don't get crazy ideas in your head,
> Just keep my words in mind.
> There's no deception in what I say,
> You don't have to analyze every word.
> For three months we have been husband and wife,
> And have you ever observed your evil wife tell a single lie?

Exit.

[Act 3]

After one scene by MOTHER *— after one scene by* JIANG SHILONG *— after* JIANG
RUILIAN *has spoken — after you have entered dressed simply:* From the time my
father cruelly tore husband and wife apart in the inn, I've never forgotten, even
for a moment, my husband, wracked by illness. Is he alive? Dead? I don't know
what my father is thinking, but every time I mention the word "student" he is
displeased: "Those miserable students never make a success of themselves!" But
no one is born as a high official to enjoy riches and glory! *Act out sighing:*

> ([ZHENGGONG MODE:] *Duanzheng hao*)
> It appears to me that those in office
> Or those who read in their study,
> Were all once upon a time helpless tigers or hibernating dragons.
> If one were to believe my father,
> No one in the world ought to pluck a branch from the cinnabar
>   cassia,
> But should save their hands to draw the carved bow.

(*Gun xiuqiu*)
If this perverse and foolish father of mine
Hears talk of ancient books,
He burns with a rage hot enough to split his skull.
No one, past or present, has been so crude or coarse.
This rich family wealth of yours—
You are afraid that I covet it with all my heart.
We will earn our luxury from the tip of his pen.
He will raise up for us a three-tiered parasol of a glorious husband
     and noble wife.
And how does it compare with that four-horse carriage, daddy's rice,
     and mommy's porridge?[12]
These two things are completely different!

After JIANG RUILIAN *speaks*: Ahhhh. I could be getting a little bit better. *After*
JIANG RUILIAN *has spoken*:

(*Tang xiucai*)
          Ah!
I have just barely managed to get through the waning of the spring,
          Hai!
Yet I look like a person haggard from sorrow.

After JIANG RUILIAN *has spoken*: If you say so, little sister. *After* JIANG RUILIAN
has spoken — after you have made up your mind:

I'm just following little sister on a stroll to dispel my depression:
But reaching the pond
And gazing quickly around
Simply makes me sigh all the more.

(*Dai guduo*)
          It's not like evening, morning, day or night, or like spring, summer, fall,
          or winter—
That sorrow-provoking scenery goes strictly season-to-season—
Look at those coin-sized, green lotus leaves floating there,
Lotus leaves that come full circle to lotus seeds.
The pond is as translucent as the face of a round mirror.[13]

---

12. This parasol was one of the regalia of high rank. A four-horse chariot was the privilege of
only the highest officials of the realm.

13. This full circle is a symbol of perfect harmony and accord, of the perfect union of husband
and wife, and of the reunion of family members.

Ah,
When will my thoughts be empty of this vexation
And my heart freed from such entanglements?
In a brass mirror just like this, reflecting my makeup,
And kingfisher-green filigree pins that stick into my chignon. . . .

[*After* JIANG RUILIAN *speaks*] *act embarrassed*: It's a good thing there is no one around, how dare you say that? This hussy! *After* JIANG RUILIAN *speaks*: I can guess what you're saying!

(*Tang xiucai*)
Don't try to rile me up with such a foul claim,
　　Whew,
It must be your spring heart that's been stirred, you witch.

After JIANG RUILIAN *speaks*: Don't worry, don't worry!

By and by on your behalf I'll tell the whole story to my father,

After JIANG RUILIAN *speaks*: You may not want me to, but if I want to, what can you do? *After* JIANG RUILIAN *speaks* — *sing*:

I'm not crazy,
I'm not addled,
If I want to, so what?

After JIANG RUILIAN *speaks*: Having no husband is fun, having a husband is suffering. *After* JIANG RUILIAN *speaks*: Let me tell you.

(*Gun xiuqiu*)
Just become attached to your husband
And all relatives start talking:
They'll say, "You are too ardent with your husband
And grow too cold toward your mother and father."
As it is, if we want clothes, the chests are filled,
If we want food, it's spread for us to eat.
When evening comes, our silken coverlets are spread out,
And there's not the smallest hook of worry on which to hang our
　　hearts.
We can sleep until, crisp and cold, incense smoke dies away in the
　　precious tripod,
Until, bright and white, the moon's image on the gauze window
　　hangs aslant.
And there's not a critical tongue.

Act out going into your room. After JIANG RUILIAN *speaks*: It's late, little sister, go on to bed. I also want to sleep. *After* JIANG RUILIAN *speaks*: Meixiang, prepare an incense table, I want to burn a stick of nighttime incense. *After* MEIXIANG *speaks*:

> (*Ban dushu*)
> You lean here on the railing overlooking the terrace
> And I will prepare some incense to burn.
> To whom can I tell the limitless secrets in my heart?
> I can only burn camphor dragon musk in the golden tripod,
> And for you devoutly pray to the moon far away in the sky,
> There's nothing else to it.

> (*Xiao heshang*)
> When, waveringly resonant, the evening horn has called its last,
> When, shiny blue, the little lamp has died out,
> My paper-thin quilt and pillow are spread out in vain.
> Crisp and cold, not as it should be,
> Endlessly idle, my body grown weak,
> Heavily depressed, how can I get through this yearlong night?

After MEIXIANG *speaks — act out burning incense*:

> (*Tang xiucai*)
>   Heaven, this stick of incense—
> I pray you pare away my father's severity,
>   And with this stick
> I pray that the husband I deserted will get better.
> There are always parents to pose obstacles;
> But, the like of mine—
> So strident
> So cruel and so mean.

Act out bowing to the moon: I pray that all loving couples are never separated and that the two of us are quickly reunited. *After* JIANG RUILIAN *speaks — act embarrassed*:

> (*Daodao ling*)
> So you've been hiding all the while deep in the flowers,
> And stealthily tiptoed up behind my back,
> To pluck, rustling light, my skirt—
> Hotly glowing, I'm so embarrassed that my cheeks burn!
>   You little witch,
> So persistent, you've found me out, oh,

You've found me out, oh,
And I have to tell you every single detail from the start.

After JIANG RUILIAN *speaks:* Sister, you can't understand. He helped me so much during the war that I can't forget him. *After* JIANG RUILIAN *speaks — after you act out grieving:* Your brother-in-law is named Jiang Shilong, he is addressed as Yantong, and is twenty-three years old right now. *After* JIANG RUILIAN *acts out grieving — act out suddenly questioning her:*

> (*Tang xiucai*)
> > Come on,
> I'm the one who should be overcome by woe,
> I'm the one who should be sobbing and sniffling.
> > But no, *you*
> Weep and sob—why is that?

After JIANG RUILIAN *speaks:*

> You must have originally been my husband's former wife or
> > concubine,
> > Yes, yes,
> It was only the difference of one individual character then,
> So I got it wrong and replied.

After JIANG RUILIAN *speaks:* Are you two really brother and sister? *After* JIANG RUILIAN *speaks — act out being overjoyed:*

> (*Dai guduo*)
> > In this way,
> We'll be even closer in the future,
> Don't think it will be like days past.
> You are both my sister and my sister-in-law,
> And I, too, your sister-in-law and sister.

After JIANG RUILIAN *speaks:* It's like this,

> My father and mother come from a clan of many branches,
> But you, sister and brother, have no relatives at all.
> From now on, don't consider yourself a child of my parents,
> But rather a relative of my husband's.

After JIANG RUILIAN *speaks:* If I talk about our separation, it will be a long story.

> (*Sansha*)
> He was struck by an epidemic fever, but his pulse was taking a turn
> > for the better

When just then
My father dragged me kicking and screaming out of the inn,
And against my will put me on a horse-drawn cart.
Who would have though that we, a dancing swallow and a warbling
    oriole,
A blue-green simurgh and a dainty phoenix,
Would run into a fierce tiger, a vicious wolf,
A poisonous scorpion, a venomous viper?
I dared not scream and weep,
Dared not intimately counsel him.
All I could do was vainly sigh and sob.
Because of that bitter pain
I was struck dumb in a second.

(*Ersha*)
On that very spot my innards and eyebrows were each tied in a
    thousand knots,
Misty rivers and cloudy mountains multiplied into ten thousand
    barriers.
He was like a raging fire driven by the wind—
So mean-hearted and vile-natured.
How could I ward off those who pushed from behind or dragged me
    ahead?
Their wild cudgels and cruel cangues?
      Ah,
Everyone has a dad,
Everyone has a father,
Everyone has a pappy,
But from the beginning of time,
None have been like this fierce daddy of mine!

(*Wei*)
He has gathered into him all the poison in the earth,
And I've tied up together all of the woe and sorrow of the world.

After JIANG RUILIAN *speaks*:

No travel money
There in the inn,
Who was there
To care for him?
So destitute,
So desolate,

Separated in life,
Left behind.
From our parting
On that day
No letter,
No news.
Lately my eyes jump, my cheeks are red, my ears are hot,
In sleep, my dreams are confused, I find no rest.
Even if your brother recovered from summer sweats and winter
    winds,
Most likely vexation and sorrow have done him in!

Exit.

[Act 4]

After WANG ZHEN, *the* LADY, JIANG SHILONG, *and* TUOMAN XINGFU *enter —
after the* MATCHMAKER *has spoken — after you have entered dressed as* WANG
RUILAN *— after* JIANG RUILIAN *has spoken:* They won't let me have my way.

([SHUANGDIAO MODE:] *Xinshui ling*)
I've gazed with expectant eyes for one full year.
You, you unjustly blame your sister, who's not free to act.
I've only just now pasted on this golden filigree hairpin
But in a blink of an eye, beside the mirror stand,
The matchmakers pressure me, again and again.

After JIANG RUILIAN *speaks:* Little sister, you don't know how lucky you are, yet
you still aren't satisfied. How can I live through it? *After* JIANG RUILIAN *speaks:*
Just how does your luck match mine? I'll tell you!

(*Zhuma ting*)
You've lucked into a love match with a man of
Torn-off bookmarks and tattered volumes—one modest and
    warm.
But I've lucked into an ill-starred union with a man of
Light bows and short arrows—one coarse and violent.

After JIANG RUILIAN *speaks:* I know for sure that I'm damned right!

Yours, for sure, when he wakes from dreams and sobers up from
    wine, will recite some poetry,
But mine, for sure, when lamplight dims and when no one is around,
    will boast of his battles.

And what's certain, by my embroidered bed curtains, he will speak
in such a terrifying way, in the end ghosts of those he slew will
appear.

After JIANG RUILIAN *speaks*: His plan is so apparent!

(*Qing dongyuan*)
He's only concerned with high station in this life,
And cares nothing about my predestined union;
He goes against my heart,
Only wanting to realize *his* desires.
Aware that "a husband and wife last a hundred years,"
He has summoned both the civil and military top graduates,
Desiring his house combine the doubled power of Prime Minister
and Generalissimo.
He pays no attention to complaints from his own;
He only wants the envy of others.

After the EXTRA *speaks — after you have acted — after* TUOMAN XINGFU *and*
JIANG SHILONG, WANG RUILAN *and* JIANG RUILIAN *have acted*:

(*Zhenjiang hui*)
See how the bridegroom of my little sister blushes
When my future husband cracks off-color jokes.
He looks me over two or three times, but I turn my newly made-up
face away.
Full of empty bluster, he goes toward the tortoiseshell mat.
Does the one who gives me away see this or not?

After WANG ZHEN *speaks —* TUOMAN XINGFU *acts out raising the cup*:

(*Bubu jiao*)
            Just look at
His mallard-green costume twilled with golden thread:
This costume won't get him a seat at the Feast of the Chalcedony
Forest.[14]
About this new First Graduate of mine,
No one will ever say, "Flowers weigh down the brim of his raven's-
gauze hat."
No longer do I dare hold up this cup of wine that seals the bond,

---

14. Given by the emperor in honor of successful graduates of the capital civil examinations.
The Park of the Chalcedony Forest was located outside of Kaifeng's western walls.

But all I can do is turn my head away and choke down half a
   mouthful.

After WANG ZHEN *speaks* — JIANG SHILONG *acts out raising the cup. Act out recognizing* JIANG SHILONG:

(*Yan'er luo*)
Are you now completely cured of your grave illness?
Is your body now completely restored to health?
When there, we were separated in the beginning.
I never dreamt that here, we'd see each other again.

(*Shuixianzi*)
Today this broken simurgh mirror has been made whole once more,
And now not a single fish letter[15] will we need to send again.

After JIANG SHILONG *speaks*: How dare you say this! *After making up your mind,
sing*:

That viciously evil father of mine forced me into a marriage,
Well, shit!
Just who talked you, Top-of-the-List Jiang,
Into accepting the silken whip as soon as you'd gotten a title?
I was always pining over you,
But you never gave anyone else a thought.
But there's a clear Heaven above for heartless scoundrels like you.

After JIANG SHILONG *speaks* — *act out speaking in your own defense*:

(*Hushiba*)
If I had mouths all over my body,
How could I defend myself?
All this turns my interminable passion, my everlasting grief into
   nothing.
During the day I couldn't eat or drink, at night I couldn't sleep.
But your sister, Ruilian, is my witness,
And if you don't believe me,
Question her when no one else is about.

After JIANG SHILONG *speaks*: Isn't that your sister Ruilian over there? *After*
JIANG SHILONG *and* JIANG RUILIAN *have recognized each other* — *act out informing* WANG ZHEN. *After* JIANG SHILONG *speaks* — *after the* OLD MOTHER

---

15. Letters from distant places were, in legend, sent in the bellies of fish or attached to the feet
of geese.

speaks — after WANG ZHEN *speaks*: You just test it out with your brother, and I'll go and try to persuade your little sister. *After* JIANG SHILONG *speaks — after* JIANG RUILIAN *speaks*: Sister, your brother and I have made up. How about you marrying that Top Graduate of the military examination? *— After* JIANG RUILIAN *speaks*: You didn't believe me, did you? *— After* JIANG RUILIAN *speaks*:

> (*Gua yugou*)
> There's a household two hundred strong laughing it up here.
> In such a secluded mansion as this,
> Don't believe what slipped from my mouth without forethought,
> "That ghosts of those he slew would appear!"

After JIANG RUILIAN *speaks*:

> On purpose then, I distorted the truth
> And faulted him in everything.
> I have no problem with his cocking the crossbow or drawing the bow,
> I never said he'd strip off his shirt to punch it out.
>
> (*Qiaopai'er*)
> That was just to demonstrate my unhappy reluctance,
> Can that be difficult to see?
> Everyday before the green window,
> I ever neglected needle and thread
> But never relaxed my brow.
>
> (*Ye xing chuan*)
> It was all because this handsome youth lay heavily upon my heart!
> You will never have a worry or a care:
> You'll ride in a high carriage drawn by four horses,
> Manage a household of servants and slaves, who—
> When you go out or when you come home—
> Will hold your spittoon and wave your fans.
>
> (*Reprise*)
> On every trip, two rows of vermilion-clad servants will line up before
>   your horses.
> But, when will my man of letters ever produce a salary?
> Just imagine Yan Yuan in his mean dwelling,
> And Yuan Xian—he of full bowl and ladle:[16]

---

16. Yan Yuan and Yuan Xian are proverbial exemplars of poor but deserving students. On Yan Yuan (also known as Yan Hui), see *Injustice to Dou E*, n. 34. Yuan Xian, another disciple of Confucius, is described in the *Zhuangzi* as being so poor he "lived in a tiny house . . . thatched

You know from your own experience what the poverty of a student is
like.

After the EXTRA *speaks*: Stop! Don't! If she doesn't want to, then stop. It makes
no sense to go on entreating her.

(*Dianqian huan*)
She's just too set on it,
She thinks doubled cushions and rows of tripods are not worth a
cent,
She's all in love with yellowed leeks and tasteless rice,
And wants to live thus until her dying day.
If you're too picky in choosing a husband,
Too concerned about your in-laws,
Then you can't blame anyone else.
True it is, marriage is determined by fate,
And our lives are linked with heaven.

After JIANG RUILIAN *speaks* — *after the* ENVOY *enters to enfeoff* TUOMAN XINGFU:

(*Gu meijiu*)
Out of the blue his official position is raised,
And in the Central Capital he's made Acting Chief of Staff
With the golden Tiger-head Plaque hung at his waist.
Seeing that imperial edict on its gold-flowered writ,
She, without rhyme or reason, now wants to be reunited.

(*Ahu ling*)[17]
Let's stop urging this girl who, for all our counsel, remains so
addlepated;
Please, my ladyship, why not wait three more years?
Since you love those blue lamps and yellowed volumes so much,
You shouldn't change your mind just because of circumstance.
Take these things here before you, which so wear you down,
And give them to others to enjoy!

---

with growing weeds, had a broken door made of woven brambles and branches of mulberry for
the doorposts; jars with the bottom out, hung with pieces of coarse cloth for protection from the
weather, served as windows for its two rooms. The roof leaked and the floor was damp. . . . "
(trans. Watson 1970, pp. 315–16); see also Slingerland 2003, pp. 153–54.

17. A name of a rarely used tune of Jurchen origin. Guan Hanqing uses it here and in another
drama that features Jurchen characters for the final tune. The metrical pattern is the same as that
of the Chinese tune *Taiping ling*, indicating that it was only differentiated by music.

After WANG ZHEN speaks — DISPERSAL SCENE.

Newly Compiled with Full Plot
A Beauty Pining in Her Boudoir: The Pavilion for Praying to the Moon

The End

4

The Autumn Nights of the Lustrous Emperor of Tang: Rain on the Wutong Tree

BAI PU

Among the playwrights of the early Yuan dynasty Bai Pu (1226–after 1307) was exceptional because of his elite background and fine education. He was originally named Bai Heng, and later adopted the sobriquet of "Master of the Thoroughwort Vale" (*Langu xiansheng*). Bai Pu lived through the traumatic period of the fall of the Jin. His father, Bai Hua (fl. 1200–50) was a high official at the court of the last Jin emperor and in the Jin capital, Bianliang (modern Kaifeng), where he made friends with his fellow Shanxi native, Yuan Haowen (1190–1257), the most famous of all Jin literati. When the Jin capital fell to the Mongols, Bai Hua was being held by the Southern Song. Bai Pu, then eight years old, was taken into Yuan Haowen's household, and accompanied Yuan's family to exile in Shandong. There, Bai Pu received a literary training at the hands of the master writer, who treated him as his own son. Four years later, when Bai Hua was able to return to the North, Yuan Haowen took Bai Pu to his father in Zhending, located in modern Hebei. Bai Pu grew up in North China in the company of the leading political figures of the time. In 1261 he was recommended for service to the court of Kublai Khan, but he declined and went southward, traveling mostly in the Hubei-Henan area. He lived many years in Jiujiang in Jiangxi Province before finally moving to Jinling, modern Nanjing. He returned to the north several times, but seems to have spent the greater part of his life in the south. The last record of his existence is in his eighty-first year, when he mentions a trip to Yangzhou. *The Register of Ghosts* remarks that Bai Pu was given several posthumous titles, including Grand Master for Excellent Counsel (*Jiayi daifu*), Chamberlain for Ceremonials (*Taichang qing*), and Chamberlain for the Court of Ceremonial Propriety (*Liyi yuan qing*). However, these appear to be the posthumous titles of his brother, Bai Que, who attained a high post in the Court of Ceremonials during the Yuan. Since Zhong Sicheng (c. 1277–1360), author of the *Register*, wrote primarily on the basis of hearsay, it probably represents a circulating, but mistaken, opinion contemporary to Zhong.

Among Bai Pu's known works were sixteen plays and a collection of free lyrics (*sanqu*), known as *The Collection of Heaven's Pipes* (*Tianlai ji*). *The Register of Ghosts* lists fifteen plays under Bai's name, and there are fragments of one other in a Ming dynasty musical formulary. Of the sixteen plays, two are extant, *Rain on the Wutong Tree*, and *One on the Wall, One on Horseback—Pei Shaojun* (like *Rain on the Wutong Tree* also based on a narrative poem by Bai Juyi). A third extant play is sometimes attributed to Bai, *The Story of the Eastern Wall* (*Dongqiang ji*), because a play by that title is listed in *The Register of Ghosts* under Bai's name. However, the style and quality of the extant play make that attribution quite unlikely, and critics agree that it is not by Bai Pu.

Bai Pu's dramatic works generally are marked by a refined literary intelligence, a style that favors the plain and unadorned, and a limited use of allusions. In traditional and modern times Bai Pu has generally been acknowledged as one of the great masters of *zaju*. He is equally well-known for his free lyrics, which reflect the influence of his teacher, Yuan Haowen, in their stylistic similarity to the two great Song lyric poets, Xin Qiji (1140–1207) and Su Shi (1037–1101). Judging from the titles of Bai's dramatic works, romantic love dominated his interest. Both of his extant plays deal with love—the first of a truncated love and the depression and angst that follows, the second with love thwarted then regained through the exercise of the heroine's determination. What shows through, particularly in *Rain on the Wutong Tree*, is his thorough immersion in the tradition of poetry, again a product of his teacher's influence. The depth of Bai's reservoir of literary knowledge is attested by Zhu Quan's comments in his *Formulary of Correct Rhymes for an Era of Great Peace*, which said that Bai's lyrics were

> like a Peng Bird gyring in the Ninefold Empyrean. His "bone and wind" (that is, vigor of his style) is one of seething depression; the fount of his lyrics is deep and broad. He is like the Great Peng's rising from the Northern Depths—with wings beating waves in the Ninefold Empyrean. He has that "ten thousand miles in every journey" ambition, so it is fitting that he be placed at the head.

The Register of Ghosts simply remarks that he was Bai Hua's son and lists the aforementioned posthumous titles. Jia Zhongming, in his continuation to the *Register*, however makes a somewhat humorous comment on the disparity between the attributed titles and Bai Pu's personality as reflected in his poetry:

Tall cap and broad belt—Chamberlain of the Court of Ceremonies,
Proud horse and light gown—the feeling of a high official,
Plucking flowers and snapping off leaves—the essence of *Feng*-style poetry.

He got a name as a ruthless cad in the green bowers,
And cleansed his inner thoughts by cutting and trimming snow and ice.
Finding interest in leisure,
And a scene outside of the objects themselves—
This was Mr. Thoroughwort Vale.

Feng-style poetry is associated with the "Airs of the States" section of the *Book of Odes*, and has implicit within it a deeply seated relationship between desire and politics. The "plucking flowers and snapping off leaves," a term for rendering beautiful poetry, is slightly redolent of a similar phrase, "plucking flowers and snapping off the gorgeous," which refers to writing romantic lyrics and dallying with prostitutes. In that case, we may also understand *Feng*-style poetry as romantic, licentious verse, a nice bridge between his official position and his reputation in the green bowers—houses of geisha. Jia's poem concludes by giving us a picture of Bai's late life: wandering around South China, making a living by managing an estate, and spending his time with high-ranking literati in the pursuit of leisure, nature, and performance.

There is a term in Chinese, *liu zuo huaba*, which means, "to leave [some knowledge of an important event] behind to become the target of talk." Any event that is redolent with significance becomes a source that will eventually generate textual and oral discourse—the stuff of legend, history, and literature—but simultaneously it also becomes a mark toward which judgments are directed. Certainly, one of the most famous and complicated of these events was the obsession of the aging emperor of Tang, Emperor Xuanzong (r. 712–56), for his young consort, Yang Yuhuan ("Jade Bracelet"), decades younger than he was and originally a secondary wife to one of his sons. In some ways, this was a common topic in Chinese literature, the repertoire of which is full of stories of emperors or other powerful men who have become infatuated with women. From the level of the family to that of the state, the ability of women to distract men from their public duties to attend to private pleasure was highly dangerous because it obscured the boundary between public and private. The intrusion of women into public space where they displaced the focus of the man's attention foregrounded the dangers of unharnessed female sexual energy. The state itself was thought of both as a healthy body and as a model of the family. Thus, losing the balance between duty and pleasure, both suitable in their proper contexts, posed a physical threat by draining male vigor, *yang* essence, from those in power, and also destroyed hierarchical systems of family governance. The harmonic balance of yin and yang that permeated every living thing and every possible event could be thrown off, causing destruction of the man, the family, the state, and even the cosmos.

It is probably no accident that the only two plays left from Yuan and Ming Northern drama that have emperors as lead characters deal with the mirror images of this complicated relationship. In *A Lone Goose in Autumn over the Palaces of Han*, a beautiful woman who has been neglected by an emperor of the Han is given in marriage to the Xiongnu Khan in order to prevent war between the two states. In this complicated story, written perhaps to respond to the negative characterization of women in *Rain on the Wutong Tree*, the emperor is deceived by a court painter who creates an ugly likeness of the woman so that she would be singled out to be sent to the cold northlands. She goes willingly, although deeply in love with the emperor, and her action compensates for the weakness and confusion of the Han emperor's ministers, who are impotent in the face of threats from outside.

The Autumn Nights of the Lustrous Emperor of Tang: Rain on the Wutong Tree (*Tang Minghuang qiuye wutong yu*), however, portrays all of the limits of imperial power and the downfall of a great monarch through his admittedly incestuous lust. Xuanzong, also known as Minghuang, "Bright Emperor," went through a complicated process to appropriate his young daughter-in-law, first having her made a Daoist nun, then lodging her in a Daoist temple within the imperial city. Later he enfeoffed her as "Precious Consort" (*guifei*), the name by which she is known best in posterity—Yang Guifei. Yang had been raised in the household of her uncle, having lost her own father in her youth. As she captured the aging emperor's attention, her family was raised to high position, and eventually a distant cousin, Yang Guozhong, was elevated to the status of Prime Minister. As the emperor became ever more infatuated with the young girl, he neglected the duties of state, tarnishing forever the brilliance of his earlier years when the empire was at the height of its military expansion and its cultural efflorescence.

Running parallel to this personal tale of love and obsession is the background of the An Rokshan[1] rebellion. An Rokshan was a general of Sogdian descent

---

1. An Rokshan's name is usually given in Chinese pronunciation as An Lushan. His original name was either Alakshan or Gelakshan, and his father's original surname was possibly Kang, which would place An Rokshan's origins in the Sogdian kingdom of Kangguo, near modern Samarkand and Bukhara. When An Rokshan's mother married a man named Aluoshan, her son adopted his stepfather's surname, An, derived from the Sogdian word for "Persian." It was a common practice for the first syllable of an Altaic name to be used as a surname in Chinese. We have chosen to transliterate the name in its approximate Tang pronunciation in a way that would show its clear Altaic roots, especially since an etymological derivation is given in the play to emphasize An Rokshan's foreignness. The text here follows the historical sources quite closely. Children took their mother's clan name as a surname. He is a "mongrel" barbarian because his mother was Turkish and his father belonged to a different group, the Kang.

who had risen high in the ranks of regional military officers, but who became involved in a political feud with Yang Guozhong. Partly out of fear that Yang would use his connections at court to ruin him, An Rokshan, then at Yuyang in charge of the defense of northeastern China, rebelled and forced the emperor to flee from Chang'an to the safety of Sichuan. But hardly had the emperor left the capital, before his troops forced him to execute both Yang Guozhong and Yang Guifei. Xuanzong's son and successor, Suzong (r. 756–61), restored the Tang as the rebellion was eventually suppressed. But the dynasty would never regain its former glory even though it survived for another century and a half. As the years passed by, the reign of Xuanzong was ever more glamorized by this tragic love story.

This story has produced hundreds of works of art—poetry, lyric poetry, dramas, narrative ballads, short stories, paintings, and ceramics. Some of these works belong to the most famous works of Chinese literature. In the early ninth century the poet Bai Juyi (772–846) wrote his "Song of Lasting Regret" ("*Changhen ge*"), a long narrative ballad about the infatuation of the aging emperor for Yang Guifei that lasted well beyond her death. The pining emperor summons a shaman to search throughout the cosmos to find the Precious Consort's heavenly abode. The ballad was accompanied by a prose account of the affair by Bai Juyi's friend Chen Hong, entitled *Tale of the Song of Lasting Regret* (*Changhen ge zhuan*). Numerous collections of anecdotes added all kinds of sentimental and titillating detail, and some of these sources include an affair between Yang Guifei and An Rokshan. On the basis of these various sources Bai Pu's contemporary, Wang Bocheng, wrote a long prosimetric narrative in the format of a *zhugongdiao* ("all keys and modes") called *Old Tales from the Tianbao Reign Era* (*Tianbao yishi zhugongdiao*). In this version, which is only partially extant, the aging emperor falls in love with a fat Yang Guifei, who deceives him with an even fatter An Rokshan; the emperor becomes very much an object of ridicule. In the final decades of the seventeenth century, the playwright Hong Sheng (1645–1704) would turn the relationship of Xuanzong and Yang Guifei into a pure and mutual love in his long *chuanqi* play, *Palace of Eternal Life* (*Changsheng dian*). These many artistic representations in general revolve around three major themes. First is the love story itself, starting from the moment Xuanzong observed the naked Yang Yuhuan as she was taking a bath at the hot springs of Huaqing Palace, and ending with Xuanzong's attempts to be reunited with his favorite concubine after her death. The second major theme is the parting and execution scene at Mawei Slope, where the limits both of infatuation and imperial prerogative are put on display; and third, a description of the emperor's loneliness upon his return to the capital, symbolized by his striking the wutong tree.

As told in our drama, An Rokshan is sent to court after a disastrous defeat for which he should have been beheaded. He wins the emperor's favor by his valor, but also by his skill as a dancer of the "barbarian whirl." He is made an adopted son of Yang Guifei, and he has complete access to the palace and to the harem. There he starts an affair with Yang Guifei before he is banished to Fanyang by the emperor. This detail of Yang Guifei and An Rokshan's affair is clearly present in the earliest extant editions, but it was removed from the edition included by Zang Maoxun in his *Yuanqu xuan*. As the latter edition is the one most widely read, this explains to some extent the variety of interpretations about the true nature of Yang Guifei.

On the eve of the Double Seven (the seventh day of the seventh lunar month) the emperor and Yang enjoy an intimate feast in the palace, where she enjoys litchis brought especially for her by post riders from southernmost China. There the emperor presents her with a silver hair ornament and an inlaid box and gives her an oath of undying love and a promise to live forever as husband and wife. Of course, the addled emperor is unaware that, as she is making protestations of love in return, An Rokshan is very much the indirect target of those comments. Later that fall, another intimate banquet is interrupted with the news that An Rokshan has rebelled and is moving toward the capital. The emperor leaves Chang'an, which cannot be defended, and starts toward Sichuan with his entourage. At Mawei Slope, his armies refuse to advance, and the general Chen Xuanli demands that Yang Guozhong be killed. The execution is carried out, but the armies still refuse to move. Then General Chen requests that Yang Guifei also be executed. The emperor realizes that he is powerless and orders the eunuch Gao Lishi to strangle her on the steps of a Buddhist monastery. The emperor retrieves from her body a sachet of perfume that she had worn about her neck as a token of rememberance. The rebellion is quelled after the emperor abdicates his throne, but he returns to Chang'an a broken man. He lives in seclusion in the western gardens, in which he hangs a portrait of his lost love. Just as he reencounters her in a dream, he is awakened by the sound of the rain on the wutong tree.

Bai Pu's play has elicited contradictory readings. One is that the play is a sentimental celebration of love. The second is that it is a critique of the failure of Xuanzong as a ruler and that the love story itself is implicated in that failure as a generalized symbol of neglect, bad judgment, and failure to heed worthy ministers. The third is that it is a political comment on the fall of the Jin, in which the splendor and happiness of the first part of the play (the older Jin rule) is contrasted with the bleak loneliness of the last (current life under the Yuan). This reading places the play within a generalized literary aesthetic of the literature of trauma and dynastic transition. Yet a fourth opinion of the play is that it is utterly chaotic and contradictory, portraying both the affair between

Yang Guifei and An Rokshan *and* celebrating the love between emperor and consort, leaving any political commentary uncertain in its focus. A more generous version of this view is that the play simply does not emphasize any one theme to the point that it provides a dominant interpretative model.

Dramatis personæ in order of appearance

Role type	Name, family role, or social role
Added Male	Zhang Shougui
Clown	An Rokshan
Servants	Servants
Male lead	Xuanzong
Imperial role	Xuanzong
Female lead	Precious Consort Yang
Gao Lishi	Grand Eunuch
Yang Guozhong	Yang Guozhong, Prime Minister
Palace beauties	Palace beauties
Extra male	Zhang Jiuling (minister); Envoy from Sichuan; Chen Xuanli (general);
Retinue	Imperial retinue
Generals	An Rokshan's generals
Zheng Guanyin	Stage name for a musician
Prince Ning	Xuanzong's elder brother, Li Xian, and master of the flute
Flowered Slave	Stage name for Li Lian, Prince of Ru'nan, master drummer
Huang Fanchuo	Huang Fanchuo, dancer and entertainer
Official	Li Linfu, Prime Minister
Minor Imperial Role	Suzong, Li Heng, reigns after Xuanzong's abdication
Li Guangbi	Military Commissioner, later defeats An Rokshan
Group	Village elders
Host of soldiers	Army accompanying Xuanzong's flight to Sichuan

The Autumn Nights of the Lustrous Emperor of Tang: Rain on the Wutong Tree

[Act 1]

(ADDED MALE, *costumed as* ZHANG SHOUGUI, *leads foot soldiers on:*)

> I sit in command of catamounts and fortify the northern frontier;
> Near the border passes I constantly receive surrendering kings.[2]
> In an era of grand peace, the garrison gates are quiet;
> Alone I grasp the carved bow and count the ranks of geese.

I am Zhang Shougui, the current Military Commissioner for the area of You.[3] When young I studied the Confucian texts and, at the same time, became fully conversant with the strategies of war. By this I've become a noted official of border garrisons and borne the heavy responsibility given a right-hand man. I am happy, too, about the past year's cessation of border beacons' alarms, and that our soldiers and officers can now rest and relax. But in the past few days the tribes of the Xi and the Khitan have rebelled and killed the [Chinese] princesses [sent to them as a marriage alliance].[4] I have ordered the Commissioner of Live Capture, An Rokshan, to lead troops in a campaign to restore order. But

---

2. This refers to actual cities constructed during the Han and the Tang to receive the surrender of border peoples; they were administrative sites charged with census, resettlement, etc. The peoples were located in six selected areas—the "six border areas."

3. Between the years 732 and 739 (Kaiyuan 20–27), Zhang Shougui was the Regional Commissioner for Youzhou, Director General for Yingzhou, and the Regional Vice-Commissioner for Hebei. The area of You includes modern Peking and the surrounding areas of Hebei and Tianjin.

4. The Xi and the Khitan were both peoples of the eastern frontier who split from the Eastern Turks in 629 (Zhenguan 2); in 745 (Tianbao 4), An Rokshan, who was Regional Commissioner for Fanyang in modern Liaodong, raided their kingdoms and Li Huaijie, leader of the Khitan, and Li Yanchong, leader of the Xi, assassinated their respective princesses and rebelled against the Tang. An Rokshan defeated them both. Earlier, in 736, An Rokshan had been defeated by another Khitan army and had been summoned for trial at that time. These two incidents (736 and 745) have been conflated here. The princesses were Tang royal daughters given in marriage alliances; the leaders of the Khitan and the Xi were also given the Chinese royal surname (Li).

there's been no news. Servants, wait outside the compound gates and if anyone arrives, inform me. (SERVANTS *speak:*) Understood. (CLOWN, *costumed as* AN ROKSHAN:)

> I'm big as a massive tree, my gall and strength are virile,
> And I'm fluent in all languages of the six foreign zones.
> If a man can follow the ambitions of his life,
> He'll prop up earth and hold up heaven to establish the great enterprise.

I am An Rokshan. For generation upon generation we have been mongrel barbarians in the land of Ying. I am originally surnamed Kang. My mother, A-shi-de, was a shamaness among the Turks. She prayed to the god of battle, Jalaksan, and then gave birth to me. When I was born, a bright radiance shone in the vault of heaven and all of the wild beasts cried out—so I was called Jalaksan in order to mark the augury. Later she married An Yanyan and I took his surname and changed my name to An Rokshan. During the Kaiyuan era, An Yanyan took me along when he surrendered and gave his allegiance to the Tang. Then we gratefully received the favor of the sagely ruler and were put under the command of Zhang Shougui, where I now bear the office of Commissioner of Live Capture and Submission. The noble Zhang, seeing that I am fluent in the languages of the six border areas and stronger than any other person, always gives me his personal commission. Because the Xi and the Khitan had recently rebelled, he sent me on a campaign to make them submit. I presumed on my own bravery to go deep into their lands. But I never thought we would be so outnumbered that my army would wind up in complete disarray. There's nothing to do now but go back and face the Marshal and devise some other plan. Here I am at the compound already. Servants, report that the Commissioner of Live Capture and Submission, An Rokshan, has come for an audience.

(SERVANTS *act out reporting.*) (ZHANG SHOUGUI:) Have him enter. (*They act out greeting.*) (ZHANG SHOUGUI:) An Rokshan, how did the campaign of submission end up? (AN ROKSHAN:) The enemy was many, we were few, my troops and officers were frightened and scared—so we wound up defeated. (ZHANG SHOUGUI:) By clear precedent, the destruction of your army and loss of the critical point in battle is unpardonable. Servants! Take him out and behead him as an example to the masses. (THE GROUP *acts out pushing* AN ROKSHAN.) (AN ROKSHAN, *shouting loudly, speaks:*) Don't you want to annihilate the Xi and Khitan, great one? Why are you killing An Rokshan? (ZHANG SHOUGUI:) Let him return. (AN ROKSHAN *acts out returning.*) (ZHANG SHOUGUI:) As for me, I cherish your skillful bravery. But the state has established laws that I dare not sell out to market my grace. I'll send you on to the capital, where we'll see what the Sage's decision is. (AN ROKSHAN:) Thank you for your Marshal's grace in not killing me.

(*Exit, escorting* AN ROKSHAN *under guard.*) (ZHANG SHOUGUI:) Well, An Rokshan has gone. I've got nothing else to attend to here, and so for the time being will go back to my headquarters.

(*Exits.*)

(MALE LEAD, *costumed as* IMPERIAL ROLE, XUANZONG OF THE TANG, FEMALE LEAD, *costumed as* PRECIOUS CONSORT YANG,[5] *enter leading* GAO LISHI,[6] YANG GUOZHONG,[7] *and* PALACE BEAUTIES.) (XUANZONG:)

> The Exalted Progenitor, seizing the time, arose in Jinyang;
> The Grand Ancestor, with divine martial skill, stabilized the borders of the state;
> Protecting their successes and continuing their control, I am cautious and attentive—
> Ten thousand miles of rivers and mountains encircle the Grand Tang.

I am Son of Heaven of the Tang. After the Exalted Progenitor, the Divine and Eminent Resplendent Emperor rose up with his troops in Jinyang, the Grand Ancestor Resplendent Emperor, with qualities of divine martial prowess, brought yellow battleaxes and white battle standards to a halt. He extinguished the dust and smoke in sixty-four places and eighteen houses that had willfully changed reign titles and thereby came to rule the world that is still Tang.[8] Then it passed down to Emperors Gaozong and Zhongzong, when the unfortunate usurpations of Wu Zetian and Empress Wei occurred.[9] In the status of Royal Prince of Linze, I led forth troops to settle the troubles, swept the court clean,

---

5. Yang Yuhuan (719–56) was originally the wife of Xuanzong's eighteenth son, Li Mao, also known as Prince Shou.

6. Gao Lishi (684–762) was head of the eunuch bureau in Xuanzong's time. He held enormous power at court and was in alliance with Yang Guozhong and Li Linfu.

7. Died 756.

8. This is a formulaic phrase found in several performing texts and refers to the various peasant uprisings at the end of the Sui and the small states formed around the periphery of the emerging Tang state. All of them were vanquished by Taizong and incorporated into the expanding Tang empire.

9. The empress dowager Wu Zetian, who set up Ruizong on the throne, forced Zhongzong off the throne in 684. Wu eventually took the reins of power herself and established the Zhou dynasty until she abdicated in 706. In 710 Zhongzong was assassinated by Empress Wei, who then ruled from the inner court. Xuanzong annihilated the cliques of both women and reestablished his father, Ruizong, on the throne.

and scoured all of the empire within the seas. My elder brother, Prince Ning, reflecting on the faults of those who had gone before, ceded the throne to me. It has now been twenty years since I assumed that throne. I am so happy that the world is at peace and that I can rely on worthy ministers like Yao Yuanzhi,[10] Song Jing,[11] Han Xiu,[12] and Zhang Jiuling,[13] to rule the state with hearts in accord. Thus, I can rest secure in my ease. There are many concubines in the Six Palaces[14] but since the death of Benevolent Consort Wu, none of them have suited my fancy. On the day of the mid-autumn festival, in the eighth month of last year, I dreamt that I roamed through the palace of the moon where I saw the face of Chang E—something seldom found in the human realm. The Consort Yang, formerly in my son Prince Shou's residence, looked just like Chang E; having already been ordered to become a Daoist nun, she has been brought into the palace, where I have given her the rank of Precious Consort. She lives in the Compound of the Most Perfected. Ever since she entered court, I have done nothing but sing and feast every day—I never miss a one. Gao Lishi, quickly send the order to prepare a banquet and have the Disciples of the Pear Garden[15] perform music so that I can wile away some time. (GAO LISHI:) Understood.

(EXTRA [MALE], costumed as MINISTER ZHANG JIULING, escorting AN ROK-SHAN, enters.) (ZHANG JIULING:)

> In the cauldron of state I mix together a proper brew to regularize yin and
> yang;
> My position arrayed among the phoenix ranks, I am seated in the halls of
> state.
> All within the four seas share peace, there is not a single untoward event—
> So morning after morning I busy my step to personally attend my lord
> and king.

---

10. Lived 650–721; minister in the successive reigns of Wu Zetian, Ruizong, and Xuanzong.

11. Song (663–737) was a grand minister in Ruizong's court; in 716 he succeeded Yao Yuanzhi as Prime Minister in Xuanzong's government.

12. Lived 673–740.

13. Lived 678–740, held many high posts including Director of the Central Secretariat. He had early on remonstrated with the emperor that An Rokshan would rebel and should be removed. The emperor disregarded his advice. He was later hounded out of office by Li Linfu and retired.

14. The "Six Palaces" was originally a metonym for the imperial palace; later it came to designate the portion of the palace where consorts and concubines lived.

15. A group of several hundred young entertainers, male and female, assembled by Xuanzong to study the performing arts and perform for his benefit.

I am the elder statesman, Zhang Jiuling, a man of Nanhai.[16] I studied the classics and histories when young and passed the examinations early on with the highest rank. I have borne the imperial grace upon my shoulders, rising clear to the position of Prime Minister. In the past few days Marshal of the Borders Zhang Shougui sent a border general who failed at the critical moment, a certain An Rokshan, here under guard. I have observed that he is fat and short, glib and accommodating in speech, and that he shows many unusual physical signs. If we retain this person there will be certain chaos in the world. I will go and see the Sage now and bring this up face-to-face. Here I am at the palace gates already. Palace eunuchs! Go and report that Zhang Jiuling desires audience with the emperor. (SERVANTS *act out reporting.*) [XUANZONG:] Tell him to come in. (ZHANG JIULING *acts out greeting and performing obeisance.*) (XUANZONG:) Why have you come, sir? (ZHANG JIULING:) A few days ago Marshal of the Borders Zhang Shougui sent a border general who failed at the critical moment, a certain An Rokshan, here under guard. According to precedents he should have been beheaded, but not daring to act solely on his own opinion, Zhang sent him here under guard to request an imperial directive. (XUANZONG:) Bring him here and let me have a look at him.

(ZHANG JIULING *exits and returns with* AN ROKSHAN *under guard.*) Here is that border general who failed at the critical moment, An Rokshan. (AN ROKSHAN *acts out kneeling.*) (XUANZONG:) What a fine leader! How good are your martial skills? (AN ROKSHAN:) I can shoot the bow left-handed and right, I am fully versed in the eighteen martial skills and am completely fluent in the languages of the six border districts. (XUANZONG:) You're so fat! What's in that barbarian belly of yours? (AN ROKSHAN:) Just a single heart red with loyalty! (XUANZONG:) Minister, we can't kill this one. Keep him as a "civilian general"! (ZHANG JIULING:) Your Majesty, this person has such an unusual physiognomy. If we let him live, there will come certain disaster. If we are to carry out the military law of Shougui, then Rokshan shouldn't be spared. (XUANZONG:) Sir, don't act as if you were Wang Yan recognizing Shi Le for what he was.[17] What are you afraid he'll do if we let him off? Servants, set him free.

(*Act out freeing him.*) (AN ROKSHAN *rises and gives thanks:*) Many thanks for my master's grace in sparing me. (*Acts out dancing.*) (XUANZONG:) And what's this?

---

16. He was from the area of modern Guangzhou.

17. As a youth Shi Le (274–333), of Tibetan descent, visited Luoyang with some merchants from his home area. Leaning on one of the palace gates and whistling, Shi was espied by Wang Yan (265–311), who told his companions that this young man's appearance and behavior marked him as one who would "disorder the empire." Wang was proven right as Shi Li went on to found the Latter Zhao dynasty in North China, where he ruled between 328 and 333.

(AN ROKSHAN:) This is the whirling barbarian dance. (PRECIOUS CONSORT:) Your Majesty, this fellow is short and fat and he can dance. Wouldn't it be wonderful to keep him here to help dissolve our cares? (XUANZONG:) Precious Consort, I'll give him to you as an adopted son. Lead him away. (PRECIOUS CONSORT:) Many thanks for our Sage's grace. (XUANZONG:) Well, nothing's happening now. I'll go on back to the rear quarters.

(XUANZONG, PRECIOUS CONSORT, AN ROKSHAN, *and* ATTENDANTS *all exit.*)

(ZHANG JIULING:) Uncle of the State, this person has a remarkable physiognomy. He'll certainly bring chaos to the house of Tang at some other date. And we who wear the caps and robes of officials will suffer in no small way. I am old, but I fear that you, Uncle of the State, will perhaps be around to see it. What's to be done? What's to be done? (YANG:) Let me bring this affair up at tomorrow's morning levee. It will be a fine thing to get rid of him. (ZHANG JIULING:) That being the case, let's return to our private residences for the time being.

(*They exit together.*)

(MALE LEAD, *costumed as* IMPERIAL ROLE, GAO LISHI, YANG GUOZHONG, *and* RETINUE *enter.*) (XUANZONG:) I've heard nothing but the sound of clamorous laughter in the rear apartments this morning. Servants, see where it's coming from. (PALACE BEAUTIES *speak:*) It's lady Precious Consort and An Rokshan performing the ceremony of washing the new baby. (XUANZONG:) Well, since it is the ceremony of washing the new baby, send a hundred taels worth of golden cash to give to them as a celebration gift. And summon An Rokshan, I'm going to invest him as an official.

(PALACE BEAUTIES *exit, carrying golden cash.*)

(AN ROKSHAN *enters and acts out greeting* IMPERIAL ROLE:) Many thanks, Your Majesty, for your generous gift. And in what capacity will you employ me? (XUANZONG:) I've summoned you for nothing else but to say that since you are now Precious Consort's adopted son, you are also mine. It is inappropriate that you should come and go in the rear palace only in commoner status. So, I am going to give you the rank of Manager of Governmental Affairs. (AN ROKSHAN:) Many thanks for your Sage's grace. (YANG:) Your Majesty! No! No! Impossible! An Rokshan is a border general who lost control of his army and by precedent ought to be beheaded. It was enough already that Your Majesty spared his life. To even have him at court in any capacity is inappropriate. By what merit has he earned the rank of Manager of Governmental Affairs? Moreover, he is a barbarian with the untamed heart of a wolf. He simply cannot be kept among your close attendants. I pray you, Your Majesty, reflect on this with your sagacity so there is no error. (XUANZONG:) You're right. An Rokshan, for the time being,

I'll make you Military Commissioner for the Yuyang Region, where you'll lead an army of foreigners and Han Chinese to guard the border. Establish your military success there so that you can be promoted out of sequence. (AN ROKSHAN:) I deeply thank your Sage's grace. (XUANZONG:) Please, sir, do not resent me. These are prescribed rules of the state. Let me explain. (*Sings:*)

([ZHENGGONG MODE:] *Duanzheng hao*) [(Wedge)]
>An Rokshan, since you
Have yet to establish any extraordinary merit,
To appoint you as a senior aide
Would make the Simurgh Chariot the point of ridicule for the whole court.
>It's clear that
It would be hard to put you in the post of Manager of Governmental Affairs,
>So on your behalf, I want
To consider this other official post.

(*Reprise*)
Hold military authority, go to Yuyang as Military Commissioner,
Smash the strong rebels, guard the region of You forever.
And when the state is as tenuous as a pile of eggs then serve to protect,
Bring the great affair to completion, plan for every exigency,
Recruit fierce generals, protect the imperial design,
Open up examinations, select famous scholars—
>Would I dare
Seal up the gates through which worthies pass?

(*Exits.*)

(AN ROKSHAN:) The Sage has returned to the palace. I'm coming out of the palace now. I can't stand that bastard Yang Guozhong, who was so rude to me in front of the emperor. My commission to become Military Commissioner of Yuyang is a promotion on the surface, but a demotion in reality. Well, the hell with everything else. All I care about is my illicit affair with Precious Consort. To be separated so far and so suddenly—I can't get her off my mind. Enough! Enough! Enough! When I get to Yuyang, I'll train my troops and feed my war-horses—I'll come up with another plan.

(*Exits.*)

❋❋

(FEMALE LEAD, *costumed as* PRECIOUS CONSORT, *enters leading* PALACE BEAU-
TIES:) I am Madam Yang, from Hongnong. My father, Yang Xuanyan, was Rev-
enue Manager in Shuzhou. In the twenty-second year of the Kaiyuan reign I
received the royal favor and was selected as a concubine of Prince Shou. On the
fifteenth day of the eighth month of the twenty-eighth year of Kaiyuan, which
was the imperial birthday celebration, I offered my congratulations at court.
The Sage Above saw that my face looked like that of Chang E and dispatched
Gao Lishi with an imperial directive, sending me to a Daoist nunnery. I lived in
the inner palaces, in the Palace of the Most Perfected, and have been given the
title of Most Perfected. In the fourth year of Tianbao I was invested as Precious
Consort and received half of the sumptuary entitlements of the empress. I have
been so favored by the emperor that my brother Yang Guozhong has been
made a Prime Minister and three of my sisters have been made ladies with
patents. Our whole house has become as glorious as possible. A few days ago
the border court sent that foreign general An Rokshan here. This guy is very
crafty and clever, and can really toady to people. He can also do the whirling
barbarian dance. The Sage gave him to me as an adopted son, and he can come
in and out of the palace at will. I never expected that this guy would take advantage of my drunkenness and ravish me. When I sobered up I didn't dare say
anything about it. And as the days passed, our affection became stronger and
stronger. My brother, Yang Guozhong, saw the signs of this affair and asked the
Son of Heaven to invest him as the Military Commissioner of Yuyang, and he's
been sent off to the border courts. I think of him all the time and the thought
that I might not see him again really vexes me. Well, today is the seventh day of
the seventh month, when Buffalo Boy and Weaving Maiden meet, and the festival when skills are sought in the human world.[18] I've already told the palace
beauties to set out our feast for seeking skills in the Palace of Eternal Life, so
that I can beseech skill. Girls, is it set out yet or not? (PALACE BEAUTIES:) It's
been ready for a long time. (PRECIOUS CONSORT:) Well, let's beseech skill then.

(MALE LEAD, *costumed as* IMPERIAL ROLE, *enters, leading a retinue of* PALACE
BEAUTIES *who are carrying lamps and props.*) (XUANZONG:) There's nothing to
do after morning court today, and my heart is thinking only of the Precious
Consort. She's already ordered a feast spread in the Palace of Eternal Life,

---

18. Weaving Maiden and Buffalo Boy are two bright stars on opposite sides of the Heavenly
River (the Milky Way). According to a popular legend, the two stars are grandchildren of the
Jade Emperor, the highest deity in the popular pantheon. The couple fell in love and so neglected
their duties. The Jade Emperor thereupon assigned them to opposite banks of the Heavenly
River, allowing them to meet only once a year, on the night of the seventh of the seventh month,
when magpies form a bridge across the Heavenly River.

where she is enjoying the festival of the Seventh Night. Attendants, lead me on. (*Sings:*)

([XIANLÜ MODE:] *Basheng Ganzhou*)
Wearied of setting in order the affairs of court,
> All I want to do is
Drink heartily in Zhaoyang Palace,
Get sodden drunk at Huaqing Springs.
> Yes, indeed
I am a fortunate man:
A Precious Consort who "can topple a state, topple a city,"
Our mutual desires fulfilled on the coral pillow,
A hundred charms displayed in front of kingfisher hangings.
At night we sleep together, together by day we walk,
Just like a phoenix and simurgh crying out in unison.
Since I have gotten Consort Yang it has been like the saying, "Every
> morning is Cold Feast, every night a lantern festival."

(*Hunjiang long*)
On the spur of the moment, late at night,
A full breast of fresh air, newly sobered up from drinking,
I loosen up the silk-knot buttons of my dragon robes,
Pull my jade belt, my red strap to the side.
The maidservants together support me into the palanquin of blue
> jade,
The palace beauties, two by two, lift up lanterns of crimson gauze.
On the wind I hear a thread of stately songs—

(*Inside are acted out the sounds of wind and percussion instruments, shouting, and laughing.*) (XUANZONG:) Where is this clamorous laughter coming from? (PALACE BEAUTIES:) Lady Precious Consort is having a banquet for beseeching skills in the Palace of Eternal Life. (XUANZONG:) You beauties! Make no noise when you walk. I want to see for myself. (*Sings:*)

Rouged beauties clustered tightly together,
Powder and kohl reveal their elegance.

(*You hulu*)
Go slow, you beauties who precede me to arrange my welcome.
I want to hear for myself.
Up these jasper steps, I move on tiptoe ever closer to the front
> columns;

Stealthily and silently, I slowly illuminate the gauze window;
Pittering and pattering, the wind shakes my shadow against the
    jeweled screen.
I was just about to walk on,
To tell a joke—
I am amazed that the parrots in their jade cage understand the nature
    of man,
And call out over and over, until my intentions are brought to light.

(*Parrot cries, made from backstage, speak:*) "Myriad Years" is here, greet the emperor! (PRECIOUS CONSORT, *startled, speaks:*) The Sage Above has come. (*Acts
out greeting the* IMPERIAL ROLE.) (XUANZONG *sings:*)

    (*Tianxia le*)
          I see
    It spread its wings, cry out "Myriad Years,"
    And startle that beauty
    Into greeting my Simurgh Palanquin.
    One confused face, makeup still unfinished, only half drawn,
    Walking in a way that makes every step alluring.
    Matured so that her every detail is pure beauty,
    Every single sound she makes resembles an oriole beyond the
        willows.

(PRECIOUS CONSORT *acts out greeting him.*) (XUANZONG *speaks:*) What are you
doing? (PRECIOUS CONSORT *speaks:*) On the occasion of the seventh of the
seventh I have assembled a feast of melon and fruit to ask the grandchild of
Heaven to bestow skills on me. (XUANZONG *acts out looking.*) (*Speaks:*) What a
fine setup! (*Sings:*)

    (*Zui zhong tian*)
    Dragon's musk burns in the golden tripod,
    Flower's blooms are stuck in the silver pitcher,
    Several tiny, tiny golden boxes planted with the five grains—
        You've even provided
    A scroll of the "Meeting of the Magpie Bridge," done in vermilion
        and bice,
    And have captured a spider as small as a grain of rice.
    Since you've just captured all of the favor that should belong to the
        whole rear palace,
        What
    Other clever skill or natural intelligence do you need?

(XUANZONG *acts out giving* PRECIOUS CONSORT *props:*) Let me give you this pair of golden hairpins and this inlaid box. (PRECIOUS CONSORT *acts out receiving them*:) Many thanks for my Sage's grace. (XUANZONG *sings:*)

> (*Jinzhan'er*)
>> I'll have
> Them covered with crimson gauze,
> And piled to the brim of the green jade plate—
> Both of these gifts are worthy of a person's respect.
>> On the occasion
> Of this early autumn's festival, I give them to you, my lovely.
> These golden hairpins set with seven jewels now seal our deep
>> feelings;
> This small box inlaid with a hundred flowers so expresses our
>> profound love.
>> These golden hairpins—Please
> Put them precariously high on top of your head.
>> This inlaid box—Please
> Bear it proudly aloft in your cupped hands.

(PRECIOUS CONSORT:) Your Majesty, this autumn radiance really stirs one. I want to stroll through the courtyard with you, my Sage. (MALE and PRECIOUS CONSORT *act out walking together.*) ([XUANZONG] *sings:*)

> (*Yi Wangsun*)
> On jasper steps the light of the moon glimmers, filtered through the
>> latticework;
> The autumn radiance of the silver candle chills the painted screens—
> Enjoying this time, the scenery of this night,
> Together with the moon, we pace through this quiet courtyard,
> Until, soaked by the moss, her stockings of wave-crossing silk turn
>> cold.

(XUANZONG:) The scenes of autumn are so different than those of the other seasons. (PRECIOUS CONSORT:) How are they different? (XUANZONG:) Let me explain. (*Sings:*)

> (*Sheng hulu*)
> The dew falls, the heavens are high, the air of the night is clear,
> The wind tosses our feathered garments until they seem weightless,
> The fragrance stirs up the tinkling of jade pendants.
> The heavens are clear and pure,

The Silver River sparkles and glimmers.
> Could we be
On one of the Three Fairy Isles?

(PRECIOUS CONSORT:) Tonight is the night that Buffalo Boy and Weaving Maiden meet. They see each other only once a year. How can they ever bear to part again? (XUANZONG *sings:*)

> (*Jinzhan'er*)
> > On this night, along the road of clouds, he
> Mounts the Phoenix Chariot,
> Across the Silver Han the Magpie Bridge lies level.
> But just as they celebrate the completion of their love,
> They suddenly hear the crowing of the morning cock.
> So soon! The sorrows of parting pulse with feeling,
> The tears of separation rain down cold and clear.
> The lengthening sighs of that fifth-watch dawn,
> > Are all due
> To this curtailed night of love.

(PRECIOUS CONSORT:) They are astral gods in the palace of heaven. They see each other only once a year. I wonder if they ever think of each other? (XUAN-ZONG *sings:*)

> (*Zui fu gui*)
> Mull over the lot of Weaving Maiden, the fate of Buffalo Boy—
> Though they might never grow old, they must still live forever.
> Separated by the Silver River, no news in the silence,
> They pass each year, enduring all the seasons in utter isolation.
> And if you inquire about them in the palace of heaven,
> You would be told that they are sick with love's longing.

(PRECIOUS CONSORT:) Since I have been honored to serve you, I have been favored greatly by you. But I fear, as my looks diminish day by day, I won't be as eternal as Weaving Maiden. (XUANZONG *sings:*)

> (*Houting hua*)
> We are not listed among the names of the constellations above,
> And were born into the dusty world below.
> The karma that brings lovers together in heaven is valued;
> The love and affection shared in the human world is disesteemed,
> But if each of us is authentic and sincere in our feelings,
> The mind of heaven must be moved to respond—
> So, why praise them alone?

(PRECIOUS CONSORT:) Buffalo Boy and Weaving Maiden see each other year after year. From time eternal it has been so. Can humans hope to match the endurance of their love? (XUANZONG *sings:*)

> (*Jinzhan'er*)
>> Every day we
> Grow drunk from rainbow beakers,
>> Every night,
> We sleep behind silver screens.
> They meet only one day, once a year, waiting expectantly for their
>> appointed tryst.
>> If it's
> The number of times that count, then we should win.
> But, even though an emperor, I still have crazy desires,
> And, even though an empress, you complain it is not enough.
>> From this we know
> That those travelers beside the constellations of the Cow and Dipper,
> Turn their heads back to ask about the outcome of their love.

(PRECIOUS CONSORT:) Like no others have I been favored and graced by you, my lord. But I fear that "as the spring fades, the flowers will grow tattered," and that your favor will be given to another, your love for me diminish. Then, I will have the same sadness as the one who wept over his fish at Longyang,[19] the same resentment as Beauty Ban penned on her fan.[20] What is there to do? (XUAN-ZONG:) Why are you saying this? (PRECIOUS CONSORT:) Please, Your Majesty, give me some secret vow by which to secure the outcome of our love. (XUAN-ZONG:) Where can we go to talk? ([THEY] *act out walking.*) (XUANZONG *sings:*)

> (*Zui zhong tian*)
>> I take her
> Head and rest it on my shoulder,

---

19. A story of Lord Longyang, who was fishing with the King of Wei. Suddenly, he began to weep as he caught a fish. When asked why, he said it was because he would throw that back and try for a bigger fish. That action made him realize that the King could cast him away as he did the fish should other suitors try to replace him. The King assuaged him and promulgated an edict that anyone whose eyes wandered from their own mates would be executed.

20. Concubine Ban (c. 48–6 BC) was a consort to Emperor Cheng of the Han who had won his favor by her consideration of his duties, her ability to recite from the *Book of Odes*, and by introducing another concubine to him. Although she had two children who died in infancy, she was finally removed from her position as the emperor's affection shifted to the legendary Zhao Feiyan, a renowned beauty. Accused of the black arts, she successfully pleaded to stay at court, where she became a handmaiden to the empress-dowager. She was also the grand aunt of the famous Han historian Ban Gu.

                    She
Raises her lovely face.
"At the western wing of the Golden Palaces, I knock on the jade door
        bolt,"
Silent and still, the winding corridors are quiet,
                Drawing near the
Shade of that wutong tree by the golden well—
        The tree that makes blue simurghs dance, that invites colorful
            phoenixes to roost—
Even though there is no one near to overhear,
            We should
Whisper our oaths and vows, eternal as the mountains and the seas.

(XUANZONG:) My consort, I will end this life with you in old age, and after our hundred years is done, we shall be husband and wife through all ages of eternity. May the gods bear witness and protect us. (PRECIOUS CONSORT:) Who is going to be the real witness for this vow? (XUANZONG *sings:*)

    (*Zhuan shawei*)
            Let our hearts be
As complete as these inlaid boxes,
Not separated like doubled hairpins of a single set.
Regard that it has been entered on the register of love's affinity
        through the ages:
"In heaven we shall be two birds joined as a single pair of wings,
On earth, grow with branches intertwined."
The moon is clear and limpid,
The Silver Han is silent,
As we speak completely of this eternal love that lasts a thousand
        autumns,
As each of us deems our will sincere.
            You say
"Who will be the real witness?"
            On this night, it is
Buffalo Boy and Weaving Maiden, who cross the Heavenly River to
        meet.

                            (*Exit.*)

                        [Act 2]

(COMIC, *costumed as* AN ROKSHAN, *leads a group of* GENERALS *and enters:*) I am An Rokshan. Since coming to Yuyang, I have trained a crack force of infantry and cavalry, composed of 400,000 men, both foreign and Han. I have a thousand battle generals. The Lustrous Emperor of Tang is now old and senile, so Yang Guozhong and Li Linfu[21] can easily manipulate the court administration. I think often of my affair with Precious Consort back in the beginning, how intimate we were, and how Yang Guozhong persuaded the emperor to send me out here. Now, under the pretext of subjugating bandits, I've raised an army and headed toward Chang'an. Only after I see the Precious Consort and only after I've wrested away the world of Tang will my heart finally be satisfied. Are the troops and horses of the left and right all ready? (GENERALS:) Everything is ready. (AN ROKSHAN:) Tell the Office of Military Affairs to first send a dispatch, saying that I have received a sealed order to suppress Yang Guozhong and the others. After that, I'll order Yin Ziqi to lead 3,000 soldiers to take Tongguan, and strike straight for the capital. Completing this great affair should be as easy as turning my hand over. Officers and men, listen to my orders: there shall be no whispering back and forth, no talking, laughing, or clamor; you shall not steal the property of others; you shall not take wives or daughters as prisoner. You shall advance with the drum, retreat with the gong. Those who disobey orders will be beheaded. It's late today, so we'll start out tomorrow. I'll go back for the time being to my tent.

(All exit together.)

(MALE LEAD *enters, costumed as* IMPERIAL ROLE, *leading* GAO LISHI, ZHENG GUANYIN,[22] *holding a pipa*, PRINCE NING, *playing a flute*,[23] FLOWERED SLAVE,[24] *playing the Tibetan drums*, HUANG FANCHUO, *holding the castanets*,[25] *and several* BEAUTIES *supporting* PRECIOUS CONSORT.) (XUANZONG:) Today is a day of fine early autumn weather. Back from morning court, I've got nothing to do today. My consort has learned how to perform the dance of the Feathered Vest and Rainbow Skirts,[26] and we're off together to Aloeswood Pavilion in the imperial

---

21. Li Linfu (d. 753) was known for his treachery, political savvy, and ability to flatter the aging Xuanzong. Often described by the phrase "honey in his mouth and a sword in his belly" (*koumi fujian*), he held absolute power as Xuanzong was lost to merrymaking and sex.

22. Master of the pipa at Xuanzong's court.

23. Li Xian, elder brother of Xuanzong and skilled musician.

24. Li Lian, Prince of Ru'nan, who was called by his childhood name of "Flowered Slave." He was particularly skilled in playing the Tibetan drum, an instrument that was imported into China during the Six Dynasties and was a particular favorite of Xuanzong.

25. Entertainer of the inner palaces.

26. A dance of nearly mythic status, introduced into China from either Central Asia or India during the Tang. Legend, however, claims that Xuanzong discovered it when he roamed on a magical trip through the palace of the moon, where the dance was performed by sylphlike immortals. Although Xuanzong tried to memorize the tune, he lost a part of it with each step across

garden to enjoy ourselves. Just look at all the phenomena that come with autumn—how it moves me. (*Sings:*)

> ([ZHONGLÜ MODE:] *Fendie'er*)
> Slate skies, lazy clouds,
> Lines of migrating geese queued across the sky.
> In the imperial gardens the scenery of summer first begins to tatter,
> The willows grow more yellow,
> Lotus leaves lose their green,
> Autumn lotus blossoms drop their petals.
> I sit near the hidden orchids exploding with fragrance, "jade-hairpin
>   flowers" splitting at the seams.

(XUANZONG:) Here we are in the imperial garden. Even though a small feast, it is really beautifully laid out. (*Sings:*)

> (*Jiaosheng*)
> I'll enjoy myself with my consort,
> At ease,
> At ease,
> As we arrange the dainties and viands in the imperial garden.
> For wine we pour out gosling yellow,
> For tea, serve up partridge speckle.

([XUANZONG]:) Bring on the wine, so I can drink with my consort. (*Sings:*)

> (*Zui chunfeng*)
> Wine's radiance glimmers in the purple metal beaker,
> Tea's fragrance floats in blue jade cups.
> Beside Aloeswood Pavilion, in the plenty of evening's coolness
> I personally select a perfect place.
> Powder and rouge laid on thick,
> Pipes and strings arrayed in order,
> Gauzy silks flit in between.

(EXTRA MALE, *costumed as* ATTENDANT, *enters:*)

> "Turn back to look upon Chang'an: it looks like heaps of embroidery.
>   On mountain peaks a thousand gates open one after another;

---

the bridge that led back to the mortal world. He immediately ordered his court entertainers to try and approximate the music and choreography.

> A single mount spurs through the red dust, a consort smiles—
> No one knows that the litchis have arrived."[27]

I am a messenger sent from Sichuan. Because lady Precious Consort loves to taste fresh litchis, I received a special imperial directive to get them here in time to present them fresh to her. Here I am outside the court. Palace eunuchs! Spread the word that the messenger from Sichuan has come with fresh litchis. (*Act out reporting.*) (XUANZONG:) Lead him in. (ENVOY *acts out greeting* XUANZONG:) I, messenger from the Circuit of Sichuan, hereby present these litchis. (XUAN-ZONG *acts out looking at them:*) My consort, you love to eat this fruit, so I have especially ordered that they be brought to court as they ripen. (PRECIOUS CON-SORT:) O what fine litchis. (XUANZONG *sings:*)

> (*Ying xianke*)
> So spurting with fragrance, their taste so sweet,
> Dripping with allure, their color just bursting,
>> Even I suspect
> They have been banished from the ninth layer of heaven to the
>> human world below.
> Hard to get in season,
> Too precious to share when gotten.
> Alas, they come from nowhere near Chang'an
>> And so I make
> Post riders trod through the red dust.

(PRECIOUS CONSORT:) The color of these litchis is so alluring and loveable. (XUANZONG *sings:*)

> (*Hongxiuxie*)
> Don't think them pretty in the metal platter,
> For they ought to be raised into view by sleeves of kingfisher green.
> Pouches of crimson gauze glisten
> As they cover the coolness of crystal.
>> And why
> Are my drunken eyes sobered?
> Is my consort's alluring face so flustered?
> Because these are rare things, seldom seen by men.

---

27. This is a poem by Du Mu (813–52) called "Passing the Palaces of Huaqing." The "thousand gates" refers to large numbers of halls and buildings constructed at the Huaqing hot springs complex outside of Chang'an.

(GAO LISHI:) Your Majesty, the wine has been served three times. Ask Lady to rise to the "jade platter"[28] and dance the dance of Rainbow Skirts. (XUAN-ZONG:) I'll petition as you desire. (PRECIOUS CONSORT *acts out dancing.*) (*All of the musicians act out playing music.*) (XUANZONG *sings:*)

(*Kuaihuo san*)
    I order you,
Court of Immortal Music: don't be lax,
   I tell you
Court Entertainment Bureau: put everything in proper sequence
    And support
The Consort of Highest Perfection to the center of the "jade platter."
Dress her finely,
And make her costume suitable for palace style.

(*Baolao'er*)
Roll back her paired sleeves, speckled with gold,
Set the tune of Rainbow Skirts from the Palace of the Moon.
Zheng Guanyin, preparing to play the pipa,
Has already attached the shark-silk band of the plectrum.
The jade flute of Prince Ning,
The Tibetan drum of Flowered Slave—
Such beautiful tones, such a panoply of sounds.
The brocade zithers of Shou and Ning,
The jade pipes of Consort Mei—
Ringing sounds chasing each other round and round.

(*Gu baolao*)
Clickety-clack, purple sandalwood opens the performance—
Huang Fanchuo moves forward with hands grasping castanets.
Softly, lowly, I cry out, "Yuhuan, my Bracelet of Jade,"
And when Consort of Highest Perfection smiles, flowers appear
  before my eyes,
The red ivory hammers beat out the five tones, striking the wutong
  lute.
A tender branch of willow, supple yet,
Wreathed in the floating sound of the jasper lute,
    Ah, my lovely, you are
Dappled by chalcedony beads of perspiration.

---

28. A stage or a dance floor.

(PRECIOUS CONSORT *acts out dancing.* XUANZONG *sings:*)

> (*Hong shaoyao*)
> Dry as wind, the sound of the waist drum,
> As her silken sleeves arch and curve
> And her clinking pendants of jade jingle and tinkle.
> > Closer and closer now
> She dances, her cloudy hair drooping low—
> Show off that waist of yours, wasp-thin,
> Your swallow shape turning.
> And when she performs "the doubled sleeves," perfumed air billows
> > out everywhere.
> > You look so tired, my lovely. Drink a cup of wine. (*Sings:*)
> I personally proffer this cup
> Of jade dew, sweet and cold,
> > You must not
> Leave the slightest bit untouched,
> > But drink until
> The night is still and the hour late.

(PRECIOUS CONSORT *acts out drinking.*) (OFFICIAL *enters costumed as* LI LINFU:)
I am Li Linfu, and now hold the post of Minister of the Left. This morning a
flying dispatch arrived, reporting that An Rokshan had rebelled. He has so
many soldiers and horses that it is impossible to go up against him. I must see
the emperor. There is no one here to report that I'm here, so I'll just go straight
in. (*Acts out greeting* IMPERIAL ROLE.) (XUANZONG:) Why are you in such a
panic? (LI LINFU:) A flying dispatch from the border passes! An Rokshan has
rebelled and an army of enormous power is killing its way toward us. Your
Majesty, the world has been so long at peace that no one knows about warfare
anymore. What shall we do? (XUANZONG:) What are you so panicked about?
(*Sings:*)

> (*Ti yindeng*)
> > This is no more
> Than a memorial that a border headquarters has erupted in revolt,
> > You should have
> Looked for an idle moment, a proper time,
> Kept on eye on what is pressing, what is urgent.
> > Couldn't you have waited
> Until the performance at my feast was done?
> > Did you have to
> Run with panting breath to offend the imperial countenance?

Come over here, you,
Guan Zhong of Qi,[29] Zichan of Zheng,[30]
You, pretending to be as loyal as Longfeng[31] and Bigan![32]

(LI LINFU:) Your Majesty, here's how it is: the traitor's armies have already smashed Tong Pass. Geshu Han[33] has lost control of the border and has fled in retreat. He is already in the capital, and the capital city is completely empty now, impossible to hold. What shall we do? (XUANZONG *sings:*)

(*Manjingcai*)
It almost
Panicked you to death, a real Dan, Duke of Zhou![34]

(LI LINFU:) Your Majesty, it's because you favored this woman too much and made slandering officials eminent. That's how you stirred up these armed troops!

You say I
Destroyed my mountains and rivers because of song and dance?
You are a fine and treacherous one.
No one can say [about you]
That "while sitting at ease with his feather fan and blue silk scarf,
He smashed the strong caitiffs, three hundred thousand strong!"

(XUANZONG:) Since the rebel armies have overrun the borders, you assembled officials work out a plan to select a general to lead a campaign against them.

---

29. Guan Yiwu (d. c. 645 BC), noted minister who helped raise Duke Huan of Qi to the position of hegemon on the basis of his policy of "resisting the barbarians and venerating true kingship."

30. Gongsun Qiao, also known as Zichan of Zheng (d. 522 BC), responsible for revitalizing the state of Zheng through the implementation of administrative reforms.

31. Loyal minister of the last bad ruler, Jie, of the Xia, who was imprisoned and killed for his remonstrance against the debauchery of his ruler.

32. Loyal minister of the last bad ruler, Zhou, of the Shang, who was likewise tortured and killed for his remonstrance against Zhou's debauchery.

33. Under the false pretext of having been ordered to capture Yang Guozhong, An Rokshan entered Luoyang in late 755 where he proclaimed his own dynasty, the Yan. Geshu Han was appointed as Grand Marshal of Infantry and Cavalry of the Crown Prince's Spearhead Army to fortify Tong Pass. Yang Guozhong pressed him to attack; he did and was captured and surrendered to An Rokshan.

34. Left with the responsibility of consolidating the power of the Zhou dynasty (1045?–256 BC) the Duke of Zhou, Ji Dan, acted as a regent for the young emperor Wen rather than seize power for himself. His name is synonymous with ethical behavior, profound political statesmanship, and the creation of parts of the classical Confucian canon.

(LI LINFU:) There are not even ten thousand troops stationed in the capital barracks. All of the generals are old and weak. When even a famous general like Geshu Han can't match up to them, who else can do it? (XUANZONG *sings:*)

> (*Manting fang*)
>> You
> Two cohorts, civil and military,
>> Make a vain display of
> Your raven-black shoes, your ivory tallies,[35]
> Your robes of purple silk fretted with gold.
> There's not a heroic man in the whole of the palace
> To sweep out the dust of this realm.
> You let that good-for-nothing Rokshan
> Pass with ease through Tongguan—
>> First defeating
> Geshu Han.
>> No wonder
> Last night, toward evening,
>> I saw no
> Beacon fires reporting eternal peace.

(XUANZONG:) Do you have any strategy to make the rebel force retreat? (LI LINFU:) The Han and foreign army under An Rokshan's control number 400,000 and each of them is worth a hundred of ours. There's no way to repel him directly. It would be best if Your Majesty would seek temporary refuge in Shu[36] to escape his vanguards and there wait until the troops of the empire assemble before making another plan. (XUANZONG:) I'll do as you suggest. Pass along my directive to get the consorts of the Six Palaces, the various royal princes, and the civilian officials ready. Tomorrow morning we shall leave for Shu. (PRECIOUS CONSORT:) Oh, what shall I do? (XUANZONG *sings:*)

> (*Putian le*)
> My vexation is inexhaustible, my sorrow without limit.
>> And alas,
> In this period of haste
>> There's no way to avoid
> Climbing ranges and ascending mountains.
> The Simurgh Chariot moves,

---

35. I.e., as they prepare to present their memorials at court.
36. Modern Sichuan, a basin surrounded by mountains and difficult passes.

Chengdu beckons,
How can I bear the west-flying geese over Chan River?[37]
Each and every sound they make urges me onto the carved saddle,
Broken-hearted for my old gardens.
In the west wind, along the River Wei,
The sun sets on Chang'an.

(PRECIOUS CONSORT:) My Majesty, can you stand the hardships of the road?
(XUANZONG:) There's nothing I can do. (*Sings:*)

(*Weisheng*)
I look closely at your "charms ascending the horse,"
How can you ever withstand the "difficulties of the road to Shu?"[38]
      I worry for you
About those steep and rugged trestle paths that run through the
    clouds:
Those who have flogged those paths before are used to it,
But how can you ever make it over Swordgate Pass?

(*All exit.*)

[Act 3]

(EXTRA, *costumed as* CHEN XUANLI, *enters:*)

For generations, benefactor of heaven's grace, I led the Imperial Armies
    And was first to know the joy and anger on the heavenly face.
      Military preparations in time of peace: none ever used;
    Who could know this wild barbarian would kick up border dust?

---

37. An adaptation of a poem by Li Qiao (645–714), called "Ballad of South Banks of the Fen River" (*Fenyin xing*), which was a lamentation of a deserted city in Shanxi where the Martial Emperor of the Han had discovered a precious tripod. The last two couplets of this long poem read,

> River and mountain are filled with moonlight, tears moisten my gown;
> Wealth and nobility, glory and splendor—how long can they last?
> Unseen, now again on the south banks of the Fen,
> All that remains, year after year, the migrations of autumn's geese.

In fictional accounts of Xuanzong's flight to Shu, he has this song performed as he leaves the capital, and once again en route. Here, the river has been switched to the Chan, which is inside the environs of Chang'an.

38. *Shudao nan*, a favorite title of poems about the difficulty of travel to Sichuan, the most famous of which is by the great Tang poet Li Bai (701–62).

I am Chen Xuanli, Right General of Dragon's Might. Recently Tongguan Pass was lost after that recalcitrant barbarian, An Rokshan, stirred up revolt. Yesterday the high ministers of state deliberated and decided that the emperor ought to seek temporary refuge in Shuchuan as a way of avoiding the rebel's thrust. A flying dispatch this morning reports that the rebel troops are not far from the capital. My sagely lord has ordered me to lead the Imperial Army and protect his passage. My men and horses have been ready now for a while, and we are waiting only for the emperor to begin the procession.

(XUANZONG, *costumed as* IMPERIAL ROLE, *enters, leading* PRECIOUS CONSORT, *and* YANG GUOZHONG, GAO LISHI, *together with* MINOR IMPERIAL ROLE,[39] GUO ZIYI,[40] *and* LI GUANGBI.)[41] (XUANZONG:) My eyes do not recognize people for what they are.[42] And so I have caused this wild barbarian to create such turmoil. And now the affair is so out of hand and pressing that I have to flee to the west to avoid his troops. It makes me so broken-hearted. (*Sings:*)

> ([SHUANGDIAO MODE:] *Xinshui ling*)
> Battle standards of the Five Quadrants flutter in the red glow at sun's
>   edge,[43]
> Clear, chill, cold, half-unfurled over the Simurgh Chariot.
> The whip I droop wearily,
> The stirrup I trod listlessly,
> I turn my head back to the capital,
> Unable to put one foot in front of another.

(XUANZONG:) I've lived my whole life in the depths of the palace, what do I know of the privation and suffering of common alleys? (*Sings:*)

> (*Zhuma ting*)
> Dark and gloomy, the edge of heaven—
> Five or six ravaged rivers and mountains destroyed.
> Lonely and desolate within the forest—

---

39. I.e., Li Heng, later to become Emperor Suzong.

40. Lived 697–781; a great Tang general, Military Commissioner of the Northern Realm, later to become a high minister under Suzong.

41. Lived 708–64, a Khitan from modern Liaoning, Military Commissioner of Hedong at this time; with Guo Ziyi, he would recapture the ten districts lost to An Rokshan.

42. Compare his criticism of Zhang Jiuling in the beginning of Act 1: "Sir, don't act as if you were Wang Yan recognizing Shi Le." This line makes reference to a well-known line spoken by Xuanzong when he was en route to Shu, "If I had listened to Zhang Jiuling, none of this would have ever happened."

43. Banners representing the four cardinal directions and capital center: green dragon, vermilion bird, white tiger, dark warrior, and ochre dragon.

Two or three homes with crumbling walls and dilapidated dwellings.
Along streams of Qin, distant trees are vague and unclear in the mist,
By the bridge at Ba, withered willows sough and sigh in the wind.
No resemblance here to the blue gauze of windows,
Or mandarin duck tiles, shimmering with fire in the morning rays.

(GROUP, *costumed as* VILLAGE ELDERS, *enter:*) Our Sage Above, the commoners of this village pay their respects. (XUANZONG:) What do you elders have to say? (ELDERS:) The palace, Your Majesty, is where you dwell; the burial mounds and ancestral temples are the graves of Your Majesty's ancestors. You are forsaking these now, but where will you go? (XUANZONG:) I have no choice but to avoid their army for the time being. (ELDERS:) If you, Your Majesty, are unwilling to stay, then we desire to lead our youngsters to follow the heir apparent to the east, smash the rebels, and retake Chang'an. If the heir apparent and our most exalted both go to Shu, then who will be master of the people of the Central Plain? (XUANZONG:) What you say is right. Attendants, summon my son before me. (MINOR IMPERIAL ROLE, *costumed as* SUZONG, *acts out approaching and greeting him.*) (XUANZONG:) These elders have explained that the Central Plain would be without a master. I am going to leave you here to return east at the head of an army to slay the rebels. At the same time, I will order Guo Ziyi and Li Guangbi to be Chief Marshals. I will split off two thousand of the rear guard to return with you. Listen to what I say now:

> (*Chenzui dongfeng*)
> I have heeded and accepted the loyal words of these elders,
> And assigned my young prince to take sole command of the
>   campaign.
>   By rights
> You should share in the anxieties of our altars of state;
>   How can we bear
> Let another rule over our mountains and rivers?
>   I leave this
> Precious seal that transmits the state to you.

(SUZONG:) I, your son, am willing to lead troops to smash the rebels, but how dare I ascend the Throne of Heaven? (XUANZONG *sings:*)

> After you have destroyed the rebel bandits
> And have saved the state,
> Why should you avoid being called "the lonely one?"[44]

---

44. I.e., the emperor, alone in his decision-making power.

(SUZONG:) Since it is a weighty matter involving our state and house, I, your son, heed the imperial directive. I will lead Guo Ziyi and Li Guangbi back. (*Acts out taking his leave of* XUANZONG.) (HOST OF SOLDIERS *acts out giving a battle cry and refusing to advance.*) (XUANZONG *sings:*)

> (*Qing dongyuan*)
> The point army ought to be moving out,
> > Why
> Haven't they started forward?

(HOST OF SOLDIERS *acts out venting their anger.*)

> After I regard this host of men, I am alarmed and full of fear.
> > Simmering with anger
> They still their whips and halt their horses,
> > Seething with hatred
> They put on battle robes, slip into their armor.
> > Flashing brightly,
> Swords are pulled from their scabbards.
> > Orderly in array,
> They line up like geese in rank;
> > One close to the other,
> They press forward as close as scales on a fish.

(CHEN XUANLI *speaks:*) This host of soldiers has explained that there is a traitorous evil in this state that has brought about the flight of your imperial palanquin. If this disaster is not rooted out from your side, then I cannot keep control of the soldiers' hearts. (XUANZONG:) What is the meaning of this? (*Sings:*)

> (*Bubu jiao*)
> > As for me:
> A myriad miles of smoke and dust;
> > As for you:
> The right reply should be a sympathetic sound.
> You presume on your strength, stand in the way to frighten me.
> This state has never stinted you in the slightest,
> So why should the army's heart so suddenly seize on the slightest
> > wrong?
> I ask you, my minister,
> > Why
> Don't you utter even a single word of understanding?

(CHEN XUANLI:) Yang Guozhong has wronged this state by his abuse of power. Now he is in contact with an envoy from Turfan and seems to be intent on rebelling. I request to execute him in order to seek pardon from the empire. (XUANZONG *sings:*)

> (*Chenzui dongfeng*)
>> In the case of
>
> Yang Guozhong, a fitting sentence is ten thousand slicings,
>> For he led on
>
> Traitor Rokshan to spread chaos in the Central Flowery realm.
>> But right or wrong,
>
> He was my right-hand man, and hard to simply cast away,
>> And, to my consort, too
>
> Bound by blood relations.
> To send him to his death
>> Would but defile
>
> The five punishable offenses of criminal law.[45]

(*Sings:*)

>> Take him
>
> And strip him of his official rank,
> And make him a common citizen—
> Is that not the same as execution?
>> To assent to this or not,
>
> Is up to General Chen Xuanli to decide.

(HOST OF SOLDIERS *acts out crying out angrily.*) (CHEN XUANLI:) Your Majesty, the heart of the army has already been swayed. I cannot control them. What shall we do? (XUANZONG:) Do what you want. (HOST *acts out killing* YANG GUOZHONG.) (XUANZONG *sings:*)

> (*Yan'er luo*)
> Rank after rank of spears crowd closely together,
> One angry shout sends the mountains a-tumble.
>> All along
>
> It was the orders of General Chen,
> That clearly finished off Yang Guozhong.

(HOST OF SOLDIERS *acts out brandishing their swords and crowding around* THE EMPEROR.) (XUANZONG *sings:*)

---

45. That is, it would be too great of a punishment. The five punishments are caning, bastina-doing, exile, banishment, and death.

(*Bobuduan*)
Jabbering and yelling,
Boisterous and chaotic,
The Six Armies do not advance, but stand firm with spear and armor
To squeeze around me on Mawei Slope—
Now what do they want?
> It scares me so much
That I quake, quiver, and tremble,
As over my body hairs are chilled to stand on end.

(*Sings* [*to* CHEN XUANLI]:)

True it is that "an army follows the transfer of power."
The orders of a general are overawing and severe.
Authority over the troops is in your hands;
The ruler is weak, the minister strong.
> Ah, sir, do you think
I fear you or not?

([XUANZONG]:) Yang Guozhong has already been slain. Why won't your armies advance? (CHEN XUANLI:) Guozhong plotted to rebel. It is not fitting for your consort to continue to serve at your side. I desire you, Your Majesty, to sever your grace for her and set it right by the law! (XUANZONG *sings*:)

(*Jiao zhengpa*)
> Gao Lishi, tell
Chen Xuanli not to destroy the distinction of high and low!
> How can he
Make my consort suffer capital punishment?
> Right now she enjoys
The rights of the empress in the Central Palace,
> And has moreover graced
My imperial couch.
She's committed no crime,

(*Sings* [*to* CHEN XUANLI]:)

> My sir,
She did not manipulate her power like Empress Lü of the Han,
Or usurp the throne the way Wu Zetian did,
Or light the beacon fires for pleasure, a Bao Si of the Zhou,
Or break anyone's shinbones to see the marrow, a Dan Ji who
  belonged to Zhou.

You've already destroyed her only brother,
And even if she were guilty of a thousand crimes,
For my sake, she should be spared.
But you've tricked me into an impossible position.

(GAO LISHI:) The Precious Consort is truly innocent! But the officers have already slain Guozhong, and how can you ever feel secure with her by your side? Please, Your Majesty, think this over carefully. If the officers are peaceful, then you, too, will find security. (XUANZONG *sings:*)

> (*Feng ru song*)
> It was no more
> Than phoenix pipes and Tibetan drums, broken now and then by the
>   pipa,
> And, hu-la-la, for clappers the red ivories were set loose.
> Even if
> We had added a *Liuyao* or a *Hushiba*,
> None of them caused the end of our state, the loss of our house.
> But now I know
> Why the last emperor of Chen was killed—
> All because he sang "Flowers in the Rear Courtyard."

(PRECIOUS CONSORT:) My death is no cause for worry; it's just that I have never had the chance to repay my lord's kindness. How can I set aside so many years of kindness? (XUANZONG:) My girl, it's hopeless now. The minds of the Six Armies have gone amok, and I cannot even save myself. (*Sings:*)

> (*Hushiba*)
> To be able to face me like this
> Means his heart has switched.
> Seeing that I love her deeply
> The "three-foot dragon-spring sword" is already in his hand.
> Even if death were the fate bestowed,
> Life or death lies in one single word from him.
> So any compunction to ask more of "Your Majesty"
> Is, probably,
> Only because he still knows enough to honor an emperor.[46]

(CHEN XUANLI:) Your Majesty, hurry and sever your grace for her and set it right by the law! (PRECIOUS CONSORT:) How can you save me, Your Majesty? (XUANZONG:) What can I do? (*Sings:*)

---

46. I.e., there was no need for Chen Xuanli to ask; he did it for the sake of form alone.

(*Luomei feng*)
> Just able to

Trim the tree of happiness,
> I resent that in my palm

I can no longer hold this "flower that knows how to speak,"[47]
Or ride forever with her astride the jade-green simurgh.[48]
How can I love her, care for her?
> Or let her be

Dragged down here below Mawei Slope?

(CHEN XUANLI:) The revolt of Rokshan was all because of the Yangs, both sister and brother. If you do not set it right by law in order to beg pardon from the empire, then when will this disastrous rebellion ever end? I beseech Your Majesty to turn over the Yangs and let the horses of the Six Armies trample their corpses. Only this can serve as a token of your sincerity. (XUANZONG:) How could she stand such a thing? Gao Lishi, take the consort into that Buddha hall and order her to kill herself. Afterwards, have the soldiers verify it by examining her corpse. (GAO LISHI:) I have a strip of white silk here. (XUANZONG *sings:*)

(*Dianqian huan*)
> She is a blossom of drooping, dangling, and delicate

Crabapple flower,
> How can she be

The unruly and riotous root of disaster that brings the state to an end?
> Never again

Will she sketch those eyebrows, arched and curving like distant
　　mountains,
Or put up in raven's black those dangling, tangled cloudlike locks.
> Can I bear to allow those violent, terrifying

Horse hooves trample her face?
It is her delicately fine and lovely neck that will be stretched.
> Already a long and twining

Strip of raw silk has been prepared—
> There

Her body will suffer its death,
> And I burn with pain,

Because of its power, alone, more than I can stand.

---

47. Once, when viewing lotuses with Precious Consort and his retinue, Xuanzong turned to his retinue and said, "Yes, but how can they compare to this flower that knows how to speak [i.e., Precious Consort]?"

48. An ancient metaphor for a happy marriage.

(GAO LISHI:) Move along, missy. You'll destroy the progress of the army! (PRE-
CIOUS CONSORT, *turning around to gaze back, speaks:*) Your Majesty! How can
you bear it so easily? (XUANZONG:) My mistress, do not resent me. (*Sings:*)

> (*Gu meijiu*)
> It's all happening so fast!
> How can I save her?
> I'm powerless.
> How can I leave her?
> Draw out the time left before her execution just a second longer—
> Scrambling to get her strangled,
> Chen Xuanli is stirring up a ruckus!

(GAO LISHI *exits, leading* PRECIOUS CONSORT.) (XUANZONG *sings:*)

> (*Taiping ling*)
> How can you so blindly curse her and accuse her by name,
> And use those warriors' golden calabashes[49] on the back of her skull?
>> Have several
> Coarse and ungainly palace ladies lead her off under guard,
> And let not that delicate and fine little lady suffer any fright.
> And when you
> See her,
> And she asks of me,
> Say, "How pitiful, the world that is Tang."[50]

(GAO LISHI *enters, carrying* PRECIOUS CONSORT's *clothes:*) The lady has already
been slain. You of the Six Armies, come forward and observe. (CHEN XUANLI,
leading a host of horses, acts out trampling her.) (XUANZONG *weeps:*) You have for-
saken me, my consort! (*Sings:*)

> (*Sansha*)
>> I never thought that you
> Would perish this morning beneath Mawei Slope,
>> There's no prospect now
> Of fulfilling those words of yesterday in the Palace of Eternal Life.

> (*Taiqing ge*)
>> I hate

---

49. A ceremonial weapon, shaped like a calabash on a long staff, carried by the imperial
guard.

50. I.e., because she has suffered a wrong, but also that she has insured his survival as emperor of Tang by her death. The question is directed at the palace women who are guarding her.

This wild wind scraping, as it rolls without feeling across the land,
Blowing down all of the palace flowers.

> I think

Of her soul, cut off at heaven's edge,
Transforming into strips of colored clouds.

> Heaven, that

Bright Consort of the Han who was married afar to the khan

> Did no more

Than weep in the western wind, her tears moistening barbarian
   pipes.[51]

> There's never been the like

Of this senseless trampling and treading

> That takes a corpse

And grinds it into the yellow sands.

(XUANZONG *acts out seizing her scarf and weeping:*) Where will she go, she who
left behind only this scarf? It breaks my heart. (*Sings:*)

(*Ersha*)

> Who has gathered up

Her embroidered leggings and narrow stockings made from the
   finest silks of Wu?[52]

> Vainly I moan over

This tear-speckled scarf of mermaid gauze that just squeezed her
   neck.[53]

(*Chuan bo zhao*)
I feel sorry for her,
Unable to fill her jade casket with quicksilver,[54]

> And lacking any

Colorful maids or palace ladies
To pull on the cotton and arrange the hemp,[55]
To pour out libations of wine, offerings of tea.

> Might as well

---

51. This is Wang Zhaojun; see *A Lone Goose in Autumn over the Palaces of Han*.

52. Sources report that old crones at Mawei picked up Precious Consort's stockings and later
sold them to passersby a strip at a time.

53. A fine silk woven by mermaids who also wept tears of pearls.

54. Mercury was added, according to various traditions, either to the casket or was poured
into a separate container to be placed in the casket, in order to ward off decomposition of the
body.

55. To wear mourning clothes for her.

Bury her temporarily in this shallow earth,
> There's no time

To pick a proper hillock in which to sink a grave.

(*Suisha*)
Yellow earth scatters and swirls, a sorrowful wind scours,
Azure clouds grow dark and dim, the evening sun falls.

(*Yuanyang sha*)
> Each leg of my journey

The rivers are green, the mountains blue,[56]
Step by step by step, through Sword Peak Pass, the Gorges of Ba.
> I cry out

Moan and sigh, full of feeling.
Scared and worried; tears scatter down.
Let me ascend from this world soon;
It's over, over. This life is over.[57]
> This

Helpless emperor,
Weeping, climbs onto his free-wandering jade flower steed.[58]

(*The whole group exits.*)

[Act 4]

(SUZONG *enters with retinue:*) I am the Suzong Emperor of Tang. After An Rokshan had stirred up rebellion, my father, the emperor, went to visit Shu. He had reached as far as Wuling when, on the request of various village elders, he turned the throne over to me. I drafted all of the horses and soldiers in the empire, returned east, and smashed the rebels. Pig Li and Guo Ziyi stabbed An Rokshan to death and Li Guangbi destroyed An Qingxu.[59] The remaining

---

56. According to one story, on the way to Shu, Xuanzong told one of his officials, "From here to Swordgate Pass, the crying of birds, the falling of flowers, the verdant tint of mountains and the green of waters—all of this will simply bolster my grief over the loss of Precious Consort."

57. A recasting of a line of Li Shangyin's poem "Mawei Slope, Number 2": "Another life as yet unknown, this life is done."

58. "Free-wandering" usually refers to the imperial palanquin. Here it seems to modify "Jade Flower," the white Arabian horse that was one of Xuanzong's favorite mounts.

59. This is historically inaccurate. An Qingxu killed his father, An Rokshan, and proclaimed himself emperor in 757 and dispatched Shi Siming, who had originally been An Rokshan's general, to recover Fanyang, from whence An Rokshan had begun his campaign. Shi Siming allied

factions of Shi Mingsi and the others have all been eradicated and now the world has been swept clean and the empire of Tang re-established. The bureaucracy and the grand ministers have set me on the throne as Emperor Suzong. I welcomed my father, the emperor, back and he has lodged in the palaces in the western part of the imperial city. I just returned from asking after his comfort this morning, and I have nothing else to do, so I might as well go back to the rear palaces.

(Exits.)

(GAO LISHI *enters:*) I am Gao Lishi. I have served in the rear palace since my youth, and because of my diligence and circumspection, I have oft been praised by the emperor and was made the Grand Eunuch, Overseer of the Six Palaces. In years past the emperor, being infatuated with the looks of Miss Yang, ordered me to take her into the palace, where she received peerless favor and was installed as Precious Consort and given the title of Most Perfected. Later that recalcitrant barbarian took up arms on the pretext of executing Yang Guozhong, thus forcing His Highness to flee to Shu. Mid-journey, the Six Armies refused to go any further. The Dragon Martial General of the Right, Chen Xuanli, put the Master on High in an impossible position when, after killing Yang Guozhong, he petitioned that the perfidy of Guozhong extended to his sister, the Precious Consort. The emperor could only go along with it, and she was strangled in the Mawei posthouse. Now the rebels have been quelled and the world is at peace. The Master on High has returned to his state, where the crown prince has become the emperor. The Master on High has withdrawn to live out his old age in the Western Palaces. But day and night, he does nothing but long for lady Precious Consort. Today he ordered me to hang up a portrait of her. He weeps for her day and night. I'd better straighten things up in case he comes. I will simply wait for him.

(XUANZONG, *costumed as* IMPERIAL ROLE, *enters:*) During the time that I went to Shu and then returned to the capital, the crown prince smashed the rebels and ascended the Throne of the Thearch. I have withdrawn to live out my old age in the Western Palaces. All I do every day is long for my consort. I had a painter paint her likeness, so that I may offer sacrifice to it. But, to face this every day only makes me more and more vexed. (*Acts out crying, sings:*)

---

himself with the Khitan and surrendered to Tang, which enfeoffed him as a Prince and made him Governor of Fanyang. Shi then restored relations with An Qingxu, and together they defeated Guo Ziyi's army. Shi Siming then assassinated An Qingxu, returned to Fanyang, and proclaimed himself emperor of the Great Yan. His own son, Shi Chaoyi, in turn, assassinated Shi Siming in 761.

([ZHENGDUAN MODE:] *Duanzheng hao*)
>   From the time
I fled to Xichuan, and then returned to the capital region,
There have been no nights of moonlight or mornings of flowers.
>   This
Last half year, I've turned more white-haired.
>   How
Can I put away this sorrowing face?

(*Reprise*)
Gaunt, gaunt, emaciated, I can't avoid provoking the laughter of all
>   those officials. . . .
Her jade likeness—raised high on the scroll,
The litchi—flower and fruit are redolent on the sandalwood table.
I stare at them and then feel the pain in my chest.

(*Acts out looking at the portrait.*)

(*Gun xiuqiu*)
>   It almost
Keels me over with heartache,
I struggle to lean on something,
I call out, call out for the Most Perfected.
But my cries are not answered so I weep tears and wail.
This Painter-in-Waiting was a man of high talent,
Painting a likeness no different from life,
But even though a skilled colorist, a capable painter,
>   He could never paint
Her dance of circling simurghs beside Aloeswood Pavilion,
Or her charms ascending the horse in front of Calyx Loft—
All her bewitching features.

(*Tang xiucai*)
>   O lady, I remember well
The feast music for the festival of my thousand autumns, held at
>   Huaqing hot springs,
Seeking skills on the seventh of the seventh month, there at the Hall
>   of Eternal Life,
>   Where an oath we did make of
Our desire to be like intertwining branches, like two birds sharing a
>   single pair of wings.
>   Who would have expected

You to rise on a rainbow phoenix and return to the Vermilion
    Empyrean, a life cut so short?

[(*Speaks:*)] The more I stare, the more heartbroken I become. Oh, what shall I
do? (*Sings:*)

> (*Dai guduo*)
> With my whole heart I wanted to build a temple to Consort Yang,[60]
> > But, alas,
> I have no power, have quit the throne, have left the court.
> I can scarce endure this life as a lonely asterism,[61]
> For the Heaven of Parting's Regret is the highest of all.[62]
> "Alive, let us share the same quilt and pillow,
> Dead, let us share the same casket and coffin."[63]
> > I never thought, instead,
> There, in the dust on Mawei Slope,
> My crabapple flower would wither and die.

[(*Speaks:*)] I suddenly feel tired. I'll go and stroll through that little pavilion.

> (*Bai hezi*)
> I move away from the palace eaves,
> And with trusting steps descend to the side of the pavilion,
> > Where I see
> Weeping willows waving osiers of greenish blue,
> And the lotus splitting buds of reddish rouge.

> (*Er*)
> Seeing the lotus, I remember her winsome face,
> Encountering the willow, recall her tiny waist.
> > Both now,

---

60. He wanted to reinter Yang in the capital, but was prevented from doing so by court officials.

61. Chinese mark time by a combination of ten earthly branches and twelve heavenly stems. Since they must combine to make a standard cycle of sixty (hours, days, months, years, etc.), not all of the earthly branches are used. He calls himself an "orphaned *chen*-branch." The implication is both that he is now alone, but also that he is unlucky and ill-starred, as well.

62. A common saying in early vernacular literature: "Of the thirty-three heavens above, the heaven of parting's regret is the highest."

63. This hackneyed quote was, indeed, that expressed by the two lovers in the Palace of Eternal Life.

As before, decorate this Shangyang Palace,[64]
> But she—

Her whole soul is desolate and lonely on the road from Chang'an.

(San)
> Often I remember her

Standing in the shade of the azure wutong tree,
Red ivory clappers chattering in her hands.
> She—

Laughing—she adjusted her raiment twilled with golden threads,
And for her dance arranged the music of Rainbow Skirts.

(Si)
> But now

Wild grasses fill that platter of jade,
Her hidden perfume has dissipated from beneath the fragrant tree.
In vain I face the shade of the wellside wutong tree,
For no face of a city-toppling beauty will appear.

[(Speaks:)] I can't stand this stroll. I'd better go back. (Sings:)

(Tang xiucai)
> All I wanted

Was to amuse myself, to pursue, in my heart, some happiness, find
    some joy,
> But instead I stirred up

Old feelings of vexation: "Heaven is wild, the earth grows old,"[65]
Unhappy and unfulfilled, I return to the quiet of phoenix
    bedhangings,
With no way to endure this night's long frustration.

[(Speaks:)] I've come back to my bedchambers, but every single thing just swells
my sorrow. (Sings:)

---

64. Imperial residence built by the first emperor of Tang in Luoyang; here simply an imperial palace.

65. It is difficult to exactly capture the intent of these lines, from a poem by Li He. They resonate with two things: first is their vow of "eternal love," which is supposed to last as long as heaven and earth; second, with the last couplet of Bai Juyi's poem, "Heaven is constant, earth endures—each will come to an end / But this hatred spins out an endless thread of silk—never a time it will snap."

(*Furong hua*)
Wispy and drifting—seal-script smoke spirals up;[66]
Gloomy and gloaming—the silver lamp shines.
The jade clepsydra drips on, and on, and on,
Yet has but reported the night's first watch.
In the dark, I peer at the pure empyrean,
Hoping that she will come to me in dreams.
The mouth sprouts heart's seed:
Over and over I call her to me, and again.

[(*Speaks:*)] I'm really drowsy. I'll try to sleep a little. (*Sings:*)

(*Ban dushu*)
One dot of heart's burning anxiety,
Four walls of insects' autumn cacophony.
Suddenly I see, tossing the curtain, the vileness of the western wind;
Far away I gaze—it fills the earth, this lid of dark clouds.
I throw on a robe, feel depressed, lean against the curtain screen;
I can't bear these cursèd eyes.

(*Xiao heshang*)
Fallen leaves, shed swirling and whirling, flutter onto deserted steps,
Fallen leaves, brushed crackling and crunching, are swept away by the
    west wind.
Whistling and whining, the wind gusts until the silver lamp sputters,
Until, clanging and banging, the palace bell sounds,
Until, rustling and clinking, the door beads move and
Ringing and tinkling, the jade horses clatter in the eaves.[67]

(*Acts out sleeping, sings:*)

(*Tang xiucai*)
Deeply depressed, I lie down with my clothes on,
Weak with fatigue, I am just now falling asleep. . . .

(PRECIOUS CONSORT *enters:*) I am Precious Consort. Today we have laid out
a feast in the halls, and your palace beauties request you, my lord, to come.
(XUANZONG *sings:*)

---

66. The light smoke of the incense burner, forming patterns like ancient characters as it
drifts slowly upward.
67. Jade horses, like "iron horses," refers to wind chimes.

I've just seen a servant in green come to report,
That Consort Most Perfected has invited me to a feast.

(XUANZONG *acts out greeting* PRECIOUS CONSORT, *speaks:*) Where have you come from? (PRECIOUS CONSORT:) There's a feast today in the Palace of Eternal Life. I invite you, my lord, to come to it. (XUANZONG:) Instruct the Disciples of the Pear Garden to prepare everything. (PRECIOUS CONSORT *exits.* XUANZONG *acts out awakening.*) Ai, it was only a dream. I saw my consort clearly in my dream and now she has disappeared. (*Sings:*)

> (*Shuang yuanyang*)
> Her halcyon-green simurgh pinions drooping down[68]
>> Were altogether like
> Her appearance that day she first stepped from the bath[69]
> And half showed her seductive beauty reflected against the mica
>> screen.
> This good dream verged on completion when I was startled awake,
> To find half of my sharkskin gauze lapels soaked by tears of passion.
>
> (*Man gu'er*)
> Frustrated, vexed,
> I ponder:
> What startled me awake was not a goose passing over the loft,
> Or winter katydids below the stone steps,
> Or jade horses before the eaves,
> Or the pheasant on its perch.
>> It was the
> Soughing and sighing of rain on the wutong tree just outside the
>> window:
> Sound by sound, sprinkling the twigs and leaves,
> Drop by drop, dripping off the cold branch tips—
> These can bring disaster to a sorrowing man.
>
> (*Gun xiuqiu*)
> This rain, it doesn't
> Rescue drought-stricken sprouts,

---

68. That is, her hair ornaments decorated with kingfisher feathers.
69. Refers to two lines from Bai Juyi's poem, paraphrased below:

In springtime chill, she was directed to bathe at Huaqing springs,
The hot springs water was smooth as it washed her skin of luster.
Serving maids helped her rise, beauty and lassitude—

This was the point from which she newly received bestowal of imperial favor.

Enrich withering grasses,
Or sprinkle the buds of flowers clean.
Who would have praised it by saying, "Autumn rains are like a balm?"
On those jade-green osiers
And lapis lazuli branches
Its sound shatters, plipping and plopping,
And increases a thousandfold as it pours in harmony on the banana
    leaves.
        It's just like
Jade scattering from a pendant string, tossing a hundred pearls.
        Uselessly,
This spilled vat, this overturned pot, pours out through the night,
Stirring up a man's heart till it burns with sorrow.

(*Daodao ling*)
        Now, in rapid succession, one after another
Ten thousand precious pearls fall onto a jade plate,
        And now, resonating like
Groups of singers and pipers in front of the tortoiseshell mat,
        Now, as clear as
A chilled spring's waterfall over halcyon-green cliffs,
        Now, as ferocious as
The thumping of war drums beneath embroidered battle-pennants.
Oh, don't vex a man to death, no,
No, don't vex a man to death. Oh,
All the forms of rain's voice grate against my ears.

(*Tang xiucai*)
        This rain—
Sheet by sheet it pounds until the leaves fall from the wutong tree,
Drop by drop it drips until a man's heart is shattered.
In vain the silver balustrade tightly circles the golden well—
        I'd be better off
To hack down these damn branches and leaves, burn them as firewood,
Saw it down!

[(XUANZONG:)] In days gone past, when my consort danced in the jade platter,
it was right below this tree. And when we made our covenant with each other,
it was facing this tree. Yet today, it is what startles me out of our dream reunion.
(*Sings:*)

(*Gun xiuqiu*)
On that night in the Palace of Eternal Life,

It listened to us offer up our promise in the winding corridor—
We should have never leaned against that wutong tree,
And spoken on and on, over and over.
On that morning by the Aloeswood Pavilion,
When she rehearsed the Rainbow Skirts, and danced the *Liuyao*,
When the red ivory sticks struck up the tune,
And the jumbled modes and keys were strident in confusion—
> It was those
Days of happy trysts that sowed the cause
That seeks me out in today's desolate chill
To secretly demand karma's debt.

(GAO LISHI:) My lord, all grasses and trees have their particular sound, can it be just the wutong tree alone? Please explain them to me, my lord. (XUANZONG:) Listen as I explain. (*Sings:*)

(*Sansha*)
Deeply enriching—the willow rain
Chills, turns drear the courtyard as it invades the pearly curtain;
Wispy fine
> The plum rain
Sprinkles dots along the river's bank as it fills towers and galleries;
The apricot blossom rain moistens the balustrade with red,
The pear blossom rain—jade-white face in loneliness,
Lotus blossom rain—a halcyon-green canopy flutters and rolls,
Bean blossom rain—the green leaves grow cold and wither.
> But none are the equal of you
Who startles the soul, smashes dreams,
Bolsters vexation, overflows sorrow,
And lasts all through the night, clear to dawn.
> Is it not
That water-goddess showing off her beauty,
Dipping the ends of willows, and shaking them off, scattering water
  to the winds?[70]

(*Ersha*)
> Bubbling and gurgling
Like auspicious animal-head scuppers spurting down into a pair of
  ponds,

---

70. The bodhisattva Guanyin, goddess of the southern seas, was thought to sprinkle dew from the end of willow branch she kept in a bottle of pure water.

> Munching and crunching
Like spring silkworms eating leaves, scattered over their frames.
Randomly you sprinkle on chalcedony steps:
Water transmitting time from the palace clepsydra;
You fly up to carved eaves:
Wine dripping from a new barrel.
> You fall until
Quilts turn chill, pillows freeze,
Lamps die out, and perfume disappears.
It is apparent:
If we are not aware in summer,
Then it will come to wash away Gao Feng's wheat.[71]

(*Huangzhong sha*)
Following the western wind it makes the silk window whistle low;
Accompanying the chill ethers it knocks frequently at the embroidered door.
> Is it not
Luan Ba scattering wine in front of the palace galleries,[72]
Or like carriage bells of our earlier passage echoing on the trestle paths of Shu?
Like Flowered Slave, beating his Tibetan drum,
Or Bo Ya playing the Water Fairy song?[73]
It sprinkles on the tender tips of bamboo by the winding hall,
Moistens the sprouts of a hundred grasses in front of the steps,
Washes the chrysanthemums,
Soaks bamboo fences,
Seeps into the deep green moss,
Topples the corner of a wall,
Washes the lakes and mountains,

---

71. A certain Gao Feng of the Han, who came from a farming family, used to read (and recite) what he was studying day and night without stopping. His wife, who took up the farming chores, had spread wheat to dry in the courtyard and had ordered him to keep the chickens away from the grain. He stood out in the courtyard, when suddenly the heavens opened up with a thunderstorm. He stood out in the rain, holding a pole to chase the chickens away and reciting the classics, unaware that the flooding waters had washed all of the grain away. He became aware of it only after his wife had returned and pointed it out to him.

72. Luan Ba (d. 168) was a Daoist recruited into the imperial court. One night at an imperial banquet, he suddenly sprinkled wine toward the southwest. Other courtiers wanted to punish him, but he replied that he had sensed that there was a fire in Chengdu, and had sprinkled the wine to start the rain there.

73. Bo Ya was a skilled lutist whose music perfectly matched the sounds of nature.

Rinses out the hollows in boulders,
Penetrates withered lotuses,
Overflows the ponds and reservoirs,
Soaks the last of butterfly's powder until it gradually disappears,
Sprinkles the floating firefly until its light goes out.
In front of the green window, the "urgers of weaving"[74] cry out.
The sounds of geese are near but their silhouettes so high in the sky.
It urges on neighborhood fulling blocks, there is pounding
    everywhere,
It bolsters this new chill, so uncommon early.
And if I really consider this one night,
Rain and man so tightly bound,
Keeping company with the bronze pot,[75] striking drop by drop—
Rain's frenzy increasing, no lack of tears,
Rain soaks the cold branches,
Tears soak the dragon's robe,
Neither is willing to relent
As the wutong tree shines beyond the screen, top to bottom, until the
    very light of dawn.

TITLE: Gao Lishi brings together and separates a pair of regal birds;
       An Rokshan rebels and weapons and spears are raised.

NAME: The bright dawns of the Precious Consort: the fragrance of the
       litchi;
       The autumn nights of the Lustrous Emperor of Tang: rain on the
       wutong tree.

---

74. The sound of the cricket was believed to imitate the click of a shuttle in the loom.
75. Of the water clock, marking the passage of time.

5

Breaking a Troubling Dream:
A Lone Goose in Autumn over the Palaces of Han

Ma Zhiyuan

Ma Zhiyuan is universally recognized as one of the great *zaju* authors. Biographical information, as in most cases of *zaju* authors, is extremely scarce. *The Register of Ghosts* limits itself to stating that he hailed from Dadu and sported the sobriquet of the Old Man of the Eastern Fence (*Dongli laoren*), a reference to the eremitic ideals of the poet Tao Qian. He held some clerical function or minor official position with the Jiang-Zhe Branch Secretariat, the provincial government at Hangzhou. Scattered information about his relations with other playwrights and songwriters suggests that he lived sometime before 1324 and that he spent at least twenty years of his life at the capital in Dadu. While in the capital he also collaborated with professional actors in the composition of the play *The Dream of Yellow Millet*.[1] This collaboration tends to suggest that he was primarily a court dramatist. In this sense he is a good contrast with Guan Hanqing, who wrote primarily for the urban theater, and with Bai Pu, whose very literary dramas seem to have been written for a smaller audience of literati for whom poetry was the core genre of literature.

Lack of hard data about Ma Zhiyuan is compensated for by Jia Zhongming's fulsome praise in a threnody appended to his revised version of *The Register of Ghosts*:

> Amidst a cluster of ten thousand flowers, the divine immortal Ma:
> After a hundred generations people will still talk of the writings of
>   Zhiyuan
> Because he is universally admired throughout the whole universe.
> In the arena for literature the Top Graduate in song:
> The renown of his name fills the Pear Garden.
> *Autumn over the Palace of Han, Tears on the Blue Gown,*
> *Lady Qi* and *Meng Haoran*—
> He was the equal of Yu, Bai, and Guan!

---

1. See the list of translations in Appendix 3.

Guan is of course Guan Hanqing, while Bai is Bai Pu. Yu is Yu Tianxi, who is credited by *The Register of Ghosts* with the authorship of fifteen plays, none of which have survived. In other contemporary assessments Ma Zhiyuan is put on a par with Guan Hanqing, Bai Pu, and Zheng Guangzu as one of the four great masters of Northern drama. *A Formulary of Correct Rhymes for an Era of Great Peace* places Ma Zhiyuan in the forefront of all other Yuan playwrights:

> The lyrics of Eastern Fence Ma are like a singing phoenix in the morning sunshine. His lyrics are classically elegant and transparently beautiful. They can be compared to the [rhapsodies on] Lingguang and the Jingfu Halls.[2] There's something in them of [a horse that] shakes its manes and whinnies loudly, in such a way that all other horses are struck dumb. On top of that, they are like a divine phoenix soaring and singing in the highest heavens. How can he be discussed in the same terms as common birds? That's why he should be put ahead of all other notables.

Such a high ranking of Ma Zhiyuan may be because of his skill at writing Daoist deliverance plays, which were extremely popular from the middle of the fourteenth to the early fifteenth century. Of the fifteen plays he wrote, a sizeable number are deliverance plays that betray a clear affinity with Quanzhen Daoism (see *Zhongli of the Han Leads Lan Caihe to Enlightenment*). On the other hand he also wrote a number of plays on students and scholars down on their luck. Seven of his plays have been preserved in whole or in part, two of which are also in Yuan printings. While the current play, *Breaking a Troubling Dream: A Lone Goose in Autumn over the Palaces of Han* (*Po youmeng guyan hangong qiu*), may be something of an exception to his general interests as a dramatist, we should keep in mind that the selfless devotion of a woman to her husband or to her country was often also used as an allegory to describe the selfless devotion of a writer, or other supplicant, to their patrons or lords. Ma Zhiyuan's popularity may also have been enhanced by the fact that he was also a very productive and respected writer of independent songs and song suites in the *qu* style.

In order to seal political relations between his empire and the Xiongnu, in 33 BC, upon a request by the khan of the southern Xiongnu, Emperor Yuandi of the Han presented him a young palace woman of good family, Wang Qiang, as a bride. Yuandi died that very year and Wang Qiang accompanied the khan

---

2. Refers to two famous rhapsodies found in the *Selections on Literature* (*Wenxuan*), the "Rhapsody on the Hall of Numinous Brilliance in Lu" (*Lu guangming dian fu*) by Wang Yanshou and the "Rhapsody on the Hall of Great Blessings" (*Jingfu dian fu*) by He Yan (d. 249), both of which are noted for their extremely detailed descriptions of the architectural splendor of the halls. See Knechtges 1982, pp. 263–302.

to his homeland in the steppes of Mongolia and there bore him a son. When he died a few years later, she followed Xiongnu custom and married his successor, a son by an earlier marriage. Wang Qiang bore this new ruler two daughters. She may have died soon thereafter. Her relatives in China continued to play an important part in Han-Xiongnu diplomatic relations for some decades, just as her children played roles in Xiongnu internal politics.

Wang Qiang, better known in literature as Wang Zhaojun, was certainly not the first Chinese palace lady to be awarded to a foreign prince. Eventually, however, she became the exemplar through which Chinese poets and painters, storytellers, playwrights, and novelists for the next two thousand years portrayed relations between China and its neighbors. She became an important figure in delineating the boundary of the worlds that existed between Chinese and foreigner, between the center and periphery, and between Chinese civilization and its counterimage. As the legend surrounding this event grew, it acquired new elements, including the famous trope about her grave, the Green Hill, which stays verdant through all seasons of the year. As her legend grew she took on the trappings of a cultural heroine, and many places in China still lay claim to being the site of her birth or her entombment.

The basic facts about Wang Zhaojun, as narrated above, are to be found in the *Documents of the Han* (*Hanshu*), the dynastic history of the Western Han dynasty (206 BC–AD 8), compiled in the first century. Throughout its history, the Western Han was confronted all along its northern border by a formidable coalition of steppe peoples, known as the Xiongnu (traditionally often mistranslated as "Huns"). Their cavalry could strike deep within Chinese territory and easily elude the pursuing Chinese infantry on the boundless grasslands of present-day Inner Mongolia. The predecessors of the Han, the short-lived Qin dynasty (221–208 BC), had attempted to secure its borders by massive defense works that would in later times grow into the Great Wall. The Han wavered between a policy of cycles of conciliation, sealed by marriages, and massive retaliation. When massive retaliation and forward military action proved to be financially exhaustive, they returned to a policy of conciliation. During such a phase, the Xiongnu king, called Huhanye, as was customary, requested a Chinese bride.

According to the *Documents of the Later Han* (*Hou Hanshu*), the dynastic history of the Eastern Han dynasty (AD 25–220), compiled in the fourth century, Wang Zhaojun assented to the marriage voluntarily. She did so because she had been a palace lady for many years without ever having been favored by the emperor. However, when the emperor saw her in all her finery at the moment of departure, he was overcome by affection and wanted to keep her. Eventually, however, he let her go in order to keep his word to the khan. The *Various Notes on the Western Capital* (*Xijing zaji*), a collection of anecdotes concerning the Western Han, stemming from the fourth or fifth century, fabricated a reason why Wang Zhaojun had never attracted the emperor's attention:

> The palace ladies of Emperor Yuandi were extremely numerous. Since he could not visit them regularly, he had painters paint their portraits, and he summoned and favored them on the basis of these portraits. All other palace ladies paid bribes to the painters, in some cases as much as 100,000 cash and at the very least, 50,000. But Wang Qiang refused to do so and so she was never received in audience.
>
> Later the khan of the Xiongnu came to pay homage and requested a beauty as his queen (*yanzhi*). On the basis of the portraits the emperor thereupon decided that Zhaojun should go. Before her departure, she was summoned and received in audience; she was the most beautiful of all the palace ladies, her repartee was quick and fitting, and her demeanor was most elegant! The emperor regretted his decision but her name had already been agreed upon. As the emperor set great store by relations of trust with foreign countries, he did not replace her with another woman.
>
> The affair was completely investigated and the painters were all executed in the marketplace. Their private possessions were confiscated: millions! Among these painters was one Mao Yanshou, who could really catch the likeness of a person, ugly or handsome, old or young. . . .

Mao Yanshou is singled out here only as the finest artist of his time who lost his life in the purge of artists following the departure of Wang Qiang, but in later legend he becomes the painter who purposely disfigured the portrait of Wang Qiang. In Ma Zhiyuan's *Autumn over the Palaces of Han*, he would eventually become the evil genius of the play. He first suggests that the emperor widely collect girls for his harem and, as an instrumental person in the selection process, he demands bribes from the families of those selected. Later, when his machinations are discovered, he flees to the Xiongnu and urges the khan to demand Zhaojun as his wife.

Paintings of Wang Zhaojun often show her at the moment she crosses the border between China and the steppe. It is a bleak winter scene and Wang Zhaojun, clad in furs, rides her horse while clutching her pipa, the loquat-shaped Chinese lute, close to her bosom. The first author to link the name of Wang Zhaojun to the pipa was the poet Shi Chong (249–300). In the preface to his poem, he noted that at an earlier departure of Liu Xijun (who had been given in marriage to the khan of the Wusun in the last years of the second century BC) musicians who accompanied her had played the pipa. He surmised that the same event probably occurred at the departure of Wang Zhaojun, and by the time of the Song dynasty (960–1279), the pipa had become an essential attribute in representations of Wang Zhaojun.

In view of the immense popularity of the theme of Wang Zhaojun in both classical and vernacular literature, it is impossible to provide a detailed survey of the development of this theme within the compass of this introduction. It has to be pointed out, however, that the story of Wang Zhaojun, certainly as treated by Ma Zhiyuan in *Autumn over the Palaces of Han*, can also be read as a foil to that other story of imperial passion, *Rain on the Wutong Tree*. In *Autumn over the Palaces of Han*, Yuandi is capable of sacrificing his love for the sake of peace and Zhaojun is capable of sacrificing herself for the political stability of the nation. In *Rain on the Wutong Tree*, however, the Tang emperor Xuanzong persists in his blind love for Consort Yang. She is having a surreptitious affair with the Sogdian general An Rokshan who eventually rebels. The emperor is forced to flee Chang'an and to agree to the murder of Yang Guifei before the imperial armies will take another step. The Tang is wracked by warfare for decades to come, causing unspeakable misery for the people at large, and in the popular mind, these political events are largely due to Xuanzong's infatuation with his Precious Consort.

Our translation of *Autumn over the Palaces of Han* is based on the edition in *Gu mingjia zaju*. In this version, the play is a regular *zaju*, consisting of a wedge and four acts. The songs are assigned to the leading male, who plays the part of Yuandi throughout the play. A number of other Yuan dramatizations of these materials are known by title from our earliest catalogues, but none of these alternative versions has been preserved.

Dramatis personæ in order of appearance

Role type	Name, family role, or social role
Secondary male	Barbarian king, Huhanye
Villain	Mao Yanshou
Leading male	Emperor Yuan
Eunuch	Eunuch
Female lead	Wang Qiang
Soldier	Huhanye's soldiers
Extras	Chancellors
Barbarian Ambassador	Ambassador from Huhanye

Breaking a Troubling Dream:
A Lone Goose in Autumn over the Palaces of Han

COMPOSED BY MA ZHIYUAN OF THE YUAN

[Wedge]

(SECONDARY MALE, *costumed as* BARBARIAN KING, *enters leading a party of chieftains:*)

> The felt tents lost among the perennial grasses in the autumn wind,
>> We listen in our yurts to mournful flutes on moonlit nights.
>> Of a million men who draw the bow, I am lord and leader,
> Knocking at the passes I declare myself vassal to the house of Han.

I am the khan Huhanye. Let us speak of our house's descent: We have long lived in these septentrional steppes and we alone dominate the northern regions. We live by shooting and hunting and carve out our enterprise through campaigns and attacks. King Wen once upon a time migrated east to avoid us, and Wei Jiang made peace with us out of fear. Xunyu or Xianyun—we change our name with every dynasty. *Shanyu* or khan—we adopt a royal title in tune with the times. When the Qin and the Han were locked in battle, the Central Plain was troubled by war while our state was strong and prosperous. With a million of armored bowmen my ancestor the *shanyu*, Maodun, besieged the High Emperor of the Han for seven days in Baideng. Thanks to the scheme of Lou Jing the two countries made peace, and a princess was married off to our state. After Emperor Hui and Empress Lü, each reign followed that precedent and sent a daughter of the imperial clan to make her home in our barbarian nation. During the age of Emperor Xuan, my brothers and I fought over the succession and the power of our state was slightly weakened.[3] Now the tribes

---

3. Khan Huhanye provides a brief historical overview of the relations between the settled Chinese and their northern neighbors. The mobile steppe inhabitants were known by different names in the course of Chinese history and it is far from clear to what extent different names referred to different ethnic groups. Moreover, the title of the kings of the steppe inhabitants varied. Whereas the Xiongnu called their king *shanyu* (and their queen *yanzhi*), the later Turkish and Mongolian tribes used the title of khan. Since the khan Huhanye here represents the Xiongnu

have raised me as their khan Huhanye. In fact I am an affinal nephew of the Han court. With a million armored troops I have migrated south, drawn near the border, and have declared myself a vassal to the house of Han. Sometime ago I sent an envoy to present tribute and to ask for a princess. Will the emperor of the Han be willing to continue our sworn pact? Today the sky is high and the air is fresh. My chieftains, let's go bow hunting in the southern dunes. Wouldn't that be great? Indeed:

> The barbarians have no productive skills,
> Bow and arrow define their existence.

(*Exit.*)

❊❊

(VILLAIN, *costumed as* MAO YANSHOU, *enters:*)

> As for my character: the heart of a hawk, the talons of an eagle;
> As for my actions: I cheat the great and oppress the little.
> I rely solely on slander, flattery, treason, and greed,
> And will never live long enough to enjoy it to the full.

I am no one else but Mao Yanshou. At present I occupy the position of Grandee of the Second Class at the Han court, at the emperor's side. Because of my hundred kinds of crafty deceptions and my single-minded sycophantic blandishments I have fooled that old fart, the emperor, in such a way that he is, O, so pleased. My words are heeded, my advice followed. Inside and outside the court, there are none who do not respect me, none who do not fear me! I have also learned yet another trick: I'll have the emperor see less of his Confucian ministers and indulge more in women and sex. Only then will my favored

---

view of the reciprocal relations, his account stresses the victories of the Xiongnu and their forebears. Sometime in the twelfth century BC King Tai (not his grandson King Wen) resettled the Zhou people at the foot of Mount Ji. Wei Jiang, a minister of Duke Dao (r. 572–558 BC) of Jin (in present-day Shanxi), urged his lord to conclude a peace treaty with his barbarian neighbors. Liu Bang, the founder of the Han dynasty (206 BC–AD 220), was once besieged by the Xiongnu in Baideng. According to one version of the later legend, the Xiongnu only retired when their queen led her troops away from the siege because she had come to fear that her husband, Maodun, might leave her upon capture of the city for a (of course much more) beautiful Chinese woman— actually, her suspicions had been roused not by an actual woman but by an artful puppet made to parade on the city walls. Emperor Hui (195–188 BC) was the nominal successor to Liu Bang, but the actual power passed upon Liu Bang's death in 196 BC into the hands of Liu Bang's wife Empress Lü, who died in 180 BC. Emperor Xuan occupied the throne from 73 to 49 BC. Khan Huhanye skips the reign of Emperor Wu (r. 140–87 BC), when the Chinese pursued an aggressive foreign policy.

position be secure. But before I have finished speaking, His Imperial Majesty has already entered. (LEADING MALE, *costumed as* EMPEROR YUAN OF THE HAN, *enters, at the head of his eunuchs and palace ladies:*)

Passed down through ten generations: the inheritance of the Fiery Liu[4]—
I alone am in charge of the cosmos, the four hundred districts.
On the borders we have since long sworn to a policy of peace,
From now on I may rest without a worry in the world.

I am Emperor Yuan of the Han. My ancestor, Liu Bang, the Exalted Progenitor, rose from amongst the commoners. Starting out from Feng and Pei, he exterminated the Qin and butchered Xiang Yu, establishing by his efforts this foundation and subsequent enterprise that has been handed down to Us—already the tenth generation![5] From the time We inherited the throne, all within the Four Seas has been secure and the Eight Directions have all been peaceful and quiet. It is not that I have any particular virtue, simply that I have been able to rely on the support of my civil officials and military officers. After the demise of the preceding emperor, all palace ladies were released from the palace and the rear quarters are lonely and desolate. What is to be done about it? (MAO YAN-SHOU:) Your Majesty, when a farmer harvests some extra ten bushels of grain, he already wants to change his wife. How much more so in the case of Your Majesty, who is exalted as the Son of Heaven, who possesses all the riches of the Four Seas. Wouldn't it be fitting to send out officials throughout the empire to select virgins? Whether from the family of a prince or noble, chancellor or minister, soldier or civilian, let her be over fifteen and not yet twenty, correct and upright in her looks and appearance, and she will be selected to fill the inner palace. What would impede this? (EMPEROR:) My minister, you are right. I hereby appoint you "Selection Commissioner," and I will provide you with an edict so you can tour the empire to make a thorough selection. Make a portrait of each you select and send it to me, so I may favor them according to these portraits. When you, my minister, return upon the completion of your mission, I will take further measures.

([XIANLÜ MODE:] *Shanghua shi*)
The Four Seas are quiet and calm, free of infantry and horse,

---

4. The Han dynasty, founded by Liu Bang, was believed to reign by virtue of the Phase of Fire.

5. Following the collapse of the Qin upon the death of the First Emperor in 210 BC, civil war broke out all over China. Initially, the most formidable contender for the imperial throne appeared to be Xiang Yu, a member of the aristocracy of the former southern state of Chu, who eventually declared himself the hegemon-king of Western Chu. In the final showdown, however, Xiang Yu lost out to Liu Bang, who came from a rather humble background.

The five grains mature into a bountiful harvest; there are no battles
   or invasions.
It is Our desire to choose virgins, to select palace beauties—
So you may not shirk the hardship and fatigue of long rides,
As you decide who is fit to be attached to an emperor's household!

(*Exit.*)

[Act 1]

(MAO YANSHOU *enters:*)

Huge nuggets of gold I grab at will;
Neither a sea of blood, nor the land's law do I fear.
As long as I have money and property while I'm alive,
Who cares if I'm spat at and cursed after I'm dead?

I am Mao Yanshou. Bearing an edict from the emperor of the Great Han, I
scour the empire to select virgins. I've already picked ninety-nine names and
each family has been more than willing to provide rich gifts. The gold and silver
I've gotten is no small amount. Yesterday I came to the subprefecture of Zigui
in Chengdu and there selected the daughter of Elder Wang. She is called Wang
Qiang, and her style is Zhaojun. Her brilliant beauty dazzles the eye, she is as
gorgeous as can be: she truly is the finest beauty of the empire! Alas, she is from
a farming family and they don't have much money or many goods. I asked for a
hundred ounces of yellow gold to pick her as the very highest. But she said that,
first of all, her family was too poor, and second, that she trusts to her exceptional looks. Actually I wanted to drop her from the selection, but that would
be doing her a favor. "As soon as one unlocks the frown of one's brows, a scheme
is born in one's heart." All I have to do is to add some blemishes to the portrait
of this beauty. After we get to the capital, she will surely be sent to the cold
palace.[6] In that way, she will suffer all her life! Yes indeed: "He whose hatred is
small is no gentleman, he without poison is no hero."

(*Exits.*)

❋❋

(FEMALE LEAD WANG QIANG *enters, leading two palace ladies:*)

---

6. Empresses and palace ladies who had lost the Emperor's favor were housed in the "cold
palace."

One day I received the summons and entered the Shangyang Palace[7]
But for ten years I have yet to see my lord and king.
So forlorn on fine nights, with no one to keep me company—
I only have this lute to summon up my endless feelings.

I am Wang Qiang. My style is Zhaojun. I hail from the subprefecture of Zigui in Chengdu. My father, Elder Wang, has been a farmer all his life. When my mother gave birth to me, she dreamt that the light of the moon entered her bosom and then fell to the ground. Thereupon she gave birth to me. When eighteen years old, I was, by the emperor's grace, selected for service in the rear palace. However, the commissioner Mao Yanshou requested gold and silver from me, and when I gave him nothing, he disfigured my portrait. Before I had even seen my lord and king, I was sent to live in the Long Street.[8] While still at home, I was very proficient in music and I could play quite a few tunes on the lute. It's such a quiet night and I'm so depressed. I'll try a tune to wile away my sorrow. (*Acts out plucking the strings.* EMPEROR, *leading* A EUNUCH *carrying a lamp, enters:*) I am Emperor Yuan of the Han. From the time I selected virgins to enter the palace, there are still many who have never enjoyed Our favor and are filled with resentment. Today We have some respite from the duties of state, so I have to make the rounds of the palace to see who is lucky enough to meet Our Person.

([XIANLÜ MODE:] *Dian jiangchun*)
The cart crushes the fallen blossoms,[9]
The jade one, beneath the moon, plays her lute, then stops.
Those palace beauties who haven't been favored—
How much have We added to their white hairs!

(*Hunjiang long*)
       I assume that their
Pearly curtains have not been furled—
They gaze toward the Zhaoyang Palace; at every single step the edge
    of heaven recedes.[10]
       Their expectations are aroused

---

7. Shangyang Palace is the name of a palace built by Emperor Gaozong (r. 650–83) of the Tang dynasty. Here it is used as a general designation of the imperial palace.

8. The Long Street is another designation for the apartments of palace ladies out of favor.

9. The emperor moved around the extensive palace grounds seated in a wheeled throne (a kind of wheelchair), pushed by eunuchs.

10. Zhaoyang Palace was the central section of the inner apartments of the imperial palace during the reign of Emperor Wu (r. 140–87 BC).

By every bamboo shadow that lacks a breeze,
> And their resentments are provoked

By windows' gauze that grows flush with the moonlight.
> Whenever they see

My jade carriage makes its rounds amid the sounds of strings and
> pipes,
> It is to them no different than

The floating raft of Zhang Qian in the sky![11]

(WANG QIANG *acts out plucking the strings.* EMPEROR:)

> I suddenly hear

From the Courtyard of Immortal Notes,
Among the sounds of strings and pipes,
In a single tune from the lute
A thousand kinds of sad resentments come!
> You must

Lightly push my embroidered axle,
Slowly turn the winding corridors
And warn that resentful woman, tell her
To receive and welcome my simurgh chair!
> Even though

You secretly transmit the imperial edict,
> Make sure not

To startle and frighten that beautiful person!
> I only fear that,

Suddenly receiving Our Grace,
She may be unable to control her heart out of fear.
We might startle the birds sleeping in the oaks of the palace,
Or the crows resting on the trees in the courtyard.

Eunuch, go see what palace houses this lady who plucks the lute just so. Transmit my wish. Tell her to come and welcome her emperor. But don't scare her! (EUNUCH *acts out informing:*) You there, which lady are you? The imperial carriage has arrived. Make haste to welcome it! (WANG QIANG *acts out hastily welcoming* [EMPEROR]. EMPEROR:)

---

11. During the reign of Emperor Wu , the Chinese official Zhang Qian (fl. 125 BC) was dispatched on a mission to the "Western regions" that took him far into Central Asia and made him a figure of legend. In due time, his name became linked with the tale of the man who was carried by a raft on the Yellow River up to the sky, where the Yellow River continues its flow as the Heavenly River (the Milky Way)—as observed from earth, his raft appeared as a new star in heaven.

(*You hulu*)
"We pardon you, who are without fault."
I will ask her myself,
> "You, there,
Under which princess's banner do you stand?
> Don't blame me
For never coming and now suddenly trespassing.
> I have come on purpose
To requite that shagreen handkerchief wiped wet with tears
And to warm and comfort those wave-treading socks chilled by
    dew."[12]
Such gorgeous looks, given at birth by heaven—
It's only fitting that I should favor them.
Tonight, below the silver stand of your painted candle,
In a trice, happy signs will pop from the wick.

Eunuch, look at the light of the gauze-shrouded candle grow brighter and brighter. Raise it up for me so I may have a better look.

(*Tianxia le*)
> Give it
Some more spirit so it will shine through the vermilion gauze!
My minister,
Just look:
> That
Emaciated shadow is so adorable!

(WANG QIANG:) If your handmaid had known that Your Majesty would deign to visit her, she should have gone out to welcome you. As I have been remiss in welcoming you, this handmaid merits ten thousand deaths. (EMPEROR:)

> At first opportunity she calls herself "handmaid";
> Repeatedly she addresses me as "Your Majesty."
> She cannot be from some ordinary common family.

I've seen her correct and upright appearance and looks—what a fine woman!

---

12. The feet of the palace ladies who do not enjoy the emperor's favors are chilled to the bone as they stand in front of the door of their apartment, sleepless through the night, desperately hoping for his arrival. "Wave-treading socks" derives from a rhapsody by the prince and poet Cao Zhi (192–232), describing his fleeting vision of the goddess of the River Luo, who appeared hovering above the waves. The erotic fascination of Chinese men for (bound) feet is well-known.

(*Zui zhong tian*)
> Two leaves

Of palace-style eyebrows has she sketched,
> And a single

Face, perfectly suited to makeup and adornment she has powdered.
For fragrant filigree ornaments, she has pasted halcyon-colored
> flowers at the corners of her brow,

A single smile has worth enough "to topple a wall."
> If

Goujian of Yue had seen her on Gusu Terrace,
That Xi Shi would have had no chance at all—
And ten years earlier he would have destroyed his state and lost his
> royal house![13]

You are so extraordinary! Whose daughter are you? (WANG QIANG:) Your handmaid's name is Wang Qiang, her style is Zhaojun, and she hails from the subprefecture of Zigui in Chengdu. Her father is the Elder Wang. From my grandparents' time we have made our living by agriculture—a common citizen from village and hamlet, I do not know the etiquette of the imperial house. (EMPEROR:)

(*Jinzhan'er*)
> To my eyes

Your brows are swept by jet,
Your locks, piled-up ebony,
Your waist, a swaying willow,
Your cheeks, the spreading dawn.
Nowhere in Zhaoyang Palace is good enough to transplant you!
> Who cares

Whether you made your living with a single plow or a pair of rakes?
> It was not because

Your lord's favor lingered over your cushion and mat,
> That caused Heaven to send

---

13. During the sixth and fifth centuries BC the southeastern states of Wu (with its capital at modern Suzhou) and Yue (with its capital at Shaoxing) were engaged in extended warfare, which ended with the destruction of the state of Wu by King Goujian of Yue in 473 BC. King Goujian had earlier presented the king of Wu with a beautiful woman, Xi Shi, in the hope that she would make him neglect his royal duties. Xi Shi succeeded completely in her mission. According to one version of the legend of Xi Shi, King Goujian then brought her back to Yue, where he himself became the next victim of her charms, causing the ruin of the state of Yue. Gusu Terrace was the location of the royal places of Wu.

Rain and dew to moisten the mulberry and hemp.[14]
> If that had not been the case, would I,

Through the ten thousand miles of my rivers and mountains,
Have searched you out until I had found those two or three thatch-
  covered cottages?

How is it possible that you, with such a figure and posture, were never favored? (WANG QIANG:) I was my father's only child. When initially the selection was made, the Commissioner Mao Yanshou requested gold and silver. Because your handmaid's family was poor and could not come up with the price, he added some blemishes below my eyes. Thereupon was I dispatched to the cold palace. (EMPEROR:) Eunuch, get me that portrait! (EUNUCH *fetches the portrait and enters.* EMPEROR *acts out looking at it:*)

(*Zui fu gui*)
> I will have

No other questions for that painter:
> Except, "Why

Did you not do justice to this face?"
> He has turned

A single inch of autumn ripples into a blemished jade.[15]
> Really,

If you are one-eyed,
He was doubly blind.
> Were I to summon forth

My eight hundred beautiful concubines to compare with her,
> They would not necessarily

Outdo my lady's painted portrait even with all its blemishes!

Eunuch, transmit my order to the commander of the guard to immediately arrest Mao Yanshou and have him beheaded! Afterwards have him report to me. (WANG QIANG:) Your Majesty, your handmaid's parents live in Chengdu Commandery, where they are registered as common people. May Your Majesty bestow your grace upon them and free them from corvée labor and grant them a few imperial honors! (EMPEROR:) That's the easiest thing to do!

(*Jinzhan'er*)
> You—

---

14. I.e., her family will receive heaven's blessings and the imperial weal because he has chosen to favor her.

15. "Autumn ripples" is a conventional metaphor for beautiful eyes, because autumn rivers are assumed to be especially clear.

In the morning you picked vegetables,
At night you kept watch over melons,
In springtime you sowed grain,
In summer, you irrigated hemp.
From the whitewashed wall near the thorn-wood gate I certainly will
    remove the corvée duties:
          Since you
Married into the Zhengyang Gate, you're not so rustic anymore![16]
          My
Office is fairly high, like that of a village chief;
          These
Courtyards are barely bigger than the district yamen,
But thank Heaven and Earth
For such a miserably poor bridegroom—
Will anyone dare abuse my parents-in-law again?

Come closer and hear my edict. I hereby appoint you as the Radiant Consort!
(WANG QIANG:) Your handmaid is not worthy of Your Majesty's grace and favor.
(*Acts out thanking him for his grace.* EMPEROR:)

    (*Zhuansha*)
    Let's enjoy the feeling of this night to the full,
    And ask no questions of the morrow.

(WANG QIANG:) I hope Your Majesty will honor me with a visit tomorrow
just as soon as you can. Here, your handmaid will anticipate your arrival.
(EMPEROR:)

    Well, tomorrow
    I will likely be intoxicated on the jade couch in Zhaoyang Palace!

(WANG QIANG:) Your handmaid's body may be lowly and insignificant but now
she has received your grace and favor, can she bear to be separated from you?
(EMPEROR:)

    Don't be upset.
    I was only teasing, but you took it for truth.
    The road my carriage took but a moment ago, I now know well.
          Could I bear

---

16. The Zhengyang Gate was the central southern gate of the imperial palace in Kaifeng during the Northern Song dynasty (960–1126). Here the term is used as a general reference to the
imperial palace.

In truth never to cross this Tall Gate again?[17]
Tomorrow night, below the western palace pavilion,
> Make sure

To welcome me with a whisper—
> I'm just afraid

All ladies in the Six Palaces will follow your example and pluck the
lute!

(*Exits.* WANG QIANG:) The emperor has returned. Servants, close the gate of
the palace, I will go to sleep.

(*Exits.*)

[Act 2]

(HUHANYE *enters:*) I am the khan Huhanye. Recently I sent an ambassador to
the Han, asking them to send me a princess as a wife. The emperor of the Han
declined on the grounds that the princesses were still very young. I felt very
upset. I think there must be no end of women in the palaces of the Han, so
what's the big deal if he gives me one? But he just dismissed my ambassador
and sent him back! I would like to raise my troops and invade the south, but
I'm also afraid of upsetting the peaceful friendship we've known for several
years. Well, let's see how the situation develops, and then figure out what to do.
(MAO YANSHOU *enters:*) I am Mao Yanshou. Because I demanded gold and silver when I selected palace ladies, I blemished the portrait of Wang Zhaojun so
she would be sent to the cold palace. I never thought that the emperor would
personally favor her and find out the truth. He wanted to have me executed! I
got a chance to escape, but now I have nowhere to flee. What's done is done—I
brought her portrait along to offer to the khan, and I will tell him to ask only
for the person in this painting. Of course the Han court will have to give her to
him! After walking for several days, I've finally arrived. Far away in the distance
I see an immense crowd of men and horses. That must be his yurt. (*Acts out asking a question:*) Chieftain, please inform your king, the khan, that a great minister of the Han wants to defect to him. (SOLDIER *acts out reporting.* HUHANYE:)
Tell him to come in. (*Acts out greeting him.* HUHANYE:) Who are you? (MAO
YANSHOU:) I am Mao Yanshou, Grandee of the Second Order of the Han court.
Wang Zhaojun, a beautiful woman now living in the apartments of the western
palace, is a beauty without peer. When earlier Your Majesty sent an ambassador

---

17. Emperor Wu banished his childhood love, Empress Chen, to Tall Gate Palace when he
was fed up with her. As a result, Tall Gate is yet another name for the palace apartments of ladies
who do not enjoy the emperor's favors.

to request a princess, Zhaojun asked to come of her own accord, but the Han ruler would not give her up and refused to let her leave. I remonstrated with him a number of times, saying: "How can you so value women and sex that you would endanger the friendship between two nations?" The Han ruler wound up wanting to kill me. This is why I have brought along the portrait of this beautiful woman to present to Your Majesty. All you have to do is send an ambassador to request the person portrayed, and you are bound to obtain her. This is the painting. (*Presents it.* [HUHANYE] *acts out looking at it.* HUHANYE:) There are no such women in this world! If I could have her as my queen, all my wishes would be fulfilled! Now I will dispatch a barbarian official with his tribal following, and write a letter to the Han Son of Heaven, demanding to seal our peace by marriage with Wang Zhaojun. If he refuses to give her up, in a matter of days I will invade the south and he will find it impossible to protect his rivers and mountains. At the same time I will lead my armored bowmen and, hunting as we go, we will enter the borders to keep an eye on developments. That will be best.

(*Exit.*)

❋❋

(WANG QIANG *enters, leading palace ladies*:) I am Wang Qiang. The Emperor began gracing me with his visits and the weeks have flown by unnoticed. His doting love for me is going to extremes: for quite a while he did not even hold audience! Hearing that he has now ascended the main hall, I'll take advantage of the time to make myself up at my toilet stand and prepare myself properly so I can serve the emperor well when he arrives. (*Acts out [making her toilet] in front of the mirror.* EMPEROR *enters*:) I am Emperor Yuan of the Han. Ever since We saw Wang Zhaojun below the western palace pavilion, We have been as though obsessed or intoxicated, and for a long time We did not hold audience. As soon as We ascended the hall today, We could not wait for it to end! I have to go to the western palace and see her!

> ([NANLÜ MODE:] *Yizhi hua*)
> Through the four seasons, rain and dew spread in due portion,
> Making ten thousand miles of rivers and mountains splendid.
> The loyal ministers all have their employment,
> We have no care or worry in the world!
> > I'm staying close
> To white teeth and sparkling eyes—
> How could We bear to leave any bright daylight unused?
> > But recently

We've been infected by some illness,
> Due half to

Our care for country and people,
> And half to

Our craving for flowers and wine.

(*Liangzhou diqi*)
> Even though

When receiving Our Prime Minister in audience
We are alike to King Wen in Our display of respect,[18]
> As soon as

We are apart from the Radiant Consort,
We turn into a Song Yu sorrowing over autumn![19]
> How can I prevent

Her natural perfume from wafting out of my dragon-gown sleeves
   when they stir?
She is adorable in everything,
She matches Our mind in all she does.
She dispels one's gloomiest depression
And keeps me company in idle roamings.
> She's perfect for

Climbing a tower beneath the pear-blossom moon,
Or playing "hiding hooks" below hibiscus candles![20]
Her figure and posture are a warm tenderness, enhanced for twenty
   years,
Our marriage bond is that of a fated pair, set five hundred years ago.

---

18. King Wen is of course King Wen of the Zhou dynasty (trad. dates, 1122–249 BC). Traditional sources describe him as the very model of the ideal ruler. Even while still a vassal of King Zhou of the Shang/Yin dynasty, King Wen attracted by his virtue two-thirds of the feudal lords to his court. King Wen showed special reverence for his prime minister Jiang Lü Wang, who was a simple fisherman of seventy when he was raised to this position. The overthrow of the Shang/Yin dynasty and the foundation of the Zhou dynasty was eventually achieved by King Wen's son and successor King Wu.

19. Song Yu, a courtier and ladies' man from the state of Chu of the third century BC, was also a poet. He is traditionally credited with the authorship of "The Nine Arguments" (*Jiu bian*) in *The Songs of the South* (*Chuci*). One of the major themes of this poem is the lament over autumn and the passing of time.

20. "Hiding hooks" was a game for which the participants were divided into two groups. While one party passed and hid a hook in their hands, the other party had to guess who was holding it.

Her face has a thousand indescribable charms,
I seek her favor—she turns coyly away:
Like the Guanyin of Potalaka Mountain, but without the willow
    branch:
Just to see her face once increases one's term of life![21]
Passion ties up my heart, never to stop,
      Unless
The very rains cease and the clouds disperse![22]

(*Acts out looking from afar and seeing her:*)

    (*Gewei*)
        How did it happen
That this resentful beauty from in front of Tall Gate should have
    become my darling,
        And wound up as
The favorite apparition of my dreams in the western palace?
        Missy is putting on her makeup!
I love her when she is done with her evening toilet—
Unpaintable,
Unportrayable,
Blushing in front of the mirror.

(*Acts out walking up to* ZHAOJUN's *back and stopping there:*)

        Now I stand
Behind this toilet stand:
        Yes, indeed

---

21. Potalaka Mountain (*Luojia shan*) on the isle of Putuo off the Zhejiang coast is sacred to the bodhisattva Guanyin, who since Song times is portrayed as a most beautiful woman. The willow branch is one of her conventional attributes. Comparing a beautiful woman to Guanyin is quite common in *zaju* literature.

22. "Clouds and rain" is the most common euphemism for sexual activity. The story takes place on Yang Terrace, also known as Gaotang, later a common metaphor for a site for a lovers' tryst. The archetypical trope of plays involving lovers is the story of King Huai of Chu and the spirit of Shamanka Mountain, recounted in Song Yu's "Rhapsody on the High Terrace." While visiting Shamanka Mountain the king took a noontime nap; a woman appeared to him, offering him a pillow, and the two made love. As she was leaving, she bade him goodbye with the following words: "I live on the sunny side of Shamanka Mountain, at the dangerous point of the highest hill. At sunrise I am the morning clouds and at sunset, the traveling rains. Morning after morning, sunset after sunset, I am below the Yang Terrace." From this story come many expressions—clouds and rain, Gaotang, Shamanka Mountain, spirit of Shamanka Mountain, Yang Terrace, even the name of the poet, Song Yu—that denote romance and the act of physical love.

Chang E in her Palace of Broad Cold
Can be found in this moon![23]

(WANG QIANG *acts out greeting the* EMPEROR.) (TWO EXTRAS, *costumed as* CHAN-CELLORS, *enter*:)

We mix and harmonize the tripods and vats, ordering yin and yang,
We hold to the axis, maintain the balance in the administration hall.
Supporting the state, comforting the barbarians—we care about nothing.
We spend our time in the Secretariat without doing a thing.

I am the chancellor Wulu Chongzong. He is the inner constant attendant Shi Xian.[24] Today, after the audience, an ambassador of the barbarian country arrived and demanded Wang Qiang to seal the peace. We have to report this to the emperor. Here we are at the western palace apartments. We'll have to go in. (*Act out having audience with the* EMPEROR:) We memorialize to our lord. At this moment the khan of the northern barbarians, Huhanye, has sent an ambassador informing us that Mao Yanshou has delivered up to him a portrait of a beautiful woman, and that he now demands the lady Zhaojun as his wife. If not, he will invade the south with overwhelming strength and it will be impossible to protect our rivers and mountains! (EMPEROR:) I've "fed the army for a thousand days and need it but for a single moment." In vain I have a court filled with civil officials and military officers. None is capable of driving back these barbarian troops—they're all people who fear the blade and flee the arrows! If you cannot even exert yourselves, how dare you ask a lady to seal the peace?

(*Muyang guan*)
Rise and fall are ever there,
Buckle and spear endure to the end.
  But isn't it true:
If one eats the salary of one's lord,
One's life hangs from the lord's hand.
During times of great peace
You vaunted your meritorious service as chancellors,
But as soon as there is trouble,
You banish my beautiful one.
  Useless now, in vain

---

23. Chang E is the beautiful goddess of the moon, where she lives her lonely life in the Palace of Broad Cold. The mirror used by Wang Zhaojun will have been a small round polished bronze mirror, which easily invites a comparison to the full moon.

24. Shi Xian (d. 32 BC) and Wulu Chongzong are both historical characters. Shi Xian was Emperor Yuan's favorite eunuch, and Wulu Chongzong belonged to his faction.

You took salary from the imperial treasury.

> Did you ever

Share the anxieties of your emperor and king?

> On that side

One who should be "chained to a tree" just wrings his hands,[25]

> On this side

One who should "clutch the railing" fears stumbling and cracking his head![26]

(EXTRA:) That foreign state says that Your Majesty is so enamored of Wang Qiang that the mainstays of the court have been neglected and thus have harmed the state. If you don't give her over, they will mobilize their troops and conduct a punitive campaign. Think how King Zhou destroyed his kingdom and lost his life because of his infatuation with Da Ji![27] (EMPEROR:)

> (*He xinlang*)
>
> > I never
>
> Constructed a Star Plucking Tower, high enough to pierce the blue welkin.[28]
>
> > Yet you do not speak of
>
> Yi Yin, who supported Tang.[29]
>
> > You speak only of
>
> King Wu, who punished bad king Zhou.[30]
>
> Someday, after you reach the Yellow Springs below—

---

25. When Liu Cong (d. 318), one of the local rulers in Northern China of the time, wanted to erect lavish buildings, a certain Chen Yuanda protested strongly. Liu Cong ordered him beheaded, but Chen Yuanda had himself chained to a tree in the palace courtyard so he could not be hauled away, and persisted in his remonstrations.

26. During the reign of Emperor Cheng (r. 32–7 BC) of the Han dynasty, Zhu Yun submitted a memorial in which he asked for the beheading of the imperial favorite, Zhang Yu. The emperor flew into a rage and ordered Zhu Yun executed, but he clung so strongly to the palace balustrade that the guards broke the balustrade when they pulled him away. Intercession by other court officials saved Zhu Yun's life.

27. King Zhou is the bad last ruler of the Shang/Yin dynasty (trad. dates, 1766–1122 BC). Tradition credited him with great debauchery and cruelty, and traced the cause of this behavior to his passion for the vixen, Da Ji.

28. The Star Plucking Tower, according to later tradition, was an excessively high tower, built by King Zhou to amuse his lady.

29. Cheng Tang, founder of the Shang/Yin dynasty, was traditionally venerated as the ideal ruler. Tang enjoyed the support of his prime minister Yi Yin, who in later tradition acquired all the traits of the ideal official.

30. King Wu founded the Zhou dynasty by destroying the debauched ruler of the Shang/Yin dynasty.

> If you encounter there
>
> Zhang Zifang,
> Will you be ashamed of yourselves, or not?[31]
>
>> You
>
> Lie on padded bedding,
> Eat from rows of tripods,
> Ride on the sleekest horses,
> Wear the lightest pelts—
>
>> You must have seen
>
> This tender willow dancing in spring winds, her palace-style waist so
>   svelte:
>
>> How can you bear to make
>
> The shadows of her girdle pendants sway in the Green Hill moon,
> Or the sounds of her lute die out in the Black River autumns?[32]

(EXTRA:) Your Majesty, at the moment neither our weapons nor armor are ready, and we have no fierce general to lead the battle. If anything should go amiss, what then? We implore Your Majesty to deny your own love, turn her over to save all the souls of your state! (EMPEROR:)

> (*Dou hama*)
>
>> I'll have you
>
> Memorialize to the lord of Han,
> Who slew until Chu itself bore the surname Liu![33]
>
>> Alas for our
>
> Marshal Han Xin, who fought the battle at Nine Mile Mountain
> And accomplished enough merit for ten generations!
>
>> And you—
>
> Inside the vermilion steps
> You uselessly wear your golden seals and purple cords!
>
>> But you—
>
> Behind your red gates
> You all dote on singing blouses and dancing sleeves!

---

31. Yellow Springs is the realm of the dead. Zhang Liang (Zhang Zifang, d. 189) was one of the great statesmen in the founding of the Han dynasty and a loyal supporter of Liu Bang.

32. These two lines are quoted from a poem on Wang Zhaojun by the Jin dynasty poet Wang Yuanjie. Green Hill is the name of the funerary tumulus for Wang Zhaojun; it has acquired this name because it is reputed to remain green all through the year. It is found to the south of modern Huhehot in Inner Mongolia. The Black River flows by Green Hill.

33. The first few lines of this song refer to Han Xin, one of the most important generals in the campaigns leading up to the founding of the Han dynasty. He commanded the Han troops in the final battle with Xiang Yu at Nine Mile Mountain.

Afraid that the border might be breached
And bring disaster, to your own families you fly in haste.
But like a goose with an arrow through its beak,
Not one among you even dares to cough!
What's vexing and upsetting Us is
That she, she, made up in red, so young of years,
Has no one to come to *her* rescue!
Why should Zhaojun deserve such vengeance, as though she had
       killed your parents?
Enough! Enough!
            It's just that
Everyone at court has become a Mao Yanshou!
I am in charge of the three thousand miles of the Lius',
Of the four hundred districts of the Central Plain,
Starting from Goose Canal.[34]
            Why is it,
A thousand troops are easily had,
But a single general is so hard to find?

(CHANCELLORS:) At this moment the barbarian ambassador is waiting outside court for your announcement. (EMPEROR:) So be it. Tell the ambassador to enter. (BARBARIAN AMBASSADOR *enters, greets with a bow, and speaks:*) Khan Huhanye has dispatched me, his minister, to the south in order to memorialize the following to the emperor of the Great Han. The northern state and the southern dynasty have for a long time sealed their friendship through marriage. Twice in the past we have dispatched someone to ask for a princess, but none has been forthcoming. Now Mao Yanshou has delivered up to our khan the portrait of a beautiful woman. I have been sent for the very purpose of demanding Zhaojun, so she may become our queen. In this way warfare between the two countries will be forestalled. If Your Majesty does not comply with our demands, we have a million brave troops and any day will invade the south in order to determine victory or defeat. May you in your sagely wisdom make the right decision! (EMPEROR:) Let the ambassador take his rest in the official guesthouse. (BARBARIAN AMBASSADOR *exits*. EMPEROR:) You civil officials and military officers deliberate! If you can offer up any plan that will make the barbarians withdraw, it will spare Zhaojun from marrying a barbarian. It boils down to this: you make light of the lady because she is meek and good. When

---

34. At one moment in the extended wars between Liu Bang and Xiang Yu, both parties agreed to a peace treaty. They agreed to divide the world between them, the border being Snow-goose Canal (Honggou), a stretch of water in present-day Henan province.

in earlier days Empress Lü was alive, none dared to contradict her as soon as she had spoken![35] But should it continue like this eventually no one would have use for civil officials or military officers, because all of the peace and security of the empire will depend only on women!

> (*Ku huangtian*)
> If you have some advice, speak up immediately!
> I've no tripods here filled with seething oil![36]
>> You
> Civil officials ought to bring security to the altars of state,
> You military officers ought to pacify by spear and halberd.
>> But all you can do
> At the head of the civil and military assembly,
> Is thrice shout "Ten Thousand Years!"
> And by your dancing steps[37] raise the dust
>> And say:
> "In sincere fear, my lord, I knock my head against the ground!"
>> Now
> On the road through Yang Pass,[38]
> Zhaojun will go out the pass.
> In earlier days, in the Weiyang Palace
> A female ruler monopolized power—
>> My civil officials and military officers, I don't believe you
> Would have dared to push Empress Lü around!
>> To no avail from this day on
> Those battles of dragons, those fights of tigers
>> Will depend on us,
> These simurgh-mates and phoenix-friends!

(WANG QIANG:) I have received Your Majesty's abundant grace so I should offer up my life in order to repay Your Majesty. Your handmaid will willingly marry

---

35. Upon the death of Liu Bang in 195 BC, his wife, Empress Lü, became the real power at court until her death in 180 BC. From behind a lowered screen, she ruled with an iron hand and did not hesitate to have some of the most meritorious officials in the founding of the dynasty executed.

36. To punish you by boiling.

37. "To dance" is the verb used to describe performing court rituals.

38. Yang pass was situated to the southwest of modern Dunhuang, at the westernmost tip of present-day Gansu province. The pass is mentioned in a famous parting poem, also known by the title "Song of Wei City" (*Weicheng qu*), by the Tang dynasty poet Wang Wei (701–61). Its name became a byword for the most extreme outpost of the Chinese realm.

the barbarian so that warfare can be halted. Moreover, she will leave a name in the historical records. But how will I be able to toss away the passion Your Majesty and I shared in the inner chamber? (EMPEROR:) Truly I cannot toss you away! (CHANCELLORS:) May Your Majesty deny his love and terminate his affection, and be concerned only with the altars of state. Send the lady on her journey as soon as possible! (EMPEROR:)

> (*Wu ye ti*)
>> Today
> She marries the khan—
> Prime Minister, don't trouble yourself so much!
> Already
> My Radiant Consort of the Han has no country she can call her
>> own!
>> And over there
> Dark clouds rise no more from the peaks of green mountains.
> Each of us, me here, she there, will stare with fixed eyes,
> Hoping for a single goose to transit the autumn.
>> It was meant to be . . .
> That We this year would gather idle sorrow,
> That Wang Qiang's fate would be to grow more haggard.
> Her headdress of halcyon feathers
> And her cord of fragrant gauze
>> Will now turn into
> A fur hat, a brocade veil,
> And sable pelts sewn with strings of pearls.

Ministers, accompany the Radiant Consort first to the guesthouse and turn her over to the barbarian ambassador. Tomorrow We will personally go out to the Baling Bridge[39] and offer her a farewell cup! (CHANCELLORS:) I'm afraid that this can't be! You will make yourself the laughingstock of all the foreign vandals! (EMPEROR:) I have agreed to everything my ministers have said, so why will you not grant this wish? For better or worse, I will see her off! Oh, how I hate that Mao Yanshou!

> (*Sansha*)
>> Oh, how I hate
> That treacherous beast that forgot all favor and bit his lord!
>> Why

---

39. Baling Bridge, to the east of Chang'an, in Tang dynasty times was a favorite spot for farewell parties.

Hasn't he been portrayed on the Pavilion that Rises above the Mists?[40]
Clerks by the Purple Terrace,[41]
You must know we are a lord and his ministers—
Whenever did I not agree with your proposals?
> How can you
So provoke my first night of dream longing?
From this time on, she will not see Chang'an, but gaze instead at the
    Northern Dipper,
As we are turned alive into a Weaving Maiden and a Buffalo Boy![42]

(CHANCELLORS:) It is not we ministers who pressure the lady to marry the barbarian! The barbarian ambassador requested her by name. Moreover, since antiquity there have been many who have ruined their state because of women and sex. (EMPEROR:)

> (*Ersha*)
> > Even though
> There have been many who have been destroyed like Zhaojun,
> > What
> Son of Heaven was ever so subject to others' summons, so little his
>   own master?
> I know in my heart she cannot master those stout, purple
>   thoroughbreds—
> > In days gone by,
> In her green jade sedan chair and fragrant palanquin
> She was too weak to lift the embroidered red curtains,
> And in mounting and descending needed help and support.
> > Who could believe
> That the moon would still shine alone in the sky or rivers still flow by
>   themselves
> When Our grief and longing goes on and on and on?

(WANG QIANG:) Your handmaid's journey may serve the grand strategy of the state, but how can I ever tear myself away from Your Majesty? (EMPEROR:)

> (*Weisheng*)
> > I fear, my lady,

---

40. The Pavilion that Rises above the Mists was erected by Emperor Taizong (r. 627–49) of the Tang dynasty. It contained the portraits of thirty-two officials who had made great contributions to the founding of the Tang.
41. The Purple Terrace is a designation of the imperial palace.
42. See *Rain on the Wutong Tree*, n. 18.

That when you feel hungry, you'll eat a lump of tasteless salted roast
>   meat,
And when you suffer thirst, you will drink a ladle of koumiss or
>   gruel.
>   I'll have
To pluck one branch of heartrending willow,[43]
And offer you a single cup to send you on your road.
>   She sees that
She will have to hurry to make today's stretch
And hasten to reach her lodging spot.
And when she, pained in her heart,
Once again looks around,
I fear
She will see no more phoenix pavilions and dragon lofts—
But for tonight at least she will lodge by the side of Baling Bridge!

(*Exits.*)

[Act 3]

(BARBARIAN AMBASSADOR *and three others enter, escorting* WANG QIANG; *they
act out performing foreign music.* WANG QIANG:) I am Wang Zhaojun. When I
was selected for the Palace, Mao Yanshou blemished my portrait and I was sent
off to the cold palace. Barely had I succeeded in receiving the imperial grace,
when Mao delivered my picture up to the barbarian king. He has now come
with his troops to demand me. If I do not go, I fear for the safety of the rivers
and mountains. So there's no way out. Let me go out of the borders and marry
the barbarian. How will I be able to stand the wind and frost of those foreign
parts? Since antiquity it is said:

>   If rosy cheeks surpass all others, one's fate oft is mean.
>   Don't blame the spring wind; you've only yourself to pity!

(EMPEROR *enters, leading party:*) Today I see the Radiant Consort off at Baling
Bridge. Here we are.

---

43. When someone left on a long journey, those who were left behind presented him or
her with a willow branch. Various explanations for this custom have been proposed, but the
most likely may well be that by presenting an "osier of a willow" (*liusi*) to those who stayed behind
gave expression to the traveler's "desire to remain" (*liusi*) or the other's desire for the traveler to
remain.

([SHUANGDIAO MODE:] *Xinshui ling*)
Brocaded sable pelts have brutally altered her Han palace attire.
> I should look only
At Zhaojun's likeness in the portrait!
Old grace—short as golden bridles,
New grief—long as the jade whip!
Originally we were a pair of mandarin ducks in a golden hall—
I never expected
We would fly apart!

You civil officers and military officials, you hundreds of officers, come up with a plan. Somehow, some way, drive back the barbarian troops, spare the Radiant Consort this marriage with the barbarian!

(*Zhuma ting*)
You, Prime Ministers, deliberate:
Send this ambassador who entered our country back to his court
   with the richest of gifts!
> We, husband and wife,
Are overcome by gloom—
Even common people who travel afar are allowed one "false
   departure."[44]
> Even now,
The ravaged willows of the city by the Wei bolster the bleak chill,
> And together with
The flowing stream below Baling Bridge, increase our anguish and
   pain.
> But the likes of you
Have no hearts to break.
> I remember how,
A whole day's sorrow was all distilled into that lady's lute.

(*Acts out descending from his horse. Acts out sharing his grief with* WANG QIANG:)
Servants, sing slowly, so slowly! I will offer the Radiant Consort a farewell cup of wine.

(*Bubu jiao*)
> Don't
Let one "Yang Pass Melody" be set free so lightly;
For us a single foot apart is as wide as the heavens.

---

44. Custom was to select an auspicious day, escort the traveler to the boat, then everyone returned together. The traveler then left whenever (s)he needed to.

Slowly, so slowly, I raise the jade goblet.
Our original intent was to draw out time over our cups,
So don't ask whether it ruins the rhythm or melody,
>   But
Sing to us, stretch it out, half-measure by half-measure!

(BARBARIAN AMBASSADOR:) Lady, let us go. It is already getting late. (EM-
PEROR:)

>   (*Luomei feng*)
>   >   How miserable we are,
>   For whom this parting is so heavy!
>   >   You may surely
>   Be in a hurry to return,
>   But Our heart has already raced ahead to Li Ling's terrace—[45]
>   As soon as you turn your head, I've already imagined it in a dream.
>   Don't ever say, "people in high places easily forget!"

(WANG QIANG:) Your Majesty! Once gone, will I ever see Your Majesty again? I
will leave my clothes from the house of Han here behind! Indeed:

>   Could I bear to wear the gown and skirt I wore for my lord,
>   >   To act the spring beauty for another?

(EMPEROR:)

>   (*Dianqian huan*)
>   >   But what to do
>   With these dancing gowns she leaves behind?
>   I fear the western wind will scatter the perfumes of earlier times.
>   >   I surely
>   Dread my palace carriage passing that moss-covered lane once more,
>   Where, suddenly reaching her peppered room,[46]

---

45. Li Ling's Terrace is found in present-day Inner Mongolia. Li Ling was a Chinese general
of the second part of the second century BC, who repeatedly gained major victories against the
Xiongnu and deeply penetrated into Inner Mongolia. During one of the wars of Emperor Wu
against the Xiongnu, however, his small body of troops was confronted by overwhelming numbers of Xiongnu and eventually he surrendered rather than committing suicide. This event took
place in 99 BC. When Emperor Wu learned of his surrender, he had Li Ling's family executed,
despite the protests of the historian Sima Qian, who suffered the penalty of castration for his
intercession on behalf of Li Ling. Li Ling remained in Xiongnu service until the end of his life.

46. The paint of the apartments of palace ladies was mixed with *fagara*, known as "Sichuan
pepper" (*huajiao*), for scent.

There at once to recall how she painted her face in front of the
    caltrop flower,[47]
Her charming appearance. . . .
And most I dread she will cross my mind abruptly once again.
Today Zhaojun goes beyond the border—
When will she, like Su Wu, return to her native land?[48]

(BARBARIAN ENVOY:) Lady, let's go. We have been waiting quite a while. (EM-
PEROR:) So be it! Radiant Consort, don't blame Us for this journey! (*Acts out
taking leave.* EMPEROR *speaks:*) I am not the Emperor of the Great Han,

(*Yan'er luo*)
    I have become
The hegemon-king of Chu, taking leave of Consort Yu![49]
    Nowhere do I see
A General Subduing the West, who guards the Jade Pass![50]
    Where can I find
A Li Zuoju, to act as go-between,
Or a Chancellor Xiao, to escort the bride to her husband's home?[51]

(CHANCELLORS:) Your Majesty should not be so upset. (EMPEROR:)

(*Desheng ling*)
    They are gone—
There are no pillars of gold and purple to span the seas![52]
In vain I've kept those armor-clad heroes on the border marches!

---

47. The backs of bronze mirrors were often decorated with a caltrop flower.

48. Su Wu (d. 60 BC) was dispatched in 100 BC as an envoy to the Xiongnu by Emperor Wu.
The Xiongnu tried to persuade him to go over to their side and when he refused they kept him
captive for many years; he was transported to the far north where he had to herd goats. The Han
court that had dispatched him believed him to have died. According to legend, the emperor only
learned that Su Wu was still alive when he shot a goose to whose leg Su Wu had attached a letter.
In 81 BC, upon a request of the Han court, Su Wu was allowed to return to his homeland.

49. On the eve of his final battle against the Han army led by Han Xin, Xiang Yu, the hegemon-king of Western Chu, realized that his situation was hopeless. His troops had deserted him
and he took leave of his concubine, the lady Yu. She thereupon committed suicide. This scene
always has been a favorite of the Chinese stage, made famous in the drama *The Hegemon Leaves
His Consort (Bawang bieji)*.

50. The Jade Pass marks the westernmost end of the Great Wall.

51. Li Zuoju, a great strategist, and Xiao He (Chancellor Xiao, d. 193 BC) were major figures
in the founding of the Han dynasty.

52. I.e., great military officials; from the saying, "Holding up the heavens, pillars of white jade
[civil officials]; bearing up the seas, beams of purple gold [military]."

You all want
Servants to do your bidding on the left and right,
So why doesn't this hold for me—
"A wife who shares bran and chaff should never be divorced."
You had but to hear "sword and spear,"
And little deer began bouncing in your hearts.
Today you have beseeched a lady for help;
You will never match this—
"A real man relies on himself."

(EXTRA:) Your Majesty let us return to court. (EMPEROR:)

(*Chuan bo zhao*)
Of course
I want to release the silken bridle,
But this is no
"Resoundingly tapping the golden stirrups with my whip."[53]
You are the ones who
Should harmonize and regulate yin and yang,
Take charge of the mainstays of the court,
Bring order to the country and peace to the state,
Extend my land and open up borders.
But if my
High Progenitor[54]
Had sent one of your simple maids
To sleep in snow and frost,
Away from home and hearth—
If she didn't think constantly of your spring breezes and painted
    halls,
I would immediately enfeoff you as a one-word prince![55]

(CHANCELLORS:) Your Majesty, don't keep calling her name. Send her on her
way! (EMPEROR:)

---

53. From a famous victory song: "Resoundingly tapping the golden stirrups with their whips, /
The men come back singing a song of victory." That is, this is no victory song we are singing going
home, but one of sorrow at parting.

54. "High Progenitor" is the posthumous title of Liu Bang, the founder of the Han dynasty.

55. During Yuan times the princes highest in rank bore titles consisting of two characters,
one character denoting the rank, one character referring to the name of an ancient kingdom.
Lower-ranking princes bore titles consisting of four characters, two characters denoting the rank,
two naming a specific area. So, one character plus a title.

(*Qi dixiong*)
Why should "Your Majesty"
Not call out
"Wang Qiang"?
      How can I withstand
That final turn of the head, that gaze as she leaves?
Or bear the fluttering and tossing shadows of banners and pennants,
    scattered by the wind and snow,
And the mournful strength of drums' sounds and bugles that shake
    the very passes and mountains?

(*Meihua jiu*)
Endless wilderness, sad and forlorn—
The grasses are already turning sere,
Their hue quickly covered with frost.
Dogs have shed until their pelts are dark,
Men raise their tasseled spears,
Horses bear the luggage,
Camel carts transport provisions.
Men begin to hunt on fields where they have formed circles.
      She
Takes leave of the ruler of the Han with pain in her heart.
      Far away, I see that he
Takes her hand and leads her across the river's bridge,
Here, before me, they have already formed my escort ranks.
My simurgh carriage returns to Xianyang,
Returns to Xianyang and passes through palace walls,
Passes through the palace walls as leaves flutter brown.[56]
As leaves flutter brown, I follow the winding corridors.
I follow the winding corridors and the bamboos produce a chill.
The bamboos produce a chill as I approach her peppered room,
As I approach her peppered room, cold cicadas[57] weep.
Cold cicadas weep by the green gauze window,
By a green gauze window, empty now of the memories of love.

(*Shou Jiangnan*)
Empty of memories of love,

---

56. Xianyang, on the northern bank of the river Wei, was the capital of the Qin dynasty. In Tang poetry, the term was often used as a designation for Chang'an.
57. "Cold" because they chirp until the weather turns cold in deep autumn.

Only a heart of steel!
But even a heart of steel
Would shed a thousand tears of sorrow!
Tonight I will hang her portrait in the Zhaoyang Palace,
And worship there, my offering
A bright burning silver candle to shine on her red attire!

(CHANCELLORS:) Your Majesty, please return, the lady has disappeared in the
distance. (EMPEROR:)

(*Yuanyang sha*)
>   If I, I
Utter only a lame excuse in front of great ministers,
>   It only is because I fear
That the brush tips of that lot will turn everything into history and
    discourse.
>   I do not see how
Her high spirit, flowerlike,
Can be set off against the scenery of those grasslands.
>   It is said:
"Long he remains standing,
Tarrying for quite a while!"
Suddenly I hear the border geese on their southward flight,
Honking loud and clear,
>   But actually it turns out to have been,
Cattle and goats as far as one can see,
>   And that
Felt-covered cart loaded with parting's grief, rattling halfway down
    the hill.

(*Exit.*)

❋❋

(BARBARIAN KING enters, *leading his party and escorting* ZHAOJUN:) Today the
Han court has not turned its back on the old treaties, but has given Wang Zhaojun to our frontier land to seal peace through marriage. I will enfeoff Zhaojun
as the Queen who Gives Peace to the Barbarians and she will be enthroned
in my main palace. How much better things are now that our two countries
have avoided warfare. My officers, transmit the order to all men to strike camp
as we depart for the north! (*Acts out traveling.* WANG QIANG:) Where are we
here? (BARBARIAN:) This is the Black Dragon River, the borderline between
the barbarians and the Han. The southern banks belong to the house of Han,

the northern banks to our frontier nation. (WANG QIANG:) Your Majesty, let me have a cup of wine so I can pour a libation toward the south. After I have taken my leave of the house of Han, we can continue this far journey. (*Acts out pouring out the wine:*) Emperor of the Han, this life has reached its end, but I will wait for you in my next existence! (*Acts out jumping into the river.*) (BARBARIAN *acts out [trying to] rescue her, and speaks:*) Now Zhaojun was unwilling to submit to the barbarians and she died by jumping into the river. So be it! Bury her here on the bank of the river and let her grave be called Green Hill. She may have died, but should I break our treaty with the house of Han? Come to think of it, it's all the fault of the machinations of that Mao Yanshou! Servants, arrest Mao Yanshou and deliver him to the Han court for punishment! As before I will conclude peace with the house of Han and forever be its nephew. Wouldn't that be best?

> In the end, good and evil cannot stay hidden:
> Out they will—it's only a matter of time!

(*Exit.*)

[Act 4]

(EMPEROR *enters, leading* A EUNUCH:) I am Emperor Yuan of the Han. Since the Radiant Consort married that barbarian, We have not held court for a hundred days. Confronted now with this desolate nighttime scene, I am overcome by vexation. I will hang up her portrait to dispel my gloomy thoughts.

> ([ZHONGLÜ MODE:] *Fendie'er*)
> Coolness arises in these precious halls,
> The night drags on; in the Six Palaces not a woman stirs.
> Facing a single cold lamp on its silver stand
> That, between cushion and mat,
> At sleeping time,
> Sheds light on just how meager is my luck!
> Ten thousand miles it is to the Dragon Courtyard,[58]
> And I have no idea where she will lodge this true soul of hers!

Eunuch, look! The incense in the brazier is gone. Add some more!

> (*Zui chunfeng*)
> We used up the incense in the imperial brazier—
> Add more yellow seal-script cakes!

---

58. The Dragon Courtyard designated the place where the Xiongnu rulers venerated Heaven.

To my mind the lady—
Exactly like the Bamboo Forest Monastery—[59]
Betrays not an inkling of her form
But leaves behind only her image,
Only her image!
But until the day I die,
As long as I am alive,
I will venerate it with unchanging passion.

I'm suddenly feeling tired. Let me sleep for a while.

[(Jiaosheng)]
Of Gaotang[60]
A dream cannot be formed—
Where are you, my love,
My love?
And why no spiritual powers to help?
　　　Why do they act as if
I am only infected lightly?

(Acts out sleeping.) (WANG QIANG enters:) I am Wang Qiang. After I had arrived in the northern lands to marry the barbarian, I secretly fled back. Isn't that my ruler? Your Majesty, your handmaid is here! (BARBARIAN SOLDIER enters:) When I dozed off for a moment just now, Wang Zhaojun immediately stole away and went back. I have come in hot pursuit and entered the Han palace. Isn't that Zhaojun? (Acts out grabbing WANG QIANG, and exits. EMPEROR acts out being startled, and speaks:) Just a moment ago I saw the Radiant Consort return, but how come I don't see her anywhere?

(Ti yindeng)
　　　Just a moment ago in this very spot
A state envoy of the khan
Shouted out the name of my Wang Zhaojun!
　　　But when We
Called "lady," she refused to answer by the lamp—
　　　It turned out,
To be only her portrait, painted in color!
　　　Suddenly I hear

---

59. The Bamboo Forest Monastery might be seen in a glimpse but could never be found.
60. Gaotang is the place where the goddess of Mount Wu shared the couch of a king of the ancient state of Chu. See note 22.

The phoenix-pipes sound from the Courtyard of Immortal Music,[61]
The *Xiao* and the *Shao*, a full concerto![62]

(*Manjingcai*)
By day I refuse entertainment,
With the result We have never once dreamt
Of a happy reunion that lasted till dawn.[63]

(*After a goose honks:*)

It turns out to be just
A goose, honking two or three times over Tall Gate palace—
I never knew
Anyone else could be so lonely and deserted too!

(*After a goose honks:*)

(*Bai hezi*)
Probably
The number of his springs and autumns is high,
So his strength and power fail;
Most likely
He lacks food and drink
So his bones and feathers have grown light.
If he wants to go back,
He worries that, South of the River, the net's silk is cast wide,
But if he goes on ahead
He fears that, North of the Passes, the carved bows will be stiff.

(*Reprise*)
He's suffering from pain, like the ruler of the Han who longs for
    Zhaojun:
As if lamenting Tian Heng, his grief-filled resentment resembles the
    song of "Dew on the Shallots,"[64]

---

61. The office in charge of music for the emperor.

62. The *Xiao* and the *Shao* are the names of musical pieces that were performed at the courts of ancient sage-rulers.

63. Because music is played at night.

64. "Dew on the Shallots" (referring to how quickly the sun makes it evaporate) is the name of a dirge that is known from Eastern Han times. Later tradition connected it to the name of Tian Heng (d. 202 BC). Tian Heng was a descendant of the royal house of Qi (present-day Shandong province). Upon the collapse of the Qin dynasty, he declared himself king of Qi, but he was soon ousted from that position and fled to an island off the coast. After Liu Bang defeated Xiang Yu

His chilling distress is like the sound of songs of Chu, sung at
   midnight,[65]
His cutting grief is like the "Yang Pass Melody," performed three
   times over.

(*After a goose honks*:)

(*Shang xiaolou*)
               To begin,
My mind was not at peace,
               Now on top of that
This fiend pesters me![66]
               He honks
Now languidly,
Now urgently,
Perfectly matching the mood of these cold watches of the night!
               Go ahead,
Circle in a gyre.
I must reply because "like sounds resonate together."
               Oh, won't this
Upset the very order of the four seasons?

(*Reprise*)
               Are you
Looking for Su Wu, seeking Li Ling?
In front of this silver candle-stand
You really make Us overcome with emotion when I see her form.
               In distant lands
That Radiant Consort of the Han may have found her fate,
               But not seeing this,
This rotten ball of feathers, at least she is spared its sound!

(*After a goose honks*:)

---

he summoned Tian Heng to his court. Tian Heng set out for the trip but committed suicide
when he approached his destination. His followers, according to legend, thereupon composed
"Dew on the Shallots."

65. During the final showdown of Liu Bang and Xiang Yu, the troops of the Han, led by Han
Xin, had surrounded the camp of Xiang Yu. Most of the troops of Xiang Yu came from the
south, the area of the earlier kingdom of Chu. At nighttime, Zhang Liang, one of the advisers of
Liu Bang, had the Han troops sing the melodies of Chu. Xiang Yu's army, believing that Liu Bang
already had conquered their homeland and drafted recruits from there, defected in great numbers, sealing the fate of Xiang Yu.

66. This term, *yuanjia*, means both "enemy" and "lover."

(*Manting fang*)
>   Nor, goose, are you
Something I love to hear—
Too much like orioles warbling in woods,
Or mountain creeks gurgling and purling.
"Mountains are long, rivers distant, and heaven is like a mirror":
>   I just fear
You have already fallen behind in your journey.
>   And have deserted
"The evening scenes of the Xiao and the Xiang."[67]
>   Who could hope to say,
"Passing by and leaving a call behind?"[68]
>   How can I bear
The eternal nights on the jasper steps?
How I hate the moon for its brightness!

(EUNUCH:) Your Majesty, don't be so vexed! Take care of your health. (EM-PEROR:) How can I not be vexed?

(*Shi'er yue*)
>   Don't say that
I am easily stirred:
>   You, my ministers,
Also detest it.
>   This is not
The twittering of swallows on carved beams,
>   This is not
The cry of cranes in brocade trees.
>   Zhaojun of the Han
Left hearth and home
On a journey of a thousand miles.

(*After a goose honks:*)

(*Yaomin ge*)
Honking, it flies across the shoal of smartweed flowers;
This lonely goose will not leave the city of emperors and kings.

---

67. The area of the Xiao and the Xiang is the region of rivers and lakes in the northernmost part of present-day Hunan province. There were "eight scenes" along the river, one of which was called *yanluo pingsha*, "Geese alight on the level sands." This scene has been dropped out because the goose is late in his journey.

68. One of two lines of a common saying, *yan guo liusheng, ren guo liuming*. "A goose passes and leaves a call behind, a person passes and leaves a reputation behind."

Under the painted eaves, iron horses[69] clink and tinkle;
In the precious hall the lord and king shivers in the chill.
In these cold, cold watches of the night
How desolate and dreary are the sounds of falling leaves!
The candle dims, Tall Gate is quiet.

(*Weisheng*)
A single sound circles the palace of the Han,
A single sound is entrusted to "the city on the Wei."[70]
Secretly it multiplies my white hairs, turns me old and sick.
      This is how
I, how I am beyond help!

(*Exit.*)

❅❅

(EXTRA, *costumed as* CHANCELLOR, *enters:*) Today, after the morning audience had dispersed, an envoy from the frontier state reached us under orders to deliver us a Mao Yanshou in shackles. He said that Mao Yanshou, by rebelling against his own country, had been the cause of our disastrous rift and the destruction of the treaty. Now Zhaojun has died and they wish to establish peace. In conformity with the emperor's edict, I have had Mao Yanshou beheaded and offered up in sacrifice to the Radiant Consort. Order the Court of Imperial Banquets to reward the envoy with a rich repast and send him back. Indeed:

> When the state is correct, the mind of Heaven will follow;
> When officials are pure, the people are naturally at peace.
> When the wife is wise, the husband meets few disasters;
> When the son is filial, the father's heart is at ease.

TITLE: Mao Yanshou rebels against his country and creates a border
        dispute;
        Emperor Yuan of the Han, as the one person, is not his own
        master.

NAME: Drowning herself in the Black River—the Radiant Consort's grief
        at Green Hill,
        Breaking a troubling dream—a lone goose in autumn over the
        palaces of Han.

---

69. Wind chimes.
70. The city on the Wei is Chang'an.

6

Dazed behind the Green Ring Lattice, Qiannü's Soul Leaves Her Body

ZHENG GUANGZU

From as early as the Ming, critics considered Zheng Guangzu to be "one of the four great masters of *zaju*," alongside Guan Hanqing, Ma Zhiyuan, and Bai Pu. Yet, we have little information on his life. In *The Register of Ghosts*, Zhong Sicheng wrote the single longest comment on Zheng:

> Guangzu, style name Dehui, was a man of Xiangling, near Pingyang [modern Linfen in Shanxi]. Even though a Confucian scholar he served as a clerk in the Hangzhou Circuit. He was straight and square with people, and did not blindly make friends with others. Therefore, many gentlemen disesteemed him, but after a while they saw that he was a man of profound feeling such that others could not even approach it. He died from an illness and was cremated in the Monastery of the Divine Mushroom [*Lingzhi si*] at West Lake in Hangzhou. Each of the mourners wrote a poem or piece of prose at the occasion. I do not need to list here all of the gentleman's works. His reputation was fragrant throughout the world; his sounds stirred up the women's quarters. Entertainers called him "Seasoned Master Zheng," and they all knew that his "virtue showed." Alas, what he wrote was too contrived to be humorous, and he could not avoid betraying the marks of laboring too hard. There is a separate criticism to be made here.

Zhong's biographical sketch of Zheng is followed by an elegy penned almost a century later by Jia Zhongming:

> (To the tune *Lingbo qu*)
> All the ointment and perfume of the cosmos enriched his skin;
> Writing that was embroidered and brocaded "filled his innards."
> From the tip of his pen were written out sentences that could startle a man.
> He tumbled through present and past
> And occupied the battlefield of the lyric; the old generals submitted:
> *Wind and Moon in the Hanlin Academy,*
> *Music from the Pear Garden*
> Truly were works of real effort.

These few words tell us virtually all we know of the life of Zheng Guangzu. He was born in one of the two most active areas for writers of *zaju* (apart from Dadu): Pingyang in Shanxi and Dongping in Shandong province. Since Zheng's name occurs in the section of the *Register of Ghosts* in which the author listed "people he knew," we can assume that Zheng was contemporaneous with Zhong Sicheng. Since the *Register* also remarks that Zheng "died from an illness," this means that his death occurred sometime before the "Preface" to the *Register* was written in 1330. From the preface of another work, Zhou Deqing's *Rhymes of the Central Plain*, we learn that Zheng was "already gone" (*yiyi*), so we can surmise that Zheng was already dead before 1324, the date of Zhou's preface. He was most likely a contemporary of Ma Zhiyuan, and a generation younger than Guan Hanqing or Bai Pu. This is also hinted at by the phrase "old generals" in Zhong Sicheng's elegy. The drama *Wind and Moon in the Hanlin Academy* draws heavily on Wang Shifu's *Story of the Western Wing*, and the drama under consideration here, *Qiannü's Soul Leaves Her Body*, which equally shows the heavy influence of that work, is also noted as a "second edition," an earlier play on the same subject having been written by one Zhao Gongfu. Wang and Zhao are perhaps specific examples of the "old generals" that Zhong Sicheng mentioned.

A total of seventeen plays are attributed to Zheng, of which seven are extant. They range from historical incidents ("tumbled through present and past") to love stories ("stirred up the women's quarters"). He has left behind only six single *sanqu* lyrics and two long lyric suites. His dramas received high praise from Yuan and Ming critics, who are more enthusiastic than Zhong Sicheng in their appreciation of his allusion-riddled writings.

The original source of *Dazed behind the Green Ring Lattice, Qiannü's Soul Leaves Her Body* (*Mi qingsuo Qiannü lihun*) is a short late Tang Dynasty tale by Chen Xuanyou, called "Story of the Departing Soul" (*Lihun ji*):

> In the third year of the Tianshou reign (692), Zhang Yi of Qinghe in Hebei was living in Hengzhou in Hunan because of an official posting. He was by nature simple and quiet and did not have many friends. He had no sons, but did have two daughters. The elder of these had died early and his younger daughter, Qianniang, was a proper beauty who had no peer. Wang Zhou of Taiyuan, Yi's sororal nephew, was young, perceptive, and insightful, and he was also a model of a handsome lad. Yi often gave him high marks, saying, "I'm going to marry Qianniang to him in the future." Each of them gradually matured and the two of them, Zhou and Qianniang, were often moved to think about each other whether awake or asleep, but none of their family knew about this circumstance.

Later on, however, someone who had been selected to receive an official appointment requested her hand, and Yi assented to it. The girl became very depressed when she heard about this, and Zhou also fell into a deep and resentful anger. On the pretext that he should be presented for selection, Zhou requested that he go to the capital. He could not be dissuaded, so he was sent off with substantial gifts. Full of suppressed anger and moved to tears by his grief, Zhou bid goodbye and, with no intent of returning, boarded his boat. By nightfall he had gone several miles into the mountains on the outskirts of the city. It had just turned midnight and Zhou was unable to sleep, when suddenly he heard someone on the bank, walking swiftly and reaching his boat in no time. He inquired who it was and it turned out to be Qianniang, walking barefoot and alone. Zhou was so startled and happy that he seemed to go crazy. He grasped her hand and asked where she had come from. Weeping, she replied, "You have been so sincere that I was moved whether asleep or eating. Now they are trying to make me change my mind, but I knew that your deep affection would never change. So I thought about suicide as a way to requite your love, but I have given up my life to elope." Zhou was ecstatic, because this was something for which he could never have hoped. He consequently hid Qianniang aboard and they fled for nights on end.

Halving the travel time by never stopping day or night, they reached Sichuan in a few months. In the five years that followed they had two sons but they had also cut off all communication with Zhang Yi. Qianniang pined for her parents all the time, and she told Wang, sobbing and weeping, "Because I could not turn my back on you in days past, I cast aside the greatest righteousness to elope with you. It has now been five years that I have been separated from their grace and compassion. How can I have the self-respect to continue on in this world?" Zhou felt sorry for her and said, "We will go back, don't make yourself so miserable." And so, they went back together to Hengzhou.

Once they reached there, Wang Zhou first went to Zhang Yi's house alone to make amends. Yi said, "Why are you lying? Qianniang has been sick in her boudoir for many years." Zhou said, "She's on the boat right now!" Zhang Yi was very taken back and sent someone off to see if it were true. And indeed it turned out that she was in the boat, happy and peaceful, and she asked the envoy, "Is my father well?" The family members thought this remarkable, and they went quickly to report to Zhang Yi. When the girl in the bedchamber heard this, she was delighted and she arose, put on her makeup and changed her clothes, laughing but wordless, and went out to greet them. The two Qianniangs immediately melded together into a single body with two sets of clothes. Her family kept this quiet because they deemed it something improper. Only close relatives knew of this secret.

Some forty years intervened before both husband and wife died. Both boys passed the highest examinations in the status of filial sons of integrity, one reaching to the rank of district magistrate, the other to that of district defender.

When I was young, I heard this tale often, but with several variants. Some said it was all empty nonsense. At the end of the Dali reign period (766–779) I met up with Zhang Zhongxian in Laiwu District in Shandong, who told me the whole tale from beginning to end. Zhang Yi was Zhang Zhongxian's paternal younger uncle. His story was very precise and detailed, so I have recorded it here.

A more immediate inspiration for the play, however, seems to be the earlier drama, *Story of the Western Wing*. Passages from *Qiannü* show direct borrowing from the stagecraft and language of *Western Wing*. Certainly one of the major themes—female desire—seems to be treated in Zheng's play in direct contrast or rebuttal to the passivity of Oriole, the female lead of *Western Wing*. Whereas Oriole remains nearly silent in terms of sexual and emotional fulfillment, Qiannü becomes an active pursuer of Student Wang who, in this play, is turned into the object of desire. Oriole's mother thwarts her promised marriage to Student Zhang, but in *Qiannü* the girl's mother assents to the union between the two lovers. Her subsequent actions, however, make her daughter fear that she may renege on the prenatal engagement promise and Qiannü, too, impatient to wait for the student's return from the examination, sets out to follow him to the capital. However, her being divides into two visible forms: an airy *hun* soul that goes with her lover, marries him and bears children, and her physical body which falls ill at home, awaking only when the *hun* soul sleeps in the physical world and returns to her body. The play is quite original in its conception of the relationship between desire, illness, and family repression, representing the fulfillment of female desire as only possible when desire is liberated from the body itself. The relationship between desire and death is more fully articulated in later plays that have adapted this motif, such as *The Peony Pavilion* (1599) by Tang Xianzu, but Zheng Guangzu's short *zaju* has rightfully been hailed as a work of stunning simplicity and power. The play is innovative in stagecraft as well, having the female lead play both the embodied soul and the physical body of Qiannü, and in having the two characters meet and merge on stage. The popularity of Zheng's play has continued to the present day. The Yuan play was performed both in London and New York in the 1990s, and there are several movie versions that follow, either loosely or closely, the structure of the Yuan play.

Qiannü's Soul Leaves Her Body consists of four regular suites of arias. A wedge consisting of two songs precedes the first long suite of songs. In the *Gu mingjia* edition the scene focusing on these two songs is not marked as a wedge as would be customary from Zang Maoxun's *Yuanqu xuan* onward. While wedges are found in many *zaju*, *Qiannü's Soul Leaves Her Body* is rather exceptional in including a final wedge: following the coda of the fourth set of songs, three more songs follow, which are sung by Qiannü after her soul and body have fused into one person again. Such "final wedges" are encountered only in a very small number of plays. This edition also identifies only one or two "padding words" (*chenzi*) in the arias by using smaller type sizes.

Dramatis personæ in order of appearance

Role type	Name, family role, or social role
Second male	Old lady, Madam Li
Male lead	Wang Wenju
Retainers	Household retainers
Meixiang	Meixiang, Qiannü's maid
Female lead	Qiannü
Ghost female	*Hun* soul of Qiannü
Comic	Zhang Qian, Wang Wenju's servant

Dazed behind the Green Ring Lattice,
Qiannü's Soul Leaves Her Body

[Wedge]

(SECOND MALE, *costumed as* OLD LADY, *enters leading* ATTENDANTS:)

Flowers will blossom on other days,
But a person knows no second youth.
Say not that yellow gold is precious,
For pleasure and security are worth the highest price!

I am Madam Li and my husband's name was Zhang. He passed away while young, leaving me just a daughter, called Qiannü. She's just seventeen but is competent in every female art of needle and hand, at household cooking and banquet fare. When my husband was still alive, he once made a prenatal pact of marriage with Vice Prefect Wang. Now the Wang family sired a son, called Wang Wenju. As this lad grew into manhood he "studied till his belly was stuffed with literature." We still haven't brought this affair to completion, and I've sent many a letter to him about it. He says now that he wants to come pay a visit to me. Servants! Keep a lookout at the gate, and if this young chap comes, report to me at once.

(MALE LEAD, *costumed as an insignificant student,* WANG WENJU, *enters:*)

All else in the world is merely crass;
Learning stands alone, first-class.

I, this humble student, am Wang Wenju. I've studied until my belly is stuffed with literature but, alas, I've yet to go on and lay claim to fame. When my father held the post of Vice Prefect of Hengzhou, unfortunately both he and my mother passed away. But when he was still alive, he made a prenatal pact of marriage[1] with a certain Zhang Gongbi, who lives here. It turned out that my mother gave birth to me, a boy, and the Zhang family had a girl, whose name is Qiannü. But my father-in-law passed away and we never finished up this marriage business.

---

1. In Chinese, "to point at the belly and make a marriage": to make a marriage contract while the mother is still pregnant.

My mother-in-law has sent me several letters to inquire about it. Now that the "spring plaque has shaken" and the examination ground opened, I'll do two things: go to Chang'an to sit for the examinations and visit my mother-in-law as well. Well, here I am already. Retainers, please report that Wang Wenju is at the gate. (RETAINERS *report, speaking:*) We report to the Madam that there is a young scholar outside who says that he is Wang Wenju.

(OLD LADY:) Well, my words have scarce left my lips and he's here already. Tell him he's welcome. (*Act out greeting.* WANG WENJU:) Your child has been so negligent in not asking after you earlier. Let me now offer you obeisance. (*Acts out making obeisance.* MADAM:) Please rise, child, and be at ease. (WANG WENJU:) Mother, I've come both to pay my respects to you and to go on to Chang'an for the examinations. (MADAM:) Son, please sit down. Servants, tell Meixiang to go ask missy to come out of her embroidery chambers to greet her elder brother. (RETAINERS *speak:*) Understood. Pass on to missy that the Madam wants her.

(FEMALE LEAD, *leading* MEIXIANG, *enters:*) I am surnamed Zhang and called Qiannü. I am seventeen now, but my father is unfortunately already dead and gone. When he was alive, he made a prenatal pact of marriage with Vice Prefect Wang. Later the Wang family sired a young man, Wang Wenju, and my family had me. I never expected Wang's mother and father to both die and leave this marriage business uncompleted. Now mother is summoning me to the fore hall. I wonder what she wants. Meixiang, go with me to see my mother. (MEIXIANG:) Sister, move it a little quicker; let's go and see your mother. (*Act out greeting.* QIANNÜ:) Mother, why did you call me? (MADAM:) Child, come forward and pay your respects to your elder brother. (QIANNÜ:) I understand. (*Acts out greeting* WANG WENJU. MADAM:) Son, this is Miss Qiannü. Now, go back to your embroidery chambers for the time being. (QIANNÜ *acts out going out the door, speaks:*) Meixiang, where did we get an elder brother? (MEIXIANG:) Sister, didn't you recognize him? That was the Scholar Wang who was betrothed to you before birth. (QIANNÜ:) If he is really Student Wang, then my mother must have had something on her mind when she had me greet him as an elder brother! (*Sings:*)

> ([XIANLÜ MODE:] *Shanghua shi*)
> He's a smart little lad with a small hat and a light gown,
> And I'm a sweet pure girl in embroidered cloaks and a perfumed cart—
> We're just a perfect match in looks and talent.
> But, on the road to Yang Terrace, my mother
> Erects a high wall to block the rains and clouds.[2]

---

2. See *Autumn over the Palaces of Han*, n. 22.

(*Reprise*)
She wants to keep that prim and proper lass from Wu Mountain out
 of reach,
But will a pining woman and wifeless man be so compliant?
Go ahead and ply your black heart—
If you hadn't tried to control me, I'd never have thought of it,
But the more you try to block me, the more I dwell on it!

(QIANNÜ *and* MEIXIANG *exit.* MADAM:) Servants, sweep out the study so my
son can stay there to hit the books and write. Don't stint on the tea and food,
either. (WANG WENJU:) Don't clean out the study, mother. I'd better be on my
way to the capital for the examinations. (MADAM:) Stay a day or two, son. Your
trip won't be delayed long. Servants! Prepare some wine and delicacies and we'll
hold a feast in the rear hall.

(*Exit together.*)

[Act 1]

(QIANNÜ *enters, leading* MEIXIANG:) I am Qiannü. Ever since I saw Student
Wang, my very soul has been stirred. I never expected my mother to go back on
the engagement and make me address him as "elder brother." I don't know what
was on her mind. Ah, it really pains me to face this autumn scene. (QIANNÜ
sings:)

([XIANLÜ MODE:] *Dian jiangchun*)
Little by little I made it through the whole autumn night,
Then suddenly started awake, the gauze window bright with dawn.
Falling leaves sough and sigh
And fill the ground, swept by none.

(*Hunjiang long*)
"Breaks a person's heart"—that's true of this late autumn turn of the
 year—
When all the cares of the heart are gathered together to rise to the
 tips of my brows.
I never gaze now at my reflection in the mirror,
And the embroidery needle I leave untouched.
Ever I regret sitting nightlong at the window, the candle shadows
 darkening—
Let that moon climb high over the hall where I make myself up at night.
This young girl within her mandarin-duck bed curtains
And that little student in his humble abode

Were matched by rights as man and wife,
But instead we are made to be elder brother, younger sister.
Let my mother block me if she will;
My feelings of love are hard to break off.
He secretly sends me words on brocade,[3]
And I surreptitiously dispatch a sachet of perfume.
And in any case, we're right here in the front house and the rear
    garden,
Not separated, as are earth and heaven, north and south.
For naught have we missed many secret meetings,
And had to pass countless darkening eves alone.
There may have been no foreordainment to bring us together,
But fate has dictated this burning anxiety.
My feelings despondent and depressed, hard to dispel, I grow bored,
Cold and forlorn, who asks about his lonely isolation?
Weighed down with sickness, nothing gained but heartache,
So thin and worn down, I am afraid my mother will find out.
Gaze far away—Heaven is wide, earth narrow,[4]
Dyed to the quick[5]—my dreams are broken, my soul is wearied.

(MEIXIANG:) Sister, fret a little less, don't worry so much. (QIANNÜ:) Meixiang, when will this all end? (*Sings:*)

(*You hulu*)
Even if he hadn't fallen sick
I would have guessed it—
Probably wasted away to nothing.
I'm so under her control and unable to vent my anger that I'm nearly
    paralyzed.
Even though this is not a case of "the road is long and distant,"[6]
Still my love follows him like the vague and distant clouds
And my tears sprinkle a rain that falls soughing and sighing.
I cannot stand by the bends in the balustrade or rest against the
    rockery.[7]

---

3. I.e., love notes.

4. He seems as far away as heaven but is, in reality, right here.

5. With lovesickness.

6. I.e., not a case of her lover traveling far away; he is in the same house.

7. To engage in romantic conversation. The language is drawn from Act 3, Play 3 of the *Story of the Western Wing*, in which Student Zhang attempts his first seduction of Oriole:

"*Chenzui dongfeng*" (Crimson sings:)
I would have said that the wind swayed evening crows in the shade of the sophora tree,

It's just like gazing far away at heaven's edge: there is a speck of green
 mountain, but small it is.

(*Speaks:*) This scholar—the poems he sent are full of enmity toward my mother.

Probably because his mind feels the unfairness,
He vents himself at will;
His heart cannot be indulged,
So in idleness he stitches these lines together.
He has shown off his every talent and feeling,
Displayed his fulsome beauty,
Boasted of the tenor of his talents.
Let me examine the structure of these lines closely,
And observe how he has wielded the hairs of his pen.

(*Tianxia le*)
He certainly does possess the high spirit of meritorious officials who
 helped found the Han—
Heaven's destiny is hard to escape.
When will he work his way through this cold and dreary fate?
We, this bachelor man, this husbandless woman, are too ill
 starred—[8]
I have made ready for mandarin ducks to nest in perfume of
 brocaded quilts,
He has looked with hope for the zither tunes of phoenix and
 simurgh crying in harmony.[9]
Could we have expected it to be like butterflies in flight, circling
 around an embroidered tree?[10]

(MEIXIANG:) Sister, Scholar Wang has turned into quite a handsome man, a
right smart fellow. And your figure, Sister, makes you a perfect match for Scholar
Wang. Relax! Don't fret. (QIANNÜ:) Meixiang, what shall I do about this fix?
(*Sings:*)

But all the while it was the raven's-gauze hat tails of the jade person.
One hides himself beside the curving balustrade;
One stands by the rockery with her back turned.
There's no polite conversation,
And neither ever addresses the other.

See West and Idema 1995, p. 309.

   8. Zang Maoxun has quite decorously changed this to "orphaned boy and orphaned girl."

   9. I.e., she has been preparing for the right man, he has hoped for the perfect marriage
match.

   10. I.e., how could our arranged marriage have just been held out as an empty promise?

(*Nuozha ling*)
I pass a whole year every single day,
And the days of joyous reunion are few.
I have looked upon all thirty-three heavens,
But the Heaven of Separation's Regret is the highest.
I have been struck by all four hundred and four illnesses
But none is as intense as that of lovesickness.

And now he's off to the examinations

To pay court at the Phoenix Gate a thousand miles away,[11]
Where in a single test he will leap over the Dragon's Gate,[12]
And receive the silk whip—[13]
There's sure to be some seductive beauties there.

(MEIXIANG:) Sister, Student Wang is a perfect match of inner talent and outer beauty. (QIANNÜ *sings:*)

(*Que ta zhi*)
From what lies within his bosom:
How heroic and bold!
From the standpoint of character:
Even loftier and more pure.
What he'll do is leap out of the yellow dust
To trod up into the blue empyrean.
He can't be compared to those swallows and sparrows that twitter at
     dawn under thatch eaves—
He's a leviathan, a giant turtle that will tug the windy waves and roil
     up the sea.[14]

Meixiang! That student.... (*Sings:*)

(*Jisheng cao*)
He spreads out the white paper, the silk from Goosecreek cocoons,[15]

---

11. The imperial capital in Chang'an.

12. To pass the Advanced Scholar examination.

13. To receive a silk whip is to assent to marriage. Young men who passed the examinations were prime candidates for marriage alliances with the houses of prominent officials. Drama and fiction are populated by stories about candidates who forsake their wives back home to remarry into high station.

14. Vague allusion to "standing on the tortoise's head": to pass the Advanced Scholar examinations with the highest ranking.

15. Writing paper from the paper mulberry, and from the silk produced in Goosecreek, located in Sichuan, noted for its high quality; especially prized by painters and calligraphers.

Dips the down of jade white rabbits from Center Mountain—[16]

He's no less than Luo Binwang, writing his "Essay on Heaven" late at
night,[17]

Will not yield to Li Bai, writing out his draft "To Quell the
Barbarians" while dead-drunk,[18]

Is better than Sima Xiangru, receiving "The Edict Summoning
Worthies" while sick.[19]

He has diligently plied book and sword for ten years in Luoyang city,

And certainly he will jut above the whole court,

And cap the whole of Chang'an Circuit.

(MEIXIANG:) Sister, Student Wang is going off to the capital to take the examinations today. The Madam wants us to send Elder Brother off at the Willow
Snapping Pavilion.[20] (QIANNÜ:) Meixiang, let's go see Student Wang off at Willow Snapping Pavilion.

(Exit together.)

(MADAM *and* WANG WENJU *enter.* WANG WENJU:) Mother, today is an auspicious day, and I had better start on my trip to the capital for the examinations.
(MADAM:) Child, you are on the verge of leaving and I want to send you off
properly from Willow Snapping Pavilion. Servants, ask my daughter to come.
(QIANNÜ *enters, leading* MEIXIANG, *and acts out greeting them.* QIANNÜ:) Mother,
I'm here. (MADAM:) Child, at Willow Snapping Pavilion today, we send your
elder brother off. Take up a cup of wine. (QIANNÜ:) All right. (*Acts out picking
up a cup of wine, speaks:*) Brother, drink fully of this cup. (WANG WENJU *acts out
drinking, speaks:*) Mother, your child has one thing to ask you as I prepare to
leave. Once, my parents made a prenatal marriage pact with you, mother-in-
law. My mother then gave birth to me and you produced this young girl. Later
on my father and mother both passed away, and the years passed quickly without this marriage business being finalized. I have come especially to offer my
respects to you, mother-in-law, to inquire about this marriage. I can't figure out

---

16. The finest rabbit hair was produced in the area of Zhongshan, in modern Hebei.

17. Luo Binwang (640–84), one of the so-called Four Eminences of early Tang poetry, wrote
a military rescript to launch an eventually unsuccessful campaign to overthrow the Empress Wu
Zetian. Even the empress admired the force of this essay and lamented that her own court had
overlooked such a man.

18. Supposedly scribbled out by the great poet at imperial request, its rhetoric intimidated
the southern tribes into submitting to the Tang.

19. Sima Xiangru (179–117 BC) was taken into the Han court because of his great skill as a
writer of rhapsodies. He was then entrusted with all imperial rescripts.

20. See *Autumn over the Palaces of Han,* n. 43.

why you want us to address each other as elder brother and younger sister. I dare not presume on my own what it might mean. I hope you will shed some of your wise light on this so that I am not mistaken. (MADAM:) Child, you are right. Why have I had you two address each other as brother and sister? It's because for three generations we've never accepted a scholar without official position as son-in-law. You seem to have a belly stuffed with learning, but as of yet you have no success in the examinations. If you return from this trip to the capital with even the slightest official position, it won't be too late to complete this marriage then. (WANG WENJU:) Well, if this is the case, I had better take my leave of you, mother, and be on my way on this long trip. (QIANNÜ:) Brother, after you get a position, you'd better not accept a silk whip from anyone else! (WANG WENJU:) Madam, rest easy. I'll be back to complete this marriage as soon as I have gotten an official position. (QIANNÜ:) Oh, how hard it is to part! (*Sings:*)

> (*Cunli yagu*)
> Those "morning rains at Wei city" of his,
> That "lingering sunlight in Luoyang"....
> Although we do not sing "The Song of Yang Pass,"[21]
> Today we send away a "Youth of Chang'an."
> Oh, don't cast me aside without a second thought,
> Or reject me out of hand
> And so leave me lonely and deserted.
> Brother, it's just that Chu marshes are deep,
> The passes of Qin are far out of sight,
> Mount Hua is high.
> I sigh over human life—so many partings, so few reunions.

(WANG WENJU:) Miss, just put your heart at ease. If I obtain a post, then you will be a noble lady. (QIANNÜ *sings:*)

> (*Yuanhe ling*)
> In this cup wine and tears have been poured to mingle,
> And I speak to you now of what is in my heart:
> It is like this pliant branch of willow at the Pavilion of Distant
>   Journeys snapped off to give to you—
> Don't have a tip at the beginning but nothing at the end.
> From this night on I will vainly pass nights to be pitied,
> For, alas, the sorrows of parting will never end.

(WANG WENJU:) I too thought about you constantly in days gone by. (QIANNÜ:) This is such a cold and biting day. (*Sings:*)

---

21. See *Autumn over the Palaces of Han,* n. 38.

(*Shangma jiao*)
Outside the bamboo windows echo branch tips of kingfisher green,
Below the moss-covered steps is deep green grass.
Your study now suddenly desolate and forlorn
And the old garden quiet and deserted—
There no one goes.
How can I dispel a rancor
That burns hottest just at this juncture?

(*You simen*)
Better to hear the sound of purple simurgh-pipes die away beyond
    colored clouds.[22]
And tonight, where will you ship your orchid oars?
Let that slip of a sail never be blocked from my view,
Nor the west wind be so cruel.
Snow-like roll the billowing waves, the shadow of the bank grows tall;
For a thousand miles, water and clouds are tossed a-scudding.

(*Sheng hulu*)
And you, don't be a swan high in the void worrying over his
    feathers;[23]
The maxim says, "Good things cannot stay as they are forever."[24]
Your body departs, but let your heart never part from me;
I tell you, sir, in the lowest whisper. . . .
"Meixiang has just reported,
That she fears mother is fretting."

(MADAM:) Meixiang, look after the cart. Tell little sister to go back. (MEIXIANG:)
Sister, get on the cart. (WANG WENJU:) Missy, go on back, I had better start my
trip. (QIANNÜ *sings:*)

---

22. I.e., "How much better to escape this world and live forever as true lovers." From an
ancient myth about two lovers, Xiao Shi and Nongyu. Xiao Shi was a "master of the pipes," able
to summon peacocks and cranes to the courtyard with his music. One of the daughters of Duke
Mu of Qin, Nongyu, fell in love with him, and he took her as a wife. He taught her birdcalls, and
after several years she could imitate the cries of the phoenix. She drew these auspicious birds
there in flocks, and Xiao built a dais for the birds where the couple also lived. After a period of
time, Xiao Shi and Nongyu flew off through the clouds with the phoenixes. Here, of course, the
line means that such a perfect marriage as that of these two mythic figures is denied our young
lovers.

23. I.e., "don't fear flying high to success, for nothing can touch you."

24. A cliché, originally based on a couplet in Bai Juyi's poem, "The Song of Jianjian" (*Jianjian
yin*): "Things of this world cannot stay as they are forever: / Colored clouds disperse too easily;
tiles that are glazed are easily smashed."

(*Houting hua*)
Here, the cart with its halcyon-green curtains: I hold back.
There, the golden stirrup: he mounts languidly.
My tears soak sleeves of perfumed silk;
His whip droops its lapis lazuli tip.
He is pained and spiritless,
Choked with rancor,
"The west wind, the old road."
Consider, this anxious man filled with passion—
This man is gone.
"And if bright heaven has any feelings—
Then heaven, too, grows weary."
The sounds of my heavy, full sighs
Cannot be controlled,
But are aided by that whirling, swirling—stirring traveler's emotion—
Wind that crazily sweeps the earth,
And those spattering, pitter-patter—streaking my makeup—
Powdered tears I fling away,
Sprinkling, fine and misty—moistening the fragrant dust—
Evening rain flies about.

(*Liuye'er*)
See it, misty and drizzling, becloud the kiosks and towers along the
    riverbanks.
I—creaking and grinding, my cart slowly passes the bridge over the
    stream,
He—clip, clop, his horse's hooves wearily set out on the road to the
    Imperial realm.
I—with every single step I become more broken-hearted,
He—there he finds it hard too,
He—each single stage of the journey is through faraway waters and
    distant hills.

(WANG WENJU:) Missy, rest easy. After I've attained office, I'll come back to
claim you. Please, get in your cart. (QIANNÜ *sings:*)

(*Zhuansha*)
From now on I need only inscribe my vexation, write it out on a
    banana leaf;[25]

---

25. The monk and calligrapher Huaisu planted thousands of banana trees near his monastery so that he could practice calligraphy by writing on them when they matured. He had used

No need to divine my dreams, or cast the milfoil stalks.
I have no heart to surround myself with pearls, encircle myself with
    green jade.
This single speck of my true-passion's soul wanders aimlessly,
And as he goes, will not leave him, but abides with him always.
If I had my way, I'd follow him until he, a Sima Xiangru, inscribes his
    name on the bridge.[26]
Oh, when will these autumn moons and spring flowers ever end?
Even if this Chalcedony Beauty has been tossed aside. . . .
If we wait expectantly for Zigao's return,
We will vainly forsake this union of phoenix and simurgh beneath
    the blue peach.[27]

(*Exits with* MEIXIANG.)

(WANG WENJU *speaks:*) Your son now takes leave of you, mother. I must make this long journey. Servants, bring my horse! Today I am off to make my name!

(*Exits.*)

(MADAM *speaks:*) Scholar Wang is gone. It won't be too late to conclude this marriage after he has gotten a position and returned home. In terms of scholar Wang's learning, he is certainly anyone's match. He's certain to get a position on this trip.

Ten years and some have passed since that prenatal wedding pact:
    A fine match as youths, a marriage vow we will enact.
    A unicorn with proud horn, he will hold a high official's place,
And a husband ennobled and a wife of honor can offer thanks for imperial
        grace.

---

up all of the mature leaves after a period of years, then began to write on the young leaves while they were still on the tree. He wrote and wrote and wrote, oblivious to the burning sun in summer or the biting cold in winter. The line may be understood, "I will constantly write out my love and frustration, over and over."

26. See *Butterfly Dream*, n. 58.

27. A certain Wang Zigao fell in love with an immortal, Zhou Qiongji ("Chalcedony Beauty of the Zhou"); they roamed together for a hundred days in Lotus City (*Furong cheng*), before being forced to part. The "union of phoenix and simurgh" refers to a lovers' tryst. Because Qiannü's mother demanded that Wang Wenju pass the examinations before granting Qiannü in marriage, the lovers have been split apart after their short time together. So now, instead of enjoying the pleasures of marriage, they must pine away for each other.

[Act 2]

(MADAM *rushes on flustered,* [*speaks*]:) "Before happiness is ended, vexation appears again." Ever since Qiannü came back from saying her goodbyes to Scholar Wang at the Willow Snapping Pavilion, she's been sick. Once down, she hasn't gotten up again. I asked a doctor to come and examine her, but she hasn't recovered and is in extremely critical condition. What can be done now? Well, just in case my child wants some hot water to drink, I'll go and check on her in her bedchamber.

(*Exits.*)

(WANG WENJU *enters,* [*speaks*]:) I am Wang Wenju, and ever since I parted from missy at Willow Snapping Pavilion, I've been grieving and upset. I've moored my boat to the riverbank now and I'll lay my zither here across my knees and play a tune to ease my depression. (*Acts out strumming zither.* QIANNÜ, *costumed differently as a separated soul, enters,* [*speaks*:]) I am Qiannü, and I've been pining so much for student Wang since we parted that I had to follow him. So, I disobeyed my mother and have chased him down. Student Wang, all you thought about was leaving, could you even consider how I was to pass my days? (GHOST FEMALE *sings:*)

([YUEDIAO MODE:] *Dou anchun*)
The man has left Yang Terrace;
Clouds have returned to the gorges of Chu.[28]
He may have anchored his boat along the Yangzi,
But how long before he passes on horseback by my gate?
Secretly and stealthily, so stealthily and secretly,
Desolate and chill, cold and lonely,
Here I tread along riverbank's sand,
Walking in moon's radiance.
I scrutinize these myriad waters and thousand mountains—
All pass by in the blink of an eye.

(*Zihua'er xu*)
Think on the vexations of parting in Qiannü's heart—
Catching up to Student Wang's orchid boat beyond the willows
Is like searching for Zhang Qian's raft floating beyond the heavens.[29]
Sweating, damp and drenched, rose quartz beads sparkle on my
     face;

---

28. See *Autumn over the Palaces of Han*, n. 22.
29. See *Autumn over the Palaces of Han*, n. 11.

Tangled, tossed, and tousled, my cloudy locks pile up black on raven's
　　black.
I've come so far my muscles are tired and worn out.
Don't you "Overnight at the wine sellers at Qinhuai?"[30]
I go down to the west, toward the broken bridge.
Rattling, rustling, and soughing—wild rice and rushes in the autumn
　　waters;
Chilling, cold and clear—reed flowers in the bright moonlight.

([*Speaks:*]) It's taken me forever to reach the banks of the Yangzi. I hear people
chattering and yelling. Let me take a look! (*Sings:*)

(*Xiaotao hong*)
Suddenly I hear the clamor and confusion of horses' snorts and
　　human speech.
I had just cocked my ear and just managed to listen,
When it scared me so much my heart went pitter-patter—it was that
　　alarming.
But it turned out only to be the clickety-clickety crack of clacking
　　clappers
For catching fish and shrimp.[31]
Here I follow the western wind, stealthily, silently listen until it's
　　gone.
Taking advantage of these heavy, weighing flowerets of dew,
I stand under this clear, bright moon,[32]
And scare the cold geese so that, squawking and honking, they rise
　　from the level sand.

(*Tiaoxiao ling*)
I tiptoe toward the sandy dike,
The sedge, slippery with frost,
Brushes the kingfisher green gauze of my silk skirt;

---

30. From a famous poem by the Tang writer Du Mu:

Mist covers cold waters, the moon covers the sand.
Mooring at night by the Qinhuai, near to wineshops—
Merchant girls do not understand the vexations of losing the state.
Across the river, they still sing "Flowers in the Rear Courtyard."

I.e., don't dally with singing girls in winehouses.
　　31. Boards beaten against the gunwales of the boat to drive the fish toward the nets and weirs.
　　32. As a ghost, she is weightless, and is weighed down by drops of dew. Student Wang never
seems to figure out she doesn't weigh anything.

The green moss soaks my "wave-crossing" stockings.
I look at evening's advent along the Yangzi—worth painting.
Enjoy this pot of ice[33] that overflows to fill heaven above and below
In a sky as severe as the autumn void—blue jade without flaw.

(*Tusi'er*)
You look at the distant inlet, the lone fulvous duck, sunset's red
     glow:
"Withered vine, old tree, sunset crows."[34]
I listen to one sound of the long flute, from who knows where:
"Ai-nai," the sound of fisherman's songs,
"Ee-ya," a scull creaks and groans.

([*Speaks*:]) That sound of the zither over there, on the boat . . . I'll bet it's Student Wang. Let me take a look! (*Sings*:)

(*Sheng Yaowang*)
I approach the smartweed hollow,
And gaze afar at the pepperwort flowers:
There are broken rushes, drooping willows, and old reeds.
I approach the water bog,
Draw next to the short raft,
Where I see "mist covering the cold waters, moonlight covering the
     sand"
And two or three thatch houses.

(WANG WENJU:) It is so late, yet I hear a girl's voice from the bank. It sounds just like my own Qiannü talking. Let me ask! (*Acts out asking*:) Isn't that Qiannü there? What are you doing here now? (GHOST FEMALE *acts out greeting him*, *speaks*:) Student Wang. I've disobeyed my mother and caught up with you here. Let's go to the capital together. (WANG WENJU:) How did you get to this place? (GHOST FEMALE *sings*:)

---

33. The moon.

34. Portions of this free lyric (*sanqu*) "Autumn Ponderings" attributed to Ma Zhiyuan have been quoted throughout the play. The poem is justly celebrated as an austere description of autumn and hardship:

Withered vine, old tree, sunset crows,
Little bridge, flowing water, human habitation,
Old road, west wind, skinny nag—
The evening sun falls west,
A broken-hearted man is at heaven's edge.

(*Malang'er*)
You're a comforting Bo Ya![35]
I have turned into your wife, left with no way out,
And you ask me why I have left my embroidered couch?
Why, to follow you to the edge of heaven!

(WANG WENJU:) Missy, I meant, "Did you come by horse or by cart?" (GHOST FEMALE *sings:*)

(*Reprise*)
I nearly
Wore myself out
Walking.
When you left on your distant journey to the capital,
This ill-fated lass was worried on account of you,
And knew I'd never get you out of my mind.

(*Luosi niang*)
From the time you discarded me
Until I had another chance to see you,
If I didn't waste away to nothing,
Then for sure love's longing would strike me.

(WANG WENJU:) What will we do if Madam finds out? (GHOST FEMALE *sings:*)

Well, if she catches up to us, what of it?
The proverb says, "Those who fear never act."

(WANG WENJU *acts out being angry, speaks:*) The ancients said, "If properly engaged, then she becomes a wife; if she elopes, then she becomes a concubine." The old lady assented to the marriage and was waiting until I had attained office and returned so she could accomplish the good union of our two surnames. Wouldn't that be proper both in name and deed? Now you have selfishly run to me here and in doing so have despoiled custom. What was the meaning of this? (GHOST FEMALE *sings:*)

(*Xueli mei*)
Student Wang, you can make faces and get angrier and angrier,

---

35. Bo Ya was a skilled zither player of the Spring and Autumn period. He was a good friend with Zhong Ziqi, who not only appreciated Bo's zither playing, but also could deduce his mental state from his playing. After Ziqi died, Bo Ya smashed his zither. A parable of perfect understanding between friends or lovers; the origin of the phrase "*zhiyin*"—"one who understands my music," i.e., a perfect match.

But I'll stare you right in the eye—I'm not going back.
I have acted out of authentic feeling—this is not to frighten you—
I've already settled my willful mind and rampant feelings.

(WANG WENJU:) Go on back, missy. (GHOST FEMALE *sings:*)

> (*Zihua'er xu*)
> You—because you were "sent off as a traveler on the wind, unfurled
>   and opened the slatted sails"—[36]
> Could only commit your depressed thoughts and troubled heart to
>   the zither,
> While I, with tears to match my sorrow, relied upon my pipa.
> Had I the heart to let the azure mists lightly encage the vermilion
>   phoenixes[37]
> Or let my kohl-dabbed eyebrows be softly swept up like paired
>   ravens?
> I would rather be like falling willow floss or flying flowers!
> No one will ask again why going far away is better than staying home.
> There's nothing else to say—
> Let the autumn wind drive our hundred-foot-high sail,
> And let spring's affairs be exhausted in a whole tree of rouged
>   blossoms.[38]

([*Speaks:*]) Scholar Wang, I caught up with you for only one reason, I just
wanted to keep you from doing one thing . . . (WANG WENJU:) What did you
want to keep me from doing? (GHOST FEMALE *sings:*)

> (*Dongyuan le*)
> If, when you have quit the imperial feast in the Chalcedony Forest,[39]
> And matchmakers stop your horse
> To raise high before your eyes portraits of beauties, bice and vermil-
>   ion set against a colored background,
> And vaunt them for being brought up in the houses of kings, nobles,
>   and Prime Ministers—
> Then you, in love with the extravagance and glory,
> Would dare hold your wedding feast within their gates!

---

36. I.e., departed happily to a new destination.

37. Vermilion phoenixes: eyes that tilt upward.

38. I.e., "set forth on your journey to success and let my beauty fade while I am with you"; collapsing her desire to follow like scattered flowers of spring follow the wind with the conceits about makeup.

39. Where the Song emperors feted new graduates of the Advanced Scholar examinations.

(WANG WENJU:) If I am successful in the examinations on this trip, I will not forget you! (GHOST FEMALE:) If you succeed in the examinations . . . (*Sings:*)

(*Mianda xu*)
You will be a "fine son-in-law" within noble gates,
Full of yourself and boastful in equal measure.
When in the houses of ministers you can be weighed down by stacks
    of glory's brocade and the embroidery of splendor,
How could you even consider "flying into an ordinary house of the
    common lot?"
When that time comes, you'll be like a fish that has leapt the
    Dragon's Gate to scatter to the corner of the seas,
You'll drink imperial wine,
Stick palace flowers in your hat,
And then, you'll stand on the tortoise's head,
Stand on the tortoise's head,
And rise to the highest class.

(WANG WENJU:) And what if I don't pass? What then? (GHOST FEMALE:) If you don't pass, then, dressed in thorn hairpins and cotton skirts, I still want to share your life, bitter or sweet. (*Sings:*)

(*Zhuolusu*)
If you are going to be like Jia Yi, in straits in Changsha,[40]
Then I will be like Meng Guang, and display my worthy virtue.[41]
Don't think I'll change my mind even a speck,
Or that I'll waffle in the slightest.
I want to "raise the tray even with my eyebrows" as I approach your
    study couch,
Live a life of coarse food, of meagerness and want,
Even though it means wearing thorn hairpins and hempen clothes.

(WANG WENJU:) Missy, since you are truly sincere, then why not go on to the capital with me? (GHOST FEMALE:) If you, scholar, are willing to take me with you, then . . . (*Sings:*)

(*Reprise*)
Summon those boatmen,

---

40. Jia Yi (201–169 BC) was a promising scholar-bureaucrat of the Han court who was slandered by jealous court officials. He was exiled to Changsha, where he was to serve as tutor to the king of Changsha. He became despondent and soon died. He later becomes a common symbol of wise talent left unused.

41. See *Injustice to Dou E*, n. 20.

Lest my family apprehend me.
I see only distant trees, cold crows,
Grass on the banks, the sand of spits.
What fill my eyes are yellow flowers,
And several strands of sunset's last.
Hurry! First raise the cloudy sail on high,
And directly under the moon's light—
Even if the east wind wildly blows—
Don't delay in the slightest, but hurry and get underway!

(WANG WENJU:) Miss, you go together with me to the capital today, there to take the examinations. If I get a post, you'll be the Lady of the District. (GHOST FEMALE *sings*:)

(*Shouwei*)
If you are indeed going to travel the road to Chang'an,
Then I will drive the chariot that lets us flee the Commandery of Shu.
I only hope that you, "a traveler in the garden of letters," will exert
    yourself at the proper time.
Then I, this wine seller from Linqiong, Zhuo Wenjun,
Desire only to serve you, this bridge-inscriber of the Brocade
    Washing River, Sima of the Han.[42]

(*Exit together.*)

[Act 3]

(WANG WENJU *costumed as official, enters*:) I am the minor official Wang Wenju. I reached the capital and there turned over my writings for examination. Before the sun even had time to move, I directly answered with myriad words. The Sage was greatly delighted and awarded me Top Graduate among those who

---

42. This aria makes use of the popular legend of Sima Xiangru and Zhuo Wenjun, who provide the prototype for scholar and beauty tales. Sima, the son of a rich family, fails in his first attempt to make a career and returns home to find the family estate in ruins. The magistrate of Linqiong, who treats him with utmost courtesy, houses him. Sima meets a certain Zhuo Wangsun, and when invited by the latter to a party, he plays the zither at his host's command. Zhuo's young widowed daughter, Wenjun, overhears the music, espies the young scholar, and falls in love with him. Sima Xiangru bribes an attendant to take her a note and they elope that night. Her father cuts her off financially, and the young couple is forced to eke out a living by running a wineshop in Linqiong. The father, embarrassed, funds the couple. In the meantime, Sima Xiangru's fame spreads until the emperor enlists his services at court. When he had left Chengdu departing for Chang'an, Sima wrote on a bridge, "If I am not riding a four-horse, red chariot, I will not pass through you!" This became later a common vow of examination-bound scholars.

passed. My wife followed me here, and now I am preparing a letter for home, telling them all is well. I will dispatch someone to report all to my mother-in-law. Servants, bring my brush and ink stone. (*Acts out writing letter, speaks:*) There, that's finished. Let me read it out loud once.

> Your son-in-law, Wang Wenju, now lodging in the capital, pays his respects before his mother-in-law. From the time I arrived at the imperial city, I placed as Top Graduate in my first try. I am now waiting until I am appointed as an official after which my young wife and I will return home together. We hope ten thousand times over for the shining bestowal of your compassion. When we return we shall kowtow in appreciation.

Now it is finished. Servants, call Zhang Qian out for me. (*Act out summoning.* COMIC, *dressed as* ZHANG QIAN, *enters:*)

> I am a servant, and the best one at that:
> I take care of all deputations snicker-snack.
> Day one I'll travel a road a hundred miles long,
> And on day two stay stretched out, asleep on the kang.[43]

I am Zhang Qian, in the employ of Wang, the Top Graduate. His Excellency has called me and I'd better go. (*Act out greeting.*) Your Excellency, why have you summoned me? (WANG WENJU:) Zhang Qian, take this letter home straight to Hengzhou, telling them all is well. Ask for the Zhang household and turn it over to them. When you see the lady of the house, tell her I've gotten an official position. Take care on your journey. (ZHANG QIANG *accepts letter, speaks:*) I understand. I'll take this letter directly to Hengzhou.

(*Exits.*)

(WANG WENJU:) Zhang Qian is gone now. I don't have anything else to do, so I'll go back for the while to the rear chambers.

(*Exits.*)

✳✳

(MADAM *enters:*) I never thought that my daughter, Qiannü, would be sick abed after parting from Student Wang. Sometimes she chats and sometimes laughs. I just don't know what these are symptoms of. I haven't seen her for these past two days, and I'd better go and look in on her myself.

(*Exits.*)

---

43. A brick structure built around a stove and on top of which blankets and sleeping mats were laid.

(QIANNÜ, *clutching herself in sickness, enters, supported by* MEIXIANG. QIANNÜ *speaks:*) After Scholar Wang left, I've been bedridden. I have but to close my eyes and I am with Student Wang. Ah! I'm being ruined by this lovesickness. (*Sings:*)

> ([ZHONGLÜ MODE:] *Fendie'er*)
> From the time we held hands, approached the fork in the road,
> I've been left only with this bout of haggardness.
> I think parting is the bitterest event in human life.
> I lack all energy and spirit when I speak,
> Don't know head from tail when I sleep,
> Know not the taste of meals—
> Such "forsaking sleep and forgetting to eat" like this
> Wears me down so much I grow thinner and thinner every day.

> (*Zui chunfeng*)
> In vain I swallow this dizzying drug, but it cures me not.[44]
> I wish I knew when I could rise from this filthy illness.
> To have it over, I must simply wait until I see him again
> To purge these symptoms caused by him, by him.
> Now floating, as if I were caught in a whirlwind,
> Now concentrating to control this husk of a body,
> Now faint and dizzy, I can't tell heaven from earth.

My eyes now see student Wang right before me, but it turns out all along it was only Meixiang. Meixiang, what season is it now? (MEIXIANG:) Now spring is near to its end, the green is dark, the red rare. Nearly the fourth month . . . (QIANNÜ *sings:*)

> (*Ying xianke*)
> As days grow longer, my sorrow stretches out,
> The red grows rare, letters even rarer.
>   Oh, Student Wang, you are so cruel!
> Spring returns so quickly, but the person has yet to return.

(MEIXIANG:) Sister, brother-in-law hasn't even been gone a year. How can you pine for him so? (QIANNÜ:)

> I would have said that we had been parted for ten years,
> I would have said that we are separated by thousands of miles.

---

44. Part of ancient medical lore was that a person should be dosed with a drug that makes one dizzy; afterward their illness would be cured along with the dissipation of dizziness.

To count the days until his return
I have notched all of the malachite stems in the bamboo garden.

(*Hongxiuxie*)
When he left: willows in westerly winds on an autumn day;
And now we've passed: pear blossoms in evening rains on Cold
    Feast.[45]

(MEIXIANG:) Sister, why not cast your fortune? (QIANNÜ:)

Well, that tortoise will divine no sure thing; it's worthless to
    consult,
The happy spider cannot be relied on,
The divine magpie is dishonest,
And there's nothing to rejoice over in the lamp's popping.[46]

(MADAM *enters:*) Here I am at my child's room. Meixiang, is your sister better? (QIANNÜ:) Who is it? (MEIXIANG:) Mother has come to look after you. (QIANNÜ:) Only Student Wang has been within the daily ambit of my eyes— why haven't I seen you, mother? (MADAM *acts out greeting her, speaks:*) Child, how is your illness?

(*Putian le*)
Ghostly lovesickness is of most concern,
Like being lost in a spring sleep from drinking too much,
Or poplar floss on the paddy paths swirling over sunlit snow.
Swallow chicks west of the tower that ride on the eastern wind
Toss aside those of us still young
And spurn the brightest days of spring.
First come separation's sorrows and those increased by plaguing
    thoughts,
How could I bear the reckless scattering of this spring scene?
My sorrowing heart—startled by a single bird's cry;
My sad life—coming to an end together with all spring's affairs,
So my fragrant soul chases after a single flower petal, flying away.

---

45. Cold Feast was held two or three days before the Clear and Bright, a day when the graves and tombs of ancestors were swept and offerings were made to them. Cold Feast, originally to celebrate the death of a hermit (Jie Zhitui) who burned to death rather than come down from his mountain retreat, was a period of three days when stove fires were forbidden, hence the name. Clear and Bright (*Qingming*) was held 105 days after the winter solstice.

46. All originally auguries of good fortune. The happy spider is the daddy longlegs, whose name (*xizi*) is homophonous with the term "happiness." The magpie is a portent of good fortune and happiness and the popping lamp is a sign that one's lover will visit.

(QIANNÜ *acts out fainting.* MADAM *speaks:*) Child, hang on! Hang on! (QIANNÜ *acts out reviving, sings:*)

> (*Shiliu hua*)
> I was already chronically ill,
> And now a new sickness is added on,
> Producing dizziness and disorientation.
> Surely the day of my death is pushing ever closer.
> This is an illness, buried deep within, unreachable by acupuncture or
>   moxibustion.

(MADAM:) I'll get a good doctor to cure you. (QIANNÜ:)

> If only *he* would come,
> That would be better than summoning Bianque, the Physician of
>   Lu.[47]

(MADAM:) I'll send someone right away to get student Wang. (QIANNÜ:)

> Better to have then made him "son-in-law of the eastern bed" than to
>   ask him to come now—[48]
> Now it is a case of too little, too late.

(MADAM:) Well, after Student Wang left, he didn't even send a single letter. (QIANNÜ:)

> He sent no news reporting a happy event,
> And why?
> I already know the two possible reasons:
>
> (*Dou anchun*)
> He attained an official post, and has married someone new,
> Or he's failed so badly he is ashamed to come back home.

(MADAM:) Child, don't dwell on it. You have to rest yourself. (QIANNÜ:)

> A thousand deaths, a thousand bad endings,
> And I'm so worn down that I am half human, half ghost.

---

47. A famous healer of the Warring States period, held up as the exemplar of physicians.

48. The "son-in-law of the eastern bed" is the famous calligrapher, Wang Xizhi. When Chi Jian sent an emissary to Wang Xizhi's father's house to search out a suitable mate for his daughter, the emissary was told to look through the eastern wing, where all of the sons lived. All of the sons vaunted their looks and talents except for Xizhi, who lay bare-bellied on the eastern bed. He was subsequently chosen. Here, more than a simple allusion, it ties Student Wang into a lineage of fine scholars (all with the same surname) and criticizes the mother, as well, for failing to recognize a person of high virtue and talent.

Why are my withered innards, shriveled up by longing, never harmed
   by hunger?
Because bitterness stuffs my whole belly!

(MADAM:) Child, drink some soup. (QIANNÜ:)

Mother, if you had consented to see this marriage through,
It would be better than eating dragon liver and phoenix marrow![49]

(QIANNÜ:) I'm getting tired and dizzy, I want to sleep awhile. (MADAM:) Meixiang, don't make any noise. Let her rest. I'm going to go back for a bit. (MADAM
and MEIXIANG *exit.* QIANNÜ *acts out sleeping.* WANG WENJU *enters in her dream
and acts out greeting* QIANNÜ. WANG WENJU *speaks:*) Missy, I've come to see you.
(QIANNÜ:) Student Wang, where have you come from? (WANG WENJU:) Missy,
I've attained a position. (QIANNÜ *sings:*)

(*Shang xiaolou*)
I just said you spurned favor and turned your back on virtue,
And so it turns out that you had obtained a post and passed the
   examinations.
You went directly to kowtow at the cinnabar steps,[50]
Won away the uniform of the court[51]
To change for your plain clothes.
Now I look closely at your face—
Compared to past days, when we parted,
You've gotten "a thousand rods more of Five Tumuli bravado."[52]

(WANG WENJU:) I'm leaving, missy. (QIANNÜ *acts out waking up, speaks:*) I clearly
saw Student Wang, and he said he had attained a post. But when I awoke, it
was simply another "Dream of the Southern Branch."[53] (*Sings:*)

---

49. I.e., especially efficacious wonder drugs made from miraculous ingredients.

50. I.e, saw the emperor.

51. I.e., official gowns prescribed by sumptuary law for each official rank.

52. Many rich and powerful families lived near the five tumuli of the Han emperors on the
outskirts of Chang'an. For the Yuan this was simply a metaphor for important and powerful
young dandies; a polite way of saying "you look like you've made it."

53. This was, first, a famous story by the Tang writer Li Gongzuo, and then a series of plays
about a person who fell asleep and dreamt that he went to a land called Acaciapeace. He married
the princess of the state, and was made Magistrate of Nanke (literally, Southern Branch), where
he enjoyed wealth and nobility. Later, he was defeated in a battle, his wife died, and he came
under the king's suspicion. Dispirited, he returned to his own home, and then awoke from his
dream, to find that Nanke District and the state of Acaciapeace were nothing more than anthills
in the roots of an acacia tree—here, of course, meant to signal that human life is nothing more
than a dream, or that a lifetime can be lived in the space of a dream.

(Reprise)
For no reason have I been puzzled for so long,
Suddenly this whole thing became clear to me:
I let my love-longing leak out,
And eagerly asked him what went on, and told him the truth,
So he quickly left.
And I bounced up,
But it was already too late to find him, to search him out—
Nothing appears now but this chillingly cold and used-up sun
     halfway up the staff.

(MEIXIANG *enters:*) Sister, what frightened you? (QIANNÜ:) I just saw student
Wang in a dream; he said he had obtained a post. (*Sings:*)

(Shi'er lou)
It turned out to all have been in one dream of the Southern Branch,
Where he knew two or three fellow scholars.
He sought instruction in the Four Categories,[54] practiced the
     important rituals of the Five Constants,[55]
Mastered the Six Arts[56] and studied until he could match the
     "Seven-pace" poetry.[57]
Relying on eight-rhyme rhapsodies and a grand pen of virile talent,
He got to follow the thunder and wind of ninefold heaven.[58]

(Yaomin ge)
I imagine that after ten years he reached the phoenix pond,[59]
Where the nine Prime Ministers and eight Grand Councilors urged
     upon him the golden cup.
To match his seven-syllable poetry,

---

54. The four areas of Confucian learning: moral action, correct language, administrative affairs, and study of the civilizing arts.

55. Those obtaining between lord-minister, father-son, elder brother–younger brother, husband-wife, and friend-friend; the basis of all human relations.

56. Rituals, music, archery, charioteering, calligraphy, and mathematics.

57. A general term for skill in poetic composition. It stems from a story of Cao Zhi and his brother, Cao Pi, who was the reigning monarch in the kingdom of Wei. Cao Zhi was ordered to come to the court and compose a poem in the length of time it took to take seven paces; if he failed, he would be executed. Cao Zhi responded with an appropriate poem that shamed his elder brother.

58. I.e., realized his ambition to succeed.

59. The "phoenix pond" was a poetic term for the Central Secretariat. "Ten years" is the time traditionally associated with a poor scholar's rise to fame.

There are few in the realm's six directions,
His five blessings are complete.[60]
Who knows where he will serve within the four sacred realms?
He has stirred up the spring thunder of the third month,[61]
His happiness first announced before the parental pair,[62]
All this because of this one list of candidates!

Meixiang, keep watch at the door and tell me if anyone comes. (MEIXIANG:) I understand. (ZHANG QIAN *enters:*) I am Zhang Qian. I am bearing the words of my master, His Excellency Wang, who sent me here to Hengzhou to deliver a letter home. I asked where Zhang Gongbi's house was, and people said it was right here. (*Acts out greeting* MEIXIANG:) Sister, greetings! (MEIXIANG:) And just who are you? (ZHANG QIAN:) Could this be the house of His Excellency, Zhang? (MEIXIANG:) This is it right here. And why are you asking? (ZHANG QIAN:) I have just come from the capital. My master, Wang, has just gotten an official post. He sent me here to bring a letter to give to Madam and the young mistress of the house. (MEIXIANG:) You stay here. I'll go tell missy. (MEIXIANG *sees* QIANNÜ, *speaks:*) Sister, Scholar Wang has gotten an official post. He sent someone here with a letter. He's waiting outside. (QIANNÜ:) Tell him to come in. (MEIXIANG *sees* ZHANG QIAN, *speaks:*) Hey, letter carrier, come here and see missy. (ZHANG QIAN *acts out greeting* QIANNÜ, *speaks:*) A fine thing this. I am from the capital. His Excellency, Wang, sent me here with a letter for the young mistress. (QIANNÜ:) Meixiang, bring the letter here and let me see it. (MEIXIANG:) Hey, fellow, give me the letter. (ZHANG QIAN *acts out turning over the letter.* QIANNÜ *acting out reciting the letter, speaks:*)

> Your son-in-law, Wang Wenju, now lodging in the capital, pays his respects before his mother-in-law. From the time I arrived at the imperial city, I placed as Top Graduate in my first try. I am now waiting until I am appointed as an official, after which my young wife and I will return home together. We hope ten thousand times over for the shining bestowal of your compassion. When we return we shall kowtow in appreciation.

So, he had a wife all the time! This really makes me angry! (*Acts out falling down from being so angry.* MEIXIANG *acts out rescuing her, speaks:*) Sister, come to. (QIANNÜ *acts out coming to.* MEIXIANG *speaks:*) It was all because of this letter

---

60. The five blessings are: to live out one's normal span, good fortune, nobility, peace and security, and many sons and grandsons.

61. A reference to the list of successful candidates; the announcement was said to rumble like spring thunder—incipient power on the horizon.

62. Here, at the family altar.

carrier! (*Acts out beating* ZHANG QIAN. QIANNÜ:) Oh, Student Wang, I'll die from hurt over you. (*Sings:*)

(*Shaopian*)
Let me go over everything right from the start—
"A hundred years of feeling"[63] amounts to no more than one long
    sigh.
In the beginning, he never mentioned any of the rituals of engage-
    ment or marriage . . .
Was it for fear that "youths will ignore the Odes and Documents?"[64]
His study beside the bamboo in the rear garden
Turned into a handy Yang Terrace
Where the clouds and rains of Wu Mountain were right at hand.[65]
But, alas, morning after morning, day after day, he was idling away
    his time.
Yet I relied on
The pure and extraordinary words of his letter,
And wrongly deemed Wu Mountain a Husband-longing Rock.[66]
I'll take these little love poems and make of them a *Collection of a*
    Broken Heart.[67]
The rain over the Xiang has just begun to darken,
Yet the hoary moon shines on the window,
For sure, "moving clouds fly all too easily away."

(*Shua hai'er*)
My mother grasped the icy silk and with scissors snipped mandarin
    ducks apart,[68]
And unable to bear our parting, I accompanied him for miles beyond
    Yang Gate.[69]
At that time I had a mind to see your journeying sail off,
I had no plans to detain your carved saddle.
But, alas, the sorrow of parting trailed after the affairs of my heart,

---

63. The hundred years of intimacy and love between a married couple who grow old together.
64. I.e., out of concern for the examinations.
65. See *Autumn over the Palaces of Han*, n. 22.
66. See *Injustice to Dou E*, n. 24.
67. The title of the Song-dynasty poetess Zhu Shuzhen's collected verses.
68. Birds thought to mate for life. The line actually reads, "she has 'scissored' them into a single male and single female duck." That is, her mother cut a pair of ducks embroidered on silk into two segments.
69. See *Autumn over the Palaces of Han*, n. 38.

Until sorrow interwove a thousand skeins of weeping willow at the
old way station,
And tears filled to overflowing a single parting cup in the setting sun.
From then on, in periods of unmatched asterisms[70] and on cold,
desolate days,
Recalling how mountain passes into my hometown were blocked by
sorrowful clouds,
I was tormented by this ghostly illness that kept me to pillow and
bed.

(*Sisha*)
This went on for a whole spring; there was no news via carp or
goose,[71]
Just now came the one sheet of a rhymed letter for which I had
hoped.
I would have guessed that his spring heart would fill the letter,
leaving it sopping with ink,
But it turned out to be only a writ of divorce in an envelope.
It makes me so angry that painful tears mixed with blood flow
uncontrollably,
And it seems the eastern wind will blow my very soul away, never to
return.
Scholars! Each poor as hell, then suddenly rich; each full of an illness
that can't be cured![72]

(*Sansha*)
This scholar ought to visit the Sangha Hall for three vegetarian
meals,[73]

---

70. See *Rain on the Wutong Tree*, n. 61.

71. A clichéd way of saying "letters," which were imagined to have been sent tied to the legs
of geese or put inside the stomach of carp.

72. I.e., they can never be satisfied.

73. Although this refers in historical fact to a scholar from the Tang, Wang Bo, popular
legend, as exemplified in Wang Shifu's drama, *The Story of the Dilapidated Kiln* (*Poyao ji*), has
adapted it into the popular legend about Lü Mengzheng's spectacular rise to fame and fortune.
The historical Lü Mengzheng (946–1011) was descended from a family of officials—both his
grandfather and father had held high office—and he was himself a man of high position, having
passed the metropolitan examinations as "head-of-the-list" in 977. Despite the factual career of
Lü Mengzheng, he was transformed in popular lore into the archetype of the poor student who
solely on account of his literary talent and perseverance eventually succeeds in the examinations.
The play is set in Luoyang, where Liu Yue'e, the daughter of a rich squire, is to select a husband
by throwing an embroidered ball from a bunted loft into the crowd below. When Liu Yue'e
hits Lü Mengzheng and refuses to repudiate her choice, her father throws her out of the house,

And ought to clean out a night's ashes from a cold stove;[74]
He ought to be made to filch his lamplight by boring through the
    neighbor's wall,[75]
Or made to stand out in the rain until it covers the wheat in the
    courtyard,[76]
Or have *his* "Stele on Sacrificing for Good Fortune" broken by
    midnight thunder.[77]
I'm not just idly venting my anger—
Even if I die, I'll die without resentment;
Should I desire to regret it, how can I?

(*Ersha*)
Qiannü—wrapped up in sickness, just hoping that heaven will take
    pity,
Meixiang—the affairs of my heart are known intimately only by
    you.
I looked toward his coming to completely reveal my true sincere
    feelings.
For half a year I've been content with my lot, mired in illness;
For days on end I've had no heart to sketch my kohl-dark eyebrows.

---

forcing the new couple to live in a dilapidated kiln outside of town. Lü Mengzheng figures out a way to get a free meal every day by joining the noontime assembly of monks at Luoyang's White Horse Monastery, but the abbot of the monastery, apparently with the intention of shaming the young man for his freeloading, has the mealtime bell struck after the repast and not before, as was usual.

74. This, too, refers to Lü, who cleaned out the kilns every night to have a place to sleep. According to legend, he returned from his unsuccessful bid to get a meal at the monastery, and recited:

> Ten times I visited the vermilion gates of the temple, nine times they were closed,
> Head covered by frost and snow, I am forced to return.
> Coming home, ashamed to face my wife face-to-face,
> I clean out a night's worth of ashes from the cold oven.

75. Another poor student, Kuang Heng of the Han, who was too poor to afford candles. He bored a hole through the wall connecting his room and his neighbor's to get enough light to read. He later rose to high office.

76. See *Rain on the Wutong Tree*, n. 71.

77. When Fan Zhongyan, the great Song statesman, was governing Boyang, a student presented him with his poems. Fan was taken by his poems and gave the student an audience. The student complained that he was the poorest person in the empire. Fan planned to help the student by making rubbings of Ouyang Xuan's famous "Stele on Sacrificing for Good Fortune," and had the ink and paper prepared. Unfortunately, thunder broke the stele before he had a chance to help the student.

I have just been able to get through until today,
When a black canopy is hoisted above his head,
And two rows of red-clothed runners are arrayed in front of his
    horse.[78]

(*Weisha*)
No one will hear of "Rejoining a broken string on the lute,"[79]
Instead "In the mountains rolls a waving flag."[80]
He has all too eagerly received the silken whip and married someone
    new—
This is what I have wound up with after giving up my life for him.

        (MEIXIANG *supports* QIANNÜ, *they exit*.)

(ZHANG QIAN:) It's all his fault. If you've taken another old lady, then fine, for-get it. But you sent me here to bring a letter that was supposed to be a letter home; instead it turns out to be a writ of divorce. You've really made missy angry. And Meixiang even beat me. Well, I think this all came from my official's being wrong.

      Just think, all this for nothing—
    Carrying a letter simply stirred up trouble.
    If he sends me out again to deliver a letter,
      Then fuck that old bald prick.

[Act 4]

(WANG WENJU, *costumed as* STUDENT WANG, *enters:*)

    Of happiness I've known none like this morning's,
    No joy I've experienced like that encountered today.

---

78. The entourage of an official.

79. I.e., broken love recaptured.

80. One explanation of this line is that this refers to the flags waved by those who clear the road in front of the entourage of an official. This is usually done in crowded areas in town to clear the path of people. To do it in the mountains suggests an unneeded gesture, hence, a futile waste of heart or mind; or perhaps it means to show off somewhere out of her sight. A second interpretation is that it refers to the spirit pennants of her funeral procession. The lines are quite ambiguous and may be read either in reference to her, as we have translated it above, or in reference to him:

No one will hear of him "Rejoining a broken string on the lute," [i.e., he'll never love me
    again]
Instead "In the mountains he rolls a waving flag." [i.e., he is somewhere out my sight]

I am the official Wang Wenju. Three years have passed since I reached the capital with my wife, Qiannü. Because I've been incorruptible, able, and upright and because I am impartial in handling affairs, the Sage has graced me with his pity and sent me to be Prefect of Hengzhou so that I can go home wreathed in glory. Attendants, get our baggage together and hook up a fine cart. My wife and I need to go to Hengzhou to take up my position and today is an auspicious day to start the trip.

> Exercising loyalty and filial behavior, I have handled the hawsers of state;
> Receiving promotion and appointment, my name is renowned within the
> four seas.
> Overcome with joy, I have been advanced in rank and raised in salary;
> Wreathed in laughter, I return home in brocade clothes.

(*Exits.*)

(MADAM *enters:*) Three years have passed since my daughter Qiannü fell sick with this chronic illness. Famous prescriptions and miraculous herbs have not been able to cure her. She seems sometimes drunk, sometimes like an idiot. She never comes to. What shall I do at this point? Servants keep watch at the door and see if anyone comes. (WANG WENJU, *together with* GHOST FEMALE, *enters:*) Missy, who would have ever thought that today I would return home in glory. (GHOST FEMALE:) Fortunately, because my husband was Top Graduate, we have been able to return home in glory. Who would have thought that today would ever come? (*Sings:*)

> ([HUANGZHONG MODE:] *Zui huayin*)
> Our baggage is simple and spare; I dally putting it in order;
> For years we have tarried here in the imperial capital.
> Beyond the flowers, the sound of the cuckoo's call[81]
> Urges the start of the homeward trip.
> When I think of the past, from the very start,
> At the core of my heart I have yet to come wide awake
> From this nightmare of "casting away my duties and rejecting my
> family."[82]

> (*Xi qianying*)
> When I think of the mind and nature of that talented man,

---

81. The cuckoo was thought to imitate the sound of the phrase, "better go home."

82. The term "casting away one's duty" usually refers to quitting one's occupation. Here, the four-character phrase probably denotes a classification of nightmares as found in oneiromantic texts.

Isn't it an intelligence purchased from the Lord of Heaven?

And even more, his inner talents and outer substance are perfectly matched.

Just seeing him once there was no way I could not be moved to passion.

So sincere—

Oh, doesn't he set my very life at risk

And lead my soul away?

(WANG WENJU:) Missy, keep your horse under control, and let's travel a little slower.[83]

(*Chu duizi*)

I ride a dragon charger, still unbroken to the bit,

To his back, I'm just like a piece of paper, even lighter.

He prances and dances, I cannot rein in his jade bridle, there comes many a false start;

So afire and fidgety he is, I cannot sit firmly in the carved saddle, I am a strange rider to him.[84]

He, haughty and headstrong—I cannot pull the bit tight—is starting to gallop off.

(*Guadi feng*)

There have been ten stretches of this road without stopping to unsaddle or feed him,

And so his very bones have grown thinner, his hooves lighter than ever.

The seasonal sights of late spring stir up a person's feelings,

And the more sights seen, the more passion born.

The whole is a road filled with blooming flowers.

Here, there, clumps of green willows or red apricots.

Here, there, pairs of purple swallows and yellow orioles,

Or matched sets of bees, matched sets of butterflies,

Each chasing after the other.

The Lord of Heaven knew what he was doing with each,

And was unwilling to let human passion be missing among them.

(*Simenzi*)

In the middle of all of this is laid a path of red fragrance,

---

83. A very nice double entendre here, since the passions are often thought of as uncontrolled horses.

84. Because, as a *hun* soul, she does not weigh anything.

Upon which we, a young husband and wife, ride our horses side by
    side.
Now we, as a pair, return to our old home in wealth and nobility,
And I finally believe, "Bringing radiance to the entire family, a glory
    of daytime brocade."[85]
When I see my mother, she will be so astounded—
Those words she spoke before showed no consideration:
Now that our houses are equal, our status commensurate,
She'll still say we acted wrongly.

(*Gu shuixianzi*)
According to the feelings between mother and child,
The fire in the Zoroastrian Temple ought never have flared up,
    flames jumping and licking.[86]
My mother took that pair of mandarin ducks on the water and,
    snicker-snack, split their twined necks apart,
Put on the carved saddle, tinkling and jingling, but left the harness
    and cinch loose,
Rattling and chattering, she sang out orders and shook the bells
    where the perfume was stolen,[87]
Ringing and resonating, the strings broke, never to be reattached on
    the blue jade koto,

---

85. A common saying, really an inversion of a cliché ascribed to Xiang Yu, the unsuccessful
contender with the founder of the Han, "If one becomes rich and noble and does not return
home [to show it off], it is like walking around at night in brocade clothing." "Daytime brocade"
later became a common saying for having achieved wealth and status.

86. A king of Shu hired a wet nurse to care for his new daughter. The nurse brought her
young son to the palace with her, but after several years, as he approached manhood, he was
forced to leave. He dwelt in a Zoroastrian temple, where he grew sick over thinking of the young
princess. She went to see him but found him asleep. She then placed in his arms some ear ornaments that they had played with as children. On awakening the boy was so distraught that he
killed himself by burning the temple down around him.

87. This is a common euphemism for illicit sexual encounters between young lovers. "Pilfer-
ing perfume" refers to an anecdote from the *Jin History* (*Jinshu*). The daughter of Jia Chong was
enraptured with Han Shou, whom she saw at a banquet. Via a maid, she communicated her
desire to Han Shou, who began to visit the girl regularly in her chambers. The emperor had given
Jia Chong a vial of perfume from Central Asia that once applied was said to stay on a person for
a month. His daughter stole it and gave it to Han Shou, who wore it among the courtiers. They
told Jia Chong of Han Shou's wonderful scent, and thus the affair was sniffed out—and ended
in marriage.

> Cracking and splintering on the fine bricks, she smashed the caltrop-
>   flower mirror,[88]
> Plunk, kerplunk, she dropped the silver pitcher into the well.[89]

(WANG WENJU:) Here we are at home already. Missy, I'll go in first. (*Acts out making greetings.* MADAM:) My son, you've come back. (WANG WENJU, *kneeling, speaks:*) Mother, I hope that you will forgive your son's wrong to you. (MADAM:) What did you do wrong? (WANG WENJU:) I should never have taken missy off to the capital without ever informing you. (MADAM:) Missy is sick and bed-ridden. She's never gone out of the house. Where do you say she is? (GHOST FEMALE *acts out greeting her.* MADAM *speaks:*) This has to be a ghostly appari-tion. (GHOST FEMALE *sings:*)

> (*Zhai'er ling*)
> I have been so bound up with sorrow every day,
> And unable to keep these tears from overflowing.
>   Now I must say I was at fault,
> And with fists pounding my chest confess to it,
> Sigh with feeling over it,
> Suffer from its hurt.
> But it was you who pushed this doltish little wronged lover
> To the point she left her home, turned her back on her village,
> Everyday vexed and worried,
> So alone and isolated in the world,
> That she could not help her sorrow turning to illness,
> Until her rotten miserable life had been forced to end.

(WANG WENJU:) Little ghost, where does your baleful spirit belong? Speak truthfully for if you don't, I'll slice you in half with my sword. (*Acts out pulling out his sword and hacking.* GHOST FEMALE *speaks:*) What are you doing? (*Sings:*)

---

88. A bronze mirror, so named for the decoration on its back; a mirror that holds a lover's image.

89. Based on a poem by Bai Juyi, "Pulling the Silver Pitcher from the Bottom of the Well":

From well's bottom, drawing the silver pitcher:
Just as the silver pitcher is about to rise, the woven cord breaks;
Upon a rock a jade hairpin is smoothed:
Just as it nears completion, it snaps in the middle.
The pitcher sinks, the hairpin snaps—do you know of it?
Like me, this morning, taking my leave of you.

This becomes a common trope for lovers forced to part. A play by this name was written by Bai Pu, author of *Rain on the Wutong Tree*.

(*Reprise*)
Out of nowhere a fierce sound like peeling thunder:
Suddenly I am so scared that my soul is set aflight.
This was all negligence on the part of my mother,
Who wants to rub out my vile reputation,
And so feigns this confusing dream babble.[90]
What kind of baleful spirit am I?
Husband, if you have any regard for our old affection,
Then you leave this miserable life of mine alone!

(MADAM:) Scholar Wang, leave her alone for a moment. She says she is no baleful spirit. Let her go into the bedchambers and see Meixiang, who used to wait on her. (MEIXIANG *supports* QIANNÜ, *who appears to be sleeping.* GHOST FEMALE *acts out seeing her.* GHOST FEMALE *sings*:)

(*Gua jinsuo*)
I suddenly enter the courtyard,
And it makes me stop, but unsteadily, walk, but not straight.
Far off I can see my jewelry, my makeup box,
And my spirit is uneasy,
My heart unsettled.
I see some little maids,
Whose mouths never cease,
Whose hands never stop
As they crowd around a half-dead beauty
Whom they cannot summon back to life,
To whom they call, with no response.

(*Weisheng*)
Abruptly my heart returns and suddenly I see clearly,
Ah, that lone lamp by the straw mattress,
Already shines on my companion but shows no clear, thin
        shadow . . .

(GHOST FEMALE *acts out joining* QIANNÜ's *body and exits.* MEIXIANG *shouts out*:) Missy, missy. Missus Wang is here! (QIANNÜ *acts out reviving, speaks*:) Where is Mister Wang? (WANG WENJU:) Where is missy? (MEIXIANG:) That girl attached herself to my missy's body, and then she revived! (FEMALE *and* WANG WENJU *act out greeting each other.* WANG WENJU:) After I attained my post, I sent Zhang Qian home with a letter. (QIANNÜ *sings*:)

---

90. Her vile reputation for eloping without proper marriage vows; "dream babble": nonsensical phrases uttered when dreaming, nonsensical utterances.

(*Ce zhuan'er*)

> Ai,
>
> You heartless, ungrateful Scholar Wang—
> Today I am gratified.
> Back then I had been hoping for a rhymed letter's arrival,
> But you posed an impossible riddle for me.

(*Zhuzhi ge*)

> I heard that you had become an official, had snapped the cassia
>   branch,[91]
> And had taken someone else, a new wife—what's the meaning of
>   that!
> Your little sister was hardly able to contain her anger,
> And that idle missive from you, brother—
> Ask that little wench there—
> I tore it into tiny little shreds.

(WANG WENJU:) But, missy, you were clearly in the capital, where we were together for three years. How can you now merge into one body? (QIANNÜ *sings:*)

(*Shuixianzi*)

> I think back on that day, when we stayed those traveling oars and
>   drank a parting cup,
> I feared only a thousand miles of passes and mountains that would
>   lie between us as well as those constant wearying dreams,
> When suddenly a miraculous communion was made and we became
>   husband and wife.
> It was if I had given birth to a self outside my self,
> Each unto itself, one of doubled beauties:
> That one went off to the examinations with him,
> This one tarried here, debilitated by a burning illness.
> Mother, this was the departed soul of Qiannü!

(MADAM:) That such a strange thing could have happened under heaven! Today is particularly auspicious; so let's complete the marriage between these two. Sister, receive the Five-colored Patent of Nobility. Nothing is more joyous in this world than the reunion of husband and wife. Slaughter a sheep, prepare the wine, and let's have a celebratory banquet!

---

91. I.e., had succeeded in the examinations.

TITLE AND NAME: At the phoenix pylons an imperial summons urges
one enlisted for the examinations;
The Song of Yang Pass sorrows one who sends the
traveler on his way;

Tuning his unadorned zither, Student Wang spells
out his vexation;
Dazed behind the green ring lattice, Qiannü's soul
leaves her body.

7

Rescriptor-in-Waiting Bao's Clever Trick:
The Record of the Chalk Circle

LI XINGDAO

The author of *Rescriptor-in-Waiting Bao's Clever Trick: The Record of the Chalk Circle* (*Bao Daizhi zhikan huilan ji*) is known only from two brief early biographical notices. There is, furthermore, no agreement on exactly what his name was. The earliest reference, in *The Register of Ghosts*, gives his name as Li Qianfu, and his style name as Xingfu, and lists the title of the play:

Li Xingfu, a man of Jiangzhou (Shanxi), whose formal name is Qianfu.

The Record of the Chalk Circle
Zhang Haitang unjustly sentenced to death; she is sent to dark prison,
Rescriptor-in-Waiting Bao's clever trick: The Story of the Chalk Circle.

Jia Zhongming later added an elegy to the text, which says:

The exalted hermit of Jiangzhou, the noble Li Qian,
Reading to cultivate and nourish his nature, his gates shut tight;
Verdant mountains, green waters, white clouds accord with him—
Cleansed of the red dust, not half a speck of stain.
Putting in ivory bookmarks in his tiny little study.
Grinding out a dew of pearls[1] that dot *The Changes of Zhou*,
Pleased with the bland taste of pickled vegetables and salt.

This is virtually all of the biographical and bibliographical information we have on Li Qianfu. We can deduce from the fact that he is listed under the section, "Those former talents already passed on who have drama scripts circulating in the world" in *The Register of Ghosts*, that he was dead when Zhong Sicheng compiled this catalogue. This allows us to place his active period sometime between the years of 1264 and 1294.

Zhu Quan's *Formulary of Correct Rhymes for an Era of Great Peace* lists the author of *The Chalk Circle* as Li Xingdao, and lists him among 150 dramatists

---

1. I.e., grinding an inkstone to make ink.

about whom Zhu Quan gives the general estimation: "They all have superior works, the best among them surpassing even the [187 Yuan writers] I have already mentioned. The force of their language is inimitable by either brush or tongue, and they are truly heroes amid the forest of writing." Zang Maoxun also attributes the play to Li Xingdao.

The main theme of the play is about the dispute between two women who claim the same child, and the wisdom of Judge Bao, who wisely resolves the case in a manner similar to that of King Solomon in the Bible. This seems to be one of those universal motifs that one finds in basic tales and fables about human morality. In the Chinese case, the story appears first as a putatively historical tale. The earliest textual record of the story appears commonly in Song texts, where it is attributed to a story in Ying Shao's (c. 150–205) *Comprehensive Meanings of Customs and Mores (Fengsu tongyi)* about two sisters-in-law who argue over a child:

> There was a rich family in Yingchuan in which two brothers dwelt together. Both of their wives became pregnant, but after several months the wife of the elder suffered a miscarriage, which she consequently concealed by staying behind locked doors. When the time for parturition came, they both went into the nursery, where the wife of the younger gave birth to a male. Because the baby was stolen that night it resulted in a three-year court case that neither the Regional Prefect nor the Commandery Governor could settle. Councilor-in-chief Huang Ba emerged and took his seat in front of the hall and had soldiers hold the child. He then separated the women by more than twenty double-paces, and then yelled at the women, "You go and take him yourself." The wife of the elder gathered up the child in a very hurried way and the child began to cry out loudly. The wife of the younger was afraid of injuring or harming him, and consequently released him and turned him over. Yet her heart was clearly miserable and broken while the wife of the elder was overjoyed. [Huang] Ba said, "This is the son of the younger brother's wife." Only after he interrogated the senior wife did she confess to [the theft of the child].

Perhaps the version most familiar to Western readers is that found in 1 Kings 3:16–28 from the Hebrew Bible, in a series of anecdotes about the wisdom of Solomon:

> Later, two women who were prostitutes came to the king and stood before him. The one woman said, "Please, my lord, this woman and I live in the same house; and I gave birth while she was in the house. Then on the third day after I gave birth, this woman also gave birth. We were together; there was

no one else with us in the house, only the two of us were in the house. Then this woman's son died in the night, because she lay on him. She got up in the middle of the night and took my son from beside me while your servant slept. She laid him at her breast, and laid her dead son at my breast. When I rose in the morning to nurse my son, I saw that he was dead; but when I looked at him closely in the morning, clearly it was not the son I had borne." But the other woman said, "No, the living son is mine, and the dead son is yours." The first said, "No, the dead son is yours, and the living son is mine." So they argued before the king. Then the king said, "The one says, 'this is my son that is alive, and your son is dead'; while the other says, 'Not so! Your son is dead, and my son is the living one.'" So the king said, "Bring me a sword," and they brought a sword before the king. The king said, "Divide the living boy in two; then give half to the one, and half to the other." But the woman whose son was alive said to the king—because compassion for her son burned within her—"Please, my lord, give her the living boy; certainly do not kill him!" The other said, "It shall be neither mine nor yours; divide it." Then the king responded: "Give the first woman the living boy; do not kill him. She is his mother." All Israel heard of the judgment that the king had rendered; and they stood in awe of the king, because they perceived that the wisdom of God was in him, to execute justice.

The play is far richer, however, than the issue of the disputed child. It is a superb investigation, through its lead character Zhang Haitang, of the pressures of family life and of the power of lust. From a good family, Zhang Haitang is forced into prostitution by the absence of a patriarch and by declining family fortunes. She is at odds with her brother, a striving and dissatisfied person for whom visible social status is more important than compassion for family members. She marries well as a second wife, and enjoys a comfortable and pleasant life with her husband. This disappears when she becomes the scapegoat for the first wife, who not only engineers her husband's death but also snatches away Haitang's child. The rationale behind the first wife's actions is, of course, a hidden affair with the local clerk. This, too, is a common motif in drama: a former prostitute who is faithful to her husband and a legitimate wife who kills him off to pursue an affair. The clerk, who has a lot of power in the local yamen office, is able to execute the murder plan or abet the affair by concealing it from higher-ups. Thus the play deals both with the pressures of domestic life and the corruption of local officials. It also, as do many dramas, scrutinizes the relationship between social status and personality, demonstrating that there is no real commensurability between person and social place. This is an important issue in a world based on social hierarchies that are presumably constructed from moral worth. In that sense, corrupt officials and pure-hearted prostitutes both betray a world in which there is no real ethical tie between person and social station. In most dramas, it is normally the second wife (usually a former prostitute) who does away with the husband and blames it on the main wife. The ethical quality of Haitang is a product of her family, a generational tradition of service to the state, but not of her actual social position. Part of the complexity and power of *The Chalk Circle* stems from both frustrating normal social perspective—prostitutes cannot be trusted—and substantiating the assumptions of that perspective. That is, Haitang belongs to a "real" family, has a "real mother" and not an adoptive madam, and has a good family tradition. A small scratching of the surface layer of social stigma shows a different hue of person.

Torture in court cases was a normal part of the judicial process and was often used to elicit a confession, because no case could be concluded without a confession. It was also a standard practice for condemned prisoners, sentenced to death, to have their cases reviewed at a higher level. The prisoner was usually sent to these higher offices under guard, wearing a cangue. In drama, the travel scene is somewhat standard: the prisoner (often female) is always escorted by two guards named Dong and Xue who try to extract bribes in exchange for better treatment. Or, as in *Rain on the Xiaoxiang* (see Appendix 3), it offers the opportunity for the prisoner to create a sympathetic bond with the guards and hence with the audience. One can conceive of the "courtroom" drama as a series of potential scenes and tropes that can be used or excluded as the story and the playwright dictate. For instance, in *Butterfly Dream* the sons are sent to Kaifeng Prefecture for review, but the travel scene is absent. Likewise, in *Injustice to Dou E* the step of higher review is elided, although this may be because the local nature of the vengeance demands that her ghost be at the spot where the seasonal and climatic abnormalities occur.

The Chalk Circle has been translated into several languages, including Japanese, German, English, and French. It was, along with *The Orphan of Zhao*, one of the plays to make its way into the Western repertoire at a relatively early date. The play was first translated into a European language in 1832 by the great French sinologist Stanislas Julien as *Hoei-lan-ki, ou l'histoire du cercle de craie, drama en prose et en vers*. In turn, Stanislas' translation was used as the basis for further translations into English and German. The version that was to have the most impact, however, was that by the German poet Klabund (pseud. Alfred Henschke), whose adaptation appeared in 1925. This led to another string of translations, including the influential English version of James Laver, which was adapted to the stage in England and America in the 1920s and 1930s. Bertolt Brecht was inspired in 1945 by the play to write his famous *Der kaukasische Kreidekreis* (*The Caucasian Chalk Circle*), which was produced first, in English, in 1948 at Carleton College, and then in German in 1954, in East Berlin. In an ironic historical twist, *The Chalk Circle* was readapted to the Peking Opera stage in 1992, carrying with it many of the dramaturgical elements introduced into modern theater by Brecht and which he claimed to have learned from Peking Opera.

Dramatis personæ in order of appearance

Role type	Name, family role, or social role
Old female	Madam Liu
Second male	Zhang Lin
Female lead	Zhang Haitang
Added male	Magnate Ma, Ma Junqing
Painted female	First wife, Magnate Ma's wife
Clown	Clerk Zhao
Household Servants	Servants
Clown	Su Shun, Magistrate of Zhengzhou
Runners	Zhengzhou yamen runners
Child	Haitang's child, Shou'er
Official	Su Shun, Magistrate of Zhengzhou
Comics	Neighbors
Clowns	Old ladies
Clown	Innkeeper
Clown	Dong Chao
Clown	Xue Ba
Second male	Judge Bao
Comic	Zhang Qian

Rescriptor-in-Waiting Bao's Clever Trick:
The Record of the Chalk Circle

[Wedge]

(OLD FEMALE, [*costumed as*] MADAM, *enters and speaks:*) I am surnamed Liu and the man I married was named Zhang. He died long ago a young man, leaving me a son and a daughter. My boy is called Zhang Lin, and I've taught him to read and write. My daughter is called Haitang—don't just say that she has only looks and a body to match—she's smart and clever, and has studied the zither, chess, calligraphy, painting; she plays wind and string instruments, sings, and dances. There's not a single skill she hasn't completely mastered. Seven prior generations had all succeeded in the examinations, but when it came our turn, our family capital was stripped away and there was no one to take care of me. There was nothing I could do but send this daughter out to earn our daily rice by selling her winsome smile. There's a moneybags in this town—Magnate Ma—who's been hanging around my place forever. He has it bad for my daughter and is always after her to be his concubine. My daughter is willing to marry him, too. But how can I bear to part with this rice bowl that keeps me in food and clothes? I'll wait until my daughter shows up and then we'll work out a long-term plan. Anything's possible. (SECOND MALE, *costumed as* ZHANG LIN, *enters and speaks:*) I am Zhang Lin. Mother, seven generations back from the time of my grandfather all have made a mark in the examinations. How can you let this little slut engage in such shameful actions? How can I show myself in front of others? (MADAM *speaks:*) What's the meaning of such trash? If you are really worried that your sister is going to bury you in shame, then *you* go on out and earn the money to support me! Wouldn't that be better? (FEMALE LEAD, *costumed as* ZHANG HAITANG, *enters, acts out greeting* [*her mother*], *and speaks:*) Brother, if you want to be a real man, then you'd support our mother. (ZHANG LIN *speaks:*) You rotten slut, carrying on so. . . . If you don't give a damn that people laugh at you, then you'd better mind if they laugh at me. You think I can't beat you, you rotten little slut? (*Acts out beating* ZHANG HAITANG.) (MADAM *speaks:*) Don't beat her; you might as well beat me. (ZHANG LIN *speaks:*) Mother, let's not have a family fight that will stir up everyone's derision and laughter. I'll take my leave of you today, mother, and go to Bianliang, find my uncle, and make my own way through the world. The proverb says, "A man must be strong himself." A strapping man like me, six feet tall, shouldn't starve if he leaves home. You little slut, you'd better take good care of mother after I leave. If anything happens, there's no way I'll let you off the hook. (*Recites:*)

All flustered, pissed off, I leave my family home,
To seek another way to earn a living and make it through the seasons;
A man who has a strapping six-foot body
Knows heaven will not let him be poor his whole life.

(*Exits.*)

(ZHANG HAITANG *speaks:*) Mother, will these quarrels ever end? You should marry me off to Magnate Ma and be done with it. (MADAM *speaks:*) You've hit it on the head, child. When Magnate Ma gets here, I'll settle this marriage thing, and it'll all be over. (ADDED MALE, costumed as MAGNATE MA, *enters and speaks:*) I am called Ma Junqing and my family hails from Zhengzhou. When young I studied the scholarly arts and became somewhat skilled in the classics and histories. But, since my family was loaded, everyone called me Magnate. In the past, being addicted to playing the rake, I have spent my emotions among the flowers and willows. Here lives Zhang Haitang, the best girl of the best house, who's been my companion for a long time. We're two people with a single mind. I want to take her to wife and—no need to say it—she often has confessed she wants to marry me. But her mother has thrown up a hundred obstacles and she's simply unwilling to say yes. I suspect that her motive is no more than a desire to squeeze me for a little more money and a few more gifts. I heard that Haitang had a loud quarrel with her brother, Zhang Lin, a couple of days ago and that he left home to go and find his uncle in Bianjing.[2] I reckon he won't be back for a while. It just so happens that today is an auspicious day, a lucky morn—I'd best put together some money and gifts and go in and see if I can press this marriage. If there's the slightest bit of affinity in the past then this fine affair will come to its rightful end! Hey, sister is standing right at the doorway. This *is* an augury of success! Let me greet her. (*Acts out greeting* ZHANG HAITANG *and performing courtesies.*) (ZHANG HAITANG *speaks:*) Magnate, you're here! I've explained to mother over and over that it would be better to assent to this marriage while brother is away. I've had to wear away half my tongue, but mother seems to be on the verge of relenting. Let's go and see her. (MAGNATE MA *speaks:*) If she really has such an intention, then the karma that I've cultivated has finally come round! (*Acts out entering and greeting her.*) (MADAM *speaks:*) Magnate, my son Zhang Lin has been unfilial enough to get into a row

---

2. I.e., Bianliang (Kaifeng).

with me. Can you dig up some cardamom for me to make soup? (MAGNATE MA *speaks:*) Mother, I am not stingy. I've prepared a hundred taels of white silver with which to seek this marriage. After she has moved to my place, I'll be the one to provide for you. I'll make sure you never worry about money again. Today is an auspicious day, mother. Accept these gifts, this money, and assent to the marriage. (MADAM *speaks:*) At any rate, if my daughter were to stay at home, I couldn't bear all that anger. Once I marry her off to someone, at least it will be quiet. But, Magnate, you have a wife at home already. If my daughter is going to be bullied after she gets to your house, then it would be better for her to stay here. I want to get it clear with you now: you'll have to persuade your wife to accept it before I'll assent to this marriage. (MAGNATE MA *speaks:*) Relax, mother. Not only am I not that kind of person, neither is my wife. When my beloved comes to my house, she and my wife will address each other as sister, and there will be no distinction in status. And if my beloved should give birth to a son, then all of my family wealth and enterprise will be under his control. Mother, don't worry about anything else. (MADAM *speaks:*) Magnate, I just wanted to set the record straight. I've received your gifts and money and my daughter is now a wife of the Ma family. Let her go to your house today. Child, it's not that I, your mother, can bear to part with you, but you are going to be someone's wife. Be no "head of the guild"[3] anymore. (ZHANG HAITANG *speaks:*) Magnate, in front of your wife, you'd better be my advocate in all the things that happen. (*Sings:*)

> ([XIANLÜ MODE:] *Shanghua shi*)
> Were I to heed that hoary-headed, weathered-faced old mother of
>   mine,
> I'd expect to stay unmarried to the very end of this life—

(*Speaks:*) Magnate, I love nothing more about you than . . . (MAGNATE MA *speaks:*) Sister, what do you love about me? (ZHANG HAITANG *sings:*)

> I simply love that your nature is soft, that your intent is true.
> Now the future that I sought is set for sure.

(*Speaks:*) I'll make all my sisters say, "It's not for aught—Zhang Haitang married Magnate Ma."

> (*Sings:*)
> From this point on, no one will deride me for bringing shame on my
>   house!

> (*Exits with* MAGNATE MA.)

---

3. A "head of the guild" is a top-class courtesan.

(MADAM *speaks:*) I've given my daughter in marriage to Magnate Ma today. The hundred taels I've accepted will be enough to keep me happy for the last half of life. There's nothing else to do now, but to find my old cronies and go off to the teahouse to have some tea.

(*Exits.*)

[Act 1]

(PAINTED FEMALE, FIRST WIFE, *enters and recites:*)

> This face of mine may be really ugly
> But everyone says I am capable of seductive beauty.
> A single pan of clear water to wash it off,
> And I'd have enough to open up a rouge and powder shop!

I am the wife of Magnate Ma. My husband took another wife, called something like Zhang Haitang, who's added a little boy to the family, and he's already five years old. I've been putting one over on the Magnate. There's a certain Clerk Zhao here who is quite the dashing man. And, he's been blessed with a tool like a mule! I've been having a sordid little affair with him. I've been scheming with my whole heart to get rid of the Magnate so that Clerk Zhao and I can be husband and wife forever. My husband isn't home today and I sent someone earlier to tell him to get over here. He ought to be arriving any time. (CLOWN, *costumed as* CLERK ZHAO, *enters and recites:*)

> My job as clerk is only a way to get drunk
> Or bed someone's old lady.
> And after all, whom shall I love?
> Any pretty face that's a match for my own.

I am surnamed Zhao and am a clerk in the yamen of Zhengzhou. People of the district, seeing that I have a modicum of ability, have given me two nicknames: Leather Shoe Zhao and Zhao the Flirt. There's a certain woman here, the first wife of Magnate Ma. One day Magnate Ma invited me to a banquet and I accidentally caught a glimpse of her. That face was truly the most perfect match for me yet born in heaven or produced on earth. Yes, a real beauty. Fascinating. She's so destroyed me that I constantly think about her both in my mind's eye and in my dreams. I never expected that she would also be taken with me. We've secretly put one over on the Magnate and have been carrying on a sordid affair. She sent someone to fetch me today. Why? I don't know, but I'd better go on over. And here I am. I'll just go straight on in. Wife! What's on your mind?

(FIRST WIFE *speaks:*) I didn't call you for "that" business. I've been thinking that our carrying on like this is no solution for the problem. I really want to mix up a batch of poisonous herbs and kill Magnate Ma. We could be husband and wife forever. Wouldn't that be great? (CLERK ZHAO *speaks:*) You're no "common whore with a like mind," but are my true mother! Sure enough, I already had come up with what you had in mind! I've had this poison prepared for a long time. (*Acts out taking out poison and giving it to the* FIRST WIFE, *speaks:*) Here's the poison. I'll turn it over to you and then go on to work at the yamen.

(*Exits.*)

(FIRST WIFE *speaks:*) Now that Clerk Zhao is gone, I'll hide this poison away and wait for the right time to set my hand to it. Ai! How could I forget? Today is the boy's birthday. I'll have someone ask Magnate Ma to come home and we'll go to the various Buddhist temples to burn incense and apply some gold leaf to the Buddha's face. Off we go.

(*Exits.*)

(ZHANG HAITANG *enters, speaks:*) I am Zhang Haitang. Five years have passed since I married Magnate Ma. My mother has passed away and I don't even know where my brother is—there's been not the slightest bit of news. The son I bore is called Shoulang. From the moment of his birth, five years ago, my elder sister has raised him. Today is my son's birthday and the Magnate and sister have taken him to various Buddhist temples to burn incense and apply gold leaf to the Buddha's face. Servants, get dinner ready so that we can eat when the Magnate and sister return home. Zhang Haitang—you've lived such a peaceful life since marrying the magnate! (*Sings:*)

> ([XIANLÜ MODE:] *Dian jiangchun*)
> Doors of moon and windows of cloud,
> Embroidered hangings and gauzy canopies—
> Who desires them now?
> I've rejected the base to follow the good,
> And bade goodbye to Tinkling Chimes Alley.

> (*Hunjiang long*)
> I'm done with that "light pouring and low singing,"
> Have forsaken those "rows of orioles and swallows lined up on the
>   stage."
> I never played up to the noble or attached myself to the rich,
> So, let others make of it what they want.

Never again to the halls of wind and moon to sell my smiles or chase
    good times,
Never again to the land of kingfisher green and red to welcome the
    new and send off the old,
And I'll never again fear the summons from high office to perform,
Never again bear the responsibility for keeping house and home
    together,
Never again let guests and friends come and go,
Never again see the jostling and wrangling in the neighborhood,
Never again worry about family fortune or business,
Never again heed the cares of worldly affairs.
Every day just one pair of intensely happy hearts and minds in
    perfect accord,
Sleeping until, meltingly warm, the three-notch-high sun casts its
    image on the silk window.
I keep company with my ardent master,
And have sent off my mother who would intercede.

(*Speaks:*) How come the Magnate and sister haven't come home yet? I'd better
go out the door and have a look. (ZHANG LIN *enters and recites:*)

    In my guts I know all to know about affairs of this world;
    In my lot lies unluckiness the equal of no one else under heaven.

After I had that quarrel with my sister, I left home to find my uncle. Who could
know that he would have gone off to Yan'an District with that Master of Strategy, Chong Shidao?[4] On the one hand, I have no one to rely on, and on the
other I'm suffering from the symptoms of a winter's epidemic. Not only do I
have no traveling money, I've even had to pawn the clothes I wear. I came back
home, but mother had died. Our house wasn't there anymore, either. What was
I to do? I learned that my sister had married Magnate Ma. He's got a fine family
business and should be willing to look out for a relative. Should be no problem
for him to take care of a brother-in-law. I'll go straight over there and throw
myself on his mercy and ask if I can borrow some traveling funds. Here I am
at the Ma house already. It just happens that my sister is at the gate. Let me go
greet her. Sister, I bow to you. (ZHANG HAITANG *greets him, speaks:*) I say, who
is this? Why, no one but my brother. Well, I see your face is nice and fat—good
thing you went abroad. (ZHANG LIN *speaks:*) Sis, is this all you can say? (ZHANG

---

4. Chong Shidao (1051–1126) was a brilliant strategist who was highly successful against the
Xixia kingdom on the Song's eastern border. He was also instrumental in the first withdrawal of
the Jurchen army's siege of Kaifeng, but later was stripped of his military offices.

HAITANG *speaks*:) Brother, did you come back to perform the sacrifices of seven sevens for mother?[5] To raise a grave mound for her? Or just to perform your filial mourning? (ZHANG LIN *speaks*:) Sis, if you can't see what I've been eating, then look what I'm wearing. I can't even provide for my own lips—what do I have to give up for the sacrifices of seven sevens or to raise a grave mound? (ZHANG HAITANG *speaks*:) Brother, after our mother died, all of the costs of the funeral clothes, casket, and coffin, were at the expense of Magnate Ma. (ZHANG LIN *speaks*:) Sister, even though Magnate Ma paid for mother's burial, I know it was all thanks to you. I know. (ZHANG HAITANG *sings*:)

> (*You hulu*)
> After losing your own father,
> Then getting rid of a mother,
> Weren't you still, after all, named Zhang?
> How could you have your sister—bringer of shame on our house,
>   destroyer of the family—take on all the responsibility?

(ZHANG LIN *speaks*:) Sis, you don't need to harp at me. I know that it was all thanks to you. (ZHANG HAITANG *sings*:)

> And finally today you prepare your sweet talk to come seek me out
>   for help.

(ZHANG LIN *speaks*:) Sis, I've come today to throw myself on your mercy. How can you turn such a cold face to me? (ZHANG HAITANG *sings*:)

> I didn't willfully create such a cold face, so hard to draw near;
> It was you who stood up, all burning with anger,
> And ran off, stewing and simmering, to the four directions.

(ZHANG LIN *speaks*:) Sis, let's not bring up what's past. (ZHANG HAITANG *sings*:)

> Well, I must say, if you have so prospered by making your mark,
> Why are you coming home in such tattered and torn old clothes?

(ZHANG LIN *speaks*:) Sis, we are from the same parents. What have I done wrong? Force yourself a bit to understand my situation. Don't list all of your resentments. (ZHANG HAITANG *sings*:)

> (*Tianxia le*)
> Brother, what self-respect can you have to appear here this morning
> And spill your guts for me to hear?

---

5. A sacrifice to the dead, made every seven days for forty-nine days.

(ZHANG LIN *speaks*:) Sis, there is nothing I can do but throw myself on your mercy. I can do nothing else. No matter how little, just give me some travel money so I can leave. (ZHANG HAITANG *sings*:)

> Every sound out of his mouth says he is at wit's end.
> Brother—if you have no money now, why did you ever go to
>   Bianliang?

(ZHANG LIN *speaks*:) Sis, don't go on and on about it. If you don't help me out with some money, who will? (ZHANG HAITANG *sings*:)

> Today you've thrown yourself on your little sister's mercy,
> And want me to give my big brother a little money.

(*Speaks*:) Say, didn't you . . .

> Didn't you say, "A man must be strong himself"?

(ZHANG LIN *speaks*:) Sister, you never forget a word. You've dumped on me enough—give me some money. (ZHANG HAITANG *speaks*:) You can't know, brother, that these clothes and hair ornaments are all gifts to me from Magnate Ma. I can't just make a personal decision to give them to someone. Except for these, what else do I have to give you? Brother, go away. Don't come to this door again. (*Acts out being rude and going inside.*) (ZHANG LIN *speaks*:) Sis, you are too cruel. You are my natural sister, and I had come just to throw myself on your mercy. You didn't give me a cent, but you ridiculed me plenty to my face. Well, I'm not going back now. I'll just wait here at the doorway until Magnate Ma comes home. Maybe he'll show some heart. Who knows? (FIRST WIFE *enters and speaks*:) I am Magnate Ma's first wife, and I've come back early from our jaunt to burn incense for our child. Ai, why is there a beggar standing at the entrance to our pawnshop? What's your business here? (ZHANG LIN *speaks*:) Don't curse me, big sister. I am Zhang Haitang's older brother. I've come to look for my little sister. (FIRST WIFE *speaks*:) So it turns out that you're Zhang Haitang's brother. That makes you a brother-in-law. Do you recognize me, by any chance? (ZHANG LIN *speaks*:) This small one does not recognize you, big sister. (FIRST WIFE *speaks*:) I am the first wife of Magnate Ma. (ZHANG LIN *speaks*:) These silly eyes of mine didn't recognize you. Please, Madam, do not take offense. (*Acts out paying obeisance.*) (FIRST WIFE *speaks*:) Brother-in-law, do you want to see your sister? (ZHANG LIN *speaks*:) I want to speak, but am afraid to. Because I'm so poor and hard up, I have nothing to get by from day to day. I wanted to find my little sister and get some traveling funds from her to use. (FIRST WIFE *speaks*:) How much did she give you? (ZHANG LIN *speaks*:) She said that all the property of the house—both inside and out—was under your control, Madam. She couldn't presume to personally decide, and so she gave me nothing. (FIRST WIFE *speaks:*) Of course, you don't know, but after your sister came here, she gave birth to a little boy. He's five now, and he's your nephew. All property in our family—major and minor—is under her control. Me, I'm childless. (*Acts out beating her breast, speaks:*) I have no luck at all. If you are Zhang Haitang's brother, then you are my brother, too. I'll go on in and ask her to give you some traveling money. If she has some, don't be overjoyed, and if she doesn't, then don't be frustrated. Just consider it fate. Just wait by the door for a minute. (ZHANG LIN *speaks:*) I understand. Now this is a kind and worthy woman! (ZHANG HAITANG *acts out greeting* FIRST WIFE, *speaks:*) Sister, you've come back first. It wore you out, I'm sure. (FIRST WIFE *speaks:*) Haitang, who is standing outside our doorway? (ZHANG HAITANG *speaks:*) It's my brother. (FIRST WIFE *speaks:*) Oh, so it turns out it was your brother. Why did he come here? (ZHANG HAITANG *speaks:*) He came to ask me for some travel money. (FIRST WIFE *speaks:*) Why don't you give him a little? (ZHANG HAITANG *speaks:*) All of my clothes and hair ornaments were given to me either by the Magnate or you, sister. How could I give them to him? (FIRST WIFE *speaks:*) If these clothes and ornaments were given to you, then they are yours. What's to stand in the way of giving them to your brother? (ZHANG HAITANG *speaks:*) I'm afraid that wouldn't be right, sister. If the Magnate should inquire after my clothes and hair ornaments, what would you have me tell him? (FIRST WIFE *speaks:*) If the Magnate asks, I'll speak on your behalf and we'll have some more made for you. Take them off and go give them to your brother. (ZHANG HAITANG *acts out taking them off, speaks:*) Since you've allowed me to do this, sister, I'll take my clothes off, take out my hair ornaments and go give them to my brother. (FIRST WIFE *speaks:*) Are you afraid I'll take what's yours? Give them to me; I'll take them out to him. (*Acts out taking the props and going out to greet him, speaks:*) Brother-in-law, even I began worrying about your travel expenses. I never expected that your little sister would be so cruel that, despite the number of clothes and hair ornaments she has, she was unwilling to give you any at all. It was just like stripping off her skin to give to you. Here are a few clothes and some hair ornaments that my mother and father gave me as a dowry. I'll give them to you as a fill-in for travel money. Brother-in-law, please don't consider this a small or unworthy gift. (ZHANG LIN *acts out accepting them, speaks:*) Many thanks, Madam. I will repay you in some miraculous way. This kind favor must be repaid in double. (*He acts out thanking her.*) (FIRST WIFE *responds politely, speaks:*) Brother-in-law, the Magnate isn't home right now and it would be improper for us to detain you here for a meal. Please don't consider it rude.

(*Exits.*)

(ZHANG LIN *speaks:*) I would have said that these clothes and ornaments were my sister's; I couldn't have guessed that they were Madam's. You are my own sister, but you wouldn't even give me a cent when I asked for traveling money. Instead, you ridiculed me to my face. That woman was a complete stranger to me, but she gave me these clothes and ornaments. I think there must be some real conflict between the primary wife and second woman. They'll wind up in a complaint or suit in court. I'll trade these ornaments for some silver and purchase a little niche as a court clerk in Kaifeng Prefecture. Sis, "may you always choose a lucky place to walk and a lucky place to sit." Just don't let our axle hubs ever rub each other. If you ever go to court and bump into me, I'll take off a layer of skin with each whack of the stick!

(Exits.)

(FIRST WIFE *acts out greeting* ZHANG HAITANG, *speaks:*) Haitang, I've given all of your clothes and ornaments to your brother. (ZHANG HAITANG *thanks her, speaks:*) I've caused you a lot of trouble, sister. But I'm still afraid that when the Magnate gets home, if he should ask me about it. . . . Please put in a word for me, sister. (FIRST WIFE *speaks:*) No problem, leave it to me.

(ZHANG HAITANG exits.)

(FIRST WIFE *speaks:*) Haitang, am I happy that your brother took those clothes and ornaments! And when the Magnate asks about them, well, I'll sorrow for you.

(MAGNATE MA *enters, leading young child, speaks:*) I am Ma Junqing. I had a boy after marrying Zhang Haitang, whom I call Shoulang. He's already five. Today is Shoulang's birthday and we went off to various temples to burn incense. I saw that the Temple of the Lady of Sons and Grandsons was decrepit and I gave them some money to repair it. That's why I have been delayed. But here I am at home already. (ZHANG HAITANG *and* FIRST WIFE *act out welcoming him home.*) (ZHANG HAITANG *speaks:*) Magnate, you're home. It must have worn you out; I'll go and fetch some tea.

(Exits.)

(MAGNATE MA *speaks:*) Wife, why have all of Haitang's clothes and ornaments disappeared? (FIRST WIFE *speaks:*) If you hadn't asked, I wouldn't have said anything. She's been really doted on since she gave birth to that child. Who would have thought that she would be keeping a lover behind your back and doing that dirty little deed? When I went with you today to burn incense, she took all of her clothes and ornaments and gave them to her lover. She was about to go and find some others in a crazy attempt to cover up her mistake when I caught her by coming home early. It was me who wouldn't let her get dressed again or put on any other hair ornaments. I simply wanted to wait until you came home so you could sort out this affair yourself. It's not that I am jealous of her—she brought this all on herself. (MAGNATE MA *speaks:*) So, it turns out that Haitang has given her clothes and ornaments to her lover. Well, that makes sense. She is a person from the world of wind and dust. But this deed really makes me angry. (*Acts out summoning* ZHANG HAITANG *and beating her; speaks:*) I'll beat you, you no-good little slut. (FIRST WIFE *acts out urging him on, speaks:*) Beat her well! Such a base person who brings shame and ruin on a house—who needs her? She ought to be beaten to death. (ZHANG HAITANG *speaks:*) Originally I wasn't willing to give these clothes and ornaments to my brother. It was she who kept urging and urging me on. Who would have thought that she would tell the Magnate that I was keeping a lover when he got home? I have a mouth, but it's hard to defend myself. Zhang Haitang, this is all something that is your own fault.

> (*Nuozha ling*)
> Back in the beginning, it was I, I harmed myself—
> I never had a clue,
> I never had a clue,
> And let my guard down,
> And let my guard down.
> She's put me in this spot.
> The more flustered my hands and feet grow as I am beaten,
> The more slander her words and phrases reveal.
> Truly, a vicious venomous person unparalleled in this world!

(MAGNATE MA *acts out being angry, speaks:*) You are my child's mother? How could you do this unchaste, shameful act? You make me so angry! (FIRST WIFE *speaks:*) Magnate, are you really angry? Only beating her to death will settle up accounts! (ZHANG HAITANG *sings:*)

> (*Que ta zhi*)
> Every vile woman in the world
> Loves to be in sole control of power,
> But who's ever seen such cur-like actions, such a wolf-like heart?
> Such maggot-ridden guts that turn the stomach?

(*Speaks:*) You're the one with the lover! And you're trying to accuse me! (*Sings:*)

> Trying to trap me into this filthy affair!

(*Speaks:*) No wonder you're trying to trap me,

> Because I am the one who refuses to belittle myself and act the
>   whore!

(FIRST WIFE *speaks:*) It's plain to see that a slut like you can't keep her old nature from resurfacing. You gave your clothes and jewelry to your lover. Trying to hide from your master that you have done the act! (ZHANG HAITANG *sings:*)

> (*Jisheng cao*)
> No other vile and venomous heartless woman
> Could match this seventh-generation bitch,
> Who claims that I tried with my whole heart to deceive the master of
>   the house.

(FIRST WIFE *speaks:*) Who asked you to take a lover in secret? And you're still defending yourself? (ZHANG HAITANG *sings:*)

> She says that I crept around in secret with a lover,
> And that I confuse the issue face-to-face with a strong defense—
> Well, if you're going to fabricate wanton infamy for me before my eyes—
> It was you, sister! You're the one who put the shit pot on his head.[6]

(MAGNATE MA *acts out feeling ill, speaks:*) I've been so upset by this slut. Wife, why do I suddenly feel so ill? Can you cook up a bowl of hot soup for me to eat? (FIRST WIFE *speaks:*) It's this slut Haitang who has made the Magnate so angry he got sick. Haitang! Hurry up! Cook up some soup and give it to the Magnate. (ZHANG HAITANG *speaks:*) All right. (*Sings:*)

> (*Houting hua*)
> Just a minute ago my backbone suffered the bastinado,
> And now I have to go to the kitchen to cook up some hot soup.
> Well, the hearts of men are hard for sure,
> And we women always wind up with the shorter life.

(*Acts out exiting and then entering to offer the soup, speaks:*) Sister, here's the soup. (FIRST WIFE *speaks:*) Bring the soup here! I want to taste it. (*Acts out tasting it, speaks:*) Too little vinegar and salt! Go and get some now. (ZHANG HAITANG *responds, exits.*) (FIRST WIFE *speaks:*) Let me take out that dose of poison from the other day and pour it into the soup. (*Acts out pouring poison, speaks:*) Haitang, come here. (ZHANG HAITANG *enters, sings:*)

> Why is she in such a fluster?
> And why does she keep on demanding vinegar and salt?

(*Speaks:*) Sister, you take it in; I'm afraid that if Magnate sees me, he'll just get angrier. (FIRST WIFE *speaks:*) If you don't go, he'll think you're upset with him.

> (*Exits.*)

---

6. I.e., made him a cuckold.

(ZHANG HAITANG *speaks:*) I understand. Magnate, have a mouthful of soup. (MAGNATE *acts out taking it and eating.*) (ZHANG HAITANG *sings:*)

> Just see him, sad and depressed, hesitate a second,
> Bitter and hurt, taste it in his mouth.

(MAGNATE *acts out dying.*) (ZHANG HAITANG, *startled, speaks:*) Magnate, wake up, come to! (*Sings:*)

> Oh, why is your face changing, turning parched and yellowed,
> And your eyes losing luster, turning white and lifeless?
>
> (*Qing ge'er*)
> Ai,
> I'm so scared my gall has scattered, my soul is lost,
> I can't keep myself from spilling thousands of tears.
> Right before my eyes your limbs grow rigid, your life is lost,
> And you've abandoned all your buildings and stores,
> Your many fields and numerous farms.
> And now, two hapless women,
> A five-year old child,
> Have no place to live, no place of comfort—
> Mothers and child—alone as orphan and widows.
> O child, who will you find to raise you now?

(ZHANG HAITANG, *weeping, speaks:*) Sister, the Magnate is dead! (FIRST WIFE *enters, weeping, speaks:*) My magnate, he's left me and gone. Haitang, you slut, the magnate was fit and fine just a minute ago. How could a mouthful of soup kill him? If you didn't poison him, who did? (ZHANG HAITANG *speaks:*) Sister, you tasted this soup, too. But it didn't kill you, just the Magnate. (*Acts out weeping, speaks:*) Oh, heaven, don't be so cruel to me. (FIRST WIFE *speaks:*) Servants, find me a place on a high plain, chop down a tree to fashion a coffin, and take the Magnate and bury him. (*Act out having* HOUSEHOLD SERVANTS *enter and take the* MAGNATE *off.* FIRST WIFE *speaks:*) Haitang, you slut, I'll take care of you in due time just as soon as the magnate is buried and gone. We'll see if you will be able to live on in this family! (ZHANG HAITANG *speaks:*) Sister, I don't have the magnate any more, and I don't want any of the family property. Just let me simply take my child and go. (FIRST WIFE *speaks:*) And just who raised this child? (ZHANG HAITANG *speaks:*) I did. (FIRST WIFE *speaks:*) You raised him? Then why didn't you nurse him yourself? He's always been with me. I am the one who kept him dry and warm, who suffered so he could prosper. I spent a lot of effort on him. He was raised in my hands. Just acknowledge that I raised the child. That will make it easier. We'll just leave it at the fact that you kept a lover and conspired with him to kill the magnate. So, do you want to settle it in public court or in private? (ZHANG HAITANG *speaks:*) What's public and what's private? (FIRST WIFE *speaks:*) If you want to settle privately, then give all of the family wealth, buildings, storehouses, and also the child to me, and you can go out the door empty-handed. If you want to settle it in public, well . . . you poisoned your husband . . . that's a nifty little crime. Let's you and I go see the judge. (ZHANG HAITANG *speaks:*) I never poisoned my husband, so what've I got to fear? I'll go with you willingly to the judge. (FIRST WIFE *speaks:*) We are clearly going to court. If you aren't afraid of a suit, then I'll take you there to see the judge. (ZHANG HAITANG *speaks:*) I'm not afraid, let's go to court. Let's go to court.

> (*Zhuansha*)
> Don't ask if you're telling the truth,
> Don't ask if I'm telling lies.
> I have at hand those old women who brought him into the world and
>   cut his fetal hair,
> Just ask them who is the real mother and who raised him later!

(FIRST WIFE *speaks:*) I am the real mother of this child, and he is my true son. He is my heart, my stomach, and the heels at the back of my feet. Everyone knows that. (ZHANG HAITANG *sings:*)

> How will you ever be able to deceive these neighbors, who witnessed
>   his birth, who saw him grow up?

(FIRST WIFE *speaks:*) You mixed the poison and plotted to kill the Magnate. I've got the goods on you! (ZHANG HAITANG *speaks:*) This poison. . . . (*sings:*)

> Was something you hid away one day
> And then secretly poured into the soup broth.

(FIRST WIFE *speaks:*) Clearly it was you who put the poison into the soup. How can it be laid on me? Surely you're going to pay with your life. (ZHANG HAI-TANG *sings:*)

> Just let whoever poisoned our husband pay with her life.
> You're simply no good
> And have trapped me into this injustice.
> Of all the first wives of all the world,
> Where is there one with as black a heart as you?

> (*Exits.*)

(FIRST WIFE *speaks:*) See, she's fallen into my trap. Now all of the family property and the child will be mine. (*Acts out pondering over something, speaks:*) Hai!

Every action requires thinking about thrice! "Avoid effort now, pay with remorse later!" You have to think this over carefully. I really didn't raise this child. She is going to call as witnesses those old ladies, the midwife and the one who shaved off the child's fetal hair, and that group of neighbors who witnessed the child being born and then saw him grow up. If we actually go to court, they won't be for me and that would be a complete waste of this opportunity. Let me think. When the pupils of their black eyes light on a tael of white silver, there's not a person who won't want it. I'd better fix this up beforehand and give each person a tael of silver. Then they'll all be on my side. But all of the officials and clerks of the yamen have to be fixed too. I wish Clerk Zhao would come so I can discuss the suit with him. How wonderful that would be!

(CLERK ZHAO *enters and speaks:*) Speak of Zhao and Zhao appears. I am Zhao the Clerk. I haven't seen Madam Ma in quite a few days and my heart is beginning to itch. I've really been thinking about her. I just can't get her off my mind. Here I am at her doorway. There's no man in her house now, so what do I fear? I'll just go on in. (*Acts out greeting* FIRST WIFE, *speaks:*) Madam, all I can do is think about you. (FIRST WIFE *speaks:*) Clerk Zhao, do you know I poisoned Magnate Ma? Now the two of us, Haitang and I, are going to court to contest control over the family fortune, and even this little kid. You go and prepare everything in the yamen, and fix everyone from high to low. The completion of this affair is now in your hands. Then I can be your wife forever. (CLERK ZHAO *speaks:*) This is simple. But that little kid wasn't ever yours. Why do you want him? Give him to her and be done with it. (FIRST WIFE *speaks:*) You seem to be a clerk for nothing, since you know nothing about the law. If I give the kid to Haitang, then someday the sons and grandsons of the Ma family will come and contest possession of the Ma family fortune and I won't be able to persuade them to give me even a cent. But she's just going to point out the old midwife and neighbors as witnesses. I've already used some silver to buy them off. Don't you worry about anything outside of the yamen. You just arrange everything for me inside the yamen. (CLERK ZHAO *speaks:*) You've hit it on the head. This being the case, you come make your complaint as soon as possible. I'll personally go to the yamen and fix it all.

(*Exits.*)

(FIRST WIFE *speaks:*) Clerk Zhao has gone. I'll seal up the doors to the house today[7] and drag Haitang off to make my complaint. (*Recites:*)

> The proverb may say, "A person has no intent to harm the tiger,
> But the tiger has a mind to injure the person."

---

7. So that nothing inside will be touched.

But I say, "When a person sees a tiger, who dares stir it up?
But a tiger who won't harm a person isn't worth a fart."

(*Exits.*)

[Act 2]

(CLOWN, *costumed as* OFFICIAL, SU SHUN, *enters leading* RUNNERS; *speaks:*) I am
the Magistrate of Zhengzhou, known as Su Shun. (*Recites in poetry:*)

Even though I hold office,
I know nothing of the law;
All it takes is just a little silver
To bring to an end any official matter.

What I find quite repugnant is that the common folk of Zhengzhou, seeing
that I am completely weak and useless have given me a nickname, "Mr. Equivocal." And because of this my name, "Equivocal Su," has been broadcast far and
wide. But then I consider that there have been many sharp people in office
lately, who freely flaunt their authority and power, and look how many people
they have harmed! Yet the likes of me, Su the Equivocal, have saved countless
numbers through our blundering stupidity—how many people in this world
are aware of that? I will begin this morning's court. Attendants, set out the
plaque of complaint. (RUNNERS *speak:*) Understood! (FIRST WIFE *enters, dragging* ZHANG HAITANG *and* CHILD, *speaks:*) Let's go see the judge. Injustice!
(ZHANG HAITANG *speaks:*) Let me go! (*Sings:*)

([SHANGDIAO MODE:] *Ji xianbin*)
Burning with rage, she grasps my clothes tightly.

(FIRST WIFE *speaks:*) You poisoned your own husband. You ought to get the
death penalty. If I let you loose that's the same as letting you flee. (ZHANG HAI-
TANG *sings:*)

You say that it's a capital offense, how can you let me flee?

(*Speaks:*) Zhang Haitang,

I thought that nine of ten who marry a good man lived a steady life,
But today I see no future, no good end in sight.
I bear this injustice, have a mouth but find it hard to speak,
And it is truly the plaintiff who "sprouts in this world."
This unexpected accusation of guilt
Can only be clearly revealed by heaven and earth.

(FIRST WIFE *speaks:*) There's no doubt you poisoned your husband, and heavenly principle will naturally see through this with divine intelligence. (ZHANG HAITANG *sings:*)

> I will pray to those divine sentient beings in the void—
> Even if "A man should come to no illustrious end,"
> It would be hard to say, "The principles of heaven do not shine and
> 　sparkle."

(FIRST WIFE *speaks:*) You little slut, here's the gate to Kaifeng Prefecture. If the court deals with you, you'll have to suffer each little step of being bound and beaten. It would be better to acknowledge it and settle it privately. There's still time to take care of it. (ZHANG HAITANG *speaks:*) I wouldn't admit to it even if I were beaten to death. I am more than willing to go to court with you. (*Sings:*)

> (*Xiaoyao le*)
> You say, "After being dealt with by official process,
> How can you withstand that caning and beating?"
> I would say, "A human life must have a place where it can find safety."
> Could I ever falsely confess to the crime of poisoning my husband?
> Or fall for no reason into the snare of another?
> Holding fast with all my life to the seven chastities and nine virtues,
> Should I fear six interrogations or the third degree?
> Let them beat me a thousand, ten thousand times!

(FIRST WIFE *cries out:*) Injustice! (SU SHUN *speaks:*) Who's yelling "Injustice" at the yamen gate? Attendants, go bring them in. (RUNNERS *perform seizing and bringing them in, speak:*) Face front! (FIRST WIFE, ZHANG HAITANG, CHILD, *act out kneeling.*) (SU SHUN *speaks:*) Who is the plaintiff? (FIRST WIFE *speaks:*) I am the plaintiff. (SU SHUN *speaks:*) Aha. Plaintiff, you kneel here. Defendant, you kneel there. (*Each acts out kneeling apart from the other.*) (SU SHUN *speaks:*) Call the plaintiff up. You speak your deposition and I'll be your advocate. (FIRST WIFE *speaks:*) I am the primary wife of Magnate Ma Junqing. (SU SHUN *acts out being alarmed, speaks:*) In that case, please rise, Madam. (RUNNER *speaks:*) She's making a complaint, how come you asked her to rise? (OFFICIAL *speaks:*) She's the wife of Magister Ma.[8] (RUNNER *speaks:*) He was no Magister. Here we call anyone with a good bit of money, "Magnate." He was no more than a rich landowner,

---

8. The term *yuanwai*, which we have consistently translated "Magnate," was adapted from an administrative title for a supernumerary court official, appointed beyond the normal quota. Here, the official takes it in its literal sense as a court official. The runner, however, explains that it has a dialect usage in Bianliang to mean "Magnate."

he held no ranked position. (SU SHUN *speaks:*) Aha! Have her kneel. Speak your deposition. (FIRST WIFE *speaks:*) That one over there is called Zhang Haitang, a good-for-nothing whom the Magnate took as a concubine. (RUNNER *acts out berating her, speaks:*) I'll bet she's a good one! (FIRST WIFE *speaks:*) You bet she's a good one. She secretly kept a lover and conspired with him to mix up some poison and, after killing her husband, wrest away the child I bore, and swindle me out of my property. I beseech you, noble one, be my advocate. (SU SHUN *speaks:*) This woman really knows how to talk. I think she's someone who is long accustomed to court suits. She just keeps blabbering on and I can't understand a thing. Go and ask the clerk to come here. (RUNNER *speaks:*) The clerk is requested to appear. (CLERK ZHAO *enters and speaks:*) I am Clerk Zhao and I was just forging a few documents in my office. The master has called me. Certainly another complaint has been lodged that he is unable to decide, and he's summoned me to help. (*Acts out greeting him, speaks:*) Master, just what is it that you can't take care of? (SU SHUN *speaks:*) Clerk, there's a case of accusation here. (CLERK ZHAO *speaks:*) Let me ask her. You, woman, what is your complaint about? (FIRST WIFE *speaks:*) I am reporting that Zhang Haitang poisoned her husband, wrested away my child, and has swindled me out of my property. Have pity, be my advocate. (CLERK ZHAO *speaks:*) Bring Zhang Haitang here. Why did you poison your husband? Quick now, confess the truth. If you don't confess. . . . Attendants, pick out a big club for me. (ZHANG HAITANG *sings:*)

> (*Wuye'er*)
> On the steps of the court,
> On bended knees—
> Listen to this humble concubine explain the facts.

(CLERK ZHAO *speaks:*) Speak, speak. (ZHANG HAITANG *sings:*)

> All these runners, lined up like wolves and tigers,
> All these clerks, set up as rows of spirits and ghosts—

(CLERK ZHAO *speaks:*) You poisoned your husband. This is one of the Ten Repugnant Crimes. (ZHANG HAITANG *sings:*)

> If I have offended the law in the least little way,
> Then, master, I am willing to take that beating for the crime of killing
>   a husband.

(CLERK ZHAO *speaks:*) What kind of family do you come from? How did you marry that Magnate Ma? Explain it to me. (ZHANG HAITANG *sings:*)

> (*Shanpo yang*)
> I reflect on how I earned our living by selling my smiles:

Originally we were an old, established family,
But because we—miserably, wretchedly poor children and mother—
    had no one on which to rely,
We barely got through from night
To morning.
I can only thank Magnate Ma, whose kindness I relied on at first sight,
Who put out his money and took me as his second wife.
So that our "oriole and swallow" relationship
Was brought to a proper end by marriage.

(CLERK ZHAO *speaks*:) So, it turns out that you were a whore and not a fine person at all. Even if you were taken into Magnate Ma's house, did you ever have a son or daughter? (ZHANG HAITANG *sings*:)

(Jinju xiang)
I suffered the "pain and weariness" of raising children for him.

(CLERK ZHAO *speaks*:) Who else is in your family? Do you still have any contact with them? (ZHANG HAITANG *sings*:)

My brother, with little food and nothing to wear, threw himself on
    my mercy,
But I had just driven him from the door when the two of them
    happened to bump into each other.

(CLERK ZHAO *speaks*:) If it was just your brother you saw, that's no problem. (ZHANG HAITANG *speaks*:) My sister said, "Haitang, when your brother came to seek help from you, you didn't have any money. Why not take off some clothes and hair ornaments and give them to him for travel money?" (CLERK ZHAO *speaks*:) Well, these words show her good intentions. (ZHANG HAITANG *speaks*:) I believed her. I took off the clothes and ornaments and gave them to my brother to take away. But when the Magnate came home and asked, "Why don't I see any of Haitang's clothes or hair ornaments?" she replied, "She's cheating on you, sir, and gave them all to her lover." (*Sings*:)

How could I know she was two-faced and duplicitous enough
To so misrepresent things to our husband?

(FIRST WIFE *speaks*:) Aiya! I am the most virtuous and worthy woman of Zhengzhou! And you say I'm two-faced and duplicitous. What did I ever misrepresent about you? (CLERK ZHAO *speaks*:) These are all little things that I'm not going to question you about. I'm only going to ask you why you poisoned your husband, why you want to wrest away her child and swindle her out of her family fortune. Confess to these, one by one. (ZHANG HAITANG *sings*:)

(*Cu hulu*)
My man had a stroke of rage,
And fell, *kerplunk*, on the floor.
When he came to, my sister herself helped prop him up.
> (*Continue in speech*:) She said, "Haitang, the Magnate wants some
> soup to sip. Go heat some up."

(*Sings*:)

And after I had heated up a hot bowl of soup, then she said it lacked
salt and soy paste.
> (*Continue in speech*:) She tricked me into getting some salt and soy
> paste.

(*Sings*:)

Who ever expected her to secretly pour in poison herbs?
> (*Continue in speech*:) And after only a spoonful or two of this soup,
> the Magnate died. Sir, think about this—

(*Sings*:)

Why did she so quickly cremate the corpse and bury it in the wilds?

(CLERK ZHAO *speaks*:) Well, it is clear the poison herbs were yours. But why did you want to snatch her child and swindle her out of her family fortune? (ZHANG HAITANG *speaks*:) I raised this child. Sir, just summon midwife Auntie Four Liu, and Great Aunt Zhang, shaver of the fetal hair, and when you ask them and all the neighbors, then you'll be clear on the whole matter. (CLERK ZHAO *speaks*:) You're right on this point. Attendants, go and round up those old ladies and the neighbors. (SU SHUN *acts out signaling with his arm.*) (RUNNERS, *going out and summoning them, speak*:) Old ladies, neighbors, and all, you are summoned to the yamen.

(TWO COMICS, *costumed as* NEIGHBORS, *and* TWO CLOWNS, *costumed as* OLD LADIES, *enter.* ONE COMIC *speaks*:) The proverb says, "Take someone's money, you must squelch their problems." Now that the big wife of Magnate Ma is making a complaint, she has summoned me to be her witness. The big wife never raised this child, but now that we've gotten her silver, we have to say that she raised it. Don't fear being beaten, just speak unclearly. (COMICS *and* CLOWNS *speak*:) We know that. (*Act out following* RUNNERS *in and kneeling.* [RUNNER] *speaks*:) Face front! (CLERK ZHAO *speaks*:) Are you the neighbors? Who raised this child? (TWO NEIGHBORS *speak*:) Magnate Ma was a rich man, and we ordinarily had nothing to do with him. Five years ago, because his first wife bore a son, each of us neighbors gave him three grams of silver as a celebratory gift.

He then invited us to the feast of the first month, where we saw that, indeed, a handsome little baby had been born. Later, every year the Magnate and his first wife would take the child out on its birthday to the various temples and monasteries to burn incense. Everyone in the city has seen this, not just the few of us here. (CLERK ZHAO *speaks:*) Aha! It is clear that the first wife raised this child. (ZHANG HAITANG *speaks:*) Sir, she has bought off these neighbors. Don't listen to what they say. (TWO NEIGHBORS *speak:*) We can't be bought off. We are telling the truth, spilling out our hearts and gall. If half a line is a lie, then let a saucer-sized chancre grow on your lip. (ZHANG HAITANG *sings:*)

> (*Reprise*)
> Bring to witness now the midwife, Auntie Four Liu,
> And Great Aunt Zhang, who shaved off his fetal hair.
> They had visited me more than ten times before my son had even
> 　　passed his first month.
> Today this rotten bitch has come to court and is conniving with
> All you neighbors—it's clear you don't accord with Heaven's way
> And have taken her "money for the mouth" to seal it up tight!

(ZHANG HAITANG *speaks:*) Sir, just ask these old ladies. They ought to know. (CLERK ZHAO *speaks:*) Ladies, just who raised this child? (CLOWN LIU *speaks:*) I am the midwife, and I deliver at least seven or eight a day. Can I remember what went on in the distant past, years ago? (CLERK ZHAO *speaks:*) This boy is just five. That's not so long ago. Just truthfully tell who raised the boy. (CLOWN LIU *speaks:*) Now, let me think. Let's see, it was dark as a dungeon in the delivery room that day. I couldn't even make out the person's face. But when I felt with my hand, well that "portal of birth" felt just like the first wife's. (CLERK ZHAO *speaks:*) Phui! Auntie Zhang, you speak. (CLOWN ZHANG *speaks:*) Well, on that day they invited me to shave that little tyke's fetal hair, he was being held by the first wife. When I saw those huge breasts, like two floppy white feed sacks, I knew for sure that only someone feeding a child could have dugs like that. So, it must have been the first wife who raised him. (ZHANG HAITANG *speaks:*) How can you old ladies be on her side? (*Sings:*)

> (*Reprise*)
> Grandma, when it was time for delivery, I whispered for you to come
> 　　into my bedroom,
> And you helped me ever so slowly up onto the birthing mat.
> Grandma, when it was time to cut the fetal hair, who burned the
> 　　incense candle in the courtyard?
> You two aren't that old, after all,
> So how can you get it all so topsy-turvy,

And in this court not separate the true from the false, the pure from
   the turbid?

(CLERK ZHAO *speaks*:) See? These two grandmas both said the first wife raised
him. It's certain that you are trying to snatch her child. (ZHANG HAITANG
speaks:) Sir, her money has bought off all these neighbors and old ladies. This
child may be only five, but he understands human affairs. You just ask the child.
(FIRST WIFE *grabs the* CHILD, *speaks*:) You say that I am your real mother and
she's the wet nurse. (CHILD *speaks*:) You are my mother, you are my wet nurse.
(ZHANG HAITANG *speaks*:) Again! My precious. . . . (*Sings*:)

> (*Reprise*)
> Ai! Son, search carefully in your heart,
> Mull it over yourself,
> See how your mother, bitterly suffering, endures these thongs of
>   thorn on her skin.
> Newly emerged from the womb, you understood human affairs,
> So you must remember the three years of nursing by your own
>   mother.
> How can we keep this heartless woman from raising hell in front of
>   you?

(CLERK ZHAO *speaks*:) This child's words aren't fully trustworthy. We should take
this group of people as the main witnesses. Only one child, yet you still wanted
to wrest him away from her! As for this swindling of the family fortune—
there's no need to go on about it. Just quickly confess to poisoning your husband! (ZHANG HAITANG *speaks*:) The poisoning of my husband has nothing to
do with me. (CLERK ZHAO *speaks*:) This perverse skin bag of treacherous bones!
If you don't beat her, she won't confess. Attendants, seize her and give her a
sound thrashing! (ATTENDANTS *act out beating her.* ZHANG HAITANG *acts out
fainting.*) (FIRST WIFE *speaks*:) Great beating, wonderful beating! It won't mean
anything to me if you beat her to death. (CLERK ZHAO *speaks*:) She's trying to
feign death. Attendants, pick her up for me. (ZHANG HAITANG *speaks*:) Sir, her
money has bought all the neighbors and old ladies off. This child may be only
five, but he understands human affairs. You just ask the child. (ATTENDANTS
act out picking her up.) (ZHANG HAITANG *acts out reviving, speaks*:) Aiyo! Heaven!
(*Sings*:)

> (*Houting hua*)
> All I can see is the club, swishing and whistling, beating me,
> Applied to my burning, throbbing backbone.
> My vital spirit deranged, convulsing in turmoil,

> My twin souls disappearing, far, far away.
> They clamp the top of my head tight . . .

(ATTENDANTS *speak:*) Phui! Confess now! Wouldn't that be better than suffering like this? (ZHANG HAITANG *sings:*)

> I hear only yelling and yammering by my ears;
> Can a clerk as evil as this ever show mercy?
> Or these vicious officials display anything but violent cruelty?

(CLERK ZHAO *speaks:*) Confess! Who was your lover? (SU SHUN *speaks:*) If she won't confess, then let me acknowledge for the moment that I was! (ZHANG HAITANG *sings:*)

> The court is pressuring me
> To point out my lover, reveal his whereabouts.
>
> (*Shuang yan'er*)
> More than once I've looked for help from those Gates of Ghosts,
> But their "following the will of humans"[9]
> Is of no use here.
> This pus and blood soaked body of mine needs retribution—
> For the rich, a snap,
> For the poor, no way to endure.

(CLERK ZHAO *speaks:*) Attendants, beat her a second time. (ZHANG HAITANG *speaks:*) I'm the daughter of a respectable family! I can't bear this torture. All I can do is confess against my will. Master, I poisoned my husband, I wrested away my child, and I cheated her out of her family fortune. O heaven, don't kill me wrongly! (CLERK ZHAO *speaks:*) It took me forever, but I've finally swindled you out of a child. Well, now that you've confessed. . . . Attendants, make Zhang Haitang sign her name, lock her up in a long cangue, appoint two escorts, and send her off under guard to Kaifeng Prefecture for sentencing. (OFFICIAL *speaks:*) Attendants, get her into that new nine-and-a-half-catty cangue to wear! (ATTENDANTS:) Understood. (*Act out putting the cangue on.*) (ATTENDANTS *speak:*) The suspect is in the cangue. (ZHANG HAITANG *speaks:*) Heaven! (*Sings:*)

> (*Langlilai sha*)
> All you officials are just too violent and cruel,
> And tyrannize us common folk.

---

9. Stems from a proverb that the domain of the spirits will respond to human pleas to rectify wrongs.

In a stupor I sign my name and confess to the crime.
Here and now I weep pitifully and complain to heaven, heaven so
    high,
For how many years must I yearn for the coming of a pure official?

(CLERK ZHAO *speaks:*) Bite your lip! When we investigate things in this yamen, the officials are pure and the law is just. Every entry and every codicil is right by the book! Is there a pure official purer than my old dad here? (ZHANG HAI-TANG, *acting out suffering, sings:*)

How will I ever, with the shitty remains of this life, endure death row?

(*Exits with* ATTENDANTS.)

(CLERK ZHAO *speaks:*) Well, this affair is done. Witnesses, go safely home. Plaintiff! Wait while the prisoner is taken into custody, and heed the dispensation proclaimed in the documents returned from Kaifeng Prefecture.

(*All kowtow and exit together.*)

(CLERK ZHAO *speaks:*) I've been interrogating this case all day, and I'm starved. I'm going home to eat.

(*Exits.*)

(SU SHUN *speaks:*) This case may be finished, but when I think on it, I realize that *I* am the chief official, yet it wasn't decided by me. Whether they are beaten or let off was all a decision of Clerk Zhao. I really am a fool! (*Recites in verse:*)

In deciding cases from this point on, I'll be less nervous,
    And right or wrong, be at the plaintiff's service.
Caned, beaten, exiled, or banished—the choice is yours to make,
    All I want is money and goods, a doubled portion mine to take.

(*Exits.*)

[Act 3]

(COMIC, *costumed as innkeeper, enters and recites:*)

The wine we sell here is so fine a batch,
    A clarity and purity none can match.
We bury our wine casks out by the privy in back,
    And strip off our pants to act as a filter sack!

I am a wine seller and run a wineshop at Tenmile Shop outside of the city of Zhengzhou. All the traveling merchants and sojourning travelers who go north or come south frequent my place to drink. Well, let me open up the gate of wine today, fire up the pot to heat up the wine warmer, and see who shows up.[10]

(TWO CLOWNS *costumed as guards and* ZHANG HAITANG *enter.*) (ZHANG HAITANG *acts out stumbling, getting up, and sitting.*) (CLOWN DONG *speaks:*) I am a famous employee of the Zhengzhou yamen, named Dong Chao, and my brother here is called Xue Ba. We're guarding this woman, Zhang Haitang, and are taking her to Kaifeng Prefecture for sentencing. Phui! Woman, move along a little faster. Observe this wind and snow and heed the hunger in our stomachs. If you have any funds for this trip, take out a little, and then after we've drunk a little wine, we can hurry on down the road.[11] (*Acts out beating her.*) (ZHANG HAITANG *acts out rising, speaks:*) Brother, don't beat me. I am a person wrongly convicted and my life lies in the balance. Where would I be able to beg even a speck of money to give to you? I only hope you'll take pity on me. (CLOWN DONG *speaks:*) Look, woman, why did you poison your husband in the first place? Or con her out of her child? Just explain it slowly and let me hear. (ZHANG HAITANG *recites* [*in ballad verse*]:)

> When will this crime be lifted from my body?
> Who will hear out my plaint of this bellyful of wrong?
> It was someone else who swindled me out of my child
> And then framed me for the murder of my husband.
> I could not stand being trussed up and beaten,
> And I met no pure incorrupt judge at the court!

(CLOWN XUE *speaks:*) When did the two of us ever see even a sliver of silver from you? Who wants your money? Are we pure and incorrupt or not? (ZHANG HAITANG *recites* [*in ballad verse*]:)

> Who sees what's right and acts on it?
> Have pity on my bitter, suffering lot.
> These sopping, soaking wet lesions—from beating—sting and
>   pain,
> These choking, catching sobs—I weep and wail over and over.
> Flat broke and lonely—nowhere to beg a single meal,
> Flappingly, flimsily thin—my clothes are tattered and torn.
> Heavy, pressing weight—iron chains and brass cangues,
> Weak, wilting, useless—old woman and wife.

---

10. The wine warmer is a pot that is filled with wine and placed in a larger vat of hot water. Chinese wine was drunk warm.

11. *Zanlu*, translated here as "hurry down the road," means specifically to make good time on the road in order to meet a specified deadline.

          Ah, how can you
Fierce, ferocious, and ruthless escort guards know,
        Brother,
That I really do suffer injustice and bear wrongs?

(CLOWN DONG *speaks:*) Well, you can talk injustice until you're blue in the face, but it wasn't us who wronged you. So how can you expect any pity from us? Move it, the snow's getting heavier. (ZHANG HAITANG *sings:*)

> ([HUANGZHONG MODE:] *Zui huayin*)
> Has the snow on my head ever stopped, even for a second?
> Pushing at the trees in the forest, a wild wind crazily blows.
> Here I am, depressed and sighing,
> Driven so hard my energy is gone and my muscles flag.
> And on top of that these itchy, scratchy, pus-filled lesions from my
>   beating are starting to ooze.

(CLOWN XUE *speaks:*) You've given us so much trouble on this journey, yet you still won't move along. (*Acts out beating her.*) (ZHANG HAITANG *sings:*)

> How can I bear this burning anger, this yammering and yelling?
> Just tread a little too slow, fall a little too far behind, and they beat
>   you with all their strength!

(CLOWN DONG *speaks:*) Well, you should have never confessed in the first place. Who made you confess anyway? (ZHANG HAITANG *speaks:*) Brother, if you don't begrudge me bothering you, then listen to me. (*Sings:*)

> (*Xi qianying*)
> Only when I ran afoul of this unfeeling field of official law
> Did I finally believe that it was an endless desert.
> How could I bear their cruel beatings?
> They squeezed me so much that I had to put my seal to the
>   document of confession.
> And it's come to this, with no one to take pity on me.
> For such injustice suffered and wrongs borne
> Have I vainly taken all I can of being bound and beaten!

(CLOWN DONG *speaks:*) Look, woman, buck up. After we get around this mountain slope, I'll let you rest a bit before we go on. (ZHANG HAITANG *sings:*)

> (*Chu duizi*)
> Here we are directly below the mountain slope,
> But I'm so frozen I have to fight to stand up.

(*Acts out stumbling, sings:*)

> I've fallen flat on my back, the tips of my feet pointing up to the sky!

(CLOWN DONG *speaks:*) Get up! (ZHANG HAITANG *sings:*)

> Have a little concern for me, my hot-tempered brother,
> It's that the ground is slippery with these slick and slippery rills of ice.

(CLOWN XUE *speaks:*) Thousands of others have walked here without slipping! But, you have to slip. Let me go ahead of you. If I don't slip, then I'm going to break your legs. (*Acts out stumbling, speaks:*) Well, it really is a little slippery here.

(ZHANG LIN *enters, speaks:*) I am Zhang Lin. I'm an attendant here at Kaifeng Prefecture now. Rescriptor-in-Waiting Bao went recently to the western borders to enlist troops, and he has dispatched me to meet him on return. What a snowstorm! Heavens! Stop for a while. (ZHANG HAITANG *acts out seeing him, speaks:*) The one who's walking over there looks just like my brother, Zhang Lin. (*Sings:*)

> (*Guadi feng*)
> From a distance, it appears that the face is his,
> If not, then my eyes are blurred with tears.
> Let me concentrate my gaze, and observe him closely,
> It was him all along. Yes! No mistake.
> I'll stretch myself here, hunch my shoulders,
> Rock back and forth, and waggle my waist.

(ZHANG LIN *acts out looking at her, speaks:*) Where are you bringing this woman in the cangue from? (ZHANG HAITANG *cries out, speaks:*) Brother! (*Sings:*)

> Brother, stay your step,
> How can you help your sister out of this mess?

(ZHANG HAITANG *cries out, speaks:*) Brother! (*Sings:*)

> You are the living avatar of the Bodhisattva Guanyin from Potalaka
>   Mountain,
> So why aren't you revealing that heart that saves others?

(*Cries out, speaks:*) Brother! Save your little sister! (ZHANG LIN *speaks:*) Who are you? (ZHANG HAITANG *speaks:*) I am your sister, Haitang. (ZHANG LIN *acts out hitting her and pushing her away, speaks:*) You rotten whore. You'll never see the day I thank you for giving me a helping hand! (*Acts out leaving.*) (ZHANG HAITANG *acts out weeping and running after him, sings:*)

(*Simenzi*)
And why does he revile me as a rotten whore time and time again?
This kind of blind anger is hard to fend off or to endure.
It did turn out to be him,
But when he saw me,
He remembered how much he hated and resented me before.
It really is him,
But when he saw me,
His anger and rage poured out with lightening speed.

(ZHANG LIN *departs, she catches up and acts out clutching his clothes.* ZHANG LIN *acts out throwing her down.* ZHANG HAITANG *cries out, speaks:*) Brother! (*Sings:*)

(*Gu Shuixianzi*)
He, he, he refuses to acknowledge me,
I, I, I risk life and limb to catch up to him,
Just, just, just able to clutch tightly at his clothes.

(CLOWN XUE *acts out grabbing the hair of* ZHANG HAITANG, *speaks:*) This woman is going to be the death of me. (ZHANG HAITANG *sings:*)

So soon, so soon, so soon dragged off by my hair!

(ZHANG LIN *speaks:*) Let go, you rotten whore. (ZHANG HAITANG *sings:*)

I beg, beg, beg you, fierce daddy, bear with me!

(ZHANG LIN *speaks:*) You rotten whore, if you knew back then that this day would come, would you have refused me a few of your clothes and hair ornaments for traveling funds? (ZHANG HAITANG *sings:*)

Her, her, her snares for trapping me were clever and crafty,
You, you, you—those were my gold hairpins you stuck in your hair,
I, I, I must suffer now because of this!

(ZHANG HAITANG *speaks:*) Those few clothes and hair ornaments are the source of my current straits. The reason that I could not give you the clothes and hair ornaments for traveling funds in the first place was precisely because I feared that that woman would come back. I never guessed that she would have me take off some clothes, which she took to you, and then would tell the Magnate when he got home that I'd been keeping a lover, and had sent *him* all my clothes and hair ornaments. It enraged the Magnate so much that he fell ill; then she secretly poisoned him to death and dragged me, your sister, off to court, where I was convicted of poisoning my husband and trying to swindle her out of a child. Heaven! Have pity on this wronged woman! (ZHANG LIN *speaks:*) Whose clothes and ornaments were they? (ZHANG HAITANG *speaks:*) Mine. (ZHANG LIN *speaks:*) Yours! That evil scoundrel told me that they were part of her father and mother's dowry! In this case, I have wrongly suspected you. There's a wine-shop ahead, let's you and I go and have a few cups. (*Acts out proceeding to the wineshop with the escorts, speaks:*) Innkeeper! Bring some wine!

(COMIC, *costumed as* HOSTELER, *enters, speaks:*) Fine, fine, fine. Please come in and sit down. (ZHANG LIN *speaks:*) Escorts, I am Head Clerk of the Fifth Kaifeng Prefectural Yamen, Zhang Lin. This is my sister. I am going back to meet Rescriptor Bao. You take care of her for me for the rest of the trip. (CLOWN DONG *speaks:*) No need to tell us more than once. Just send us back, correctly certified, as soon as you return to the Prefecture. (ZHANG LIN *speaks:*) That's easy enough. Sister. I would have said that that woman was saintly and wise. But it turns out all along that she was vicious and evil. How can you be done with her? (ZHANG HAITANG *sings:*)

> (*Gu zhai'er ling*)
> That rotten woman's face was all made up—
> You'd say, "She's virtuous and able in all she does,"
> But she stirred things up so much that my husband interrogated me.
> And later she showed her clever lips,
> Used her clever teeth,
> And face-to-face, told three lies:

> (*Gu shenzhang'er*)
> She said that I had poisoned my man,
> And also said that I had complete control of the family wealth,
> And that I wanted to swindle her out of her child.
> So she dragged me off to the district yamen where she made her
>   complaint,
> And there was no concern there for what was hard to endure,
>   hard to suffer:
> It was one long taste of wrongful torture and wrongful beating
> That sent me to a living death at the tip of a sword, under its
>   blade.
> And who was it that sent this wronged person to her death?
> None other than that maggot that makes my stomach churn.

(*Speaks:*) Brother stay here, I want to go relieve myself.

(*Exits.*)

(CLERK ZHAO *enters with* FIRST WIFE, *speaks:*) I am Clerk Zhao. This is how it is: when I sent Zhang Haitang off to Kaifeng Prefecture under escort, I thought to myself—Haitang has no relative to plead for her life, and so it would be better to finish her off on the road. How clean that would be. So, I picked two particularly able men, Dong Chao and Xue Ba, to escort her. As they were preparing to leave, I gave each of them five taels of silver and told them, "Doesn't need to be far off, set your hand to it in any out-of-the-way, quiet place." But there's been no news yet, and I suspect something has gone wrong. So, it's better to find out for myself, in the company of my old lady. (FIRST WIFE *speaks*:) Traveling so far on such a snowy day has made me cold. Let's go into that wineshop for a spell and buy a bowl of wine. We can go on after warming up a little. (CLERK ZHAO *speaks*:) Well spoken, dear. (*Act out entering the wineshop.* ZHANG HAITANG *acts out seeing them, speaks*:) All right! She and her lover have caught up with us. Wait until I tell brother. (*Sings*:)

> (*Jiejie gao*)
> This vile woman is absolutely vicious,
> And entirely foolhardy.
> We've caught up with each other here—
> Well, how are we to settle this once and for all?

(*Speaks*:) Brother, the adulteress and her lover are here in the wineshop. Let's seize them. (ZHANG LIN *speaks*:) Brothers, give me a hand to catch that adulteress and her lover. (ZHANG HAITANG *sings*:)

> Go on out quickly,
> Don't frighten them away,
> Seize them quickly—
> This is a case of "those really in love are those who will suffer the
>   punishment!"

(ZHANG LIN *and* ZHANG HAITANG *go out to apprehend them.*) (DONG *and* XUE *wave their hands to set them aflight.*) (ZHANG HAITANG *acts out tightly clutching* FIRST WIFE.) (FIRST WIFE *acts out escaping and fleeing with* CLERK ZHAO.) (ZHANG HAITANG *sings*:)

> (*Gua jinsuo*)
> I had grabbed her clothes tightly here,
> But was pulled straight down the steps by her,
> And because of this, that vile woman was set free.
> I've made a useless scene,
> And for nothing caused my brother
> To expend every ounce of his energy.
> I hate those escorts, who signaled with their hands,
> And will surely say that I let my lover loose!

(ZHANG LIN *speaks:*) Escorts! You animals, you pure donkey seeds! You're from the same yamen as he is, you signaled him to flee! I am Head Clerk of the Fifth Kaifeng Prefectural Yamen. I'll beat you—let's see if you inform on me! (*Acts out administering a beating.*) (CLOWN XUE *speaks:*) If you, a constable, from a higher office can beat me, then I can beat this woman, who's a prisoner under my control. (*Acts out beating* ZHANG HAITANG.) (ZHANG HAITANG *sings:*)

> (*Weisheng*)
> They are officially deputed to see me securely there under guard,
> But on the road you, both sides, squabble over the precedence of
> 　your mission. . . .

(ZHANG LIN *acts out grabbing* CLOWN DONG's *hair.*) (CLOWN DONG *acts out grabbing* ZHANG HAITANG's *hair.*) (ZHANG HAITANG *sings:*)

> And so destroy me, this worn-out prisoner under sentence.

(INNKEEPER *acts out blocking them:*) You guys pay up your wine debt. (CLOWN XUE *speaks:*) Phui! What wine debt? (*Acts out kicking him down, exit together.*) (INNKEEPER *speaks:*) Just look at my bad luck. I waited half the day in front of my shop, until three or four people came to buy some wine. I don't know why they started fighting, but it drove away a couple of good customers. They didn't even buy a dollar's worth of wine. I'm not going to run a wineshop anymore; I'll see what else I can find to make a living. (*Recites in verse:*)

> No fun at all, this livelihood, no fun;
> Seems I'm always owed money by someone.
> Now I'll strike down the wine flag and shut the gate.
> Better to string up some wild ducks to sell for ready cash.

(*Exits.*)

[Act 4]

(SECOND MALE, *costumed as* JUDGE BAO, *enters leading* the COMIC, ZHANG QIAN, *and* BAILIFFS.) (ZHANG QIAN *shouts:*) Oyez! All horses and people in the yamen—now be still! Bring forward the cases. (JUDGE BAO *recites:*)

> In years gone by, I personally received the Imperial Commission;
> 　My hands grasp the Golden Plaque and the Sword of Power.
> 　I exhaust the way of justice in the Southern Yamen;
> No need for the Soul-frightening Dais at the Eastern Marchmount.

I am Bao Zheng, known as Xiwen, the one from Codger Village, in Four Vista County, Golden Measure Commandery, Lu Prefecture. Because I keep a mind

of purity and uprightness and hold firm and fast to integrity, I have always bus-
ied myself with the state's affairs, never shaming myself by grubbing after profit
or personal gain. I keep company only with the loyal and filial and never mix with
slandering toadies. I thank the sagely grace that took pity and granted me the
position of Rescriptor-in-Waiting at Dragon Design Pavilion and Academician-
in-Waiting at the Hall of Heaven's Splendor. I have been given the assignment
of Prefect of the Southern Yamen of Kaifeng Superior Prefecture. An imperial
order has bestowed on me the Golden Plaque and Sword of Power, and I seek
out excessive officials and corrupt clerks, alleviate injustice to the hundred surnames and right their wrongs. I have been allowed "to behead first and memorialize afterward." For this reason, families that presume on their wealth and
power, hearing my name, all rein in their hands; bullies who are violent and
treacherous, seeing my shadow, all have a chill in their hearts. I knot together a
rope at the boundary plaque to make a pen, and by the screen of justice draw a
circle in the earth to act as my jail. Officials and bureaucrats are upright and
solemn, and on the stone of warning is engraved, "By Imperial Order." My retainers are numerous and severe; below the steps are writ two words, "Keep
Silent." In the shade of the sophora are arrayed twenty-four long cangues with
ends shaped like magpie tails and in front of the Hall of Compassionate Administration are several hundred wolf-toothed cudgels. (*Recites:*)

In the Yellow Hall no dust dare enter all the day long;
There is only the shade of the sophora encroaching on the main street.
Do any from outside dare stir up a clamor?
Even magpies and crows fly by in silence.

I saw a report from Zhengzhou yesterday that said some woman named Zhang
Haitang had killed her husband because of a lover, had kidnapped a son from
the primary wife, and had swindled the family fortune. This is a major infraction of the Ten Repugnant Statutes and brooks no delay. . . . Let me think. . . .
An evil woman who has poisoned her husband—that's no rare affair. But to
steal a child from the primary wife? Is the child so wonderful that she had to
steal him? And there's no lover concretely pointed out. Perhaps there is some
injustice in this case. I've already sent someone secretly to fish up the original
plaintiff and all those witnesses involved. Let's wait until they get here and examine them to reopen the case. This is precisely where I'm fairest. Zhang Qian,
go and set out the plaque that says "Court in Session." Then send in, one by one,
all of the accused sent here from other prefectures and counties. I will pronounce
their sentences.

(ZHANG HAITANG, GUARDS, *and* ZHANG LIN *enter.*) (ZHANG LIN *speaks:*) Sis,
he'll question you for sure when you go into court. All you need say is, "Injustice,"

and Judge Bao will overturn your case. If you can't get it all out, then you just purse your lips and I'll speak up on your behalf. (LEADING FEMALE *speaks:*) If I don't lay plaint today about my injustice, then when? (CLOWN DONG *speaks:*) Daddy judge went into court a while ago and we want to deliver you when the plaque goes up. So hurry on in. (ZHANG HAITANG *sings:*)

> ([SHUANGDIAO MODE:] *Xinshui ling*)
> Who can fathom this injustice that I carry in my belly,
> That wells up as I wail and weep, to fall in two streams of passionate
>   tears?
> How angry I am that earlier I didn't see what was going on,
> So that now the regret seems so drawn out.
> They pull me from the front, push me from the back,
> And never say, "Rest a moment."

(ZHANG LIN *speaks:*) Sis, we're in front of Kaifeng Superior Prefecture already. Let me go in first and you come in with the guards. Judge Bao is a round, bright mirror that is suspended from above. The things he asks about he sees as clearly as with his own eyes. You need only pump up your courage to go defend yourself. (ZHANG HAITANG *speaks:*) Brother, (*Sings:*)

> (*Bubu jiao*)
> You say he is a bright mirror suspended on high inside the Southern
>   Yamen,
> And if I bravely report all the circumstances, he'll simply cleanse my
>   feelings of injustice.
> So then, what do I fear?
> Just this—belted with chains, bearing a cangue, I can't muddle up
>   what I have to say,
> If by one chance in a thousand I don't match his expectations,
> Brother, then you must step in and rescue your own little sister.

(ZHANG LIN *acts out going in first.*) (ZHANG HAITANG *and* TWO CLOWNS *act out kneeling and having an audience.*) (CLOWN DONG *speaks:*) One female prisoner, named Zhang Haitang, dispatched from Zheng Prefecture, is hereby delivered. (ZHANG QIAN *speaks:*) Head clerk for capital cases, ratify the guards' documents and send them home. (JUDGE BAO *speaks:*) Keep them here until we have reviewed the case, and then send them back. (ZHANG QIAN *speaks:*) Understood. (JUDGE BAO *speaks:*) Zhang Haitang, why did you poison your husband, kidnap the primary wife's child, and scheme for the family fortune all for the sake of a lover? Tell me the whole story, step by step, from the beginning. (ZHANG HAITANG *acts out pursing her lips and looking at* ZHANG LIN.) (ZHANG LIN *speaks:*) Sis, can't you speak? Hai! From her birth she's never seen an official. I'll speak for you. (*Kneels and speaks:*) I petition you, father, this Zhang Haitang is a weakly woman who would never dare poison her husband or be involved in such an evil affair. (JUDGE BAO *speaks:*) You are a bailiff in the court, how can you petition on behalf of an accused? (ZHANG LIN *acts out rising.*) (JUDGE BAO *speaks:*) You, woman, speak your deposition. (ZHANG HAITANG *acts out pursing her lips a second time.*) (ZHANG LIN *kneels and speaks:*) I petition you, father, this Zhang Haitang had no lover and she never poisoned her husband, nor stole a child, nor schemed for the family fortune. It was that first wife who kept Yamen Clerk Zhao as her lover. And that same Clerk Zhao was in charge of the case when it went to court. It is true that they wrongly elicited a confession from her. (JUDGE BAO *speaks:*) You scoundrel, who asked you? Zhang Qian, seize him and beat him thirty times. (ZHANG QIAN *acts out seizing* ZHANG LIN *and beating him.*) (ZHANG LIN *kowtows and speaks:*) This Zhang Haitang is my own little sister. She's never seen a high official before, and I think she's too terrified to speak the real facts of the case. I am laying plaint in her stead. (JUDGE BAO *speaks:*) So, it is the bond of feeling between brother and sister that has made him speak out of turn in this court. If not, then I'll bring out a brass cleaver and slice up this ass's head. Woman, tell me the truth in detail and I will be your advocate. (ZHANG HAITANG *speaks:*) Daddy, (*Sings:*)

> (*Qiaopai'er*)
> I hurriedly bend down upon my knees here before the court,
> From whence you've passed your sagely instructions to tell the whole
>   truth.
> How can I face these vicious and fierce lions and wolves, these court
>   clerks all in a row?
> Daddy, listen as I tell you the inner workings little by little, bit by bit.

(JUDGE BAO *speaks:*) Zhang Haitang, what kind of family do you come from, and how did you come to marry Magnate Ma as a concubine? (ZHANG HAITANG *sings:*)

> (*Tianshui ling*)
> I am from the willowy paths and flowery lanes,
> Where I sent off the old and welcomed the new,
> Where I was a dancing beauty, a singsong girl.

(JUDGE BAO *speaks:*) Ah, so you are a singsong girl. Did that Magnate Ma treat you well? (ZHANG HAITANG *sings:*)

> We loved each other with all our hearts and became man and wife.

(JUDGE BAO *speaks:*) This Zhang Lin says he is your big brother, is that right? (ZHANG LIN *speaks:*) Zhang Haitang is my little sister. (ZHANG HAITANG *sings:*)

> My brother, just a year ago,
> Had little to eat and nothing to wear,
> And sought me out for help.

(JUDGE BAO *speaks*:) And so, you gave him a little for travel money? (ZHANG HAITANG *sings*:)

> Right, right, right! He took away some of my head ornaments and robes and gowns.

(ZHANG LIN *kowtows and speaks*:) The money that I used to buy my position here was what came in exchange for these head ornaments and clothes. (JUDGE BAO *speaks*:) Surely your husband asked you where these things went? (ZHANG HAITANG *speaks*:) Daddy, my husband did ask me, yet the first wife, who had urged me to give them to my brother and who took them to him herself, told the Magnate that I had sent them behind his back to my lover. And so she succeeded in making him burn with anger. (*Sings*:)

> (*Zhegui ling*)
> She made my man so angry that he shouted and stormed until he got sick—

(JUDGE BAO *speaks*:) Since she was the one who killed her husband, why did she go to court? (ZHANG HAITANG *sings*:)

> All of a sudden, she took me to court where I suffered the six interrogations and three questionings.

(JUDGE BAO *speaks*:) Your husband died, but why did you kidnap the child? What do you say to that? (ZHANG HAITANG *sings*:)

> On the one hand my master was dead, and then, snicker-snack, mother and child were to be split apart.

(JUDGE BAO *speaks*:) Which wife raised this child? (ZHANG HAITANG *sings*:)

> They believed the thousandfold envy buried in her evil heart!

(JUDGE BAO *speaks*:) But all the neighbors, and those old ladies, they all said it was hers. (ZHANG HAITANG *sings*:)

> She paid off all the neighbors, and the ones who had served my son all went along, too.

(JUDGE BAO *speaks*:) And I suppose the clerks never inquired any further? (ZHANG HAITANG *sings*:)

> The officials and clerks never even asked a single "Who's right," or "Who's wrong?" "Who's telling the truth," or "Who's lying?"

(JUDGE BAO *speaks:*) If it's as you say it was, then you shouldn't have confessed. (ZHANG HAITANG *sings:*)

> I didn't want to mark the paper and bear the confession,
> It's just that I couldn't stand the constant pressure of club and cudgel.

(JUDGE BAO *speaks:*) Just how did those officials and clerks in Zheng Prefecture pressure you? (ZHANG HAITANG *sings:*)

> (*Yan'er luo*)
> How could I withstand that "The official is not awesome, but his
>   tooth and claws are."
> And they never asked who was guilty and who was not.
> From the very beginning there was an enemy in the court,
> And I was sandwiched between those attendants for no reason.

> (*Desheng ling*)
> Yah! Each shout before the steps was like a peal of thunder;
> On my back each stroke of the club peeled away one layer of skin.
> Here, the one who was beaten couldn't bear the pain;
> There, the one who wielded money suffered no loss.
> I was beaten until I passed out in oblivion,
> Stroke after stroke fell until my spine was smashed to smithereens.
> Those who raised the cudgels were all of one mind,
> Each and everyone one had wrists of strength.

(ZHANG LIN *petitions, speaks:*) The additional convoy of suspects from Zheng Prefecture has arrived all together. (JUDGE BAO *speaks:*) Send them in.

(FIRST WIFE *and* CHILD *enter together with the neighbors and old ladies and act out kneeling.*) (ZHANG QIAN *speaks:*) Face the court. (JUDGE BAO *speaks:*) You, woman, who raised this child? (FIRST WIFE *speaks:*) I raised this child. (JUDGE BAO *speaks:*) Neighbors, old ladies, who raised this child? (THE GROUP *speaks:*) It was truly raised by the elder wife. (JUDGE BAO *speaks:*) Well, it must be so. Send Zhang Lin out. (*Acts out signaling* ZHANG LIN, *who acts out going out, exits.*) (JUDGE BAO *speaks:*) Zhang Qian, bring some chalk and draw out a circle below the steps. Put the child in the circle and have the two women pull him out. The one who is really his mother will pull him out of the circle. The one who isn't won't be able to pull him out. (ZHANG QIAN *speaks:*) Understood. (*Acts out drawing a chalk circle and making the* CHILD *stay in it.*) (FIRST WIFE *acts out pulling* CHILD *out of the circle.*) (ZHANG HAITANG *acts out not being able to pull him out of the circle.*) (JUDGE BAO *speaks:*) Woman, I observe that each time you don't exert all of your energy to pull the child out. Zhang Qian, beat her with the large cudgel. (ZHANG HAITANG *speaks:*) I beseech you, Daddy, hold your thunderlike anger, and stop your tiger- and wolf-like power. From the time I married Magnate Ma and gave birth to this child, I bore him ten months in the womb and nursed him for three years. I swallowed the bitter to spit out the sweet for him, and don't know how much I've suffered over the years to care for him. The five years I've raised him were spent for his sake only. "When two people contest violently, anyone in the middle will be harmed." This child is so young and small. If I were to wrench or break one of his arms, then you would beat me to death. So, I dared not use all of my force to drag him. I hope you will have pity on me. (*Sings:*)

> (*Gua yugou*)
> How could a real and feeling mother do this?
> > (*Continues in speech:*) Daddy, just try and see this:
> The arms of this child are as thin as dried hemp stalks,
> She's a heartless old woman, what does she care?
> How come you cannot see through her wiles?
> She has plied her crafty mind,
> And I've suffered this filthy humiliation.
> Don't let a contest of our two hard hearts
> Cause harm to this child's bones or tear his skin.

(JUDGE BAO *speaks:*) "The intent of the law may be distant, but the feelings of the person can be deduced." The ancient one said, "Look at what a man does; observe the source of his actions; investigate wherein he ceases—can a man hide his character? Can a man hide his character?"[12] Observe how formidably this chalk circle holds all secrets within it. That woman's original intent was to monopolize the family wealth of Ma Junqing, so she wanted to seize that child as her own. She never suspected that the truth and falsehood of it all would come clear by itself, with no help. (*Recites in verse:*)

> She wanted to swindle her sons and grandsons out of their family fortune,
> > But the chalk circle was able to bring out what was false and true.
> Her outer appearance was mild and soft, her heart evil and venomous—
> > It was the real parent, all along, who was acting as the parent.

I've already sent Zhang Lin to arrest her lover. I wonder why he isn't here yet.

(ZHANG LIN *enters holding on to* CLERK ZHAO; *acts out kneeling, speaks:*) Oyez! I've brought Clerk Zhao here. (JUDGE BAO *speaks:*) You, Clerk Zhao, you've picked a fine law case! Tell me truthfully every single fact about the lovers who killed Ma Junqing, the stealing away of the child, the swindling of the family

---

12. From *Analects* 2.10.

fortune, and how the neighbors and old ladies were bought off to be perjured witnesses. (CLERK ZHAO *speaks:*) Aiyo! I'm a clerk and I'm from the yamen—don't I know the law? It's all because of that magistrate, called Equivocal Su. The case was carried out under his hand—I was just a big thumb scratching an itch wherever he told me to. If there was some mistake in taking down the deposition, what does it have to do with a lowly clerk? (JUDGE BAO *speaks:*) I'm not asking you about mistakes in the deposition. I'm asking you if you poisoned Ma Junqing because of your lover. (CLERK ZHAO *speaks:*) Perhaps your honor hasn't really observed that that woman's face is completely covered with powder. If you wash off this powder you'll see what an ugly face she has. If she were thrown down by the wayside, no one would want her. How could I have an affair with her? Or commit such an act? (FIRST WIFE *speaks:*) In private you said that I was just like Guanyin. But now you've brought me down so that I'm not even a person. Such a cheat! (ZHANG LIN *speaks:*) In that snowstorm yesterday, Clerk Zhao and the first wife caught up with us on the road and exchanged some words with those escorts. How can he not be the lover? Just interrogate those escorts and it'll all come clear. (CLOWN DONG *speaks:*) So, even we've been implicated. (JUDGE BAO *speaks:*) Zhang Qian, take Clerk Zhao down, pick out a big club, and beat him. (ZHANG QIAN *speaks:*) Understood. (*Acts out beating* CLERK ZHAO.) (ZHANG HAITANG *sings:*)

> (*Qing xuanhe*)
> So, you thought you'd be husband and wife forever with First Wife
>   Ma,
> And that you'd send me away, never to return.
> Otherwise, why did you try to catch up to us midway here?
> Let's have it out, face to face,
> Face to face.

(CLERK ZHAO *acts out dying.*) (JUDGE BAO *speaks:*) He dares feign death? Zhang Qian, pick him up and spew some water on his face. (ZHANG QIAN *spews water,* [CLERK ZHAO] *acts out reviving.*) (JUDGE BAO *speaks:*) Confess quickly! (CLERK ZHAO *speaks:*) Well, my congress with that woman was certainly more than a single day. According to the codicils of law, you've uncovered only my co-adulteress. This carries no death penalty. As for the poisoning—it was never my own idea to go out and purchase the poison. That woman, herself, put the poison herbs into the soup and killed her husband. As for stealing away the child—I told her from the start that we didn't want one raised by someone else. And it was that woman, again, who said that if we got the child then we had easy claim on the family fortune. I'm just a poor clerk. I don't have any silver to use to buy off those old ladies or neighbors. That woman bought them off, too. And it was that woman who ordered the escorts to kill Haitang on the road.

(FIRST WIFE *speaks:*) Ha! You, who beg for your life, have already confessed. What's left for me to say? I did it all, I did it all. There's no great disaster except death. I hope that you kill the both of us, so we can be husband and wife forever in the Yellow Springs.[13] Wouldn't *that* be nice? (JUDGE BAO *speaks:*) Everyone, listen to my decision: Magistrate of Zhengzhou, Su Shun, has wrongly violated the criminal code. He is stripped of his official cap and robe and made an ordinary citizen, never to be selected for employment again. Neighbors and old ladies should not have accepted bribes for their testimony and become perjured witnesses at court. Each shall be bastinadoed eighty times and sent into exile three hundred miles from their homes. Dong Chao and Xue Ba, as members of the official ranks, should never have accepted any bribes for anything. They shall be judged one step in punishments above an ordinary person, and are to be bastinadoed one hundred times, then sent far away to some miasmic place where they shall serve in the army. The adulterer and adulteress should not have plotted the death of Ma Junqing by poison, or stolen away the child, or swindled the family fortune. They shall suffer slow slicing. Take them to the execution grounds and let each die by 120 slices of the knife. All family wealth shall be given to Zhang Haitang to manage, and the child, Shou'er, shall return home to be raised properly. Zhang Lin is ordered to live with his sister, and his official obligations are forgiven. (*Recites in ballad verse:*)

> Because Clerk Zhao sold his charms and practiced adultery
> Zhang Haitang bore grave injustice.
> I made a plan with a chalk circle,
> And was able to deduce the principles behind the case with clarity.
> Additionally, every person who received any profit has been exiled,
> And the chief conspirators have been beheaded before the steps.
> Only by relying on Zhang Lin to raise his sword to help,
> Could mother and child be reunited.

(ZHANG HAITANG, *with* ZHANG LIN, *acts out kowtowing, sings:*)

> (*Shuixianzi*)
> Neighbors—didn't you say that you were telling the truth with all
>   your hearts?
> Grandmothers—didn't you say you could not remember because of
>   your advanced years?
> Clerk—didn't you say that officials were pure, laws just, and every-
>   thing was by the book?
> Elder sister—didn't you say you were the number one virtuous saint?

---

13. I.e, the Chinese equivalent of Hades.

Today, based on the causes brought out by Kaifeng Prefecture's
  investigation,
These few here are exiled to wild borderlands,
These two are punished by death in the noisy marketplace.
Grandfather Bao, this *Record of the Chalk Circle* will be spread
  beyond the four seas for all to know!

TITLE: Zhang Haitang is unjustly sent to Kaifeng Prefecture.

NAME: Rescriptor-in-Waiting Bao's clever trick: the record of the chalk
  circle.

8

Zhongli of the Han Leads Lan Caihe to Enlightenment

Anonymous

Zhongli of the Han Leads Lan Caihe to Enlightenment was probably written between 1250 and 1320. While neither *The Register of Ghosts* nor *A Formulary of Correct Rhymes from an Era of Great Peace* mentions a play with this title, a general dating can be derived from internal evidence. Many plays on the topic of enlightenment stem from the last half of the thirteenth century, and the names of the six (or seven) other dramas that Lan Caihe enumerates in Act 1 can all be dated reliably to that period.

Three of the characters in this play belong to a group called "The Eight Immortals": Lan Caihe, the protagonist; Zhongli Quan, who guides Lan Caihe to his immortal state; and Lü Dongbin, a disciple of Zhongli Quan who helps in a charade to open the recalcitrant Lan Caihe's eyes to the terror and impermanence of the human realm. The set number of the group has always been eight, but its constituent members have changed over time. The Eight Immortals in their modern configuration are:

Name	Depiction
Zhang Guo lao (Old Zhang Guo)	Riding a donkey, carrying a fish drum
Zhongli Quan	Bare-bellied, holding a fan
Lü Dongbin	Dressed as a scholar, sword on his back
Tieguai Li (Iron Crutch Li)	Iron crutch
He Xiangu (Immortal Lady He)	Carrying a lotus flower, holding a fly whisk
Cao Guojiu (Imperial In-law Cao)	Dressed in court robes, carrying castanets
Han Xiangzi (Young Han Xiang)	Carrying or playing a flute
Lan Caihe	Carrying a basket of flowers, wearing one shoe, hoe over his back

He Xiangu, the only confirmed female, did not appear in earlier formulations of the eight, and in the Yuan her place was occupied by Xu Shenweng (Holy

Codger Xu), a historical twelfth century Daoist known both for his uncanny prognostications and his outspokenness. His name appears in the play in Act 2 (the song *Dou hama*), although not explicitly as one of the Eight Immortals.

The distinguishing accessories of each member and their rank within the group were also not stable. For instance, the protagonist of our play, Lan Caihe, is usually portrayed with a flower basket (*lan*, his surname, is synonymous with the word for "basket"); but in earlier representations, Han Xiangzi is shown carrying such a basket. In modern times Lan Caihe is also portrayed either as a male or female. This androgynous representation is clearly a later phenomenon. In Yuan times, he is shown as a male, wearing only one boot and carrying a huge set of castanets that were called "Yunyang clappers." The name of the clappers is challenging, since the term Yunyang can refer in dramatic literature either to the execution grounds or to a propitious tree spirit that could be summoned by reciting that name. Lan Caihe is also commonly represented as trailing a long string of cash, which he hands out freely to onlookers and the many children that follow him. Likewise, the lineage of master-disciple relations within the group changes according to the texts in which they are presented.

The name Lan Caihe first appears in the area of Nanjing during the latter Tang dynasty (923–936). "Foot-stomping" songs lamenting the impermanence of life and praising the pleasures of the immortal were extremely popular at that time, and their opening line usually included the three syllables *lan cai he*. There is a debate about whether these were simply nonsense syllables, like *tra-la-la* in English, or whether they could possibly be an adaptation of a synonymic phrase, "basket gathering grain," and refer to an ancient agrarian ritual. Whatever the case, the phrase metamorphosed into a personal name and by the middle of the tenth century, Lan Caihe had been converted into a Daoist transcendent in a hagiography by Shen Fen, the *Continuation of the Biographies of Transcendents* (*Xu Xianzhuan*):

> Nobody knows where Lan Caihe came from. He always wore a tattered blue gown with six clasps and a belt of black wooden pieces that was over three inches wide. He wore a boot on one foot, but the other was naked. In the summer he would pad his gown with floss, but in the winter he would just lie in the snow and the vapors would rise from him just as if he were being steamed. He always traveled singing through the city, begging for handouts, and carried a large set of clappers that were over three feet long. He often got drunk and stomped and sang, and old and young followed him to look at his performance. He was clever and quick-witted, and when someone asked him something, he answered quick as an echo, and everyone would double over

with laughter. He pretended to be crazy but he was not. When he walked, he would shake his boot and sing the "Stomping Song":

Stomping song, stomping song,
Lan Caihe,
How long will the world of time and space last?
Ruddy faces—a tree at the height of spring,
Flowing years—a single throw of the shuttle.
The ancients a muddled mess, gone to never return;
Moderns a profuse plethora, come in growing numbers.
In the morning I ride the phoenix to the azure sky;
At nightfall watch the fields of mulberries turn to whitecap waves;[1]
The bright radiance of eternal light is at the verge of the void,
Palaces and pylons golden and silver rise high and towering.

There were many, many different lyrics for the song, but they all had to do with becoming a transcendent, although none could guess their import. But they would just give him coppers that he would string on a long rope and trail behind him as he walked. If they fell off, he never paid attention to them; if he saw a poor person, he would give him some. Once when he was drunk, there were clouds and cranes and the sound of reed organs and pipes. Suddenly he was lightly lifted into the clouds, and he threw down his boot, his gown, his belt, and his clappers and slowly disappeared.

While the drama we have translated below is the first work to actually portray Lan Caihe as an actor, this short passage already identifies him as a kind of street entertainer who sings and dances for cash. There are at least ten poems written about Lan Caihe in the thirteenth and fourteenth centuries, several of which are about his portrait, presumably those in albums or scrolls that picture all eight immortals. These poems are all congruent in the sense that they describe his image as blue-gowned, trailing a string of cash, and being surrounded by children scrambling to pick up the falling coins. The only source to call him an "actor" is a song suite written by a contemporary, which includes the two lines, "Zhongli Quan was originally a lead commander, / Lan Caihe was an actor all along." This is the only direct link established between the drama and his early hagiography, but we can see in all the documents a gradual evolution of Lan as an entertainer—a quick-witted singer of songs of enlightenment, a busker who performs for cash. It would not be too far of a leap in the popular

---

1. Long periods of time in which mulberry fields turn to oceans; upheavals of time, etc.

imagination to cast him as an actor, the lead player of worlds within a world that he was destined to leave.

Lan Caihe belongs to a distinct subgenre of Northern dramas called "deliverance plays" (*dutuo xi*). There are ten plays still extant, of which eight are Daoist and two Buddhist:

> Daoist:
> Anon., *Zhongli of the Han Leads Lan Caihe to Enlightenment*
> Anon., *Lü Dongbin in Peach and Willow: A Dream of Ascending to Immortality* (*Lü Dongbin taoliu shengxian meng*)
> Gu Zijing, *Lü Dongbin Thrice Leads the Willow South of the City to Enlightenment* (*Lü Dongbin sandu chengnan liu*)
> Ma Zhiyuan, *Lü Dongbin Gets Drunk Three Times in Yueyang Tower* (*Lü Dongbin sanzui Yueyang lou*)
> Ma Zhiyuan, *Ma Danyang Thrice Leads Crazy Ren to Enlightenment* (*Ma Danyang sandu Ren fengzi*)
> Ma Zhiyuan, Li Shizhong, Hua Lilang xueshi, Hongzi Li Er, *Gaining Enlightenment at Handan: The Dream of Yellow Millet* (*Handan dao xingwu huangliang meng*)
> Yang Jingxian, *Ma Danyang Leads Head of the Guild Liu to Enlightenment* (*Ma Danyang dutuo Liu hangshou*)
> Yue Bochuan, *Lü Dongbin Leads Iron Crutch Li Yue to Enlightenment* (*Lü Dongbin dutuo Tieguai Li*)
>
> Buddhist:
> Li Shouqing, *The Monk of Moon's Light Leads Liu Cui to Enlightenment* (*Yueniang heshang du Liu Cui*)
> Zheng Tingyu, *The Monk with a Burden and the Story of "Patience"* (*Budai heshang renzi ji*)

The term "deliverance" (which we translate as "leading to enlightenment") is a shortened form of a common Buddhist phrase, "to be delivered by transcending the world and liberated from the cycle of transmigration" (*chaodu jietuo*). The convertible use of the term between Buddhism and Daoism can be explained by the fact that this era witnessed a syncretist movement in which the terminology and doctrines of the three basic modes of thought (Confucianism, Daoism, and Buddhism) were united under the banner of "three teachings united as one" (*sanjiao heyi*). Some of the Daoist deliverance plays are, in turn, intimately related to the sect of the Perfectly Realized Way (*Quanzhen dao*), a school that came into ascendency in the Jin and Yuan dynasties and continues to the present time. The Eight Immortals always figure prominently in these plays. This is because the Quanzhen School included among their Five Patriarchs not only a primeval mythical figure, Lord of the East (*Donghua dijun*), who is often seen as the male counterpart to the Queen Mother of the West, ruler of Daoist paradise, but also two of the Eight Immortals, Zhongli Quan and Lü Dongbin; along with two early Quanzhen masters, Ma Dongyang and Liu Haichan. The "deliverers" in the Daoist plays known to us are Zhongli Quan, Lü Dongbin, and Iron Crutch Li from the Eight Immortals, Wang Chongyang, the human patriarch of the Quanzhen school, and his disciple Ma Danyang.

We can see a distinct lineage of transmission of the Way reflected in the plays themselves. From their contents, we can establish the following line of transmission: Zhongli Quan→Lü Dongbin→Wang Chongyang→Ma Danyang. These plays did not form part of the urban, commercial repertoire, and may have been solely performed at court or at private birthday celebrations. From this point of view, Lan Caihe's conversion on his own birthday within the play reveals the irony of such a venue: on the day in which one marks the passage of one's life toward eventual death, one is prodded into the awareness that the only way to transcend that end is to deliver oneself into the timeless world of the immortal. In the same manner, the time lapse of some thirty years between Acts 3 and 4, in which Lan Caihe does not age, reinforces the message that life can be prolonged indefinitely. We can surmise that these were private celebrations from the fact that, of the seven plays set in the environment of an acting troupe that enumerate dramas that can be performed on the urban stage (as Lan Caihe does in Act 2), none mention deliverance plays. In fact, the list of plays in *Lan Caihe* is the only such list of all of the dramas to include the title of a deliverance play.

In all respects this drama follows the conventions of deliverance plays. A Daoist master becomes aware that a certain person is destined to become an immortal, but on his first encounter is rebuffed by the mortal being, who refuses to acknowledge either the master or the message of transcendence. The one who is to be transformed eventually undergoes some form of reversal of fortune and is saved from torture and death by the master. The disciple then leaves his family only to be confronted by them after years of wandering. He then repudiates them and is led off, in a grand finale, to the land of Jasper Pools and peaches of immortality, to live forever in the company of the Queen Mother of the West and other immortals. The person being converted often is at the very bottom of the social ladder, and butchers and prostitutes seem to be the favorite occupations. The mortal can also sometimes be a banished immortal who has been sent away from Daoist paradise for some minor infraction. A peculiar turn on this motif is that some souls are first made into tree spirits, from which they had to be turned into human form before being liberated.

The value of *Lan Caihe* to the history of the early theater lies specifically in its detailed description of everyday life in an acting troupe through the eyes of its manager and lead player. Specifically, it provides knowledge about the organization of family troupes, preparations for performance, and staging in an urban environment. It also details the relationship between actors and the public, officials, and authors. It can profitably be compared to the mural of Zhongdu Xiu's troupe found in the Introduction (Fig. 1), where one can see a visual representation of the elements of the stage as described in the play. There are some caveats, however, to accepting this information uncritically. First is that the theme of the deliverance play itself demands a family that the disciple must repudiate. Lan Caihe's troupe is composed primarily of blood and marriage relatives, but other plays on the theater indicate that this is not always the case. Second, the portrayal of Lan Caihe himself as a brash, arrogant, and self-assured person who hobnobs with high society is a necessary background for his initial rebuffing of Zhongli Quan. His supreme confidence in his worldly position and his belief in the economic viability of his troupe are a precondition for his eventual reversal. Thus, when we see how the troupe's fortunes decline when their lead actor is gone, we may see a reflection of a real phenomenon, but we may also be seeing a mirror reflection between those who choose enlightenment and those who do not.

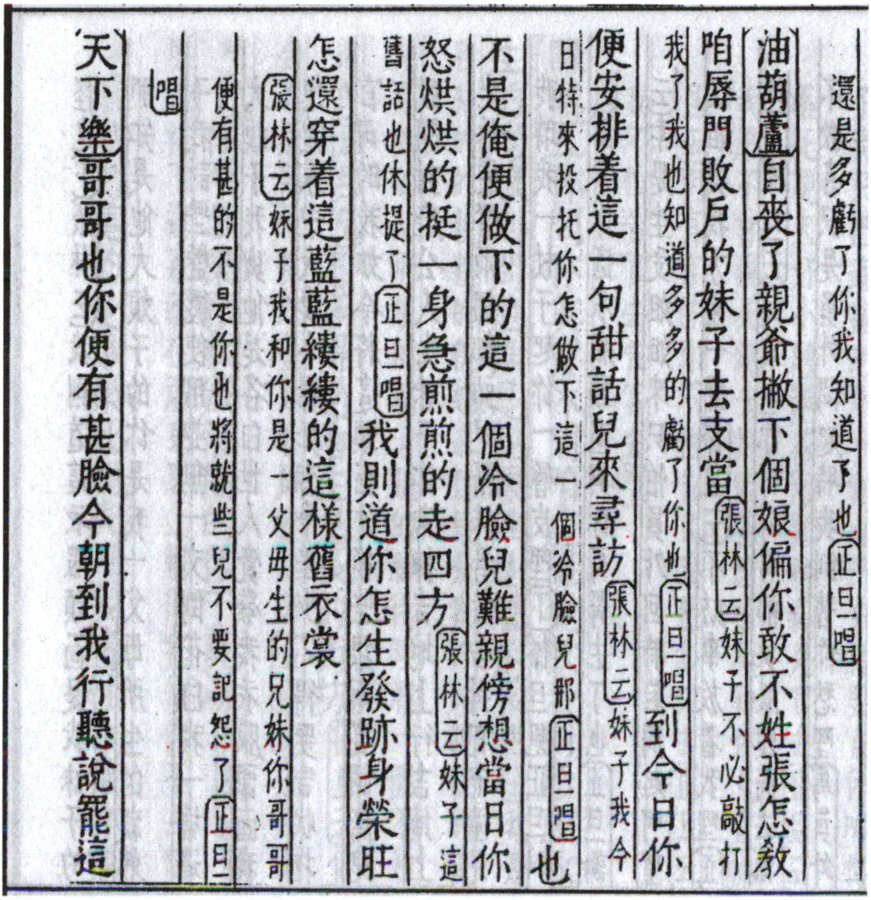

還是多虧了你我知道下也〔正旦唱〕

油葫蘆自袭了親爺撤下個娘偏你敢不姓張怎教咱辱門敗戶的妹子去支當〔張林云妹子不必敲打我了我也知道多多的虧了你也〔正旦唱〕到今日你便安排着這一句甜話兒來尋訪〔張林云妹子我今日特來投托你怎做下這一個冷臉兒那〔正旦唱〕也不是俺便做下的這一個冷臉兒難親傍想當日你怒烘烘的挺一身急煎煎的走四方〔張林云妹子這舊話也休提了〔正旦唱〕我則道你怎生發跡身榮旺怎還穿着這藍藍縷縷的這樣舊衣裳〔張林云〕妹子我和你是一父母生的兄妹你哥哥便有甚的不是你也將就些兒不要記怨了〔正旦唱〕

〔天下樂〕哥哥也你便有甚臉令朝到我行聽說罷這

Fig. 3. The tunes *You hulu* and *Tianxia le* from Act 1 of *The Record of the Chalk Circle* (page 249 in this volume), from Zang Maoxun's *Selection of Yuan Plays*

Dramatis personæ in order of appearance

Role type	Name, family role, or social role
Second male	Zhongli Quan
Female lead	Xiqianjin, Lan Caihe's wife
Extra female	Lan Caihe's sister
Child	Little Caihe
Clown	Bandleader Wang
Clown	Thinhead Li
Male lead	Lan Caihe
Runners	Yamen runners
Official	Lü Dongbin
Children	Children

Zhongli of the Han Leads Lan Caihe to Enlightenment

[Act 1]

(SECOND MALE, *costumed as* ZHONGLI *enters, recites:*)[2]

> The gate of our birth is the door of our death,
> Yet how many get it, how many become enlightened?
> The hardest of men should ponder this when night falls—
> Undying eternal life is a product of man himself!

This humble Daoist is surnamed Zhongli, named Quan, and styled Cloud House.[3] My designation in the Way is the Master of Upright Yang. I was just returning from a vegetarian banquet in Heaven when I saw a shaft of blue light from the lower realm stream up against the Ninth Empyrean.[4] I looked for a long time then saw an actor in the Liangyuan Playhouse[5] in Luoyang, Xu Jian, who is known by his stage name as Lan Caihe. This man already possesses half of what it takes to be an immortal. I might as well go straight down to the Liangyuan Playhouse and lead this person across. I'll see to it that

> King Yama remove Lan's life *and* his death from his Register,[6]
> In order to establish his name in the Palaces of the Purple Precinct;[7]

---

2. The original identifies characters by the role type of the actor or actress who performs a specific role. We have followed standard convention in designating the speakers and singer.

3. A term that designates the home of an eremite or otherworldly being; high in the clouds of the mountains or the clouds in the sky.

4. The highest point of heaven; the abode of Daoist immortals.

5. Liangyuan originally referred to a mansion of a royal prince of the second century BC that was located near modern Kaifeng. There the prince housed many literary retainers in his houses and gardens. It later becomes a stock designation for a place of sumptuous intellectual and material life. In light of the subject matter of the play, we can assume that the author chose this as the name of the playhouse because of the proverb, "Liangyuan may be wonderful, but it is not the place for which I long," meaning that a foreign place may be fine, but it is never as good as home.

6. The judge of the underworld, assigned to deciding the fate of the dead in keeping with the Register of Life and Death.

7. "Purple Tenuity," the constellation that is located above the North Pole.

I will point him toward that road to the corner of the sea at Heaven's edge,
And guide that deluded one down the Great Way.

(*Exits.*)

(FEMALE LEAD *together with* EXTRA FEMALE, CHILD, *along with two* CLOWNS *dressed as* WANG *and* LI *enter,* WANG *speaks:*) One of us is Bandleader Wang, the other Thinhead Li, our elder brother is Lan Caihe. We all perform on the stage in Liangyuan Playhouse. This is our sister-in-law. We're going on ahead to set things up on the stage. . . . Let me open the door and see who shows up. (ZHONGLI *enters:*) I'll go straight down on my cloud to the lower realm and onto the stage in Liangyuan Playhouse. Here I am already. (*Acts out seeing the musician's bench and sits down.* CLOWN *speaks:*) Okay, Reverend, go on up to the bleachers or to the side seats to watch. This is where the women perform, not a place for you to sit. (ZHONGLI *speaks:*) Is that famous male lead Xu Jian home? (WANG *speaks:*) Old master, he'll be here by and by. Did you have something you wanted to say to him? (ZHONGLI *speaks:*) I'll wait until he gets here to talk to him personally. (WANG *speaks:*) Well, master, just sit here for a bit. Brother will be along any time.

(MALE LEAD, *dressed as* LAN CAIHE, *enters and speaks:*) I'm Xu Jian, called Lan Caihe in the theater. My wife is Xiqianjin,[8] and we have a son, Little Caihe, whose wife is called Lanshanjing.[9] Bandleader Wang is married to my elder sister and Thinhead Li to my younger. We all perform here on the stage of Liangyuan Playhouse. Yesterday we hung out our spangled advertisements, and my two brothers have gone on ahead to make everything ready. I'd best get to the stage. I believe that the life of an actor is no easy thing! (*Sings:*)

> ([XIANLÜ MODE:] *Dian jiangchun*)
> I transmit these old texts on and on
> To give face to our itinerant performers.
> Practiced in the arts of the guild,
> Telling my jokes like a monk seizing the moment of enlightenment,
> Exhausting this meager art, I now understand the depth of its
>   significance.
>
> (*Hunjiang long*)
> Just look at how I have carefully stitched together this livelihood,

---

8. This is obviously a stage name. *Qianjin*, literally "a thousand gold," can mean "a lot of money," and "rich and noble," the elegant daughter of a rich family (used as a honorific designation for someone else's daughter), as well as the title of a medical book by a famous Daoist.

9. Another stage name, meaning something like "vista of blue mountains."

And in this Liangyuan city[10] have already passed twenty years since
    here I first set foot,
Always doing what people want,
Treating every customer like a king.
For every new farce that tells of passionate love or urges virtue and
    piety,
I eke out a few coppers to keep the household comfortable and save
    us from hunger and cold.
But it surpasses any other district or county,[11]
And studying just a portion of these meager arts
Is far better than owning a thousand acres of fine fields.

(LAN *speaks:*) Here I am at the theater. Are there spectators, brothers? Look at the time! Hurry and get things ready. (WANG *speaks:*) When I opened up the door to the stage, there was a reverend sitting there on the music bench. I said, "Reverend, go on up to the bleachers or to the side seats to watch, this is where the women who perform sit." But he cursed me instead. (LAN *speaks:*) You probably ruffled him. I'll attend to it myself. (LAN *acts out greeting him, speaks:*) Respectful greetings, old master. (ZHONGLI *speaks:*) Where have you been loitering around? (LAN *speaks:*) You're giving me a bum rap! You don't understand— some fine men in the city asked me to have a cup of tea with them. That's why I'm late. (ZHONGLI *speaks:*) Well, I've been sitting in this theater all day and you finally show up. "It's better that the music wait on the guests than the guests wait on the music!" I have come just to see you perform a comedy. Whichever piece you pick to perform, I'll watch. (LAN *speaks:*) Master, what comedy would you like to see? (ZHONGLI *speaks:*) Just name off the ones you know by heart. (LAN *speaks:*) Okay, listen to these few. (*Sings:*)

> (*You hulu*)
> Please, beneficent patron, pick out any that strikes your fancy!

(ZHONGLI *speaks:*) Isn't this being a bit presumptuous? (LAN *sings:*)

> How could we, these itinerant performers, dare be
>   presumptuous?
> These are all newly composed by the poets' writing clubs.

(ZHONGLI *speaks:*) Well, since they're by poets, I'm listening. (LAN *sings:*)

---

10. Cf. note 5; Liangyuan city normally means Bianliang, modern Kaifeng.

11. Here meant in two senses. Luoyang is more lucrative than other places, but also his earnings as a performer in a stable location are better than those of itinerant performers who "run the counties and travel the prefectures."

I'll play *Yu Yuzhi: Inscribing Sadness on a Red Leaf at Golden Stream,*
Or *Zhang Zhongze: The Jade Girl's Sadness of the Loquat Guitar.*

(ZHONGLI *speaks:*) How many bare-chested comedies can you do?[12] (LAN *speaks:*) I'll try to list off a few. (LAN *sings:*)

I can do *The Old Commander: Sword against Sword,*
Or *The Young Yuchi: Whip against Whip,*
Or *The Three Princes Consolidate Governance at Linhu Hall.*

(ZHONGLI *speaks:*) I don't want these. Do another. (LAN *sings:*)

Nothing is better than *Poetry and Wine in the Garden of Radiant
   Spring.*

(*Tianxia le*)
Or perhaps I could do *Snow Packs Lan Pass: The Horse Cannot
   Go On.*

(ZHONGLI *speaks:*) Do something else. (LAN *sings:*)

I am afraid that my talent truly is not up to it,
Thank you deeply, patron, for your kind consideration.

(LAN *speaks:*) Bandleader Wang, put up the flags, valances, spirit pictures, and backdrop for me. (WANG *speaks:*) I already did. (LAN *sings:*)

Here the flags and valance are raised,
There the backdrops are hung.

(LAN *speaks:*) And when that audience catches sight as they arrive, they will let this be known outside: the male lead Lan Caihe is performing on stage at Liang-yuan Playhouse. (*Sings:*)

And I expect the whole world will glorify my name!

(LAN *speaks:*) Old master, go on over to the side seats to watch. This music bench is no place for you. This is where the women who perform sit. (ZHONGLI *speaks:*) No, I'll just sit here. (LAN *speaks:*) This spiteful reverend is really boorish. I see you're not from around here, but you're a cloud-roving reverend who washes in the river, sleeps in temples, lives in a dilapidated kiln, and doesn't even have a convent. I'm not laughing at you, since you've never seen a stage in your life. (ZHONGLI *speaks:*) And just what kind of oh-so-famous guild player

---

12. These are martial plays, in which the fighters in the challenge strip down to their pants to do battle.

are you? (LAN *speaks:*) And I suppose you're some kind of Master Guangcheng[13] or Zhongli of the Han? Don't take into account what you eat—just look at what you're wearing. So just "drop that sheep's skin of yours!" (*Sings:*)

> (*Nuozha ling*)
> Judging from the fact that your mouth has escaped the fate of eating
>   dregs and chaff,
> And that your body has met its cloud conveyance and cap of thin
>   rattan slips,[14]
> I would say that you are sitting firmly astride the transcendent's
>   crane bound for Heaven!

(ZHONGLI *speaks:*) I've been all over the world, but I've never seen a male lead like you! (LAN *sings:*)

> In perfect peace you insert yourself into the wine stalls,
> And roam all over the world
> Until that pair of those feet of yours silently cry out, "Mercy on me."

(ZHONGLI *speaks:*) The only reason that you take the stage to perform is to swindle people out of their money. (LAN *sings:*)

> (*Que ta zhi*)
> You say I swindle people out of their money
> And guilefully perform these dramatic scripts.

(*Speaks:*) Only officials, the high class, and the rich come to the theater to relieve their minds; I've seen no reverend watch a play in my lifetime! (*Sings:*)

> Have you ever seen a clump of singers and dancers
> Produce an arhat or a spiritual transcendent?

(*Speaks:*) You go door to door to beg, and no one has anything good to give you. (*Sings:*)

> You point to believers and beg a few scraps and odds and ends.

(*Speaks:*) And from those contributions you patch together a tidy sum, and when you see how much money it is, your desire for profit has already begun. (*Sings:*)

---

13. A famous Daoist master of antiquity who is reputed to have instructed the Yellow Emperor in the Way.

14. In visual representations Daoist "realized ones" are represented riding clouds and wearing a hat made out of thin strips of rattan vine.

And you don't even put it into Buddha's pocket,[15] but whisk it away
for your own use!

(ZHONGLI *speaks:*) Well, the only reason you have to perform every day is because of your own "burning guild."[16] When will it end? You don't understand
the pleasures we who have left the family enjoy. (LAN *speaks:*) Well, we of the
vulgar world have a hundred flavors of the rarest foods when we want to eat,
and a thousand baskets of silks and damasks when we want to put something
on. I've seen what you who "leave the family" enjoy. (*Sings:*)

> (*Jisheng cao*)
> You, not I, eat bland food and endure yellowed cabbage;
> I, not you, pick out just what to put in my mouth, change from
>   outfit to outfit.
> Everyday you wind through teahouses, wineshops, and theaters,
> Carrying an earthenware bottle, a wooden begging bowl, and a
>   white ceramic can
> To beg some noodle-leavings scraped from the bottom of the
>   press.

(*Speaks:*) They push you out of a wineshop here, run you out of a teahouse
there.... (*Sings:*)

> Eat just a little bit of a singsong girl's wine and food,
> And you'd probably think it was a banquet of Queen Mother's[17]
>   sacred peaches from the Jasper Pool.

(*Speaks:*) Look, you vile reverend, get out of here! You've spoiled a whole day's
performance. (ZHONGLI *speaks:*) I'll see the performance. I'm not leaving. (LAN
speaks:) Since he won't get out, Bandleader Wang, lock up the theater gates.
(WANG *speaks:*) You've hit it on the head, brother. I'll lock up the gate and see
what he's going to do when he's locked inside! (LAN *speaks:*) Listen here, you
spiteful reverend, you've harassed us today so that we never got to perform. If

---

15. That is, he has no permanent monastery to which he can contribute what he begs.

16. A double entendre on the term *huo yuan*: (1) "Your companions in the guild": the people
who rely on him as the lead performer; (2) "your burning guild": akin to the Buddhist term "sea
of bitterness," the trials and tribulations of being in and attached to the vulgar secular world.

17. The Queen Mother of the West lives near the Jasper Pool in the westernmost mountains
of the world. There she presides over a court of beautiful immortal maidens. Her peaches, which
grow in the orchard of Langyuan and ripen only once in three thousand years, confer immortality upon the eater. In some novels, the Eight Immortals are brought together to visit the Queen
Mother, and they are given a banquet of rare delicacies and entertained by the Queen's five
daughters.

you show up again tomorrow and get in the way of our livelihood, I'll pick out a few big toughs and beat you senseless. (*Sings:*)

> (*Zhuansha*)
> You'll never match the clever subtlety of the truly wise,
> And I can't be concerned about another person's "face."
> When will you get to the fairy isle of Penglai or Langyuan
>   Orchard?[18]
> When will you escape the six realms of recurrent incarnations?[19]
> That crazy, mad behavior of yours will do no good!

(*Speaks:*) Let me lock up the stage doors and see how you get out. (*Sings:*)

> Go ahead and ride your cloud chariot,
> Ascend to the Heavens in broad daylight,
> Will you dare "twaddle before my face again?"[20]

(*Speaks:*) Bother me again and I'll keep the doors closed for ten days and starve you to death. (*Sings:*)

> That physical body of yours is so weak
> Your body will fold over[21] and you will not be able to see.

(*Speaks:*) And since you're already someone who has left the family, instead of seeing a play, (*Sings:*)

> Go ahead and imitate that Realized Lord Xu, who ascended to blue
>   Heaven in broad daylight![22]

> (*Troupe members all exit together.*)

(ZHONGLI *speaks:*) I came here today to enlighten Lan Caihe, but his dull brows and carnal eyes did not recognize me. Do you think I can't go out just because you closed the stage doors? Gates, open! If this guy doesn't have something bad

---

18. Penglai is one of Three Isles of Immortals in the eastern sea.

19. Literally, the "six paths of reincarnation." According to Buddhism, all living creatures must travel a path through one of six realms into which karma dictates they will born: the path of heaven, the path of humans, the path of frightful demons, the path of animals, the path of hungry ghosts, and the path of hell.

20. Based on the proverb, "speak no lies in front of the realized one!"

21. The text gives the very rare character *xue* here, but it may be a scribal error for *zhepi*, "the skin folds"; i.e., there is nothing left inside to keep the body from folding. For instance, when one cannot hold up one's head, it is called *zhebozi*, a folded neck.

22. One of the customary designations of the Daoist master Xu Xun, who ascended to Heaven in 375–76. According to one source, he was 136 years old at that time; and in another source, he ascended with forty-two members of his household.

happen to him, he'll never be willing to leave his household. Tomorrow is his birthday. Quick! Dongbin, come down to this lower realm. (*Recites:*)

> If I do not liberate him from his ties to dust-blown custom and the world
> of the vulgar,
> How will he know that inside he is an immortal?
> When his practice of merit has reached its full, he can ascend to the
> transcendents' realm,
> And then, at that time, he will rise to blue Heaven in the white light of day!

(*Exits.*)

[Act 2]

(LI *and* WANG *enter, speak:*) Today is Brother Caihe's birthday. We brothers have brought along a few gifts, have prepared a banquet, and will wish him long life today. (LAN *enters with* WIFE, *speaks:*) It's my birthday today, and my fellow guild members have brought some presents to wish me long life. Hang up the portrait of the Longevity Star, and make our offerings in front of him. Set up the incense, and on this happy occasion today, let us slowly drink a few unhurried cups. (*Sings:*)

> ([NANLÜ MODE:] *Yizhi hua*)
> A white lotus is stuck in the jade vase,
> Yellow seal-script incense[23] is placed in the golden tripod;
> Pour out a cup of long-life wine,
> Hang up a portrait of the Star of Longevity,
> And come wish me long life.
> I am deeply moved by your respect,
> When I consider just what my own humble capabilities are.
> I am such a trouble to you, my companions and neighbors near
>   and far,
> I thank you for your good wishes, my relatives, friends, and
>   colleagues.

(*Speaks:*) Since you have already come to pay your respects to me, don't leave now. Let's take our time and drink some wine. (*Sings:*)

> (*Liangzhou*)
> Let's drink until that falling red wheel sinks in the west
> And that sparkling jade hare rises in the east.

---

23. This is incense made in the shape of complicated archaic characters, which took quite a while to burn and was used to measure time. Here, of course, a symbol of wishes for long life.

It's a common saying, "One understands the Mandate of Heaven only
 after fifty,"[24]
My years have now passed that half of a hundred,
And I have experienced all kinds of things.
A man has his sentient nature,
Just as birds know how to rise in flight.
The aphorism says, "Even things that wriggle have sentience,"[25]
So wherever one performs, who dares relax or rest?

(*Speaks:*) We in this guild have figured out the power of water. (*Sings:*)

We, we, we produce feelings from the circumstances when we
 perform,
You, you, you risk your life and gamble your fate when you rise to
 high position;
We, we, we only grasp profit or vie for reputation when we go
 anywhere.
And should we meet
A rival troupe,
How do we dress ourselves up to dominate the stage?
We put our trust in a line of four or five "powdered noses,"
Rely on the benevolence of the writers' guilds, from whom we seek
 text and songs.[26]

(*Speaks:*) "The Gentleman applies himself to the roots; when the roots are established the Way will grow."[27] (*Sings:*)

And so need not worry about the future.

(WANG *acts out taking up a cup, speaks:*) Drink a cup of birthday wine, brother.
(ZHONGLI *enters and speaks:*) It's Lan Caihe's birthday today, and I'll lead him
across to enlightenment now. Here I am at the gate already. (*Acts out sobbing three
times, laughing three times.* LAN *speaks:*) Did you hear that, Bandleader Wang?
Who's making all that racket at the doorway? (WANG *speaks:*) Don't bother
yourself about little things, brother. Who knows? Let's just drink. (LAN *sings:*)

---

24. Slight changes to *Analects* 2.4, "At fifty I understood Heaven's mandate."

25. Cf. *Butterfly Dream:* "Even things that wriggle have sentience; all possess the Buddha
nature."

26. The term *yixie benling*, which we have translated as "text and songs," may be a simple
mistake for a homophonic phrase that simply would mean "inspiration (or talent)."

27. *Analects* 1.2. There is a pun here. The same character we have translated as "roots" can also
mean "text." Therefore, "The good actor works on the script; if the scripts are good, then business
will be good."

(*He xinlang*)
Who is that weeping and wailing?

(*Speaks:*) I'll just open the door. Oh, it's just that vile reverend. You are crazy.
(*Sings:*)

> You've put a curse on our house!
> You really fan the flames of the common folk's suspicions.

(ZHONGLI *speaks:*) Go ahead, take me to court, I'm not afraid of you. You are
crazy. (LAN *sings:*)

> Well if we did sue you in court, I'm afraid neither of us would get
>   off clean—

(*Speaks:*) If I wanted to make a complaint against you, then the old folks would
certainly say, "You're a leading male on the stage, but you're no wiser than that
crazy old reverend." (*Sings:*)

> But because it's my birthday I'm not going to quarrel with you.

(*Speaks:*) Today is my birthday, and I am under the Star of Longevity, so I'm
going to let this go. (ZHONGLI *speaks:*) Who is the Star of Longevity? (LAN
speaks:) I am. (ZHONGLI *speaks:*) You might be the Star of Longevity today, but
tomorrow you'll be under the Star of Calamity. (LAN *speaks:*) You really lack
any sense of decency to say such unpropitious things. (*Sings:*)

> Quit this wild name-calling and crazy behavior.

(ZHONGLI *speaks:*) These words wouldn't hurt you either! (LAN *sings:*)

> These aren't words you should use;
> These aren't words fit to listen to.
> Are you doing more than begging some blandly spiced soup
> To temporarily stuff that skin sack of yours?

(ZHONGLI *speaks:*) I see you're enjoying yourself! (LAN *sings:*)

> Yes I am! I'm eating big old buns and long broad noodles;
> You're eating some vegetable filling and bland leek soup.

(*Speaks:*) This vile reverend is spoiling our banquet. Bandleader Wang, close up
the gates. Brothers, sit down, let's just drink our wine. (ZHONGLI *speaks:*) Will
anything make him see the light? If he doesn't experience some kind of awful
situation, he'll never leave his family. Look, Xu Jian, if you leave your family and
go away with me right now, roam about in leisure and freedom, happy and carefree, you'd really find its hidden pleasures! (LAN *speaks:*) I know about the kind

of path you immortals trod! (ZHONGLI *speaks:*) Since you know all about it, let me hear it. (LAN *sings:*)

> (*Dou hama*)
> I've seen households set out a vegetarian feast,
> Invite you reverends to recite a penitence or a sutra:
> Right in front is hung a scroll of the Three Purities,[28]
> And the patrons recite a sutra.
> Busily they prepare a vegetarian feast,
> Then take down the picture of Laozi[29]
> And hang up a scroll of the Ten Kings of Hell,[30]
> And that painter knew well the ways of the world,[31]
> And when he tells about how retribution fits the experience,
> It's also painted out there frighteningly cruel.
> Who can stand to look at these representations?
> All I have to do is remember how lifelike the paintings are in the
>   Temple of the City God—
> Boiling pots and pans of oil,
> And stuck there inside
> So many souls,
> Each one of us from the secular world.
> Among the lot neither a single monk
> Nor a Daoist reverend, nor a Spiritual Codger Xu.[32]
> It is said, "There is no clean escape,"
> But this sentence is unheeded—
> Either by me, this male lead, or by you, this reverend.

(ZHONGLI *speaks:*) Quick! Bring disaster on this man!

(Exits.)

---

28. The three Daoist sages who inhabit the three realms of clarity: the Venerable Celestial One of the Primordial Beginning in the Realm of Jade Clarity, the Celestial Worthy of Nuninous Treasure in the Realm of Highest Clarity, and the Celestial Worthy of the Way and Its Virtue, the Highest God of Great Clarity.

29. The third of the sages above.

30. Both popular Buddhism and Daoism believe in ten judges in the ten courts of the netherworld.

31. The "painter," *daizhao*, is a general term in drama for any particular specialist. Xu Jiang's *Quan Yuan qu* understands it as fortune teller. In this case, he would be interpreting the paintings of the ten courts of hell as part of the process of explaining systems of retribution that would figure in how one's life was shaped.

32. A historical Daoist, Xu Shouxin (1033–1108), who was honored at the court of Huizong, in the late Northern Song.

(RUNNERS *enter and speak:*) Lan Caihe, open up! The magistrate summons you to perform your official service. (LAN *speaks:*) Who's that calling at the gate? (RUNNERS *speak:*) The magistrate is summoning you to perform your official service. (LAN *speaks:*) This is a special day for me, take Bandleader Wang. (RUN-NERS *speak:*) We don't want him. You have to go. (LAN *speaks:*) Take Thinhead Li. (RUNNERS *speak:*) We don't want him either. (LAN *speaks:*) Have Bandleader Wang take some female roles along and go. (RUNNERS *speak:*) We don't want any of them. We only want Lan Caihe. (LAN *speaks:*) I have twenty people under my care, and I get stuck with it. All right! All right! I'll go fulfill my official service.

(*Exit together.*)

(LI *and* WANG *speak:*) Go ahead and get the banquet ready, when brother gets home we'll all eat together.

(*Exit.*)

(OFFICIAL, *dressed as magistrate, enters and speaks:*) I am the Daoist Lü Dong-bin. I received the command of my master, Zhongli, and have disguised myself as the Prefect because of an entertainer in this place, called Xu Jian. He has a stage name of Lan Caihe and has it in his fated lot to be an immortal transcendent. Zhongli attempted to enlighten him and lead him over, but he couldn't see the light. Because he has been too slow to fulfill his official service, I've had some people go and fetch him here under arrest. Servants, bring in that Lan Caihe. (LAN *enters, speaks:*) Oh, no! What should I do? I screwed up my official service, and have been deemed guilty by the magistrate. Now I've been summoned and I'd better go see him. (*Acts out kneeling in audience.* LÜ DONGBIN *speaks:*) Are you aware of your crime? You did not respect the office. You were late in performing official service. Take him down into the courtyard and beat him forty times! Get the heavy clubs ready! (LAN *sings:*)

> (*Ku huangtian*)
> It scares me so much that I seem dumbstruck;
> Away, away flies my sentient soul,
> And all I can hear is someone calling my actor's name on the
>   musician's dais.
> It scares me so much that my three souls have become lost far,
>   far away,
> And I can perceive not the slightest bit of motion.
> I arrogantly missed the time of my official service,
> So I'll hurry to smooth it over,
> And if necessary to confess.

Those thick and thin thorns and staffs will be laid upon my body,
More painfully than the simulated fights on the stage!

(LÜ DONGBIN *speaks*:) Beat him forty times in the courtyard! Lay it on! Lay it on! (LAN *sings*:)

This is so much more thorough than a "Judge Bao,"[33]
No one has ever seen members of the guild "carrying thorns."[34]

(LÜ DONGBIN *speaks*:) Beat him forty times in the courtyard! Lay it on! Lay it on! (ZHONGLI *enters and speaks*:) He's good and scared now. (LAN *speaks*:) Who will save me? (ZHONGLI *speaks*:) Lan Caihe, have you seen through it all now? You didn't believe me when I told you, but what about now? (LAN *sings*:)

(*Wu ye ti*)
This reverend's words are truly to be believed,
Indeed he said, "The Star of Longevity will turn into the Star of
      Calamity."
My eyes wide open, I dare not move ahead,
I dare not reveal to sight or hearing what I feel.
Who dares say this is just to bear enough to get through it all?
I thought we were all in the ranks of Confucius;
I never would have said that I would break the laws of Xiao He.[35]

(*Speaks*:) It seems that none of the words spoken by the Sage are to be believed! (LAN *sings*:)

Each and every one
Is hard to rely one,
They are all wild words and lies,
Spurted out without any thought.[36]

---

33. He is referring here to the performance of beatings in Judge Bao plays (such as *Butterfly Dream*).

34. He may be referencing the famous play *The Black Whirlwind Li Kui Carries Thorns*, in which one of the heroes of the *Water Margin* atones for a crime by carrying thorns on his back.

35. Lived c. 193 BC. One of Liu Bang's lieutenants, instrumental in the founding of the Han, he also drafted the law code for the new dynasty. "The laws of Xiao He" is roughly equivalent to "the law of the land."

36. "Words spoken by the Sage": An uninflected language, Chinese often does not indicate number. This may be "sages," a general reference to all sages of the past. But it may also refer to the Sage, Confucius, whose words uttered on the spot were collected into the ethical canon, the *Analects*. This would seem to make sense here, following on the line, "ranks of Confucius," and would make a nice counterpoint for Lan Caihe's conversion to Daoism.

(ZHONGLI *speaks:*) Why are you here? (LAN *speaks:*) I missed the appointed time for my official service, and the magistrate is going to give me forty strokes in the courtyard. Save me, master. (ZHONGLI *speaks:*) If I save you, will you follow me and leave your home? (LAN *speaks:*) Save me and I will follow you with all my heart. (ZHONGLI *speaks:*) Stay here for a minute. (*Acts out seeing* LÜ DONGBIN, *speaks:*) Your Excellency. (LÜ DONGBIN *speaks:*) If I had known earlier that you, master, were coming, I would have met you at some distance. Please do not consider my lack of a proper welcome a crime. (ZHONGLI *speaks:*) What crime did Lan Caihe commit? (LÜ DONGBIN *speaks:*) He was remiss in fulfilling his official service, and he should be charged according to the law. (ZHONGLI *speaks:*) Are you willing to turn him over to me to become my disciple? (LÜ DONGBIN *speaks:*) Whenever you want him I'll gladly turn him over to you. Servants, bring him over here. You there, Lan Caihe—you really are lucky. If the master had not shown up, I would have given you forty in the courtyard. The master wants you for a disciple. I'll forgive your crimes, and you go off with the master. (LAN *speaks:*) Thank you both, I'll leave my home today and follow the master! (*Sings:*)

> (*Shawei*)
> No longer will I lead those dozens of companions of the guild,
> But stride alone ever more on the twelve-tiered Terraces of Jasper.
> Former wealth dispersed, friends gone, I've turned my back on old
>   feelings,
> Back where they raise a shout, start the music
> And call out my stage name in the theater.
> I'm now confused, beclouded, yet more awake.
> Lan Caihe's vile reputation runs through every prefecture and town,
> But have they ever seen a comedy-playing actor become enlightened
>   first?
>
> (*Exits.*)

(ZHONGLI *speaks:*) Since Lan Caihe has had a change of heart today and will leave the family, I will wait until his merit is complete and his disciplines are finished, and then we can go off together to the Langyuan Orchard and the Jasper Pool.

(*Exits.*)

[Act 3]

(LAN'S WIFE *enters and speaks:*) I am Lan Caihe's wife. On that day my man was celebrating his birthday with a little wine and was summoned away for his official service. He never came back, and someone said that he had gone off with a Daoist master. Nothing left to do now but summon my two younger brothers-in-law and discuss all this. (LI *and* WANG *enter and speak:*) No one knows where brother went after he was summoned for official service. If he really has left the home, what are we going to do? Let's go look for him today.

(*Exit together.*)

(LAN enters, *playing the clappers, leading* CHILDREN, *speaks:*) Everything has been so serene since I went off with master. [(*Recites:*)]

> The old country of Jinling
> Was originally my home,
> So I went there many times
> And remonstrated once with the Princes Li,[37]
> But they did not listen,
> And I feared stirring up trouble or calling down misfortune.
> So I stayed not in Jinling,
> But went straight off to Bianliang,
> Where I was enlightened in the theater,
> And never went again into the ranks of performers.
> My gentry cap worn aslant,
> I set loose my Yunyang clappers;[38]
> Around my waist I tie a plaited rope
> Circling my long robe with dancing sleeves.

Ah, there is no greater serenity. (*Sings:*)

> ([ZHENGLÜ MODE:] *Duanzheng hao*)
> Around my waist I drag a hundred coppers,
> On my head I wear a gentry cap.
> I dance in my blue robe, clack the clappers, and sing out loud,

---

37. Li Jing and Li Yu, the two rulers of the Southern Tang (937–46). This poem may be seen as recounting his life: originally from Jinling (modern Nanjing), Xu Jian (Lan Caihe) remonstrated with the two rulers of the Southern Tang and then moved to Bianliang in order to avoid punishment. This would imply that he was a court entertainer in the Southern Tang. Actors at court were very free with criticism, usually cloaked in a form of humor. But, given the lavish life styles of, particularly, Li Yu, he could also be speaking about himself as a Daoist immortal, like Zhongli Quan, pointing out the uselessness of the world's attachments.

38. Yunyang is a common designation for the execution ground. The use of the term as the designation for his clappers is also commonplace. Are they meant to signal a sudden sound that startles people into the realization that the whole world, where people cling foolishly to pleasure, is an execution ground?

Heading for the streets every day.
How many can recognize my true worth?[39]

(*Gun xiuqiu*)
Ai!
Why do you little devils
Keep on pestering me?
I never really summoned them together—
Those who run into me laugh happily, *ha ha ha.*

(*All of the* CHILDREN *pull at him,* LAN *sings:*)

You snatch at my clappers,
And I'm afraid my string of cash will loosen.
You've nearly ripped my green gown to shreds;
You beat and grasp as soon as you see me.
This group of ruddy little faces covered with the stench of mother's
    milk
Is pestering Lan Caihe, who's just escaped from the twelve links in
    the chain of causation![40]
How will I ever perfect my nature through meditation?

(CHILDREN *speak:*) Master, give us a copper!

(LAN'S WIFE *enters and speaks:*) There's Lan Caihe! Where have you been?
Come home! (LAN *speaks:*) Pleased to meet you. Who are the lot of you? (LAN'S
WIFE, ENSEMBLE *speak:*) I am your wife! We are your brothers! This is your
child! (LAN *sings:*)

(*Tang xiucai*)
I no longer heed the cacophony of chatter that passes my ears,
Sons and daughters are just golden cangues and jade shackles,
Isn't it said, "the more sons and daughters, the more karmic
    pain?"
When I'm enjoying myself, I pick up my clappers;
When I am troubled, I sing out loud.
No one is as happy as me!

---

39. Literally, "physiognomize me correctly."

40. They are: (1) *avidyā*, ignorance, or unenlightenment; (2) *saṃskāra*, action, activity, conception; (3) *vijñāna*, consciousness; (4) *nāmarūpa*, name and form; (5) *ṣaḍāyatana*, the six sense
organs, i.e., eye, ear, nose, tongue, body, and mind; (6) *sparśa*, contact, touch; (7) *vedanā*, sensa-
tion, feeling; (8) *tṛṣṇā*, thirst, desire, craving; (9) *upādāna*, laying hold of, grasping; (10) *bhava*,
being, existing; (11) *jāti*, birth; (12) *jarāmaraṇa*, old age, death.

(LAN'S WIFE *enters and speaks:*) You come home! We'll get the theater ready, do a couple of performances to raise some living expenses for the family, and then you can go out again. (LAN *sings:*)

> (*Gun xiuqiu*)
> I will be alone ever after,
> Don't think now about how I lived then.
> Never again will I put on a costume, or keep the beat to the musical
>   performance.
> I'll never open or close another performance on stage, ad-libbing on
>   the spot.

(*Speaks:*) There, where we performed, you wanted me to yell at Bandleader Wang and Thinhead Li, "Hurry up!" "Faster, faster." (LAN *sings:*)

> And yell at my sisters-in-law, the whole group:
> "Faster, hurry up! Go make up, put on your costumes!"
> And I would still need a nice round of applause from those elders
>   when I perform.

(WANG *speaks:*) No one comes to the theater anymore now that you've gone, brother. (LAN *sings:*)

> Why is the audience so pitifully small?
> If you don't hit it off with them, a single line is too much.

(WANG *speaks:*) What kind of crazy nonsense was that? (LAN *sings:*)

> I'm not the crazy one!

(LAN'S WIFE *speaks:*) I've tried to make you go home, but you won't. What have you studied with your master? (LAN *speaks:*) What my master taught me to sing was the "Song of Blue Skies," and what he taught me to dance is the "Stomping Song." (LAN'S WIFE *speaks:*) Perform them for us and let us hear them. (LAN *acts out dancing, recites:*)

Stomping Song,
Lan Caihe,
How long is a human life?
Red faces: a tree of "third spring,"
Flowing light: a shuttle once thrown:
Those buried are buried,
The bearers bear them.
An adorned casket, a colorful hearse—what use are they?
Wrapped in a mat, carried by a pole—what can a person do?

Alive, before, they refused to chase after happy laughter,
Dead, afterward, they let others sing the burial dirges.
When you have a chance to drink, drink;
When you find a place to cool your heels, cool your heels.
Don't go around depressed with saddened brow,
Just laugh out loud with opened mouth.
You work and work all day long, greedy for fame and profit,
Paying no attention to mortal life—how long can it last?
How long can it last?
Stomping song,
Lan Caihe.

How incredibly serene!

(LAN'S WIFE *speaks:*) Don't leave the family! Follow me home! (LAN *sings:*)

> (*Kuaihuo san*)
> And if death should come, what then?

(*Speaks:*) Lady, go away! (*Sings:*)

> Now I've got a place to cool my heels, and I'll cool them for a while,
> And study that song of Zhuangzi, beating on the tub—[41]
> I've realized the disasters that will cause my death.

(LAN'S WIFE *speaks:*) Since you've already left home to become an immortal, how about letting me go with you? (LAN *speaks:*) You can't leave home.... (*Sings:*)

> (*Chao Tianzi*)
> The guild members all accumulate a shared pot of money to get by.

---

41. From the *Zhuangzi*, an anecdote commonly used in drama to represent leaving the mundane world and "entering the Way" of Daoism:

Zhuangzi's wife died. When Huizi went to convey his condolences, he found Zhuangzi sitting with his legs sprawled out, pounding on a tub and singing. "You lived with her, she brought up your children and grew old," said Huizi. "It should be enough simply not to weep at her death. But pounding on a tub and singing—this is going too far, isn't it?" Zhuangzi said, "You are wrong. When she first died, do you think I didn't grieve like anyone else? But I looked back to her beginning and the time before she was born. Not only the time before she was born, but the time before she had a body. Not only the time before she had a body, but the time before she had a spirit. In the midst of the jumble of wonder and mystery a change took place and she had a spirit. Another change and she had a body. Another change and she was born. Now there's been another change and she's dead. It's just like the progression of the four seasons, spring, summer, fall, winter. Now she's going to lie down peacefully in a vast room. If I were to follow after her bawling and sobbing, it would show that I don't understand anything about fate. So I stopped." (Trans. Burton Watson, *Complete Works of Zhuangzi*, pp. 191–92.)

(LAN'S WIFE *speaks:*) We are all in a single guild. Bring out some coppers for us, and I'll make sure they get divided equally. (LAN *sings:*)

> What's this "You die so I can live?"

(LAN *speaks:*) Everyone else runs around day and night, struggling and scrimping to get by, telling themselves lies so they can do what they are forced to do. (*Sings:*)

> None of them can make it by following their own fates or going along
> with what the world offers.

(LAN *speaks:*) When I have a moment now, I read *The Way and Its Virtue*,[42] and when I'm tired, I sleep soundly. (*Sings:*)

> When I get a chance to close my eyes, I close them,
> When I get a chance to lie down, I lie down in the clothes I wear.

(LAN'S WIFE *speaks:*) Here, line them up and take a look—your brothers, your son, his wife, all these relatives—how can you go off and leave us? (LAN *sings:*)

> Line them up in a row, my son, his wife, all the grandsons—

(LAN *speaks:*) But, on that day, when I heard "For missing official service, give him forty licks in the courtyard"—if it hadn't been for my master saving me.... (*Sings:*)

> If I had met an untimely death, who would have substituted
>   for me?

(LAN'S WIFE *speaks:*) If that's the way it is, then lead me across and out of the family too! (LAN *sings:*)

> Hold on! It's not proper to lead you across.

(LAN'S WIFE *speaks:*) Go on back! This doesn't help anything. (LAN *sings:*)

> Truly, I'm also "stuck in the ditch"![43]

(LAN'S WIFE *speaks:*) Go home! It looks like you'll never get the true rewards of becoming an immortal. (LAN *sings:*)

> (*Weisheng*)
> Even if I don't get the true rewards,
> Or lead you, my worthy wife, across,

---

42. The *Daode jing*, also known as the *Laozi*.
43. Roughly equivalent to the English, "in a pickle."

If you will just happily keep to your lot for me, go along with what
   the world offers
And wind up with a single day's peace—wouldn't that make me
   ecstatic!

(*Exits.*)

(LAN'S WIFE *speaks:*) If you won't go home, we will.

(*Exit together.*)

[Act 4]

(LAN'S WIFE *enters with* LI *and* WANG. WANG *speaks:*) Thirty years have gone by
since Lan Caihe left the family to follow his master. I'm now eighty, Thinhead
Li is seventy, and sister-in-law is ninety. We're all old and incapable of making
a living anymore. So now the younger ones perform, and we drum for them.
I'll go and get the drums ready, and we'll see who comes along. (LAN *enters and
speaks:*) Thirty years now since I left with the master. The master said my exer-
cises are finished, and today we are going off together to Langyuan Orchard
and the Jasper Pool. Oh, how serene it all is. (*Sings:*)

> ([SHUANGDIAO MODE]: *Xinshui ling*)
> The rules and rituals of the Daoist Way I have refined and to them I
>   hold fast.
> My master has now enlightened a disciple of the stage.
> Clearly and brilliantly my master exercised the law of the Way,
> Secretly explaining the workings of meditation.
> Now he wants to go to the Jasper Pool together—
> Could I have ever hoped for this day?

(*Speaks:*) I just passed the mountain pass and see a garden of fruit trees, with
apricot flowers opening in their brilliance. Turning my head—a whole pond
of fine water chestnuts, then the whole place filled with fine frost, and then a
whole stretch covered with fine snow. Let me think—apricots are spring,
water-chestnuts are summer, frost is autumn, and snow is winter. How can all
of the seasons come at once?

(WANG *and* LI *enter and act out playing music.* LAN *sings:*)

> (*Qing dongyuan*)
> There's a group of noisy people there—

(*Speaks:*) Oh, it's the sound of music! (*Sings:*)

It's a group of hick itinerant performers.
I suppose they are in that public square
Holding up their spears, knives, swords, and halberds,
Gongs, clappers, drums, and flutes.
They already set up the valance and some flags.
I wonder which troupe of the guild they are?
Probably nobody famous.

(*Speaks:*) So, it turns out to be a troupe from the guild. I'll ask, "Which family troupe are you?" (LAN'S WIFE *speaks:*) Lan Caihe's. (LAN *speaks:*) Which members of Lan Caihe's troupe are you? (LAN'S WIFE *speaks:*) I am his wife. Those two are his brothers, Bandleader Wang and Thinhead Li. (WANG *speaks:*) It's been thirty years since our elder brother left, and now I'm eighty, brother here is seventy, and our sister-in-law is ninety. Boy, are we old. (LAN *sings:*)

(*Gu meijiu*)
Sigh over how unceasingly it changes from light to night,
Moan over how bitterly swift the days and months flee by,
And lament that our lives seem to pass but in a dream.
I am awakened now:
No life, no death, cut free from fame or profit.

(*Taiping ling*)
You must be my brothers,
The pack I ran with when young.
But it was nothing more than studying the arts when given place and
    opportunity,
From which comes these various years:
This one says seventy,
That one eighty,
The lady says ninety—
It may have been hard, but they have all lived to a ripe old age.

(WANG *speaks:*) And who are you? (LAN *speaks:*) Well, I am Lan Caihe. (WANG *speaks:*) You've been gone for thirty years, but you're still not old. You still look the same. (LAN *speaks:*) I've only been gone for three—how did you get so old? (WANG *speaks:*) We're all old now. You're still middle-aged. Wouldn't it be great if you'd go once more to the theater and do a day or two of comedies? (LAN *sings:*)

(*Chuan bo zhao*)
You want me to do some comedies,
To act out some dynasty's rise and fall, to judge what's right or wrong.

You want me to drum, or play the flute,
Drum up business, put things in order.
"Don't stop for a rest!""Be a little more diligent!"
"Get busy!""Don't dawdle!"

(*Qi dixiong*)
In those days
When I faced a rival—
And I'm not bragging—
I made them laughingly set out new clothes and fancy hats.
The old skits and farces I knew well,
And understood every trick of my colleagues on stage.

(*Meihua jiu*)
How could they attain my skill?
As a director, none was my match.
I had no rival in creativity,
I knew every musical tempo.

(WANG *speaks:*) Brother, all of the costumes and accessories from your old comedies are still in good shape. Brother, just lift up the curtain and take a look. (LAN *sings:*)

My heart delights after hearing this,
And I unconsciously smile,
Let me just lift the curtain . . .

(*Acts out lifting the curtain.* ZHONGLI QUAN *and* LÜ DONGBIN *are sitting inside.* ZHONGLI *speaks:*) Xu Jian, your mortal mind is not completely gone! (LAN *sings:*)

That scares me so much my souls go flying far, far away,
I would have sworn they were my brothers,
My sisters and sisters-in-law—
It's just like coming back from the dream of the Southern Branch.[44]

(*Shou Jiangnan*)
Ah, it was founder of the sect, teacher of the doctrine Zhongli of the
    Han all the time,
Accompanied by master Dongbin at his side.
I drop my Yunyang clappers and climb the steps,
You're all here—
The Eight Immortals now lead me off to the Jasper Pool together.

---

44. See *Qiannü's Soul*, n. 54.

(ZHONGLI *speaks:*) Xu Jian, you are no mortal, but are now Lan Caihe of the Eight Immortals! Your practices finished, you can ascend to the immortal realm. Just listen:

Xu Jian, have no doubt in your heart,
Listen carefully as I explain:
Here is Dongbin, in the Dao designated Master of Pure Yang,
And I am called the Roaming and Loafing Zhongli of Han.

TITLE: Leading the children, he laughs heartily wherever he goes;
The Old Immortal claps his hands and drunkenly sings out a loud song.

NAME: Lü Dongbin transforms a traveler in the actor's world;
Zhongli of the Han leads Lan Caihe to enlightenment.

9

Newly Compiled:
A Leopard Monk Returns to the Laity of His Own Accord

ZHU YOUDUN

Zhu Youdun was by far the most prolific playwright of the first century of the Ming dynasty (1368–1644). He was the eldest son of Zhu Su, the fifth son of the dynasty's founder, Zhu Yuanzhang. Zhu Su (d. 1425) had been enfeoffed as Prince of Zhou and resided at Kaifeng, the city that once had been the capital of the Northern Song dynasty and also the capital of the Jin from 1213 to 1232. Zhu Su was a full brother of Zhu Yuanzhang's fourth son Zhu Di (1360–1424), who had been enfeoffed as Prince of Yan at Beijing. In 1399, when Zhu Di rebelled against his nephew, the newly installed Jianwen Emperor, Zhu Su was stripped of his title and banished with his family to Yunnan. But when Zhu Di took the throne following the death of the Jianwen Emperor in 1402, he reinstated Zhu Su to his original position. A grateful Zhu Su soon would capture a *zouyu*, a mythical animal shaped like a white tiger that was believed to appear in this world only during the reign of a sage emperor. He presented this supernatural sign of Heaven's approval to his elder brother, whose usurpation had created widespread resentment in literati circles.

The capture of a *zouyu* in 1403 provided the young Zhu Youdun with the subject for his first play. Zhu Youdun was not unique in the imperial family in his interest in Northern drama. His uncle Zhu Di had been an active patron of dramatists when he was the Prince of Yan, and his uncle Zhu Quan (1378–1448), the Prince of Ning, is known as the author of *A Formulary of Correct Rhymes for an Era of Great Peace*, a study of writers and the prosody of *qu* songs, as well as a *zaju* playwright. Zhu Youdun succeeded his father as Prince of Zhou in 1425, and his descendants would succeed to the title to the very end of the Ming dynasty.

Zhu Youdun's thirty-one *zaju* may be divided into two groups. Half may be best characterized as elaborate court pageants that were written for the celebration of annual festivals and princely birthdays. These plays often required a very large cast and made use of elaborate and spectacular stage effects. Some of these plays provided scripts for annual rituals such as the New Year's lion dance or the exorcist Dance of Zhong Kui at the end of the year, while others provided entertainment for flower-viewing parties or birthdays. Those written for performance at royal birthdays are all deliverance plays (see *Zhongli of the Han Leads Lan Caihe to Enlightenment*), and many of these may only have been performed once. Later in life Zhu Youdun tended to write a new deliverance play each year for performance at his own birthday celebration. Since many of his plays were produced only once, Zhu Youdun may have been stimulated to preserve them in print. In contrast to the plays printed in the Yuan dynasty, which are minimalist editions meant only for the main role type, Zhu Youdun printed his plays "with full dialogue" (*quanbin*). Despite this claim, these plays remain far less complete in terms of writing out the full text of the dialogues than those that later emerged from the imperial palace. This is because Zhu still allowed actors considerable leeway for improvisation and also did not write out well-established routines.

The remaining half of Zhu Youdun's dramatic oeuvre consists of regular Northern dramas that could be easily staged by a small cast and performed either inside or outside the court. Many were written in praise of loyal courtesans and probably served two purposes. First, Zhu Youdun's devotion to drama may well have been intended as a conspicuous display of lack of political ambition in order to allay ever-present imperial suspicions. Second, the plays simultaneously could allegorically declare his loyalty to the reigning emperor in the timeworn convention of casting political loyalty in the guise of a love relationship. But Zhu Youdun also wrote a number of comedies including one, *Liu Jin'er Becomes a Singsong Girl Again*, about the antics and adventures of a conspicuously disloyal courtesan-actress who repeatedly dumps her husband for a richer partner, until she is reassigned to the status of courtesan again by an irate judge.[1] In the final years of his life Zhu Youdun devoted two plays to the noble bandits of the Liangshan marshes, whose adventures later would be written up as the famous novel *Water Margin* (*Shuihu zhuan*). But while writing about colorful characters like Lu Zhishen, Li Kui, and Yan Qing, he still felt a need to defend this choice of subject in his prefaces as an example of "playful writing" (*xibi*).

Zhu Youdun's plays all are preserved in editions produced during his lifetime. His plays are distinguished by well-made plots, lively dialogue, and expertly crafted songs. They are eminently performable and so enjoyed considerable popularity in the fifteenth and sixteenth centuries. But once modern scholarship increasingly came to view Northern drama as the genre solely representative of the Yuan dynasty, Zhu Youdun's works were increasingly ignored. Even though Zang Maoxun included numerous other works by early Ming authors in his *Yuanqu xuan*, he completely neglected Zhu Youdun. In the People's Republic of

---

1. See Appendix 3.

China the Marxist view of literature that dominated scholarship until the last years of the twentieth century also contributed to a critical neglect of Zhu Youdun because he was seen as a representative of the ruling feudal class. An unbiased reader, however, will find much to enjoy in his plays.

The tales of the outlaws of the Liangshan marshes have been popular from at least the thirteenth century to the present. In the early decades of the People's Republic the tale was turned to political use, hailed by Marxist critics as an epic of peasant rebellion. The cycle of stories may well derive from a kernel of historical truth. Chronicles refer to the exploits of the bandit Song Jiang in the general area of Kaifeng during the last years of the reign of Emperor Huizong (r. 1101–25). After his surrender to imperial forces, he and his men were dispatched to the south to fight the rebel Fang La. Moreover, a list of topics popular with professional storytellers in Hangzhou during the Southern Song dynasty includes the names of several heroes who, in later versions of the saga, are also listed as members of Song Jiang's band. The most likely hypothesis, however, seems to be that many originally independent so-called "greenwood stories" (stories of bandits) gradually amalgamated into a single cycle of stories that centered on the Liangshan marshes in western Shandong. The earliest coherent account of the adventures of the band is found in the *Anecdotes of the Xuanhe Reign* (*Xuanhe yishi*), a narrative that may date from the second half of the thirteenth century. But the adventures of Song Jiang and his men occupy a mere few pages in this work, which is centered primarily on the contrast between Huizong's dissipated life while on the throne and the misery of his captivity after the Jurchen conquered the Northern Song in 1126–27.

Eventually, the oral saga grew into a huge novel that became known as *Shuihu zhuan* (*The Water Margin Story*). Traditionally, authorship of the novel is ascribed to one Shi Nai'an, about whom no reliable information can be found; some accounts also credit the playwright and novelist Luo Guanzhong (second half of the fourteenth century) with a hand in its composition. Modern scholarship, while admitting that the novel contains many earlier materials, tends to favor an early sixteenth century date for its full maturation. The earliest preserved editions date from the second half of that century and show great discrepancies in style and content. The rather late date of the novel's compilation is supported by the fact that Zhu Youdun shows no knowledge of it. Rather, he claims in a preface to one of his plays that *Xuanhe yishi* provides the fullest account of the *Water Margin* bandits' activities. The novel lists many more heroes by name than does the *Xuanhe yishi*: whereas the latter work lists thirty-six leaders in the band, the novel increases their number to 108. The most popular edition of the novel during the Qing dynasty, prepared by the critic Jin Shengtan (c. 1610–61), cut the final third of the novel, a section that details the collective activities of the fully formed band. Jin retained the first two-thirds, in which the career of individual bandits and the circumstances under which they came to rebellion are recounted.

The outlaws of the Liangshan marshes also provided substantial material for Yuan playwrights. Unfortunately, only six of the more than thirty *zaju* dealing with the bandits' individual and collective adventures are still extant, all preserved in late Ming editions that clearly show the influence of the novel in their final redaction. Remarkably enough, none of the stories dramatized in these early plays made it into the novel, with the exception of *The Black Whirlwind Li Kui Carries Thorns* (*Li Kui fu jing*) by Kang Jinzhi (fl. 1250–1300).[2] This play features the three most distinctive and heroic of the outlaws: Song Jiang, Li Kui, and Lu Zhishen. Song Jiang, the leader of the band, is a former district clerk who had extensive contacts in the world of local ruffians and outlaws. He was forced to give up his lucrative position and flee to the greenwoods after killing his former paramour Yan Poxi. Li Kui, a former prison guard, is distinguished by an enormous physique, dark complexion, and a mercurial disposition toward violence. His simple sense of justice at times clashes with his total devotion to the wilier Song Jiang. Lu Zhishen is a former army officer who became a Buddhist monk after killing a local bully. His conversion did not rob him of his voracious appetite or easy irascibility. The ugliness of his massive tattooed body is brought out even more clearly because he continues, like Friar Tuck of the Robin Hood stories, to wear his vestments and shave his head while an outlaw.

The action of *Li Kui Carries Thorns* takes place after the band has reached full strength. Two common ruffians, who pass themselves off as Song Jiang and Lu Zhishen, abduct the daughter of an old wineshop operator. When the old man tells his sad tale to Li Kui, who happens to pass by, the latter takes him at his word and sets out for the band's stronghold in a towering rage (Act 1). Back at the stronghold, Song Jiang and Lu Zhishen strongly deny the accusation, but Li Kui wagers his head that they did it (Act 2). Li Kui takes them to see the girl's father and the old man is forced to admit that Song Jiang and Lu Zhishen are not the abductors of his daughter (Act 3). Back at the stronghold, Li Kui appears before Song Jiang with a bundle of thorns on his back, imploring his mercy, but Song Jiang shows himself adamant and insists on the terms of their wager. But when the old man comes to the stronghold with the information that the original two scoundrels have returned and drunk themselves into a stupor, Song Jiang allows Li Kui to redeem himself by capturing them. Accompanied by Lu Zhishen, Li quickly succeeds in his task (Act 4).

---

2. See Appendix 3.

While in the *Water Margin* Li Kui embodies anarchistic rebelliousness and brute violence, Yuan playwrights, starting with Kang Jinzhi, were more interested in the rather stark contrast between Li Kui's outwardly huge and ugly physique and his delicate inner sensibility and keen sense of justice. Li Kui was so popular with Yuan playwrights that his name occurs in fourteen titles of greenwood plays (seven alone by the Shandong playwright Gao Wenxiu). He is the protagonist in three of the six preserved Yuan dynasty *zaju* about bandits and appears in both of Zhu Youdun's plays on that subject. He is a subsidiary character in *A Leopard Monk Returns to the Laity* and the protagonist in *Black Whirlwind Li Spurns Riches out of Righteousness*.

Lu Zhishen has a more active part in another early *zaju*, entitled *Lu Zhishen Enjoys Chrysanthemum Valley* (*Lu Zhishen xishang Huanghua yu*). The title of this anonymous play is recorded in the *Continuation of the Register of Ghosts*, which suggests that it was in existence by the early fifteenth century, the date of the *Continuation*'s compilation. In this play, the young scholar Liu Qingfu and his lovely wife Li Younu return home from a pilgrimage to the Eastern Marchmount of Mount Tai. When they stop at an inn, she entertains her husband with a song. A local bully named Cai then commands her to sing for him, and when the indignant Liu Qingfu protests, Cai has him tied up. Yang Xiong, one of the outlaws of the Liangshan marshes, frees the couple but the bully Cai later kidnaps Li Younu (Act 1). Liu Qingfu comes to the bandits' stronghold and requests their help, whereupon Li Kui volunteers to track down the villain by disguising himself as a peddler (Act 2). Li Kui finds Cai and gives him a sound beating (Act 3). When Cai consequently flees to his family's Buddhist temple in Chrysanthemum Valley, he runs smack into Lu Zhishen, who gives him another beating. Song Jiang brings the play to an end by condemning the lecherous bully to death (Act 4). Zhu Youdun not only explicitly refers to the story of this earlier play in his *A Leopard Monk Returns to the Laity* (*Baozi heshang zi huansu*), but the plot of *Black Whirlwind Li Spurns Riches out of Righteousness* also bears a strong resemblance to it.

Lu Zhishen is mentioned in the *Xuanhe yishi* only as an afterthought, as if to fill out the number of thirty-six leaders: "Then there was the monk Lu Zhishen who rebelled and also joined Song Jiang." The *Water Margin*, however, devotes a number of chapters to his exploits prior to his joining with the band in the Liangshan marshes. We first encounter him as an army major in the western province of Gansu. Here he saves a destitute young singer from the clutches of another local bully, butcher Zheng. After the damsel and her father have made their escape, Lu kills Zheng with three punches of his fist. He now has to flee, and when he arrives in northern Shanxi, the new patron of the young singer pays for his ordination as a Buddhist priest in the great monastery of

Mount Wutai, where he adopts the religious name of Zhishen ("deep wisdom"). While he may have donned the habit, however, he remains a stranger to monastic discipline. One day, he leaves the monastery, gets drunk, and wrecks a little pavilion halfway down the mountain; when he gets back to the monastery, the doorkeepers refuse to let him in and Lu beats the gate down to force his way in. On another occasion he goes down to the village at the foot of the mountain, orders a sixty-two-pound iron staff and a sword from the local blacksmith, and again gets totally drunk. When he arrives in his sodden state at the monastery, he finds the gate closed and proceeds to smash the statues of the four guardian deities in front of it.

The abbot at Mount Wutai, the novel continues, now finds it impossible to keep him and sends him off with a letter to the great Xiangguo Monastery at Kaifeng. On his way to the capital, Lu Zhishen stays one night at a manor, where he learns from his host that that very night a local bandit is going to force an old man to hand over his daughter as a bride. Lu Zhishen takes the place of the bride inside the bed-curtains and gives the lascivious bandit a sound beating. When the monk later arrives in Kaifeng, the abbot of the Xiangguo Monastery puts him in charge of the monastery's vegetable gardens, located in the suburbs outside the city walls. Here Lu quickly overawes local ruffians who were in the habit of roundly abusing his predecessor. His demonstration of martial skills in this episode also attracts the attention of Lin Chong, a martial arts instructor in the imperial guards. Later, Lin Chong is framed by his superiors and condemned to banishment to Cangzhou, south of Tianjin in modern Hebei. Lu Zhishen discovers a plot by Lin's two escorts to take Lin's life and saves him from murder. Lu also sees Lin safely to Cangzhou, but because of this involvement with Lin Chong, he has to flee Kaifeng. On his peregrinations, he first kills an evil Buddhist monk and an equally evil Daoist priest who had ruined a once-flourishing monastery, and then takes over a bandit stronghold by killing its chief. Eventually, he and his colleagues join forces with Song Jiang. These episodes also show the favored representation of Lu Zhishen on stage—a violent drunk who punishes those who stand in his way, a man with strong principles, a tenaciously loyal friend who operates out of a strong sense of righteousness.

Written in 1433, *A Leopard Monk Returns to the Laity* is carried by a plot of Zhu Youdun's own invention. It shows a Lu Zhishen who is sincerely penitent of his life as an outlaw and wants to find peace in a monastic existence. The *Water Margin* makes a point of stating that Lu Zhishen had no relatives whatsoever. In the play, however, he not only has a close friend in Li Kui, but also a wife, a son, and a mother. Zhu Youdun's play is the only source to refer to a second attempt by Lu Zhishen "to leave the family" and become a Buddhist monk. The first attempt, common to his portrayal, was only a ploy to escape from the law. The emphasis on a real desire to become a monk makes *A Leopard Monk Returns to the Laity* a mirror image of the ordinary deliverance play. As in *Zhongli of the Han Leads Lan Caihe to Enlightenment*, translated above, a Daoist priest or Buddhist monk usually tries to convert someone who has a comfortable material life to give it up and become an ascetic. *A Leopard Monk* provides instead a threefold effort to persuade the monk to give up his calling and return to lay life. And while Lu Zhishen is capable of cutting off the ties of friendship, his love for wife and child, and any concern for his reputation, he cannot get beyond his feelings of filial piety, the basic virtue in traditional Chinese thought. When his mother is abused, he breaks his vows in order to protect her. In this respect, this play foreshadows the novel, in which many heroes may be indifferent to women but will go to extremes in their devotion to their mother.

A Leopard Monk Returns to the Laity is in most ways a regular *zaju*. The four suites of songs are assigned to a male lead who plays the part of Lu Zhishen. The anamolous feature of the play is the fact that a short suite of two songs, to the tune *Qiong hexi*, and a coda follow the regular suite of songs that constitute Act 3. The two songs are separated by a recited passage in octosyllabic lines. The construction of this scene is unique: it is not a wedge, because it neither precedes a suite nor uses standard wedge tunes. Neither is it a final demi-act (as in *Qiannü's Soul Leaves Her Body*), since it concludes the third not the last suite.

This curious structure supports the scene in which Lu Zhishen, after deciding he will take care of his mother by lodging her with his patron Goodman Zhang, sets off with her from the monastery for Goodman Zhang's village. When his mother voices her misgivings about the backwoods where he may be taking her, he describes the joys of country life to her at length. The recited passage enumerates all the shops and trades in the village, with a special emphasis on the trades practiced by women. The entire passage has the air of an independent performance routine, only minimally adapted for inclusion in this play. Such routines were a common feature of variety performances of the Song and Yuan.

A Leopard Monk is preceded by a short preface in which Zhu Youdun argues that not all literature has to be didactic, pointing out that many ancient luminaries and staunch Confucians at times took up the brush only to display their erudition or to indulge in a pleasant pastime:

As far as texts of this world are concerned, there are those that are tied up with the teaching of morals, and there are those that are not tied up with the teaching of morals. Those texts that are tied up with the teaching of morals . . . all accord with principle and human nature; smartly and subtly, time and again, they never fail to enlighten and awaken later students so they can know the Way of human nature and of fate. For this reason they are of help to the world.

As for those texts that are of no help to the world and are not tied up with the teaching of morals . . . what happened is that great Confucians and eminent gentlemen, in the overflowing fullness of their learning, wrote these texts for fun; they simply wished to give free rein to the fine splendor in their bosoms.

In my days of leisure I remarked that some authors of the Yuan had composed plays on outlaws. The depictions and descriptions in them gave a complete picture of the bandits' demeanor. This is just a case of writing for fun to "display the elegant texts nurtured in one's bosom." Now, for a leisure pursuit, I have imitated their style to compose a play on bandits and called it *A Leopard Monk Returns to the Laity*. I also had actors perform it and watched their demeanor simply as a form of amusement that can urge one to drink. A gentleman is ashamed if there is but one thing he does not know. It is my wish that later students may broaden their erudition by it.

Dramatis personæ in order of appearance

Role type	Name, family role, or social role
Extra	Song Jiang
Bandits	Bandits
Male lead	Lu Zhishen
Added male	Li Kui
Underlings	Bandits
Female lead	Wife of Lu Zhishen
Child	Lu Zhishen's child
Old female	Mother
Acolyte	Acolyte
Goodman Zhang	Zhang Shanyou, Zhang Yuanliang, a villager
Little females	Goodman Zhang's daughters

Newly Compiled

A Leopard Monk Returns to the Laity of His Own Accord
With Complete Dialogue

[Act 1]

(EXTRA, *dressed as* SONG JIANG, *enters leading* BANDITS.) (SONG JIANG *recites:*)

> In Liangshan Moor we make our home
> And have never planted a field our whole life long.
> We've polished our knives till the wind-quick blade is keen,
> And tempered our axes till the moon-sickle edge is round.
> We have limitless stratagems for coercion and robbery,
> And all the courage needed to break and enter:
> Thirty-six brothers have I altogether—
> Each and every one strives to be first!

I am Song Jiang, known as Gongming. I am an outlaw bandit of the Proclaiming Peace era of the Song dynasty. Since that night in Yuncheng when I killed Yan Poxi, I've been on the run.[3] Banding together with friends in the greenwood, I've sworn brotherhood with thirty-six men. We live deep inside Liangshan Moor and make a living by robbing people of their money and property. Let me try and count all the names of my thirty-six brothers! (SONG JIANG *recites:*)

> Number one: Strategy Star Wu Jialiang;
> Number two: Iron King Chao Gai;
> Number three: Jade Unicorn Li Yi;
> Number four: Blue-faced Beast Yang Zhi;
> Number five: River-roiling Dragon Li Hai;
> Number six: Black Whirlwind Li Kui;
> Number seven: Nine-patterned Dragon Shi Jin;
> Number eight: Cloud-piercing Dragon Gongsun Sheng;

---

3. In a fit of rage, Song Jiang, a government clerk, killed his former lover, the courtesan Yan Poxi, after she had tried to blackmail him with incriminating evidence concerning his connections to the very criminals he was supposed to be hunting down.

Number nine: White Jumper in the Waves Zhang Shun;
Number ten: Living Yama[4] Ruan Xiaoqi;
Number eleven: Thunder Fire Qin Ming;
Number twelve: Erect Disaster Ruan Xiaowu;
Number thirteen: Fierce Erlang[5] Ruan Jin;
Number fourteen: Broad Sword Guan Bisheng;
Number fifteen: Leopard-head Lin Chong;
Number sixteen: Little Whirlwind Chai Jun;
Number seventeen: Master of the Golden Lance Xu Ning;
Number eighteen: Sky-grabbing Eagle Li Ying;
Number nineteen: Red-bearded Ghost Liu Tang;
Number twenty: One-smash-through Dong Ping;
Number twenty-one: Winged Tiger Lei Heng;
Number twenty-two: Fine Beard Zhu Tong;
Number twenty-three: Divine Guardian Dai Zong;
Number twenty-four: Guan Suo's Rival[6] Wang Xiong;
Number twenty-five: Yuchi's[7] Trouble Sun Li;
Number twenty-six: Little Li Guang[8] Hua Rong;
Number twenty-seven: Featherless Arrow Zhang Qing;
Number twenty-eight: No Barrier Mu Heng;
Number twenty-nine: Yan Qing, The Dandy;
Number thirty: Iron Whip Huyan Chuo;
Number thirty-one: Eager Vanguard Suo Chao;
Number thirty-two: Acolyte Wu Song;
Number thirty-three: Reckless Erlang Shi Xiu;
Number thirty-four: Fire Ship Attack Zhang Cen;
Number thirty-five: Cloud-groper Du Qian.[9]

Now these brothers are all here except for that Tattooed Monk Lu Zhishen. Because he took it on himself to kill an ordinary citizen, I gave him forty strokes of the big rod. Because he couldn't bear the affront, he ran off to the Clear Still-ness Monastery in Clear Brook Harbor, where he shaved off his hair and became

---

4. King Yama is the highest judge in the courts of the underworld.

5. Erlang is the name of a fierce deity in popular mythology.

6. Guan Suo (or Hua Guan Suo) is a son of Guan Yu, one of the heroes of the Three King-doms saga, and a formidable fighter in his own right, whose legendary exploits were the materials of prosimetric ballads in the fifteenth century.

7. Yuchi Gong (Jingde, 585–658) was one of the most formidable generals in the founding of the Tang dynasty. In later ages, he was commonly venerated as one of the door gods.

8. Li Guang (d. 119 BC) was a Chinese general who scored major victories against the Xiongnu on China's northern border.

9. This list is practically identical to the list provided in the *Xuanhe yishi*.

a monk. I've sent people there time after time to persuade him to come back, but he's refused. It's been more than half a year now. I remember when we became sworn brothers—we swore an oath, saying:

> We come as thirty-six,
> And leave as eighteen pairs.
> If even a single one is missing,
> Go home? None of us dare![10]

How can I go against my oath? Today we lack only him. Which of my many brothers dares go and persuade him to come back to become a robber again? (ADDED MALE, *dressed as* LI KUI, *speaks:*) I, your brother Mountain Lad Li, want to go!

> (*After further dialogue all exit.*)

(MALE LEAD, LU ZHISHEN, *dressed as* A MONK *with the palms of his hands pressed together, enters, recites and speaks:*)

> Each and every phenomenal dharma
> Is like a dream, an illusion, a bubble, a shadow,
> Is like the dew, or a lightning bolt:
> One should consider it all "like this."[11]

What superb words! I, this poor monk, am surnamed Lu; my lay name used to be Zhishen. Originally I was a monk in the Monastery of Extensive Wisdom in Nanyang but because I did not strictly follow the monastic rules in my youth, my master scolded me angrily and I returned to the laity as a common citizen. I fell in with brother Song Jiang at Liangshan Moor and became an outlaw. I brought my decrepit mother along so I might look after her early and late. But last year when I was given forty strokes of the big rod by brother Song Jiang, I couldn't tolerate his anger and ran off to the Monastery of Clear Stillness in Clear Brook Harbor. I "left the family" and became a monk. If you ask me, I think people who practice austerities and mind the Way are far better off than those who are bandits! (LU ZHISHEN *sings:*)

([XIANLÜ MODE:] *Dian jiangchun*)
> I now have
> Packed away my reckless behavior,

---

10. When the thirty-six members of the band had been united, tells the *Xuanhe yishi*, they went together on a pilgrimage to the Eastern Marchmount Mount Tai; on the date of their departure, Song Jiang inscribed this poem on their banner.

11. "Like this" is the phrase that usually opens a sutra lecture, for instance on the evanescence and illusory nature of life. Paraphrased, it means "we should adapt a Buddhist outlook on life."

And cleaned up my violent bullying
To become a monk.
>> So now I
Loudly recite sutras and spells,
>> And, each day I
Sit upright on my meditation bench.

(*Hunjiang long*)
>> When I recall
My old doings:
>> My body, clothed in
A short tunic and tight trousers,
>> My hands, holding
A black oiled lance;
>> When the wind was high,
I murdered and set fires ablaze,
>> When the moon was dark,
I bored tunnels and dug through walls.
>> In those days, I recall
Mustering my courage, being fearless, displaying daring and might,
>> But still I had
To hunker down, walk tiptoe, hide myself in the dark.
>> In those days
Sleep was never a real rest or ease,
And when awake I was always afraid and frightened.
>> Each night
I traveled by stars and moonlight,
>> And day after day
I slept in snow and frost.
>> But now I've turned into
A carefree, untrammeled monk:
>> In the morning
I sweep the ground before the temple gate,
>> And at night
I burn incense in the Buddha hall.

(ADDED MALE, *dressed as* MOUNTAIN LAD LI, *enters.*) (*After acting out greeting, he acts out trying to persuade* LU ZHISHEN.) (LU ZHISHEN *sings:*)

(*You hulu*)
>> Many thanks to you,
Brother Black Whirlwind, for all your kind questions.

(LI KUI *speaks:*) Brother Song Jiang has ordered me to come and fetch you. Why not come back to our mountain stronghold? (LU ZHISHEN *sings:*)

> You say
> It is Song Jiang,
>> But, even if you were
> An evil King Yama, pursuing souls and snatching away life,
>> How could you cajole
> Lu Zhishen into entering the Liangshan wilds again?
>> All for nothing he made you, Li
> The Mountain Lad, come to Clear Brook Harbor,
>> Because I have already accepted
> A master who insists on the rules,
>> And become
> A fine, bald-pated monk!

(LI KUI *speaks:*) You've forgotten that you were a monk once before but came along with us to be a bandit. (LU ZHISHEN *sings:*)

>> I can't be compared to that
> Heroic Tattooed Monk of earlier days,
>> Don't look here for the
> Bad behavior a bandit does!

(LI KUI *speaks:*) Come with me! We bandits have gold and silver. We fine fellows get other people's possessions without turning a hand. (LU ZHISHEN *sings:*)

> (*Tianxia le*)
>> Take Liu
> Daozhi's[12] family tradition, and think it over carefully,
> Examine it closely:
>> What kind
> Of fine business is that?

(LU ZHISHEN *speaks:*) You bandits live in constant fear and worry. It's hush-hush here and hush-hush there. You jump across someone's wall, but when they are on to you, you have to turn around and jump back over. And if you don't escape, you get caught. (LU ZHISHEN *sings:*)

---

12. In the *Zhuangzi*, the character of Robber Zhi (*Dao Zhi*) is introduced as a ferocious highwayman and bandit and identified as the younger brother of the proverbial paragon of virtue, Liuxia Hui (720–621 BC). Zhu Youdun here treats *Dao Zhi* as his personal name, Daozhi, and provides him with the surname Liu.

People like you
Who are robbers one day get caught and sentenced on the spot!

(LU ZHISHEN *imitates the posture of someone wearing a cangue, sings:*)

A big, heavy
Cangue is clamped around your neck
And thick hemp cords
Tie your hands behind your back.
Now you are
"A real man who relies on his strength!"[13]

(LI KUI *speaks:*) You monks live a tough life every day. What's so great about keeping fasts and eating vegetarian food? We bandits have a great time. We amass a fortune, get food and clothing, and never touch our own money. I'll just have to say that it's better being a bandit. (LU ZHISHEN *speaks:*) We monks live a life of carefree pleasure. Just listen to me! (LU ZHISHEN *sings:*)

(*Nuozha ling*)
I beg
A tile shard full of grain—
Onions or meat I never taste.[14]
I wear
Two lengths of linen cowl—
Lance or sword I never raise.
I receive
Donations from every direction,
So never worry about money or goods.
My desire to be a bandit
Turned into a heart that minds the Way,
My fierce and evil look
Has turned to one of compassion.
You might break into prison cells but that's no match
For lonely vigils I keep in my own little cell.

(LI KUI *speaks:*) Sitting in meditation and practicing austerities is just suffering and being bored for no reason at all. What's the big deal? We bandits have it better—come with me! (LU ZHISHEN *sings:*)

(*Que ta zhi*)
You only want

---

13. A cliché roughly meaning "a real man knows how to take care of himself."
14. In addition to meat, Chinese vegetarians usually eat no onions or garlic.

To sit on a bench in jail,
> I just love

To sit on the meditation bench.
> You

Burn incense on the Eastern Marchmount,[15]
> I

Burn incense in the Buddha hall.

(LU ZHISHEN *speaks:*) You bandits do all the evil things I did once. (LU ZHISHEN *sings:*)

> You'll only

Bide your time to carry out evil, set your mob free to plunder!

(LU ZHISHEN *speaks:*) When you enter someone's house, you stoop over, creep to the left, then to the right, whisper here, whisper there. . . . (LU ZHISHEN *sings:*)

> It's always

Hush-hush whispering, hiding in the dark.

(LI KUI *speaks:*) You are just a wimp, a sissy. You're no real man. In all those years you never contributed anything to our success of robbing camps and strongholds, committing murder and arson! (LU ZHISHEN, *angrily tucking up his sleeves, speaks:*) Who says I did not contribute to your successes? Who says I am a wimp and a sissy? (LU ZHISHEN, *striking postures, sings:*)

> (*Jisheng cao*)
> You relied on me to

Employ heroic fierceness,
Show off powerful strength!
> You relied on my

King of beasts posture, that could uproot mountains and lift
> tripods,

My kraken dragon capacity, that could make rivers roll and oceans
> roil,

My gibbonlike nature that could fly along the eaves and run across
> walls.

---

15. Taishan (Mount Tai) in Shandong was believed to be the seat of the Great Emperor of the Eastern Marchmount, the ruler of the underworld. He was one of the most popular deities of early premodern times and his main temple in "the holy land of Tai'an" was a center of pilgrimage. According to the *Xuanhe yishi*, in addition to the trip led by Song Jiang, Chao Gai, the original leader of the band, also led an earlier pilgrimage to the same site.

(LU ZHISHEN, *rubbing his head twice with his hand, speaks:*) Wow, I almost forgot I'm a monk now! (LU ZHISHEN *speaks:*) Blessings on you! (LU ZHISHEN, *not striking postures anymore but pressing the palms of his hands together, sings:*)

> I never again desire to
> Dismiss the dangers of life, brave my own death, suffer turmoil!
> For I've wound up in a position where I can
> Cultivate the true, nurture my nature, exist without hindrance.

(LI KUI *speaks:*) Come along with me, brother. Song Jiang is expecting you at the mountain stronghold. (LU ZHISHEN *speaks:*) Blessings on you! I'll never be a bandit again! (LI KUI *speaks:*) You're just afraid to die. You've grown old and don't have the guts to go. But even if you went, you'd enter not a single success on the ledger of merit! (LU ZHISHEN *again acts out being angry.*) (LU ZHISHEN, *striking postures, sings:*)

> (*Reprise*)
> You say that I
> Have grown too old;
> I say that my
> Gall is unyielding.
> Once upon a time
> I blocked a bandit in a great fray in Chrysanthemum Valley,
> Once upon a time
> I wasted a monkey-bitch[16] during a nighttime raid with Black
>   Whirlwind,
> And once
> I raised the golden pitchfork on the sly with Red-bearded Ghost![17]

(LU ZHISHEN *again rubs his head twice with his hand and speaks:*) I forgot again that I am a monk now! (LU ZHISHEN *speaks again:*) Blessings on you! (LU ZHISHEN, *not striking postures anymore but pressing the palms of his hands together, sings:*)

> Don't mention again—
> With wide-open eyes and vertical brows—
> Being

---

16. Standard pejorative for a prostitute-performer; the monkey was the finest symbol of unbridled lust.

17. It is not quite clear to which two adventures Lu Zhishen is referring here in the last two lines. It should be remembered that the adventure of Lu Zhishen in Chrysanthemum Valley has only been preserved as a *zaju* and was not included in the later novel.

a murderous robber,
> I'll always—

In a squared gown and a round pate
> Be

> the perfect picture of a monk!

(LI KUI *speaks:*) What's the big deal in being a monk here? What are your enjoyments? (LU ZHISHEN *speaks:*) Small chance a bandit like you can understand my pleasures! (LU ZHISHEN *sings:*)

> (*Zui zhong tian*)
>> In this stretch of
>
> Misty and foggy blue, this tall screen of a cliff
>> I live in a
>
> Dark and dusky green little mountain cell.
> I lie on a bed of clear shade, cool in the hottest days of summer,
> And listen to ten thousand valleys sound out the wind in pines.[18]
>> Whenever at leisure,
>
> I fetch water from the creek and brew up tea of a taste, Oh, so
>> fragrant!
>
> A situation of free and easy leisure,
>> Where feelings of right and wrong
>
> Intrude not the least!

(LI KUI *acts out dragging* LU ZHISHEN *back.*) (LU ZHISHEN *speaks:*) Blessings on you! I, this poor monk, won't go! (LU ZHISHEN *sings:*)

> (*Zhuanwei*)
>> Since I have jumped out
>
> Of the arena of murder,
>> Why would I want to fall again into
>
> That net of law wide as heaven?
> Report this to brother Song Jiang for me!

(LU ZHISHEN *speaks:*) Don't drag me! Boy, haven't I practiced the austerities right! The signs are appearing. (LU ZHISHEN *points once to the east and once to the west.*) (LI KUI *speaks:*) What are you pointing at? (LU ZHISHEN *sings:*)

> Now
> For half a year I have practiced austerities well enough to make signs
>> appear!

---

18. The harmonic sound of nature thought to emanate from deep valleys.

(LI KUI *speaks:*) What signs? Tell me! (LU ZHISHEN *sings:*)

Right above my head there are a myriad rays of light![19]

(LI KUI *speaks:*) There are no rays of light! It must be the glittering of the lamps in the Buddha hall. (LU ZHISHEN *sings:*)

> You say I don't
> Radiate a halo of light,
> > That it is
> The glittering of the lamps:
> > You really
> Ruin the finest affair of us monks!

(LI KUI *speaks:*) Listen to me. Come back, be a bandit. How can you stand this boring life? (LU ZHISHEN *sings:*)

> I'm not willing again to go
> Drill holes, jump across walls,
> Twirl the lance, make the staff dance.
> > That's no match for my
> Sitting cross-legged, palms together, on the meditation bench!

(*Exit.*)

(LI KUI *speaks:*) Even I can't talk any sense into him. So now I will go back to our mountain stronghold and report to brother Song Jiang.

(*Exit.*)

[Act 2]

(SONG JIANG *enters with* UNDERLINGS.) (SONG JIANG *speaks:*) I sent the Black Whirlwind, Mountain Lad Li, to go get Lu Zhishen. I wonder where he is. (LI KUI *enters.*) (*Following* the *conversation,* SONG JIANG *speaks:*) I have a plan! You go get his wife and child to call him back. He'll be willing to come then. (LI KUI *calls for* WIFE, *who enters leading* CHILD. *Following conversation they exit.*)

(LU ZHISHEN *enters, recites and speaks:*)

> Each and every phenomenal dharma
> Is like a dream, an illusion, a bubble, a shadow;

---

19. The bald pate of monks is a source of unlimited fun in China. One of the words for "bald" is *guang,* which also means "shining"; here it also refers to the halo of light that surrounds those who have attained the Buddha nature.

Is like the dew, or a lightning bolt:
One should consider it all "like this."

What fine words those are! I, this poor monk, am Lu Zhishen. Ever since I arrived in this temple, my life has been one of carefree pleasure. Just look at these green mountains and blue rivers: what a beautiful landscape! (LU ZHISHEN *sings:*)

([YUEDIAO MODE:] *Dou anchun*)
>>Arranged in a single row
The green mountains behind the temple,
>>Hidden by two ranks
Of verdant willows in front of the gate:
>>I've planted five seedlings
Of dark-blue pines down at the creek,
>>And trimmed a few
Azure bamboos in the garden.
>>I listen awhile to
The call of the crane and the cries of the gibbon,
>>And watch awhile
The flight of the crow, the race of the hare.[20]
>>When at ease,
I have a zither,
>>When sleepy
A pot of tea.
>>And eating
Bland rice and yellow pickles
>>Still beats
The fattest sheep or finest wine!

(LU ZHISHEN *speaks:*) Now I practice austerities and don't involve myself in right or wrong. What a pleasure! (LU ZHISHEN *sings:*)

(*Zihua'er xu*)
>>All I want is to
Put my hands up the sleeves of my monk's robe,
Give my body ease in this bare cell,
Hide my head in my tattered hood,
Unaware of summer and winter,
Mindless whether it's autumn or spring—
Ended, done with it all!

---

20. In Chinese mythology the sun is inhabited by a crow, the moon by a hare.

> I've done away
>
> With slender profit and empty fame in a single stroke!
>
> I'm like
>
> The clouds in the wilds emerging from the rocks,[21]
>
> Stretching and contracting without intent—
>
> Oh, what wonderful freedom!

(LU ZHISHEN *speaks:*) Let me lock the door of my cell and sit in stillness for a while on my meditation bench. (WIFE *enters, leading* CHILD, *acts out calling out to him to open the door.*) (LU ZHISHEN, *startled, speaks:*) This must be some fiendish Māra[22] or heretic, who has noticed how I practiced my austerities to the point of very perfection and now comes to disturb me! (WIFE *again acts out calling out to him to open the door.*) (LU ZHISHEN *speaks:*) This is the voice of a woman. It must be some patron at the foot at the mountain, inviting me to an early vegetarian meal. (LU ZHISHEN *sings:*)

> (*Jin jiaoye*)
>
> Who is it
>
> Who knocks so long on my grass-weave door, my brushwood gate?

(LU ZHISHEN *acts out opening the door, sings:*)

> It turns out to be
>
> My baby boy and rustic wife who've come to visit!

(WIFE *speaks:*) You've been here for six months. Your child has even learned to walk. (LU ZHISHEN *sings:*)

> Well, I'll be damned, the child has learned to walk!
>
> And how is she, that dear old white-haired mother of mine?

(WIFE *speaks:*) Your mother is fine but she is longing for you and has grown old. (LU ZHISHEN *acts out weeping.* WIFE *speaks:*) And this silly little child of yours also longs for you every day. Since you've been here—well, I'm just a woman— I've nowhere to go for food. You're so cruel. Left us without any concern for wife or child! (LU ZHISHEN *hugs* CHILD.) (LU ZHISHEN *sings:*)

---

21. While here a metaphor for illusion and reality, it was believed that clouds were created from rocks, as attested by another name for rocks: *yungen*, "cloud roots."

22. Māra was lord of the sixth heaven, the heaven of desire. He attacked the Buddha, about to attain enlightenment, as he feared that the Buddha by his teaching would end his domination of the world. When the attack of Māra and his heavenly hosts had failed, Māra's daughters tried to seduce the Buddha with their charms. When the Buddha turned these beautiful young girls into ugly old hags, Māra admitted defeat.

(*Xiaotao hong*)
With tear-filled eyes I hug my child
> And ask why, since our separation,
My deserted wife has grown so thin?

(LU ZHISHEN *feels his head twice with his hand and speaks:*) Again I forgot that I have left the family. Woman, step back and don't pull at me! (LU ZHISHEN *puts down the* CHILD *and pushes him toward* WIFE.) (LU ZHISHEN *sings:*)

> I myself
Have seen right through all the tangled affairs of this sordid world!

(LU ZHISHEN *speaks:*) Blessings on you! (LU ZHISHEN *sings:*)

> So this should stop!

(WIFE *speaks:*) If you don't come back, the family will have no firewood, no rice. The house is leaking too. How am I going to live? (LU ZHISHEN *sings:*)

> I don't care whether
You have no firewood, no rice, whether the house leaks!

(WIFE *steps forward and clutches him.* LU ZHISHEN *sings:*)

> Don't grab my collar,
> Don't clutch at my sleeves,
>> Don't think you can
> Talk me into changing my mind!

(WIFE *speaks:*) If you won't go back, I will leave this damned child with you. When you have taught him how to be a bandit, send him back to me so he can take care of me! (WIFE *pushes the* CHILD *toward* LU ZHISHEN.) (LU ZHISHEN *speaks:*) I won't teach him that! Give him to brother Song Jiang for instruction! (LU ZHISHEN *pushes the* CHILD *toward* WIFE.) (WIFE *in turn pushes the child toward* LU ZHISHEN.) (*After further conversation,* LU ZHISHEN *again pushes the* CHILD *toward* WIFE.) (*After further conversation,* WIFE *speaks:*) You really want to practice austerities and not come back? (LU ZHISHEN *sings:*)

> (*Tiaoxiao ling*)
>> Now I
> Am able to cultivate myself,
> Delight in pure seclusion,
>> Now I have
> Stored away the basket, put away the peck![23]

---

23. Units of measure, hence, to care no more for worldly gains.

> So what I fear are
> The red-dust, blue-sea battles of dragon and serpent,[24]
> The endless, unending rights and wrongs!

(WIFE *speaks:*) You're practicing austerities all by yourself. Who is keeping you company? (LU ZHISHEN *sings:*)

> Now I
> Read my sutras and recite Buddha's name, together with friends of
>   goodness,
>> And each and every day
> I keep company with my tile-shard bowl and earthenware cup.

(CHILD *cries out, speaks:*) Daddy, listen to mommy! Come home! Daddy, since you came here, I haven't had any big buns or long date cakes to eat! Mother and I are dying of hunger! (LU ZHISHEN *acts out wiping his tears, steps forward and takes* CHILD *in his arms.*) (LU ZHISHEN *sings:*)

> (*Tusi'er*)
> I carry my child in my arms.

(LU ZHISHEN *acts out weeping, sings:*)

> I also imagine my old mother, beset by sorrow!

(WIFE *again acts out urging* LU ZHISHEN *to go back.*) (MALE *sings:*)

>> And she
> Keeps on and on and on, urging me, never shutting her mouth!
>> It's really
> Hard to come to a decision—
> Tears surge
> To fill my eyes!

(WIFE *grabs* LU ZHISHEN *tightly and speaks:*) If you refuse to go back, how can I take care of this child at home, find any food to eat? If you really want to practice your austerities, write me a writ of divorce, so I can marry someone else, find a place to get clothes and food to eat! (LU ZHISHEN *sings:*)

> (*Sheng Yaowang*)
>> There, she
> Demands a divorce.
>> But how can I
> Give you a divorce?

---

24. Battles for power and profit.

> She only wants to find some other way out,
>
> Some way to provide her lifelong clothes and food.

(LU ZHISHEN, *after feeling his head with his hand, sings:*)

> I would like
>
> Not to care
>
> But of course I care!
>
> We should be
>
> Husband and wife, share fifty years of perfect accord.

(LU ZHISHEN *speaks:*) Let me go! (LU ZHISHEN *sings:*)

> I really
>
> Have a hard time giving up my phoenix-mate!

(WIFE *speaks:*) How can I find food to eat when I go back if you won't give me a divorce? Keep this damned child here with you. When you teach him how to be a bandit, send him back so he can take care of me. (WIFE *pushes the* CHILD *toward* LU ZHISHEN.) (LU ZHISHEN *speaks:*) I am someone who practices austerities. It would look bad if I were raising a child in the monastery. You'd better take him home! (LU ZHISHEN *pushes the* CHILD *again toward* WIFE.) (*After* WIFE *has spoken some lines, she pushes him again toward* LU ZHISHEN.) (*After* LU ZHISHEN *has spoken some lines, he pushes him again toward* WIFE.) (*After pushing the* CHILD *back and forth seven or eight times,* LU ZHISHEN *sings:*)

> (*Qingshan kou*)
>
> We push the child
>
> Over here,
>
> Over there:
>
> How can the child
>
> Stand all that?

(CHILD *cries out.*) (*After* LU ZHISHEN'S WIFE *has spoken some lines,* LU ZHISHEN *sings:*)

> Just listen to her,
>
> Blabbering about every single thing known to man!

(LU ZHISHEN, *after feeling his head twice with his hand, speaks:*) Right here, in this temple courtyard. . . . A woman like you comes running in wailing and weeping to Heaven and Earth—this is no way to act! (LU ZHISHEN *sings:*)

> I am
>
> So ashamed, too ashamed, really ashamed!
>
> This rotten old woman can't rescue me.

Just look at
Her disgraceful behavior—
Impossible to put her in her place!
Walk, sit—she comes racing after,
Here, there—she grabs me tightly.
She rails and rants off the top of her head—
Always at cross-purposes
And bringing out all my ferocity!
Keep her, keep her—no way I'll keep her!
Divorce her, divorce her—I will certainly divorce her!
Don't ask for reason or cause,
Let's do it, divorce in writing.
   No more will I think
Of the depth of our love and affection:
   Today, on this day,
A single stroke finishes it off!

(LU ZHISHEN *speaks*:) Get me paper and brush and I will write you a writ of divorce, so you may go! (WIFE *speaks*:) No way I'll accept your writ of divorce! I was just trying to trick you into returning. But since you refuse to go, I will go back to report to brother Song Jiang. (*Exits.*) (LU ZHISHEN *sings*:)

(*Weisheng*)
When I'm back in my cell, go ahead, knock on the gate all you want:
I have cut off all those feelings of love, once and for all!
   Constantly will I
Practice austerities here, in Clear Stillness Monastery;
   Never will I
Flee there, to Liangshan Stronghold!

(*Exit.*)

[Act 3]

(SONG JIANG *enters leading* UNDERLINGS. SONG JIANG *speaks*:) I sent Lu Zhishen's wife and child off, and they haven't reappeared. (WIFE *enters, leading the* CHILD. *After she has spoken some lines,* SONG JIANG *speaks*:) If I sent anyone else, they wouldn't be able to talk him around. There's nothing left to do but to send his mother to persuade him. This brother of mine is nothing if not filial and obedient. When he sees it's his mother who's come to fetch him, he is bound to come back together with her. (*Acts out calling for* MOTHER. MOTHER *enters. After some dialogue,* [MOTHER *and*] SONG JIANG *exit.*)

(LU ZHISHEN *enters, recites and speaks*:)

> Each and every phenomenal dharma
> Is like a dream, an illusion, a bubble, a shadow;
> Is like the dew, or a lightning bolt:
> One should consider it all "like this."

What superb words! Today Goodman Zhang, a patron at the foot of the mountain, has invited me for a vegetarian feast. I'll go there for a bit. I'll instruct my little acolyte to look after my room.

(Exits.)

(*After* ACOLYTE *enters, after some lines of speech,* MOTHER *enters.*) (*After she has acted out greeting* ACOLYTE *and after she has spoken some lines,* ACOLYTE *speaks*:) My master isn't at home. Some patron down at the foot of the mountain invited him over. Madam, why don't you sit down in his cell, he'll be along anytime now. (LU ZHISHEN *enters, speaks*:) Early this morning Goodman Zhang invited me for a vegetarian feast. Now I am hurrying back. This mountain road is hard going and it's getting late, too. (LU ZHISHEN *sings*:)

([ZHENGGONG MODE:] *Duanzheng hao*)
> Over high ranges at the edge of far heaven I see, vividly blue,
>> lambently green, the gradually
> Dispersing mists of many colors;
>> Down in the hollows of western hills refulgently verdant at the rim of
>> evening clouds, shines, shimmeringly radiant
> A sinking red wheel—
>> I'm walking on
> A rough and rocky mountain road where stones are sharp and pines
> rise high,
>> My only fear that that stupid little
> Monk, that silly acolyte, will close the monastery gate with a
> thudding bang,
>> And therefore all panicky and out of breath,
> I've run until I haven't a thread of energy left!

(LU ZHISHEN *speaks*:) That good Goodman Zhang invited me over to eat my fill of his vegetarian feast! (LU ZHISHEN *sings*:)

(*Gun xiuqiu*)
> This morning I ate a full begging bowl of tangy-and-tartly sour,
>> honeyed-and-sugar sweet,
> Yellow vegetable pickles,

        Two bowls of slippery smooth and watery cold
Vegetarian ravioli;
        And I also ate some explodingly fragrant, mounded and quivering
Mushrooms and soft tofu, mixed in a half basin of clear broth.
        And then there were those fresh and tenderly crisp, spicy and
            pungently hot
Dried, vinegar-soaked mustard greens and radish.
        Roundly, tightly inflated, I've filled up
This big belly of mine,
        And with exploding blasts of breath, I've let loose
Any number of burps and belches,
        Barely managing to move this lethargically lumbering, packed to the
            gills, immovable
Dead weight of a body.
        This vegetarian feast
Was quite unlike
        The trembling bodies and quailing hearts
            at banquets of Empress Lü.[25]
        By the time that I, this walking-stealthily-in-a-pitch-black-cave
Monk, return to my *dhyana* cell, where flower scent is so light,
        That dripping, trickling bright, shimmering, glimmeringly radiant
Moon will have already reached the cold window where bamboo
    shadows move
        And by their rustling
Startle sleeping birds to flight.

(LU ZHISHEN *speaks*:) Here I am outside my cell. Who is to blame for this open door? (MOTHER *acts out moaning, speaks*:) Ah! Alas! (LU ZHISHEN *acts out listening*.) (LU ZHISHEN *sings*:)

    (*Tang xiucai*)
        Who is that in my monk's cell
Moaning and groaning?

---

25. Empress Lü was the wife of Liu Bang, the founder of the Han dynasty (206 BC–AD 220). Once Liu Bang had completed the conquest of the Chinese world, the empress played a decisive role in executing some of the ablest generals who had supported her husband in founding the dynasty. Following the death of her husband in 195 BC, she became the most powerful person at court and ruled with an iron hand. On one occasion she tried to murder one of her guests at a banquet by ordering him to drink poisoned wine; on another occasion she enforced the rules of a drinking game as martial law. One of her relatives was promptly executed when he broke the rule. As a result, the expression "a banquet of Empress Lü" came to mean "a situation fraught with danger."

It must be some
Bewitching demon or baleful ghost from a mountain temple!

(LU ZHISHEN *speaks:*) I'd say it's a ghost, but it isn't. (LU ZHISHEN *sings:*)

I'd say that it is
A bandit who late at night bores through walls and tunnels holes,
But I have no
Precious goods whatsoever,
Nor any
Really fine stuff,
So what would he steal from me?

(MOTHER *speaks:*) Aiya! Aiya! (LU ZHISHEN *speaks:*) This must be some baleful ghost. I will chant a few true words to catch it. (*After* LU ZHISHEN *has struck postures and recited a complete spell,* MOTHER *speaks again:*) Aiya! Aiya! (LU ZHISHEN *speaks:*) My first incantation hasn't caught it. The subduing power of the Buddha power won't touch it. (LU ZHISHEN *again strikes postures and recites his spell, speaks.*) (MOTHER *speaks again:*) Aiya! Aiya! (LU ZHISHEN *speaks:*) Weird! How come two incantations won't catch it? Let me recite my spell once more. This time I will catch it for sure! (*After* LU ZHISHEN *again has struck postures and recited the spell,* MOTHER *again speaks in raised voice:*) Aiya! Aiya! (LU ZHISHEN *speaks:*) This incantation is worthless! I'd better go into my cell and hit it over the head with my tin-tipped staff! (LU ZHISHEN *acts out entering into his cell, raising his tin-tipped staff, about to strike.*) (MOTHER *cries out, speaks:*) Don't hit me! I'm your mother! I've come to visit you! (*After* LU ZHISHEN *throws down his tin-tipped staff, kneels down, and weeps, tightly clutching* MOTHER, LU ZHISHEN *sings:*)

(*Gun xiuqiu*)
I, your child,
Am just too unruly!
I didn't know that my aged mother
Had come to this place!
Mommy, how did you ever make it,
Such a long, long way?
Mommy, did you
Get a meal tonight to dampen your hunger?

(MOTHER *speaks:*) I've had my meal, don't worry. I came to urge you to come back with me. Your brothers don't blame you anymore. (LU ZHISHEN *sings:*)

Mommy, you urge me
To return quickly,

> But how on earth
Can I return?
> Each and every one of those robbers provides a ready
Example, far and wide, of wrongdoing.
> If ever taken,
Could they stand the six questionings, three interrogations?

(LU ZHISHEN *speaks:*) Arrested by the authorities, those robbers won't be able to stand up to torture and under duress will confess to their stolen booty. They will be paraded through all the main streets of town, wearing heavy cangues. And then while prison guards and executioners on both sides keep them under close guard, it's "three rolls on the drum, and one rap of the gong!"[26] (LU ZHISHEN *sings:*)

> After looking at those
Two rows of swords and lances swinging in front,
> Don't mistake *that* for
"A band of flutists and singers follows when they leave and return!"[27]
> Mommy, under those conditions, even
You'd weep and wail!

(MOTHER *speaks:*) If you refuse to become a robber, at least return to the mountain stronghold to live; you could be a watchman and guard the camp. (LU ZHISHEN *speaks:*) That wouldn't do either. (LU ZHISHEN *sings:*)

> (*Tang xiucai*)
> Should I
Guard the robbers' camp,
> I couldn't forestall
Those bandits dragging me in, implicating me.

(LU ZHISHEN *speaks:*) If they were just thieves and pilferers, small-time hoods, I could still escape, but if they are armed robbers or murderers, no distinction is made between mastermind and accomplice—all have to die. (LU ZHISHEN *sings:*)

---

26. Announcing the execution.

27. This line is repeated in one of Zhu Youdun's plays on singsong girls, *Liu Jin'er from Xuanping Ward Becomes a Singsong Girl Again*, where it is used to refer to the past glories of courtesans of renown. It appears to be a common expression for any kind of glory heaped on a person; both the actual group of singers that announce one's arrival and departure, but also the fuss that attends one of high accomplishment or station.

Even those guarding the camp
Are bound to see their garments splattered with blood at Yunyang.[28]
> So I've taken my bandit's heart

And changed it forever,
> Taken my bandit's ways

And reined them all in
> To become a little monk:

I've seen through right and wrong.

(MOTHER *speaks:*) Monks suffer misery. What's the big deal? Come back with me, so you can take care of me at the mountain stronghold. (LU ZHISHEN *speaks:*) Mommy, it's not good to be a bandit, it's much better to be a monk! (LU ZHISHEN *sings:*)

(*Gun xiuqiu*)
> We monks,

From the time we get up
Till late at night,
> Constantly recite

Para Gati.[29]
> And those

Roots and sprouts of goodness
> Widely sow the seeds of

Buddha fruit and *bodhi.*[30]
> What we eat

Is food from our patrons,
> What we wear

Are clothes from our patrons:
> We never squander

A cent of our own, capital or interest.
> Wherever there is

A vegetarian feast
> We're sure to get

A few gifts bestowed.

---

28. From the time that Li Si (d. 208 BC), Chief Minister of the First Emperor of the Qin, was executed in the marketplace at Yunyang, this has become a standard metaphor for the execution ground.

29. *Para Gati* is a spell from the *Prajñā-pāramitā sūtra,* or *Heart Sutra,* one of the most popular sutras in East Asia.

30. *Bodhi* means "perfect wisdom."

And the
Rice and noodles won by begging
   Are truly
Better than any stolen.
Money and goods won without effort—
   Compared to those stolen—
Are a big return on a small investment.

(MOTHER *speaks*:) My child, when you were young, you were a real man. But now you have become such a weakling. Your brothers at the mountain stronghold all make fun of you. They say you have grown weak and frail and that you never contributed to their success. That you never contributed to their success—unlike Black Whirlwind, Mountain Lad Li! (LU ZHISHEN *speaks*:) Who said I never contributed to their success? (MOTHER *speaks*:) At the stronghold they all say you never contributed to their success—unlike Black Whirlwind, Mountain Lad Li! (LU ZHISHEN *acts out being angry*.) (*After* LU ZHISHEN *has taken off his cassock, he strikes a posture and sings*:)

  (*Dai guduo*)
    This vexes me until
  I can't control my thumping rage!
    There's no way—
  Weak and feeble!
    I don't believe
  That this Tattooed Monk, Zhishen
    Is any less than
  That Black Whirlwind Li Kui!
    Talk about
  A fight with whip or club—it's I who can use them!
    Discuss
  Lance or sword—I master both!
    Stir me up and, crashing and banging,
  I can reverse the very axis of the earth!
    And, boiling and roiling,
  I stir up all the waters of the deep blue sea!

(*After* LU ZHISHEN *feels his head twice with his hand, he speaks*:) Again I forgot that I practice austerities and have left the family. Again I act this way! (LU ZHISHEN *hastily puts on his cassock and speaks*:) Mommy, blessings on you! Mommy, as a monk I am not concerned with valor and daring anymore! (LU ZHISHEN *sings*:)

(*Zui taiping*)
> All I want is

To flee from the right and wrong of the red dust,
Perch quietly on a verdant ridge,
Where a little cell suits me well—a low paper window,
Hemmed around with a bamboo fence.
My carefree body fallen into a sound and undisturbed sleep,
Impoverished cassock and begging bowl untainted by rank smells.
A plain life in friendship with mountains and clouds,
After all, how long is a human life?

(LU ZHISHEN *speaks:*) Mommy, you shouldn't go back either. Leave the family!
(LU ZHISHEN *sings:*)

(*Reprise*)
After all, how long is a human life?
Just watch the race of the hare and the flight of the crow![31]
> In the snap of the fingers

The white hairs at our temples urge us to age:
Fine times are like flowing streams!
Yesterday—we happened to meet our own brothers,
Today—we send off our youngest relations,
Tomorrow—we have lost our oldest friends.
Can we not sigh in grief?

(LU ZHISHEN *speaks:*) Mommy, I have seen through all the affairs of this world.
(LU ZHISHEN *sings:*)

(*Weisheng*)
> I know

The affairs of this world are like chewing wax: truly without taste.
> I fear

These days and months, passing faster even than a shuttle thrown.
> The proverb says:

"Empty the limited cups of this life;
Don't bend your mind toward clever schemes."
Just find pure quietude, be free of "right and wrong,"
And the road you trod to practice austerities will never be in doubt.
> I've done away with

---

31. See note 20.

All that snail's-horn, fly's-head fame and profit,
And laugh scornfully in a veritable painting of mountains and clouds!

(MOTHER *speaks*:) Judging by how you talk, I see you won't go. Who will look after me? (LU ZHISHEN *speaks*:) Mommy, don't go back to the mountain stronghold! But you can't stay in this monastery either. Around here we have a certain Goodman Zhang. He is really a good man, and is a good friend of mine, as well. I've received his gifts many times. I will now take you to his house and there find a room for you to live in. And every few days I will come down from the monastery to visit you. (MOTHER *speaks*:) How can I live in such a desolate village, such a backwoods hamlet stuck away in the mountains, where no people are living? (LU ZHISHEN *speaks*:) This place is much better than the mountain stronghold. Let me tell you! (LU ZHISHEN *sings*:)

> (*Qiong hexi*)
> I implore you, my mother, don't go back!
>> You may
> Live forever in the house of my patron.
>> They all are
> My closest friends who know me well.
> You now must leave this monastery—
> I dare not keep you here any longer.
> This monastery is too lonely and desolate,
> But in that village you'll find clothing and food.

[*Recites in ballad verse:*]

> The house of Goodman Zhang is truly large,
> The farm of patron Li sees few robbers.
> In the market of Dogvillage live many people,
> In the shop of Magnate Chen are pearls and jewels.
> Outside the gate of Mister Zhao is the clearest wine:
> Two hundred cash for a couple of bowls and you're drunk as mud!
> Little Liu the butcher sells the fattest mutton:
> One string of cash buys you the lot, complete with head and hooves!
> Greens from the gardens of Hunchback Guo are delicious,
> In the inn of Lame Wang Two are found tea and rice.
> The baked cakes of Muslim Ma are, oh-so-large,
> The tofu of Southerner Huang tastes fresh and rare.
> Immortal Dame He reads your physiognomy as clear as a mirror,
> Big Sister Yang is the best for telling your future.
> Woman Ding is expert in weaving cloth, a family tradition,
> And Sister Qin Two is a specialist in medicine.

Witch Chu is number one for going into a trance,
Auntie Zheng's steamed dumplings are without equal in this world.
Eighth Aunt Shen peddles everything cheaply,
And Little Sister Lu's needle seems to fly.
Old Woman Liu is a most reliable midwife
And everyone listens to Matchmaker Su.

[*Sings:*]

(*Sha*)

> Over there

The harvest is fine, the bounty great, the customs are true,
The water is sweet, people are good, happy to make friends.
I'm not lying,
Or making this up.
I'm not trying to trick you:
This is really the truth!

> Mommy,

Don't worry, don't grumble,
Don't fret, don't be suspicious!

> Mommy, if you

Are just willing to settle down,
You'll be as carefree as can be:
You'll have something to eat, something to wear,
Be free from right, free from wrong—
A hundred years of fun and pleasure,
A lifetime of pure quietude!

> Thanks to

Heaven's happy blessing,
And the compassion of the Buddha,

> All his children

Will be united forever!

> Only then will I be able to show

That your son, the Tattooed Monk
Never, ever lacked the Way of filial piety!

(*Exit together.*)

[Act 4]

(SONG JIANG *enters, leading* UNDERLINGS. SONG JIANG *speaks:*) I am Song Jiang.
Half a month ago I told Lu Zhishen's mother to go and call her son back but I

have yet to see her return. Yesterday his wife told me that he kept his mother there with him and that now she was living with a family at the foot of the mountain close to the monastery. I have a clever scheme that is bound to talk him into coming back. I will order two underlings to dress up as merchants, go to that village and without any cause collect debts. When they get to the place where his mother is staying they will find some excuse to beat his mother up. When Lu Zhishen hears that people are beating his mother up, he is bound to come to her rescue. I will personally follow later. I'll get him to come back, one way or the other! (*Calls for* UNDERLINGS; *after he has instructed them, all exit.*)

(GOODMAN ZHANG *enters, speaks:*) My name is Zhang Yuanliang. People, aware that I love goodness and revere the Buddha, call me Goodman Zhang. Half a month ago Monk Lu of the Clear Stillness Monastery brought his mother to my house to live here. My two unmarried daughters keep her company. Today we have made some noodles and I have asked Madam Lu over. I'll tell my daughters to have some noodles with her. (MOTHER *and* DAUGHTERS *enter.*) (*After some dialogue,* UNDERLINGS *enter, dressed as merchants, and speak:*) This is the house of Goodman Zhang. They said that old lady Lu is living here. Sure enough, we get here and she's sharing a meal in the main room. (*After* UNDER-LINGS *have acted out greeting her,* OLD LADY *asks:*) Where are you two merchants going? (UNDERLING *speaks:*) We have come to this village to collect debts. We gave you a cotton comforter on credit, but you, you old bitch, went back on your promise and haven't paid us! (OLD LADY *speaks:*) I'm only living here temporarily, I am not from this village! (UNDERLING *speaks:*) You rotten old cunt! (GOODMAN ZHANG *speaks:*) Brothers, brothers, I don't know you either. Why are you so abusive? (UNDERLING *speaks:*) Abusive, abusive? We're not demand-ing something for no reason! (MOTHER *speaks:*) Sir, why are you so violent? (UNDERLING *speaks:*) Violent, violent? We never turned you upside down, bitch! (GOODMAN ZHANG *speaks:*) We are good folk and have never done anything to offend you, so please go! (UNDERLING *speaks:*) This woman shows no respect! Why did she curse us? (UNDERLINGS *act out beating the* OLD LADY.) (ZHANG *acts out coming to her rescue.*) (*Acts out calling out to* ZHANG THE SECOND *to come to their rescue.*) (UNDERLINGS *act out knocking them down and begin to curse* MOTHER *loudly.*) (OTHER PEOPLE *enter, act out imploring them earnestly.*) (UN-DERLINGS *speak:*) Let's first help ourselves to these noodles, and then beat that woman! (LU ZHISHEN *enters, speaks:*) Since I took my mother half a month ago to the house of Goodman Zhang, I've visited her a number of times. Today I'm on my way to the village by this small road. Mountain roads are hard going. Just look at these mountains: how steep they rise! (LU ZHISHEN *sings:*)

> ([ZHONGLÜ MODE:] *Fendie'er*)
> The mountain path is rocky and rough,

I cross a mountain creek, a mountain spring: sounding jades,
I see mountain sights, mountain colors: just right for a painting!
I step over mountain peaks
And pass over mountain ridges
       And when I get
To this deepest spot in mountain cliffs,
       I run into
Mountain rains, just clearing away.
       And there arises a gust
Of wind to fan the mountains and blow away the clouds and mists
    that cover them!

(LU ZHISHEN *speaks:*) What fine scenery here in the mountains! (LU ZHISHEN
sings:)

    (*Zui zhong tian*)
       I only see
Mountain leaves, a confusion of green,
Mountain flowers, so fragrantly red.
       And too, those
Mountain peaches, mountain apricots covering mountain peaks!
       On mountain slopes immortal cranes
Dance,
Dance!
       From the branches of mountain trees hang
Mountain gibbons drinking from the creeks,
       In the mountain forest I listen to
Mountain birds announcing spring
       And on the mountain slopes lie
Mountain deer seeking the sun.

(LU ZHISHEN *speaks:*) Over there I see the house of Goodman Zhang. Faster,
faster, faster! I'm almost there. How come such a crowd of people is gathered
together? (LU ZHISHEN *sings:*)

    (*Hongxiuxie*)
       All I see is
Dust rising, blocking the house from view!
       How come
The village people crowd around the gate?

(LU ZHISHEN *acts out stepping forward and listening.*) (LU ZHISHEN *sings:*)

How come
There's all this shouting in a good man's house?

(LU ZHISHEN *acts out greeting them.*) (LU ZHISHEN *sings:*)

It turns out to be
Violent merchants,
Who are truly
Damned good-for-nothings!
How come they
Maltreat an old person like this?

(*After* LU ZHISHEN *hastily steps forward to* ZHANG *and unties his cords, after* LU ZHISHEN *hastily takes off the upper garment of his cassock, he strikes postures and sings:*)

(*Shiliu hua*)
This vexes me so my mind is in turmoil,
My arms and legs shake like mad,
Ethers of rage stuff my breast!
I just want to
Clench my fists, roll up my sleeves, and beat these damned
good-for-nothings!
Only now I believe
"A man without poison is no man at all!"

(*After feeling his head twice with his hand,* LU ZHISHEN *speaks:*) I practice austerities. Enough, enough! (LU ZHISHEN *sings:*)

I'm afraid that,
Ignoring my fast and breaking prohibitions will make it impossible
to cultivate blessings,
And therefore provisionally,
I will bear it, and hesitate of my own accord.

(LU ZHISHEN *kneels down and sings:*)

(*Dou anchun*)
I implore you,
Revered elder brothers in my previous life,
Don't scare
This old mother of my present existence!

(UNDERLING *speaks:*) Who are you? What's your name? (LU ZHISHEN *sings:*)

> I
> Have been a monk from long ago,
>> And my family
> Used to be called Lu.

(UNDERLING *speaks:*) You deserve a beating! Let's also beat up this guy! (LU ZHISHEN *speaks:*) Sir, still your rage! (UNDERLING *speaks:*) *You* owe *us* money that you don't pay back and *you* tell *us* to still *our* rage? (LU ZHISHEN *sings:*)

> The more I try to convince them, the more evil they become!
> You can't tell "a" from "z"!

(UNDERLING *speaks:*) You curse us for not knowing "a" from "z". You call me a stupid lout who is illiterate? Well, an "a" is an "a" and a "z" a "z"! You deserve a beating! (LU ZHISHEN *sings:*)

>> Who in this village
> Owes you money?
>> I will go myself
> To get it for you in person!

(UNDERLING *speaks:*) I recognize this woman. I gave her cotton on credit but she doesn't pay up! (UNDERLING *acts out stepping forward, about to beat* MOTHER.) (LU ZHISHEN *grabs him and speaks:*) Sirs, you two better beat me up! (LU ZHISHEN *sings:*)

> (*Shang xiaolou*)
>> All they want is
> To bastinado my mother,
>> How come
> They pay no attention to me?

(LU ZHISHEN *speaks:*) Sirs, you better beat me up! (LU ZHISHEN *sings:*)

>> You are free
> To kick my breast,
> To grab my hair,
> To clutch my clothes!

(GOODMAN ZHANG *acts out stepping forward and urging them to stop.*) (UNDERLING *speaks:*) If this woman is your mother, what kind of relation is she to Goodman Zhang? (LU ZHISHEN *sings:*)

>> She is
> My mother,

His aunt!
> This isn't like being at home where
You batter your wife, beat up your old lady!
> He is
A good man—
> How can you
Call at his gate and abuse him?

(LU ZHISHEN *speaks*:) You aren't listening to me! I'm getting pissed! (LU ZHISHEN *sings*:)

(*Reprise*)
> So pissed that
My rage is pounding!
> I control myself
Till I'm awash with sweat:
> How I'd like
To crush their skulls,
Snap them at the waist,
Trample their chests!

(ZHANG *acts out grabbing* LU ZHISHEN *and urging him to desist, speaks*:) Don't get rashly carried away! Please still your rage! (LU ZHISHEN *sings*:)

> You tell me
"Don't get carried away,"
"Please still your rage."
> But how
Do you want me to still my rage?
> Even if you had
Four Diamond-demons,[32] they couldn't keep me back!

(UNDERLING *speaks*:) You are a monk. You're not prepared to beat us up. (LU ZHISHEN *speaks*:) Because of my mother and my feelings of filial piety, I cannot successfully conclude my practice of austerities. So be it! (LU ZHISHEN *acts out fighting with the* TWO UNDERLINGS.) (LU ZHISHEN *sings*:)

(*Shi'er yue*)
You want to pull out the tree by its roots,

---

32. The Four Diamonds or *Mahārāja-deva*s are venerated throughout China as the guardian deities of Buddhist monasteries; their ferocious images are displayed at the entrance.

But I am truly
The "evil purple that displaces vermilion!"[33]

(UNDERLING *speaks:*) We don't believe that we can't best you! (LU ZHISHEN *sings:*)

> Don't brag
> That you are strong and I am weak,
> Let's just see
> Who wins, who loses.
> I'll smack this bastard for his flippant overstepping of bounds,
> And smack this one for his gutsy and audacious manner.

(*Yaomin ge*)
> This one
> I lift by his collar and throw him down smack, flat on his face,
> Grab his clothes and pull him until they are torn, tattered in ruins.
> I'll punch his nose until he is smeared with blood,
> Take his face, and beat it until his lips are all puffed up.
> I ask you:
> Do you admit defeat or no?
> Are you now
> Afraid or not?

(SONG JIANG *and* LI KUI *enter hurriedly and pull back* LU ZHISHEN's *hand,* [SONG JIANG] *speaks:*) Brother, don't beat them! You'd break your fast! (LU ZHISHEN *sings:*)

> Shit! Haven't you
> Ruined my path to *bodhi!*[34]

(SONG JIANG *speaks:*) Brother, come back with us to the mountain stronghold! I will tell you the truth: these two merchants are just a couple of lackeys. I tricked you by strategy! (LU ZHISHEN *sings:*)

(*Qitian le*)
> My brother's

---

33. *Analects* 17.18. "The Master said: 'I hate that purple has usurped the place of vermilion, that the tunes of Zheng have been confused with classical music, and that the clever of tongue have undermined both state and family.'" See Slingerland 2003, pp. 207–8. According to the traditional interpretation of this passage, vermilion is the pure color, while purple is a mixed color.

34. See note 30.

Hundred schemes or so
>Were so
Cleverly dissembled.
Alas,
You worked your wiles
>Even in
This backwoods hamlet, this little village,
Ensnaring me!
You secretly found your way to my cell,
Of course they were no money lenders!
>Secretly
He has explained his cunning scheme,
>Clearly
Exposing this bit of sham!

(LU ZHISHEN *kneels down in front of* SONG JIANG *and sings:*)

>Now I'll
Return with my mother!
I forgive my brothers.
Let us now, as soon as possible, get on the road.

(SONG JIANG *speaks:*) Are you willing to change your mind and come with us?
(LU ZHISHEN, *kneeling, sings:*)

>(*Hongshan'er*)
I will not stay on in Clear Brook
But go straight back to Liangshan!
>Now I'll
Puff out my chest,
Puff out my chest,
To be a robber once more
And return to the laity,
And return to the laity.

(LU ZHISHEN *speaks:*) Brother, there was nothing else I could do! (LU ZHISHEN *sings:*)

Let others laugh at me as much as they want!

(SONG JIANG *speaks:*) Now you take your mother with you and all together we will return to the mountain stronghold! (LU ZHISHEN *sings:*)

>(*Reprise*)
I'll be reunited with my old mother

And we brothers will live all together:
An eternal joy!
An eternal joy!

(SONG JIANG *speaks*:) You were too rash and impetuous. No more killing or injuring wives of common folk! (LU ZHISHEN *sings*:)

No need to go on and on—
I've changed my careless behavior,
I've changed my careless behavior:
Never again will I kill a respectable woman!

(SONG JIANG *speaks*:) Today you brothers are all here. The reunion of the thirty-six at our mountain stronghold is now completed. Let's slaughter ten sheep and prepare a great banquet in celebration. Now my life's wishes have been fulfilled! (LU ZHISHEN *sings*:)

(*Wei*)
   I will take this
Monastic garb, and return it to the monastery,
Give this vegetarian food back to my patrons.
   On that
Eight-hundred-mile-long road to Liangshan by Reedflower Rapids
   I'll have those
Who act against conscience and are blind to their natures
   All taste
     my tempered metal ax!

TITLE: Practicing austerities and minding the Way: a monk is a
     monk;
     Getting in a fight and battling each other: bandit versus
     bandit.

FULL NAME: Tiger skin merchants collect debts in a crazy way;
     A leopard monk returns to the laity of his own accord.[35]

---

35. A tiger skin is used to frighten people, and robbers dress up in a tiger skin. Also cf. the expression "a tiger's skin but a sheep's nature." The meaning of the term "leopard" in combinations like these is a matter of dispute; some scholars prefer the meaning "ferocious," others opt for the interpretation "fake, counterfeit."

10

Newly Compiled:
Black Whirlwind Li Spurns Riches out of Righteousness

Zhu Youdun

As if unnerved by his own temerity in writing a play that lacks a positive moral message by showing the tricks by which an outlaw chief forces a reluctant member of his band to return to a life of banditry, Zhu Youdun followed up the composition of *A Leopard Monk Returns to the Laity* almost immediately by the composition of *Black Whirlwind Li Spurns Riches out of Righteousness*. Also written in 1433, this play emphasizes the basic humanity of the bandits by showing how they come to the aid of a damsel in distress and then surrender to the government to aid in the suppression of rebellion. The moral message is clearly spelled out in the preface to *Black Whirlwind Li Spurns Riches out of Righteousness*:

> Stories often record that people like Song Jiang lived in the days of Emperor Huizong of the Song. They were also righteous outlaws. But one named Li Kui was especially capable of spurning riches out of love of righteousness. Later they all surrendered to the Song, were given the rank of military grandees, and were assigned as deputies to the various provinces. On account of his merit in the suppression of Fang La, he [Song Jiang] was later raised to the rank of governor. This is all recorded in great detail in the *Anecdotes of the Xuanhe Reign* (*Xuanhe yishi*).
>
> And so I wrote for fun a play on these bandits and had actors perform it. Even though it is meant only as an aid to urge one on to drink, it may still cause people to realize that those vile and ignorant good-for-nothings were capable a modicum of humanity and righteousness, of loyalty and obedience. If they are so capable, can any gentlemen of this age suffer to swerve even a hair's width from humaneness and righteousness, loyalty and obedience?

The plot of *Black Whirlwind Li Spurns Riches out of Righteousness* is more complicated than that of *A Leopard Monk Returns to the Laity*, and it would also appear to be much more derivative. The action of the first three acts—Li Kui and Yan Qing coming to the aid of a damsel in distress, in this case a poor peasant's daughter who is desired by a low official—shows a remarkable similarity to the plot of *Chrysanthemum Valley*. The fourth act shows Li Kui and Yan Qing disguised as peddlers, and a final fifth act is devoted to a description of their contribution to the victory over Fang La.

Li Kui comes to the aid of the girl by dressing up as the bride and taking her place first in the bridal chair and then in the bridal chamber. He does so accompanied by his sidekick, Yan Qing, who disguises himself as the matchmaker. It is a common motif in early vernacular literature to have a blushing bride replaced by a hulk of a man. In the *Water Margin*, a naked Lu Zhishen hides within the bed-curtains of the bridal room (see the introduction to *A Leopard Monk Returns*). In another anonymous *zaju*, *A Duel of Wits across the River* (*Ge Jiang douzhi*), Zhang Fei takes the place of Liu Bei's bride in her sedan chair in order to scare off pursuing troops. Likewise, it is a common motif in early vernacular literature to have the protagonist disguise himself as a peddler. In the *Water Margin*, Yan Qing dresses up as a peddler and Li Kui assumes that disguise in *Chrysanthemum Valley*.

Yan Qing is the main protagonist in one Yuan *zaju*, in which he is portrayed as an expert wrestler. In *Water Margin*, Yan Qing is distinguished by his sharp mind; he is repeatedly selected for sensitive missions that require sophistication and savoir faire for their success rather than brute strength or physical courage. As his nickname, The Dandy, suggests, Yan Qing makes the perfect foil to Li Kui in both appearance and behavior.

Black Whirlwind Li Spurns Riches out of Righteousness (*Hei xuanfeng zhangyi shucai*) departs from *zaju* conventions in two important respects. First, two separate male leads, playing the parts of Li Kui and Yan Qing, share the lead and are often instructed to sing together. When not singing together and when it is not specified who is singing, it seems more likely to assume that the *mo* playing Li Kui is expected to perform alone. A second exceptional feature of this play is that it consists of five suites of songs. *Black Whirlwind* is one of three plays by Zhu Youdun to contain five suites and all share the feature of having two singing leads. In *Black Whirlwind*, the fifth suite constitutes a "messenger act." In such acts the male lead plays the part of a messenger and narrates in song an action that, as a rule, has taken place offstage. This is usually provoked as a reply to questions posed by the extra male lead who then resumes the narrative by reciting poems or passages of parallel prose. In the present case, the male lead narrates the contribution of the reformed outlaws to the victory of the government's troops over Fang La. Zhu Youdun had a clear affinity for the messenger act: he used it in seven of his thirty-one plays. A difference in *Black Whirlwind*, however, is that the songs stand alone and are not followed by recited text.

For this anthology, both *A Leopard Monk Returns to the Laity* and *Black Whirlwind* were translated on the basis of the woodblock edition prepared during Zhu Youdun's lifetime. For *Black Whirlwind* we also have a manuscript version from the late sixteenth century, based on an adaptation for performance at the Imperial Court. In this version, the play has been heavily edited and regularized—all songs are assigned to a single male, and the last two suites of song are deleted and replaced by a single act that is closely modeled on the final act of *Chrysanthemum Valley*. From a parable on the perfectibility of all men, the play was turned into yet another simple outlaw adventure. Paradoxically, it is this version as performed at the imperial palace that would seem best to meet the requirements of the Marxist critics: the outlaws now are merciless in their struggle against the oppressors of the people, and there is no talk of surrender.

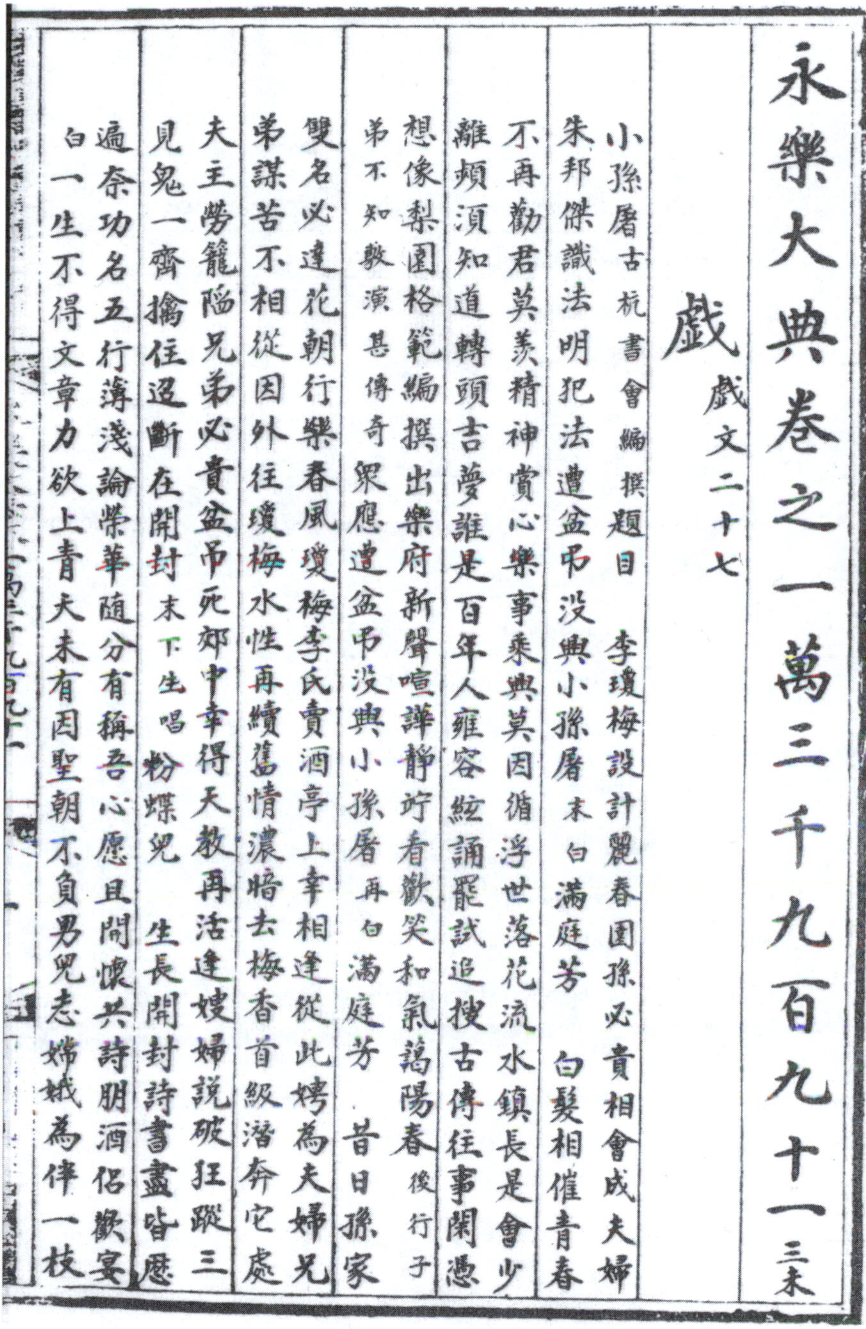

戲

戲文二十七

小孫屠　古杭書會編撰　題目

李瓊梅設計麗春園　孫必貴相會成夫婦

朱邦傑識法明犯法遭盆弔沒與小孫屠（末白）滿庭芳　白髮相催青春

不再勸君莫羨精神賞心樂事乘興莫因循浮世落花流水鎮長是會少

離頻須知道轉頭吉夢誰是百年人雍容絃誦罷試追搜古傳往事閒憑

想像梨園格範撰出樂府新聲喧譁靜听看歡笑和氣藹陽春（後行子

弟不知敢演甚傳奇聚遭盆弔沒與小孫屠（再白）滿庭芳　昔日孫家

雙名必達花朝行樂春風覽梅李氏賣酒亭上幸相達從此烤為夫婦兄

弟謀苦不相從因外往瓊梅水性再續舊情濃暗去梅香首級潛奔它處

夫主勞籠陷兄弟必貴盆弔死郊中幸得天教再活逢嫂說破狂蹤三

見兔一齊擒住迸斷在開封（末下生唱）粉蝶兒　生長開封詩書盡皆懨

遍奈功名五行薄淺論縈華隨分有稱吾心願且閒懷共時朋酒侶歡宴

白一生不得文章力欲上青天未有因聖朝不負男兒志姊娀為伴一枝

FIG. 4. The first page of *Little Butcher Sun* (page 395 in this volume), from the *Grand Canon of the Reign of Perpetual Joy*

Dramatis personæ in order of appearance

Role type	Name, family role, or social role
Villain-official	Sheriff Zhao
Runners	Yamen runners
Extra	Straight Arrow Li, Li Biegu; messenger-questioner
Old woman	Li's wife, Missus Cui
Female	Li's daughter, Qianjiao; woman who purchases rouge and powder
Child	Li's son, Li Kuan
Child	Li's son, Li Yu
Male	Li Kui, The Black Whirlwind; Messenger
Male	Yan Qing, The Dandy
Bullies	Bullies
Bandit	Bandit
Matchmaker	Played by Yan Qing
Added villain	Cook
Military official	Zhang Shuye, Commander of Song Army
Guard	Guard
Poster distributor	Poster distributor

Newly Compiled

Black Whirlwind Li Spurns Riches out of Righteousness
With the Complete Dialogue

[Act 1]

(VILLAIN-OFFICIAL, *dressed as* SHERIFF ZHAO *and leading* RUNNERS, *enters, opens, and speaks:*) I'm Sheriff Zhao. I have been ordered by my superiors to go into the countryside to speed up the collection of autumn tax grain. (*Acts out calling for* RUNNERS, *who enter.*) (SHERIFF ZHAO *speaks:*) Companions, when we go down into the countryside to collect taxes this time, we should really interrogate those farmers who have defaulted and squeeze them for some money!

(*Exit.*)

(EXTRA, *dressed as* STRAIGHT ARROW LI *and leading* OLD WOMAN, *costumed as* MISSUS CUI, FEMALE, *costumed as* QIANJIAO, *and* TWO CHILDREN, *costumed as* LI KUAN *and* LI YU, *enters and speaks:*) I am surnamed Li and I live in Liu Family Village of Dongping Prefecture. Because I'm always direct and honest, people call me Straight Arrow Li. This is my wife, Missus Cui. We have three kids. This is my daughter Qianjiao, just eighteen. And these two are my boys Li Kuan and Li Yu. One is twelve, the other eleven. Because I am poor, I've let my grain tax drag on until it is now more than fifty stones. The authorities are pressuring us to pay, and I'm at wit's end. I'll take these two little boys to Dongping and sell them. There I can exchange the money for grain to hand over to the authorities. We're only half way there and it's already getting dark. Oh, there's an old temple over there. Wife, let's stay overnight in the temple and go on into town tomorrow. (*After they act out arriving at the temple,* SHERIFF ZHAO, *dressed as* OFFICIAL *and leading* RUNNERS, *enters and speaks:*) I am Sheriff Zhao. I'm here to speed up the delivery of tax grain. It's getting late and there's not a house around, so let's take a rest in that old temple. (*Acts out noticing* STRAIGHT ARROW LI.) (*After he questions* STRAIGHT ARROW LI *and* [STRAIGHT ARROW LI] *tells him everything in detail,* SHERIFF ZHAO *speaks in an aside:*) Suddenly, getting tax grain isn't so important! What a fine girl! (SHERIFF ZHAO *asks:*) Old fellow, what's your relation to this girl? (*After* STRAIGHT ARROW LI *speaks, after* SHERIFF ZHAO

asks about her marital status, after STRAIGHT ARROW LI *speaks,* SHERIFF ZHAO
speaks:) Forget about those fifty-odd stones of grain you owe! I will spread the
grain you still owe over other families and they'll pay in your place. But I have
a request I hardly dare to utter. (STRAIGHT ARROW LI *speaks:*) Sir, please speak
freely! (SHERIFF ZHAO *capers about and speaks:*) Old fellow, I want to take your
daughter Qianjiao to wife. What do you think? (STRAIGHT ARROW LI *speaks:*)
I only have this one daughter and she is still very young. You've come to pressure us for grain tax and I certainly have to forfeit the grain I owe. How can I
sell my daughter off just to purchase the connivance of you authorities? And, if
I don't turn in the grain, then my load is spread over others. That's just hurting
other poor folk. Sir, there's just no way I can comply with this! (SHERIFF ZHAO
gets angry, speaks:) Companions, string up that old fool! (*Act out stringing him
up.*) (SHERIFF ZHAO *speaks:*) Companions, bring out wine, call that girl Qianjiao over here to pour my cups herself! (*Acts out drinking wine.*) (TWO MALES,
dressed as BLACK WHIRLWIND LI KUI *and* THE DANDY YAN QING, *enter and* [LI
KUI] *speaks:*) I am Song Jiang's younger brother Mountain Lad Li and this is
The Dandy, Yan Qing. Brother Song Jiang ordered us to go to Dongping to buy
some grain. We bought more than a hundred stones and are transporting it in
five big carts. It's getting late and no inn lies ahead. In the clear moon of autumn, the landscape along the road is quite fine. (LI KUI *and* YAN QING *sing:*)

([XIANLÜ MODE:] *Dian jiangchun*)
> We have looked at
This one swath of green mountains
And those doubled rows of white geese.
The autumn void turns toward evening:
Maple leaves wither and wilt,
Chrysanthemums along the fence burst open to the frost.

(*Hunjiang long*)
A level dike, an old shore—
In the little boat the fishing rod has been laid aside in leisure.
Yellow rushes along overgrown rivers,
Pink smartweed by sandy rapids—
Hearing the distant barking of dogs, a traveler grows happy,
And sitting backward on his buffalo's back, the herd boy returns.
Taking advantage of the last rays of the setting sun, we urge on carts
    that fell behind,
Looking for the lighted lamps of some homes, we search for a village
    ahead.
> Just now
Tired birds seek to return to the woods
And idle clouds emerge from the peaks.

(LI KUI *speaks:*) The road is long, the carts heavy—what an effort! (LI KUI *and* YAN QING *sing:*)

> (*You hulu*)
> Racing and spurring over a thousand miles—temple locks are
>   speckled gray.
> The wind and the dew are cold
>> But this still beats
> "The misty waves of fame or profit," where everyone suffers.
>> We have followed
> The twist and turn of ancient roads, doubling our daily march,
>> We have seen
> The wind and moon above our horse, our "poet's horsewhips"
>   drooping.[1]
>> Wild rocks are piled
> On steep high ridges,
>> A broken bridge spans
> A twisting shallow creek.
>> As we face
> Evening in the wild wastes where yellow leaves cover the river
>> We are worn out,
> And lean against our precious carved saddles.

(LI KUI *speaks:*) It's dark now. There's no inn ahead. For now, set the draught animals free to eat the grass in front of this old temple, and we can start out early at midnight. (LI KUI *and* YAN QING *sing:*)

> (*Tianxia le*)
> Time and again we sing out loud, tapping on our swords
> As we enter the gate.

(LI KUI *acts out looking around and sings:*)

>> When I look from afar
> Inside the temple hall,
> I see a beautiful girl from a rustic inn raising cups—
>> Some foolish fellow
> Is being deluded by song and wine
>> And a fine flower
> Is abused by wind and rain:
>> Each and every one of the others
> Has sorrow-wrinkled brows and eyes awash with tears.

---

1. I.e., a nice joke; this term usually refers to the horsewhips used by poets as they travel. Here, roughly, "too tired to sing about our journey in poetry."

(LI KUI and YAN QING act out entering the temple and speak:) Sir, why have you strung old and young up in the trees? (SHERIFF ZHAO speaks:) This is none of your business, so keep your nose out of it! (LI KUI then questions STRAIGHT ARROW LI.) (After STRAIGHT ARROW LI has spoken, [STRAIGHT ARROW LI] speaks again:) Because he wants my daughter and I refuse to hand her over—that's why he strung us up! (LI KUI speaks in an aside:) This guy really has no morals! The ancients said: "If you happen to see an injustice done, pull your sword to help the victim." I'll step forward and get him to back off. (LI KUI steps forward and addresses SHERIFF ZHAO.) (LI KUI speaks:) This old fellow is my kinsman. I have a hundred of stones of grain with me. If I pay fifty stones of grain here and now on his behalf, won't you please let him go? (SHERIFF ZHAO speaks:) You're his relative? Then you can guarantee this marriage and tell him to give his daughter to me as wife. (LI KUI speaks:) Sir, if you want her, just wait till he has paid his taxes and then send a matchmaker around to arrange this marriage. Wouldn't that be the best? (SHERIFF ZHAO speaks:) How will I be able to wait until tomorrow? I want to couple with her now, right behind this temple! I don't want him to pay off a single stone of rice! (LI KUI and YAN QING angrily speak:) He really wants to ravish this maiden! No morals at all! (LI KUI and YAN QING beat SHERIFF ZHAO and sing:)

> (*Zui fu gui*)
>> Let's beat him up, this too,
> Too lecherous and greedy, corrupt official
> Who bitterly savages the hundred surnames![2]
> Go ahead and speed up the delivering of tax grain!
> But no one told you to abuse your power to rape the wives and
>> daughters of common folks!
>> This is the way
> You handle public affairs?

(SHERIFF ZHAO speaks:) Companions, come and save me! They are beating me up! (LI KUI sings:)

>> Let's beat up
> His servants, those sycophantic parasites
>> Who have never
> Saved anyone from distress!

(RUNNERS come and fight but are all beaten back by LI KUI and YAN QING.) (After each of them flees, LI KUI and YAN QING sing:)

---

2. The "hundred surnames" is still a widely used term for the common people.

(*Jinzhan'er*)
> We saw a few dozen of them
Flaunt their vicious stupidity,
> But in one or two rounds
We beat them all into a pulpy mess.
> Since our
Reckless fists have no eyes,
> We beat them til
They scattered in all four directions, as if in convulsions,
> Until
All in a panic they hunted for their ghostly warrens,
And now quick as a flash hastily bow before the altar shrine!

(SHERIFF ZHAO *speaks:*) God of this temple, help me out! May your golden whip show me the road! May your divine hand protect and defend me! (LI KUI *and* YAN QING *sing:*)

> Uselessly he calls for
The golden whip to show him the road,
The divine hand to protect and defend him!

(SHERIFF ZHAO *and* PARTY *all exit, fleeing. After* LI KUI *and* YAN QING *have untied* STRAIGHT ARROW LI *and* THE CHILDREN, STRAIGHT ARROW LI *bows and speaks:*) Sirs, if you two hadn't saved me, that official surely would have beaten me to death and abducted our daughter Qianjiao! May I ask what your name is and where you're from? (LI KUI *and* YAN QING *speak:*) We are younger brothers of Song Jiang from Liangshan Stronghold. I am Mountain Lad Li and he is The Dandy Yan Qing. Since you and I are both surnamed Li, we will here and now swear brotherhood. Uncle, accept my four bows! (*Acts out bowing.* LI KUI *speaks:*) Uncle, go on home; and take these two carts of grain to pay your grain tax. Don't go into town to sell your sons! (STRAIGHT ARROW LI *speaks:*) Sirs, many thanks! You two are my benefactors! But I'm afraid that that Sheriff will come back to my place and raise hell. (LI KUI *and* YAN QING speak:) If he attempts to come back to ravish your daughter, go to Liangshan Fortress and tell brother Song Jiang. He'll take care of the matter for you. (LI KUI *and* YAN QING *sing:*)

(*Zhuanwei*)
> Our only wish
Is to rescue the orphaned and the poor,
> All our life
We've aided those in danger and need.
> We'll never
Slacken in our intent to spurn riches for righteousness:

Just look how Mountain Lad just now
> Made that rotten

Scoundrel's gall quake and shake and his heart grow cool!

(YAN QING *speaks*:) I'm sure brother [Song Jiang] will blame us for giving that grain away to people when we get back! (MOUNTAIN LAD *sings*:)

When we return,
> Our brother will

Smile happily with joyful face!
> Even if we had given up

Fifty stones of grain,
He'd find nothing strange in that!

(STRAIGHT ARROW LI *speaks*:) Dare I take this grain home? (LI KUI *and* YAN QING *speak*:) It's fine. Take it with you! (LI KUI *and* YAN QING *sings*:)

> And if that scoundrel again wants your daughter

To lift the tray or pass the cup,
> If again he tries

To ravish or molest her. . . .

(LI KUI *and* YAN QING *continue in speech*:): You come and tell brother Song Jiang, who will dispatch us (LI KUI *and* YAN QING *sing*:)

> And we will turn the corrupt yamen of Sheriff Zhao

Into the very gates of Hell!

(Exit.)

[Act 2]

(SHERIFF ZHAO, *leading* TWO BULLIES, *enters.*) (SHERIFF ZHAO *speaks*:) Just the day before yesterday at that old temple I noticed that that Straight Arrow Li had a fine daughter. All I could think of was taking her, but suddenly two completely unknown fellows came by. They beat the hell out of me and then untied Li and his children. Today I will take a gang along with me to his home. No matter what, I want to get his daughter!

(Exit.)

(STRAIGHT ARROW LI *enters with* QIANJIAO, MISSUS CUI, LI KUAN, *and* LI YU. STRAIGHT ARROW LI *speaks*:) The day before yesterday those two brothers saved my daughter. They also gave me fifty stones of grain and told me to pay my taxes. I have to take these fifty stones of grain into town and pay up. Wife, if those two brothers of Song Jiang come to visit, make sure you treat them well. I'm off to pay the taxes. (STRAIGHT ARROW LI *exits first.*) (SHERIFF ZHAO, *leading* BULLIES, *enters.*) (SHERIFF ZHAO *speaks:*) The day before yesterday those two bandits gave me a sound whipping. Now that I've arrived at Li's house, I will abduct his daughter for sure. (*He acts out greeting* MISSUS CUI. *A conversation ensues,* MISSUS CUI *speaks:*) Sir, please wait until my husband comes back from paying his taxes. Wouldn't it be much better to marry her properly through a matchmaker? (*After she has explained a number of times that she does not agree,* SHERIFF ZHAO *speaks:*) This woman is right. I'll be back in a few days to fetch your daughter. (SHERIFF ZHAO *exits.* MISSUS CUI *speaks:*) Daughter, hurry and send a relative to town and tell your father to go to Liangshan Moor to tell Song Jiang.

(*Exit.*)

([ACTOR,] *dressed as* SONG JIANG, *enters and speaks:*) The day before yesterday my brothers Mountain Lad Li and The Dandy Yan Qing went and bought grain. On the road they ran into an old peasant who owed taxes, and whose daughter Sheriff Zhao had forcibly demanded. The two of them saved that peasant and helped him out with the grain we had bought. I am very pleased. Today I have arranged for a banquet and I will call for these two brothers so I can drink a few cups with them as a token of my appreciation. (*Acts out calling for* LI KUI *and* YAN QING.) (LI KUI *and* YAN QING *enter and sing:*)

> ([ZHONGLÜ MODE:] *Fendie'er*)
>> These last couple of days
> We've been hanging out in our mountain lair.
>> All of a sudden I hear someone calling:
> "Mountain Lad Li," and I immediately shout out a reply.
>> My iron ax I have
> Honed till it vies in brilliance with the dazzling sun—
>> Doesn't matter if I'm sent to
> Reconnoiter government troops,
> Spring someone from jail,
> Or save somebody's life,
>> There's no way I'd
> Dare to dilly or dally.
>> Hurriedly I
> Bind this crimson turban around my head!

> (*Zui chunfeng*)
>> Right here I have
> Prepared my black oiled lance

And straightened out my long red gown
To go outside.
> Shit! I don't smell
A single whiff of a bloody stench on the wind,
> That would let me
Display the depth of my courage,
Courage!

(*Others again act out calling for* MOUNTAIN LAD *and* YAN QING. LI KUI *and* YAN QING *sing:*)

> Right over there they keep on calling
"Yan Qing, The Dandy,"
> And call too
The name, "Mountain Lad."
> I can't stand
Such urgent urging!

(*After* LI KUI *and* YAN QING *act out greeting* BANDIT, BANDIT *speaks:*) Just guess why I called you. (LI KUI *and* YAN QING *sing:*)

> (*Hongxiuxie*)
> Because
We must leave this watery stronghold to fight others?

(BANDIT *speaks:*) No, that's not it. (LI KUI *and* YAN QING *sing:*)

> Because
We must go down from Liangshan to reconnoiter the mood of the
> people?

(BANDIT *speaks:*) No, that's not it. (LI KUI *and* YAN QING *sing:*)

> Because
Someone has suffered injustice, lodged a complaint, or seeks redress?

(BANDIT *speaks:*) No, that's not it. (LI KUI *and* YAN QING *sing:*)

> Because that rebel Fang La
Is wreaking havoc?[3]

---

3. The historical Fang La led a rebellion that broke out in Zhejiang province in 1120. The rebellion quickly spread and at one time extended over fifty-two counties; the rebels even occupied the great city of Hangzhou. After the government raised a large army in Northern China, the rebellion was eventually suppressed after 450 days.

(BANDIT *speaks*:) No, that's not it either. (LI KUI *and* YAN QING *sing*:)

> Because Grand Preceptor Cai
> Is misbehaving too much?[4]

(BANDIT *speaks*:) No, not it. (LI KUI *and* YAN QING *sing*:)

> Because the Great Jin
> Is invading the border regions?[5]

(BANDIT *speaks*:) You've guessed all wrong. Guess again! (LI KUI *and* YAN QING *sing*:)

> (*Reprise*)
> To protect
> Our Emperor of the Song, honoring Li Shishi with a visit?[6]

(BANDIT *speaks*:) Nope, nope, that's not it either. (LI KUI *and* YAN QING *sing*:)

> To protect
> Our Emperor of the Song, visiting some inn incognito during the
>   Lantern Festival?

(BANDIT *speaks*:) That's not the reason. (LI KUI *and* YAN QING *sing*:)

> Because we need to protect our Emperor of the Song,
> Listening to a performance on the zither in some clandestine
>   bordello?

(BANDIT *speaks*:) No, that's not it. (LI KUI *and* YAN QING *sing*:)

> Because we must protect our
> Emperor of the Song at the house of Zhao Xuannu
> Where they tell short stories?[7]
>   Or the house of Supreme Commander Yang,
> Where they perform new tunes?[8]

---

4. Grand Preceptor Cai is Cai Jing (1047–1126), the most powerful minister during the reign of emperor Huizong. In later legend he was depicted as an arch-villain.

5. The Great Jin is the Jin dynasty, that had been founded by the Jurchen in 1115.

6. The story of how Emperor Huizong once incognito visited Li Shishi, the most famous courtesan of Kaifeng, is related in detail in the *Xuanhe yishi*.

7. Zhao Xuannu was a famous storyteller.

8. Supreme Commander Yang is Yang Jian (d. 1121), a eunuch who rose to the highest military offices at the court of Emperor Huizong. Later legend blamed him and his cronies for the military debacle of 1126. According to the *Xuanhe yishi* he was the person who suggested to Emperor Huizong to visit the pleasure quarters of Kaifeng.

(BANDIT *speaks*:) Nope, all wrong. You just can't guess! (LI KUI *and* YAN QING *sing*:)

> If that's not the reason, why do you keep on summoning your
Black daddy?

(BANDIT *speaks*:) It's brother Song Jiang who is calling for you two. What have I got to do with it? (*They act out going over and greeting each other*,.) (*After* SONG JIANG *speaks, after drinking wine, after* UNDERLINGS *have sung and danced, after* STRAIGHT ARROW LI *and* MISSUS CUI *lodge their complaint, after they speak some lines and explain everything in detail*, LI KUI *and* YAN QING *sing*:)

> (*Shiliu hua*)
> > Hearing this, in a towering rage
> Hatred rises from our gall:
> > He simply
> Abuses the common folk too much!
> > Even if you
> Use your position of power to throw your weight around,
> > There still are
> The three matchmakers, the six ceremonies,[9]
> And the proposal has to be duly accepted!
> > Even if he's just
> A poor farmer who dares not disobey your commands,
> You still should show him natural decency and human feeling!
> > How could you simply
> Walk on over, send no betrothal gifts of red?
> > And out of the blue
> Abduct a comely little lass?
>
> (*Dou anchun*)
> > Really, that Sheriff Zhao's
> Misdeeds are hard to brook!

(SONG JIANG *inquires and speaks*:) Do you dare to go and right this wrong? (LI KUI *sings*:)

> This wrong I, Mountain Lad Li,
> Personally want to right!

---

9. The "three matchmakers" refer to the matchmaker from the bride's side, the matchmaker from the groom's side, and the matchmaker who acts as witness; the "six ceremonies" refer to the various steps from the first contacts between the two parties to the final conclusion of the marriage.

(SONG JIANG *inquires and speaks:*) Who will go with you? (LI KUI *sings:*)

> I'll take along
> The Dandy Yan Qing!

(SONG JIANG *speaks:*) How are you going to save her? (LI KUI *sings:*)

> I have
> Secretly prepared a subtle scheme.

(SONG JIANG *speaks:*) And what subtle scheme do you have to save her? (LI KUI *sings:*)

> I'll dress up as a lovely maiden on bound feet walking
> And take her place in the bridal chair.
> > For a time I'll learn
> To put on paint and daub on rouge
> > And temporarily be one of those
> Oily heads and powdery necks!

(SONG *speaks:*) First perform for us how you will seize him! (LI KUI *and* YAN QING *sing:*)

> (*Shang xiaolou*)
> > That guy is bound
> To be waiting for me in his yamen
> > And I
> Will keep the shades tightly pulled down.
> After I get inside the front gate,
> And reach the central courtyard,
> I'll be seated behind a curtained screen.
> Once the guests are assembled to the sounds of music
> And wedding gifts fill all the lanes,
> > Just look how demurely and shyly I
> Will ride the saddle across the doorsill!

(SONG *speaks:*) Go on, show us how you will seize him! (LI KUI *and* YAN QING *sing:*)

> (*Reprise*)
> > But as soon
> As he's lifted my veil,
> And seen my ugly visage,
> > With one hand
> I'll grab him by his topknot,

Dash him down the steps,
And bash his skull to smithereens!
>   I will cause
Such a scare that all of the town will be in turmoil till dawn!
But he will never learn who did it—
>   And the following day,
Completely at ease, I'll report on my mission to you!

(SONG *speaks:*) You two brothers are surely filled with indignation and desperately want to help old Li to save his daughter. Old Li better go quickly with the two of you. (LI KUI *and* YAN QING *sing:*)

(*Shua hai'er*)
>   This time
We'll right the wrong and take revenge without respite!
>   We'll beat that corrupt official
Until he drops out of sight and disappears!

(SONG *speaks:*) I'll detail some underlings to accompany you down the mountain. (LI KUI *and* YAN QING *sing:*)

>   We need no underlings
To accompany us down the mountain road,
>   There's only need for
Black Whirlwind and The Dandy Yan Qing.
If, in a crowd
>   We see him,
We'll give a shout—roiling and roaring rivers and seas will rage!
If, in the town
>   We meet up with him,
We'll jump on him—rumbling and thundering hills and mountains
>   will quake!
>   We will rely on
Our doubled fists of iron,
>   Our single lance
That can defeat spirits and pulverize ghosts,
>   And our one ax that
Calls up the moon and raises storms!

(*Weisheng*)
>   No way
Is Mountain Lad Li just talking big,
Or sly Yan Qing boasting—

> If you want him alive, he'll be
> Tied and trussed like a hungry wolf, incapable of any resistance,
> If you want him dead, he'll be
> Dragged back like a dead dog, to wait at the foot of the stronghold!

(*Exit.*)

[Act 3]

(SHERIFF ZHAO *enters and speaks:*) I am Sheriff Zhao. Yesterday I sent some of my servants to the house of Straight Arrow Li to fetch his daughter. They're still not here. Let me call for a matchmaker, to urge them even more! (*Acts out ordering someone to call for* A MATCHMAKER.) (YAN QING, *dressed as* A MATCH-MAKER, *enters and speaks:*) I'm The Dandy Yan Qing. I have learned that Sheriff Zhao is looking for a matchmaker, so I have dressed up as one to fetch him his bride. (*After acting out greeting* SHERIFF ZHAO, *and after some dialogue, exits.*) (SHERIFF ZHAO *acts out calling for* THE COOK *to prepare the banquet.*) (*After one scene by the* ADDED VILLAIN, *dressed as* THE COOK, SHERIFF ZHAO *speaks:*) How come I still don't see my bride? (LI KUI *and* YAN QING *enter.* YAN QING *supports* LI KUI *in female costume, who enters and sings:*)

> ([ZHENGGONG MODE:] *Duanzheng hao*)
>> I've been plastered and painted
> Till my cheeks are all red,
>> And trussed up so tightly
> I've a waist like a wasp,
> And I have learned the bashful glance of a girl.

(LI KUI *acts out descending from the sedan chair and sings:*)

> But down from the chair I jump with the force of a hundred stones—
> I cannot suppress my heroic might!

> (*Gun xiuqiu*)
>> I'm dressed up
> As a woman
>> And follow hard behind
> This leopard matchmaker.[10]
>> How can I muster up "spring in painted halls"—
> That collection of charming seductions?
>> I'm not used

---

10. "Leopard" is explained both as "counterfeit" and as "ferocious."

To making a living out of skirt and girdle!
    Just look: these road slappers[11] of mine
Are a full foot in length,
    These dirty old claws
Are black as a stick of ink!
    This veil covers up
My thickly matted and full-grown beard—
    My figure is no
"Jade-white bones or ice-like skin" of a "state-toppling beauty."
    It's more like
Marrying a demon-king's daughter in front of a monastery
    gate![12]
    Actually I am
A leopard wife, born and bred in the Liangshan Stronghold,
    What do I know
About all these fucking female frills?

(MATCHMAKER *acts out supporting him in paying obeisance to the ancestors in the* *hall.* LI KUI *acts out bowing in male style. After* MATCHMAKER *has spoken some* *lines,* LI KUI *sings:*)

(*Tang xiucai*)
When bowing before the ancestors
    I almost forgot
How a woman is supposed to act!

(*Acts out drinking the marriage cups of wine.* LI KUI *sings:*)

While joining cups, I can't conceal my boorish manner of acting.

(SHERIFF ZHAO *acts out capering about and smiling,* LI KUI *sings:*)

    With
A smiling face he meets my angry scowl:
    I've never seen
Such impatient carnal lust!
This damned creature!
Where are your morals?

---

11. "Road slappers" is our lame translation of a slang term for broad, flat feet.

12. The four demon-kings (*Mahārāja-devas*) are venerated as the guardian gods of Buddhist monasteries; their ferocious images are displayed in the entrance gate.

(MATCHMAKER *acts out supporting* LI KUI *into the bridal chamber.* LI KUI *sings:*)

(*Gun xiuqiu*)
As soon as I
Have entered the embroidered curtains,

(SHERIFF ZHAO *acts out taking off clothes,* LI KUI *sings:*)

He already
Has taken off his clothes!

(SHERIFF ZHAO *acts out wooing her,* LI KUI *sings:*)

I can't stand those lascivious words of
Tender passion, great affection!
Among the wedding guests
Must be some matchmaker to "sprinkle the curtains!"[13]

(SHERIFF ZHAO *speaks:*) Of course there is! Matchmaker! Hurry over here and sprinkle the bed-curtains! Then I will get what makes me happy! (LI KUI *sings:*)

You say
"On this very spot,
I'll get what makes me happy."
Come on, come on, come on, right here at the chamber's door.
I'll show you some acrobatics:
I've kept myself under control until
I'm dripping with a hot sweat!

(*After* MATCHMAKER *lifts the veil,* SHERIFF ZHAO *acts out being afraid.*) (LI KUI *takes out his sword and sings:*)

After you've seen Black Daddy
Hastily raising his three-foot blade of autumn streams,[14]
Don't think I'm some lovely lass,
A single span of spring breeze jade for you to feast on with your eyes—
Your remorse is too late in coming!

(MALE [*who plays the part of*] MOUNTAIN LAD LI *takes off his girl's costume;* MALE [*who plays the part of*] YAN QING *takes off his matchmaker's costume. They sing:*)

---

13. "Sprinkling the bed-curtains," i.e., throwing all kinds of things over the bride and bridegroom seated inside the bed-curtains, used to be a part of the marriage ceremony, as it was believed to express the wish for many sons.

14. "Autumn streams" is a common description of the cold glimmer of a polished sharp blade.

(*Daodao ling*)
> As for us—
The one who acted the girl has taken off his gauze sleeves;
The one who acted the matchmaker has dropped his oily wig.
> That bunch of
Wedding guests are so terrified they can only stand there dumb-
> struck and stupid;
> You, who acted
The bridegroom, can't show off that bright and shining cap!
> We step forward
To give this guy a beating, oh yes!
To give this guy a beating, oh yes!
> A beating because
He oppressed the poor by abusing his official powers!

(LI KUI *and* YAN QING ACT *out beating* SHERIFF ZHAO.) (LI KUI *and* YAN QING *sing:*)

(*Ban dushu*)
> You, you, you,
Come on over here, don't try and hide!
> We, we, we
Cannot suppress the anger in our heart!
> We'll beat him till
His flesh puckers, his skin splits, and he'll have not a shred of
> strength!
> We'll beat him till
He'll panic and plead, beg for mercy and throw himself prostrate on
> the floor!
> We'll beat him till
Every word from his mouth cries, "I know I've done wrong!"
> He, he, he
Plops down to kneel by the steps!

(*Xiao heshang*)
> We'll beat him till
Soft as a jelly he'll be unable to rise!
> We'll beat him till
Silent and still he'll have nothing to say!
> We'll beat him til
Arms and legs all curl up just like he was soundly sleeping!
> We, we, we, we'll beat him till

His face is disfigured,
> We, we, we, we'll beat him till

His skin splits!
> Come on, come on, come on, let's truss him up

To give every other corrupt official a public warning!

(*After* LI KUI *and* YAN QING *truss up* SHERIFF ZHAO, *and after they truss up* A
FEW RUNNERS, *who act out lying on the ground,* LI KUI *and* YAN QING *speak:*)
Let's search his house for the booty he got by harming the people! (LI KUI *and*
YAN QING *exit unobtrusively. They reenter carrying some four or five boxes.* LI KUI
and YAN QING *speak:*) When we looked into these boxes, they turned out to be
filled with gold and silver, goods he obtained by terrorizing the people. We
didn't come here as bandits looking for booty. Because he abused his official
position to harm the people, we wanted to make a stand for them, to vent our
indignation. Now we will write "Sealed by Mountain Lad Li, the Black Whirlwind" on these ten-odd boxes and place them in the courtyard. We won't kill
Sheriff Zhao either, but truss him up and also put him in the courtyard. Tomorrow, when the authorities come to investigate, they will punish him for his
crimes. Brother Yan Qing, light a torch and find me a brush. I will write down
four lines on a white wall in this courtyard. When the authorities arrive tomorrow, they'll want the truth. (LI KUI *acts out writing, recites:*)

> The Sheriff abused his power and maltreated the people:
> He sold exemptions of official tax just to marry a gorgeous gal.
> Should you want to know exactly what happened here tonight,
> Come to the Liangshan Stronghold and ask for Mountain Lad!

(LI KUI *speaks:*) I've written down these four lines. Now let's get out of town!
(LI KUI *and* YAN QING *sing:*)

> (*Weisheng*)
> > We have
>
> Carried outside a dozen or so boxes of gold and silver
> > That he
>
> Had scraped together by savaging the common folk!
> > We don't
>
> Love your possessions or act as thieves,
> > Nor will we
>
> Kill you off, you lascivious, corrupt official!
> We haven't come here because we covet your money,
> But because that mean heart of yours is too tyrannical:
> > You
>
> Subject an elderly father to torture,

> You
Abduct a beautiful girl to be your wife!
> You don't fear:
"The meek may be abused by man but they are not abused by
      Heaven,"
> You don't fear:
"From time immemorial retribution is certain, come early or late!"

(SHERIFF ZHAO *and others cry and speak:*) We'll never dare to do it again! Please set us free! Sir, you may take all these goods with you, please! (LI KUI *and* YAN QING *sing:*)

> Now
You have been exposed, what's the good of remorse?
> Tomorrow
Upright officials will reach a just verdict—
I can't imagine they'll easily let you off.
> And if they ask you for the name
Of the bandit who roughed you up,
> You tell them that Mountain Lad Li
Of the three hundred miles of Liangshan Moor paid you a visit!

(*Exit.*)

[Act 4]

([ACTOR,] *dressed as* MILITARY OFFICIAL, *enters and speaks:*) I am Zhang Shuye, Commander in Chief of the Great Song.[15] A military dispatch came from Dongping Prefecture today, saying that Sheriff Zhao had been beaten and gravely injured by the bandits Mountain Lad Li and Yan Qing because he abducted a young girl of the common people and sold people relief from tax obligations. These bandits tied him up at his house and also sealed up his gold and silver, his money and goods without touching a thing. The emperor has dispatched me here to Dongping prefecture to grant amnesty to Song Jiang and his band of bandits and welcome them into the army. These thirty-six people are all very brave and fierce—most are expert boxers and stick-fighters. Now I'll distribute posters, to the effect that if they are willing to surrender of their own accord, we

---

15. The historical Zhang Shuye (d. 1127) was a high official of the Song dynasty. When in 1126 the Jin troops encircled Kaifeng he served in a provincial post, from where he led his troops to the capital. He followed Emperor Huizong in captivity, eventually committing suicide out of loyalty. According to the *Xuanhe yishi*, Song Jiang and his followers were induced to surrender by Zhang Shuye, "the scion of a hereditary house of generals."

will give them an official position and forgive their crimes. We will appoint them to the rank of captain and dispatch them to the front to capture Fang La. Servants, put up the notices of surrender and pardon!

(*After* SERVANTS *have replied, all exit.*)

(LI KUI *and* YAN QING, *now dressed as* KNICKKNACK PEDDLERS, *enter and speak:*) We are Mountain Lad Li and Yan Qing. Since we beat up Sheriff Zhao a few days ago, we haven't kept up with what has been happening in Dongping Prefecture. Brother Song Jiang has dispatched us there to check up on recent developments. We have dressed up as peddlers and shouldering our carrying pole we go on into town. (LI KUI *and* YAN QING *sing:*)

> ([SHUANGDIAO MODE:] *Xinshui ling*)
> > Shaking
> And sounding our snakeskin drum we enter the city gate,
> > We are dressed
> As peddlers—we never shirk from hardship or toil.
> Wearing green breeches
> And on our head sporting black turbans
> > We sell
> A hundred kinds of novelties!
> Now that we're going into town, we're sure we'll get questioned.

(LI KUI *shakes drum and speaks:*) Finely mixed standard powder! Beeswax-base rouge! A piss pot gourd and a ladle for thin porridge! (SOLDIERS *who guard the gate order them to stop, speak:*) Where are you two peddlers going? (LI KUI *and* YAN QING *sing:*)

> (*Zhuma ting*)
> > Each day we
> Hit a hamlet, go door to door,
> We've run the round of the villages to the south and those to the
> > north!
> > We simple folk
> Accept our poverty, keep to our station:
> For every tael's worth of goods we sell,
> Ten cash is all we keep.

(GUARD *speaks:*) Go on into town. (LI KUI *and* YAN QING *sing:*)

> > We turn around
> This little corner
> And storefronts are evenly arrayed.

On the
Ornamental Arch Avenue we may walk at ease.

([ACTOR,] *dressed as* A FEMALE *leading* A CHILD, *enters and acts out calling for them.*) (LI KUI *and* YAN QING *speak:*)

We suddenly see
A bewitching creature,
Leaning against her door, summoning us for rouge and powder.

(FEMALE *inquires about each article separately.*) (LI KUI *and* FEMALE *haggle.*) (LI KUI *sings:*)

(*Yan'er luo*)
I have
Headdresses of true pearls, with clouds of kingfisher feathers!
And
Cornelian cups, streaked with luminous threads!
And
Combs of tortoise-shell, inlaid with gold!
And
Interlocking seals, carved of jade!

(*Shuixianzi*)
I also have
Beads of glass just like pearls!
And
Clasps of pewter, white as silver!
As well as
Phoenix-head shoes, with soles barely three inches long!
And
Rouge made of wax and fragrant oyster powder!
Then there are
Dongting oranges that spurt fragrance on your hands,
Qingzhou dates
As sweet as honey,
Zhengzhou pears
That weigh a pound,
And Shanzhou onions
Complete with leaves and roots!

[LI KUI *and*] FEMALE *haggle for a while.* [(LI KUI *sings:*)]

(*Gu meijiu* followed by *Taiping ling*)
>I also have

Musk-fragrant tea of every quality!
>And

Medicines sweet to the mouth, all of a warm disposition!
>And

Bathing bean-boxes[16] and basins for washing one's face!
>And

Towels from Songjiang!
>And

Long-headed combs and osmanthus oil!
>And

Old mirrors of green bronze, made in Yangzhou!
>I also have

Multicolored gauze skirts, embroidered in Fujian!
>And

Ivory-handled knives with points quite sharp!
>I also have

Filigree hairclips rubbed with gold!
>Lady,

Make your own choice, that's good enough for me!
>But the price you give

Has to be fair:
Just name it, and everything else will go as it should!

(FEMALE *speaks:*) I only want this pair of hairclips. Wait till my husband comes home and he'll give you your money! (LI KUI *inquires and speaks:*) Lady, where did your husband go? (FEMALE *speaks:*) He's gone off to read some poster. (LI KUI *speaks:*) What kind of poster? (FEMALE:) A few days ago two bandits robbed Sheriff Zhao. Now the authorities have issued a poster offering them amnesty—if they surrender, their crimes will be pardoned! (LI KUI *speaks:*) What kind of bandits were they? (FEMALE *speaks:*) They were Black Whirlwind Mountain Lad Li and The Dandy Yan Qing from Liangshan Moor. The increased security at the four city gates these last few days also is because of those two damned bastards! (LI KUI *speaks:*) Don't curse them! Let's go and have a look too.

(*They exit unobtrusively.*)

---

16. Bean-boxes are little boxes for beans that are used as soap.

([ACTOR,] *dressed as* A POSTER DISTRIBUTOR, *acts out putting up a poster.*) (*Four or five people act out reading the poster.*) (LI KUI *and* YAN QING, *carrying their carrying poles, enter, inquire.*) (*After the crowd speaks at length,* OTHERS *speak:*) That black motherfucking scoundrel! Because he spent a whole night stirring up Sheriff Zhao's household, the gates have been sealed tight the last few days. Not a single load of vegetables has been brought in! How come you two were lucky enough to get in! (LI KUI *speaks:*) Who is that black motherfucking scoundrel? (OTHERS *speak:*) It's that Mountain Lad Li from Song Jiang's band! They should cut off his head and hack him to pieces, scrape out his marrow, and rip out his tendons! If they arrest him tomorrow, we'll hack him to paste! (LI KUI *sings:*)

> (*Chuan bo zhao*)
>   I suddenly hear
> Them tell the whole story:
>   They curse that
> Mountain Lad Li fiercely!
>   They curse and swear they'll
> "Hack at his bones, dismember his body,
> Scrape out his marrow, rip out his tendons!"
>   It really makes
> My ears grow hot enough to burn my lobes![17]
> The anger starts to swell up—
> Ahchoo!
> Ahchoo!
> I keep on sneezing!
>   That's okay,
> Black daddy, control yourself!

(OTHERS *exit.*) (LI KUI *and* YAN QING *act out reading the poster; then, on the verge of returning,* STRAIGHT ARROW LI *enters and speaks:*) I am Straight Arrow Li. Because of his run-in with my daughter the Sheriff has been hunting bandits in our village the last few days. I heard a poster was issued, so I came to read it. (*Acts out running into* LI KUI *and* YAN QING, *first not recognizing them and only recognizing them after inquiring.*) (LI KUI *and* YAN QING *speak:*) In the mountains we lead a life of pleasure. When the wind is high, we commit arson, and when the moon is dark, we commit murder. We are our own bosses, our own masters! Why would we be willing to leave all that and surrender, even with the promise of amnesty and a position? (STRAIGHT ARROW LI *speaks:*) Sirs, you

---

17. One's ears feel hot when one's name is mentioned.

have the wrong idea! I have been frank and honest my whole life and am incapable of deceiving people by flattery. Moreover, you two are my benefactors. What I am going to tell you is well intentioned. You thirty-six fine fellows all have skill and great daring, and you are all fine fellows. Someone like Star of Strategy Wu Jialiang has great strategic insight. Why don't you use this opportunity to surrender yourselves to the authorities, so you can exhaust your loyalty on behalf of the emperor? Campaigning in the south or fighting in the north, you'll achieve merit and become high officials. Your wife will be ennobled, your son will inherit your rank, and you will eat the finest food and drink the choicest wines! Isn't that much better than living in leather tents and committing murder every day, without ever feeling safe? When will you ever rid yourself of that name of "bandit"? Fang La is creating havoc right now in the south! Go on back and talk it over with Song Jiang. It's really the best solution to surrender to the authorities, exert yourself on behalf of the emperor and show your undivided loyalty for the dynasty! (LI KUI *and* YAN QING, *after having bowed to* STRAIGHT ARROW LI, *sing:*)

> (*Meihua jiu*)
>> As I
> Listen to his disquisition
> A happy expression floods my face.
> We'll go out through the city gate
> And walk with proud steps through the red dust,
> Change our ways and start all over!
> At the mountain stronghold we'll persuade elder brother
> To surrender of our own accord and become good citizens!
> I think it over by myself—
> I thought it over by myself:
> I want to join the army.
> I want to join the army,
> And pay back deep favor shown;
> Pay back deep favor shown
> By going to the land of Min;[18]
> By going to the land of Min
> And fighting those barbarians;
> And fighting barbarians
> I will perform great deeds;
> Performing great deeds

---

18. The land of Min refers to the area of present-day Fujian province. The northern part of this area was affected by the rebellion of Fang La.

Victory will be reported;
Victory being reported
To the imperial palace;
From the imperial palace
We will receive an edict;
Receive an edict
That makes us all officials.
And when we are officials
We'll sit on doubled cushions;
Sitting on doubled cushions,
We'll be gifted with gowns of office as well as high pay!

(STRAIGHT ARROW LI *speaks:*) Wouldn't it be better to show some remorse for your deeds? (LI KUI *and* YAN QING *sing:*)

> (*Shou Jiangnan*)
>   Yes, here will apply:
> "As long as the Emperor reigns we will be his ministers!"
>   Relying upon
> Our capacity to fight and our willingness to struggle, we'll clean away
>   all mist and dust!
>   We'll see to it
> That "the four directions are at peace, happiness lasts a thousand
>   springs!"
> The thirty-six of us
> Will capture Fang La alive to show our mettle!

(STRAIGHT ARROW LI *speaks:*) Now return and surrender quickly! You all will be appointed as captains! (LI KUI *and* YAN QING *sing:*)

> (*Weisheng*)
>   As captains
> Our office demands loyalty and obedience.
>   So much
> Safer than digging tunnels and boring through walls!
>   From now on
> When bandit meets bandit, we'll show no mercy!

Uncle, we leave you now to go back. (MALE *sings:*)

>   In my case
> Favor repays favor: a full restitution!

                              (*Exit.*)

[Wedge]

([ACTOR,] *dressed as* MILITARY OFFICIAL, *enters and speaks:*) I am the Commander in Chief Zhang Shuye. I have been appointed by the emperor to lead our troops to the south and capture that pirate Fang La. Yesterday we gave battle but won no victory. Now he has challenged us to battle again. Who dares go? (VILLAIN *dressed as the minor general* CAI SHOUJIAN *speaks:*) I am Cai Shoujian. I want to go and defeat those bandits!

(*After dialogue,* OTHERS *exit.*)

([ACTOR,] *dressed as* FANG LA *enters.*) (CAI SHOUJIAN *enters, acts out doing battle and being defeated.*) ([ACTOR,] *dressed as* SONG JIANG *enters with party.*) (LI KUI *sings:*)

> (*A Wedge: Shanghua shi*)
> This is no boasting on the part of Mountain Lad Li:
> I regard those rebellious troops as a children's game!
> I need at most a second, half a moment
> To scourge them with my whip, beat them with my cudgel—
> > It will be like
> A gale rolling up the last few lingering clouds!

(*Acts out fighting a battle and winning.*) (LI KUI *sings:*)

> (*Reprise*)
> The victorious army and officers grow braver and more powerful,
> The defeated rebel soldiers are almost scared to death—
> It's like cleaving a gourd,
> Like cutting a melon!
> Now I've captured Fang La
> And will deliver him to the Song Emperor!

(*Exit.*)

[Act 5]

([ACTOR,] *dressed as* EXTRA *who questions the messenger, enters.*) (*After some lines of speech,* MESSENGER *enters and sings:*)

> ([HUANGZHONG MODE:] *Zui huayin*)
> On horseback, hunching my shoulders, puffing and panting—
> I've raced on for who knows how long!
> > I crossed

High ridges,
Wide plains,
And now I have arrived before the troops
To tell the whole tale again in full detail!

(*Xi qianying*)
                    Both generals
Faced off with battle chargers—
                    Just look at how our
Black Whirlwind Li shows off his martial arts in our army!
                    Then there's
Song Jiang with all his clever schemes,
                    And
Wu Jialiang, too, whose daring and strategy are both complete!
Orders are transmitted,
Drums and horns resound
And millions of valiant fighters form tight circles.
Before the array
A wild wind scrapes up the earth,
A darkening rain of dust obscures the sky!

(*Chu duizi*)
                    With those
Southern barbarians[19] they engage in battle:
                    Alas for us,
We first lose Cai Shoujian!
                    But then I saw
Broad Sword Guan Sheng daring to take the lead,
The Dandy Yan Qing pressing his horse into the fray—
                    And with them were
Li Hai and Zhu Tong, unmatched in their heroics![20]

(*Reprise*)
                    Each one of them
Turns like a pint, swivels like a peck!
Huyan Chuo uses his iron whip,
The Divine Guardian whirls like a cyclone,
White Jumper in the Waves occupies the ships.

---

19. "Southern barbarians" (*nanman*) is a common curse word for Chinese who live south of
the speaker.

20. All of the names that follow are those of Song Jiang's band from Liangshan Moor.

And
Red-bearded Ghost Liu Tang grabs them by the throat!

(*Guadi feng*)
Thunder Fire Qin Ming rolls up the clouds and fog!
> Each one of them:

A tiger's arms, the shoulders of a bear!
The rebellious troops are slain, there's nowhere to turn,
Scattered they flee across the plain!
> Lance against lance:

The cold flash is like lightning!
> Sword meets sword:

The snowy points resemble whitest silk!
The bows are drawn full circle,
Triggers release the strings:
> Right through golden helmets—

They shout when their arrows hit their marks!
They pierce through battle dress, penetrate armor plate!
> I saw the southern barbarians

Lie all over the level plain!

([EXTRA] *questions and speaks:*) Did they capture the head of the rebels, Fang La? (MESSENGER *sings:*)

(*Simenzi*)
Black Whirlwind never stopped, knew no fatigue,
When the battle drums sounded, he pressed forward again.
Searched through every battalion of the barbarians,
Unwilling to let that rebel Fang La escape!
Through gullies and creeks he trod,
Through woods and waves he bored:
Killed the remnant troops, swept them away like a whiff of smoke!
His horse was exhausted,
He was panting,
Watching how far our army was away!

(*Shuixianzi*)
By the bank of a river he met up with him:
In iron ring-mail armor he was fully dressed.
He reined in his horse and bravely took the lead.
> Brightly gleaming—from his quiver decorated with beasts

He drew an arrow, nocked it on the fully drawn bow.
> I saw in a flash

The fire-pointed lance
Hurriedly stab at his sides and his belly,
   I saw that grating
Long-bladed sword
    Cleave the scalp,
Ears and all, right to the shoulder,
    Saw that whistling
Tiger-eyed whip fall like an arrow on both his arms.
   I saw in one fell swoop
Fang La lifted alive from his brocade saddle!

(*Weisheng*)
   This time
He swept away all mist and dust and established his merit:
From now on the four seas will be at peace.
   And
The name of Black Whirlwind Mountain Lad Li will be yet more
  famous!

TITLE: Sheriff Zhao tries to force a pretty lass to marry;
    Straight Arrow Li heaves heavy sighs, broken-hearted.

NAME: Zhang Shuye puts up posters to pacify the barbarians;
    Black Whirlwind Li spurns riches out of righteousness.

Newly Compiled: *Black Whirlwind Li Spurns Riches out of Righteousness*

II

Little Butcher Sun

The Writing Club of Hangzhou

Little Butcher Sun is the only example in this anthology of a Southern play. As stated in the Introduction, the examples of early Southern plays that have been preserved are not necessarily representative of the genre as it flourished in the thirteenth and fourteenth centuries. *Little Butcher Sun* violates some of the formal rules associated with Southern drama. First, even though it is, with twenty-one scenes, much longer than a *zaju*, it would appear to be very short for a Southern play, which could easily run to over fifty scenes. Second, it dispenses with the clown (*chou*), the single character most closely associated with slapstick, humor, and knave and butt skits, and only uses the following role types: young male (*sheng*), female (*dan*), comic (*jing*), male (*mo*), extra (*wai*), old woman (*po*), and maid (*meixiang*). This may be partially due to the serious nature of the *mo* role in this particular play. While the *mo* comes on stage to report the title of the play, he also appears as a friend of Sun Bida and as a minor clerk in the yamen. But, most of the time he plays the part of Sun Bigui, the butcher, and he has a singing role reminiscent of that of the male lead in Northern drama. In fact, he sings all of the northern melodies in the play sung by a male character, including a long suite in the seventh act of mixed Northern and Southern tunes. Thus, there is some indication that portions of this play are in fact derived from a Northern comedy. Early bibliographies list a late *zaju* bearing the name and title of *A Pure Official Wisely Investigates a Wild and Licentious Woman: A Lawbreaking Prison Guard Binds and Strings Up Little Butcher Sun*. While this now-lost play is not necessarily directly related to our Southern drama, it is a fact that many dramas by different authors, but with the same titles, were produced in the north during the Yuan and Ming periods. The intertextual borrowing between forms of performance literature is well-known, and the same stories can sometimes have the same lines under different authorship, a process that confirms the corporate nature of early drama. Since the story of *Little Butcher Sun* is clearly a bifurcated tale, one can easily imagine that the parts directly related to *Little Butcher Sun*—which are sung either in Northern mode or in the mixed Northern and Southern style that characterized late comedy—stem from an earlier Northern source.

Since the action of *Little Butcher Sun* is resolved in a court of law, the play also may be classified as a "courtroom play." *Little Butcher Sun* uses the conventions of courtroom drama to bring together two quite separate strands of the plot. One is the story of love and betrayal centering on Li Qiongmei, the other, the relationship between filial behavior and popular religion as exemplified in the death and rebirth of butcher Sun. Each of these two subplots seems to be able to stand on its own as an independent story. The language and register of each is quite different, divided between what the Chinese would call *ya*, refined and elegant, and *su* or *bense*, earthy and even a bit vulgar. Furthermore, each of these stories is basically told only through one person's eyes (Li Qiongmei and butcher Sun), each of whom carries the weight of a major singing role. This supports the argument that at least the sections dealing with filial piety and with the Temple of the Eastern Marchmount, sung in Southern and Northern music by the *mo*, are based on a preexisting Northern play. In the early *xiwen* this role type never sings as a main character.

If we look at the courtroom scenes at the end of the play as a process to restore familial and social harmony, then the function of the doubled story within the play becomes clear. The climax in the courtroom resolves a tension between desire, which can wreak havoc on a family, and filial piety, which becomes an active, even practical, agent in restoring the proper ethical categories that govern family life. The first part of the play revolves around Sun Bida, the elder brother, and his pursuit of Li Qiongmei, a prostitute whom he meets in a garden on the western side of the capital, Bianliang. He pursues her, bribes a corrupt yamen clerk to have her name removed from the tax roles as a prostitute, and marries her as a legal wife. Unfortunately, he loves the wine pot more than he does her, and he soon neglects her for the company of his male friends. She rekindles an affair with a sleazy yamen official, Zhu Bangjie, and they hatch a plot to free her from the marriage. She proposes that they behead her maid, Meixiang, dress the corpse in her clothes, and frame her husband. The plot appears to work beautifully.

However, when she had first moved into the house, she immediately aroused the antagonism of the younger brother, Sun Bigui, who is certain that she cannot change her stripes. The mother, playing the role of peacemaker, suggests that the family make their triennial pilgrimage to Mount Tai to repay the gods for their good fortune. While they are en route, and as the plot to murder Meixiang is simultaneously carried out, the mother dies. Sun Bigui returns home quickly, but finds the house sealed up and his brother in jail. At this point in the text, part of the play is missing. It appears that the younger brother, in a filial act of brotherly love, changes places with his elder brother and is executed for the crime. The gods at Taishan revive him because of his deep filial piety, restore him to life, and together with his brother and the ghost of Meixiang, they

confront the conspirators and take them to court in Kaifeng, where Li Qiongmei and her paramour are executed.

The love story itself is an expansion and reworking of two standard features
of drama. In the first instance, it elaborates on what is usually a set scene of
adultery between a greedy, dissatisfied wife and a local yamen lackey. In this
stock plot, they usually conspire to have the husband either sent away or killed
so that he is no longer an impediment to their affair. In one sense, the story of
Li Qiongmei is a rather brilliant retelling of this tale that goes into detail about
the curious mixture of desire, boredom, and rejection that lies behind such a
decision. In this case, Li Qiongmei is portrayed quite sympathetically at first.
Her desire to be wed seems to lead her down the path to proper behavior. But
when Sun Bida leaves her at home, lonely and bored, while he carouses with his
friends, this desire turns to rage and violence. It results in the murder of her
own maid, the incarceration of Sun Bida, the death of Sun Bigui, and eventually her own death. But the play gives a long and sympathetic portrayal of a
woman forced to deal with the overwhelming place of male homosociality in
traditional society. For Sun Bida, the sexual excitement of Li Qiongmei soon
dwindles away, and sensual excitement is once again sought within or through
a circle of males in which drinking, sex with other women, and play are the foci
of activity. He seems to be either sleeping, drunk, or absent from the home after
the marriage. While the second part of the story returns to the more or less
stereotyped portrayal of the scheming and rapacious woman, the audience finds
itself in a much more ambiguous world of motives that can lead to murder.

In the second instance, it turns one of the favorite plots of Southern drama
on its head. Many of the early plays are about "heartbreakers" (*fuxin han*), students who marry hometown girls in their youth but reject them as soon as
they pass the examinations. They prefer a new marriage and new alliance with
families of power and prestige. In the oldest extant play we know, *The Top
Scholar Zhang Xie*, said student even resorts to murder to remove his former
wife from the scene. But other plays, as well, work over this theme. In this case,
Sun Bida is a failed scholar, or at least a minor talent, who gives up the quest for
fame to indulge in drink. Certainly, part of the interest of this play in its own
time must have lain in how it turned these old themes into complicated and
ambiguous issues about desire and responsibility. Moreover, by exploring the
lack of feeling and insincerity as outcomes of sexual passion in marriage on the
part of males, it makes them complicit in the creation of such stereotypes as
the harridan wife. The critique of the failed scholar also suggests that rejection
does not occur only by students who leave home to make their mark in the
world, but also by those who stay close at hand. This opens up an interesting
schism between the supposed lessons of the classical canon, in which ethical
development is the central theme, and the exercise of such ethics by people

whose self-image has been fashioned to represent them as masters of those texts and their contents.

The second major subplot of the play involves the issue of filial piety and popular religion. As in *Immolating One's Son to Save One's Mother* (*Fen'er jiumu*), an anonymous *zaju* only preserved in a Yuan printing, in *Little Butcher Sun* filial piety is linked both to extraordinary acts of self-sacrifice on behalf of one's senior family members, and to the veneration of the Great Emperor of the Eastern Marchmount (*Dongyue dadi*). This particular subplot is redolent with issues of justice, and how such justice is meted out in popular religion. Judge Bao, an historical person who became a legendary sage of justice, a veritable Solomon, delivers judgment in the courtroom and is also the President of the Court of Speedy Retribution in Mount Tai, where one's merits and demerits are requited in necessary fashion. (For a more detailed description of Judge Bao, see the introduction to *Butterfly Dream*). In essence, the delivery of justice occurs in the realm of Taishan, when the spirits reward Butcher Sun for his great filial piety—both to his mother and, we presume, to his elder brother—by restoring him to life. This part of the play constructs an effective counterpoint between commercial interests, represented by the butcher, and the privilege of the learned class, represented by the elder brother. The names of the two brothers, Bida, "one destined to be successful in terms of prestige," and Bigui, "one destined to be noble (or rich)," betray the quality of *su*, earthiness or vulgarity. They represent a kind of middle-class aspiration for success that a person of culture would never express in a name. Part of the interest in the play is developed from the fact that the elder, "destined for prestige," and supposedly a student of the Classics is, by all accounts, a failure. His younger brother, while not a fully formed character in the play, seems far smarter, but is forced through his inferior status to work as a butcher, a despised trade in that period. He does so happily, and is deeply enmeshed both in caring for his mother and in earning enough money to support the family. It is difficult, in fact, not to read this portion of the play in a larger social sense as a critique of the disparity between talent and status. In that sense, it offers a sympathetic portrayal of a younger brother, one who works hard at keeping his mother happy and the family together, while his elder brother enjoys a privileged lifestyle. Sun Bida relies on the status that even his degraded form of mediocre learning affords as an entrée into a social world in which he can squander the family fortune.

The temple at Taishan was both a site devoted to the repayment of vows of filial piety and also a place where merchants showered gifts on the gods as a reciprocal gesture for granting them good business. In that sense, it grounds filial piety not necessarily in its moral position as the foundation of all other Confucian ethics and the cornerstone of family life, but in the practical realm of earning enough money to make sure that one's elders were taken care of. Too often, the play seems to suggest, those who rely on learning are incapable of providing either emotional or financial support for their family. Indeed, because of the association of learning with wine, poetry, and aesthetic sensitivity as well as ethics, the danger always lurked that it would lead one astray onto a path of refined hedonism. Here, says the play, is the center of interest: desire for sex, for drink, for play, if not contained by ethical value or (as in the case of Sun Bigui) by just good common sense, will eventually lead to murder, adultery, and eventual collapse of the family. The only hedge against the financial and ethical toll that it will take is hardheaded common sense and a deep belief in the fundamental necessity of filial acts.

Dramatis personæ in order of appearance

Role type	Name, family role, or social role
Male	Announcer; unnamed friend; Sun Bigui; Aide Zhang
Young lead	Sun Bida
Comic	Unnamed friend of Sun Bida; Zhu Bangjie; Matchmaker; Old lady Wang; Prison guard
Female	Li Qiongmei
Serving girl	Meixiang
Old woman	Mother Sun
Extra	Judge Bao; Unnamed friend of Sun Bida; Prince of Taishan

Little Butcher Sun

Composed by the Writing Club of Hangzhou

TITLE

Li Qiongmei Sells Wine in the Garden of Gorgeous Spring,
Sun Bida Meets Her and They Become Man and Wife.
Zhu Bangjie, Knowing the Law, Consciously Violates the Law;
Bound and Strung up, Out of Luck: Little Sun the Butcher

[Scene 1]

MALE *enters, declaims:*

> (*Manting fang*)
> White hairs urge us on,
> Youth does not come twice.
> I urge you, gentlemen, don't hoard your energies.
> Enjoy yourself, find pleasure in what you do;
> Don't dilly-dally when spirits are on the rise.
> This floating world is but "falling flowers and flowing rivers";
> True it remains, "Meetings are few, separations frequent."
> Be aware—
> Turn your head to look back, and it will have been only a happy
>   dream:
> Who among us lives to a hundred?
> Sedate deportment and musical recitation of the classics over and
>   done,
> We searched our way through ancient legends,
> Idly sighing over things long past.
> We imagined them in the conventions of the Pear Garden,
> Composed new melodies to sing them to.
> So, hush your clamor now,
> Be still, watch, enjoy, and laugh,
> Let the mellow air of harmony infuse this glorious spring!

Disciples of the rear rank, what story are we going to perform? *All reply: Bound and Strung Up,*[1] *Out of Luck: Little Sun the Butcher. Declaim again:*

> (*Manting fang*)
> Once upon a time a certain Sun,
> Who had been given the name Bida,
> Took his fun on the Morn of Flowers[2] in the winds of spring.
> Miss Li Qiongmei
> Sold wine in the pavilion where, by fortune, they met.
> From that time on, through proper ritual they became husband and
>   wife,
> And the younger brother's dire warnings were not heeded.
> Because he went away,
> Qiongmei, of slippery virtue,
> Took up again in hot passion with her former lover.
>
> They secretly removed the head of the servant girl,
> And surreptitiously fled to another place,
> While her husband and master was caged up.
> They framed little brother, Bigui,
> And he was bound, strung up, and died on the outskirts of town.
> Fortunately, Heaven restored him to life,
> And, running into his sister-in-law, he exposed her wild deeds.
> Three ghosts appeared,
> All were apprehended together,
> And sent to Kaifeng for sentencing.

MALE *exits.*

[Scene 2]

YOUNG LEAD *costumed as* SUN BIDA *sings:*

> (*Fendie'er*)
> Born and bred in Kaifeng,

---

1. This is explained in some detail in the *Water Margin*: "In the evening, he'll fix you two bowls of dried yellowed granary rice and some stinky fish and give it to you to eat. Then, while you're full, he'll drag you down into the jail and wrap you up tight with a rope. Then you'll be rolled up in a straw mat, have all of your orifices plugged tight, and strung upside down by the wall. It won't take more than an hour or so and your life will be over. This is what we call 'being bound and strung up.'"

2. A set day in the second civil month, falling somewhere near the fifteenth, when people turned out in city gardens to view flowers, hold banquets, drink wine, etc.

The *Odes* and *Documents* I've all perused.
But alas, merit and fame are meager enough in my Five-Element
  fate.[3]
Yet, riches and glory,
Mine by lot,
Balance out my heart's desire.
So, for now, I'll enjoy myself,
And feast with my comrades of verse, my companions of
  wine.

Declaims:

My whole life has been denied the power of writing;
Though I desire to ascend the blue heavens, there is no cause yet.
This sagely reign will not turn its back on a real man's ambition.
Chang E will be my companion—my sprig of spring;[4]
When they promulgate the imperial summons at the Phoenix Hall,[5]
I will seize my spot on the Leopard and Tiger List.[6]
I sigh to myself, "if a green robe is hard to hang upon my frame,[7]
Who are those belted with gold and clad in purple?"[8]

I am Sun Bida and we have lived in Kaifeng for generations. Unfortunately my
father died and only my mother still lives, as old as she is. I have a younger
brother, Sun Bigui—so we are only three close relatives. I thank old Heaven for
its blessings that allow us to live in security. And now, fortunately, the times are
bountiful, the harvests full, the days clear, and the breeze is mellow. I've invited
several friends to take our pleasures as the season allows—why aren't they here
yet? (COMIC *and* MALE *enter — perform a greeting, asking after each other, making
jokes —* SUN BIDA *sings:*)

---

3. The "Five Elements" or Phases of the flow of yin and yang (metal, wood, water, fire, and
earth) were matched to the cyclical signs of earth and heaven to determine one's fate.

4. This most certainly refers to "snapping the cassia branch," a common saying in drama for
success in the examinations; women of pleasure (also one "sprig of spring") will substitute for success in the examinations.

5. When local officials announce the list of provincial candidates selected to go on to the
examinations in the capital.

6. A somewhat self-deprecating remark—the plaque announcing the Advanced Scholars
was usually called "the dragon and phoenix plaque." The reference to tigers and leopards is to a
second level of success—not as good as dragons and phoenixes, but "better than remaining a dog
or sheep."

7. Green robe: robe worn by a newly enfranchised "advanced scholar."

8. High officials.

(*Xi Nujiao*)
We go out together west of town,
Listen to baby orioles on the branches,
Chirping all as one.
They bind up one's feeling, stir up vexation,
As though reporting to people "how enchanting and lovely."[9]
How suitable, indeed,
To slip by twos and threes through the flowers,
And pass around the cups to reciprocate our joyous feelings.

In chorus:

You and I take advantage of our youth,
Day after day drink and feast,
Deeply drunk before the flowers.

COMIC:

We gather in happiness.
Grasses tender, light, and yellow
Ply thread by thread to secretly weave
A thousand strands of remembered heartache.
The young peaches unfurl their brocade,
Burning candles that give off neither smoke nor flame.[10]
Look closely—
Ten thousand blossoms vie to open, spring becomes silken gauze.
What a pleasure to tread through the fragrant outskirts of town.

Chorus as before — MALE *sings:*

(*Jinyi xiang*)
See the dandies,
Idly playing around,
Next to such gorgeous women!
Idly playing around,
Chasing jade bridles and golden saddles,
Seeking out the finest spots together—
A small bridge, fragrant grasses, a dike of willows' shade,
A bubbling overflow of pipes and songs,

---

9. "Enchanting and lovely" refers both to the scenery and to women.

10. An alternative reading of this line is, "When there is no smoke or fire they burn like candles." "Neither smoke nor flame" refers to the period known as "Cold Feast," when cooking fires were prohibited.

Dropped hairpins, forgotten ear ornaments.
Delighting in the scenic wonders of rivers and hills,
Our very selves seem to exist inside a painting.

Chorus:

Horses whinny where the grass is fragrant,
Powdered butterflies zigzag,
Coming and going, pair by pair.
Roamers are thick as ants.

MALE:

Orioles fly near willows' edge,
Crossing the small bridge,
Next to the green stream.
Clumps of peonies—Wei purples and Yao yellows—
Compete with each other to unfurl their silky gauze.
Branches of the crabapple are tinged with rouge—
Whose compound is this?
Swallows come and go,
Guiding along dandies in the height of youth,
As little "darkheads"[11] race to see who can weave the most kinds of
     grass into baskets.

Chorus:

Look at the swings erected pair by pair—
Hidden laughter bubbles over whitewashed walls.

Sing together:

(*Jiangshui ling*)
Of the four seasons, spring's radiance is most beautiful,
So, let us enjoy it together, tarry no further!
Warm breezes day after day, the finest of weather,
Don't let them go by unnoticed
And uselessly feel sorry for yourself.
Where flowers are deep
Hangs the wineshop sign.
Can we begrudge undoing our sable hats, leaving our belt ornaments
     behind?[12]

---

11. Servants.
12. In pawn for drink.

> We will have fun together,
> Fun together,
> We will go home happily drunk together.
> Helping each other home,
> Helping each other home,
> We will carry fine sprigs of flowers.

SUN BIDA:

> Don't turn your back on the enchanting scenery, this sky of seductive
> yang,

COMIC:

> Don't give a second thought, squander thousands on the outskirts
> west of town;

MALE:

> Flowers may fade but bloom again another day,

Together:

> But men grow old and never have a second chance at youth.

Exit together.

[Scene 3]

(FEMALE *costumed as* LI QIONGMEI *enters:*)

> (*Pozhenzi*)
> I pity myself, since birth so poor of fate,
> This one body wrongly fallen into the wind and dust.
> I often think—if former karma lacks a portion of fortune,
> In this life husband and wife will lack true love.
> When will I ever find a match for my heart?

Declaims: I am Li Qiongmei, top-rank courtesan of the prefecture of Kaifeng. I am upset that this body is just like willow floss—unfeeling, fruitlessly married off to the eastern wind. My appearance may be like a spring flower, but I vainly sigh over the sunlit days I've wasted. How many times have I muttered silently, flicked away powdered tears, or wept for no reason in front of others, grieving that I am so full of passion? Confronting this fine weather in the third month of spring, I'll sell my fragrant wine in this Garden of Gorgeous Spring here in the western outskirts. On the one hand, I'll take advantage of the pleasures of the season and on the other, hope to run into a lover. Heaven will provide us this convenience. I have only a single serving girl, Meixiang, with me here. I'll have her take care of arranging the wine implements. True it is,

> Orioles and flowers particularly fear the aging of spring's radiance,
> And will let no person pass spring in vain.

LI QIONGMEI *sings*:

> (*Pozhenzi*)
> If heaven were to pity the hardships of being alone,
> It would allow me to meet a good man in front of the wine cups.

MEIXIANG *continues the singing*:

> The spring radiance that fills my eyes is capable of inspiring poetic
>   sentiments,
> So don't blame the eastern wind alone for tears that seem to pour—
> I'll just stand at the wine stove to dispel my feelings.

LI QIONGMEI:

> Unfortunately, my body fell in among the misty flowers,

MEIXIANG:

> Life's bitterest lot is sighed over all the more in spring.

Together:

> On willow paths, seeking fragrance, people are as thick as ants,
> On whitewashed walls are written "vexations"—the characters dark
>   as ravens.[13]

LI QIONGMEI *sings*:

> (*Yujia ao*)
> Constantly, I moan that I pass the spring in vain, betraying vermilion
>   cheeks;
> Sorrowfully, I listen to sounds of a yellow oriole in weeping willows
>   of others' courtyards.
> My secret hidden from others, two brows lock up new sorrow and
>   vexation—
> I'm too lazy even to look at myself in the simurgh mirror.
> Alas, because Heaven is too slow to grant my wish,

---

13. They are both ink-black and as numerous as evening rooks flocking to trees.

I am forever a rain of tears or clouds of sorrow,
Facing the eastern wind, tears trickling as new sorrow intermingles
     with old.[14]

MEIXIANG *sings*:

(*Ti yindeng*)
Spring hills reflected in autumn ripples[15] secretly arouse passion,
So why foresee only lonely blankets, and one unused pillow?
If the wine is fragrant and the road is long, someone will buy a drink;
If a face is bewitching, the style comely, there will be a romantic
     rogue to match.
Day in, day out,
To share pleasure, to drink together,
Is far better than being like Chang E, who never has sex.

LI QIONGMEI *sings*:

(*Di jinhua*)
So listless I just lightly brush the locks of my raven-black clouds,
Lazily dot my crimson lips.
Mindlessly tend the wine stove to imitate Wenjun.[16]
But if I think to myself about Wenjun—
When will I ever meet one who knows my music?
Who has a full heart of faithful love?
Alas, Heaven never follows the desire of man.

Sing together:

(*Mapozi*)
I faced this scenery, vainly inscribed my own "vexation,"[17]
But won nothing but heart's onset of depression.
Only in sorrow, sorrow alone passes our green spring
As this flowering of the year inwardly compels us on.
I earnestly turn my head and ask the Lord of the East,[18]
"Peach blossoms open only to fall upon encountering spring;
I know for sure that my looks grow older—
When will I meet that man?"

---

14. Both physically, as new tears over old tear stains, and emotionally, by new passion aroused.
15. Autumn ripples: eyes.
16. See *Qiannü's Soul*, n. 42.
17. I.e., on the aforementioned wall.
18. Spirit of spring, master of love.

LI QIONGMEI *declaims*: Meixiang, surely some fine gentlemen out to enjoy the spring will come to buy wine. Set out the wine implements for me and arrange them nicely.

MEIXIANG *exits*.

SUN BIDA, COMIC:

> (*Shuidi yu'er*)
> Willows are green, flowers red,
> So much scenery in famous gardens!
> Apricots blossom like brocade and embroidery;
> Tender peaches seem to spurt fire.
> Noble gents and fine ladies
> With happy smiles share the joy of the feast.
> Seeking out the fragrance, picking up the kingfisher feathers,
> With abandon they empty the cups and grow deeply drunk.

SUN BIDA, MALE, *and* COMIC *perform greeting her and playing drinking games* —
FEMALE *sings*:

> (*Qiao hesheng*)
> All the flowers have burst their buds,
> Burst their buds, red and white compete to adorn them—
> Limitless radiance of spring is enchanting.
> My fragrant brew is smooth and oh-so-special;
> There's no need to reject it or refuse.

Chorus:

> We accompany each other in laughing chatter,
> And if you have a mind to,
> Then be my painted fence, become the master of this flower.[19]

MEIXIANG *sings*:

> Gentlemen, just look—
> See how bees and butterflies, pair by pair,
> Chase each other amid the flowers, roaming and sporting.
> What holds you back, right now,
> From unrestrained drinking until deeply drunk?

Chorus, as before. SUN BIDA *sings*:

---

19. I.e., enclose me within the garden of your protection and keep me for yourself.

(*Tete ling*)
The swallows twitter, conversing on the carved rafters,
Who knows what they tell each other?
I think they should be describing
Their inner feelings like this:
"The two of us will fly always as a pair,
Coming as a pair, a pair,
Going as a pair, a pair."
Ah, when shall we be like you?

MALE:

How many people do you reckon live to a hundred?
If we don't take our happiness now, will we ever?
Altogether, it's only thirty-six thousand days.
And why not, when encountering flowers, encountering wine,
Drink in front of the flowers,
Get drunk under the flowers?
Let us, free from care, allow ourselves to relax.

LI QIONGMEI *sings*:

(*Hongxiuxie*)
I thank you, my Lord of the East, for being so interested,
So interested
That you would come buy my goblets of sunset red to make you
     tipsy,
Goblets of sunset red:
Appreciating their aroma and fragrance,
You treasure what the flower signifies.
You can do what you want
Inside the brocade screens—
Don't let anyone else
Crazily reach up to snap off your blossom.

SUN BIDA:

How fortunate that flower and [bee] have met,
Have met.
Just like Student Cui asking for water,[20]

---

20. Cui Hu, an examination candidate in Chang'an, was enjoying the spring sights at the height of spring, during the Festival of Clear and Bright, when he got thirsty. He stopped to ask

Asking for water,
Surely after I leave
I'll remember this time next year.
Peach face, peach flower,
Each go their separate ways.
And what time, what season,
Will we meet again?

All sing together:

(*Guagu ling*)
The shadows of the flowers inexorably move,
The red sun is on the verge of sinking.
Facing these flowers, abandoning ourselves to drunkenness,
We stick sprigs of flowers in each other's hats.
The flower-bedecked palanquins exude a fragrance smooth and rare,
In the shade of flowers, below the willows, people gradually
     disappear.
Song, wine—we are soused enough to
Make people say, "They stagger home drunk."

SUN BIDA: How much for the wine? LI QIONGMEI: It doesn't matter, whatever
you want to give, sir. SUN BIDA: Here's some loose silver, perhaps it's enough. LI
QIONGMEI and MEIXIANG: Many thanks, sir. SUN BIDA: Ma'am,

When deep in drink, and people scatter drunk, they help each other home;
   Lithe willows, cloud-light, hang down to brush the ground below.
            But when will we be as intertwining branches?

LI QIONGMEI: Sir,

              The peach is voluptuously beautiful,
             The apricot is voluptuously beautiful,
     But first they must find a fence to protect them all around,
              Before they will bear any fruit!

SUN BIDA: Ma'am, you need give it no more thought. If you don't reject me, I'll
take pearls and gold enough to the government bureau, and there ply it among

---

for water and was greeted by a beautiful young woman. The next year, remembering his encounter,
he returned to find her, but she was gone. Disappointed, he inscribed the wall with this poem:

   Last year and today in this very doorway,
   A face and the peach blossom shared red's reflection;
   But now, where has the face gone?
   Like before the peach blossom laughs in the winds of spring.

ranks high and low to get you removed from the registry so you may marry a respectable citizen. What do you think about that? LI QIONGMEI: I'm sure I could never be so fortunate. But if you, sir, protect me in such a way, it wouldn't be too late to give myself up to spend the rest of my life with you. SUN BIDA: Your humble servant takes his leave. COMIC *performs supporting him in his drunkenness — sing together*:

> (*Fendie'er*)
> A thousand goblets in a single bout,
> Snockered and soused, we help each other down the road,
> Stewed and pickled, how can we put one foot in front of the other?

LI QIONGMEI:

> He loves the flower's heart—
> I must entrust myself
> To the protection of this fence.

SUN BIDA:

> Vexed now by a heart made soft,
> I must turn back nine times, look back a thousand.

> *Exit together.*

[Scene 4]

MOTHER SUN *sings*:

> (*Jinji jiao*)
> Old age urges me on;
> The affairs of my youth grown dimmer, gone like flowing water.
> Praying that my family will be without worry or care,
> Morning and night, I offer pure incense,
> One stick each, to thank Heaven and Earth.

Declaims:

> The dissolution of our family fortune is not yet worth a worry,
> So for now I will trust in karma to pass my years.
> When the moon goes past the fifteenth, its light diminishes,
> When a person reaches middle age, the myriad affairs cease.

I am a citizen of Kaifeng. My husband, Mr. Sun, passed away several years ago, and I just have two sons. When my husband died, the eldest, Bida, taught himself a few lines of the ritual teachings of the *Odes* and *Documents* and so became a Confucian scholar. My youngest, Bigui, is intelligent but strong-willed. He only wants to raise the knife and wield the ax, so he's a butcher here in the neighborhood, and that's how he supports me. Today I learned that second son wants to go out of town to try and make some money. I wonder if it's so? When he gets here, I'll just give him a few words of advice. SUN BIGUI *enters and declaims*:

> Returning from my buying and selling, sweat soaks my shirt;
> Only after settling accounts do I realize how hard it is to raise a family.

My surname is Sun and I am second in the family. I make my living as a butcher in this neighborhood, so everyone just calls me Little Sun, the butcher. There's been no business in the past few days, so I've been thinking about buying some presents and making the rounds to throw myself at the feet of some out-of-town acquaintances. But first, I have to tell my mother.

SUN BIGUI *greets her* — MOTHER SUN: Child, I've heard someone say that you're going out of town to raise some money. As long as you can get by at home, why do you need to leave? SUN BIGUI: Mommy, as the proverb says, "If you sit and eat, the cupboard gets bare." I'll go and find a stake and then come back. Mother, don't worry. MOTHER SUN: My child,

> When the heart is already gone, the mind is hard to keep behind,
> To keep you behind would only create an enemy.

I can't stop you from going, but you must come back as soon as possible. SUN BIGUI: Your child will be back soon. MOTHER SUN *sings*:

> (*Huaqiao'er*)
> In the past you've traveled a lot,
> And have experience on the road.
> But on this journey today,
> Be sure not to get distracted.
> This is going to make me so burn with worry, morning and night,
> That I will look for you until my eyes wear out.
> Hearts of child and of mother,
> Will each be on tenterhooks, here and there.

Chorus:

> To where the swan flies but cannot reach,
> Men are pulled by profit and fame.

SUN BIGUI:

> I tell you, mother,
> Don't worry or fret.

People say, "Small fortune stems from fate,
Great fortune stems from Heaven."
Getting security and happiness is a matter of prior karma,
But if you just sit and enjoy it, it will not last forever.
So, I'll leave home for a while,
But return as soon as I can.

Chorus:

Wherever you go, wherever you stay, don't tarry or linger,
Your mother will look for you until her eyes are worn out!

To where the swan flies but cannot reach,
Men are ever pulled by profit and fame.

Both exit.

[Scene 5]

SUN BIDA *sings:*

(*Tianxia le*)
One kind of love longing gathers between two brows
Just because a lovely face suits me to a T.
So I can only squander a thousand gold to purchase her,
And remove her name from the register of flowers.

Declaims:

Even the very edge of heaven, the corners of the seas, can be reached;
Only love's longing goes on without cease.

Every day at home, I study my books, peruse the histories, and wait upon my beloved mother. But there was that one day when I went roaming in spring in the Garden of Gorgeous Spring; there, where the apricot flowers were the thickest, I chanced upon Li Qiongmei, who was tending her wine stove and selling government wine. She has turned out to be a woman with skin that sparkles like snow on a chalcedony terrace, with cheeks fresh and alluring as red apricot petals. I saw her, and before I realized it, the desire to become a mandarin duck pair was stirred up and I lusted after the pleasures of simurgh and phoenix. Then she told me, "If you can get my name removed from the registers, I'm willing to be your wife." Now, there was nothing left to do but to spend more gold and silk, go off to the yamen, look up my old buddy, Zhang, the Prefect's Aide, and get him to go and talk to the Prefect personally.

AIDE ZHANG *enters and declaims*: I took care of that affair that Sun Bida entrusted to me last night, and turned it over to the magistrate. Today I've come here just to let him know. AIDE ZHANG *performs greeting* SUN BIDA — SUN BIDA: Prefect's Aide Zhang, what about that affair I turned over to you yesterday? MALE: I fixed it up with the Prefect, himself, last night. Brother, go ahead. SUN BIDA: Well, I don't have much, but here's an advance of two blocks of silver to use for those places high and low. I must personally show you my deepest gratitude, as well. AIDE ZHANG: There's no need for that. SUN BIDA *sings*:

> (*Guangguang zha*)
> Beloved brother, heed what I have to say,
> Bring it to completion by any means necessary.
> If I get your full support,
> My gratitude won't be shallow at all.

AIDE ZHANG:

> Husband and wife is a predestined bond,
> I'll work it all out for you.
> Relax, set your worries aside,
> I'll see to it that you wind up married.

Declaims:

> My eyes will watch for the pennants of victory to be displayed at the gate,
> My ears, listen for the sound of good news.

Exit together.

[Scene 6]

JUDGE BAO *sings*:

> (*Xidi jin*)
> I, this humble official, am fair-minded and upright;
> My lowly office puts me in charge of Kaifeng.
> Just because the people sing for a thousand miles that I am fair and
> just,
> I repay them rightly with spring breezes of harmonious ethers.

Declaims: My authority ranges for a thousand miles and my office puts me in charge of Kaifeng. The space of my heart is transparent and clear, simply not bothered by thoughts outside of the public interest. The rarest and strangest administrative cases I judge with an authority that accords exactly with principle.

True it is, those infused by the imperial grace all delight in their work, each and every day families are protected, enjoy peace and security. This heart is as fragrant as an orchid, as level as a balance. True it is, when I travel I tell them not to clear the road with loud shouts lest they startle the villagers beyond the woods. Let the Head Clerk on duty present himself. COMIC *costumed as* ZHU BANGJIE *performs entering, declaims:*

> Generals and ministers are not born as such;
> A real man must vaunt his own strengths.

I am Zhu Bangjie, the regular Head Clerk of this prefecture, and all around town I'm known as Esquire Zhu. Last night Prefect's Aide Zhang came to see me about this affair of Li Qiongmei. Today, the Prefect holds court, so I'll wrap up the case for Zhang. *Performs calling* LI QIONGMEI *after greeting* JUDGE BAO — LI QIONGMEI *enters and sings:*

> (*Fengma'er*)
> Hearing that I'm going to be raised from my status, my heart is happy
> As I arrive at the court to hear His Honor's verdict.

MEIXIANG *continues the singing:*

> You, Madam, now escape the wind and dust,
> And hereafter will be spared
> Everyone snapping off the tips of your willow branches.

Performs greeting JUDGE BAO *and being removed from the register* — LI QIONGMEI *sings:*

> (*Eya manduchuan*)
> I thank you, my beneficent Honor,
> For releasing me from being a whore.
> Such an act of grace and virtue
> Is something I can never forget.
> When will I ever be able to do anything to repay you?

Chorus:

> Hereafter my names are removed from the registers,
> I have been issued proof of this and now may leave.
> No more resentful sighing;
> From the glazed-tile well,[21]
> By good luck I've escaped!

---

21. Called in another song "a glittering prison, this glazed-tile well."

JUDGE BAO:

> Heretofore always impartial....
> Because of your beauty
> You fell among the misty blossoms,
> And this is not reasonable.
> Reform quickly, speedily, as fast as you can—too slow, then, we'll
>   reopen the case.[22]

Chorus as before — ZHU BANGJIE:

> Your names are removed today,
> All thanks to my grace and virtue.

LI QIONGMEI:

> A person is not earth or wood;
> I would not dare forget your grace and righteousness.

Chorus:

> By fortune alone I have managed to escape from the gates of flowers,
> And with delighted, happy heart, become one of a pair of mandarin
>   ducks.
> No more drunken lust,
> A face like a flower
> Now relinquishes the wind and rain.

JUDGE BAO:

> The nature of my own mind
> Means that affairs follow impartial principle.
> I kick you free of all of this,
> And there must be some hidden virtue in this act.

Chorus as before — MEIXIANG:

> I consider that mistress of mine[23]
> Was the daughter of a respectable family.

---

22. This is a difficult passage to understand. The magistrate has been moved to grant her the wish partly on the basis of her beauty, which was the cause of her original fall from being a member of a "good family." The hesitation in the first line, which we take to be an incomplete thought, refers to him mulling over the sources for this apparently special dispensation he is making. The last line, then, may be a reference to the fact that he is acting against what he knows to be right.

23. The term *nu* (used here in the phrase *nian nuniangzi* that we have translated as "I consider that mistress of mine") is a humble term ("servant") by which a woman refers to herself. But it

At the earliest opportunity prepare some fine incense,
And reply with thankfulness to Heaven and Earth.

Chorus as before — ZHU BANGJIE:

Don't forget that once upon a time we drank to each other.

JUDGE BAO:

Li Qiongmei, your flower name has been removed.

Together:

If one in power does not provide favors for others,
It is like entering a mountain of gold and returning with empty
    hands.

Exit together.

[Scene 7]

In Northern music — SUN BIGUI *sings the* Yizhi hua [*suite*] *as he enters, en route to seek help from his guild*:

The mountains stretch on and on, the rivers and streams are long,
My family is far away, the edge of Heaven is near.
I travel along, ascending the purple paths,
And wind my way as I tread through the red dust.
From the time I left my home and village,
I've been alone—no one cares.
Day after day, sorrow and depression wear me away.
And, although I'm willing to travel this road,
At heart, I am still unsettled.

In no time at all—old road, western wind, steep ridges,
What I've crossed—evening sun, flowing streams, isolated villages,
And now, dust follows the horse's hooves—what year will it end?
Always driving oneself to exhaustion—
There's no comparison to ordinary toil.
Every backward turn of the head
Is a loss of my very soul

---

also, when combined with the word we have translated as "think" (to form Niannu), is the name of a famous singer of the Tang, and later a common metaphor for beautiful courtesan entertainers. In that case, we could understand this line as "This lovely singer." It is quite ordinary for these terms to be used in a way that retains a double level of meaning.

Because, at home, my compassionate old mother
Has no one to wait on her, morning or night.
I know clearly that filial duty and obedience are the great beginnings
    of a man,
And when I think of how she suffered to nourish me and keep me
    whole,
I cannot just drop my business to take it easy.
As I was leaving on my trip
I expressed to my brother
That he should be in constant attendance, and not be negligent.
I'm just afraid my brother didn't take me seriously
And has been lost in his lust for red skirts.

I've not yet encountered any thunderstorm signs from the Heavenly
    Han,[24]
But one day I'll be able to return to the peach-spring paradise of my
    hometown hamlet.
At the very moment I return from making my rounds
I'll pay my respects to mother,
Express my gratitude to the gods,
And so enjoy the true rewards of this racing around.

Exits.

[Scene 8]

MOTHER SUN *sings:*

(*Fengshichun*)
Success and failure, flourish and decay all lie in our fate,
Does Heaven not dictate this affair of husband and wife?
Now my child has become a husband to a wife,
And if we discuss this karmic bond,
The whole affair must have been predetermined.

Declaims: "When a man is grown, he must marry; when a woman is grown she must find a home." But my eldest son, Bida, had never taken a wife. About half a month ago, the matchmaker came to arrange a marriage, and in just a few words the affair was completed. We have selected today as an auspicious day to fetch her and bring her home. But, there's just one thing. My younger child,

---

24. "Heavenly Han" is the Milky Way; here used as a synecdoche for Heaven. He has yet to have any success finding help.

Bigui, hasn't come back from making his rounds. Moreover, he's a butcher, and he will surely have something to say when he gets home. Well, no matter. Why haven't I seen the matchmaker yet? COMIC *costumed as* MATCHMAKER *comes out and declaims:*

> I but open my mouth and they become a perfect pair;
> I but raise my voice and they are united as simurgh and phoenix.

SUN BIDA *sings:*

> (*Ying xianke*)
> Thank you, my wife,
> For all your help—
> I must have met you in an earlier life.
> Swallows fly by twos,
> And form a perfect pair.

Chorus:

> One must conclude that karmic bonds
> Are not easy things to unite.

LI QIONGMEI:

> I consider that I am[25]
> A daughter to a respectable family,
> By fortune I've met you, so rare in talent and looks.
> Like simurgh and phoenix,
> We'll form a perfect pair.

Chorus — MOTHER SUN:

> My child,
> You're so smart and intelligent,
> Having taken a wife, everything will now be fine.
> And as sweet as Zhengzhou pears,
> You'll form a perfect pair.

As before. MEIXIANG *enters and sings:*

> My mistress,
> You're so alluring and seductive,
> And by fortune you've met a master who's handsome and fine.

---

25. "A lovely singer, / Daughter to a respectable family" is an alternative translation of these two lines.

Like mandarin ducks,
You'll form a perfect pair.

Chorus as before — SUN BIDA:

A perfect couple created by heaven join in harmony,

LI QIONGMEI:

And now I realize that the whole house is filled with joy.

MOTHER SUN:

When encountering the chance to drink wine, you must drink;

All together:

When finding a place to sing out loud, then go ahead and sing.

MATCHMAKER *exits first —* MOTHER SUN *sings*:

(*Xiudai'er*)
Heed well, my child, the words of your mother:
For me, the sun draws near the mulberries and elms;[26]
Now that you've finally tied the knot with a girl right at the hairpin
    age,[27]
Your mother's heart is relieved of its worry.
Overjoyed, I hope you will grow old in harmony to a full hundred
    years,
And if you achieve glory and fame, my heart will be content and
    happy.

Chorus:

Truly rare and exceptional—two beauties in a single pair,
Set out the banquet, and as a pair, let them imitate phoenixes in
    flight.

SUN BIDA:

I, Bida, address my mother:
Karmic bonds are hard to find,
But today, our love for each other is in perfect accord.
So, Mommy, you can be relieved of worry.

---

26. The sunset of one's life.

27. Just reached adulthood; fifteen *sui* by Chinese calculation of years—somewhere between
thirteen and fifteen years old, depending on month of birth.

So hard to equal—
Her gorgeous makeup and seductive face are so comely and fine,
Only a Xishi could be like this![28]

Chorus as before — LI QIONGMEI:

In my earliest years I was the daughter of a respectable family,
And I thank you, sir, for bringing me to this place.
You did not reject me, and I will gladly hold dustbin and broom;
I only wish to be like branches intertwined to the end of old age,
And with you
Live in harmony for a full hundred years
Without second thoughts.

Chorus as before — MEIXIANG:

Please heed this serving girl's respectful address:
Having arrived at this point through luck has been no easy thing,
But today, your concern for each other is in perfect accord—
Thanks to our patron for parting with a thousand gold to purchase
    this flower's release, to become her master.
It must be
That fate brought you together in this heavenly union.
I hope that, in your hundred years, you will always be like fish in
    water.

Chorus as before — SUN BIGUI *enters and declaims*:

No joy can ever match this morning's,
No happiness can ever equal that of today.

Well, Bigui, you've been very successful. I must be grateful for the presents of
my many acquaintances in the guild that allowed me to return in such joy. Just
a moment ago I met a couple of friends outside of the city walls and we drank
a few cups of wine. Now, I'd better go home and see my mother. *Performs greeting* MOTHER SUN *and kneeling* — [MOTHER SUN:] You're back, my second son.
Congratulations. SUN BIGUI: What congratulations? MOTHER SUN: Your brother
got married, you've got a sister-in-law. SUN BIGUI *performs greeting* SUN BIDA
and LI QIONGMEI — SUN BIGUI *sings*:

(*Zhu ge'er*)
Please heed your brother's respectful address:
She is surely a misty blossom, a rotten whore—

---

28. An archetypal beauty.

Has she ever been one in control of slippery virtue?
What background does she have to become a man's legal spouse?
If you won't listen
To your own brother's advice,
Then you should observe the examples of those who've gone before.

SUN BIDA:

There's something to what you say, my brother,
But now she is really removed from the registers.
I consider her trustworthy and honest and so brought her home as a
   wife.
I will rely on her to care for our mother, who is now so old.

Chorus:

On this very day
They marry in love and joy,
So don't blabber on with such a sharp tongue.

LI QIONGMEI:

Brother-in-law, you're way off base;
I was originally the daughter of respectable folk.
Could I have controlled how I fell among the misty blossoms?
When you curse me like this, my teardrops trickle down.

Chorus as before — MOTHER SUN:

I urge you, my child, don't act like this.
Your sister-in-law seems worthy and virtuous to me.
From now on, our whole household should be in harmony.
On another day, I'll find a wife for you, too.

Chorus as before — MEIXIANG:

Don't listen to idle theories of good and bad,
And I urge you, my mistress, do not be so irritated.
There's no rhyme or reason for all this bickering,
If anyone else overhears, then what will it look like?

Chorus as before — SUN BIDA:

My brother's nature is just too wild and rash:

SUN BIGUI:

How can we bear such a mismatch in status?

MOTHER SUN:

> On this day husband and wife complete the great ritual;

All together:

> As a group we guide them off into the orchid chamber.

> *Exit together.*

[Scene 9]

COMIC, *costumed as* ZHU BANGJIE, *enters*:

> For no reason at all pleasant prospects were halted,
> But when the sun comes out, things will happen again.

What I personally remember about this Miss Li is that I used to frequent her place in earlier days and spent a lot of money there. Later on, though, we had a silly argument and my foot never crossed her threshold again. Now, the elder Sun has taken her to wife, but I've been told that he is drowned in his cups every day. Now his wife is upset about that; moreover, she's been squabbling with the younger Sun. I really want to go see her but I don't have a pretext. Really, "A single dot of sorrow on the brows can never be wiped away." When we were together before, this woman borrowed three silver ingots worth of money from me. To be honest, she's already returned it to me, but I never gave her the IOU back. Now, I'll take this IOU and under the pretext of getting my money back, I'll go on over to her place. I'm sure that our karmic bond has not been completely broken and that a few words will get us back together. True it is,

> If you don't use a scheme as unfathomable as an abyss
> You'll never snatch the pearl from the black dragon's chin!

> *Exits.*

LI QIONGMEI *enters and sings*:

> (*Liangzhou ling*)
> One pair, a simurgh and a phoenix, should share their festive joy,
> But I am vexed that I am rejected and picked on day after day.
> This lover of mine shouldn't believe all the bad-mouthing,
> And throw everything away—
> Me,
> My love, and favor, too.

Declaims:

> Mandarin ducks have always had the nature of migrating birds,
> Nurture them as you will, in the end they have no love for home.

When I married into the Sun family, I believed that we would be like fish and water and that we would imitate the simurgh and the phoenix. I didn't know he would consider the close love of newlyweds no more than tasteless water. He never comes home. Is he seeking fame or striving for fortune? Or is he lusting after wine and being led astray by blossoms? It makes me sad and weary, listlessly reclining on the embroidered couch. How can I wile away this gloom?

LI QIONGMEI *sings*:

> (*Wutongshu*)
> Just to think of it brings depression to my heart.
> He is gone without shadow or trace.
> Just like the willow floss with the wind, inconstant, unreliable—
> No correspondence to his heart of earlier days.
> He ruins my fine nights; alone, I tend the lonely lamp.
> Counting every single tally of the watch, deep in the long night, after
>   people have stilled,
> Makes me hate that "alive-but-dead unformed thing."[29]
> I've no desire to ply the embroidery needle
> Because my heart is unsettled the livelong day.
> All I'm left with is an anxious fear; I am made a lonely widow
>   by him.
> All day I try to imagine what his feelings might be.
> I endure until dusk, until the moon climbs and my small window
>   grows bright;
> Through the night, I wipe my teary eyes until my mandarin duck
>   pillow is soaked,
> And at daylight, I listlessly face the lonely-simurgh mirror.[30]

---

29. Complicated to render in English, literally "live early death." It is roughly comparable to cursing someone as a "dead fetus," in the sense that he or she is a living reminder of the death of something that had potential to develop.

30. A certain prince had captured a simurgh and put it into a cage. Despite the fact that he lavished attention and food on the bird, it went three years without singing. His wife suggested that the bird was lonely, so he put a mirror up next to the cage. The simurgh thought that he had seen his real mate and he killed himself trying to fly out of the cage to be with her.

EXTRA *performs supporting* SUN BIDA *and calling out to open the gate.* LI QIONG-
MEI *performs opening the gate.* [EXTRA *exits.*] SUN BIDA *performs falling asleep
and shouting.* LI QIONGMEI *sings:*

> (*Northern music: Xinshui ling*)
> He has just trod over "Courtyard-Filling Fragrant" grasses and
>   "Returned from Viewing the Blossoms";
> I "Resent my Prince" for not thinking of "Plucking the Cassia
>   Branch."
> Every day he "Ascends the Small Loft" to "Buy Fine Wine,"
> Inside "Gold Fretted Curtains" they pass the cups together.
> Drinking deeply of his wine, he is "Helped Home Drunk";[31]
> I cannot but be hurt and wrapped in bitterness.

Sings again:

> (*Southern music: Feng ru song*)
> I remember our feast of days gone by, with green ants[32] floating—
> We were to be husband and wife, together forever like intertwined
>   branches;
> Who would have thought that you would lust after trysts?
> And be so soused you'd give no thought to coming home?
> Who shares your wonderful time there
> While you make me stay within lonely bed-curtains here?

Sings again:

> (*Northern music: Zhegui ling*)
> How often have I guarded fast these scented chambers,
> Tossing, sleepless, my emotions like one obsessed?
> I wept until the smoke of the crimson candles disappeared,
> The shadow of the silver toad sank below the horizon,
> The aroma of the precious seal-script incense grew faint.
> Barely had I heard the sound of the cricket weaken along the four
>   walls
> When I heard the neighbor's cock crow in the last starlight to
>   announce the dawn.
> My single shadow orphaned and desolate,

---

31. The phrases in quotation marks are the titles of Northern tunes. This is a set performance
in which the titles of the song patterns are fretted into a clever aria.

32. I.e., little bubbles of wine froth.

My heart, broken and sad.
One pinch of bitter sorrow
Is compressed between sorrowed brows.

Sings again:

(*Southern music: Feng ru song*)
With my whole heart I had hoped you would set to your books,
And wanted you to change our family status.
But now, I am something to be tossed away—
Every day I look for you, every day you never show up.
It makes me feel sad under these mandarin duck coverlets,
With one pillow of mine left unused.

Sings again:

(*Northern music: Shuixianzi*)
Wuling Creek[33] becomes an obstruction for *this* fine marriage,
Because you have turned your back on our "tryst under the moon
  and before the flowers."
Colored clouds disperse too easily, the glazed tiles are fragile—
No unfaithful lover is as bad as you,
Who set aside the joys of newlyweds!
Don't wrong my true heart, my true love,
And make it so that I, who want to keep you warm, shield you from
  the cold,
Cannot match you stride for stride.

Sings again:

(*Southern music: [Feng ru song] Adapting the tremolo.*)
I remember how intelligent and quick he was,
How clever,
How sardonic his wit—
But why is he now like this?
And when I think how seductive I am,
How completely elegant,
How witty and clever—
Who will take me by the hand?

---

33. Originally the way to the famous Peachspring Paradise of Tao Yuanming, it later becomes a standard metaphor for the way to any paradise or utopia, including trysts with beautiful women.

Sings again:

> (*Northern music: Yan'er luo*)
> Who will share oriole and swallow trysts?
> Who will spread the mandarin duck coverlets?
> Who will now pour a pair of parrot goblets?
> Who will be paired with me as simurgh to phoenix?

Sings again:

> (*Southern music: Feng ru song*)
> If I think too much about it, it makes my tears fall,
> Makes me waste these fine times.
> I listlessly enter the embroidery room and pick up the needle—
> And all day long, I am distracted and numb.
> Time after time beside the pillow and screen, I call "Where are you?"
> But feelings of hope turn quickly into silence.

Sings again:

> (*Northern music: Desheng ling*)
> How I laugh at myself, this Zhuo Wenjun, just too obsessed,
> But he's under the spell of the Demon King of Sleep.[34]
> He only thinks of the huge cosmos of yin and yang that lies inside
>   drink,
> And pays little thought to trysts of clouds and rain among the
>   flowers.
> Against this screen surrounding me he may lean,
> But at whose feet does his dream soul now lie?
> The addiction to wine is hard to cure,
> And this morning he comes slowly to.

Sings again:

> (*Southern music: Feng ru song*)
> Well I think Liu Ling,[35] when half sobered up from wine,
> Was no match for you, drunk as a lump of mud.
> Li Bai once wrote about it,
> But he had to meet the emperor of the Tang.

(*Declaims:*) When Li Bai was drunk, Yang Guifei held up his inkstone for him,
Gao Lishi removed his boots, the dragon's hand wiped away Li's spittle with his

---

34. I.e., the power of wine.
35. A prodigious drinker of antiquity, who refused his wife's summons to quit.

personal handkerchief, and with the imperial hand, mixed Li's stew.[36] You are drunk, too, today,

> But it just makes me tell you in a hundred different ways:
> Find someone else to loosen your belt.[37]

ZHU BANGJIE *enters and declaims*: "Don't let things get to you, if they do you'll go nuts!" Here I am at the gate of Sun Number One's house. *Performs calling at the gate.* LI QIONGMEI: Who's calling my name? ZHU BANGJIE: It's me, Zhu Bangjie. LI QIONGMEI: So it turns out to be Clerk Zhu. *Opens gate.* Clerk, why this rare visit? ZHU BANGJIE: Why, I've come especially to offer you congratulations. LI QIONGMEI: Clerk, you may say this, but today I am not of the same station I was before. ZHU BANGJIE *performs*: You borrowed money worth three ingots from me earlier and haven't paid me back yet. LI QIONGMEI: I have already paid you everything back. ZHU BANGJIE *performs*: I never got anything. LI QIONGMEI *performs an aside*: The clerk must be using this as a pretext and has come here on some other purpose. ZHU BANGJIE *performs*: Who's that asleep there? LI QIONGMEI *performs*: My husband. ZHU BANGJIE: What shall we do? LI QIONGMEI: No problem, he's drunk. ZHU BANGJIE *performs*. LI QIONGMEI: Clerk,

> Don't cling to the idea that only home and hearth are fine,
> Wherever favors are found in plenty—there can be your home.

LI QIONGMEI *sings*:

> (*Shiliu hua*)
> From a tender age I drifted into the windy dust,
> And have shared pillow and mat with you many times.
> Now I've kicked myself free and became a decent citizen,
> But who would know when I reached this stage,

---

36. A conflation of many stories of the famous "wine immortal" poet, Li Bai. Once, when en route to climb Mount Hua, he drunkenly rode by the Prefect on his donkey. The Prefect got angry and pulled him into court, asking him, "Just who do you think you are that you dispense with correct ritual?" Without giving his name to the Prefect, he wrote out his confession, "Once the dragon's (emperor's) own handkerchief wiped off my spittle, the imperial hand mixed my soup, Yang Guifei held up my inkstone, and Gao Lishi took off my shoes. In front of the gates of the Son of Heaven, I could ride my horse, but here on the northern side of Mount Hua, I can't even ride my donkey!" Li Bai was summoned to appear before the emperor to compose some poems, but he had been drinking in the marketplace. He sobered up enough to write them, with the help of the cast of characters that included Emperor Xuanzong of the Tang, his famous courtesan Yang Guifei, and the eunuch Gao Lishi.

37. I.e., she's neither the wife of Liu Ling nor the emperor of the Tang; if he wants to get out from under the curse of drink, then someone else will have to help him, because she won't.

I would doubly suffer such painful emotions.
Thank you, sir, full of solicitous ardor, for coming—
I think our karmic bond must have been knotted tight.

Chorus:

We feast and sport in front of the flowers, in pleasure united;
You and I are both of a single mind.

[ZHU BANGJIE:]

Your face is beautifully whitened,[38] your locks like piled up clouds,
Your makeup and hairstyle are so artfully done.
Your three-inch golden lotuses are just too light and dainty,
And your conversation and behavior so elegantly refined.
My face so young,
Young and handsome,
People will say, "Indeed. What a perfectly matched pair!"

Chorus as before:

SUN BIGUI *enters and declaims:*

Wildflowers are not planted, but sprout up every single year;
   Vexation has no roots, but it is renewed every single day.

I had a good quarrel with that woman that day. We both had a lot to say. I'm gone from early in the morning to late at night, but I can still see she has problems. I heard today that my brother went out to drink with some buddies, so I will go on home. *Performs the action of listening.* "Murder is forgivable, but impropriety is unpardonable." Who's here drinking while my brother is gone? SUN BIGUI *kicks open the door.* ZHU BANGJIE *flees and exits.* SUN BIGUI *performs trying to carry out murder.* SUN BIDA *sings:*

(*Zhuma ting*)
Deep, deep in a drunken stupor,
In my sleep I hear people fighting.
This startles me violently, wakes me with a start,
And I feel my whole body
Shake, shiver, quiver, and quake.
Just as I become aware enough to ask what the reason is,
I suddenly see my younger brother holding a knife,

---

38. That is, she has applied a layer of white lead.

And yelling over and over.
Wasn't elder sister deferential or respectful enough?

SUN BIGUI:

Let me tell you the reason:
She's after all a woman from a bordello—
And when she peeked in and saw you, brother, passed out asleep,
She shared her pillow and coverlet
Voluntarily with someone else.
I was about to take this knife with the intent of catching that
    adulterer,
But I almost killed my own brother.

LI QIONGMEI: If I have a lover, why don't you grab him? SUN BIGUI:

Are your words worth listening to?
This court case will astound others.

LI QIONGMEI:

I beg you, my lord, listen:
I was just about to go to bed in my room,
And didn't expect that my brother-in-law would come here
And, uttering clever words and sweet phrases,
Grab hold of the lapels of my gown.

SUN BIGUI: Sun the second is not that kind of person! LI QIONGMEI:

Because I wouldn't give in, he got angry
And wanted to kill you with his knife.

SUN BIGUI: Brother, don't listen to her! I wouldn't dare. LI QIONGMEI:

I'll have to call the neighbors,
For you'll drive me out, with nowhere to go!

SUN BIDA:

There's nothing to rely on in this incident,
When both are so at variance, how can I get it clear?

SUN BIGUI: Brother, what's unclear? She's got a lover. LI QIONGMEI:

With every breath my brother-in-law says,
"She's keeping a lover."
But can you say who that lover is?

SUN BIGUI: She's clearly keeping a lover! LI QIONGMEI:

> Brother-in-law, you just look down on people too much.

SUN BIGUI: You say you don't have one. Dare you swear to it? LI QIONGMEI *spits*:
On my life! LI QIONGMEI:

> In the azure blueness above, heaven will be my witness.

SUN BIGUI: Do you dare say you have never once had one? LI QIONGMEI: None!
SUN BIGUI:

> Don't try and pull the wool over our eyes;
> Willow floss and watery things have no stable measure.

SUN BIDA:

> Family filth is never bandied beyond the doors;

LI QIONGMEI:

> Who could know that flesh and blood fight like cats and dogs?

SUN BIGUI:

> Let everyone fly, pure as a phoenix, to the top of the wutong tree;

Together:

> There will always be a bystander to gossip about them!

[Scene 10]

MOTHER SUN *sings*:

> (*Zhuanshanzi*)
> Why are quarreling voices filling the house?
> I hear every word spoken is at cross-purposes.
> If I trust my own heart, I feel I'm being suspicious,
> And I'm not sure yet just what kind of misfortune it is.
> I'll go into the main room to find out
> So that I won't be wondering about it all the time.

Declaims: If you don't think ahead, troubles will be right at hand! I wonder
what the quarrel was here last night? Let me call out Little Sun, the butcher,
and ask him about it. "Butcher Sun, where are you?" SUN BIGUI *enters and declaims*: "If you should speak, but don't, you're close-mouthed; if you shouldn't
speak, but make yourself do so anyway, then you're impudent." Didn't I almost
do something bad last night because of that bitch? This affair ought to die away

by itself. Mother is calling me, so I'd better go. *Greets her.* MOTHER SUN: What was all the quarreling about last night, son? Tell me. SUN BIGUI: Mommy, what are you talking about? Mommy, you let brother have his way back then, so he married this woman and now there's all these problems. So don't ask about it. MOTHER SUN: My child, don't make such a fuss. He's already married her, and since she is what she is, don't talk about her like this. When your father was still alive, I made a promise to go on pilgrimage to the Eastern Peak for three years. I've gone for two years, and this will make the final year. Child, pack the luggage for me, and come along with me to repay my vow, and then you can avoid this bickering at home. SUN BIGUI: Mother, you're right. I'll go and pack our luggage. Say a word to brother and have him send us on our way and then come back home. MOTHER SUN: Go on now and get the luggage ready.

Have no fear of range after range or mountains beyond mountains.

[SUN BIGUI *exits.*]

MOTHER SUN *remains on stage.* MOTHER SUN *sings:*

> (*Guazhen'er*)
> It's a long way to the holy shrine of the Eastern Peak,
> But to fulfill my vow I must go on.
> I just worry that at home
> There will be no one to look after things. . . .
> Let me call out my child and tell him what he has to do.

SUN BIDA *enters and sings:*

> Contented newlyweds, we united in joy;
> How can we bear even a parting of a single step?

LI QIONGMEI *enters and sings:* I've suddenly learned that mother has sent for us, and together we will pay our respects in the main room. MOTHER SUN *sings:*

> (*Naizi hua*)
> Since the Emperor of the Peak's birthday is drawing near,
> I want to go with you to burn incense and paper offerings.

SUN BIDA:

> We'd better prepare the luggage and go on,
> But I'm very concerned about the family business.

LI QIONGMEI *sings:*

> It'll surely be hard for him to leave if he's thinking of family business;
> You should tell my brother-in-law to go on ahead.

Chorus:

> Just have Bigui prepare the luggage,
> See you safely there, then come back.

MOTHER SUN:

> Well, we should be on our way now.
> I entrust the family affairs to you.

SUN BIDA:

> Mommy, go on the road with heart at ease,
> And let's not worry about each other.

LI QIONGMEI:

> Mommy, you must get back as soon as you can,
> And you'd better be careful on the road.

Chorus as before:

SUN BIGUI [*enters*] *and sings:*

> (*Zhuan*)
> I hear mother has sent for me
> And wants to leave quickly for the Eastern Peak.

LI QIONGMEI:

> I hate these partings,
> Because there's no one home to take charge of me.

SUN BIDA:

> I will now see my mother off beyond the district border,
> Then turn around and come back home ahead of them.

SUN BIGUI:

> Let's not tarry any longer.

[LI QIONGMEI:]

> I'll tell the maid to prepare a few cups.

MEIXIANG:

> I hear my mistress calling me.

MEIXIANG *sings*:

> (*Hong shaoyao*)
> Today they're off to the Eastern Peak,
> And a single cup aids in bringing peace.

MOTHER SUN:

> You, maid and young wife, should stay within your chambers,
> And be sure to mind the family business.

LI QIONGMEI:

> You three must be careful on the road,
> And it would be best to plan an early return.

Chorus:

> With one stick of fine incense, we beseech the gods,
> "May our whole family be protected from harm."
> We pour out wine in the eastern outskirts, and are already tipsy;
> In front of the gate the palanquin awaits;
> We hope you come home in a day or two.[39]

Declaims:

> That eastern peak, Mount Tai, is awesome and efficacious;
> One candle of fine incense takes care of our devout sincerity.
> Don't wear yourself out over all the mundane things;
> Just raise your head three feet in the air, and all the gods are there.

> SUN BIDA, SUN BIGUI, MOTHER SUN *exit*.

LI QIONGMEI *remains on stage and declaims*:

> Falling blossoms desire to follow flowing water,
> But flowing water has no mind to embrace the fallen blossoms.

Meixiang, I had originally hoped that he and I would be constant company and never a step apart. Who could have guessed that today he would turn his rudder with the wind and be gone with the first gust? In vain he leaves half the mandarin duck cover unused. Ah, when will he come back to me? MEIXIANG: Mistress, no need to fret or worry. LI QIONGMEI *sings*:

---

39. Perhaps these last three lines are all sung by the female.

(*Wuye'er*)
I want to talk about it,
But who will listen?
He never remarks what I tell him in secret.
He's gone with the first gust,
Just like duckweed on the water.
And all love is held
Just as light as a single wutong leaf.

MEIXIANG:

Mistress, don't worry,
Just ease your mind.
Why do you have to put yourself in such a state?

LI QIONGMEI:

Even though he'll come back as soon as he goes,
It'll be really chilly in my bedchamber.
I heave sigh after sigh,
Because he's as hot as fire and I'm as cold as ice.

LI QIONGMEI:

I shouldn't
Long for them,
"Be nice to whoever strikes your eye."
I don't need to be so impatient,
Someday my wish will be fulfilled—
So don't you treat my love like ice.

Declaims: Meixiang, now that he's gone, I'm bored and listless. Go on in and put out a few cups of wine, and keep me company while I wile away the time. MEI-
XIANG: All right,

Three cups harmonize all mundane affairs,
A single episode of tipsiness dissolves a thousand cares.

MEIXIANG *first exits*. COMIC *costumed as* ZHU BANGJIE *enters and declaims*:

In quietness I carefully examine my life's events,
And when idle I search out those things I did myself.

If I hadn't run as fast as I did the day before yesterday, I'd have been beaten up
by Little Sun, the butcher. I've been told now that the old lady and the two

brothers have gone off together on a pilgrimage, and that no one's home but that woman. I just can't stay away. *Performs greeting* LI QIONGMEI. LI QIONG- MEI: Head Clerk Zhu, you've come just at the right time today. I'm just setting out a few cups of wine, and we can drink them together. COMIC: I was really in danger the day before yesterday. LI QIONGMEI: If you hadn't been sharp-eyed, he'd have done it to you. Today, they've all gone off on a pilgrimage, and it'll be a few days before they get back. Now, we might as well have Meixiang bring the wine out. MEIXIANG [*enters*]:

> Drink wine when you meet friends;
> Recite poetry to those who understand it.

Here's your wine. MEIXIANG *performs greeting* ZHU BANGJIE. LI QIONGMEI: This gentleman is my brother. Go and fix us some food. At the same time, go and lock the outside gate, so the gentleman and I can drink a few cups of wine. MEIXIANG: In heaven and on earth, making it all go smooth is the first order. MEIXIANG *first exits.* LI QIONGMEI *sings:*

> (*Taojin ling*)
> The lamp reported blessings,
> And the magpie cried out happiness before the eaves—
> Being able to see you today,
> Was certainly no easy thing.
> I pour out wine lightly, softly I sing,
> Release a little tender silliness,
> Fearing no wind or rain at the tip of the flower.
> Giving it all my effort,
> With one cup of wine, I beseech you sir, mark this well—

Chorus:

> Holding white hands,
> And leaning shoulder to fragrant shoulder,
> Together we enter the gauze bedhangings to imitate twining branches.

ZHU BANGJIE:

> Matching the halves of this karmic bond
> Can be counted no easy thing.
> One pair, two beauties,
> Even I become adorable.
> We'll never be split,
> Never be separated....

Chorus as before. ZHU BANGJIE *declaims:* And now we should call Meixiang here, now's the time to do it. LI QIONGMEI: You're right. Meixiang, come here! MEIXIANG *enters and sings:*

> (*Taoli zheng fang*)
> Since I've heard them call, "Meixiang,"
> I'll have to go to the main hall and get my orders.

MEIXIANG *declaims:* Sister, who is this guy? Why are you so intent on keeping him here to drink? LI QIONGMEI: It's none of your business. ZHU BANGJIE *acts out killing* MEIXIANG *and costuming* MEXIANG *as the corpse of* LI QIONGMEI. *Performs removing* MEIXIANG's *head.* LI QIONGMEI *and* ZHU BANGJIE *declaim:*

> If you don't use a scheme as unfathomable as an abyss
> You'll never snatch the pearl from the black dragon's chin!

> *Both exit.*

[Scene 11]

JUDGE BAO *enters:*

> (*Meizi huangshiyu*)
> Pure and upright, I wield authority,
> Fair and transparent without tiring.
> People suffer no injustice, and families do no wrong.

Declaims:

> Under my command ten ingots, five ingots of ink,
> Have sketched out a thousand branches, ten thousand branches of trees—
> So enticing that the birds of the forest come in droves,
> But unable to roost on the branches, they emptily go back.[40]

I am in charge of all of the folk of Kaifeng. There was quite a commotion outside the gate at morning court today, and I don't know why. Servant, come here.

---

40. This is a complicated poem, which may roughly be based on another verse that was attached to a wall painting of an ancient pine, "I ground out one or two ingots of ink, / And brushed out a thousand, ten-thousand-year-old pine. / When the moon is bright rooks and magpies fly to it by mistake, / But unable to alight on its branches, they fly away in vain." There are several rare characters, all of which seem to be close structurally to characters in the original poem. Its use as an entrance poem here has puzzled commentators (and us), although we believe it to be a clever reshaping, involving "costuming," or "deceit"; expectations perhaps of bribery, all of which are to no avail.

ZHU BANGJIE, *costumed as Head Clerk Zhu, performs entering, explains [to the audience] the plot about the murder:* "Better to deceive the gods above than to lack logic in the world of men." The official in court has summoned me; it's about the murder case involving the elder Sun. I'd better go. *Performs greeting* JUDGE BAO *and explaining the plot.* JUDGE BAO: This is a case involving human life and no trifling matter. No confession without beating! ZHU BANGJIE: I've beaten him. *Performs bringing* SUN BIDA *in.* SUN BIDA *sings:*

> (*Jintian le*)
> Please still your might,
> I beg you, your compassionate Honor, to show some mercy.
> Yesterday my mother left on pilgrimage,
> And I came home after escorting her halfway there.
> Who conspired to murder my wife?
> Her head is gone and she's covered in fresh blood,
> I beg your compassionate Honor to grant me your enlightened
>   autopsy.
> I turn it over in my mind,
> Now, I'm innocent—
> So why should I suffer this unjust punishment?

Sings again:

> (*Shang xiaolou*)
> The clerks and runners are arrayed in rows on both sides,
> And involuntarily my heart is alarmed and my gall trembles—
> How can you employ these iron chains, this heavy cangue, and the
>   hempen hammer and finger presses?
> I've suffered all I can of this burning torment,
> Even if my heart were made of iron,
> Like an oven, the laws of this court would melt it.
> Don't grieve that I am wrongly accused,
> That I'll die without resentment.
>
> Even right now I don't know
> What has made me a criminal!
> I hope for even a little clemency,
> The proverb says, "Within courtroom doors one should do good
>   deeds."
> People are easy to scare,
> But Heaven is bound to see.
> You've tortured me in a thousand ways, my soul and spirit are
>   disordered.

Even though the sun and moon shine brightly in the heavens,
They shed no light on what's under an overturned pot.
Even if I confess and become a ghost, I will carry a grudge after
   death.

(*Hongxiuxie*)
They have thrashed me until my spirit flies away and my soul
   dissipates,
And beaten me until my flesh turns to pulp and my skin is worn
   away.
I tell you clerks who investigate with such clarity—
I beg you to help me out.
You are a document of imperial pardon,
Flying down from the nine-layered heaven.
How can I avoid
This penalty of death?

SUN BIDA *performs making a complete confession.* JUDGE BAO: Since he's already confessed, confine him in prison in a cangue to wait until the head is found, and then I will sentence him. JUDGE BAO *sings:*

(*Sibian jing*)
Recite in full his short oral statement,
Look thoroughly over his written deposition.
"Don't follow the feelings of others,[41]
But proceed on your own according to the law."

Chorus:

This punishment
Is inescapable.
He has confessed on each and every point,
And will have three years to wait for a decision.

SUN BIDA:

Who could foretell my fate would run so foul,
And that I would suffer these punishments today.
You have spared me being trussed up and put on public
   display,
And for this my gratitude is not shallow.

---

41. This line can also mean, "Don't act according to bribes."

Chorus as before. ZHU BANGJIE:

> Clearly it was *you* who murdered your wife,
> So how can you speak such nonsense?
> Of course being beaten and strung upside down
> Is inescapable now.

Chorus as before. SUN BIDA *sings:*

> (*Yicuozhao*)
> I have eaten the bitter root,
> But to whom can I tell the bitterness in my heart?[42]
> I've nowhere to protest,
> Can't even complain to blue heaven.

JUDGE BAO:

> The cangue has been put on,
> And tomorrow you will return for further interrogation.
> The facts of the case,
> If truthfully told, will help you out.

SUN BIDA:

> How can I stand cangue and shackles?
> Even with a heart of iron, one's tears would flow without end.
> And the bitterest feeling of all,
> Is that my body has ended up in prisoners' lockdown.

JUDGE BAO *declaims:*

> Day after day, interrogate with no delay;
> We only seek what is fair and just and desire no money.

SUN BIDA:

> My brother's not back; who will take care of me?
> Who will take a message to my mother?

ZHU BANGJIE:

> In the beginning he thought that only fine writing was to be respected,
> And only now does he realize that prison guards are strict.

All exit.

---

42. From the common saying, "When a dumb person eats bitter root, his own mouth cannot express the bitterness of his heart."

[Scene 12]

MOTHER SUN *enters*:

> (*Wangyuan xing*)
> We have left our home village
> And are worn out by traversing the hilly roads.
> We overnight by rivers, dine in the winds,
> How can we get through these travails of travel?

SUN BIGUI:

> On that day as we were leaving home,
> I never thought I would be turning my head toward my
>   home—
> For now, with slow steps we set out on the road.

MOTHER SUN:

> (*Sifan lameihua*)
> High mountains, range upon range; the road is long.
> When will we reach the Halls of the Eastern Peak
> And repay our vows with a brazier of incense?
> People are few and far between,
> And I am frightened and flustered
> Because there are only the two of us, son and mother, traveling
>   together.
> We hurry toward the travelers' inn,
> Everywhere I look, mountain flowers line the sides of the road.

Chorus:

> If we meet flowers or wine on our journey,
> Then we naturally dilly-dally,
> And turn one leg of the trip into two.

SUN BIGUI:

> In the evening we overnight in a village inn, and in the morning set
>   out again.
> Relax, take it easy, and let's not be unhappy or disconsolate,
> But repay our vow with a brazier of incense.
> Healthy and hale,
> We will return to our native village,
> Traveling by day and stopping by night—a son and his mother.

With all my heart I want to imitate
The one who danced before his parents in his colored clothes.[43]

Chorus as before. MOTHER SUN *declaims:* Son, I'm not feeling at all well. Find us a place to rest soon. SUN BIGUI: Mommy, there's a thatched inn at Strawbridge just ahead. Let's rest there. We can go on to the temple tomorrow to repay our vow. [MOTHER SUN:] Son, quickly find an inn where we can stay the night. A healthy body is a limitless blessing! We can go home as soon as we repay our vows.

Exit together.

[Scene 13]

LI QIONGMEI *enters* [*with* ZHU BANGJIE] *and sings:*

(*Ye xing chuan*)
When a perfect couple, husband and wife, meet a second time,
It is bestowed by heaven, not something given by people.

ZHU BANGJIE *continues singing:*

If one does not enter the deep abyss,
And the terrifying breakers and waves,
Can one seize the brightest pearls from the great ocean?

LI QIONGMEI *declaims:* If one does not enter the terrifying waves . . . ZHU BANGJIE: Then it's hard to meet a satisfying fish. LI QIONGMEI: Head Clerk Zhu, if I hadn't come up with this plan, then how could you and I be together today? ZHU BANGJIE: Many thanks, madam. LI QIONGMEI: Sir,

Stop listening to songs of love longing in this world,
But finish instead these cups of wine of eternal youth.

LI QIONGMEI *sings:*

(*Xiu ting zhen*)
From that day on,
As mandarin duck mates were driven asunder, I have ceaselessly
    sighed,
The gauze of my sleeves soaked red by tears of rouge,
Sorrow brought on by his very mention.

---

43. I.e., Lao Laizi, who was so filial that, at seventy years of age, he dressed up in multihued children's clothing, and cried and cooed like a baby to please his aged and senile parents.

Thank heaven for opening its eyes to provide us a little ease—
By employing a little scheme, we seized the opportunity.
From now on we will not be a single step apart,
In heaven we want to fly together,
And on earth be as intertwining branches.

ZHU BANGJIE:

Trysts of rain and rendezvous of clouds—
Most bitter it was to be apart when our passion was thickest.
How to bear a full heart lusting for your mandarin duck quilts,
When a single foot away from you was like a thousand miles?
I could not imitate Zhuangzi dreaming of the butterfly,
But I wanted to fly right to you,
To sit with you, walk with you, and sleep together with you.

LI QIONGMEI:

I want you to be in charge—
Don't wait until the right and wrong of it is settled in bystanders'
    discussions.
Within gauze bedhangings the embroidered quilt is fragrant and
    warm
And I want our love to be just as it was before.
Talk as you will of morning clouds and evening rains on Yang
    Terrace,[44]
But they're no match for my tender care and joyful pleasure—
I want never to be separated from you.

ZHU BANGJIE:

When I look at your beautiful face,
Your amazing autumn ripples make a man obsessed.
Face, peach blossom red in the dew, cherry lips, bewitching.
No one else comes close to your lightly sketched curving brows:
You're just like a bud forming in spring's radiance
Which, to my fortune, I pluck inside the screen and bedhangings.
From now on it will not be easy to match the two halves of this
    karmic bond,
So henceforth we will strike out all idle sorrow,
Steel our hearts, and again never mention right or wrong.

---

44. See *Autumn over the Palaces of Han*, n. 22.

LI QIONGMEI *and* ZHU BANGJIE *declaim:*

> In heaven we go back together to the azure vault,
> Entering the earth, we will return together to the yellow springs.

Exit together.

[Scene 14]

SUN BIGUI *enters and declaims:*

> Of all the sad and grievous affairs of this world,
> Nothing is worse than separation in life or by death.

How awful! When I set out, I left with my mother, but now I return all alone. I didn't expect my mother to die suddenly in the inn as soon as she repaid her vow. Now, I can only carry her bones back home. And to my joy, I'm back home now. But as soon as I start thinking about it, my heart hurts as if it were pierced by thorns and my tears spill out like pearls. *Sings:*

> (*Northern music: Duanzheng hao*)
> On that day, I left the capital with keen intention,
> And never thought, sunk in sorrow and depression,
> I would be hurrying back, depressed and alone with my tears.
> When we set out, we were happy and overjoyed, as my mother
>   climbed the mountain ridges.
> But now I return
> Bearing this sad box of bones on my back.

Sings:

> (*Southern music: Jinchandao*)
> I rush along journey's way,
> Mourning and wailing without stop.
> I can't stop my pearly tears that spill out.
> I raise this paper pennant,[45]
> That, fluttering, spreads my painful grief.
> This box of bones is now light,
> Now, oh-so-heavy.
> Is it not that my mother shows her mighty power,
> As she supports me, follows me,
> And assists me back to the imperial capital.

---

45. That leads the soul back.

As soon as I get home,
And see my brother I'll tell him how it happened.

Sings:

(*Northern music: Tuo bushan*)
By light of day there are rains of tears and clouds of sorrow,
And by evening my dreaming soul is wearied and worn.[46]
It's all because my sister-in-law cursed me by name—
If mother had died at home, then the appropriate rites could have
    been held.

Sings:

(*Southern music: Shuazi xu*)
When I think on it in my heart,
I resent my mother's oh-so-unhappy fate.
If you had died at home,
Then we would have carried out the seven-times-seven-day masses,
And would have invited several monks.[47]
But, I could only arrange a few nights of masses,
And have several chapters of confessional texts and the *Heart Sutra*
    read.
I am well aware that everything had to be done too hastily,
As our funeral procession went out of the western gate.

Declaims: Hurrah! To my joy I've arrived outside the walls. But, I'd better not go home in this way. I'll place this box of bones in the Monastery of Perfect Virtue outside the city gates. I'll go on home then and let my brother know and we'll request some monks go fetch her bones. *Performs depositing the box of bones. Performs returning home. Performs action of coming upon a sealed door:* The proverb says, "Good fortune never comes paired, disaster never strikes alone." Why have we been sued and our doors sealed up? I'll have to go to our neighbor, old lady Wang, who lives next door and ask her about it. SUN BIGUI *calls out.* COMIC *costumed as* OLD LADY WANG *comes out of the house:* Coming, coming! Who is it? SUN BIGUI *and* COMIC *act out greeting each other.* COMIC: Sun Two, didn't your mother come back? SUN BIGUI: I'll tell you about it, but it's a long story. When mother and I had reached Strawbridge Inn on our journey, my mother wasn't feeling well. After she had repaid her vow and had reached the inn, she died. Ma'am, do you know why we have been charged by the courts

---

46. By dreams of his mother.
47. I.e., to read scriptures for the dead.

and had our doors sealed up? COMIC: Your brother didn't listen to anyone's advice and married that woman. She did something bad, I don't know what, and your brother killed her. The officials have now arrested him and concluded the case. He's locked up in prison. SUN BIGUI *sings:*

> (*Suo nanzhi*)
> Ma'am, listen to me,
> And I will relate it all.
> I went to the Eastern Peak along with my mother.
> Who would believe that halfway there,
> My mother would suddenly give it all up.
> The bones of her corpse
> I have brought home myself.
> But when I got home,
> Why had the gate been locked?

NEIGHBOR:

> Listen to me tell you what has happened—
> Unexpectedly tears fall in silence—
> You went away with your mother to repay the vow,
> And alas, your brother
> Began to quarrel with his wife.
> He killed her,
> And was arrested and held,
> And at the present
> Is locked up in jail.

SUN BIGUI *declaims:* Can you tell me how I can see my brother now? NEIGHBOR: Now, the only way you can see him is to say you're bringing him food. SUN BIGUI: I came home completely broke. *Acting out giving him food,* NEIGHBOR: I tell you, child, if you see your brother, don't get upset. SUN BIGUI: All right.

> When I see him, I dare not wail with raised voice,
> Lest others hear and have their hearts broken.

Exit together.

[Scene 15]

SUN BIDA *enters, singing* (*Jinlongcong*), *and carrying the cangue:*

> In pure and impartial heaven and earth,
> It is my unjust death that is hard to countenance—

I sob quietly, tears welling out.
No news of my mother,
Is she somewhere together with my brother?
They can't know that I have wound up in jail.

SUN BIGUI *enters and declaims:*

> Trust not the counsel of good people,
> And wind up with today's troubles.

This has been proven true today! Here I am at the jail gate and I can only shout, "Bringing food!" *Performs the action of knocking on the gate. Performs greeting* SUN BIDA, *bringing him food, and feeding him.* SUN BIGUI *sings:*

> (*Xiaoshun ge*)
> It's your fault, brother,
> So whom else can you blame?
> It's hard to find anyone as obsessed and deluded as you.
> The good advice of your younger brother
> You smugly dismissed
> As wind passing your ears.
> She, in wind and dust,
> Was a misty blossom, a rotten whore.
> You took her as a wife,
> Never expecting to encounter this day.

SUN BIDA:

> You're right in what you say,
> And it makes my tears fall in silence.
> When I first brought her home
> I thought she would behave well.
> But who knew?
> When affairs came to a head
> There was no way to get a handle on it.
> I've suffered the worst torture,[48]
> And now there's nothing to do but regret it.

SUN BIDA *acts out asking about his mother.* SUN BIGUI: I'll tell you about it, brother, but it's a long story. When mother and I had reached Strawbridge Inn on our journey, she wasn't feeling well. By the time she had repaid her vow, she was dead.

---

48. The term is "slow slicing," the most feared of all punishments; but clearly here it simply means the worst torture imaginable.

SUN BIDA: Oh, no! SUN BIDA *sings*:

> (*Yi duojiao*)
> My heart truly grieves,
> My pearly tears drop in silence.
> I didn't know my mother is now a ghost below,
> Who will take care of her son in jail?

Chorus:

> Disaster never strikes alone,
> Oh! Mother, how can you know how bad I feel?

SUN BIGUI:

> You acted
> Without checking the facts.
> How can I save you now?
> But don't worry about getting fed.

Chorus as before. ZHU BANGJIE *shoving* SUN BIGUI *aside and escorting* SUN BIDA *off*:

> Even though human hearts are like iron,
> They can't escape the furnace of the law.

> SUN BIDA *exits.*

SUN BIGUI *stays on stage, acts out greeting* ZHU BANGJIE *and promising him goods*:

> Today I've gotten your kind support
> So that he doesn't have to lie in the muck and mud.

> *Exit together.*

[Scene 16]

LI QIONGMEI *enters [together with* ZHU BANGJIE] *and sings*:

> (*Linjiang xian*)
> Disguised feelings turned into a plan, and now I here live;
> Clearly people have fallen into my snare.

ZHU BANGJIE:

> In this life I have realized my heart's desire,
> Happy pleasures make the nights too short.
> Few indeed who know such joy!

LI QIONGMEI: Just as I escaped those flowery gates and willow doorways to become the legal wife of Mr. Sun, I had hoped to grow old with him for the hundred years of this life. But I didn't expect him to be sodden drunk day and night. If I hadn't come up with the plan to murder Meixiang. . . . Whatever it takes to live together with Head Clerk Zhu! ZHU BANGJIE *performs relating the old lady's death.* ZHU BANGJIE: I'll kill the elder Sun today and then you and I can share the happiness of simurgh and phoenix, enjoy forever a hundred years of pleasure. LI QIONGMEI:

> If the scheme succeeds, we can snatch the jade hare from the moon,
> If the plan works out, we can capture the golden raven in the sun.

Exit together.

[Scene 17][49]

SUN BIGUI *enters, acting out counting out the objects. Performs seeing the chest.* ZHU BANGJIE *enters, apprehends* SUN BIGUI, *and speaks:*

> If your whole body were mouths, you could not speak;
> If your whole shape was lined with teeth, you could not talk.

Exit.

JUDGE BAO *enters and sings:*

> (*Xi Nujiao*)
> I administer justice here in Kaifeng.
> Hearts of those who unjustly accuse others are as stubborn as iron,
> But in vain, since once put into the furnace of the law, they melt of
>   their own accord.[50]

ZHU BANGJIE *enters and performs relating the plot.* JUDGE BAO: Sun Bida, that chief conspirator in murder has already been arrested. I'll let you off today to go home and wait for news. SUN BIGUI *enters carrying the cangue. Performs greeting* SUN BIDA. SUN BIDA: Alas! O Heaven! SUN BIDA *sings:*

---

49. There is a large portion of text missing between the last scene and the beginning of this one. Several anomalous facts present themselves here: first, Sun's house was sealed when the murder was committed, yet this scene takes place in the Sun household; second, the significance of looking at the chest and counting out the items has been lost as well (although there is a general antecedent in Scene 15); third, the comic is now Zhu Bangjie; fourth, the elder brother has made an entrance. Perhaps Little Sun switched places with his brother in prison, or confessed in his place and was executed?

50. Ruminating about the fact that he had sentenced the wrong brother to death?

(*Hong na'ao*)
I didn't think carefully enough at the start,
And when I met this "enemy of mine"[51] I was like a drunken idiot.
And the bitterest thing is that my mother has left us,
And our family fortune has been destroyed—too late now for
    remorse.
Today he[52] will be unjustly killed,
Who can understand this bitter pain?
I am willing to brave death in the Yellow Springs,
And set this case right in the courts of hell.

SUN BIGUI:

I pray you stop your tiger- and wolf-like might,
Head Clerk Zhu, abuser of the good citizens.
How can you be an exemplar when you work wrongful harm on
    common folk?
People below may easily be bullied, but can Heaven be deceived?
I've fallen into the net,
But who is the real murderer?
I'm quite willing to stand in brother's stead,
And be a ghost of the knife or die by being bound and strung up by
    my feet.

SUN BIGUI *performs.*

Exit together.

[Scene 18]

MEIXIANG *enters as a ghost, singing*:

(*Gaoyang tai*)
One dot of invisible soul,
A whole breast of the bitterness of wrong—
In the unending limitless dark, I suffer my grief,
Fresh blood flows red,
Pain and tears drip, mix together, and fall.
Resentment over my wrongful death batters against heaven and earth:
I hate that person so much I am speechless, and heave long sighs.

51. Usually this term means a lover; here it is obviously used with both meanings in mind.
52. Little Sun, the butcher.

Wrongs are always righted,
The only question is, how soon, how late?

Sings again:

> (*Shanpo yang*)
> The ethers of resentment batter against heaven, and stuff everything
>   on earth,
> My wronged soul is lost in darkness.
> Dripping, dropping fresh blood soaks my sleeves.
> Li Qiongmei—
> You and your deceitful feelings,
> Murdered me so you could enjoy a love of intertwining branches.
> Eternity past[53] holds no foe hated more than you—
> My enemy,
> When it's all over I'll meet you yet!

Sings again:

> (*Houting hua*)
> It makes me hate you so much,
> My soul can find no place of rest.
> This injustice is impossible to vent,
> Azure heaven cannot be relied on to act in time.
> You kept it secret
> From all others,
> Employed clever, crafty schemes.
> Used vicious knowledge,
> And quickly did in my life.

Sings again:

> (*Shuihonghua*)
> I harbor wrong, am filled with hatred, my bitterness incapable of
>   remedy,
> You got the best of me.
> Where sad winds stir,
> My hidden form leans on nothing, relies on nothing.
> What's most heartrending
> Is a light drizzle at dusk,
> All on the tips of banana leaves.

---

53. Literally, 10 thousand kalpic cycles. A *kalpa* is a Sanskrit term for a period roughly equal
to 16 million years.

My resentful soul flies,
And this grieving person's tears fall like pearls,
Oh, alas.

Sings again:

> Don't think I'll take this lying down,
> There will come a day in the cyclical transmigration of heaven and
>   earth,
> When I remember to repay all past wrongs.
> You are truly bereft of compassion and righteousness,
> Li Qiongmei,
> And when you get to the court of hell,
> You'll be tortured with ten thousand slicings.

[*Exits.*]

[Scene 19]

COMIC, *costumed as* PRISON GUARD, *enters, opening the gate and dragging out* SUN BIGUI. COMIC *exits.* EXTRA *enters, costumed as* PRINCE OF TAISHAN, THE EAST-ERN PEAK, *and singing* (Shaonian you).

> In the single glance of an eye,
> In a blink the whole world is arrayed before me.

Declaims:

> Do not deceive Heaven and Earth, do not deceive your heart,
>   If you do not deceive others, disaster cannot strike;
>   Do good deeds twenty-four hours a day,
> And the star of calamity will pass you by, the star of fortune shine upon you.

I, this humble god, am Prince of Taishan, the Eastern Peak,

> I urge you, sir, do not do things that make you feel guilty.
> At the Eastern Peak, I have been appointed Officer of Speedy Retribution.

I have just noticed that that slut Li Qiongmei has murdered someone and that Sun Bigui has unjustly died on the outskirts of town. It is commendable that this man has been filial all his life. But today he has such a misfortune. The Emperor of Heaven has announced his orders and commanded me, this humble god, to let several drops of sweet rain fall and revive this man, Sun Bigui.

> Sweet rain soaks your body, your soul will awake from its dream,
>   And when you awaken, injustice will become clear by itself.

Out of the air I stretch my cloud-snatching hand,
And raise up this man caught in heaven's net and earth's web.

EXTRA *exits*.

SUN BIGUI *performs coming back to life*. SUN BIGUI *sings*:

(*Northern music: Xinshui ling*)
In my dream all I could hear was the soft drizzle of rain.
Actually, this is where I parted from life.
My whole body is smashed and broken,
How did I withstand this pain?
       Zhu Bangjie,
What did I ever do to you?
May heaven take pity on Little Sun, the butcher.

(*Suo nanzhi*)
My spirit and soul in chaos,
My hands and feet are numb,
Just another moment and I would have died.
If old Heaven had not helped me out....
Sweet rain fell from the sky,
And in my soul's dream,
Sprinkled on my face.
Now I am revived,
And I sigh.

Performs looking at a club.

(*Northern music: Tianshui ling*)
This stave by my side—
Who dropped it here?
My hands so a-tremble, how can I pick it up?
Wavering and reeling side to side,
How can I rouse myself up?
My energy so flagging and failing,
I can't seem to move.

(*Xiang Liuniang*)
I wonder where brother is—
"Don't you know
That your brother died on this very spot?"
There were no inns in the Yellow Springs,
So where will I lodge tonight?

My life was covered by the yellow sands,
But now I stir myself
And pick up this stave
As my soul flies and my spirit is stunned.[54]

SUN BIDA *enters with a hoe and paper money, and performs. Performs seeing* SUN BIGUI: A ghost! SUN BIGUI: Brother, I'm not a ghost. In prison I was strangled and strung up, and they threw me out on the outskirts. But thanks to the sweet rains that heaven sent down, I was revived and saved. Brother, I am not a ghost, I am a human. SUN BIDA: Brother, are you really a human? Brother, slowly get up and walk, support yourself on this stave. Press on until you get home and then we'll figure a way to handle it. LI QIONGMEI *enters and sings*:

(*Hua'er*)
Toward evening in the deserted outskirts,
As stars and moon gradually appear and the sun sinks in the west.
Carts and horses of roamers gradually disappear,
And I walk with secret steps, tied by mutual love.

Performs seeing SUN BIDA *and* SUN BIGUI, *declaims*: A ghost! SUN BIDA *and* SUN BIGUI: Are you a ghost or a person? LI QIONGMEI: I am not a ghost, I am a person. SUN BIDA *and* SUN BIGUI: If you aren't a ghost, then who was killed? LI QIONGMEI: The one who was killed was Meixiang. When the two of you left, I talked it over with Head Clerk Zhu and we murdered Meixiang, cutting off her head. We made her out to be my corpse and falsely accused you of murdering me. We put you brothers in jail, planning on doing away with you. This was a conspiracy between Head Clerk Zhu and me. SUN BIDA *and* SUN BIGUI: So, it was you, you bitch, and Head Clerk Zhu who conspired to do us in. Where is Head Clerk Zhu now? LI QIONGMEI: In a village five miles down the road. SUN BIDA *and* SUN BIGUI: Take us there, and now

For all the deeds you've done before,
Misfortune will come in a single swoop.

Exit together.

[Scene 20]

ZHU BANGJIE *enters and declaims*: Achoo! My eyes are jumping today. There's something wrong. Why hasn't Li Qiongmei shown up yet? What's she up to?

---

54. At being brought back to life.

SUN BIDA, SUN BIGUI, *and* LI QIONGMEI *enter. Perform catching* ZHU BANGJIE.
SUN BIDA *sings:*

> (*Nian Fozi*)
> After hearing this,
> I know it's true:
> You murdered Meixiang and fled,
> You dressed up the corpse to lure me into your snare.

LI QIONGMEI:

> I have listened and taken in your opinion;
> It's so laughable that you're so wrong.
> Just because I look like your wife,
> You've nabbed us one after the other.
> Because I just happened to pass by here,
> And I suddenly saw that your form looked like a ghost's,
> I was flustered and my heart turned to water.

SUN BIDA *and* SUN BIGUI:

> You clearly
> Have told us the true facts,
> So how can you so crazily deny it now?
> And right now you'll have a hard time explaining your way out of
>   this.
>
> (*To the same tune*)
> Li Qiongmei,
> We reckon the crimes you've done
> Have come to full measure and ought to be punished:
> How can we spare you now?

LI QIONGMEI:

> This is for the way I acted in other days,
> For a single moment of conspiracy,
> I submit myself today that I was wrong.

SUN BIDA *and* SUN BIGUI:

> (*Same tune as before, with different beginning*)[55]
> By good fortune we ran into you.

---

55. We assume that the ghost of Meixiang enters at this point.

No one expected ghosts to appear three times
And in a single swoop catch them both.
We were imperiled in a thousand different ways,
But fortunately, Heaven, Heaven came to our rescue.
Could those two have grown wings?
Even if mouths covered their bodies, could they talk their way out
    of it?
Right and wrong—
We'll wait for judgment below the steps of Dragon Design.[56]

SUN BIDA, SUN BIGUI, *and* MEIXIANG *grab* LI QIONGMEI *and* ZHU BANGJIE
tightly and declaim: Today we'll take you to the court of Dragon Design, where
it'll all be settled. True it is,

> Never say you'll fish forever in the autumn rivers,
> For a time will come when you have to reel in your line and hooks.

Exit together.

[Scene 21]

JUDGE BAO *sings*:

> (*Qiniangzi*)
> My verdicts and sentences are strict and clear,
> I administer justice in the world of men, and in the gloom and dark
>   of the courts of hell.
> Whoever suffers injustice or harbors wrongs,
> Will be judged with impartiality.
> My heart knows no bias or prejudice; it is as clear as a mirror.

Declaims: A secret whisper in the world of men is heard like thunder in heaven.
I am Bao Zheng. I have received the edict that descends from the clouds, ordering me to sit in judgment over Kaifeng. By light of day I judge the world of
yang, and at night the world of yin. I assure that every single person will suffer
no wrong and make sure that each individual suffers no injustice. Far, far away,
I see a little group of people coming. I fear someone has been remiss and that
things are not right. Staff, come here. SUN BIDA, SUN BIGUI, *and* MEIXIANG
enter, and perform holding LI QIONGMEI *and* ZHU BANGJIE. SUN BIDA *and* SUN
BIGUI *sing*:

---

56. Judge Bao.

(*Zisu wan*)
I would have never thought that your false heart would injure
others—
Li Qiongmei, now you're caught.

MEIXIANG:

In the world of yin I harbored resentment for being wronged, was
hurt by sad grief.

ZHU BANGJIE *and* LI QIONGMEI:

Who would expect that injustice would repay injustice and all its debts!

JUDGE BAO *declaims:* I reckon you have a case of injustice, so let each of you give
an oral deposition from the start. SUN BIDA *sings:*

(*Lülüjin*)
She originally sold wine
And entertained fine customers.
I had her name taken off the register of flowers
And made her a decent person.
I took her as a wife,
But her watery nature had no fixed standard.
She murdered Meixiang and eloped,
Leaving me to wrongfully suffer punishment,
Leaving me to wrongfully suffer punishment.

LI QIONGMEI:

Sir Dragon Design,
Listen to the facts:
From a tender age I
Lived in the wind and dust.
I was taken as a wife into his house,
But my heart was not fixed.
I eloped with mutual intent with Zhu Bangjie,
And we robbed Meixiang of her life,
Robbed Meixiang of her life.

SUN BIGUI:

Brother there
Took her as a wife.
Who knew her heart was a turning wheel
That would forget all favor?

She joined Zhu Bangjie,
And shared the mandarin duck pillow with him.
She murdered Meixiang, made innocents suffer,
And left me wrongfully buried in the gloomy darkness,
Left me wrongfully buried in the gloomy darkness.

JUDGE BAO:

Zhu Bangjie,
Li Qiongmei—
After killing Meixiang,
You lived in adulterous lust.
You wrongly accused these brothers
Who were locked up in jail.
Murdering one's husband and killing his brother is no light crime.
The two of you will have to pay with your lives,
The two of you will have to pay with your lives.

JUDGE BAO *declaims his verdict:* Zhu Bangjie upholds the law and violates the law; Li Qiongmei conspired to murder and committed murder. You conspired to murder Meixiang, and falsely accused elder Sun of killing his wedded wife. This falls under premeditated murder of a husband in order to commit adultery and entrapment of his younger brother—this is one of the abominable crimes. Now award Zhu Bangjie's wife and all family possessions to elder Sun and his brother as recompense, and escort Zhu Bangjie and Li Qiongmei to the marketplace, there to pay for the life of Meixiang. SUN BIDA *sings:*

(*Shanhuazi*)
This morning we thank our exalted and enlightened ruler,
Who bestows on us gold and acts as our protector.
Li Qiongmei turned against her conscience and acted wrongly,
Secretly conspiring with him in this scheme.

Chorus:

We are moved by Dragon Design's verdict in this case,
We were aggrieved by being parted in life and separated by death,
But now Meixiang is spared being a resentful ghost,
And injustice is avenged by justice—
Fortunately we have escaped from its cycle.

SUN BIGUI:

You slut, you've always been a whore,
But my brother raised you up and led you home.

He did not understand that willow floss can't be caught
And that your deeds would betray his decency.

Chorus as before. LI QIONGMEI:

My heart shivers, my gall is shattered,
I am filled with remorse over the wrong of my deeds.
I should never have conspired with him,
It was all for a momentary passion.

Chorus as before. MEIXIANG:

You never considered my past service to you,
And only hoped to live with him in this life.
Who could have thought you would come up with such crazy plans,
And conspire with your lover to murder me.

Chorus as before. JUDGE BAO:

Li Qiongmei was easily moved and forgot old favor,
Zhu Bangjie was neither humane nor righteous.
According to my impartial verdict, they should be escorted through
the streets,
And suffer death by slow slicing.

Chorus as before. ZHU BANGJIE:

I should have never conspired in the beginning,
I beg Your Honor to show me mercy and clemency.

JUDGE BAO:

Don't blabber such nonsense—
Take them away.

Chorus as [before]:

On the postal route we apprehended the younger brother;
In the room in the inn, a mother passed away.
She had not a speck of the matrimonial love and respect,[57]
He was a full breast of evil, a poisonous heart and innards![58]

---

57. Li Qiongmei.
58. Zhu Bangjie.

Appendix 1

A Note on the Translation and Study of Early Chinese Drama in Europe and the United States

Zaju was one of the earliest genres of Chinese literature to be translated into European languages. In the early eighteenth century Joseph de Prémare, a Jesuit missionary in Beijing and an excellent linguist, produced a French translation of the prose dialogues of Ji Junxiang's *Zhaoshi gu'er* (*The Orphan of Zhao*) to assist one of the mission's patron's in Paris in his study of vernacular Chinese. This text was published in 1735 by Jean Baptiste du Halde in his *Déscription de la Chine* as a "tragédie chinoise." As the first Chinese play ever to be translated into a European language it exerted considerable influence and was repeatedly adapted for the stage in a variety of European languages. The most famous adaptation eventually was Voltaire's *Orphelin de la Chine* of 1755, which was produced all over Europe in the following decades.

French sinologists of the early decades of the nineteenth centuries were very much interested in the study of Chinese drama. One of the reasons for this interest was that plays, along with novels, provided a window into daily life in China, which at that moment was still closed to foreigners. For their study of *zaju*, French sinologists based themselves, like Prémare, on Zang Maoxun's *Yuanqu xuan* (see pages xxvii–xxxi). The most influential of these French scholars was Stanislas Julien. He not only provided a new and full translation of *Zhaoshi gu'er*, but also translated Li Xingdao's *Huilan ji* (*The Chalk Circle*) into French, perhaps attracted to the subject matter because of the similarity to one of King Solomon's judgments. Throughout the following century this play would continuously be retranslated and readapted to the stage. Eventually it would be one of the inspirations for Bertolt Brecht in writing *Der kaukasische Kreidekreis*. Stanislas Julien also was the first sinologist to offer a translation of Wang Shifu's *The Story of the Western Wing* (*Xixiang ji*), which is still the only version of that play available in French.

Once China was opened to Westerners following the Opium War of 1839–42, drama and fiction lost much of their status as a privileged window into daily life in China. Sinologists, as the level of their scholarship increased, also became increasingly aware of the relative low status of drama and fiction in the literary universe of traditional China. European sinology took a distinctively philological turn by the end of the nineteenth century, and had lost practically all interest in fiction and drama during the first half of the twentieth century. Paradoxically, during this same period, Chinese scholars and intellectuals had abandoned the traditional notions of literature and came to embrace the vernacular genres of the past as a "living literature" and a forerunner of their own modern vernacular fiction and drama. *Zhaoshi gu'er* and *Dou E yuan* were now hailed by the pioneering scholar of Chinese drama Wang Guowei as Chinese examples of tragedy, in his eyes the highest mode of literature.[1] Western scholars who studied with modern Chinese scholars introduced this new canon of Chinese literature to their home countries. This was especially successful in the United States, which witnessed a considerable expansion of Chinese studies in the 1950s and 1960s in Departments of East Asian Languages and Literatures.

One of the most inspiring teachers of early drama in the United States was James I. Crump, who also trained numerous Ph.D. students in this field. Crump was first of all a gifted translator, whose playful renditions still are a joy to read. From his first publication on drama in 1958 on the "Elements of Yüan Opera" to his later years as a scholar, he produced a remarkable body of material on the staging and literary merit of Yuan drama. Because of Crump and others such as Shih Chung-wen, Dale Johnson, and George Hayden, the 1970s and 1980s witnessed the publication of a considerable number of studies and translations. Students' interest shifted to other subjects, however, when China opened up to the West in the 1980s and contemporary Chinese culture started to manifest all of its rich vibrancy. Students and scholars interested in theater now could not only study texts but also performance, which made living theatrical traditions much more attractive as objects of study. Recent years, however, have seen a renewed upsurge of interest in early drama, particularly in its relationship to China's emergence as a nation state and its modernization in the late nineteenth and early twentieth centuries.

---

1. See He Yuming 2007 for the first Western study (written in 1998) of Wang Guowei's role in establishing Chinese drama as an academic field.

Appendix 2

Bibliography and Suggested Readings

General Studies

Chen, Fan Ben. 1997. "Reunion with Son and Daughter in Kingfisher Red County." *Asian Theatre Journal* 14.2: 157–99.

Crown, Eleanor H. 1980. "Jeux d'Esprit in Yüan Dynasty Verse." *CLEAR* 11 (2): 182–98.

Crump, J. I. 1958. "The Elements of Yuan Opera." *Journal of Asian Studies* 17: 417–34.

———. 1971. "The Conventions and Craft of Yüan Drama." *Journal of the American Oriental Society* 91 (1): 14–29.

———. 1980. *Chinese Theater in the Days of Kublai Khan*. Tucson: University of Arizona Press.

———. 1990. *Chinese Theater in the Days of Kublai Khan*. Ann Arbor: Center for Chinese Studies, University of Michigan.

———. 1994. "The Monk Budai and the Character for Patience." In *Columbia Anthology of Traditional Chinese Literature*. New York: Columbia University Press. 1223–78.

Dolby, William. 1976. *A History of Chinese Drama*. London: Paul Elek.

———. 1978. *Eight Chinese Plays from the Thirteenth Century to the Present*. London: Paul Elek.

———. 1997. "'Tea-Trading Ship' and the Tale of Shuang Chien and Su Little Lady." *Bulletin of the School of Oriental and African Studies* 60 (1): 47–63.

Doleželová-Velingerova, Milena. 1991. "Traditional Chinese Theories of Drama and the Novel." *Archiv Orientalni* 59 (2): 132–39.

Fei, Faye Chunfang, and Richard Schechner. 1999. *Chinese Theories of Theater and Performance from Confucius to the Present*. Ann Arbor: University of Michigan Press.

Forke, Alfred, and Martin Gimm. 1978. *Chinesische Dramen der Yüan-Dynastie: 10 nachgelassene Übers entzungen von Alfred Forke*. Wiesbaden: Steiner.

Hawkes, David. 1971. "Some Remarks on Yüan *Tsa-chü*." *Asia Major*. New Series 16 (1–2): 69–81.

———. 2003. *Liu Yi and the Dragon Princess: A Thirteenth Century Zaju Play by Shang Zhongxian*. Hong Kong, London: Chinese University Press.

He Yuming. 2007. "Wang Guowei and the Beginnings of Modern Chinese Drama Studies." *Late Imperial China* 28 (2): 129–56.

Idema, W. L. 1984. "The Story of Ssu-ma Hsiang-ju and Cho Wen-chün in Vernacular Literature of the Yüan and Early Ming Dynasties." *T'oung Pao* 70 (1/3): 60–109.

———. 1987. "Poet versus Minister and Monk: Su Shi on Stage in the Period 1250–1450." *T'oung Pao* 73 (4/5): 190–216.

———. 1989. "The *Tsa-juh* of Yang Tz: An International Tycoon in Defense of Collaboration." In *Proceedings of the Second International Conference on Sinology*. Taipei: Academia Sinica. 523–48.

———. 1990a. "The Founding of the Han Dynasty in Early Drama: The Autocratic Suppression of Popular Debunking." In W. L. Idema and E. Zürcher, eds., *Thought and Law in Qin and Han China: Literature*. Leiden: E. J. Brill. 183–207.

———. 1990b. "Emulation through Readaption in Yüan and Early Ming." *Asia Major*. Third Series 3: 113–28.

———. 1990c. "The Remaking of an Unfilial Hero: Some Notes on the Earliest Dramatic Adaptations of the 'Story of Hsüeh Jen-kuei.'" In Erika de Poorter, ed., *As the Twig Is Bent . . . Essays in Honour of Frits Vos*. Amsterdam: J. C. Gieben. 83–111.

———. 2001. "Traditional Dramatic Literature." In Victor Mair, ed., *The Columbia History of Chinese Literature*. New York: Columbia University Press. 785–847, 1126–31.

———. 2004. "Banished to Yelang: Li Taibai Putting on a Performance." *Minsu quyi* 145 (9): 5–38.

———. 2006. "Something Rotten in the State of Song: The Frustrated Loyalty of the Generals of the Yang Family." *Journal of Song-Yuan Studies* 36: 57–77.

———. 2007. "Madness on the Yuan Stage." *Horin vergleichende Studien zur Japanische Kultur* 14: 65–85.

Idema, W. L., and Stephen H. West. 1982. *Chinese Theater, 1100–1450: A Source Book*. Wiesbaden: Steiner.

Jing, Anning. 2002. *The Water God's Temple of the Guangsheng Monastery: Cosmic Function of Art, Ritual and Theater*. Leiden: E. J. Brill.

Johnson, Dale R. 1980. *Yuarn Music Dramas: Studies in Prosody and Structure and a Complete Catalogue of Northern Arias in the Dramatic Style*. Michigan Papers in Chinese Studies 40. Ann Arbor: Center for Chinese Studies, University of Michigan.

———, trans. 1985. "Qiao Mengfu, 'The Golden Coins.'" *Renditions* 24 (Autumn 1985). 130–54.

———. 2000. *A Glossary of Words and Phrases in the Oral Performing and Dramatic Literatures of the Jin, Yuan, and Ming*. Ann Arbor: Center for Chinese Studies, University of Michigan.

Kao, George. 1998. "Guan Hanqing: 'A Sister Courtesan Comes to the Rescue.'" *Renditions* 49: 7–41.

Keene, Donald. 1965. "Autumn in the Palace of Han." In Cyril Birch, ed., *Anthology of Chinese Literature*. New York: Grove Press. 422–56.

Knechtges, David R. 1982. *Wen Xuan, or, Selections of Refined Literature*. Vol. 3. Princeton: Princeton University Press.

Li, Tche-Houa. 1963. *Le signe de patience et autres pièces de théâtre des Yuan*. Paris: Gallimard.

Liu, James. 1958. *Elizabethan and Yuan: A Brief Comparison of Some Conventions in Poetic Drama*. London: China Society.

Liu, Jung-en. 1972. *Six Yüan Plays*. Harmondsworth: Penguin.

Ma, Qian. 2005. *Women in Traditional Chinese Theater: The Heroine's Play*. Lanham, MD: University Press of America.

Mair, Victor. 1994. *The Columbia Anthology of Chinese Literature*. New York: Columbia University Press.

————. 2001. *The Columbia History of Chinese Literature.* New York: Columbia University Press.

Owen, Stephen. 1996. *An Anthology of Chinese Literature: Beginnings to 1911.* New York: Norton.

Shih, Chung-wen. 1976. *The Golden Age of Chinese Drama, Yüan tsa-chü.* Princeton: Princeton University Press.

Sieber, Patricia. 2003. *Theaters of Desire: Authors, Readers, and the Reproduction of Early Chinese Song-Drama.* New York: Palgrave MacMillan.

Slingerland, Edward, trans. 2003. *Confucius Analects.* Cambridge, MA: Hackett.

Song, Geng. 1999. "Wax Spear-head: Construction of Masculinity in Yuan Drama." *Tamkang Review* 30 (1): 209–54.

Tan, Tian Yuan. 2004. "Prohibition of *Jiatou Zaju* in the Ming Dynasty and the Portrayal of the Emperor as Sage." *Ming Studies* 49: 82–111.

Wang, C. K. 1984–85. "Lü Meng-cheng in Yüan and Ming Drama." *Monumenta Serica* 36: 303–408.

Wang Pi-tuan, H. 1978. "Chi Chün-hsiang: 'The Revenge of the Orphan of Chao.'" *Renditions* 9: 103–31.

Watson, Burton. 1970. *The Complete Works of Chuang-tzu.* New York: Columbia University Press.

Wei, Shu-chu. 2003. "Staging: A Comparative Study of the Chinese Yuan and English Renaissance Theaters." *Dong Hua hanxue* 1: 175–206.

West, Stephen H. 1977. "Jurchen Elements in the Northern Drama, Hu-t'ou-p'ai." *T'oung Pao* 63: 273–95.

————. 1982. "Mongol Influence in the Development of Northern Drama." In J. D. Langlois, ed., *China under Mongol Rule.* Princeton: Princeton University Press. 434–65.

————. 1986a. "Drama." In W. Nienhauser, ed., *Indiana Companion to Chinese Literature.* Bloomington: Indiana University Press. 13–30.

————. 1986b. "Tsa-chü." In W. Nienhauser, ed., *Indiana Companion to Chinese Literature.* Bloomington: Indiana University Press. 774–83.

————. 1997. "Playing with Food: Food, Performance, and the Aesthetics of Artificiality in the Sung and Yuan." *Harvard Journal of Asiatic Studies* 57 (1): 67–106.

————. 2005. "Meng Yuanlao, 'Recollections of the Northern Song Capital.'" In V. H. Mair and P. R. Golden, eds., *Hawai'i Reader in Traditional Chinese Culture.* Honolulu: University of Hawai'i Press. 405–22.

West, Stephen H., and Wilt L. Idema. 1991. *The Moon and the Zither: Wang Shifu's Story of the Western Wing.* Berkeley: University of California Press.

————. 1994. "Innocence and Allure: The Characterization of Oriole in Wang Shifu's Story of the Western Wing." *The Paradox of Virtue in Traditional Chinese Vernacular Literature.* Hong Kong: Chinese University of Hong Kong Press. 57–75.

————. 1995. *The Story of the Western Wing.* Berkeley: University of California Press.

Yang, Richard F. S. 1972. *Four Plays of the Yuan Drama.* Taipei: China Post.

Yu, Shiao-ling. 1978. "Ma Chih-yuan: 'Tears on the Blue Gown.'" *Renditions* 10: 131–62.

————. 2005–6. "From Revenge to What? Seven Hundred Years of Transformation of *The Orphan of Zhao*." *Chinoperl Papers* 26: 129–48.

Yuanben and *Zhugongdiao*

Ch'en, Li-li. 1972. "Outer and Inner Forms of *Chu-kung-tiao*, with Reference to *Pien-wen, Tz'u* and Vernacular Fiction." *Harvard Journal of Asiatic Studies* 32: 124–49.

———. 1973. "Some Background Information on the Development of *Chu-kung-tiao*." *Harvard Journal of Asiatic Studies* 33: 224–37.

Chen, Fan Li Ben. 1992. "Yang Kuei-fei in *Tales from the T'ien-pao Era: A Chu-kung-tiao Narrative*." *Journal of Sung-Yuan Studies* 22: 1–22.

———. 2007. "Translations from Wang Bocheng's *Tales of the Tianbao Era* (Tianbao yishi): Genre and Eroticism in the *Zhugongdiao*." *Chinoperl Papers* 26: 149–70.

Crump, J. I., and Milena Doleželová-Velingerová. 1971. *Ballad of the Hidden Dragon (Liu Chih-yüan chu-kung-tiao)*. Oxford: Oxford University Press.

Dong, Jieyuan, and trans. Li-li Ch'en. 1976. *Master Tung's Western Chamber Romance (Tung Hsi-hsiang chu-kung-tiao): A Chinese Chantefable*. Cambridge, New York: Cambridge University Press.

Idema, Wilt L. 1978. "Performance and Construction of the *Chu-kung-tiao*. *Journal of Oriental Studies* 16: 63–78.

———. 1984. "Yüan-pen as a Minor Form of Dramatic Literature in the Fifteenth and Sixteenth Centuries." *CLEAR* 6: 53–75.

———. 1993. "Data on the 'Chu-kung-tiao': A Reassessment of Conflicting Opinions." *T'oung Pao* 79 (1–3): 69–112.

———. 1995. "Satire and Allegory in All Keys and Modes." In H. C. Tillmann and S. H. West, eds., *China under Jurchen Rule*. Albany: SUNY Press. 238–80.

West, Stephen H. 1977. *Vaudeville and Narrative: Aspects of Chin Theater*. Wiesbaden: Steiner.

On Editions

Besio, Kimberly. 2005–6. "The *Moheluo Doll* Revisited: Yuan Drama in the Late Ming." *Chinoperl Papers* 26: 25–46.

Idema, Wilt L. 1988. "The Orphan of Zhao: Self-sacrifice, Tragic Choice and Revenge, and the Confucianization of Mongol Drama at the Ming Court." *Cina* 21: 159–90.

———. 1990. "Emulation through Readaptation in Yüan and Early Ming Drama." *Asia Major*, Third Series 3: 113–28.

———. 1994. "Some Aspects of Pai-yüeh-t'ing: Script and Performance." In Tseng Yong-yih, ed., *Proceedings of International Conference on Kuan Han-ch'ing (Guan Han-qing guoji xueshu yantao hui lunwen ji)*. Taipei: National Taiwan University, College of Liberal Arts. 57–77.

———. 1996. "Why You Have Never Read a Yuan Drama: The Transformation of *zaju* at the Ming Court." In *Studi in onore di Lanciello Lanciotti*. Napoli: Istituto Universiatorio Orientale, Dipartimento di Studi Asiatici. 765–91.

———. 2004. "Zang Maoxun as a Publisher." In I. Akira, ed. *Higashi Ajia shuppan bunka kenkyū: Niwatazumi*. Tokyo: Nigensha. 19–29.

———. 2005a. "Educational Frustration, Shape-Shifting Texts, and the Abiding Power of Anthologies: Three Versions of *Wang Can Ascends the Tower*." *Early Medieval China* 10–11.2: 145–83.

———. 2005b. "The Many Shapes of Medieval Chinese Plays: How Texts are Transformed to Meet the Needs of Actors, Spectators, Censors, and Readers." *Oral Tradition* 20 (2): 320–34.

———. 2005–6. "Li Kaixian's *Revised Plays by Yuan Masters* (*Gaiding Yuanxian chuanqi*) and the Textual Transmission of Yuan *zaju* as Seen in Two Plays by Ma Zhiyuan." *Chinoperl Papers* 26: 47–66.

Idema, Wilt L., and Stephen H. West. 1982. *Chinese Theater 1100–1450: A Source Book*. Wiesbaden: Steiner.

West, Stephen H. 2004. "Text and Ideology: Ming Editors and Northern Drama." In Paul Jakov Smith and Richard von Glahn, eds., *The Song-Yuan-Ming Transition in Chinese History*. Cambridge, MA: Harvard East Asia Center. 329–73.

Guan Hanqing

Dolby, A. E. William. 1971. "Kuan Han-Ch'ing." *Asia Major*. New Series 16: 1–60.

———. 1994. "Kuan Han-ch'ing's *San-ch'ü* of Reclusion." In Tseng Yong-yih, ed., *Proceedings of International Conference on Kuan Han-ch'ing*. Taipei: National Taiwan University, College of Liberal Arts. 399–408.

Idema, Wilt L. 1994. "Some Aspects of *Pai-yüeh-t'ing*: Script and Performance." In Tseng Yong-yih, ed., *Proceedings of the International Conference on Kuan Han-ch'ing*. Taipei: National Taiwan University, College of Liberal Arts. 57–77.

Johnson, Dale R. 2003. "Courtesans, Lovers, and Gold Thread Pond in Guan Hanqing's Music Dramas." *Journal of Song Yuan Studies* 33: 111–54.

Kalvadová, Dana. 2005–6. "The Story of the Haunted Grave Mound." *Chinoperl Papers* 26: 67–70.

Liu, Wu-chi. 1990–92. "Kuan Han-ch'ing: The Man and His Life." *Journal of Sung Yuan Studies* 22: 163–88.

Oberstenfeld, Werner. 1983. *China's bedeutendster Dramatiker der Mongolenzeit (1280–1368), Kuan Han-ch'ing*. Frankfurt: Peter Lang.

Shih, Chung-wen. 1994. "The Images of Women in Kuan Han-ch'ing Plays." In Tseng Yong-yih, ed., *Proceedings of the International Conference on Kuan Han-ch'ing*. Taipei: National Taiwan University, College of Liberal Arts. 291–302.

Sieber, Patricia. 1994a. "Comic Virtue and Commendable Vice: Guan Hanqing's *Jiu Feng Chen* and *Wang Jiang Ting*." *Ming Studies* 32: 43–64.

———. 1994b. "Rhetoric, Romance, and Intertextuality: The Making and Remaking of Guan Hanqing in Yuan and Ming China." Ph.D. diss., University of California. 145–225.

Yang, Hsien-yi, and Gladys Yang, trans. 1958. *Selected Plays of Kuan Han-ch'ing*. Shanghai: New Art and Literature Publishing House (reissued as *Selected Plays of Guan Hanqing*. Beijing: Foreign Languages Press, 1979).

Crime Plays

Hayden, George A. 1974. "The Courtroom Plays of the Yüan and Early Ming Periods." *Harvard Journal of Asiatic Studies* 34: 192–220.

Hsu, Dau-lin. 1970. "Crime and Cosmic Order." *Harvard Journal of Asiatic Studies* 30: 111–25.

Meng, Hanqing. 1980. "The Mo-he-lo Doll." In J. I. Crump, ed., *Chinese Theater in the Days of Kublai Khan.* Tucson: University of Arizona.

Perng, Ching-hsi. 1978. *Double Jeopardy: A Critique of Seven Yüan Courtroom Dramas.* Ann Arbor: University of Michigan.

Ptak, Roderich. 1979. "Die Dramen Cheng T'ing-Yüs." Thesis (doctoral). Klemmerberg, Ruprecht-Karl-Universität zu Heidelberg, Bad Boll.

Wolff, Ernst. 1972. "Law Court Scenes in Yuan Drama." *Monumenta Serica* 29: 193–205.

Injustice to Dou E

Hwang, Mei-Shu. 1990. "The Deaths of Cordelia and Tou E: Morality or Theatricality." In Y.-T. Luk, ed., *Studies in Chinese-Western Comparative Drama.* Hong Kong: Chinese University Press. 167–75.

Shih, Chung-wen. 1972. *Injustice to Tou O (Tou O Yüan).* Cambridge: Cambridge University Press.

West, Stephen H. 1991. "Zang Maoxun's Injustice to Dou E." *Journal of the American Oriental Society* 111 (2): 283–302.

Butterfly Dream

Judge Bao

Bauer, Wolfgang. 1970–71. "The Tradition of the 'Criminal Cases of Master Pao,' *Pao-kung-an (Lung-t'u kung-an).*" *Oriens* 23–24: 433–39.

Hanan, Patrick. 1980. "*Judge Bao's Hundred Cases* Reconstructed." *Harvard Journal of Asiatic Studies* 40 (2): 301–23.

Hayden, George A. 1975. "The Legend of Judge Pao: From the Beginnings through the Yüan Dynasty." In L. Thompson, ed., *Essays in Felicitations of the Seventy-fifth Anniversary of Professor Ch'en Shou-yi.* San Francisco: CMRASC. 339–55.

———. 1978. *Crime and Punishment in Medieval Chinese Drama: Three Judge Pao Plays.* Cambridge, MA: Council on East Asian Studies, Harvard University, distributed by Harvard University Press.

Idema, Wilt L. 2009. *Judge Bao and the Rule of Law: Eight Ballad Stories from the Period 1250–1450.* Singapore: World Scientific.

Ma, Y. W. 1975. "The Textual Tradition of Ming Kung-an Fiction: A Study of the Lung-t'u kung-an." *Harvard Journal of Asiatic Studies* 35: 190–220.

———. 1979. "A Study of the Lung-t'u king-an." *T'oung Pao* 65: 200–59.

Schmoller, Bernd. 1982. *Bao Zheng (999–1062) als Beamter und Staatsmann: das historische Vorbild des "weisen Richters" der Volksliteratur.* Bochum: Studienverlag Brockmeyer.

Shi Yukun. 1998. *Tales of Magistrate Bao and His Valiant Lieutenants: Selections from Sanxia wuyi.* Trans. Susan Blader. Hong Kong: Chinese University Press.

Shi Yukun and Yu Yue. 1997. *The Seven Heroes and Five Gallants.* Trans. Song Shouquan. Beijing: Panda Books.

Butterfly Dream

West, Stephen H. 1994. "Law and Ethics, Appearance and Actuality in 'Rescriptor in Waiting Pao Thrice Investigates the Butterfly Dream.'" In Tseng Yong-yih, ed., *Proceedings of the International Conference on Kuan Han-ch'ing.* Taipei: National Taiwan University, College of Liberal Arts. 93–112.

Praying to the Moon

Idema, W. L. 1994. "Some Aspects of the Pai-yüeh-t'ing: Script and Performance." In Tseng Yong-yih, ed., *Proceedings of the International Conference on Kuan Han-qing.* Taipei: National Taiwan University, College of Liberal Arts. 57–77.

Bai Pu and *Rain on the Wutong Tree*

Cavanaugh, Jerome. 1975. "The Dramatic Works of the Yüan Dynasty Playwright Pai P'u." Ph.D. diss., Asian Languages and Literatures. Stanford University.

Chen, Fan Ben Li. 1984. "Yang Kuei-fei: Changing Images of a Historical Beauty in Chinese Literature." Ph.D. diss., East Asian Languages and Cultures. Columbia University.

———. 1990–91. "Problems in Chinese Historiography as Seen in the Official Records on Yang Kuei-fei." *Tang Studies* 8–9: 83–96.

Chen, Fan Pen. 1992–93. "The Many Faces of Yang Guifei in Chinese Drama." *Chinoperl Papers* 16: 95–132.

Forke, Alfred. 1978. "*Wu-t'ung-yü (Der regen am Wu-t'ung Baum)* von Po P'u." In M. Gimm, ed., *Chinesische Dramen der Yüan-dynastie, zehn nachgelassene Übersetzungen von Alfred Forke.* Wiesbaden: Steiner. 186–242.

Hong Sheng. 1955. *The Palace of Eternal Youth.* Trans. Tu Pien-pu. Beijing: Foreign Languages Press.

Kroll, Paul. 1985. "The Flight from the Capital and the Death of Precious Consort Yang." *Tang Studies* 3: 25–53.

———. 2003. "Nostalgia and History in Mid-Ninth Century Verse: Cheng Yü's Poem on 'The Chin-yang Gate.'" *T'oung Pao* 89: 286–366.

Levy, Howard S. 1958. *Harem Favorites of an Illustrious Celestial.* Taiwan: Lin Yun-p'eng.

Lin Lüzhi. 1981. *Le règne de l'empereur Hiuan-Tsong, 713–756. Mémoires de l'Institut des hautes études chinoises.* Trans. Robert Des Rotours. [Paris]: Collège de France.

Matsuda, Shizue. 1974. "Rain on the Wutong Tree (Acts III and IV)." *Renditions* 3: 53–61.

Nakagawa Masako. 1998. *The Yang Kuei-Fei Legend in Japanese Literature.* Lewiston, NY: Edwin Mellen Press.

Owen, Stephen. 1996. "Xuan-zong and Yang the Prized Consort." In *An Anthology of Chinese Literature: Beginnings to 1911*. New York: Norton. 441–58.

Panish, Paul. 1976. "Trembling Pearls: The Craft of Imagery in Po P'u's 'Rain on the Wu-T'ung Tree.'" *Monumenta Serica* 12: 355–73.

Ma Zhiyuan

Idema, Wilt L. 2005–6. "Li Kaixian's *Revised Plays by Yuan Masters* (*Gaiding Yuanxian chuanqi*) and the Textual Transmission of Yuan *Zaju* as Seen in Two Plays by Ma Zhiyuan." *Chinoperl Papers* 26: 47–66.

———. 2007. "Madness on the Yuan Stage." *Horin vergleichende Studien zur Japanische Kultur* 14: 65–85.

Wang, Linda G. 1995. "Autumn Moon over Dongting Lake: Twenty-four *Sanqu* Lyrics to the Tune *Shou yang qu*." *Renditions* 43.

Yen, Yuan-shu. 1975a. "Yellow Millet Dream: A Translation." *Tamkang Review* 6: 205–39.

———. 1975b. "Yellow Millet Dream: A Yuan Dynasty Play by Ma Chih-yuan." *Echo* 13–23, 94.

———. 1975c. "Yellow Millet Dream: A Study of Its Artistry." *Tamkang Review* 6: 241–49.

Autumn over the Palaces of Han

Besio, Kimberly. 1997. "Gender, Loyalty, and the Reproduction of the Wang Zhaojun Legend: Some Social Ramifications of Drama in the Late Ming." *Journal of the Economic and Social History of the Orient* 40 (2): 251–82.

Demiéville, Paul. 1973. "Quelques traits de moeurs barbares danse une chantefable chinoise des Tang." In *Choix d'Études sinologiques 1926–1970*. Leiden: E. J. Brill. 307–21.

Eoyang, Eugene. 1982. "The Wang Chao-chün Legend: Configurations of the Classic." *CLEAR* 4 (1): 3–22.

Idema, Wilt L., and Beata Grant. 2004. "Banished beyond the Border: Liu Xijun and Wang Zhaojun." In Wilt L. Idema and Beata Grant, eds., *The Red Brush: Writing Women of Imperial China*. Cambridge, MA: Harvard University Asia Center. 91–94.

Kwong, Hing Foon. 1986. *Wang Zhaojun, une héroïne chinoise de l'histore à la légende, Préface de Jean Pierre Diény*. Paris: Collège de France, Institue des Hautes études Chinoises.

———. 1991. "L'évolution du théâtre populaire depuis les Ming jusqu'à nos jours: Le cas de Wang Zhaojun." *T'oung Pao* 72: 179–225.

Lei, Daphne. 1996. "Wang Zhaojun on the Border: Gender and Intercultural Conflicts in Premodern Chinese Drama." *Asian Theatre Journal* 13 (2): 229–37.

Ma, Zhiyuan. 1965. "Autumn in the Palace of Han." Trans. Donald Keene. In Cyril Birch, ed., *Anthology of Chinese Literature*. New York: Grove Press.

———. 1978. *Han-kung ch'iu*. In A. Forke, ed., *Chinesische Dramen der Yüan-dynastie, zehn nachgelassene Übersetzungen von Alfred Forke*. Wiesbaden: Steiner. 60–108.

Yu, Ying-shih. 1986. "Han Foreign Relations." In Denis Twitchett and M. Loewe, eds. *The Cambridge History of China: The Ch'in and Han Empires, 221 B.C.–A.D. 220.*

Qiannü's Soul Leaves Her Body

Chen, Xuanyou. 1985. "Tale of the Disembodied Soul." In K. Gao, ed., *Classical Chinese Tales of the Supernatural and the Fantastic: Selections from the Third to the Tenth Century.* Bloomington: Indiana University Press.

———. 1991. "Ch'ien-niang." In A. Manguel, ed., *Black Water 2: More Tales of the Fantastic.* New York: Random House/Clarkson & Potter.

Falaschi, Isabella. 2002. *"Le Mal d'amour de Qiannü ou l'âme qi se sépara de son corps": Comédie en prose en vers.* Trieste: Università degli Studi.

Hsiung, S. I., trans. 1968. *The Romance of the Western Chamber.* With a "Critical Introduction" by C. T. Hsia. New York: Columbia University Press.

Lu, Tina. 2001. *Persons, Roles, and Minds: Identity in* Peony Pavilion *and* Peach Blossom Fan. Palo Alto, CA: Stanford University Press.

Tang, Xianzu. 2002. *The Peony Pavilion: Mudan ting.* Trans. C. Birch. 2nd ed. Bloomington: Indiana University Press.

West, Stephen H. 2009. "Intertextuality and Desire: Mimesis in *The Story of the Western Wing* and *The Departed Soul of Qiannü.*" Paper read at International Conference on Performing Literature in Honor of Yu Ta-kang's 100th Birthday, at Ilan.

West, Stephen H., and Wilt L. Idema. 1995. *The Story of the Western Wing.* Berkeley: University of California Press.

The Record of the Chalk Circle

Chow, Shu P'ing. 1975. "Bertolt Brecht's the Caucasian Chalk Circle and Li Hsing Tao's the Chalk Circle: A Comparative Study." Thesis (doctoral). Tamkang College of Arts and Sciences.

Du, Wenwei. 1995. "*The Chalk Circle* Comes Full Circle: From Yuan Drama through the Western Stage to Peking Opera." *Asian Theatre Journal* 12 (2): 307–25.

Hall, Katherine Wai-Hing. 1973. "The Chalk-Circle: From Li Hsing-Tao to Bertolt Brecht." Thesis (doctoral). University of Hong Kong.

Klabund [Henschke, Alfred]. 1952. *Der Kreidekreis: Spiel in fünf Akten nach dem Chinesischen.* Neuauflag, Zurich: Phaidon-Verlag.

Klabund [Henschke, Alfred], and James Laver. 1929. *The Circle of Chalk: A Play in Five Acts.* London: W. Heinemann.

Li Xingdao. 1832. *Hoei-lan-ki, ou l'histoire du cercle de craie, drama en prose et en vers.* Trans. Stanislas Julien (1797–1873). London: Printed for the Oriental Translation Fund of Great Britain and Ireland, sold by J. Murray.

———. 1876. *Hoei-lan-ki. Der Kreidekreis. Chinesisches Schauspiel in vier Aufzugen und einem Vorspiel.* Trans. A. E. Wollheim da Fonseca. Leipzig: Phillip Reclam.

———. 1926. *Der Kreidekreis, in der Übersetzung von Alfred Forke.* Leipzig: Phillip Reclam.

————. 1953. *Der Kreidekreis: Ein Spiel in sechs Bildern nach dem Altchinesischen (Li Hsing-tao)*. Trans. Johannes Guenther. Stuttgart: Reclam-Verlag.

————. 1954. *The Story of the Circle of Chalk: A Drama from the Old Chinese*. Trans. Frances Hume. London: Rodale Press. From the French of Stanislas Julien.

Yang, Peter. 1998. *Theater ist Theater: ein Vergleich der Kreidekreisstücke Bertolt Brechts und Li Xingdaos*. New York: Peter Lang.

Lan Caihe

A Double Issue on the Eight Immortals. 1975. Taipei: Echo Magazine Co.

Eskilden, Stephen. 2004. *The Teachings and Practices of the Early Quanzhen Taoist Masters*. Albany: State University of New York Press.

Hartman, Charles. 1995. "Stomping Songs: Word and Image." *CLEAR* 17: 1–49.

Idema, Wilt L. 1985. "In Celebration of Life." In *The Dramatic Oeuvre of Chu Yu-tun (1379–1439)*. Leiden: E. J. Brill. 63–93.

————. 1990. "Some Notes on a Clown with a Clapper and Foot-Stomping Songs (*T'a-ko*)." *Han-hsüeh yen-chiu (Chinese Studies)* 8 (1): 655–64.

————. 2007. "Madness on the Yuan Stage." *Horin vergleichende Studien zur Japanische Kultur* 14: 65–85.

Idema, W. L., and Stephen H. West. 1982. "Chung-li of the Han Leads Lan Ts'ai-ho to Enlightenment." In *Chinese Theater 1100-1450: A Source Book*. Wiesbaden: Steiner. 299–340.

Katz, Paul. 1994. "The Interaction between Ch'üan-chen Taoism and Local Cults: A Case Study of Yung-le Kung." Paper read at International Conference on Popular Beliefs and Chinese Culture, at Taipei.

————. 1996. "Enlightened Alchemist or Immoral Immortal? The Growth of Lü Dongbin's Cult in late Imperial China." In R. W. Meir Shahar, ed., *Unruly Gods: Divinity and Society in China*. Honolulu: Hawai'i University Press.

————. 1999. *Images of the Immortal: The Cult of Lü Dongbin at the Palace of Eternal Joy*. Honolulu: University of Hawai'i Press.

Kwok, Man-Ho, Joanne O'Brien, and Philip Lamantia. 1990. *The Eight Immortals of Taoism: Legends and Fables of Popular Taoism*. New York: Meridian.

Lai, T. C., Po-ch'uan Yüeh, and Yeh Lü. 1972. *The Eight Immortals*. Kowloon, Hong Kong: Swindon Book Co.

Wiedmann, Earl. 1975. "An Analysis of the Eight Immortals in Literature." *Echo* 75: 72–86, 93.

Wu Yuantai. 1993. *Pérégrination vers l'Est*. Trans. Nadine Perront. Paris: Gallimard.

Yang, Erzeng, and trans. Philip Clart. 2008. *The Story of Han Xiangzi: The Alchemical Adventures of a Daoist Immortal*. Seattle: University of Washington Press.

Yao, Tao-chung. 1980. "Ch'üan-chen Taoism and Yüan Drama." *Journal of the Chinese Language Teacher's Association* 15: 41–56.

————. 1986. "Ch'iu Ch'u-chi and Chinggis Khan." *Harvard Journal of Asiatic Studies* 46 (1): 201–19.

Zhu Youdun

Idema, W. L. 1980a. "Shih Chün-pao's and Chu Yu-tun's Ch'ü-chiang-ch'ih: The Variety of Mode within Form." *T'oung Pao* 66 (4/5): 217–65.

———. 1980b. "Zhu Youdun's Dramatic Prefaces and Traditional Fiction." *Ming Studies* 10: 17–21.

———. 1980c. "Zhu Youdun's Dramatic Prefaces and Traditional Fiction: An Addendum." *Ming Studies* 11: 45.

———. 1982. "Chu Yu-tun as a Theorist of Drama." In R. P. Kramers, ed., *China: Continuity and Change.* Zürich: Hausdruckerei der Universität. 223–63.

———. 1985. *The Dramatic Oeuvre of Chu Yu-tun (1379–1439), Sinica Leidensia.* Leiden: E. J. Brill.

Idema, W. L., and Stephen H. West. 1982. "Theater in the Time of Chu Yu-tun (1398–1439)." In *Chinese Theater 1100–1450: A Source Book.* Wiesbaden: Steiner. 344–425.

Water Margin Story and Tales of Violence

Coyaud, Maurice. 1975. *Les opéras des bords de l'eau: théâtre Yuan, 1280–1368: traduction et étude linguistique.* Paris: Éditions du Centre national de la recherche scientifique.

Ge, Liangyan. 2001. *Out of the Margins: The Rise of Chinese Vernacular Fiction.* Honolulu: University of Hawai'i Press.

Hayden, George A. 1976. "A Skeptical Note on the Early History of Shui-hu-chuan." *Monumenta Serica* 32: 374–99.

Hennessey, William O. 1981. *Proclaiming Harmony.* Ann Arbor: Center for Chinese Studies, University of Michigan.

Hsia, Chih-tsing. 1968. *The Classic Chinese Novel: A Critical Introduction. Companions to Asian Studies.* New York: Columbia University Press.

Idema, W. L. 1985. "Outlaws and Townspeople." In *The Dramatic Oeuvre of Chu Yu-tun (1379–1439).* Leiden: E. J. Brill. 176–209.

Irwin, Richard Gregg. 1953. *The Evolution of a Chinese Novel: Shui-hu-chuan.* Cambridge, MA: Harvard University Press.

Kang, Jinzhi. 1980. "Li K'uei Carries Thorns." In J. I. Crump, ed., *Chinese Theater in the Days of Kublai Khan.* Tucson: University of Arizona Press. 201–46.

Plaks, Andrew H. 1980. "Shui-hu Chuan and the Sixteenth-Century Novel Form: An Interpretive Reappraisal." *CLEAR* 2 (1): 3–53.

———. 1987. "Shui-hu-chuan: Deflation of Heroism." In *Four Masterworks of the Ming Novel.* Princeton: Princeton University Press. 279–360.

Porter, Deborah. 1993. "Toward an Aesthetic of Chinese Vernacular Fiction: Style and the Colloquial Medium of *Shui-hu chuan.*" *T'oung Pao* 79 (1/3): 113–53.

West, Stephen H. 2006. "Crossing Over: Huizong in the Afterglow, or the Deaths of a Troubling Emperor." In *Emperor Huizong and Late Northern Song China: The Politics of Culture and the Culture of Politics.* Cambridge, MA: Harvard University East Asia Center. 565–608.

Wu, Yenna. 1996. "Outlaws' Dreams of Power and Position in *Shuihu zhuan.*" *CLEAR* 18: 45–67.

Little Butcher Sun

Fu, Hongchu. 1999. "The Cultural Fashioning of Filial Piety: A Reading of 'Xiao Zhangtu' (Little Zhang the Butcher)." *Journal of Song Yuan Studies* 29: 63–90.

Idema, Wilt L. 1997. "The Pilgrimage to Taishan in the Dramatic Literature of the Thirteenth and Fourteenth Centuries." *CLEAR* 19: 23–57.

Idema, Wilt L., and Stephen H. West, "Wind and Moon in the Courtyard of Purple Clouds." In *Chinese Theater 1100–1450: A Source Book.* 236–78.

Llamas, Regina. 2007. "Retribution, Revenge, and the Ungrateful Scholar in Early Chinese Southern Drama." *Asia Major.* Third Series 20 (2): 75–101.

Sun, Mei. 1996a. "Reconsidering *nanxi*'s Position in the History of *xiqu. American Journal of Chinese Studies* 1: 22–30.

———. 1996b. "Performances of Nanxi." *Asian Theatre Journal* 13 (2): 141–66.

———. 1999. "The Division between *nanxi* and *chuanqi.*" *American Journal of Chinese Studies* 5 (2): 248–56.

West, Stephen H. 2008. "Shifting Spaces: Local Dialect in *A Playboy from a Noble House Opts for the Wrong Career.*" *Journal of Theater Studies* 1 (1): 83–107.

Zbikowski, Tadeusz. 1974. *Early Nan-hsi Plays of the Southern Sung Period.* Warsaw: Wydwnictwa Universytetu Warszawskiego.

Appendix 3

A Partial List of Modern English Translations of Early Drama

Northern Drama

Anonymous

Ding-ding dang-dang pen'er gui 叮叮當當盆兒鬼
Ding-ding Dong-dong: The Ghost in the Pot
  Hayden 1978: "The Ghost of the Pot"

Han Zhongli dutuo Lan Caihe 漢鍾離度脫藍採和
Zhongli of the Han Leads Lan Caihe to Enlightenment
  Idema and West 1982: "Chung-li of the Han Leads Lan Ts'ai-ho to
    Enlightenment"

Jinyun tang anding lianhuan ji 錦雲堂暗定連環計
At Embroidered Cloud Hall: Secretly Setting the Stratagem of Interlocking Rings
  Liu 1972: "A Stratagem of Interlocking Rings"

Bai Pu

Tang Minghuan qiuye wutong yu 唐明皇秋夜梧桐雨
The Autumn Nights of the Lustrous Emperor of Tang: Rain on the Wutong Tree
  Yang 1972: "Rain on the Wu-t'ung Tree"
  Matsuda 1974: "Rain on the Wutong Tree (Acts III and IV)"

Gao Maoqing

Cuihongxiang ernü liang tuanyuan 翠紅鄉二女兩團圓
A Reunion with Son and Daughter in Kingfisher Red County
  Chen 1997: "Reunion with Son and Daughter in Kingfisher Red County"

Guan Hanqing

Bao Daizhi Chenzhou diaomi 包待制陳州糶米
Rescriptor-in-Waiting Bao: Selling Rice in Chenzhou
  Hayden 1978: "Selling Rice at Chenzhou"

Bao Daizhi sankan hudiemeng 包待制三勘蝴蝶夢
Rescriptor-in-Waiting Bao Thrice Investigates the Butterfly Dream
  Yang 1958: "The Butterfly Dream"

Bao Daizhi zhizhan Lu Zhailang 包待制智斬魯齋郎
Rescriptor-in-Waiting Bao Cleverly Executes Court Gentleman Lu
  Yang 1958: "The Wife-Snatcher"

Deng Furen kutong ku cunxiao 鄧夫人苦痛哭存孝
Deeply Grieved, Lady Deng Laments Cunxiao
  Yang 1958: "Death of the Winged-Tiger General"

Du Ruiniang zhi shang Jinxian chi 杜蕊娘智賞金線池
Du Ruiniang Wisely Appreciates Gold Thread Pond
  Johnson 2003: "Gold Thread Pond"

Gantian dongdi Dou E Yuan 感天動地竇娥冤
Moving Heaven and Shaking Earth: The Injustice to Dou E
  Yang 1958: "Snow in Midsummer"
  Liu 1972: "The Injustice Done to Tou Ngo"
  Shih 1972: "The Injustice to Dou E"
  Yang 1972: "Tou O Was Wronged"
  Ma 2005: "Injustice to Dou E"

Guan Dawang dandao hui 關大王單刀會
The Single-Sword Meeting of Great Prince Guan
  Yang 1958: "Lord Kuan Goes to the Feast"

Wangjiangting zhongqiu qiekuai dan 望江亭中秋切鱠旦
Riverside Pavilion at Mid-Autumn: A Female Slicing Fish
  Yang 1958: "The Riverside Pavilion"

Wen Taizhen yu jingtai 溫太真玉鏡臺
Wen Taizhen and the Jade Mirror Stand
  Yang 1958: "The Jade Mirror-Stand"

Zhao Pan'er yanyue jiu fengchen 趙盼兒烟月救風塵
In Mist and Moonlight Zhao Pan'er Rescues Her from the Windblown Dust
  Owen 1996: "Rescuing One of the Girls"
  Kao 1998: "A Sister Courtesan Comes to the Rescue"

Ji Junxiang

Zhaoshi gu'er 趙氏孤兒
The Orphan of Zhao
  Liu 1972: "The Orphan of Chao"
  Wang 1978: "The Revenge of the Orphan of Zhao"

Kang Jinzhi

Liangshan po Li Kui fujing 梁山泊李逵負荊
At Liangshan Marsh Li Kui Carries Thorns on His Back
  Crump 1980: "Li K'uei Carries Thorns"

Li Haogu

Shamen dao Zhangsheng zhuhai 沙門島張生煮海
At Shaman Island Student Zhang Boils the Sea
  Liu 1972: "Chang Boils the Sea"

Ma Zhiyuan

Handan dao xingwu Huangliang meng 邯鄲道省悟黃粱夢
On the Road to Handan, Awakening from a Dream Dreamt While Cooking Millet
    Yen 1975a: "Yellow Millet Dream"

Lü Dongbin sanzui Yueyang lou 呂洞賓三醉岳陽樓
Lü Dongbin Gets Drunk Three Times in Yueyang Tower
    Yang 1972: "The Yüeh-yang Tower"

Po youmeng guyan hangong qiu 破幽夢孤雁漢宮秋
Breaking a Troubling Dream: A Lone Goose in Autumn over the Palaces of Han
    Keene 1965: "Autumn in the Han Palace"
    Liu 1972: "Autumn in Han Palace"

Jiangzhou sima qingshan lei 江州司馬青衫淚
The Overseer of Jiangzhou: Tears on the Blue Gown
    Yu 1978: "Tears on the Blue Gown"

Meng Hanqing

Zhang Ding zhikan Moheluo 張鼎智勘磨合羅
Zhang Ding Cleverly Investigates the Moheluo Doll
    Crump 1980: "The Mo-ho-lo Doll"

Li Taibai pipei jinqianji 李太白匹配金錢記
Li Bai Arranges a Marriage: The Story of the Golden Coin
    Johnson 1985: "The Golden Coins"

Shang Zhongxian

Dongting hu Liu Yi chuanshu 洞庭湖劉毅傳書
At Dongting Lake Liu Yi Transmits a Letter
    Hawkes 2003: "Liu Yi and the Dragon Princess"

Shi Junbao

Lu daifu Qiu Hu xiqi 魯大夫秋胡戲妻
The Grandee of Lu Qiu Hu Comes on to His Wife
    Dolby 1978: "Qiu Hu Tries to Seduce His Own Wife"

Fengyue ziyun ting 風月紫雲亭
Wind and Moon in the Courtyard of Purple Clouds
    Idema and West 1982: "Wind and Moon in the Courtyard of Purple Clouds"

Wang Shifu

Cui Yingying daiyue xixiang ji 崔鶯鶯待月西廂記
Oriole Cui Waits for the Moon: Story of the Western Wing
    Hsiung 1968: "Romance of the Western Chamber"
    West and Idema 1995: "Story of the Western Wing"

Yang Xianzhi

Linjiang yi Xiaoxiang qiuye yu 臨江驛瀟湘秋夜雨
At Linjiang Hostel: Autumn Night Rains over the Xiao and Xiang Rivers
   Crump 1980: "Rain on the Hsiao-hsiang"

Zheng Guangzu

Mi qingsuo Qiannü lihun 迷青瑣倩女離魂
Dazed behind the Green Ring Lattice, Qiannü's Soul Leaves Her Body
   Liu 1972: "The Soul of Ch'ien-nü Leaves Her Body"
   Yang 1972: "Ch'ien-nü's Soul Left Her Body"
   Ma 2005: "Qiannü's Soul Leaves Her Body"

Zheng Tingyu

Bao Daizhi zhikan houtinghua 包待制智勘後庭花
Rescriptor-in-Waiting Bao's Clever Trick: The Flower in the Rear Courtyard
   Hayden 1978: "The Flower of the Back Courtyard"

Budai heshang renzi ji 布袋和尚忍字記
The Monk with a Burden and the Story of the Word "Patience"
   Mair 1994: "The Monk *Pu-tai* and the Character for Patience"

Zhu Youdun

Liu Panchun shouzhi xiangnangyuan 劉盼春守志香囊怨
Liu Awaiting Spring Remains Loyal: Perfume Sachet Grief
   Idema and West 1982: "Liu Awaiting Spring Remains Loyal: Perfume Sachet
      Grief"

Xuanping xiang Liu Jin'er fuluo chang 宣萍巷劉金兒復落娼
Liu Jin'er from Xuanping Ward Becomes a Singsong Girl Again
   Idema and West 1982: "Liu Chin-erh from Hsüan-p'ing Ward Becomes a Sing-
      song Girl Again"

Southern Drama

Anonymous

Huanmen zidi cuoli shen 宦門子弟錯立身
A Playboy from a Noble House Opts for the Wrong Career
   Dolby 1978: "Grandee's Son Takes the Wrong Career"
   Idema and West 1982: "A Playboy from a Noble House Opts for the Wrong
      Career"

Index